P9-BYX-454

ALSO BY JULIAN MAY

Jack the Bodiless

Intervention: The Surveillance

Intervention: The Metaconcert

The Adversary

The Nonborn King

The Golden Torc

The Many-Colored Land

A Pliocene Companion

DIAMOND MASK

DIAMOND MASK

< A NOVEL BY >

JULIAN MAY

BOOK TWO

OF THE GALACTIC MILIEU TRILOGY

ALFRED A. KNOPF

New York

1994

THIS IS A BORZOI BOOK
PUBLISHED BY ALFRED A. KNOPF, INC.

The author is grateful for permission to quote from "Caledonia" by Dougie MacLean, published by Limetree Arts and Music, 29/33 Berners St, London W1P 4AA.

Library of Congress Cataloging-in-Publication Data

May, Julian.
Diamond mask : a novel / by Julian May.—1st ed.
p. cm.—(Galactic milieu trilogy ; Book Two)
ISBN 0-679-43310-4
I. Title. II. Series: May, Julian. Galactic milieu trilogy ; Book Two.
PS3563.A942D53 1994
813'.54—dc20 93-37802
CIP

Manufactured in the United States of America
First Edition

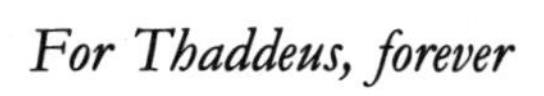

For Thaddeus, forever

Every culture gets the magic it deserves.

DUDLEY YOUNG, *Origins of the Sacred*

A mask tells us more than a face.

OSCAR WILDE, *Intentions*

Sancta Illusio, ora pro nobis.

FRANZ WERFEL, *Star of the Unborn*

DIAMOND MASK

[PROLOGUE]

KAUAI, HAWAII, EARTH
12 AUGUST 2113

He knew it had to be some kind of miracle—perhaps one programmed by Saint Jack the Bodiless himself. The misty rain of the Alakai Swamp ceased, the gray sky that had persisted all day broke open suddenly and flaunted glorious expanses of blue, a huge rainbow haloed Mount Waialeale over to the east . . . and a bird began to sing.

Batège! That bird—could it be the one? After four futile days?

The tall, skinny old man dropped to his knees in the muck, slipped out of his backpack straps, and let the pack fall into the tussocks of dripping grass. Muttering in the Canuck patois of northern New England, he pulled his little audiospectrograph from its waterproof pouch with fingers that trembled from excitement and hit the RECORD pad. The hidden songster warbled on. The old man pressed SEEK. The device's computer compared the recorded birdsong with that of 42,429 avian species (Indigenous Terrestrial, Indigenous Exotic, Introduced, Retroevolved, and Bioengineered) stored in its data files. The MATCH light blinked on and the instrument's tiny display read:

O'O-A'A (MOHO BRACCATUS). ONLY ON ISL OF KAUAI, EARTH. IT. VS.

The man said to himself: Damn right you're Very Scarce. Even rarer than the satanic nightjar or the miniature tit-babbler! But I gotcha at last, p'tit merdeux, toi.

The song cut off and a discordant *keet-keet* rang out. Something black with flashes of chrome yellow erupted from the moss-hung shrubs on the left side of the trail, flew toward a clump of stunted lehua makanoe trees twenty meters away, and disappeared.

The old man choked back a penitent groan. Quel bondieu d'imbécile—he'd frightened it with some inadvertent telepathic gaucherie!

And now it was gone, and his feeble metapsychic seekersense was incapable of locating its faint life-aura in broad daylight. Everything now depended upon the camera.

Taking care to project only the most soothing and amiable vibes, he hastily stowed away the Sonagram machine, uncased a digital image recorder with a thermal targeter attached, and began anxiously scanning the trees. Wisps of vapor streamed up, drawn by the tropical sun. The sweet anise scent of mokihana berries mingled with that of rotting vegetation. The Alakai Swamp of Kauai in the Hawaiian Islands was an eerie place, the wettest spot on Earth, a plateau over 1200 meters high where the annual rainfall often exceeded 15 meters. The swamp was also home to some of Earth's rarest birds, and it attracted hardy human students of avifauna from all over the Galactic Milieu.

The old man, whose name was Rogatien Remillard, knew the island well, having first come to it back in 2052, when his great-grandnephew Jack, whom he called Ti-Jean, was newborn with a body that seemed perfectly normal. Jack's mother Teresa, rest her poor soul, had needed a sunny place to recuperate after hiding out in the snowbound Megapod Reserve of British Columbia, and the island afforded a perfect refuge for the three of them.

Rogi had returned to Kauai many times since then, most recently four days earlier, for reasons that had seemed compelling at the time.

Well, perhaps he'd imbibed just a tad too much Wild Turkey as he celebrated the completion of another section of his memoirs . . .

Crafty in his cups, he had decided to get out of town before his Lylmik nemesis could catch up with him and force him to continue the work. He'd done a damned good job so far, if he did say so himself—and he might as well, since only God knew when any other natural human being would ever get to read what he'd written.

Even though he was drunk as a skunk, Rogi had wit enough to toss a few clothes and things into his egg, climb in, and program the navigator for automatic Vee-route flight from New Hampshire to Kauai. Then he had passed out. When he awoke he found his aircraft in a holding pattern above the island. He was hungover but lucid, with no idea why his unconscious mind had chosen this particular destination. But not to worry! His old hobby of ornithology, neglected for more than a decade, kicked in with a brilliant notion. He could backpack into the Alakai Swamp, where he might possibly see and photograph the single remaining indigenous Hawaiian bird species he had never set eyes upon. He landed the rhocraft at Koke'e Lodge, rented the necessary equipment, and set out.

And now, had he found the friggerty critter only to lose it through gross stupidity? Had he scared it off into the trackless wilderness of the swamp, where he didn't dare follow for fear of getting lost? He was a piss-poor metapsychic operant at best, totally lacking in the ultrasensory pathfinding skills of the more powerful heads, and the Alakai was a remote and lonely place. It would be humiliating to get trapped armpit-deep in some muck-hole and have to call the lodge to send in a rescuer. Still, if he was careful to go only a few steps off the trail, he might still snag the prize.

He skirted a pool bordered with brown, white, and orange lichens, then peered through the camera eyepiece from a fresh vantage point. The luminous bull's-eye of the thermal detector shone wanly green in futility. Despair began to cloud his previous mood of elation. The very last bird on his Hawaiian Audubon Checklist, forfeit because he'd failed to control his doddering mindpowers—

No! Dieu du ciel, there it was! He'd moved just enough so that the infrared targeter, preset to the parameters of the prey, could zero in on it as it sat mostly concealed behind the trunk of a diminutive tree. The bull's-eye blinked triumphant scarlet. The old man cut out the targeter, cautiously shifted position once more, and the bird was clearly revealed in the camera's viewfinder: a chunky black creature 20 cents long, seeming to stare fiercely at him from its perch on the scraggly lehua tree. Tufts of brilliant yellow feathers adorned its upper legs like gaudy knickers peeping out from beneath an otherwise somber avian outfit. The bird flicked its pointed tail as if annoyed at having been disturbed and the old man experienced a rush of pure joy.

It was the rarest of all nonretroevolved Hawaiian birds, with a name that tripped ludicrously from the tongues of Standard English speakers: the elusive o'o-a'a!

Nearly beside himself, the old birdwatcher used the imager zoom control, composed his shot, and pressed the video activator. Before he could take a second picture the o'o-a'a repeated its double-noted alarm call almost derisively, spread its wings, and flew off in the direction of Mount Waialeale.

The rainbow had faded as a new batch of dark clouds rolled in from the east. In another fifteen minutes or so the sun would set behind the twisted dwarf forest and the Hawaiian night would slam down with its usual abruptness. He had barely found the bird in time.

He touched the PRINT pad of the camera. A few seconds later, a durofilm photo with exquisite color detail slipped out of the instrument into his hand. He stared at the precious picture, now curiously dispassionate, and heaved a sigh as he unzipped his rain jacket and tucked the trophy into the breast pocket of his shirt.

A voice spoke to him from out of the steamy air:

What's this, Uncle Rogi? In a melancholy mood after your great triumph?

Rogatien Remillard looked up in surprise, then growled a half-hearted Franco-American epithet. "Merde de merde . . . so you couldn't let me celebrate my hundred-and-sixty-eighth birthday in peace, eh, Ghost?"

The voice was gently chiding: You have done so—and received a fine present besides.

"You didn't!" the old man exclaimed indignantly. "You didn't chivvy that poor little bird here on purpose, just so I'd find it—"

Certainly not. What do you take me for?

"Hah! I take you for an exotic bully, mon cher fantôme, that's what. Not even a week since I turned off the transcriber, and here you are breathing down my neck. Go ahead: deny that you came to nag me to get on with my memoirs."

I don't deny it, Uncle Rogi. And I realize that the work is hard for you. But it's necessary that you resume writing the family chronicle without delay. It must be completed before this year is out.

"Why the tearing hurry? Does your goddam Lylmik crystal ball foresee that I'm gonna kick the bucket come New Year's Eve? Is that why you keep the pressure on? I've had a sneaking suspicion about that ever since I finished the Intervention section. You and your almighty schemes! What's the plan? You squeeze my poor old failing brain like a sponge, then toss me on the discard heap once you get what you want?"

Nonsense. How many times must I tell you? You are immune to the normal processes of human aging and degenerative disease. You have the self-rejuvenating gene complex, just as all the other Remillards do.

"Except Ti-Jean!" Rogi snapped. "Anyway . . . I could always be destined to die in some accident that you and your gang of galactic snoops in Orb prolepticate, and *that's* why the mad rush."

The sky was completely overcast again and the tussocks of sedge and makaloa grass rippled in the rising wind. More rain was imminent. Turning his back upon the region from which the disembodied voice came, Rogi went squishing through the mire to retrieve his abandoned backpack. He hauled it up, mud-splattered and dripping.

"Damn slavedriver. If you really did give a hoot about me, you'd do something about this mess."

The pack was instantly clean, dry, and as crisp and unfaded as the day Rogi had purchased it from the outfitting store in Hanover, New Hampshire, eighty-four years earlier. His initials newly adorned the belt buckle, which had once been homely black plass but now appeared to have been transmuted into solid gold.

The old man let loose a splutter of laughter. "Show-off! But thanks, anyway."

De rien, said the Ghost. Consider it a small incentive. A birthday present. Hau'oli la hanau!

Rogi frowned. "Seriously, though. My bookshop business is getting shot all to hell with me taking so much time off for writing. And I don't mind telling you that rehashing this ancient history is getting more and more depressing. There's a whole parcel of stuff I'd just as soon forget. And if you had a scintilla of pride, you'd want to forget it, too."

The personage known to Rogi as the Remillard Family Ghost and to the Galactic Milieu as Atoning Unifex, Overlord of the Lylmik, was silent for some minutes. Then It said:

The truth about the Remillards and their intimate associates *must* be made available to every mind in the Galaxy. I've tried to make this clear to you from the very beginning. You're a unique individual, Uncle Rogi. You know things the historians of the Milieu never suspected. Things that even I have no inkling of . . . such as the identity of the malignant entity called Fury.

The old man paused in adjusting his pack straps and looked over his shoulder with an expression of blank incredulity. "You don't know who Fury was? You're not omniscient after all?"

Rogi, Rogi! How many times must I tell you that I am not God, not even some sort of metapsychic recording angel—in spite of the silly nickname that was given me! I am only a Lylmik who was once a man, six million long years ago. And I have very little time left.

"Jésus!" Rogi's eyes widened in sudden comprehension. "*You!* Not me at all. You . . . "

Abruptly, the rain began to fall again; but this time it was not the gentle drizzle called ua noe that usually cloaked the Alakai Swamp but a hammering tropical deluge. Rogi stood stark still in the midst of the downpour, transfixed by his invisible companion's words, seeming to be unaware that he had neglected to pull up the hood of his rain jacket. Water streamed from his sodden gray hair into his eyes.

"You," he said again. "Ah, mon fils, why didn't you tell me before, when you came to me at the winter carnival after the long years of silence? Why did you let me rave on, resisting your wishes, making a fool of myself?"

The mind of the Lylmik Overlord erected a transparent psychocreative umbrella over Rogi, but tears mingled with rain continued to flow down the old man's cheeks. He reached out awkwardly to the empty air.

The Ghost said: Keaku Cave is nearby. Let's get out of the wet.

Rogi was conscious of no movement, but he found himself suddenly within a fern-curtained grotto, sitting on a chunk of weathered lava in front of a small, brisk fire of hapu'u stems. Outside, a torrential storm battered the high plateau, but he was miraculously dry again. What was more, the profound grief that had pierced him seemed to have receded and he felt embraced by a great peace. He knew that the paradoxical being who had haunted him since he was five years old—the person whom he both loved and feared—had meddled once again with his mind, short-circuiting emotions that would have interfered with Its plans.

The lava cave the Ghost had brought him into was the site of ancient mysteries sacred to the local Hawaiians, all but inaccessible to foot travelers. None of the hikers or birdwatchers or botanical hobbyists who came to the Alakai Swamp dared to visit the place. It was kapu—forbidden—and said to be protected by powerful operant Hawaiians claiming descent from the kahuna magicians of ancient Polynesia.

Rogi had entered Keaku Cave only once before, not quite fifty-nine years ago. On that day in the fall of 2054, just after the Human Polity had finally been granted full citizenship in the galactic confederation, he and the teenaged Marc Remillard and young Jack the Bodiless had flown to the Alakai in a rhocraft, accompanied by the kahuna woman Malama Johnson. Their mission was to remove the ashes of the boys' mother that had been sequestered in the cave a year earlier according to Malama's solemn instructions. Rogi and the boys had found the interior of Keaku Cave mysteriously decorated with leis of gorgeous island flowers and fragrant berries. The box containing Teresa Kendall's ashes was as clean and dry as it had been when they left it.

Sitting in the cave now, knowing that the unseen Lylmik Overlord lurked close at hand, the old man seemed once again to smell the anise scent of mokihana. He remembered Marc, a stalwart sixteen-year-old, and Ti-Jean, apparently only a precocious toddler, on their knees beside the small polished pine box holding their mother's remains. They had asked Rogi to carry the urn to their waiting rhocraft, since he had been her protector during the greatest crisis of her life.

Teresa's ashes had been scattered over the green tropical ridges and canyons on a day of resplendent rainbows. In the years that followed, Jack the Bodiless returned often to the island of Kauai, visiting his great friend Malama and eventually making his home there, bringing his bride to the place he loved more than any on Earth. But Marc Remillard had never set foot on the island again.

"Are you glad?" Rogi asked abruptly. "Glad it's almost over?"

The Ghost's reply was slow in coming:

I had feared that I was fated to live until the very consummation of the universe. Fortunately, it didn't come to that, even though God knows I richly deserved it.

"Tommyrot! You sincerely believed that the Metapsychic Rebellion was morally justified. Hell, so did I! Back then, lots of decent people had serious doubts about Unity. Maybe not to the point of going to war, but—"

My principal motive for leading the Rebellion had nothing to do with the Unity controversy. I instigated an interstellar war because the Milieu condemned my Mental Man project . . . because it rejected my vision for accelerating the mental and physical evolution of humanity. With me, Unity was only a side issue.

Rogi looked up from the fire in surprise. "Is that a fact! You know,

I never was too sure just what that Mental Man thing was all about."

The Ghost's tone was ironic: Neither were most of my Rebel associates. If they had known, they might not have followed me.

"And the Mental Man project was—was so wrong that—"

Not wrong, Rogi. *Evil* . . . There's a considerable difference. It took me many years to recognize how monstrous my scheme actually was, to understand just what kind of galactic catastrophe my pride and arrogance might have brought about.

"It didn't happen," Rogi said very quietly.

No, said the Ghost, but there remained a grave necessity for me to atone, to make up for the damage I had done to the evolving Mind of the Universe. My sojourn in the Duat Galaxy was a partial reparation, but incomplete. The evil had taken place here, in the Milky Way. The Duat labors were exciting, satisfying—joyous, even—because Elizabeth shared them with me and helped me to fully understand my own heart. Before we came together, my self was unintegrated; I had no true notion of what love meant.

"I don't agree," the old man said stubbornly. "Neither would Jack."

The Ghost was not to be sidetracked. It continued:

When the Duat work was done, Elizabeth was weary and ready to pass on. She begged me to follow her into the peace and light of the Cosmic All . . . but I could not.

Instead, I felt compelled to return here. Alone, cut off from every mind that had loved me and from the consoling Unity I had known in Duat, I undertook what I judged was my true penance: to assist the maturation of our own Galactic Mind.

Through years that seemed without end I guided one promising planet after another, cajoling civilization from barbarism, altruism from savagery. Of course I could not truly coerce the developing races of the Milky Way. I only assisted the inevitable complexification of the World Mind that accompanies life's evolution.

I made many ghastly mistakes.

Can you conceive of the doubts that assailed me, Rogi, the fear that I might have succumbed to a hubris even more immense than that which originally obsessed me? No . . . I see that you can't understand. Never mind, mon oncle. Only believe me. It was a terrible time. Le bon dieu is as silent and invisible to the likes of me as he is to any other material being. I could not help but ask myself if I was committing a fresh sin of pride in thinking that my assistance was needed.

Was I helping the Galactic Mind, or merely meddling with evolution again, as I had been when I tried to engender Mental Man?

Our galaxy has so many planets with thinking creatures! Yet so few—so pathetically few!—ever achieved any sort of social or mental maturity under my guidance, much less the coadunation of the higher mindpowers that leads to Unity. But finally, perhaps in spite of my efforts rather than as a result of them, I found success. The Lylmik were the first minds to Unify, and I adopted their peculiar race as my own. Then, aeons later, the Krondaku also achieved coadunation.

After that came a great hiatus, and I feared that my infant Galactic Milieu was doomed to eventual stagnation and death. But le divin humoriste elevated the preposterous Gi race to metapsychic operancy against all odds (the Krondaku were deeply scandalized) and not long after that the Mind of the engaging little Poltroyans matured as well. The Simbiari were accepted into the Milieu next, even though they were imperfectly Unified. And suddenly there seemed almost to be an evolutionary explosion of intelligent beings, burgeoning on planet after planet—not yet ready for induction into our confederation, but nevertheless making great progress.

One of the less likely worlds in this group was Earth.

Knowing what I do, I overruled the consensus that rejected the human race as a candidate for Intervention. The result was the Metapsychic Rebellion, a towering disaster that metamorphosed into triumph. And now the Mind of this galaxy stands poised at the brink of a great expansion you cannot begin to imagine . . .

"Are you going to tell me about that?" Rogi asked.

I cannot. My own role in the drama is nearly complete and my proleptic vision fails as my life approaches its end. Assisting you to write the cautionary family history will be my last bit of personal intervention. Others will oversee the destiny of this Galactic Mind henceforth and guide it to the fullness of Unity that is so very, very close.

. . .

The old man fed the fire with an armful of tree fern stalks as Atoning Unifex fell silent. The swirling smoke seemed to slide away from a certain region near the cave entrance. Out of the corner of his eye (his mental sight perceived nothing) Rogi caught occasional hints of a spectral form standing there.

"What next, mon fantôme? You gonna snatch me back to New Hampshire through the gray limbo like you did the last time, on Denali?"

Would you rather write the Diamond Mask story here on Kauai?

Rogi brightened. "You know, I think I would! She and Ti-Jean did honeymoon here, after all."

There is also the matter of the Hydra attack that took place here.

Rogi's brow tightened. "Maudit—why'd you have to remind me about *them*?" He fumbled with the side compartment of his backpack and took out an old leather-bound flask. Unscrewing the cap, he tossed down a healthy slug of bourbon. "To do a proper job on Dorothée's early life, I'll have to tell all about those poor, perverted bastards. Just remembering 'em turns my stomach." He took another snort.

The Ghost said: I can alleviate your gastric distress more efficiently than whiskey can, if you'll permit the liberty.

Rogi gave a bark of nervous laughter. "And will you be able to flush my skull of Fury dreams, too?"

The Lylmik's thought-tone was wry: I've had experience with them myself, as you may recall. I'll build you a protective mental shield—

"Hey! Now wait just a damn minute!"

The Ghost was insistent: It can be done while you sleep, so you'll have no experience of invasion whatsoever. I can leave all your precious neuroses intact, but you must permit me to install the dream-filter. It would be the height of ingratitude on my part if your writing chores precipitated anxiety and a fresh bout of alcohol abuse. You will suffer no nightmares, I promise. We Lylmik are the most skilled redactors in the universe.

"Oh, yeah? Then where the hell were you when Fury and his Hydras were doing their metapsychic vampire act back in those thrilling days of yesteryear?"

Our interference would not have been appropriate at that time. The crimes of those entities, heinous as they were, were necessary to the evolution of Higher Reality, just as the Metapsychic Rebellion was.

"I," the old man declared wearily, "do not give a rat's ass for the Higher Reality. Or the Lower, for that matter." He lifted the flask again.

Rogi—

"All right! Go ahead and fix my brain so I don't go apeshit after dredging up those old horrors. But don't you dare try to do me any favors plugging in Unity programs or any other Lylmik flimflammery."

The phantom in the cave's darkened entrance now seemed to be approaching the fire, and Rogi stared in fascination at the way the smoke wafted about the invisible form. As the Lylmik mind spoke soothingly and the liquor did its work, the old man suddenly caught his breath. For an instant, he thought he'd glimpsed a man's face there in the shadows—one he remembered all too clearly. He surged to his feet, calling out a name, and tried to throw his arms about the evanescent shape; but he embraced only a cloud of smoke. His eyes began to sting, and he pulled a bandanna handkerchief from his hip pocket and blew his nose, subsiding back onto his rocky seat.

The Ghost said: Vas-y doucement, mon oncle bien-aimé! Think only of the memoirs. When you complete them, I'll be able to go in peace.

The old man mopped at his eyes. "Batège! Who'd have thought I'd get all soppy over *you*? A goddam figment of my goddam booze-pickled imagination! That's what Denis and Paul always said you were. Merde alors, it makes more sense for me to believe that than the cosmic bullshit you've been dishing out."

If it makes you more comfortable, by all means believe it.

"I'll make up my own mind what to believe," the old man muttered perversely. Then he asked: "Where do you think I should settle in to do the writing? Down at the old Kendall place in Poipu?"

I have a better suggestion. How about Elaine Donovan's lodge near Pohakumano? It's at a high enough elevation to be cool, and no vacationing Remillards are likely to bother you there, as they well might down at the coast. The house is isolated and it has been kept in excellent condition by caretakers, even though Elaine has not visited it for many years. You'd find it very comfortable and much quieter than Hanover in the summertime.

"Elaine . . . " Rogi's face stiffened. "I didn't know she had a vacation house on Kauai. But she was Teresa's grandmother, of course."

I can arrange to have your transcriber and any other personal items you might need brought over from New Hampshire. Even your cat, Marcel, if you like.

"I—I don't think I better stay at Elaine's place."

The thought of her still brings you pain?

"No, not anymore."

Then use her house. You know she wouldn't mind.

The old man sighed. What did it matter, after all? "All right. Whatever you say. Bring my stuff and old Fur-Face, too. And a stock of decent food and liquor." He stretched, easing his aching muscles. It had been a long day, and now it was pitch black outside and the rain was pouring down harder than ever. "I don't suppose I could spend the night here in the cave, could I?"

Do you wish to?

Rogi shrugged. "It feels real good in here. Metasafe! If I'm going to stay on the island, I guess I'll have to ask Malama Johnson to tell me more about this place. Funny thing—when you and I first brought Teresa's ashes here after the funeral Mass at St. Raphael's in the cane fields, Malama seemed to think you'd been here before."

[Laughter.] Kahunas know too much. They are an anomalous type of human metapsychic operant, as any Krondak evaluator will tell you . . . And now, why don't you make yourself something to eat and then get some sleep. I have other matters to attend to and I must leave you for a time. I'll come and collect you in the morning.

"Suit yourself," said Rogi, and opened his backpack.

Even though there was no discernible physical manifestation, the old man was aware that the Family Ghost had abruptly vanished. Shaking his head, Rogi took out packets of gamma-stabilized food and a tiny microwave stove and began to prepare a Kauaian-style supper of chicken-feet appetizers, fried rice, Spam, pineapple upside-down cake, and lilikoi punch. As he ate, the small mystery of why he had been drawn to Kauai also seemed to resolve itself. The birds, of course. The island had always been a magnet for amateur ornithologists like himself.

And like Dorothea Macdonald, the subject of this next part of his memoirs.

It had been *her* doing that brought him here—or perhaps that of her memory abiding deep within his own unconscious. Dorothée. Saint Illusion. The woman who always wore a mask, even in her youth, when her face was bare.

Much later, when he was snug in his sleeping bag and the fire had gone out and the continuing rain had freshened the air, Rogatien Remillard let the tranquil ambiance of Keaku Cave lull him to sleep. The air was fragrant again now that the smoke had dissipated; but oddly enough the scent seemed not to be that of mokihana berries but rather of a certain old-fashioned perfume called Bal à Versailles.

How did I know that? Rogi asked himself drowsily. More huna magic? Or are the Family Ghost and Dorothée still playing games in my head?

A moment later he was fast asleep, dreaming not of the monster named Fury and its attendant Hydras, nor even of Diamond Mask. Instead he dreamed about a woman with silvery eyes and strawberry blonde hair who had first smiled at him on top of Mount Washington in New Hampshire, years before Earth knew that the Galactic Milieu even existed. It was a sweet dream, without remorse.

In the morning, Rogi had forgotten it completely.

[1]

FROM THE MEMOIRS OF ROGATIEN REMILLARD

Unity!

God, how we Earthlings were afraid of it, in spite of all that Paul and Ti-Jean and Dorothée did. Quite a few normals still have their doubts—and so do I. A minority of one: the only uncoadunated meta head still at large.

I'm still a Rebel. The very last unconverted human operant, shunning Unity's consolations, thumbing my nose at the Coadunating Noösphere, evading all that magical, mystical superstuff that the Milieu confers on good little minds who participate in Teilhardian ultracerebration. All the other human operants live in Unity. Even those odd young people—some of them my own kin—who escaped the Pliocene Exile have undergone the initiation and signed on as conditional uniates. But not me. No siree! I'm not much, but what there is, is straight up and 190 proof Everclear.

What's more, the Milieu can't do a thing about it. Up until the reappearance of the Family Ghost and my embarking upon these memoirs, I thought the Unanimity Affirmers had just overlooked me. After all, I'm no high-powered meta, just an unimportant old bookseller making no particular use of my meager powers . . . unless I'm really backed into a bad corner.

But that isn't the reason I escaped.

At this late stage of the game I realize that my apparent immunity was all part of the Family Ghost's plot. I was allowed to evade the Unity net so that the really outrageous deeds I had witnessed or perpetrated wouldn't be exposed to public scrutiny too soon, as they would have been if I had been forced to Affirm and hang out all my mind's dirty laundry during the initiation.

Earlier on, especially during the crucial decades immediately following the Metapsychic Rebellion, the time just wasn't ripe for the revelations contained in these memoirs. The Remillard family—even the ones who were dead or otherwise removed from the chessboard by then—were still too important to the grand game to be accidentally traduced by the likes of me.

Now those considerations are moot. Even the most scandalous doings of my illustrious family can be revealed in these chronicles because the tenure of Atoning Unifex, Overlord of the Lylmik and founder of at least two Galactic Milieux, is finally at an end. I have been assured that uncounted billions of entities as yet unborn will study these processed words of mine, making God knows what of them. I have *not* been told what consequences will fall upon me, their author, once the memoirs are published and the cat's out of the bag.

C'est une bizarrerie formidable, mais c'est comme ça et pas autrement!

And it's probably wiser not to think about it.

[2]

HANOVER, NEW HAMPSHIRE, EARTH
9 MAY 2062

Nineteen days before the murders would take place in Scotland, at a little past two on Tuesday morning, Fury prowled the campus of Dartmouth College.

Only an occasional groundcar moved along North College Road in front of the School of Metapsychology. There were no pedestrians. The elegant buildings of the meta complex were set on a wooded slope, where the spring foliage of spreading sugar maples and tall mutant elms gleamed in the light of old-fashioned iron standard lamps set along paved walkways. At this hour the buildings themselves were mostly dark. There was a single pair of lighted windows in the office block and several more in a line on the second floor of the Cerebroenergetic Research Laboratory further uphill, which had been established less than two years earlier with a generous (and still controversial) endowment by the Remillard Family Foundation.

For a moment Fury paused to survey the scene. Long ago, before the Great Intervention, a ramshackle old gray saltbox building scheduled for imminent demolition had given grudging shelter to the college's infant Department of Metapsychology, and its workers had been regarded with bemusement and a fair amount of uneasiness by fellow academics of more traditional scholarly disciplines. These days, the Dartmouth School of Metapsychology was one of the premier research establishments for higher mindpowers in the Human Polity of the Galactic Milieu, and a favorite object of Fury's scrutiny.

Tonight the monster's mission was more urgent than usual.

Fury proceeded to insinuate itself into the faculty offices. Its virtual presence was imperceptible to the senses of normal people, to the metafaculties of operant humans and exotic beings, and to the sensors of mechanical security systems and janitorial robotics.

19

In the single lighted suite it found Denis Remillard, Dartmouth's nonagenarian Emeritus Professor of Metapsychology and living legend, sound asleep at his desk with his blond head cradled on his arms and his perennially youthful face touched by a gentle smile. He had dozed off while scribbling annotations on a durofilm printout of a chapter for his latest book, *Criminal Insanity in the Operant Mind.* The project had occupied most of the great man's time during the past five years, for reasons that Fury knew only too well.

The MESSAGE WAITING telltale on the desktop communicator was blinking unheeded—perhaps with a plea from the professor's wife, Lucille Cartier, that he come home and go to bed. (Formidable personality that she was, Lucille would never have dared to disturb her husband's work with a telepathic summons.) Denis's dreams, Fury noted, were innocuous, even banal, involving the cultivation of bizarre strains of orchids in his home greenhouse.

The egregious twit!

On another night, Fury might have invaded those dreams to give Denis a personal taste of the horrors madness might evoke in the metapsychic personality . . . but not tonight. There was more urgent business to attend to.

After scrutinizing the newly written book chapter and sneering at the worst of its misperceptions, Fury used the professor's computer terminal to access a highly confidential file of galaxy-wide cerebroenergetic research projects. Having no physical voice, the monster activated the input microphone by means of psychokinesis. It had learned this trick, and certain others, by observing Jack the Bodiless. In an encrypted delete-protected volume tagged RESTRICTED ACCESS: BY ORDER OF HUMAN MAGISTRATUM was an updated précis of the research being done at Edinburgh by Robert and Viola Strachan and Rowan Grant.

Fury studied this data with mounting dismay. Damn them! They were moving in the very direction it had feared. The monster cursed the circumstances that had prevented it from checking out the update sooner. If the Scottish workers managed to publish their findings, there was a good chance that Marc's dicey E15 cerebroenergetic project would be shut down in the ensuing uproar over operator safety.

That would have to be prevented.

Erasing the dangerous data files and replacing them with innocuous material would be easy. Ensuring that the three Scots did not discover the fiddle and raise a flaming row was more difficult—but Fury already had a notion how the problem might be resolved.

First, however, a brief check on the E15's progress.

Eliminating all trace of its illicit access to Denis Remillard's computer, Fury gave the professor a final glance of contempt and then abolished its presence in the administration building. It reappeared an instant later on the second floor of the CE lab. There, inside a chamber crowded with workbenches and racks of apparatus, two scientists were totally absorbed in their work.

The elder was a very tall, powerfully built man twenty-four years of age. His name was Marc Remillard and he was the grandson of the eminent Denis. In addition to holding the Marie-Madeleine Fabré Chair of Cerebroenergetic Research at Dartmouth College, he was conditionally acknowledged to have the most powerful farsensory, metacoercive, and metacreative faculties in the Human Polity. He had just been nominated a Grand Master and Magnate of the Galactic Concilium. His acceptance, as well as the affirmation of his mental status, was still pending.

Fury had yet to decide whether Marc was a true antagonist or a potential ally in its grand scheme.

The enigma sat now at the console of a late-model Xiang analytical micromanipulator, intent upon the holographic display. The command headset of the machine was nearly buried in his untidy black curly hair, and its two short, hornlike antennae projected vertically above his temples, giving him an uncanny resemblance to a young Mephistopheles. His eyes were the luminous gray of brushed steel, set deeply in shadowed orbits, and his brows had a winglike shape, being narrowest just above the distinctive aquiline nose that characterized so many members of the Remillard family. Marc wore a faded green twill shirt over a white cotton turtleneck, a pair of tattered Levi's, and muddy Gokey chukka boots. Caught at the edge of one pocket flap by its barbless hook was a tiny artificial fly that Fury recognized as a Number 18 Black Gnat.

Marc's unofficial colleague, also dressed in grubby outdoor clothing and perched on a high stool, was a ten-year-old boy. From time to time he attempted to explain to his elder brother what he was doing wrong, only to be sedulously ignored. Jon Remillard was a child prodigy, a prochronistic mutant whose intellect was arguably the most powerful of any entity in the Galactic Milieu—always excepting members of the ineffable Lylmik race. Marc and the other members of the Remillard family vacillated between regarding the boy as a potential saint or a world-class pain in the ass. To Fury the wretched child was the Great Enemy who would have to be destroyed eventually, no matter what the cost.

Two rod cases and a pair of battered Orvis tackle bags lay on the floor beside the micromanipulator. The two brothers had evidently come to the lab directly from a session of evening flyfishing, and had felt impelled to burn the midnight oil.

The object of their attention, invisible within the machine, where it was being worked upon by means of microscopic tools controlled by telepathic transmissions from Marc's command headset, was a tiny synorganic intraventricular enhancer. The SIE, less than a millimeter in length, was both a computer and an endocrine-function stimulator. It was designed to be inserted, together with similar units of slightly different design, into the hollow spaces within the human brain. Externally energized SIEs were capable of triggering neurochemical production and causing other profound changes in brain activity, greatly augmenting that organ's own processing abilities. The effect was described by lay people as "mind-boosting," and by metapsychic professionals as cerebroenergetic enhancement.

Fascinated, Fury hovered behind the oddly matched pair and watched the split holodisplay above the console. In the left-hand section was the 200x image of the SIE itself, looking like a gnarled and leafless bush with a myriad of finely looped branchlets. It was hung about with several dozen multicolored objects called electrochemical initiators that bore a resemblance to quaint Christmas ornaments. A single ECI was targeted with a red circle. The further magnified image of this particular device, opened like a Fabergé egg of outlandish design, filled the right-hand side of the display. Tiny testing probes and quasi-living miniature tools guided by Marc's thoughts had latched onto the innards of this minute object. Graphical and numerical analyses of its output flickered continually beside the image as Marc attempted to fine-tune the program of a newly modified gallium-lanthanide operating module that controlled the ECI's complex neurostimulation effects.

"That revision of the glom's not going to mesh with your changes in my SIECOM program," said the ten-year-old, after his brother had completed a certain painstaking adjustment. "Look what's happening to the simulated NMDA functions. They really suck."

"Ferme ta foutue gueule, ti-morveux," Marc said pleasantly. "Je m'en branle de ton opinion."

Distracted for a moment by the fascinating new French obscenity, the boy's face lit up. "You do *what* to my opinion? Shake? . . . No, it means something really filthy! Tell me, Marco! Or just open your mind so I can translate."

Marc's laugh was wicked. "Not a chance, pest." Another level of his mind continued feeding program changes into the ECI.

"Please! It's the very latest fad among Dartmouth undergraduates, cussing in one's ancestral tongue. It's very important that I be au courant in Franco slang. It enhances my prestige and helps compensate for the fact that I'm so much younger than the other freshmen."

"Ask Uncle Rogi. I learned my stuff from him."

"But he won't teach me the really interesting old vulgarisms. He says I'll have to wait until I'm a teenager. And I can't sneak into him to root out the phrases on my own. His mind is curiously impenetrable to redactive infiltration, in spite of the fact that he's such a weak meta otherwise. Of course I'd never coerce him—"

"Quiet! I've nearly got this damned thing ready."

"It's not going to work right. You deviated too far from my original infusion parameters. That's what I've been trying to tell you."

"Programming the ECIs my way will give us more efficient feedback to the third-ventricle SIECOMEX when all twenty-six of these little hummers are cooking. Ah . . . there we are. Finished at last."

"But, Marco—"

Ignoring the child's flood of revisionary expostulation, Marc's mind said to the machine: Integrate and consolidate all modifications. Open test path to SIECOMEX. Energize. Ready for Mode One ECI operational simulation. And now *GO* you bastard!

The boy shook his head gloomily as the analyzer began its model cerebroenergetic operation. "You'll get better feedback, all right, but you'll also mess up the brain's limbic functions—destabilize the model CE operator's mental equilibrium as his creativity is enhanced. Look where the NMDA factor's going! You know that this config of the E15 is already marginal for operator safety. Your cobble is going to push it right smack over the edge."

"Give it a chance, dammit! It's only started to run."

But after only three minutes of simulation had passed, the projection showed that any CE operator whose analog brain held the modified SIE would suffer acute schizophrenia—and very likely have epileptic seizures as well.

Fury bespoke an imperceptible curse.

Marc groaned and said, "Welcome to Shit City."

The little boy said, "I told you so. The simulation's going into grand mal and it's crazy as a bedbug."

Marc halted the test, took off the command headset, and massaged his aching temples. "It looks like you were right after all, shrimp. I was trying for too much, too fast in this configuration . . . I should have stuck to the original concept you dreamed up on the river this evening instead of trying to embroider it. Now we're well and truly fucked. Nearly five hours of work wasted."

"Just backtrack," the child urged. "Kill the divagination starting from CAH Path 83.4. We'll still be able to crank up creativity by a factor of more than thirty if we reprogram the glom and fix the ECI infusors my way."

Marc glanced at his wrist-chronograph and flinched. "My God, look at the time. Almost half past two, and you've got three seminars tomorrow! Grandmère Lucille's going to kill me if she ever finds out I kept you up so late. We'll have to pack it in, kiddo, and get you back to the dormitory. You can do your own mind-wipe of the proctors."

The boy's face crumpled in disappointment. "I *really* want to see if this will work, and you know I always get more sleep than I really need. Let me take the comset! I can do the fix lots faster than you can. Please!"

"Oh, no you don't. You know you're not supposed to use this equipment. Officially, you're only an observer in this lab, even if Tom Spotted Owl did give you free run of the place."

"Uncle Tom'll never know. And it's not as if we were really doing anything wrong. It's only a technical infringement of college regulations. Not even as bad as my staying out after hours."

As Marc hesitated, Fury damned the young scientist's puritanical rectitude, together with the stubborn pride that did not want to concede that his little brother had been right after all. The monster was as keenly interested in seeing whether this experiment succeeded as the abominable child was. Its own long-range plans required that powerful new cerebroenergetic equipment be available to its Hydra component; and if these two had actually achieved a major breakthrough with the E15, then it would be imperative to squelch the Scottish spoilers immediately.

Might metacoercion work on Marc? His brain was deeply fatigued after hours of unrelenting concentration and possibly vulnerable— given that the violation of his principles was so minor. Although the Great Enemy had never been allowed to use the micromanipulator, he knew every nuance of its complex operation even better than Marc did. There was no danger that the child might damage the equipment or harm himself.

Fury said: < *Give Jack the machine's comset.* >

Marc blinked, then uttered a weary expletive and handed over the command headset to the little boy. He started to rise from his seat in front of the console.

With a crow of glee, Jack hopped from his stool. "Just stay there, Marco. You don't have to get up. I'm going to de-bod so I can give the job my full concentration!"

Marc sat immobile, his face expressionless and his mind tightly shuttered, as Jon Remillard—Jack the Bodiless—began blithely to disincarnate before his eyes.

Jack had been born with the body of a normal infant, but before he reached three years of age his mutant genes accomplished a metamorphosis that was both ghastly and wonderful. Leaping millions of years of evolution, he became what other members of the human race would eventually become in the far distant future: a being Marc had dubbed Mental Man. Neither Marc nor any other person knew how the little boy felt about his unique condition; he had always cheerfully deflected any inquiries into his fundamental mind-set or mental health, and he was immune to mechanical or metapsychic probing. Only a handful of people outside the Remillard family knew of Jack's awesome condition, for while his intellect was prodigious, emotionally and socially he was still a child, with a child's emotional vulnerability.

Jack had instinctively clothed himself in the guise of normal humanity from the time that his mutation stabilized. The disguise served to spare the sensitivities of others as much as to keep him from being shunned as an inhuman freak. He maintained a simulacrum of human shape nearly all of the time, even when he slept. But sometimes—most notably with his older brother Marc and with his eccentric great-granduncle Rogi—the boy let himself assume his true form.

Jack's disincarnation was a phenomenon that Marc had witnessed many times before, but he had never managed to get used to it.

Fury found it supremely disgusting—especially when compared to its own ingenious reification procedure.

"You keep those damn volatile sulfur compounds under control this time," Marc warned the child. "I'm in no mood for a pong-up. And for God's sake, no puddles on the floor or gooey blobs floating around in the air. Keep your shit together so you can take out what you came in with when we leave here."

"I'll be neat, I promise."

Jack's clothing, unfastened by psychokinesis, fell away. Then his realistic shell of pseudoflesh—the warm skin, the black wavy hair, the eyes, teeth, fingernails, and all that his unrivaled metacreativity had concocted from air, atmospheric water vapor, dust, and other odds and ends—became tenuous and ectoplasmic. His body streamed and dripped away like thick fog, the internal quasi-organs needed for certain imitative human activities dissolved, and his face melted into smoky wisps, with the excited grin and the bright blue eyes lingering longest.

In moments, the discarded solid and liquid portion of Jack's corporeal envelope re-formed into a gently quivering pinkish spheroid of organic soup about the size of a large grapefruit. It rested on the laboratory floor, right between a pair of small empty sneakers with muddy socks still in them. What remained of the boy, suspended in midair and looking mysteriously elegant rather than repulsive, was a glistening, silvery-gray naked brain that housed a mind preeminently operant in all of the metafaculties. In this form Jack processed input only through his ultrasenses, communicated via telepathy, and acted by means of psychokinesis and the metacreative function. His life-processes were self-sustained redactively by direct interaction with the atmosphere and photons of light. Jack the Bodiless was invulnerable to most injury, immune to disease, and could, at any time, refashion for himself a new human form or any other material housing that struck his fancy.

Fury could neither inflict physical damage upon Jack nor penetrate his perfect mental screen with a coercive-redactive ream. Nevertheless, if this experiment succeeded, the first step in the ultimate destruction of the Great Enemy would have been taken.

The micromanipulator comset that had been hovering above the floating brain settled into place. Since the device had a noninvasive brainboard interface and could respond to thought input, it was as easy for Jack to use as it was for an embodied person.

Nervous telepathic giggles bubbled in the aether. Jack said: First the wipe & then TheBigTweak!!!

He began the modification and the holographic imagery of the improperly modified ECI seemed to go wild. Displays indicating the progress of the work turned into a featureless blur as tools darted in and out of nowhere at lightning speed, plucking at the electrochemical unit, tearing it down and building it up again. Microscopic organelle supply-slaves zipped hither and yon in the fluid of the model brain ventricle like demented bacteria, carrying tiny bits and pieces for insertion or disposal. When the ECI modification was finished, a glom command fleck completely reprogrammed by Jack through molecular-beam epitaxy was married to the SIE's central processor.

Marc watched incredulously as the operations that had taken him hours to accomplish were done in less than twenty minutes by his mutant brother. His admiration was frankly tinged by the envy that had lately begun to undermine the compassion he felt for young Jack's grotesque physical condition. Was Mental Man really to be pitied—or was *he*, the embodied one, the true unfortunate? What would it be like to be free of nearly all of the body's needs and limitations? To be able to channel all vital energies toward cerebration? Jack did require a limited amount of sleep, but most of his other physical functions were automatic. When he wore a body, he ate and drank only to be sociable.

He never experienced physical pain because he had not bothered to fashion the receptors within his pseudoflesh. His mind's function was hardly ever skewed or limited by the biochemical deterioration that occurred in an ordinary person's body during the course of a day's work. He would never be driven to irrational actions by turbulent sex hormones—

Jack said: There that's done let's run a full Mode2 simulation shall we?

"Yes," said Marc aloud. "Go ahead with a regular helmet test." Whatthehell we might as well know whether we've got a hot new CErig here or just another bloodybonkerbucket.

In actual operation, a complete set of the newly redesigned SIEs would be incorporated into a CE helmet having an external energy source. When a person donned the helmet and gave the proper telepathic command, his skull and cerebral tissue would be penetrated by a series of hair-thin electrodes nicknamed the "crown of thorns," the tips of which would come to rest within the cerebral and diencephalic ventricles, three fluid-filled hollow places in the operator's brain. The drilling procedure was only minimally uncomfortable as the scalp was pierced, since the brain itself was insensitive to pain. At another command, 26 SIEs with their two supervisory SIECOM units would emerge from the electrode-tips and bloom within the right and left lateral ventricles. A single master SIECOMEX unit would unfold within the third ventricle, above the brainstem. When the CE equipment energized, the operator's mental potential would, in theory, be greatly multiplied. Unfortunately, certain other brain activities might also be augmented by improperly tuned implants, leading to side effects that ranged from mildly annoying to fatal. The risk to the CE operator increased in direct proportion to the amount of mental enhancement generated by the equipment, especially in metacreativity designs.

When Jack the Bodiless began his test, the image of the newly modified SIE tree with its baroque ornaments seemed to glow within its bath of artificial cerebrospinal fluid. Responding to Jack's initiation command, the single unit triggered a complex flood of mind-boosting neurosecretions to a model operator-brain roughly equal in mental assay to that of a grandmasterclass operant. For a few seconds, the executive processor let the new cerebroenergetic enhancement "cook," activating certain portions of the cerebral cortex that were ordinarily unused. Then the SIECOMEX phased in the equivalent of 25 additional SIE units also having the modification. At this point Jack commanded the fully equipped brain simulation to evaluate itself in the metacreativity mode, and the most critical part of the test began.

Marc said: Neurometrics looking good mondingofrelot damngood.

Jack said: Limbics okay this time both hemispheres syncing on creative parameters feedback beautiful I'm going to ask for the overall evaluation now Marco letusPRAY!!

The holodisplay changed abruptly to a flickering mass of graphical analysis that almost defied Marc's ability to keep up with it. In less than six minutes, the analyzer simulated an hour of CE equipment use by a metapsychic operant of high mental status. While there was increasing minor dysfunction in certain areas, the psychoresultant showed an upgrade in creative metafaculty output somewhat greater than Jack had originally anticipated.

IT WORKS! shrieked the enraptured boy-mind.

"Yes," Marc said. "It certainly does. In theory." He watched the continuing simulation for some time with a slight, one-sided smile. Then he reached out and shut down the machine. "The new design is practicable and all I have to do is build it and tune it and test it on a meat-brain."

How long do you think that'll take?

Marc shrugged. "Seven months—maybe less. I'll be the guinea pig, of course."

ME TOO pleaseMarcoPLEASE—

"Don't be silly. You can help with the helmet design work in your spare time, but that's all. Testing this new rig will be dangerous and expensive, and there are also tricky political considerations that'll need juggling. The college administrators are getting more and more antsy about the project."

But—

"Don't argue! You're only a kid, Jack. A brilliant and talented and bizarro kid—but in the eyes of the law and of Dartmouth College you have no business messing around with hazardous equipment. Now put yourself back together again and let's get the hell out of here."

29

. . .

Fury paid no attention as Jack the Bodiless reassumed his former aspect of a ten-year-old child. Jubilant at what it had just witnessed, the monster had already abolished its presence in the laboratory and was soaring eastward over the Atlantic Ocean toward the British Isles, indulging in delicious speculation.

Until now, the practical applications of cerebroenergetics had been relatively prosaic, and not particularly useful to Fury. For over half a century, simple CE devices had been used for recreational romps in various virtual-reality environments; but the potentially addictive amusements were now hedged about with legal restrictions and forbidden to children altogether, while CE equipment incorporating more elaborate technology was widely utilized, even by normals, for specialized education and for operating sophisticated machinery.

CE augmentation of the metapsychic functions was still in its infancy, however. It was a uniquely human endeavor that the five other races of the Milieu viewed with both awe and misgiving. Exotic critics judged the new technology to be just one more way for upstart humanity to endanger the stability of the Galactic Mind.

Redactive CE was sometimes used by operants performing delicate psychosurgery or retroevolutionary genetic engineering. Psychokinetic boosting had been applied to macromolecular synthesis and complex nanotechnology such as the building of elaborate electronic, photonic, or bionic flecks. Lately, even more powerful "barber-chair" CE requiring life support as well as brain implantation had been used to boost the mental capacity of PK operants working on subatomic projects. Similar equipment, potentially very hazardous to the operator, had been used by farsensory adepts probing the gray limbo of hyperspace in search of experimental evidence for the three hypothetical "matrix fields" that were believed to form the ultimate basis of reality.

Significant augmenting of the creative metafunction, the higher mindpower that might theoretically have the greatest impact upon the physical universe, was thought by many Milieu authorities to be of dubious potential, not only because of the inherently grave risk to the mind utilizing the technology, but also on account of the danger of misapplication.

The latter, of course, was what most intrigued Fury.

Marc Remillard had no doubts whatsoever about the practicability of creativity enhancement. He had experimented with different types of brain-boosting for years, and he persisted with his research into the far frontiers of creativity magnification when more conservative workers in the CE field held back. His work was given academic respectability under the aegis of Dartmouth College, and the papers he published were acknowledged to be brilliant. But certain powerful faculty members of the Department of Metapsychology had objected strenuously to the E15 project on ethical grounds, also intimating that young Professor Marc Remillard was arrogant, high-handed, contemptuous of his more prudent colleagues, and insufficiently sensitive to the metapsychic Pandora's box his work might open.

Marc pooh-poohed the timidity of his critics while loftily ignoring slights to his character. Greatly enhanced creativity was not for every mind, that went without saying. In his opinion, only the most powerful grandmasterclass operants of proven mental stability were suitable candidates. As for the ethical questions, he maintained that they could be confronted and dealt with once the E15 equipment was operable, at the time that individual CE creativity projects were proposed. It was the *misuse* of the technology, not the technology itself, that might be adjudged immoral. Application guidelines should be and would be developed for creativity augmentation, just as they had been developed for nuclear energy and even for metafunction itself, which had posed similar ethical problems.

When Jack the Bodiless became secretly involved in the experiments of his elder brother, he confessed that he was seriously concerned about the moral dilemma; but he was only a child, after all, with limited experience in matters of good and evil in spite of his towering intellect. Marc's arguments in favor of the E15 research had been very persuasive.

It had taken the two strangely compatible colleagues a little over a year to proceed from bare-bones theory to this monumental breakthrough. Beyond a doubt they would now continue to work together unofficially, attaining even greater success in times to come.

Fury was quite proud of the brothers, even though they were flawed and unlovable. All unawares they had furthered the monster's grand scheme.

If only Fury could have used the new CE technology itself! But that was a fundamental impossibility, since the entity presently lacked a genuine physical presence, being even less substantial than the Lylmik. It was Fury's Hydra component, tucked away in a safe corner of Earth for a number of years while slowly maturing, that would be the proper beneficiary of creativity enhancement.

Wearing this new E15 helmet, even nonoperants might find their natural creative gifts producing novel inventions, worthy artwork, or spectacular stratagems for altruism or villainy—provided that the brain of the operator was strong enough to withstand the device's potential. A metapsychic possessing strong natural creativity, as the Hydra-units did, would be able to accomplish deeds that normal humans would deem godlike: complex material synthesis; geophysical alteration; massive ionic accumulation, discharge, and control. Transforming matter into directed energy would be child's play to such an operator, who would command the equivalent of a gigawatt mental laser.

The Hydra would eventually have to increase and multiply in order to take full advantage of the breakthrough, but that was also part of Fury's great plan. After suitable training, the CE-equipped creature, acting in metaconcert with Fury, need utilize no other weapons save its augmented multiplex brain in order to destroy the present galactic confederation and establish a Second Milieu . . .

Provided that this new E15 technology was not suppressed by meddling regulatory officials, to die aborning.

The Scottish threat to Marc's project, the nearly completed adverse statistical report on long-term CE operator safety that would very likely bring *all* human creativity-boosting research to an abrupt halt, must now be neutralized without delay.

Obliterating the data was not the answer. The Edinburgh team would simply reconstruct it. There was only one way to make certain that Marc's project was not endangered: all three of the Scottish researchers would have to die. And Hydra, Fury's creature and its only safe link to the matter/energy-space/time lattices, was the only one who could do the job.

Taking out three masterclass metapsychics without a trace was well within the Hydra's competence; but it would still be a tricky operation, especially if it was done in the environs of the University of Edinburgh, that teeming hive of leery and powerful Celtic operants. A misstep (the Hydra-units were still very young and overconfident, and some sort of cock-up was all too likely) and the creature itself might be imperiled.

That would be totally unacceptable. Fury was severely limited in the physical sphere without Hydra, and its work was further complicated by periods of enforced dormancy. As a matter of fact, the present window of activity was about to close, and soon Fury would have to withdraw; but there was time yet to set Hydra on the track of its prey.

Clever, precious Hydra! The units were twenty-two years of age now, and while they had not stinted in supplying themselves with their primary source of mental nourishment, the killings had been done at decent intervals with admirable ingenuity. No suspicion had ever fallen upon the four disguised entities. The Hydra now was well educated, polished to a reasonably sophisticated luster, and very nearly ready to operate in the arena of the Galactic Milieu.

This particular executive action would be good training for similar exercises in the future. The three Scottish researchers would have to be lured out of their sanctuary at the university, then eliminated without a trace. Once they were gone and their data destroyed, Marc would face no significant opposition to his project. No other CE safety-study groups on Earth or on human colonial planets posed any imminent danger.

The monster hovered above the British Isles for some time, studying various aspects of the situation together with the dramatis personae involved. Then at last it called.

< Hydra! Dear little one, listen! I have wonderful news for you. >

Fury? . . . FuryFurydearestFury is it YOU after allthistime?

< Yes my little love it is I. >

But what happened not single word from you not a farsqueak for more than 3years!

< My silence was necessary. And you were busy enough with your education. >

But Godalmighty 3years 3friggingyears I thought you'd forgotten ME/us thought your grandscheme was ruined thought the GreatEnemy might have won thought UncleFred/you might *really* have died—

<Be silent. I shall never die and I shall never stop loving you and caring for you as long as you follow my commands faithfully. This long exile of yours and even my silence was necessary but now it is about to come to an end. My grand scheme for a Second Milieu has received a great thrust forward.>

!!Tell ME/us!!

<I shall. And even better—soon you will have a great feast. A feast of *masterclass* operant lifeforce! Open your MIND/minds in welcome for I am here and ready to lead you to the consummate joy.>

[3]

INNER HEBRIDES, SCOTLAND, EARTH, 25–26 MAY 2062

During the brief rhocraft flight from Edinburgh to the west coast of Scotland, the five-year-old child who called herself Dee studied the durofilm sea chart that Gran Masha had given her. They were going to travel to their holiday destination in a very special way—not in an ordinary inertialess egg-bus but on an old-fashioned ferryboat nearly a hundred years old.

From the air, the boat looked like a strange toy, its contours dimmed by mist; but then the egg landed at the dockside pad and Dee and the others disembarked and were able to see the ancient vessel closely. It was huge, looming there in the drizzle, as unlike the small pleasure boats of Granton Harbour near Dee's home as Edinburgh Castle is unlike a regular townhouse. The ferry had a scarlet funnel and a black-and-white hull and an earsplitting whistle that echoed from shore to shore in the rainswept narrow sea-loch. It seemed to urge those on shore to get aboard quickly or be left behind.

Mummie took one of Dee's hands and Aunt Rowan took the other. Loudspeakers on the ferry broadcast an eerie bagpipe melody as they went up the gangplank. Tall, imposing Gran Masha in her smart green tweed walking suit led the way, towing Dee's brother Ken, and Uncle Robbie brought up the rear carrying their bags.

"This is weird," Ken said, as they all arrived on the wet and windy deck. Pennants were flapping, passengers in raingear were laughing and taking pictures, and a ship's officer was directing people to move along. "Maybe," the boy added, "we'll have a good time on this holiday after all."

"An inquiring mind," said Mummie tartly, "will find things to enjoy no matter what place it finds itself in."

"It's going to be fun," Gran Masha declared. She gave Ken's hand an encouraging squeeze and smiled at Dee, who cringed as the ferryboat whistle gave another deafening hoot. Then the gangplank rose, the mooring lines were cast off, and they were on their way.

Groundcars bound for the Western Isles had been driven up a ramp into the hold and abandoned there; but the humans and the handful of exotic tourists making the voyage rode in the upper part of the ferryboat, where there were places to eat, and places to sit and look out of the windows at the gray sea, and a game room, and a souvenir store, and even tiny cabins to sleep in if you were traveling to one of the Outer Hebrides that were depicted on Dee's chart, all connected to each other and to the Inner Hebrides and to the mainland of Scotland by a web of red lines that signified the Vee-routes of the egg transports. Only a handful of the Western Isles were served by the picturesque old ferries, whose routes were shown by black dots.

One of those islands was Islay.

By the time Dee and Ken finished exploring the vessel with Uncle Robbie and rejoined the three women, who had settled down with coffee in the spacious forward saloon, the ferryboat had come to the end of the protected waters of West Loch Tarbert and entered the rough open sea. The deck began to tilt in an alarming fashion, huge waves rolled past like gray mountains on the march, and the Scottish mist changed to heavy rain that splattered the saloon windows as though a giant hose had been turned on.

Ken thought that was exciting. "Maybe this big old tub will sink, and we'll get to ride in the lifeboats!"

"The ferry will not sink," Mummie said firmly. "Don't be ridiculous, Kenneth."

Dee was terrified that her older brother might be right. Gripping the arm of a seat to keep from losing her balance, she felt her stomach give an ominous leap. She took a deep breath and commanded it to stop that. No one must suspect how frightened she was!

Ken asked how long the trip would take. "Only two hours," said Robert Strachan. "It's about fifty kloms from the terminal at Kennacraig to Port Askaig on the eastern shore of Islay where we'll be landing."

"I hope the rain lets up soon," Rowan Grant murmured. Like her husband, she wore a rain-resistant grintlaskin sportsuit. Hers was wine-colored and his was royal blue with white stripes up the arms and legs. Petite Viola Strachan was more elegantly dressed in gray woolen slacks, a black silk blouse, and a repelvel Burberry.

"The forecast promises fair skies by this afternoon," said Masha.

"I still wish we'd gone to the Elizabethan Immersive Pageant," Ken said. But his mother cut him off, handing him a credit card.

"That's quite enough, Kenneth. You and Dody may go and get something to eat if you wish. Or find someplace to sit and read the guide-plaques you brought. We grownups have some academic matters to discuss in private."

"Oh, boy! Food! Come on, Dee!"

Ken went lurching off happily, but Dee felt much too queasy to eat. Her stomach was not obeying her order to behave itself and she was becoming dizzy as well. Fortunately, Mummie and the others never noticed her distress. She was very glad of that. It would be inconsiderate to bother them when they wanted to talk about really important things. While her brother headed for the ferry snack bar, she crept away to the other side of the passenger saloon and huddled alone in a leather seat. She had with her a small plaque with two book flecks installed, one a descriptive guide of the island and the other entitled *Birds in Islay*, with an electronic notebook for entering species observed. She loved birds, especially the bold merlins and kestrels and peregrines that were common in the countryside around Edinburgh. Gran Masha had said that they might catch sight of a sea eagle on Islay, and there would surely be many other interesting birds to look at—razorbills, puffins, and fierce skuas.

A few gulls accompanied the ferryboat now, dodging easily among the enormous ocean swells, but Dee felt too ill to look in her book and identify them. She had never seen such monstrous waves, like heaving crags streaked with foam. At first she waited, stiff with dread, for one of them to crash down on the boat and kill them all, praying to her guardian angel to take her to heaven when she died. But none of the big waves ever broke over the rail. The ferry rolled and wallowed and creaked, but it kept pounding sturdily onward, miraculously immune from being swamped, while the jaunty birds soared alongside and Dee felt more and more dazed and miserable.

I'll die, she thought. Or even worse—I'll spit up my breakfast and everyone will call me a baby! Oh, angel, help me.

She clung to the chair-arms with white-knuckled hands. There was a sour taste in her throat and the giddiness was getting worse.

I won't throw up! I won't! I won't . . .

Ken was suddenly there, holding a glass of ginger beer. "Gran Masha says this'll help calm your stomach." He held out the drink.

"My—my stomach is fine," she mumbled mulishly. Only troublesome children complained.

"Come on. Take it. You must be broadcasting subliminal barf-vibes. Those three Gi sitting over there came twittering to Mummie and said that her poor darling little girl was getting ready to toss her cookies. Gran called me on my wrist-com and told me to bring you this."

On the far side of the saloon, near where Mummie and the others sat, engrossed in telepathic conversation, the trio of friendly long-necked nonhumans waved their silly feathered arms at Dee and whooped and simpered.

Chagrin at being betrayed darkened the girl's eyes. "It's none of *their* business how I feel. The hateful snoopy-minded things."

"Gi are supersensitive to emotions. You're probably making them feel like woofing their custard, too. Come on, drink this."

Ken was two years older than Dee. The lank hair falling over his brow was the color of oatmeal porridge, and his brown eyes seemed too large for his waxen, fine-featured face. He wore corduroy trousers tucked into Nesna lobben-boots and a thick Fair Isle sweater. He had left his tan anorak with the grownups.

Dee took tiny sips of the spicy, bubbling ginger beer, but it only seemed to make the nausea worse. Any minute now, she was surely going to vomit and disgrace herself. "If only the boat would stop tipping from side to side," she moaned. "Then I'd be all right."

"You think this is bad?" Ken gestured at the rampaging sea. "You'd feel a million times worse if you were on a starship popping in and out of hyperspace. You probably don't remember, but Mum says you squalled like a piglet during every limbo-leap on the trip from Caledonia to Earth."

"I was only a little baby then. And I bet *you* cried twice as much, you rotten old dumb doofus!"

Ken shrugged and flashed a gap-toothed grin. "Look," he said kindly. "I read about motion sickness. It's all in your head. Your inner ear is sending wrongo signals to your brainstem's upchuck switch because it thinks you're off-balance and not in control of your environment. What you gotta do is show the brain that you *are* still in control. Take a good gargle of your beer and redact the pukes away."

"I can't," she sobbed miserably. "I already tried. You know my mindpowers are no good."

Ken bent closer. "That's not true. We've both got really strong powers even if we're latent, and sometimes they *can* be used if we really need them. Especially redacting—the healing power. Try hard. I did once and it worked for me."

Dee stared at him through bleared, skeptical eyes.

"When I was really small," he continued, "I used to wheeze and pant all the time. It was a thing called asthma. Sometimes I could hardly breathe. Do you remember?"

Dee shook her head listlessly.

"I didn't think you would. I got it just after we first came to Earth. I took medicine and a Master Redactor tried to cure me, but it didn't help much. The doctor said something deep inside my mind was causing it. The asthma was really bad. I couldn't run or play ball or anything without losing my breath. Then one night when I was about your age I woke up all of a sudden feeling like I was strangling. I couldn't breathe at all. My eyes were popping out of my head and I saw all sorts of spinning crazy lights and I kicked and tried to yell and no sound came."

"And then what?"

"I started to die."

Dee felt her chest constrict. She discovered that she was holding her own breath, willy-nilly. For a moment, her churning stomach was almost forgotten. "How did you know?"

Ken was whispering. "I stopped hurting and choking and I went floating up like a kite. I could still see me down below in my bed thrashing around and turning blue, but—*I really wasn't there.* I was going away to die. It felt soooo good! . . . But then I remembered that Uncle Robbie was taking me to a grownup rugger game the next day, and I decided I didn't want to die after all. I got mad and I told myself, Cut that out! You can breathe if you really want to. No more of this stupid asthma shit. No more!"

"What happened?"

"I saw my body heave this big sigh and stop flopping about. Then all of a sudden there was a kind of no-noise explosion and I was back in bed. Sucking in air. The asthma was gone. *And it never came back.* Mum and Gran said I cured it with self-redaction." He poked her midsection with one finger. "You can do the same thing, Sis. You really can. Try!"

Dee squeezed her eyes shut, shaking her head wildly. She was afraid to do as Ken asked. The grownups were always trying to make her use her latent higher mindpowers—trying to push their way into her mind, too, so they could *force* her to be operant. But even though she was a precocious and obedient child who tried very hard not to be trouble-some and inconvenient, she had always resisted giving in to the adults in this very personal matter. What was hidden in her mind belonged to her, even if it was scary. The only way she could keep herself safe was to make sure that no one else ever got inside and messed about with what was there.

She thought of the innermost part of her head as a dark and secret cellar full of strange boxes with special locks on them, the kind that wouldn't open until you spoke a code word to their tiny internal computers. Inside the boxes, which were glassy but not quite transpar-ent, were all the awful mindpowers that Mummie and the meta thera-pists had tried in vain to coerce out of her during the painful therapy sessions. The imprisoned powers shone dimly in different colors—blue, yellow, green, violet, rose—and moved about within their boxes like ghostly and dangerous sea creatures trapped in murky containers, darting at her in treacherous appeal, squirming and scrabbling against the walls of their traps like blobby, glowing starfish or demonic hands.

The angel kept her safe from them. This friendly guardian was invisible even to her mind's eye and quite mute; but Dee was certain that he was the custodian of the dangerous boxes. They were hers and there was no getting rid of them, but the angel was the one who prevented the things inside from escaping and harming her.

Only once, long before she had found out about guardian angels, when she was still a toddling baby terrified by the adult minds trying to batter their way in and control her, had she dared to open one of those mysterious containers. *Someone* (it was a while before she realized who!) had told her the secret word enabling her to free the cool, midnight-blue shielding faculty. The power had seemed to flow out and enclose her entire mind and body like an impervious, completely transparent shell, protecting her from mental attackers.

By now the faculty—which the frustrated preceptor-therapists told her was called the self-defensive aspect of metacoercion—was so much a part of her that she hardly noticed it. She had overheard Mummie and the other adults talking about her mental screen once, saying how different it was from Ken's puny one, marveling at how wonderfully strong it was, and how it must be guarding other metafaculties of hers that were probably even more amazing . . . if they could just discover how to pry them out of her.

But she knew her latent powers were more than amazing. They were terrible, and they must never be allowed to escape. No matter how the therapists and Mummie tried, hurting her for what they said was "her own good," Dee resisted their attempts to invade her and open the other boxes. The things inside were hers, not theirs, and so was the angel who guarded them. She didn't want to be an operant like Mummie. Nobody could make her do what she didn't want to do.

Especially not Mummie.

Ken said softly, "You stupid pillock—she doesn't even have to know. None of 'em have to know! Just do it for yourself. Open the self-redaction box and keep the power . . . inside."

Dee almost screamed out loud from shock and terror. Ken had heard her thoughts!

"Well, I could hardly help it, could I, the way you were howling at me."

She opened her eyes. He sat on the edge of a seat facing her, and his eyes were wide and black. He knew about the boxes, knew she had deliberately shut the adults out when they tried to force her into operancy. What else did he know?

She cried: *Stop looking and listening! I just want you to leave me alone! I want everybody to leave me alone!*

He backed away from her, as shocked as she was by the unexpected telepathic transmissions on his intimate mode. "Okay, okay! You let your screen crack while you were thinking about those things. I couldn't help hearing. Then your mind almost knocked my socks off shrieking at me."

"Can you read my mind now?" she whispered suspiciously. She was back in control.

"No. No more than you can read mine. We're *not* True People, Sis. We're deadheads. The farspeak and the other stuff only works when it feels like it—not when we want it to." He got up and moved away, taking his drink. "But I'm not like the others, you know."

She watched him go. He had told the truth. He was a terrible tease, but unlike the grownups, he never pushed her to do things that hurt or frightened her. He was just Big Brother Ken—sometimes rude, very often snotty and superior. But never a threat.

Cautiously (for she was still buffeted by the whirlpool of motion sickness) she descended into the mental cellar. She greeted the angel and contemplated the boxes.

Yes, Ken was right. If she opened only the smallest rosy-glowing box, the one that now throbbed so eagerly, the redactive power she set free would behave as the friendly blue mind-screen had, remaining safe within her head. No one would ever notice if she redacted only herself—except maybe the grockly old Gi, and there were never too many of them around to worry about. Most Big Birds were too daft and giggly to teach or study at Edinburgh University, unlike the Green Leakie Freakies and the Wee Purple Poopers and the horrible Krondak monsters, who seemed to be all over the place. But those other kinds of exotics couldn't see past her mind's blue mask any more than True People could, so she would be safe most of the time.

. . . I will be safe, won't I, angel?

But he did not reply. He never did, even though she was quite convinced of his existence. The angel was mute. She would have to decide all by herself.

She took a deep breath. She said to the angel:

Yes. I'll do it! No more seasickness, no more painful latency therapy, no more colds, no more hurting when I stub my toe or fall down and skin my knees because *you* forgot to look after me! My new power will be able to fix all kinds of things like that. And no one but you and I and Ken will ever know.

How stupid she had been not to think of this before! But when you were five years old, you couldn't help doing a lot of stupid things, even though the grownups said you were a mental prodigy.

She reached for the imaginary box with the shining red thing inside and touched it with a trembling, imaginary finger. The secret code word revealed itself to her in an instant. It was not a word a person said. You had to think it.

She did. And the rosy squirming thing slipped joyously from its prison and swelled and grew, becoming as beautiful as a gigantic flower with shining petals. The rose enfolded her, turned to liquid light, to a calm lake glowing in the sunset that washed away all her sickness. She floated on it, completely at peace, and closed her eyes. Through closed lids, she was aware of the redness brightening, becoming dazzling white, becoming part of her. She felt no more fear, no more discomfort, no more helplessness. The new power belonged to her and filled her with its healing warmth. It was good.

She opened her eyes, lowered her feet to the carpeted deck, and got up. She stood there easily, letting her body sway and compensate for the motion of the ferry. Her self-redactive metafunction let her take complete command.

Ears, listen to me! I'm not off balance and I'm not going to fall. I'm just fine. Do you hear that, brain? You can stop telling my stomach it has to throw up. Nothing is wrong. I'm going to Islay on holiday, and I'm not going to be sick or even afraid anymore.

Do you understand me, brain? I will tell you what to do.

You will not tell me.

Every trace of the seasickness was gone.

Dee looked at Ken and nodded solemnly. Smiling, he gave her the thumbs-up sign. On the far side of the saloon, the three outlandish Gi were yoo-hooing and fluting incomprehensible things at her. They probably knew! But Mummie and Gran Masha had blank faces, as they always did whenever Dee or Ken made any sort of a scene, while Uncle Robbie and Aunt Rowan and the other human operants among the passengers looked puzzled. Dee was certain that they had no idea what had happened. She would never tell and she would make certain that Ken didn't tell either, or she would hate him as long as he lived!

Dee went to the nearest door leading to the ferry's outer deck, slid it open, and quickly went outside.

The rain had stopped. There were six or seven bundled-up adults standing at the ship's rail. Herring gulls and blackbacks soared overhead calling, and sunlight was beginning to pierce the ragged clouds. Ahead, two large islands loomed above the choppy sea. The one on the right was stark, rocky, and dramatic, with two glistening conical mountains humping up from the interior. The one on the left was gently rolling and its slopes were a brilliant green. Oddly, there were peaceful vibes coming from the place with the weird mountains, while the prettier island seemed to have a faint aura of menace.

Which one, Dee wondered, activating her plaque-book, was Islay?

Hydra's laying of the groundwork for the fateful trip had been flawless.

When Professor Masha MacGregor-Gawrys returned home to Edinburgh after six months of bodily rejuvenation, her mental screen was understandably a bit woolly at first, easily penetrated by the subtle coercive-redactive ream that the Hydra knew how to use so well. The idea for taking a brief holiday that came stealing into her mind through the tiny aperture was both gratifying and pleasant, and Masha accepted it as her own without demur.

Hydra withdrew from the professor's unconscious and patiently orchestrated the next step in its plan.

A few days later, Masha held a small tea party in her townhouse in the Willowbrae district of Edinburgh and invited those who were closest to her—her daughter-in-law Viola Strachan, Viola's gifted children Dorothea and Kenneth Macdonald, Viola's brother Robert Strachan, and Robbie's wife Rowan Grant.

Also attending, but unnoticed by the professor and her guests, was the Hydra.

Masha served little crustless sandwiches, homemade spongecake and sweet whipped cream, and scones with butter and raspberry jam. She and the others sat round a cheery fire eating and drinking while rain rattled on the new leaves of the plane trees outside the sitting-room window . . . and on the roof of the Bentley groundcar parked across the square, where the Hydra lurked and watched with its farsight.

It took some time for the two children to get over their surprise at the remarkable change in their grandmother's appearance. When they had last seen her half a year ago she was very old—fifty-two!—but now she seemed to be younger than Mummie. She no longer looked tired and wrinkled, and her tall frame was straight and slender instead of slumping and slightly too large for her clothes. Her hair, in the familiar coronet of braids, now shone like polished copper. Only her dry voice and her vivid emerald eyes, glowing with metapsychic power, seemed the same.

Dutifully, Dee and Ken told Gran Masha what they had been doing in school during the months she had floated switch-off in the regen-tank. Ken had won a prize for a story he had written, and he produced this and read it aloud to judicious appreciation. Then, prompted by Viola, Dee admitted that she had begun taking lessons on the scrollo keyboard. When Viola insisted, she unrolled the instrument, pecked out "Loch Lomond," and then fled to the bathroom, overcome by shyness as the adults clapped.

Masha sighed. "I hoped Dorothea would have grown out of that tiresome habit by now." She frowned a little as she poured more tea for her daughter-in-law. "How is her latency therapy coming along?"

"Not very well. Dr. Crawford found no progress after the latest round of tests. We'll continue the preceptive exercises, of course, but Crawford thinks it unlikely that Dody will ever attain operancy. Her superior intellect certainly understands what the therapists are trying to do, but apparently she lacks the strength of will that would enable her to break the bonds of latency and finally become one of us."

"Now, Vi," her brother said. "It's not completely hopeless." Robert Strachan was a natty man of small stature, only slightly taller than Viola. His dark eyes glittered and his hair was combed back, making him look sleek as an otter. He exuded the self-confidence of a highly adept metacreative operant. He was an Associate Professor of Psychophysics at the University of Edinburgh, director of the CE Operator Safety Research Project that also involved his wife and sister.

Viola rounded upon him with surprising bitterness. "You're right, as usual, Robbie. Occasionally, children with Dody's form of latency have broken through after suffering some great mental or physical trauma. So we can always hope the child will be in a car smash or some such thing—and become a True Person in spite of herself."

"Vi!" said Masha sharply, and her eyes flicked to young Kenneth, who was listening openmouthed. Both women fell silent, but it was plain that the acrimonious exchange continued telepathically.

The boy toyed with his sandwich, now completely expressionless. Rowan Grant tried to distract him with a lecture on the wonderful things rejuvenation technology had done for his grandmother. "Someday your Mum and Uncle Robbie and I will also have ourselves made young again through genetic engineering," she concluded brightly. "So will you! And if any of us should have an accident and be badly hurt, the regen-tank would make us well again."

"But it's no good for us," Ken muttered. "Not for little kids. I learned about it in school. A person can't go into the tank until he's at least twelve or thirteen, because up until then kids don't have all the special body chemicals that make the regen thing work . . . And even if Dee and I wait until then, the tank can't make our *normal* brains meta."

"Well—no," Rowan admitted. "Thus far, regeneration technology has been unable to benefit those with latent metafunctions. The human brain is so complex that we don't yet understand all of the genes involved in its operation. But you musn't fret about it, dear. Things will surely change in the future. Someday, we'll have the means to make every human being an operant. Why, even if it takes another hundred years, you can be rejuvenated over and over again until—until it *happens*."

Ken said calmly: "But meanwhile, we'll be deadheads."

"Of course not!" Rowan Grant's plain, kindly face was horrified. "Wherever did you hear that awful term? You must never call yourself that, Ken—or let anybody else do it, either. We all belong to the World Mind and we're all important to the Galactic Milieu—operants and nonoperants alike. And you know that we love you and your sister very much, whether you're full metas or not."

Ken's gaze fell. Making no reply, he abandoned his sandwich, took a piece of spongecake, and began to pile on honeyed cream until it dripped from the side of the plate onto the carpet. Viola noticed what was happening and uttered a sharp exclamation of annoyance, but a warning thought from Masha brought her up short. She pressed her lips together and rose from her chair.

"I'd better see what's happened to Dody. And you, Kenneth—take a serviette and wipe up that disgusting mess at once." She left the room.

"Hurry back," Masha called. "I have an important announcement to make. My great surprise!"

When Viola finally returned with her daughter, Masha addressed them all with determined good humor. "Now, my darlings, I'm very happy to have my strong new body, but I'm not quite ready to go back to work. First, I need to spend some time with all of you to catch up on what's been going on in the world while I was growing young again. So I'd like you to join me on a whirlwind holiday. Let's fly away tomorrow and spend the whole weekend together at some interesting place getting to know one another all over again. Please say that you'll come!"

The other adults, after a brief startled pause, made encouraging noises.

"But where will we go?" Dee asked, bewildered.

"Anywhere you like," Masha said. "Dorothea, you're the youngest. You may choose the place. Just a moment while I get something out of the credenza."

The four components of the Hydra sitting tense in the Bentley let out their collective breath in relief. The scheme of coercive manipulation they had hatched in response to Fury's orders hovered on the brink of bearing fruit. The professor was following the unconscious compulsion they had implanted. Now there was only the child to deal with.

Masha produced a large durofilm map of the British Isles, which she spread on the rug in front of the fire. She handed a silver CAD stylus to her granddaughter. "Stand up, Dorothea. Now close your eyes and I'll spin you round. Then you must kneel down and point to the map while still keeping your eyes shut, picking our destination."

"But what if Dee picks someplace awful?" Ken wailed. "Like Dundee or Wolverhampton?"

"Then those of us who have creative ingenuity will use it to make the holiday rewarding," Viola retorted. Poor Ken flinched.

Dee took the stylus and closed her eyes, trying not to let her nervousness show. Very often she "saw" things when her optic nerves no longer received photon stimuli—not ultrasensory images, as a True Person might perceive, but pictures drawn by her own imagination. As she was turned round and round she had quick little visions of English castles and Irish horse farms and Parisian toy stores. She caught glimpses of the Elizabethan Immersive Pageant at New Kenilworth that Ken had enjoyed so much, and Disney Cosmos, and Buckingham Palace, and Elfinholm, and the great zoo at Glentrool with its strange animals from the colonial planets. She saw place after place that she and Mummie and Ken had visited on holiday. Places she would love to see again—

She stopped spinning.

"Now point with the stylus," ordered Gran Masha.

Hydra acted in full metaconcert.

Into the mind of the little girl flashed a different kind of mental picture, like a Tri-D suddenly turned on in a dark room. She drew in a startled breath and almost exclaimed out loud because the scene was so real, so unlike any inner vision she had ever experienced before.

It was a place. A beautiful place with fields of bright wildflowers, green hillsides above a seashore, and a palace on an islet in the midst of a sparkling loch. She knew at once that she had never been there in her life, and she also knew that the place was real.

"Choose, Dorothea!" Gran Masha urged gaily.

Choose that place! something else commanded.

Slowly, Dee knelt with her eyes still tightly shut, reached out with the stylus, then let it gently descend, still seeing the same picture in her mind.

"Well, I'll be gormed!" said Uncle Robbie.

"Oh!" Mummie's voice was full of dismay.

Aunt Rowan said, "It must be synchronicity—or something."

Dee opened her eyes. Both Mummie and Gran Masha looked flustered and none too pleased. The silver stylus rested squarely on a sizable island off the Scottish coast, almost directly west of their home in Edinburgh.

Masha sighed. "Well, it's my own fault for letting the child decide."

Viola's face tightened. "Dody can pick another place."

"No." Masha was firm. "We'll go there. The children should see the lands that their clan once ruled, and the places where their great-great-grandfather and grandfather were born."

"Izz-lay?" Ken was peering closely at the map in puzzlement. "Dee picked out an island named Izz-lay where . . . *who* ruled?"

"You pronounce it EE-luh," Gran said briskly. "Islay was the place where the Lords of the Western Isles had their seat of government in the fourteenth century. From there they held sway over all the Hebrides for two hundred years. Your ancestors—Clan Donald."

"Oh." Ken spoke very softly and looked at his little sister out of the corner of his eye. "Dad's people."

Their father Ian Macdonald was a shadowy figure who was seldom spoken of by Gran or Mummie. From his home on the faraway "Scottish" ethnic planet, he ordered presents that were sent to Dee and Ken from a big Edinburgh store on their birthdays and at Christmas. The gifts had brief notes attached, handwritten by some anonymous personal shopper according to Ian's transmitted instructions and signed "Love, Dad."

Ken, who had been three when his parents were divorced on Caledonia, had only the most distant memory of his father, while Dee had none at all. There were no holopix or Tri-D recordings of him in Viola's house; but Ken had discovered a single durofilm photo with *I.M.—2055* written on the back, buried in a drawer full of miscellanea in his mother's desk. He had stolen the picture and hidden it, and from time to time he would take it out and look at it, and sometimes show it to Dee. The picture was badly scuffed and faded, and showed a dashing young man in a shiny environmental suit with the mask and helmet doffed, standing beside some kind of odd aircraft. The scenery was unearthly and the children had decided that the picture must have been taken on the Scottish planet.

"Islay is a lovely place for our holiday," Aunt Rowan was saying with an encouraging smile. "Wild and strange, with a beautiful reconstruction of the medieval palace of the Lords of the Isles that serves as a museum. Your great-great-grandfather Jamie MacGregor, who was a pioneer metapsychic, was born there, and so was your grandad, Kyle. The island is a bird sanctuary as well. I think it's an excellent place for us to visit."

Dee was dubious. "But if Mummie doesn't want to go there—"

"Of course we'll go," Viola snapped. "Why on earth not?"

Masha arose and began to gather together the tea things. "You children help me clear up. Then we'll order some flecks about Islay that you can take home to read tonight."

When the professor and her grandchildren had left the room, Viola Strachan said to her brother: "That was a very eerie performance by

Dody. Enough to make one wonder whether Crawford's diagnosis is entirely correct. I wonder if the child could be crypto-operant."

Robert Strachan left his chair and began to poke up the fire. "What makes you think that?"

"Robbie . . . *I was thinking of Kyle Macdonald's birthplace when Dody made her choice.*"

"She couldn't have read your mind, Vi. You're a masterclass adult, as Rowan and I are. Even if the child were crypto-operant she'd be unable to penetrate your social mind-screen—much less the inner defensive barrier."

"But—"

"I was thinking of Islay, too," Rowan interrupted, her eyes wide with astonishment. "Only I thought of it as the place Jamie MacGregor came from. Now what do you make of that?"

Robbie frowned. "God damn it all, I believe I might have had a flicker about the place myself! But for no reason that I recall." He pondered the puzzle for a minute, then his brow cleared. "Masha! Of course—it has to be Masha who did it. She's fresh from the regen-tank and her brain hasn't quite settled yet. She must have had some stray thoughts of Islay. A Grand Master Creator-Redactor like her could inadvertently zap all our minds with an imaginative icon that just popped into her head. She could even penetrate a latent youngster if the erratic was heavily energized."

Rowan nodded. "And anything that Masha's unconscious mind associated with that bloody fool husband of hers *would* carry a considerable emotional charge. Her superego would have tried to reject any thoughts of Kyle Macdonald as fast as they formed, and—pow!"

"I suppose you're right," Viola said. "It's the only logical explanation. But . . . I still wish we weren't going to Islay."

But you are, the Hydra observed, and the game is afoot!

The Bentley groundcar that had been parked outside Professor MacGregor-Gawrys's townhouse then drove away briskly through the rain, heading for the George Hotel. Fury had insisted that the Hydra travel first class on its initial foray away from its place of exile, and the quadruplex mind had been delighted to comply.

. . .

The ferryboat was now very close to the narrow channel between the two large islands. Some people were taking pictures or making videos, some sat in floppy canvas deck chairs that crew members had brought outside once the rain stopped, and some scanned the spectacular scenery with powered oculars. Dee stood at the rail, consulting her descriptive plaque from time to time. She was just barely tall enough to peer over the rail's top if she stood on tiptoe, looking more like a solemn miniature adult than a child of five in her red hooded anorak and new slacks woven in the somber tartan of Macdonald of the Isles.

Her continuing sense of vague disquiet about Islay could not be cured by self-redaction as the earlier seasickness had been. But she kept the uneasiness walled away inside her and there were no creepy Gi about to betray her private feelings, only humans out there with her on the windy, swiftly drying deck.

The ferry was traveling almost due north now, moving into the narrow strait that separated Islay from the neighboring island of Jura. The sea was nowhere near so rough as before and strengthening sunlight had turned it from dull gray-green to deep blue. The steep face of Islay rose on the left. Cliffs and skerries had creamy surf boiling around them, and the hanging glens and rounded green heights were emerging from low-hanging clouds.

Using the plaque-guidebook, Dee studied Islay's modest mountains and found out the names of the highest ones, saying them softly out loud:

"Beinn Uraraidh, Beinn Bheigeir, Glas Bheinn, Beinn na Caillich, Sgorr nam Faoileann . . . Boundary Mountain, Vicar's Mountain, Gray Mountain, Mount of the Old Woman, and Steep Hill of the Seagulls."

"You pronounce the Gaelic very well," said a man who stood at the rail a couple of meters away from her.

Unlike most of the other holidaymakers, he and the dark-haired woman beside him, who had come out on deck from the saloon a few minutes earlier, were dressed in city clothes. He wore no hat and his blond hair was wildly tousled by the wind, making a strange contrast to his crisply starched shirt, red silk cravat, charcoal-gray Beau Brummel suit with black velvet collar and cuffs, and shining jockey boots. He smiled at Dee with the cool friendliness of a condescending cat, showing teeth that were extremely white. His nose was fine-bridged and prominent, and his eyes were the color of shadowed ice. He was a metapsychic operant, and Dee shivered as she felt his coercive-redactive probe sweep over her impervious mind-screen, light in its touch as a drifting spiderweb and more powerful than those of any other adults she knew. But he made no real effort to delve into her.

"Do you know," the man added, with a lordly wave of his hand, "that the Old Woman who gives that mountain its name is actually the Great Goddess, who was worshipped by the ancient people of the island?"

"No. I didn't know that." Dee was polite. "Thank you for telling me. Some of my ancestors lived there, and that's why we've come on holiday."

"That's interesting. I have a home on Islay myself." The man looked away toward the misty hills. "You'll find there are all kinds of fascinating things to be seen. The reconstruction of Finlaggan Palace, excavations of prehistoric forts, the Kildalton Cross that dates back to the ninth century, flowering bogs and high cliffs and sea-caves alive with birds. You must be sure to visit the great cave at Bholsa! We even have a kind of demon called the Kilnave Fiend hanging about who's supposed to make people disappear—but that's just a folktale, of course."

"I'd like to hear it," Dee said, with a grave little smile. "I love stories like that. Please don't think I'd be frightened. I'm only five years old, but I'm a child prodigy and very mature for my age."

The attractive stranger burst into laughter, and his woman companion looked up from her own plaque-book, seeming to notice Dee for the first time. She was quite beautiful, and her face seemed as smooth and pale as eggshell, with rose-tinted lips and sapphire eyes framed by thick dark lashes and narrow arched brows. Her black hair was unusual, having auburn glints that were almost crimson. It was pulled tightly into a knot at the nape of her neck and crowned by a small scarlet turban that revealed a pointed widow's peak at her brow. She wore thigh-high black boots with red heels, and a fitted coat and short skirt that were the same brilliant scarlet color as her hat. The coat had golden buttons and a golden Celtic brooch pinned to the shoulder. Its sleeves were pushed up to accommodate long black leather gloves.

"What's your name, little Miss Mature-for-Your-Age?" The woman was smiling, but her voice had a keen edge.

"Dorothea Mary Strachan Macdonald. And you?"

The man gave another bark of laughter, and this time Dee sensed that his amusement was not directed at her. A mental thrust stronger than any Dee had ever experienced before lanced into her mind-screen, which held firm. The woman's eyes widened momentarily and then she inclined her head, as a queen might when acknowledging another royal personage. Her voice became soft and compelling, with a lilt that made her seem to be half singing when she spoke. "I am Magdala MacKendal, and this is my husband, John Quentin."

"How do you do," said Dee. "Now may I please hear the story of the Kilnave Fiend?"

"Come sit down with me," said Magdala MacKendal, "and I'll tell it to you." Dee obediently plopped down into a canvas chair, while the man and woman sat on either side of her.

Long ago [Magdala MacKendal said] during the late 1500s, when the Lords of the Isles had fallen on hard times and had lost their sovereignty to the Kings of Scotland, there lived on Islay a wicked dwarf called the Dubh Sìth, which means "the Black Fairy." He had a twisted little body and bent legs, and only his arms were strong. Black hair grew down to his eyebrows and an ugly black beard nearly covered the rest of his face, except for his pointed nose.

The Dubh Sìth lived deep in the forlorn bogs and savage heaths of Kilnave Parish in the northwestern part of Islay, and people were very much afraid of him because of his frightful appearance. But he was also the best bowman on the island, and it was said that his arrows never missed their target. He eked out a living shooting swans and geese and other wildfowl, and bartered them for clothing and other things he could not make for himself.

Now in those days the Macdonalds of Islay and the MacLeans of the island of Mull were quarreling bitterly over some land on Islay that the MacLeans claimed was theirs. Big Lachlan MacLean decided one day in 1598 that the time was ripe for an invasion of his neighbors and a taking by force of what was his. A local witch heard about his plans and told him he was sure to win out—provided he didn't go on a Thursday and didn't drink from a famous well near Loch Gruinart on Islay.

Big Lachlan was not impressed by witches. He sailed to Islay on Thursday because stormy winds prevented his going on Wednesday, and he landed at Ardnave in the shallow bay of Loch Gruinart on the north shore. The day was hot and sultry, and as he and his army marched inland along the Kilnave track to attack the Macdonalds, Big Lachlan stopped to take a drink at the forbidden well. Not long afterward, a strange sight met his eyes. Sitting atop a rock at the pathside was a horrible-looking creature all in black, with a head of snarled hair and a face almost invisible behind a filthy beard. It was the dwarf Dubh Sìth.

"Good day to you, Big Lachlan," said the little man. "I've come to offer my services, for I'm the finest bowman in Islay."

The giant chieftain of the MacLeans roared with laughter. "I'd not have such an ugly runt as you for love nor money," said he. "Now begone before I set my deerhounds on you."

The Dubh Sìth melted away into the heather and bracken. Then he went by one of the secret underground ways that he knew to the place at the head of Loch Gruinart where Sir James Macdonald was waiting with his outnumbered force of defenders. The dwarf presented himself to Sir Jamie and made the same offer.

"Well, we don't have much of a chance, and you'll never get your pay if we lose," Sir Jamie said, "but I'll hire you gladly."

"Let me worry about that," said the Dubh Sìth. "And now farewell, for you won't see me again until the battle's won."

The army of MacLeans now fell howling upon the Macdonalds in the marshlands of Gruinart Strand, and the fighting was fierce and bloody for there were three times as many invaders as there were defenders. Before long the Macdonalds began to notice that more and more of their enemies lay fallen with black arrows through their throats or sticking from their eyes. But never a sight of the dwarf archer did they see.

The MacLeans took note of their arrow-shot comrades, too, and word began to pass among them that the Dubh Sìth was lurking invisible, killing man after man and laughing like the Devil himself. Lachlan MacLean tried vainly to rally his force, but they were now stricken with fear and reminded him how he had disregarded the witch's warnings. Many of them declared that they wanted to retreat.

Big Lachlan threw his head back and cursed the witch with ringing shouts, and cursed the Dubh Sìth, and cursed his men for a pack of low cowards. But just then a black arrow came flying and pierced his throat above the steel gorget, and he crashed to the ground stone-dead near a hawthorn all covered with milk-white blossoms.

Suddenly, a small shape leapt out of the thorn tree, shrieking with glee, and began capering around the fallen chief. It was the Dubh Sìth who had killed Big Lachlan MacLean, as well as scores of his men, by shooting them from his hiding place among the white flowering branches.

When they saw the enemy chief fall, the Macdonalds took heart and shouted their battle cry and fought with fresh vigor. By the end of the day the marsh was heaped with three hundred MacLean bodies, and the invaders knew that they were beaten.

They took up their wounded and began to flee back along the Kilnave track, toward the place where they had left their boats. Then a great storm broke and rain poured down in torrents. A crowd of MacLeans took shelter in the ancient church of St. Nave on the seashore, but the Dubh Sìth, who had followed the fugitive army through his secret underground tunnels, found out where they were hiding. He soaked rags in seal oil, tied these to his arrows, set the oil alight, then shot dozens of flaming missiles onto the wood-and-thatch church roof.

In spite of the rain the roof blazed up, and the Dubh Sìth danced about madly while the trapped MacLeans burned to death in the sacred building.

Now some of the victorious Macdonalds came on the scene, and they were horrified and disgusted at what the wicked dwarf had done.

"Pay me!" the Dubh Sìth cried. "Pay me my weight in gold! For I slew Big Lachlan MacLean and sixty-three of his best fighters with my black arrows, and I have made a merry bonfire of this lot!"

"You are no ally of Clan Donald," the leader of the Islaymen said. "You have desecrated a holy church through wanton murder and you are fit only for the company of the Foul Fiend, Satan himself. You shall receive your payment for tonight's work in hell."

The two strongest Macdonald men seized the Dubh Sìth by his arms and legs and began to swing him back and forth, for they intended to fling him into the inferno. "If I burn, then so shall ye," cried the dwarf. "So shall ye all!"

The Macdonalds gave a mighty heave and sent him flying through a window into the blazing church, and he uttered one last terrible cry before he disappeared into the roaring flames.

But that was not the end of the Dubh Sìth.

From time to time during the past four hundred and fifty years, people walking or riding in the lonely northern places of Islay have caught glimpses of a small, scuttling black figure. They came to call it the Kilnave Fiend, for very often after it was seen a person would disappear, and later a body would be found, burnt to a cinder.

There are those who put the blame for those awful deaths on lightning, while others believe that the Dubh Sìth himself is responsible. They say that his ghost still prowls the bogs and moors of the island, and he pops in and out of the secret tunnels and caves that only he knows, laughing and taking his terrible revenge.

"Dee? Are you asleep? Wake up! The ferry's almost ready to dock."

She opened her eyes and saw Ken. Only Ken, standing over the deck chair she lay in, looking down at her with a condescending big-brotherly smirk.

Slowly, she pulled herself to her feet and stretched. Had she really fallen asleep? It seemed that the melodious coercive voice of the woman named Magdala MacKendal still echoed in her ears. She remembered the vivid scenes her imagination—or something—had conjured up to accompany the story: the marshy battleground, the fighters in their breastplates and helmets, Lachlan MacLean bareheaded and gigantic, urging his men on, the flowery thorn tree with the hideous dwarf leaping out of it, the stormy night and the flaming church . . .

She still felt unaccountably uneasy, even though the tale of the Kilnave Fiend was really rather tame when compared to *Frankenstein* or *Aliens* or *Moon of the Undead* or some of the other classic horror shows she had seen on the Tri-D.

The ferryboat was pulling into its berth at Port Askaig, a steep little town with quaint whitewashed stone buildings and a great number of flower beds. Dee looked about the deck, but none of the women who now crowded the rail wore an elegant scarlet outfit, and none of the men were tall and blond and dressed in a gray Beau Brummel suit.

"Come on," Ken said. "They're waiting for us." He gestured to the deck beside the canvas chair. "And don't forget your book-plaques."

Dee looked down in surprise. The small plaque was hers, of course, but the other was probably the one the dark-haired woman had been reading. Its title was *Folktales and Fairy Lore of Islay and the Inner Hebrides.* When Dee touched the corner activator she discovered that the book was handsomely illustrated in full color.

In the table of contents she found "The Kilnave Fiend at the Battle of Gruinart." When she called up the story and swiftly scanned it, she saw that the pictures exactly matched those she had "dreamed."

The ferryboat hooted.

"Come *on*!" said Ken.

Dee tucked both plaques into the kangaroo pouch of her anorak as she followed Ken back inside the passenger saloon. Perhaps she would see Magdala MacKendal again sometime during the holiday weekend, and she would be able to return the book.

[4]

FROM THE MEMOIRS OF ROGATIEN REMILLARD

She was called by so many different names . . . and that, too, was part of her mask.

Dorothea Mary Strachan Macdonald was christened in the year 2057 at the tiny chapel of St. Margaret the Queen in Grampian Town on the continent of Beinn Bhiorach on the planet Caledonia, the first "Scottish" ethnic colony. Her mother, the operant psychophysicist Viola Strachan, called her baby girl by the nickname of Dody. So did the monster known as Fury, in its later attempts to intimidate and destroy her.

Her father, Ian Macdonald, called her Dorrie, a name that she did not like very much because (she told me years later) it seemed as though it properly belonged to a pretty little doll-faced girl with golden ringlets and melting eyes who was the apple of her doting Daddy's eye.

But her hair was an unexceptional brown, and her face was plain but pleasingly heart-shaped. While her eyes were an interesting hazel color, they were also close-set, piercing, and disconcerting—and they did not weep easily, nor did they readily reveal the secrets of the mind behind them. Her troubled father Ian did undoubtedly love her in his fashion, but the little girl finally realized that he would much rather have had a brawny second son who would have assuaged his disappointment over Kenneth. Even worse, she had hidden within her tremendous mental faculties that Ian feared . . . almost as much as she feared them herself.

Her beloved older brother Ken called her Dee, and this was also the first name she called herself, because it could have belonged to either a male or a female—or even to something that was not a person at all. Janet Finlay, Ian Macdonald's crusty factotum, called her Doro. The nonborn fosterlings and the hired hands at the family airfarm teased her by calling her Dodo in her early years, when her mindpowers were still mostly latent. Much later they would respectfully style her Dirigent, after she assumed the metapsychic leadership of Caledonia.

Her grandmother, the colorful Rebel stalwart Masha MacGregor-Gawrys, never called her anything except Dorothea.

To the awesome Lylmik, who were her tutors and ultimately her canonizers, she was Illusio, the evasive one, because the physical perception of her gave no hint of her true nature.

Jack the Bodiless, himself a profound human anomaly, gave her the name Diamond—at first ironically, then later in the clear blaze of newfound love.

I, who am an antediluvian Franco-American, obstinately clinging to remnants of the tongue of my Québecois forebears, always called her Dorothée, which a speaker of Standard English would pronounce dor-oh-TAY. She said she liked that name best of all. But perhaps she was only trying to be kind to an old man who loved her even before she showed me what lay behind her mask.

It was none other than the Family Ghost who directed me to introduce the grandparents of Dorothée, and it was through them that I eventually came to know Diamond Mask herself.

Kyle Macdonald was a charming, hard-drinking author of popular science fiction novels and Tri-D scripts. He was no littérateur, only a competent journeyman writer with a fine comic flair who made a lot of money at his trade and frittered most of it away at the night spots and casinos of Earth and the cosmop worlds.

We first met in 2027, when Kyle was only twenty-one and enjoying the controversy provoked by his first outrageous novel, *Prometheus Regnawed.* We chanced to be lubricating ourselves side by side in the hotel bar at a World Fantasy Convention in Sydney, Australia, when a trio of well-sloshed local fans let their literary criticism get offensively verbal (Macdonald's novel featured a blockheaded Aussie character) and then physical. My innate Franco chivalry resented the odds against the embattled young author, who was brawny but unskilled in the martial arts, and I lent him moral support and a friendly fist or two to scatter the ungodly.

We celebrated our victory with triple drams of Lagavulin 16, discovered that we had compatible bibliophilic tastes, and I wound up promising to help him dispose of some valuable Roger Zelazny collector's editions he had inherited. Kyle lived in Scotland, so we only managed to get together at the occasional fantasy or science fiction con to lift a jar, but we gossiped rather often over the teleview. I helped him with literary research, and from time to time he purchased rare old paper-printed fantasy items by mail from my antiquarian bookshop in New Hampshire.

Kyle Macdonald was not a metapsychic operant like me. He was, as were some 26 percent of humanity at that time, a normal possessing significant MP latencies, meaning that he carried the genes for higher mindpowers and had potentially strong metafaculties tucked away deep within his cranium—but for various reasons the powers were unusable. Sometimes latents were spontaneously raised to operancy by severe psychic trauma, but the more usual means involved specialized therapy by meta preceptors, using techniques pioneered by Catherine Remillard and her late husband Brett McAllister. But Kyle Macdonald's enormous font of latent creativity proved to be quite inaccessible—except insofar as it fueled his imagination and enabled him to earn a living as a writer of fantastic fiction.

My friendship with Macdonald might have remained casual if a certain Ghost had not intervened, commanding me to attend the 2029 World Fantasy Convention in London. I was ordered to make certain that Kyle met a young woman named Mary Ekaterina MacGregor-Gawrys, whom I myself would have to squire to the con and introduce to him.

Of all the humans possessing metapsychic powers in the mid twenty-first century, three families stood out: my own Franco-American clan, headed by Denis Remillard and his wife Lucille Cartier, the MacGregors of Scotland, and the Gawrys-Sakhvadzes of Polish-Georgian descent, who at that time lived mostly in England. Mary MacGregor-Gawrys, who was usually called Masha, was then a student at Oxford, where her parents Katharine MacGregor and Ilya Gawrys headed an important metapsychology research group at Jesus College. I had no acquaintance with Masha, but more distinguished Remillards than I—notably my nephew Denis—knew the MacGregor and Gawrys clans well. Once I had determined that the young woman enjoyed reading fantasy, I was able to trade shamelessly upon Denis's name and concoct a scheme that successfully lured her to the convention and to her destiny with Kyle Macdonald.

In spite of the fact that their minds were disparate, the two young people fell instantly in love. Brilliant, operant Masha, who had lived only for her studies up until then, was enchanted by Kyle's dynamic personality, his roguish good looks, and his screwball sense of humor. He in turn thought she was the loveliest creature he had ever seen, with a cascade of shining red hair, eyes like living emeralds, and a passionate temperament that she had successfully kept under control until Kyle Macdonald inspired her to cast restraint to the winds.

To the horror of her academic family, Masha dropped out of Oxford to spend the winter with the dashing Scottish scribe in his cruck-frame cottage on a windswept, romance-laden Hebridean island. The following spring the pair announced that they would marry. Masha was carrying Kyle's child, a boy of great metapsychic potential whom they planned to name Ian. The Gawrys and the MacGregor families gritted their teeth, shielded their thoughts well, and professed to be delighted. The newlyweds planned to move into more civilized digs in Edinburgh once the baby was born. Meanwhile, Kyle finished writing his second madcap transmedia best-seller, *Nijinsky Takes a Quantum Leap.*

Ian was born three months prematurely, but he was a sturdy child and he throve under intensive neonatal care, seeming little the worse for his abbreviated tenure in the womb . . . except that his substantial metafaculties, like those of his father, proved to be intractably latent.

When it became evident that her firstborn son would not achieve operancy, Masha fell into a profound depression and seemed to lose interest in the baby. A nanny was hired and the young mother enrolled at the University of Edinburgh. There she resumed her studies under the benevolent eye of her maternal uncle, Davy MacGregor, who would later be appointed Planetary Dirigent of Earth.

During the next five years Masha and Kyle had three more children, Lachlan, Annie Laurie, and Diana, all powerful operants. Kyle's comic novels continued to top the best-seller lists and four of them were converted into blockbuster Tri-D shows. The most notable, *Cream Cheese for Birkhoff's Bagel,* was nominated for an Academy Award in 2036, and only lost because of the enduring prejudice of the Hollywood cinéaste establishment against any production smacking of sci-fi.

Masha earned doctorates in medicine and metapsychology, eventually deciding to devote her talents to latency research. At the same time, her relationship with her husband grew stormier and stormier as a widening gulf opened between operant wife and nonoperant husband. Their quarrels were Homeric, especially when Masha took Kyle to task for neglecting his writing in favor of the more amusing perquisites of authorship—parties, travel, and the occasional overly attentive female fan. He was also an enthusiastic tosspot (one of the reasons we two got on so famously). The pressures of Kyle's celebrity, Masha's increasing impatience with his frivolous behavior, and her preoccupation with her own important work eventually caused the marriage to break down. They separated in 2044, but over the years there would be reconciliations, and they were never formally divorced.

Happy-go-lucky insensitive egotist that he was, Kyle had never considered the possibility that Masha would actually abandon him and take the children. His writing career faltered, and for six years after she chucked him out of their Edinburgh home he produced nothing, passing the time in drinking, gambling, sexual dalliance, and touring colonial planets of the Human Polity, supposedly in search of inspiration.

In 2051, when he was nearly broke, he attempted to pull himself together and wrote another novel, *Mustangs of the Sombrero Galaxy.* After this proved to be an excruciating flop, he emigrated with his tail between his legs to the Scottish ethnic world of Caledonia, where he became Writer in Residence at the colony's small University of New Glasgow. He taught creative writing classes to earn bed and board in the faculty apartments and spent most of his free time in seedy pubs, ranting against perceived injustices in a Galactic Milieu run by elitist operants such as his perfidious wife, and cadging free drinks from science fiction fans who remembered his days of glory. When the Rebel faction expanded to include normals as well as metapsychic operants, he became one of its most eloquent literary proponents, achieving polity-wide notoriety as well as an improved bank balance by writing dark satires traducing the Milieu.

Through the years of his separation from Masha, Kyle Macdonald faithfully sent loving and hilarious letters to his four children back on Earth, describing his largely fictitious adventures on far-flung worlds and latterly on the interesting Scottish planet. Ian, Lachlan, Annie Laurie, and Diana grew up believing that their father was a colorful adventurer living a fascinating life, while their mother seemed to place them second to her duties as a researcher at the University of Edinburgh and an Intendant Associate for Europe.

The three younger, operant Macdonald children eventually took degrees in metapsychology from Edinburgh's medical school. But Ian, even then a Rebel, matriculated instead at the North of Scotland Agricultural College in Aberdeen. Upon receiving his degree in xenohusbandry he emigrated to the planet Caledonia just as his father had done and filed a homestead application for an airfarm on the rugged northern continent of Beinn Bhiorach, which had just been opened to settlement.

About that time Kyle and Masha attempted a reconciliation. She had been chosen to be a magnate, and both of them attended the inaugural session at Concilium Orb when the Human Polity first took its seats. But the old conflicts between them resurfaced more virulently than ever, exacerbated by Kyle's envy of Masha's success. At the end of the inaugural session she washed her hands of him and returned to Earth while Kyle slunk back to Caledonia and went on an imperial toot.

Ian Macdonald, hoping to lift his father out of his despondency, invited Kyle to join him in working the airfarm. Although Kyle hastily declined (he was not a man fond of hard physical labor, except in the pursuit of pleasure), he was touched by his eldest son's gesture. He and Ian saw each other frequently during the two years it took to get the new enterprise established, and Ian became sympathetic to the Rebel cause his father had espoused.

Then, in 2054, Ian Macdonald visited Earth for the awarding of his brother Lachlan's first degree. At the ceremony in Edinburgh Ian met the woman who would become his wife and the mother of Diamond Mask.

Poor Masha, observing the divine thunderbolt strike her eldest son and the fledgling Doctor of Psychophysics, Viola Strachan, must have suffered a sickening attack of déjà vu. Once again a brilliant, scholarly, operant young woman with a distinguished career ahead of her had fallen hopelessly in love with a handsome, latent, completely unsuitable man. That the man was Masha's own flesh and blood was quite irrelevant. She did everything she could to break up the romance, even revealing to Viola intimate details of her own unhappy marriage to Kyle. But her efforts were unavailing.

Viola Strachan was not a conventionally beautiful woman, but she was vivacious and possessed of an intense personal magnetism, an adjunct of her coercive metafaculty. Young Ian's romantic colonial background, his air of taciturn mystery, and his compelling sexuality overcame all Masha's appeals to logic. The couple was married at St. Patrick's Church, Cowgate, and immediately returned to Caledonia, where the reality of life on a colonial planet hundreds of lightyears from Earth only gradually became evident to the starstruck bride.

Caledonia has an austere magnificence and is richly endowed with natural resources, but no one has ever called it an immigrant's paradise. Few of the so-called ethnic worlds are, being more marginal in human preferenda and harder to colonize than the more appealing cosmopolitan planets that are open to settlers of any Earth nation. To encourage people to live on the more difficult worlds, the Milieu allows human ethnic groups that it judges to have sufficient "dynamism" to found colonies almost exclusively populated with their own stock. In contrast to the motley human culture of the cosmop worlds, the people of the ethnic planets make a special effort to reflect the heritage of their Earthling ancestors. For instance, an ethnic colonial government may encourage the day-to-day use of an old native language or dialect now severely restricted on Earth, provided that the citizens are equally fluent in the Standard English of the Human Polity. Ethnic costume (authentic and colorfully bogus), native arts and crafts, traditional occupations and the like are also de rigueur, insofar as they are not contrary to civilized usage, economically detrimental, sexually repressive, incompatible with the mandated Milieu standards of education and social justice, or xenophobic.

Thus, it is meet and just for Caledonians to speak the Gàidhlig or mangle the Guid Scots Tongue, wear tartans (whether entitled to them or not), idolize golf, go flyfishing with Spey rods for naturalized Caledonian salmon, celebrate Highland Games, distill and guzzle Scotch whisky, eat cullen skink, cock-a-leekie, bashed neeps, cranachan, and mutton, make pets of collies, Scottish terriers, long-horned Highland cattle, and Shetland ponies, play bagpipes, and designate "Westering Home" as the planetary anthem. But they are forbidden excesses of ethnic fervor such as clan blood feuds, the humiliation or massacre of Sassenach (English) visitors, passing laws requiring all inhabitants to eat haggis, or forcing children to do manual labor rather than go to school.

Since Caledonia was one of the earliest ethnic worlds settled after the Great Intervention in 2013, its population was already fairly large—approaching a million people—when Viola Strachan arrived in 2054. Many of the first generation of settlers had come from the Hebrides and the Scottish Highlands, but there were also citizens of Scottish blood who had emigrated from the Lowlands, from other parts of Britain, from Canada, the United States, Australia, New Zealand, and elsewhere. As might be expected in a group having strong Celtic genes, there was a sizable community of stalwart metapsychic operants, as well as many lower-grade metas with more modest mind-powers. In accordance with the social engineering policy of the Milieu, over half of the normal populace were high latents like Ian Macdonald, who carried genes for strong metafunction and might be expected to engender operant descendants in good time.

The bias favoring meta colonists on the ethnic worlds, which seemed reasonable and proper to nonhuman Milieu policymakers desiring to encourage coadunation of the Human Mind and its eventual embrace of Unity, was destined to be one of the significant factors in the Metapsychic Rebellion of 2083. When Viola Strachan first set foot on the Scottish planet twenty-nine years earlier, its nonoperant element (including her husband and father-in-law) was already flirting with sedition, while the metas were mostly enthusiastic supporters of the exotic-dominated Galactic confederation.

Caledonia's star, a solar-type G2 V, is 533 lightyears away from Earth. Its inhabited fourth planet is a trifle larger than Earth but nearly as massive, covered with a vast hydrosphere (laconically known as The Sea) in which smallish continents and many volcanic island arcs are sprinkled. A large Earth-type moon travels in an orbit rather close to the planet, causing very high tides. The mountainous north and south temperate-zone landmasses have glaciers that constantly give birth to icebergs. An extensive mantle of clouds, together with smoke and airborne ash from the abundant active volcanoes, makes the climate generally chillier than Earth's, while the ocean is comparatively warmer and shallower, with teeming aquatic life.

The native flora and fauna of Caledonia have not evolved much beyond the equivalent of our Mesozoic Era. Its genome is terrestrial-equivalent, and minimal ecoengineering by the exotic races rendered the place compatible to introduced Earth crops, fish, and domestic livestock. The most advanced native animal species are the myriad gorgeous birdlike creatures and a class of ferocious invertebrate predators bearing an embarrassing resemblance to the Krondaku. (Members of that ancient, ultraintelligent race rarely visit Caledonia for this reason, in spite of its unique geology, superlative fossils, and outstanding local booze.)

Most of the colonists live in twelve continental states: Orcadia, Nessie, Cairngorm, Ardnamurchan, Atholl, Strathbogie, Katrine, Argyll, St. Andrews, Caithness, Beinn Bhiorach, and Clyde—site of New Glasgow, the capital, and Wester Killiecrankie Starport.

The economy of the planet is largely dependent upon exports, and when Viola lived there it was still not totally self-sufficient. A much-sought-after renewable resource are the exquisitely beautiful Caledonian pearls, fashioned by native artisans into high-priced jewelry much coveted by the Poltroyan race as well as by humankind. Fully automated mines produce industrial diamonds, inexpensive gem-quality diamonds of many colors, fiber graphite, buckyball carbon, lanthanides, and gold. Some continents have extensive sheep ranches, where bioengineered animals yield fine wool famed throughout the Human Polity. In the cities there are fabric mills and garment-making establishments, although a lot of handweaving and knitting is also done as a cottage industry in the more remote regions. Glom components, nanotech equipment, gourmet honey, and the better brands of Caledonian single-malt whisky were at that time exported to the nearest human cosmop world, Okanagon, then a populous Milieu Sector Base and the home of the Twelfth Fleet. In those days Caledonia also enjoyed extensive tourist trade from Okanagon, which was only nineteen lightyears away, and from the "Japanese" ethnic world Satsuma, twenty-seven lights distant.

By far the most interesting aspect of the local economy, and one unique to this single human colony, is the cultivation of native balloon-flora that yield peculiarly valuable biochemicals. In the mid-twenty-first century, airfarming was the fastest-growing commercial enterprise on Caledonia, but one that was risky as well. Ian Macdonald was already experiencing difficulties due to undercapitalization when he brought his new bride Viola to Glen Tuath Farm, a primitive homestead nestled amidst precipitous crags at the head of a great fjord on the northern end of Beinn Bhiorach.

The continent is roughly dumbbell-shaped, measuring some 1200 kilometers from north to south and 400 at its widest from east to west. It lies a good 9000 kloms from Strathbogie, the nearest landmass to the southeast. In 2054 it boasted only a single municipality that could be dignified with the title of "city"—the state capital of Muckle Skerry on the southern coast. This place had a large biochemical plant, a brand-new shopping mall, a medical center, governmental and law enforcement offices, and a fast-proliferating gaggle of grog-shops, clip joints, bordellos, and recreational drugstores that catered to the hardworking miners, ranch hands, agriworkers, airfarmers, fisherfolk, and other dwellers in the sticks who egged into town on weekends to whoop it up in a civilized setting. There were no institutions of higher learning or metapsychic research in Muckle Skerry or anywhere else in Beinn Bhiorach. The other twenty-one permanent settlements of the frontier continent were very small, ranging from market towns and fishing hamlets to lonely trading posts in the interior mountain ranges. The only settlement within 300 kloms of Glen Tuath Farm was Grampian Town, population 2200, a center for barley-growing and the site of two important distilleries and a brewery.

Ian worked his holding with the help of seasonal contract workers, some of whom owned their harvesting aircraft. Viola, an energetic young woman, willingly took over the bookkeeping and purchasing, supervised the airfarm's domestic robotics and ground personnel, and spent long hours transforming the bleak collection of prefabricated buildings into an oasis of dramatic beauty. At the same time, she gestated the couple's first baby, Kenneth, who was born—regrettably frail of body and metapsychically latent—in 2055.

Like her mother-in-law Masha before her, Viola Strachan compensated for her disappointment in the nonoperant child by turning once again to neglected academic pursuits. The branch of psychophysics that had been her specialty involved a good deal of mathematical analysis that required no other equipment than her own talented brain and a computer with satellite-linkage that put her in touch with the University of New Glasgow. Through that institution, Viola could communicate with fellow researchers on worlds throughout the galaxy. Early on, she began to specialize in statistical cerebroenergetics, with a special emphasis upon the potentially injurious effects of mind-boosting equipment upon CE operators.

Ian was more than willing to have his wife resume her scientific career, even if it meant that he would have to hire a domestic manager to take over her erstwhile duties. He worshipped Viola, finding it almost incredible that such an exceptionally talented woman would have agreed to marry him, bury herself in a colonial wilderness, and have his children. He was so deeply in love that he would have done almost anything to please her. For two years they seemed to be happy, in spite of the fact that little Kenneth was a sickly child who failed to thrive. The meta therapists in New Glasgow declared that there was no chance that he would ever achieve operancy, even though his intellect was exceptional.

Then Dorothea was born in 2057—also latent but quite healthy—apparently having a prodigious mentality, with truly extraordinary suboperant metafaculties that might conceivably be released if the appropriate stimuli were applied. Unfortunately, Caledonia did not then have the facilities to handle the baby girl's case properly. For accurate evaluation and treatment she would have to be taken to Earth.

Viola was bitterly disappointed that this second child, like the first, was not an operant. She began to reassess her marriage and saw her handsome husband in a new, much less flattering light. It seemed clear to Viola that the meta shortcomings of their children were a result of his genetic input, and she felt increasingly stultified by the intellectual isolation of farm life as well. She became withdrawn and cool to Ian and began to exert her considerable coercive power upon him, urging him to sell the airfarm and return to Edinburgh with her and the children, so that their daughter at least might have a chance to reach her enormous mental potential.

Ian at first agreed. The farm was going through an especially rocky period and he was discouraged and overworked. He would be able to get some kind of job Earthside, and Viola had already been offered a good research position at her alma mater. But then Ian's father Kyle Macdonald caught wind of what was about to happen, egged over to Beinn Bhiorach from Clyde, and in an impassioned man-to-man dialogue managed to change his son's mind.

Viola was thunderstruck when Ian then flatly refused to sell Glen Tuath. All of Masha's warnings about the impossibility of an operant woman having a successful marriage with a normal man now came home to Viola. She finally looked at her husband with complete objectivity . . . and decided that she no longer loved him.

Less than a year after Dorothea's birth, Viola Strachan told Ian Macdonald that she was going to divorce him. She returned to Earth on an express starship, taking Kenneth and Dorothea with her. At first she moved in with her sympathetic mother-in-law Masha, who was then a full Professor of Clinical Metapsychology at the University of Edinburgh as well as a Magnate of the Concilium. Later Viola rented a townhouse of her own and the children were cared for during the day at a nursery school.

For the next four years Viola worked in the university's Department of Psychophysics together with her older brother Robert Strachan and his wife, Rowan Grant, until all three of them were slain on a day that changed the history of the Galactic Milieu.

[5]

ISLAY, INNER HEBRIDES, SCOTLAND, EARTH, 26–28 MAY 2062

There were many other tourists at Dun Bhorairaig besides Professor MacGregor-Gawrys and her party, but all of them were adults except Dee and Ken, and so the student archaeologist who was their guide pitched her lecture at a rather rarefied level. The dun was an ancient stronghold on a knoll high above the Sound of Islay. It had been extensively excavated and it featured a small museum with dioramas and exhibits in addition to the partially restored ruins. The two children liked the museum, but they soon became bored by explanations of the diggings and wandered off by themselves. Ken was eager to snoop through the rubble in hopes of finding some treasure that the scientists had overlooked. But Dee was feeling odd again, and all she wanted was to stand quietly at the edge of the parapet, staring down the long rough slope leading to the seashore.

Even in bright sunlight, with the expanse of water shining and birds warbling in the heather, she could not escape the feeling that something very bad was going to happen. By instinct, she connected the premonition with the strange aetheric atmosphere of Islay itself, which had made it seem so much more sinister than neighboring Jura when she had viewed both islands from the ferry. She had never felt this way before, and it was very unpleasant.

Closing her eyes, she set about to delete the disagreeable sensation with her new self-redactive faculty. She greeted the invisible, silent angel, took up the proper box, opened it, freed the soothing redness, and let herself float effortlessly upon it.

There, she said to herself. Now nothing can hurt me. It's all right. Yes—

"Dee! Look at this! D'you think it might be ancient?"

The spell broke and her eyes flew open. It was Ken, holding what looked like a rusty bit of crinkled wire under her nose.

She gave a cry of consternation. "I was trying to use my new power and you spoiled it!"

Ken grimaced. "You fixing to upchuck again?"

"No! I just . . . feel funny." She looked at him sidelong. "Don't you get weird vibes from this place?"

"No." He was clearly uninterested. "I'm going to show this doodah I found to the archaeologist. It could be important."

Smoldering with indignation, Dee watched him go back toward the crowd of tourists. Boys! A grungy old piece of wire was important—but she wasn't. It would serve Ken right if the terrible thing happened to *him*.

But as soon as the thought passed through her head, she repented of it. Not Kenny, she prayed. Please, angel, don't let anything happen to my big brother.

Her malaise was forgotten. She trotted off after him, calling: "Wait for me!" She caught Ken up just as the archaeologist was examining his find and pronouncing it to be a hairpin of late-twentieth-century vintage. The adults gathered round were laughing and Ken's pale features had gone bright pink with embarrassment.

"Don't fash yuirsel', laddie," said a stout middle-aged man wearing a marmalade-colored sports jacket and trews in the gaudy Buchanan tartan. He was standing with Gran Masha and the other members of the family. "Losh, at least yuir een were sharp enow to identify the wee whatsit as a human artefack. That's verra commendable."

Gran Masha said, "How kind of you to say so, Evaluator. May I present my grandson Kenneth Macdonald and his sister Dorothea . . . Children, this is Evaluator Throma'eloo Lek, who is a Visiting Fellow in Forensic Metapsychology at Edinburgh University. He is also here on a holiday visit."

Dee said "How do you do" and shook the Evaluator's very clammy hand. But Ken stared at him, dumfounded.

"Kenneth!" Mummie chided him. "Your manners."

With great reluctance, the boy held out his hand. After the greeting had been exchanged, the Evaluator winked and said: "Noo, that wasna sae gruesome, was it?" Then he exchanged a few more jovial words with Gran Masha and took his leave, saying he was on his way to visit the usquebaugh works.

"What a surprise, finding him here," Rowan said. They all began heading back to their rented groundcar, a spacious blue Audi.

Robbie laughed. "Not really, when you consider that Islay is probably the most renowned producer of single malts on Earth. It would be odd if old Lek and his ilk *didn't* make the pilgrimage."

Ken was still looking shocked. Dee stared after the departing Evaluator. There was something creepy about him. But what? He looked very old, but lots of people didn't want to be rejuvenated. Was it his fakey use of Scots dialect when he was obviously not Scottish at all?

"What do you say we follow Throma'eloo's example?" Robbie suggested. "There's plenty of time to visit the Bowmore establishment before we're due at Finlaggan for this evening's festivities. It would be a pity if we didn't come home from Islay with a few well-aged souvenirs." When his stern-faced sister looked as though she were about to object, he laughed. "Oh, come on, Vi. Lighten up. It isn't as though the bairns were going to absorb the product by oz-bloody-mosis."

"Unless the gene is dominant," Viola said bitterly. "Oh . . . very well. If Masha can stand it, so can I."

They climbed into the car, the professor spoke the destination, and they drove off. What with the strange old man and the incomprehensible byplay among the adults, Dee felt totally mystified. But Ken was sitting in the front seat between Mummie and Gran and there was no way she could question him about what was going on without the grownups hearing, and she was too proud to admit her ignorance to them. So she sat back and looked out of the window while the car traveled at a sedate pace along the narrow roads, heading southwest and eventually reaching Lochindaal, the great arm of the sea that nearly divided Islay in two. The threatening feeling Dee had experienced at the dun had vanished.

Bowmore, the unofficial capital of the island, was a tidy village with slate-roofed white houses and an unusual round church at the head of its broad main street. On the southern outskirts of town was some kind of sizable factory with shiny onion-shaped "pagodas" towering above its buildings. A peculiar odor filled the air, and when Dee asked what it was, Masha replied crisply. "Burning peat, fermenting barley water . . . and fine single-malt Scotch. We are going to tour one of the places where Islay whisky is made, because liquor from this small island is famed throughout the entire Galaxy."

At first Dee enjoyed the Bowmore Distillery tour very much. The pagodas turned out to be ventilators on top of peat-fired kilns for roasting malted barley. In another building they watched the sweet-smelling dried malt ground up and turned into porridge. Sugary liquid drained off the porridge was mixed with yeast, and fermentation eventually turned the sugar water to a kind of barley beer having a low percentage of alcohol. This was carefully heated to concentrate the spirits through distillation.

Dee was especially intrigued by the stillroom with its huge copper vessels shaped like gnome hats. Numbers of other trippers were staring at the stills as well. The things were very old, and the tour guide began an elaborate explanation of how they operated . . . but suddenly Dee could no longer hear him.

It was back.

The threat of impending danger had abruptly returned. Even worse, Dee felt something prying at her mind, something cold and horrid and fearfully powerful, quite different from any human coercive-redactive prober she had ever encountered. She froze where she stood, unable to call out to Mummie or the other grownups who stood several meters away listening to the guide. There was only her brother close by, and four or five innocent-looking strangers.

Then she saw them.

They were lurking amongst a group of human beings who had just entered the stillroom: the three Gi from the ferryboat! In a flash she understood everything. Her fear turned to hot anger and indignation. She gave a mighty mental push, banishing the would-be intruder from her head, then poked her brother and whispered, "Kenny, look! Those awful Big Birds are here."

"So what?" he muttered. He had been unusually quiet ever since they had left Dun Bhorairaig.

"They're trying to probe my mind and they're making me feel all spooky. I think they were sneaking about on the dun, too! If they keep following me, the holiday will be spoiled."

"Why should the Gi follow you? You're bonkoid! What's the matter—are you afraid they'll tell Mummie about your new power?"

Dee shook her head. "It's not that at all. I've felt that something bad was going to happen ever since we got to Islay. And just now somebody really, really strong was trying to dig into my mind! It's not one of the True People. It felt different. So it must be an exotic—"

Ken grasped her arm and squeezed an urgent warning. "Shh! Pipe down. Didn't you know? There's another nonhuman here on the tour with us! Over there. That geeky professor or whatever he is that Gran Masha made us shake hands with. It must be *him* drilling at your mind-screen."

Dee followed her brother's eyes and saw the man dressed in the orange nebulin sports jacket and funny pants. He was staring up at the row of gigantic copper pot stills. The expression on his face was one of religious awe.

Dee was bewildered. "But he's just a grownup!"

"He's not," Ken said, with stark conviction. "He's a ruddy great thumping Krondaku Grand Master! Metacreatively disguised. They do that sometimes when they go prowling on other folks' planets and don't want to be recognized."

Dee stared. Was it possible that that ordinary-looking person was actually a great warty tentacled monster with six eyes and a funnel mouth full of sharp fangs? She, like most very young Earthlings, was terrified by the supremely intelligent exotic beings, whose coercive and mind-probing powers were legendary. "But why would a Krondaku care about me?" she whimpered.

Ken shrugged. A sly smile touched his pale lips. "Maybe he wants you for a snack."

But Dee was having none of that. "The Krondaku don't eat people, silly!"

"Then maybe he wants you for a stupidity specimen."

She very nearly punched him. But that would have meant losing control. She took a deep breath instead and spoke with complete calmness, even though her eyes blazed with anger. "Now you listen, Kenny! I'm not fooling. Something really *is* messing with my mind."

Ken's attitude changed from mocking to sober in an instant. "You could tell Mum or Gran Masha," he began. But his tone was dubious. He knew that the Evaluator must be a very important person, not to be lightly accused of the unauthorized mental probing of a child.

Everyone knew that was a serious crime under the laws of the Galactic Milieu.

"No." She shook her head stubbornly. "I'm not even sure that he's the one. Maybe it's the Gi."

"It could be your imagination."

"It's real! It felt like the mind-ream the latency therapists use, only ever so much stronger. And exotic."

"If you say so. But I don't know what we can do about it—short of telling the oldies."

Dee's face had gone stony. "I'll be all right. Whoever's doing it, *I'm not going to let him in.* But—"

"What?"

"Can I hold your hand?"

He sighed. "Gaw! What a complete dragola. You know what? You're turning into a faffing beanbag."

But he held on to her tightly until they were safely back in the car, and by then the queer sensations had once again disappeared.

Early in the evening they visited the expertly restored seat of the Lords of the Isles, built on an island in Loch Finlaggan. It was both a museum and the scene of a "medieval feast" presided over by costumed actors, with fourteenth-century entertainment accompanying the meal. Ken was very taken with the Macdonald castle and its pageantry; but Dee found the ambiance disturbing and once again felt unaccountably ill at ease, although this time there was no outsider attacking her mind-screen.

All throughout the feast she felt as though someone were watching her. She whispered her suspicion to Ken and they studied the crowd of dinner guests carefully, but there was no sign of the three Gi or the camouflaged Krondaku. It was a relief to Dee when the bards sang their last song and she and her family walked back to the car park across the torch-lit lake causeway. The feeling of danger melted away completely as they drove to Bridgend, where they spent the night in a handsome inn.

On Saturday morning they hiked up to see the "Giant's Grave," an important prehistoric site on Beinn Tart a' Mhill. Then they visited the

Museum of Islay Life in Port Charlotte, where there were exhibits of simple family dwellings ranging from Neolithic huts to homesteadings of the late nineteenth century. After that Masha, Viola, and Rowan drove off together to see the great Celtic cross and the carved grave slabs at Kildalton Chapel while Robbie and the children attended a lively little agricultural fair near Bowmore. Many of the other tourists (including the three Gi) were also at the gathering, buying up island handicrafts and homemade goodies and watching demonstrations of traditional folkways.

The fair turned out to be an occasion of pure fun for Dee. There was no trace of her former feeling of foreboding as she and her brother and her good-natured uncle mingled with the happy crowd. Collie dogs showed off their shepherding skills; shaggy little West Highland cattle, lyre-horned Ayrshires, and other pampered pet live-stock were paraded before critical judges by their proud owners; and there was an old-fashioned shearing contest with hand clippers that demonstrated the way wool was taken in the days before a simple pill that temporarily interrupted the hair-growing cycle caused sheep to drop their fleeces as neatly as unzipped fluffy coats.

After spending that night at the Dower House Hotel in Kildalton, they went on Sunday morning to look at the little whitewashed cottage on the nearby Lochindaal seashore where their grandfather Kyle Mac-donald had been born in 2006. The place had long since passed out of the family and become someone's summer home. There was no possibility of going inside. Nevertheless Dee and Ken insisted upon getting out of the car and walking round the locked and deserted building.

"Well, do be quick about it." Viola's irritation was plain. "Gran Masha and your aunt and uncle and I would much rather have our picnic than sit here in the car waiting for you two."

"We won't be long," Dee said. "But we *really* want to see Grandad's house."

It had never really come home to the two children before that their grandmother had had a husband and a family. Dee and Ken mostly thought of Gran Masha as a professor at the University and a very important person—who coincidentally happened to be a rather jolly elderly relative. That she could also have been a wife to someone named Kyle Macdonald and a mother to Ian, their mysterious father, was something they had never really thought about before.

"Grandad's on Caledonia with Dad," Ken said. "He writes books. I heard Uncle Robbie say so." They were out of sight of the car, walking through the house's back garden that faced the sea. Pinks and sandwort grew amidst the coarse grass, and the dog roses were in bloom. Beyond the strand, the wide sea-loch was almost as calm as green glass. The sky had become hazy.

"Both Dad and Grandad are latent," Ken added in a low voice. "Like us. That's why Mum and Gran Masha never talk about them."

"I wonder if Grandad wore a kilt when he was little and lived here?" Dee tried to peer into one of the back windows, but the interior of the house was too dark for her to see anything.

Ken gave a scornful laugh. "Not likely. He was born just before the Great Intervention. Kids back then wore clothes pretty much like ours . . . " He broke off, suddenly uncertain. "But I read that people on Caledonia wear kilts a lot, so maybe he does now. And Dad, too."

"I wonder if Grandad's nice? I really wish we could visit him and Dad. Do you think we ever will?"

"Mum will never take us. That's a dead cert."

"No," Dee agreed gravely. "She thinks Earth is the best place to live."

"I'm not so sure about that. When I grow up, I'm going to go to Caledonia and see for myself."

"Take me with you!" Dee begged.

Before Ken could reply, his wrist-communicator peeped softly. With a sigh, he pressed the RECEIVE pad. Mum's voice, incisive and not to be ignored, ordered the two of them back into the car at once.

Suddenly Dee's eyes were fierce. Both her fists were clenched. "Kenny—please! Please promise you'll take me to Caledonia."

"Stupid git," he said, but his voice was kind. "Oh . . . all right. I promise. Now let's go back to the car before Mum comes after us and starts frizzing our ears."

The last activity Masha had planned for them before they caught the late evening shuttle bus back to the mainland was a picnic followed by a leisurely walk along the wild northwestern shore of the island, where they would be able to explore the cliffs and sea-caves and perhaps catch sight of some rare birds. The car carried them north to the Gruinart Flats that formed Islay's narrow "waist." Long ago the flats had been drained dry for crop planting, but now they had reverted to their original wetland state and were set aside as a bird sanctuary.

"Islay once had over fifteen thousand people living on it," Gran Masha said, "and much of the native wildlife was killed. But when the Great Intervention opened the way to the stars, many of the inhabitants went away and helped to colonize new planets, just as human beings in other parts of the Earth did. Those who still live here on Islay are very careful to take good care of the land and the plants and animals, so that the island will remain beautiful forever."

"Did some of the people who went away go to the planet Caledonia?" Dee asked.

"Yes," Gran Masha said shortly. Then she changed the subject, and began talking about the Battle of Gruinart.

By now, everyone—even Ken—had already read the story of the Kilnave Fiend from the book that Dee had picked up on the ferry. (But when Robbie Strachan checked with Islay Telecom, there was no listing for subscribers named John Quentin or Magdala MacKendal, so Dee was allowed to keep the plaque.) Viola had been very dubious about the tale of the Fiend. She had taken the time to consult with the Keeper of the Islay Museum and found out that there was no evidence whatsoever that the dwarf known as the Dubh Sìth, a genuine historical character, had been responsible for the fiery massacre of the MacLeans. As for the notion that the Kilnave Fiend still stalked the moors dealing fiery death to the unwary, the Keeper had laughed and called it sensational rubbish. Viola had said that she suspected as much, and she used the occasion to lecture the children on the virtue of healthy skepticism.

They spent a brief time looking over the scene of the 1598 battle, a glistening spread of salt marsh alive with waterfowl. Dee entered the birds that she could recognize into her Day List of species observed. Then the car headed up the road on the west side of Loch Gruinart toward Kilnave. After about five kilometers they came to a discreet notice board on their right that directed them down a short dirt track to a roofless stone church overlooking the sandy shallows. Everyone got out of the car, and Aunt Rowan took her camera and made a Tri-D video as they explored the scene of the ancient atrocity.

The church of St. Nave was built of massive gray slabs stained with yellow lichen. A stone cross with dim carvings stood outside. Dee hated the place, in spite of the colorful wildflowers that surrounded it. Her earlier feeling of uneasiness had returned more strongly than ever during the drive north. She refused to go inside the decaying stone-arched door of the ruin, which reminded her of a mouth with snaggleteeth, and she was the first to climb back into the car when Gran Masha said it was time to move on.

Beyond Kilnave the road led past some abandoned farmsteadings and then turned inland, away from Loch Gruinart, and skirted Loch Ardnave, a small body of freshwater that was alive with nesting ducks and grebes. They stopped briefly so that Dee could enter the birds in her notebook. Eventually they reached the road's end at the sea, where there were several stone picnic shelters in niches among the sand dunes of Tràigh Nòstaig. Two other groundcars were in the parking area and a few people were visible down by the shore. The sky had partly clouded over again and great waves were crashing onto the beach. But it was pleasant inside their shelter, where Aunt Rowan and Uncle Robbie unpacked the lunch and set it out on the salt-bleached wood of the rustic table. A flock of gulls immediately appeared, evidently having designs on the food, and some of the bolder birds began buzzing the picnic grounds.

Ken set out to chase them, but Gran Masha urged him to sit down and then used her strong coercion to shoo the pests away. Dee got out her bird plaque, ran through the gull pictures until she identified the correct species, then soberly entered them in her Day List with a tap of her fingernail: HERRING GULL. GLAUCOUS GULL. COMMON GULL. LESSER BLACK-BACKED GULL. LITTLE GULL.

"Very good." Viola nodded in approval. "And do you see that large, dark bird soaring above the sea?"

"Yes, Mummie."

"It's a pomarine skua. Rather uncommon. Find it in your book."

Obediently, Dee pressed the plaque's upper right-hand corner until the image of the marine predator appeared—

And then it happened again.

Dee's face froze into a blank mask. The mind-prober was back! This time the digging was very gentle and cautious and she almost had not noticed it. Once she did, she had no trouble resisting the would-be intruder. But Mummie mustn't know!

"Well, aren't you going to enter the bird?" Viola asked rather testily.

"But—but I have to identify it *myself* to put it on the list. And I can't see it well enough to be sure it's not a gray allan or some other kind of skua. You forgot, Mummie . . . I don't have farsight." Hold fast! The mind-prober can't get in. Angel! Help me keep my barrier strong!

Uncle Robbie pulled a little pair of binoculars out of his jacket pocket. "Use these, lass. My own farsight's nothing special, and I always carry them when birding."

Dee peered blindly through the glasses and then silently tapped the plaque. POMARINE SKUA appeared on the checklist.

"I'm glad that's finally official." Viola smiled tightly. "Shall we eat?"

The hotel had packed sandwiches of Islay cheese and thin-sliced roast beef spread with crunchy mustard. There were also celery and carrot sticks, crisp green New Zealand apples, and gingerbread. The children drank cold milk, and a Zojirushi bottle brewed sweet hot tea for the adults at the touch of a button. After they had finished eating they got their daypacks from the car, and then Gran Masha programmed the vehicle and sent it away on autopilot. They would find it waiting for them at the end of the hike.

"Do you think we'll be able to visit the old MacGregor place when we get to Sanaigmore?" Aunt Rowan asked.

Masha shook her head. "I inquired at the hotel this morning. The farm is privately owned and not open to the public. But we can see it from the cliffs and perhaps get a closer look when we return to the car." She buckled her small pack. "Well, let's be off."

No one noticed that Dee had eaten almost nothing. She put on her own daypack like a person in a trance, paying no attention to the shorebirds running about on the strand. The mind-prober was still slyly at work.

Later, Dee would remember very little of the first hour or so of the hike, during which the assault on her mind continued. Then, to her great relief, it stopped. She was still safe behind her strong blue armor and now she felt much less frightened. Whoever the prober was, he could not get in. Dee was very proud of herself and when she was able, she told Ken all about her mental victory.

"I'm only five years old," she boasted, "but I'm strong."

"Then carry my pack," Ken demanded.

She only stuck her tongue out at him and ran off ahead of everyone along the rough, high shore, saying the triumphant words over and over again to herself:

I'm strong I'm strong I'm strong!

The path dipped to cross a little burn in a rocky hollow, and it was there that Dee saw something moving among the tumbled boulders and stopped short. She thought at first it was an animal and eagerly pulled Uncle Robbie's binoculars from her anorak pouch to get a good look at it.

It was not an animal.

Scrambling faster than a monkey, it whisked into a crevice between two huge rocks almost as soon as she got it into focus. But she had seen it clearly for the merest instant: a person nearly as small as her brother Ken, having bandy legs and arms that were disproportionately long. He was dressed in black clothes and he had frowsy black hair and a black beard.

The Dubh Sìth.

No! It's only a story! He can't be real. Oh, angel . . .

The adults and Ken found her standing petrified, with the binoculars still held to her eyes.

"Have you discovered something interesting, Dody?" Mummie inquired.

Slowly, she lowered the glasses. "I thought—but it's gone now, whatever it was." She handed the binoculars back to Uncle Robbie, keeping her renewed fear carefully concealed behind her mental mask. From then on she walked close to the adults, and now and then she stopped and quickly turned around to scan the landscape behind them. But there was never anyone there.

They came to a medium-sized sea-cave full of nesting rock doves and discovered the most interesting bird they had yet seen. It was a large gyrfalcon perched on a nearby rock, watching the doves fly in and out of the cave. Dee was enchanted as she viewed it through the binoculars. She had watched Tri-Ds about these rare birds and she had seen a live gyrfalcon of the dark-colored Icelandic race once before, at a considerable distance. But this was a Greenland gyrfalcon, nearly white.

Abruptly the splendid bird of prey took wing, soaring high above the sea, and a moment later it was back almost overhead. It stooped, diving with incredible speed, and seized one of the hapless doves in a shocking explosion of feathers. Then it flew off seaward with the limp body, heading toward some skerries that thrust darkly from the foaming breakers.

Dee slowly let out the breath she had been holding. The beautiful bird had killed in order to eat. She knew falcons did that, but never before had she seen it happen right before her eyes. It saddened her that some creatures should be born to kill, should need the lives of others in order to survive themselves. She entered both the rock dove and the gyrfalcon on her list, gave the field glasses back to Uncle Robbie, and then walked along at his side, brooding.

People also killed animals for food. Why, the roast beef in their sandwiches had once been part of living cattle! Some of Dee's mates at kindergarten ate only vegetables out of respect for animal life; but when Dee had spoken about this interesting idea to Mummie, she had only frowned and called it sentimental tommyrot and told Dee to finish her pork chop. Of course, the domestic meat animals didn't suffer at all when they died, the way the poor dove killed by the falcon must have.

Or had it? Dimly, she remembered a wildlife program in which the narrator had asserted that creatures seized violently by predators went almost instantly into a state of shock and felt no pain. Could that be true? It would be kind of God to make it so—especially since he had made the meat-eaters in the first place . . .

Thinking about this and other mysteries, Dee nearly forgot her fear.

In midafternoon they came to Sanaigmore Bay, where there were numbers of ruined stone crofts looking forlorn beneath the gray sky. While they rested among the sandhills and had a snack, Uncle Robbie told the story of the Clearances during the 1800s, when small tenant farmers who lived in the Hebrides and on the Scottish mainland were forced to leave their homes because the rich people who owned the lands wanted to create huge sheep runs.

Dee was appalled. "But, couldn't the little farmers *do* anything?"

Uncle Robbie shook his head. "They were powerless. The rich people had the law on their side in those days, and the law said that property was more important than people. So the poor farmers lost their homes and livelihood and had to go live somewhere else, like North America. There was a lot of suffering. The people who stayed and managed the sheep were the lucky ones—and some of them were Jamie MacGregor's ancestors." He smiled at Dee and Ken. "And yours."

Gran Masha pointed out the place where the MacGregors had lived, which lay some distance uphill from the bayshore. There were no sheep on the land now and the farmhouse had become a luxurious private home.

As she studied the distant buildings with the wind-blasted trees and ornamental shrubbery surrounding them, Dee felt a sudden deep pulse of dread. *That place* . . . She knew with sick certainty that it was the source of all the evil feelings that had plagued her throughout the holiday. But when she went to Ken, who was throwing stones into the surf, and told him her discovery he refused to believe her.

"Everybody knows that Jamie MacGregor was one of the greatest men who ever lived." He did not bother to conceal his scorn. "He forced the normals in the world to be fair to True People. His old house just couldn't be giving off bad vibes."

"Not the house," Dee said. Her lips were trembling and it was all she could do not to burst into tears. "The people inside! . . . Kenny, it was *them* trying to ream my mind, not the Gi or the Krondaku. I'm certain!"

"You said the probing was exotic—"

"It was. Maybe exotics live in the house. Bad ones! And I saw the Kilnave Fiend, too, when we were back on the cliffs—"

"You're stone doolally! You know? Completely batshit!" He turned away from her, and she felt his own sudden terror now, overlaid with strong denial. "Leave me alone! Tell Mum if you're so scared. Now naff off!"

But of course she couldn't tell Mummie or any of the other grown-ups. It was just impossible. Nor could she allow them to see her afraid, for humiliation would make everything worse. She covered her face with her hands, praying to the angel, submerging herself in the sweet rosy pool of redaction. Then Mummie called and they set off again on the final leg of their walk, heading for the heights of Tòn Mhór. There were sure to be guillemots nesting in the cliffs, Gran said, and kittiwakes and razorbills. And if they were very lucky, they might even see puffins!

Damn that brat!

Fucked it up did you luv?

I followed her nearlyanhour used every trick in my armamentarium and had no more luck than you did. That incrediblypowerfulmindscreen of hers has been strengthened somehow since we played our little map game with her back in Edinburgh. A strong redactivefactor has been added to it. The child has *grown.* She's still latent as far as any external manifestation of metafaculties goes but I'm convinced that she actually senses Hydra while the boy and the 3masterclass adults and GrandMasterMasha don't.

She could be dangerous Maddy.

Yes . . .

Jeopardize our plan.

Bullshit youguys! She's only a kid. Fury would have warned us if she posed any real threat.

Fury might not have known.

FurydearFury knows *everything*!

Cele he only outlined the plan to us broadly how could he have suspected that a latent child would have grandmasterly screening ability to say nothing of the psychosensitivity to detect Hydra? Maddy&I softened her up on ferryboat tried to get into her skull to neutralize her but no luck.

. . . Parni? [Anxiety.] We'll still have the feast won't we?

Don't sweat it Celebabe. But Quint&Maddy are probably right. As usual. Sounds like we'll have to modify the plan of attack a skosh that's all.

Both the girl *and* the GrandMaster must be bypassed.

I agree. Our metaconcert might not be strong enough to take her+masterclass adults.

Aw shit! Why not let me hide at the top of the geodh

and just *push* the kid over? No coercivemetaconcert needed—just a flick of the wrist. She'll go down with the three adults and shock+physical injuries will cancel her screeningability and we'll have her cold.

Oh yes let's do it Parni's way I'd so hate to miss out on the girl! [Wistful longing.] She'd be exceptionally delicious you know. The strong latencies would provide a lovelytang that would offset the bland taste of immaturelifeforce.

[Laughter.] Celebabe you are too much!

Wait until I've dined and I'll show you what TOO MUCH can be lover . . .

Will you two stop acting like fools? Parni your idea is out of the question. All units of the Hydra *must* be down in the geodh ready to receive the 2Strachans&RowanGrant and get them quickly into the cave. They must be completely subdued before they can give a telepathic shout or press the alarm buttons on their wrist-coms. Let me remind you that the 3researchers are the ones Fury instructed us to eliminate. The girl is extraneous.

Maddy's right.

Maddy's always fuckingright . . .

It will still be a glorious meal. I'm so starved I'm actually weak—

Well you damnwell better pull your weight in the metaconcert this time Cele no bubblebraining or other wrongnotes. And you too Parni or your ass is grass. This kill won't be easy. There must be NO OUTCRY no other hint that they're being harmed the others must think they've simply wandered off.

[Truculent assent.] What about the boy?

I've been thinking that over. We'll have to let him live too.

Ohhhhhhh . . .

I agree with Quint. If GrandMasterMasha is encumbered with two small children it will be that much longer before she becomes alarmed at the disappearance of the others.

Ohhhhhhh . . .

Hey Celebabe doncha worry we'll still have the best goodies since we got stuck here on this damnisland. Three masterclass operants! It'll be megaloendorphic! We'll blast into solar orbit.

[Reluctant acceptance.] But you *know* I like young ones.

Quint have you scanned the area thoroughly? We must make certain that there are no other grandmasterclass metas in the vicinity when we implement the ambush. The professor is a fairly inefficient farsensor I don't think she'll be able to see through the dense Precambrian rocks into the cave but a more talented GrandMaster might.

There are a few other birdwatchers and hikers at the cliff nesting sites right now. Only two lowpoweredheads amongst them. More people will probably show up by the time our friends arrive but it shouldn't affect our plans. I've found only 6 other GrandMasters on the entireisland and 3 of them are Gi. None are anywhere near our area.

Good. Let's get into position then.

Bon appétit everyone!

Celebabe you are TOO MUCH.

The climb up to the headland of Tòn Mhór was a steep one and Dee was exhausted when they finally reached the top—not only physically weary, but also mind-numb from the ebb and flow of fear that had afflicted her all throughout the weekend. She still felt an evil exotic presence nearby and it was as scary as ever. But it hadn't *done* anything except try to see inside her. She knew she could keep it out—so why should she care about it anymore? What she really wanted was to rest.

The others had gone immediately to the lookout at the cliff's edge in search of birds, but Dee plumped herself down on a small patch of grass in the lee of a great rock and didn't move. Clouds were racing overhead. She could hear the rumble of waves pounding at the base of the cliffs and the shrill cries of kittiwakes. Ken and the grownups were peering over the fenced precipice a dozen meters away, and a number of other people were also busy with cameras and viewing devices. Dee heard voices exclaiming over something and after a few minutes, Gran Masha came looking for her.

"We've found puffins and razorbills nesting, Dorothea," Gran said heartily. "Come and use Uncle Robbie's field glasses."

"I'm really very tired." She tried to keep her voice steady. Gran Masha hated whining. "I've had enough birdwatching for today. I'd like to go back to the car, please. I'm sure I could find my way by myself. You could tell me the car's door code, and I could wait for you inside."

The professor frowned, her face showing concern rather than annoyance. "Poor baby. It has been a long walk, hasn't it? But we've just come to the best birding place on all Islay. And there's wonderful news! One of the people we've just been talking to says that a small flock of retroevolved great auks have been spotted swimming off the rocks just a klom or so further west along the cliff track. Your mum and Uncle Robbie and Aunt Rowan are eager to be off at once."

"Great auks? . . . "

"A black-and-white flightless bird that looks something like a huge penguin. They stand nearly a meter high. They were exterminated in 1844. But genetic engineers used DNA from some skins preserved in the British Museum to bring them back again about ten years ago. The breeding colonies are still very small and rare, and we'll be very lucky to see them."

Dee turned away. In spite of all her resolution, tears had begun to slide down her cheeks. "Granny, I don't feel well. I'm sorry to be so tiresome. Maybe I could just sit here by myself and wait while the rest of you go and see the auks."

"No, that wouldn't do, Dorothea." Masha sighed, then smiled at the sight of Dee's woeful face. "Don't worry, dear. I'll wait with you, and you can try to take a little nap. When you wake up, you'll probably feel much better. I don't mind staying. I've already seen the great auk. I'll just tell the others, then come right back."

Dee closed her eyes.

Oh, angel, I really would like to go to sleep and forget this horrid feeling! Why am I so sure that something awful is going to happen? Should I tell Gran Masha about the bad exotics in the farmhouse? Should I tell her about the mind-reamer? . . . But I don't want anybody to think I'm a silly baby! I only want to hide. Hide behind my strong blue wall and float on my nice rosy pool and be safe. That's all I want. Can't I just do that—?

"There, now. It's all settled."

Dee opened her eyes. Gran stood there together with a very glum-faced Ken. "The three of us will wait here while your Mum and aunt and uncle go see the great auks at Geodh Ghille Mhóire."

"I wanted to go!" Ken said peevishly.

Masha undid her pack, took out a cushion, and pinched it to inflate it. "You're tired, too, Kenneth. The walk to the geodh is strenuous and you're better off staying here, as your Mum said. Sit here beside me on the cushion. It seems there's only enough grass for Dorothea."

Still grumbling, Ken settled down.

"What's a gyo gilmore?" Dee asked sleepily.

"It means 'Gilmour's Chasm.' It's a steep cleft in the northwestern corner of the island, and once a terrible shipwreck happened there. But never mind about that. I'm going to tell you another story—one I heard when I first came to Islay many years ago." Masha put one arm around Ken and the other around Dee. Since her rejuvenation, Gran wasn't quite as soft and comfy as she used to be, but it still felt very good to be cuddled next to her.

"Did you hear the story from Grandad?" Ken asked.

"Yes. Now hush and listen: The story is about the great cave at Bholsa on the other side of Loch Gruinart. It's the biggest cave in the west of Scotland. For centuries people used it as a shelter and even kept sheep in the area around the entrance. But they were afraid to go very deep inside because it was said that its tunnel led straight to the fiery underworld."

"You mean, like hell?" Ken asked doubtfully.

"Yes. Now let me tell the tale. One day a brave piper said he was going to find out for himself what was inside the great cave, and he marched in playing 'MacCrimmon's Lament,' with his little dog following after . . ."

Dee closed her eyes again and let the calm voice of her grandmother fill her mind, overwhelming everything else.

. . .

She dreamed she was a white gyrfalcon, flying high above the rocky headland, following Mummie and Uncle Robbie and Aunt Rowan. As the three tiny figures approached a long, deep cleft in the rocks they began to hurry. Strange noises came faintly on the wind. Was it the great auk? The gyrfalcon lofted high, curving out over the churning sea and then turning back to fly up the geodh.

The three figures reached the lip of the chasm.

And one by one, as the falcon watched in helpless horror, they leapt into empty space. They tumbled slowly, slowly down, as gently as falling leaves, neither their minds nor their voices crying out, until they landed on a rocky shelf. There the waves boomed and hissed as the sea surged into the cleft, reluctantly retreated, then came roaring back again to wash over the bodies lying there.

In the cliffside was a dark hole, and from it came a scuttling dwarfish thing that moved as quickly as a spider.

The Kilnave Fiend.

Plummeting down, the gyrfalcon cried a warning. At the sound of the bird's scream the three people lying on the drenched rock slowly lifted their heads and caught sight of the horrid thing approaching.

Get up! the falcon cried. Run! Run!

But the adults seemed paralyzed—or else they did not understand her. She swooped past their listless faces and hurtled toward the Fiend himself, talons outstretched and beak agape.

Instantly, the dwarf changed, expanding into a huge, ungainly black beast larger than an elephant, having four misshapen heads. Its eight eyes blazed blue-white like a constellation of evil stars, and its red mouths had pointed tongues thrusting in and out. Four long, supple necks bent over Uncle Robbie and the many black limbs held him fast.

Slimy lips pursed. The thing began to suck out his life.

She flung herself at the monster telling it: NO NO STOP STOP—

Pain.

The most awful pain she had ever felt. It lasted only an instant, and when it stopped the four-headed monster had vanished. Dee seemed to see two men and two women deep inside the wet green cave, laughing. On the rocky floor were three smoking dark mounds that might have been large heaps of half-burnt seaweed. Mummie and Uncle Robbie and Aunt Rowan were gone.

"Go away!" the red-mouthed bright-eyed people said. "Go away, you stupid bird, and find your own food! There's nothing at all left here. Nothing but ashes."

She knew then what the smoking piles must be. She screamed and flew at the four adults in a rage of sorrow. But before her talons struck, the people turned again into the ravening monster. Its black arms spread wide. It seized her and the four laughing mouths got ready to suck and once again there was horrible pain . . .

Dee woke from the dream, crying out. Ken, somewhere nearby, was also shrieking at the top of his lungs.

She was not a gyrfalcon but her own self. And the pain was real. Her head was covered by something, and she was being squeezed so tightly that she could hardly breathe. She kicked and struggled until finally she tore herself free and scrabbled about in the stony dust, dazzled by the sudden daylight, sobbing and gulping and gasping as she regained her breath. She crawled a short distance away, still hearing Kenny's screams, feeling giddy with shock.

It was some moments before the dizziness passed. And then Dee saw that it had not been the Kilnave Fiend of her nightmare trying to crush her. It was Gran Masha!

Her grandmother sat with her back to a large rock, her youthful features so distorted that she was hardly recognizable. Her eyes were shut tightly and her mouth was twisted awry. She was making an inhuman rhythmic groaning noise, as though every breath she took was unbearable agony, and she clutched Kenny, flailing and howling, to her breast. His head was partially muffled by her open jacket.

Dee heard Masha's mind shouting: *Holdyouholdyou notletyougo never letyougo you FIEND!*

Dee was nearly paralyzed with fear. What was wrong with Gran? "Let him go!" she screamed. "Gran, let Kenny go, you're hurting him!"

Had the Kilnave Fiend somehow got inside Gran's mind? Dee tried to shout again but found that she was unable to utter a sound. It was not until she thought to close her eyes and summon the healing redness that she regained any strength. She climbed to her feet then and staggered toward the cliff overlook.

"Help! Somebody help!"

But no one was there. She turned back, heading for the steep path that led down to the car park, trying not to hear Ken's weakening cries and the ghastly sounds made by her grandmother.

"Help! Help!" She stumbled down the trail, tripping over heather roots and exposed rocks, pulling herself back up, canceling out the pain, shouting again, going on and on—

CHILD. STOP.

She was brought up short, coerced to a standstill, nearly fainting, certain that the four-headed monster who had driven Gran crazy was now taking hold of her with its deadly mental power.

No, little girl. You are safe. I will not harm you. I am an official of the Galactic Magistratum. A kind of policeman. Open your mind to me and tell me what is wrong. OPEN.

A vast indigo wave swallowed her. Coercion. Almost overwhelming her protective shield, yet failing at the last. She was still safe! But Gran Masha and Kenny . . . She looked into the face of an elderly man who held her by the shoulders as he knelt in front of her.

He was wearing a garish orange sports jacket.

"My g-granny . . . my b-brother . . . " she stuttered. Then she seemed to see him properly for the first time, and she whispered: "You!"

Be still, Dorothea Macdonald. I will not hurt you. I will help you if I can. [By the All-Penetrant! What a mind-screen this infant weaves! I don't believe I can force it.] "Little one, tell me in verbal speech what is wrong. Are you hurt?"

"No . . ." It was the Krondaku, all right, but no longer talking like a fake Scot! "My granny—the Kilnave Fiend's got her. And my brother. Up there." Dee pointed, then she pulled herself loose from the exotic's illusory hands and began to run back the way she had come. "Come on!" she shouted, and was lost to view behind a rock outcropping.

"Wait. Trust me. Open your mind. It will be so much quicker!"

But the child ignored him, and so Evaluator Throma'eloo Lek thrust forth his seekersense, located the madwoman with the half-throttled boy far up the slope, smote her with his coercion to force her to turn the lad loose, poured the balm of redaction upon the suddenly released victim, and was astounded to realize that he knew the deranged operant female who now lay thrashing weakly among the rocks at the top of the headland of Tòn Mhór.

"Sacred Aperiodicity! It's Professor Masha MacGregor-Gawrys! And what's this in her mind? . . . I cannot believe it. All *three*? And branded with those peculiar radially symmetrical patterns of ash? Extraordinary!"

Earth's gravity was twice the optimum for the Krondak species and the planet was oxygen-deprived as well. Lacking the vulgar metafaculty of psychokinesis that might have sped him on his way, the Evaluator could only struggle up the path with ponderous slowness. Finally, in order to conserve his fast-dwindling energies, he shed the superficial guise of humanity and slithered au naturel to the scene of the disaster, pushing aside with his tentacles the sharp rocks and obstructing plant life. His primary optics glowed bright blue.

The little girl uttered a shriek when the exotic apparition first came into view, but she stood her ground beside her collapsed brother, an expression of fierce resolution on her face. Masha and the little boy lay about two meters apart. Ken was coughing and weeping, while the professor still rolled feebly in the throes of her seizure.

"Stand back, Dorothea. Do not touch your grandmother. I will take care of her. You may assist your brother if you are able. Give him some water. See that he does not aspirate it—choke on it."

Uncertain, Dee stared at the hideous being for a moment, then nodded. She unzipped one of the daypacks that had been flung aside by Gran's struggles, took out a water bottle, and knelt beside Ken.

The exotic sent out several urgent farspoken communications. Then he supported Masha's lolling head with one tentacle while a second pressed against her forehead. Instantly, the paroxysms ceased and she fell back in a faint. The Krondaku gently lowered her to the ground and placed the air cushion beneath her head. After a few moments she opened her eyes and moaned softly.

"Be at ease, dear colleague. It is I, Throma'eloo Lek."

"Lek?" Masha's voice was hoarse. "Oh, thank God. I *tried* to hold it for the authorities, but . . . Did—did you see in my mind what happened? In the sea-cave?"

"Yes." His voice was solemn and portentous. "This is a very grave situation. More serious even than you realize, for I know what kind of entity has done this terrible thing." Masha mydearfriend are you capable of mental speech? I do not want to traumatize the children further by speaking of this in front of them.

Lek! I hurt poor little Dorothea&Kenneth! I didn't mean to nonono I was deluded thought they were the THING ohGod as the three of them began to die to give up their lifeforce in that hideous way the vision burst into my farsight and I saw them burn and I tried to seize the THING I thought I had it but . . . but . . .

[*Peace.*] I am afraid that you suffered a violent brainstorm. Perhaps it was indeed triggered by the draining of the lifeforce from the persons who were beloved by you. Perhaps it was caused by . . . something else. I have repaired some of your mental damage but you will require additional treatment later. The two children are well. I redacted their minor injuries.

Lek! Call the Magistratum fortheloveofGod Viola&Robbie&Rowan were burnt beyond recognition beyond any hope of regeneration how in Christ'sname could it have happened CATCH THE THING THE KILNAVEFIEND BEFORE IT GETS AWAY—

I regret to say it is already gone. The local police are on their way and I have summoned investigators of the Human Magistratum from both Edinburgh and Concord. And also the First Magnate of the Human Polity.

Paul Remillard? But—

This tragedy concerns him personally. And his family.

"I don't understand." Masha spoke aloud. Slow tears had begun to streak her dusty face. Her hair lay in sweaty strands, which a gentle tentacle brushed back from her forehead.

"Gran Masha?" Dee stood there, hesitantly offering the water bottle. "Would you like a drink, too?"

"You poor children," Masha whispered, turning aside, refusing to look at Dee. Her voice caught in a sob. "Oh, sweet Jesus. Lek, be sure that they don't—" A tentacle touched her lips and she fell silent. Her eyes closed.

Dee said to the Krondaku, "It got away, didn't it."

"So you know that much," the exotic murmured. "Remarkable."

Gran Masha seemed to be sleeping. Dee knew the Krondaku had done that to help her. The awesome exotic body now began to shimmer, to shrink. He was fuzzing her mind and putting on his human illusion again, but the pressed-down outline of his bulk in the dust remained the same.

"I knew something awful was going to happen," Dee told him. "But I didn't know what, and I was afraid nobody would believe me if I said anything."

"It is a metafaculty called prolepsis, Dorothea Macdonald. Even latent humans like you may have it. The power is not well understood."

Dee nodded. "I dreamed the monster was coming after me."

"A delusion. Your mind, like that of your grandmother, was affected by the death throes of your loved ones. You were never in danger."

But Dee was not so sure about that. She knew who the Kilnave Fiend was. She had seen all four of the beast's human faces. Two she knew already: the man and woman she had met on the ferryboat. The others had been strangers but she would never forget them.

Ken had got to his feet and was standing behind her. Fading bruises, ugly purple and yellow marks, discolored his face. The Krondaku's healing was not completely instantaneous.

"You children will have to be brave," Throma'eloo Lek said. His human face was kind and very sad. He reached out to them, took their hands, and poised his redaction again, ready to calm them once more if it was required. "There has been a most melancholy occurrence. Your mother and your uncle and your aunt have died."

Ken uttered a choked gasp and burst into tears. Dee spoke with soft intensity. "Do you know *who* killed them?"

The Krondaku frowned and did not respond to her question directly. "It may take some time to discover how they died. I am very, very sorry."

Dee nodded, pulling her hand free. The Krondaku did know about the monster—but he thought she did not. Very well . . .

Ken was weeping bitterly. It did not occur to Dee to wonder why she felt calm and unafraid. Certainly it was not because of the Krondaku's mental power, which she had shut out of her mind. She was quite certain that the Kilnave Fiend was gone. The aetheric aura of Islay was now peaceful.

How very strange, she thought, that all of a sudden I can't remember Mummie's face, or Aunt Rowan's, or Uncle Robbie's. But I remember *them.*

"What's—what's going to happen to us?" Ken's voice was desperate.

"Your grandmother will soon recover," Throma'eloo said. "She will love you and care for you."

Dee looked down at the sleeping woman. Gran Masha probably did love them, but she was always so very busy. Now that she was young again, she would be even busier. It would be a great bother for her to have to take care of two little children, and Dee did not want to be a bother. Besides, there was a better place for them to go.

"No," she told the Krondaku, "we won't be staying with our granny. We're going to live with Daddy. On the planet Caledonia."

FURYFURYFURY answerpleaseansweranswer FURYFURYFU—

<Yes. [Tranquillity.] My dear Hydra I am here . . . !! But what are you doing at the Unst Starport—>

GettingthehelloffEarth. Don't worry I did job got you decrypt and the 3subjects are extinct but there was unforeseenproblem. [Image.]

<A *Krondaku*? A high official of the Galactic Magistratum? You integral imbecile!>

He was on Islay incognito both mind&body disguised. How could I have known? He never perceived my identity I left as soon as I had fed but he did find the burnt bodies deep inside the cave you *know* how those octopoid brutes can see through rock I was going to return to destroy them after I had . . . celebrated . . . but when I checked the cave out after an hour or so it was swarming with cops and the bodies were discovered and I decided to blast off—

<Yesyes. Enough! . . . You say that you have the mental key to the encrypted files?>

Yes. [Data.] There it is fresh out of RobbieStrachan's skull you've got plenty of time to wipe out the dangerous shit and substitute whitebread nobody will ever suspect a thing.

<Excellent . . . Do you think that the Krondak Evaluator has identified the killer as Hydra yet?>

I'm sure of it he's the same one who interrogated Marc when I whacked old BrettMcAllister years&years ago he recognized the 7ashen chakras on each bod and the goddamkid DorotheaMacdonald had some mixedup EE perception of Hydra too she'll tell Krondaku&cops about Sanaigmorehouse they'll find MY/our DNA odds&sods all over the fucking place I'm completely blown I delayed leaving Earth only until I could contact you I thought you'd *never* answer!

<This is a nuisance. But by no means a catastrophe. [Cogitation.] Where had you planned to go?>

Elysium. You set up corporation there. Lose myself in the booming cosmop scene—

<I think not. I have a better idea. [Image.]>

There? But aren't you afraid—

<Be silent. As it happens there will be useful work for you to do on this particular world. But you must not embark from Unst Starport. Take a shuttle to Anami-o-Shima at once. I will have tickets waiting for you there and I will modify the transport records so that the Magistratum will never discover where you have gone. However the contretemps on Islay necessitates the utmost discretion from now on in your feeding activities even when you are away from Earth. You will take only enough lifeforce to maintain your identity—>

Shit!

<—and henceforward you will destroy the bodies promptly! No more procrastinating "celebrations"! Is this understood?>

Yes. Fury I'm sorry . . . Do you still love me?

<Dear Hydra. Of course. It is only the thought of losing you [having my grand scheme for the Second Milieu fail!] losing the dear ones I created with so much loving care that vexes me. It is true that you could not have anticipated the presence of the Krondaku. You did your very best. *Know* that I love you!>

Everything I/we owned was left behind at Sanaigmore . . .

<You will lack for nothing when you reach your new home. I will see to it. Unfortunately I am not at the present time able to reprogram your mental signatures. That will have to wait. But it should cause no problem at the present time. When you arrive at Anami-o-Shima Starport you will find that new identities in these names [image] have been entered in the Human Polity vital statistics database. Your emi-

gration formalities will have been taken care of. I will provide you with new credit cards. Ample funds will be transferred to a new corporate bank account. Do not attempt to use the old corporation. You are now to operate under the aegis of Lernaeus Limited—a purveyor of biochemicals—as well as penetrating the planetary government.>

Whatever you say. Only . . . pleaseplease don't ever leave me completely alone again.

<We will commune whenever it is practicable. I will give you further instructions when you reach your new home. Now however there are many things that I must do so farewell.>

Goodbye Fury. Goodbye . . .

[6]

FROM THE MEMOIRS OF ROGATIEN REMILLARD

I was there when death gave life to them, both Fury and the creature called the Hydra. It happened on Good Friday in the year 2040 in the little town of Berlin, New Hampshire, on the day that Victor Remillard finally died.

It had been the custom of my nephew Denis, Victor's older brother, to assemble the immediate family each year on that date, ostensibly to pray for Vic's recovery and for the salvation of his soul. I had never participated in the annual ritual before, judging it to be futile and possibly even dangerous; but that year Denis's wife Lucille was unavailable and so I was dragooned to complete the metapsychic minyan.

There were fifteen of us gathered around the bed of the criminal genius who had unwittingly helped to precipitate the Intervention. After he had tried and failed to murder me and nearly three thousand of Earth's leading operants, he had been struck down—perhaps by me, perhaps by the entity I call the Family Ghost—and lapsed into a mysterious coma that deprived him of all sensory input and of all his metafaculties except self-awareness. His body, having the Remillard self-rejuvenating gene complex, had remained healthy for nearly twenty-seven years while he endured the ultimate solitary confinement. But finally, at long last, Victor seemed to be sinking toward natural death.

Present for that last Good Friday prayer session were all seven of Denis and Lucille's adult grandmasterclass children together with their operant spouses—the so-called Remillard Dynasty. The oldest was Philip Remillard, with his wife Aurelie Dalembert. She was the only wife who was not pregnant at the time. The other Remillards were Maurice, with his wife Cecilia Ashe; Severin, with his wife Maeve O'Neill; Anne Remillard, who was unmarried, although she did not become a Jesuit until some years later; Catherine Remillard (enceinte), with her husband Brett McAllister; Adrien, with his wife Cheri Losier-Drake; and the most brilliant of the lot, Paul Remillard, with his wife Teresa Kendall.

When Denis attempted to link me into the metaconcerted "prayer," I balked. Frankly, I was scared shitless, wanting to have nothing whatsoever to do with Vic, who was the most evil man I have ever known. Pray for him? Maybe if I was shamed into it I might have squandered a two-bob candle in some nice, bright church, on the off chance that Jesus knew something about Vic that the rest of the world did not and was willing to forgive and forget. But in no way was I going to be involved in any interactive mental shenanigans concerning that thoroughgoing bastard. My charity does not easily embrace a man who had attempted to turn me into his zomboid stooge—and when that failed, who was ready to drain my lifeforce like a bottle of Heineken.

So when Denis tried to incorporate me into his metaconcert I slithered out. And since I was his foster father, with all of the operant parent's usual metapsychic perks, not even his paramount coercion could force me to stay. Thus it was that my mentality stood aside somehow, unable to perceive what transpired among Victor and the others, and I became aware that an entirely new actor had come onstage.

Who are you? I asked.

I am Fury.

Where did you come from?

I am newborn. Inevitably.

What do you want?

All of you. I require assistance. And I'll take you to start with. Silly, flawed old Rogi! But you'll be useful . . .

I knew in a lightning stroke of insight that it was a demon, a mind-devourer conjured somehow by the dying Victor. It didn't get me because the Family Ghost saved my pathetic ass, telling Fury to do what it had to do, but not with me. In the dream, or vision, or whatever the hell it was, I clung to a gigantic simulacrum of the key-ring charm that I call the Great Carbuncle and was towed back to reality.

Where I discovered that Victor was dead.

The Dynasty and Denis and I were all safe, and so was baby Marc, Paul's son, who had been left in an adjacent room with a nurse.

Victor's body was cremated, and on Easter Monday of the year 2040 Denis went to Anticosti Starport and handed a leaden box containing the compacted ashes to the captain of the CSS Saul Minionman, outward bound to the planet Assawompsett. Before the starship left our solar system, the captain launched the remains of Victor Remillard on an impact trajectory into the sun.

That seemed to be that . . . until Fury's creature, the Hydra, fed for the first time in 2051, and it seemed that Vic had somehow been reborn.

Brett Doyle McAllister, Catherine Remillard's husband, was Hydra's first victim. His body was hideously charred, and along the spine and on the head were seven peculiar ashen patches like intricately drawn wheels or flowers: chakra symbols. In Kundalini Yoga the chakras are subtle force-centers that are intimately connected to the vital lattices infusing the human body. But what had been done to Brett had no basis in pranic healing or any other ancient discipline; it was instead a kind of metapsychic vampirism that only one person was ever known to have used before.

Victor.

In 2013 I was an eyewitness when he murdered Shannon O'Connor, whose body was branded like Brett's. Hours later, Shannon's villainous father, Kieran O'Connor, was killed in an identical manner when he tried to foil Vic's plans on the night of the Great Intervention. Only a handful of people, all nonoperant save for Denis and me, ever realized that Vic had killed O'Connor and his daughter in a completely unique manner, by draining their lifeforce through the chakra points.

When Brett McAllister was murdered in the same way, Victor had been dead for eleven years.

Hydra, Fury's agent, was to remain nameless for some time to come; but the next action that could be directly attributed to Brett McAllister's killer was an attempt on the life of Margaret Strayhorn, the wife of the famous metapsychic scholar and politician Davy MacGregor.

She was attacked later that same year, 2051, while attending a dinner party at the home of Dartmouth College's president, Tom Spotted Owl. Margaret survived the assault, but a single distinctive chakra burn on top of her head linked her assailant to that of Brett.

Two months later, Margaret Strayhorn disappeared from her apartment in Concilium Orb, the administrative center of the Galactic Milieu, apparently a suicide. There was only a single clue that hinted at murder: her farspoken cry, *Five,* which her husband perceived at the moment of her death. Davy MacGregor was convinced that whoever had attacked Margaret before had finally managed to kill her and destroy her body completely.

On the face of it, there was no obvious motive for either murder. However, Brett McAllister had managed to convince his wife Catherine Remillard to turn down her nomination to the Galactic Concilium shortly before he was slain, and the family had been extremely disappointed. With Brett dead, Cat decided to accept. This, together with certain other suspicious circumstances, led the Magistratum to conjecture that a criminally ambitious Remillard might have murdered Cat's husband.

The entire Dynasty, plus thirteen-year-old Marc, underwent rigorous mental probing by a Krondaku-Simbiari forensic team. The family all seemed to be exonerated; but the exotic officials had already begun to suspect that the seven adult Remillard siblings and Marc—and perhaps other powerful human metas as well—were able to screen their innermost thoughts from the usual kinds of coercive-redactive interrogation used by the Magistratum, thereby avoiding self-incrimination.

At that time, the Human Polity was still under probation and had not yet been admitted to full citizenship in the Galactic Milieu. The suspicion that Earthlings might be able to circumvent the justice system of the Milieu—plus the possibility that our planet's most famous and powerful metapsychic family might harbor a mental Dracula—was enough to cause some of the exotic Concilium members to demand that the Great Intervention be nullified and *all* humanity quarantined forthwith, with interstellar travel permanently prohibited.

There had been serious opposition to letting us join the Milieu in the first place. We Earthlings were considered to be a mentally immature and barbaric lot, and only a summary veto by the almighty Lylmik

Supervisors had prevented our world from being passed by. The Fury-Hydra hullabaloo brought the old objections to the fore once again, and once again the Lylmik saved our bacon. They insisted that the induction of humanity into the Milieu proceed as scheduled. Furthermore, no action was to be taken against any Remillard unless there was ironclad proof of criminal activity.

One possible motive for Margaret Strayhorn's murder, even more tenuous than that advanced for Brett's, also seemed to point the finger at the Dynasty. Margaret's husband Davy MacGregor was the only serious opponent to Paul Remillard in the election contest for First Magnate of the Human Polity. A widower who had taken thirty years to recover from his first bereavement, Davy had recently discovered that his dearly loved second wife was carrying their child. Her death might have been expected to cause Davy's emotional breakdown and the withdrawal of his candidacy, leaving the field wide open for Paul. Instead, Davy held up adamantly after Margaret's murder and vowed to track down her killer.

MacGregor narrowly lost the election and Paul became First Magnate; but Davy was appointed Planetary Dirigent of Earth, and took advantage of his august position to reopen the stalled investigation of the Dynasty. He acquired a fair amount of damning evidence by coercing *me* six ways to Sunday.

I was forced to tell him about my first encounter in 2040 with the monster called Fury. I told him how the same malignant entity seemed to show up at the birth of Jon Remillard in 2052, apparently hoping to devour the prodigious newborn mind before being thwarted somehow by me.

I told him how five other metas—including Adrien Remillard's oldest daughter Adrienne—had mysteriously disappeared during that same summer in the immediate vicinity of the family beach house on the Atlantic coast. The girl's death and the presence of seven chakras on her incinerated body had actually been perceived metapsychically by baby Jack as the murder was committed. The naïve infant, not realizing what he had witnessed, described Addie's assailants to his brother Marc as "a Hydra" controlled by "Fury." Ti-Jean was otherwise unable to identify the perpetrators and poor Addie's remains were never found.

Paul Remillard now deduced that Margaret Strayhorn's dying

thought, *Five,* referred to the number of minds that had combined in pernicious metaconcert to form Hydra; but it seemed quite incredible that five members of the Dynasty—six, if you counted Fury—were killers somehow possessed by Victor's demoniac passion.

Paul was torn between his innate desire to see justice done and his fear that the Human Polity might be expelled from the Galactic Milieu because members of his family, the most powerful human minds in the galaxy, were possibly criminal lunatics. I confessed to Davy MacGregor how Paul finally allowed Addie's death to be attributed to sharks, as the four earlier disappearances of operants had been. There was no corroborating proof, after all, that little Jack's appalling vision had been anything except infantile fantasy, no proof that entities called Fury and Hydra existed at all.

Nevertheless, in his heart Paul remained convinced that Fury and Hydra were real—and somehow intimately connected to the Dynasty.

My evidence, even though given under duress, supplied Dirigent MacGregor with legal grounds for a new interrogation of the Remillards, this time utilizing the recently invented Cambridge mechanical mind-probe, a horrendous piece of equipment that the Spanish Inquisition would have awarded five stars in the agony category. It was supposed to reveal the infallible truth when yes-or-no questions were posed to the examinees. The Dynasty and their spouses, Denis, his wife Lucille, and young Marc were all hooked to the machine and asked the following questions:

1. Are you the entity called Fury?
2. Do you know who or what Fury is?
3. Are you the entity called Hydra, or a part of that entity?
4. Do you know who Hydra is?
5. Do you know who or what killed Brett McAllister?
6. Do you know who or what killed Margaret Strayhorn?
7. Do you know who or what killed Adrienne Remillard?
8. Do you know who or what killed the four operants who disappeared in the vicinity of the New Hampshire seacoast last summer?

9. Do you know for a fact that Victor Remillard is alive?

10. Do you suspect that the Fury-Hydra murders of McAllister, Strayhorn, Adrienne Remillard, and the others have some connection to the Remillard family?

Everyone answered "No" to the first nine questions and the machine affirmed that they told the truth. All of the Dynasty wives answered "No" to the tenth question and told the truth. Lucille Cartier said "No" to the tenth question and lied. Denis Remillard, his seven adult children, and young Marc answered "Yes" to the tenth question and told the truth.

Davy MacGregor asked the Lylmik Supervisors to rule upon whether or not the results of the questioning gave him grounds to continue his investigation of the Dynasty. The Lylmik decreed that they did not. Because the interrogation had been done confidentially, according to the discretion of the Dirigent, no record of it was released to the media or the Human Magistratum. The Galactic Magistratum in Orb did retain a file, however, and the *fact* of Fury and Hydra's existence soon became the worst-kept secret among influential metas of the Human Polity—including the then-clandestine group of Magnates of the Concilium and other respected operants who would form the nucleus of the Metapsychic Rebellion in 2084.

The Rebels were the first to speculate that Fury, controller of the Hydra assassin, might be a Remillard suffering from a malignant multiple-personality disorder, possibly triggered by some deathbed mental contact with the evil Victor. His or her "normal" persona would have no inkling that a deviant Fury aspect also existed, and this meant that Fury could never be exposed by any conventional form of mental interrogation. Only a probing of the deep unconscious—a tricky and often inconclusive procedure where Grand Master metapsychics were concerned—might manage to ferret the monster out.

No one expected the Remillards to volunteer for further mental examination very soon.

The next assault by Hydra was not prompted by Fury at all, but by the jealousy of the creature itself. Earlier, Hydra had suspected that Fury was seeking ways to incorporate the powerful mind of young

Marc Remillard into its mysterious grand scheme. Hydra sought to prevent being overshadowed by trying to destroy Marc, in defiance of Fury's orders. Hydra botched the job, but it was ready to try again in 2054, when Marc had just turned sixteen. Once again Marc survived . . . but this time one unit of Hydra's multiplex mind died. Fury was in a towering rage at its creature's stupidity and had to initiate drastic damage control.

Events now rushed to a climax. At first only Marc, Ti-Jean, and I knew why Gordon McAllister, the fourteen-year-old son of Catherine Remillard and her late husband Brett, had tried to murder his cousin Marc. But the boys and I mistakenly believed that Gordo alone was Hydra.

Fury decided that we three had to die, so that the surviving Hydra-units and the monster itself would not be exposed. I was to be eliminated first. But I was saved in spite of myself, discovering in the process that the other heads of Hydra included four other children: Celine Remillard, daughter of Maurice; Quentin Remillard, son of Severin; Parnell Remillard, son of Adrien; and Madeleine Remillard, daughter of Paul, and Marc's own younger sister. They were all fourteen years old. Later we deduced that the Hydra-children had been in utero as their mothers prayed around the deathbed of Victor in the year 2040. Somehow, as the family's most flagrant black sheep expired, he had been able to *tempt* those intelligent, precocious fetuses—and win them for his successor, Fury.

Escaping from Hydra's attack with a little help from a friend, I rushed to help Marc save baby Jack, who was confined to the Dartmouth Medical School's Hitchcock Hospital with (as we then believed) terminal cancer. But Fury got there ahead of us and set Ti-Jean's room on fire. The miracle of the child's rescue was described in the previous volume of my memoirs.

The four youngsters who comprised the Hydra had disappeared, but by their brazen attack on me, they had given themselves away as homicidal cat's-paws. The Dirigent of Earth and the Galactic Magistratum conducted intensive investigations after the Hydra-children's identities were discovered, hoping to unmask Fury. Because the Lylmik insisted upon keeping the reputations of the Remillard magnates unsullied until indisputable proof of criminal activity was obtained, everything was handled with exquisite discretion. As far as the media were concerned, the attack on Marc by Gordo McAllister was an act of adolescent insanity, and the fire in Jack's hospital room was an unfortunate accident that had a gloriously happy ending.

But behind closed doors, all of us Remillards—including me, but not the newly reincarnated Ti-Jean, who was too young to endure the trauma—were subjected to interrogation conducted by the Milieu's premier mind-reamer, Evaluator Throma'eloo Lek. By coincidence, this official had also put Marc to the question back in the days when the boy was suspected of having drowned me and his mother.

No fresh data were obtained as a result of the Evaluator's best efforts. We all checked out innocent as lambs. The Hydra-children had apparently vanished off the face of the Earth—and there was no trace of them on any other Milieu world, either. This meant that they were dead . . . or that by some unimaginable virtuoso maneuver Fury had managed to alter the mental signature—the unique brain-pattern that is registered at the birth of each operant child—of its four young minions. Backtracking, the investigators learned that the Hydra-units had indeed been in the vicinity of each chakra murder and attempted murder. But no adult Remillard could be similarly placed at every single crime scene, so none could be pinned positively with the Fury label. This did not prove their innocence, however. Not if the monster really was a family member with a split personality.

In the end, there was nothing Davy MacGregor and the Magistratum could do but abandon the investigation. Neither Fury nor the Hydra were heard from again until eight years had passed, and even then they might have escaped notice had it not been for Evaluator Throma'eloo Lek and little Dorothea Macdonald.

Fury had made an excellent choice when it decided to hide its creature on Islay in the Scottish Hebrides. By the mid twenty-first century the island had only about four thousand permanent inhabitants. Because of the Milieu's social policy of compelling the best and brightest of humanity (especially those with metafaculties) to achieve their highest potential, only a handful of elderly, invalid, and intransigent metas were allowed to continue living on the remote island. Every one of these possible threats to Hydra's security died conveniently of "natural causes" not long after the fourfold creature took up residence on Islay.

The possibility of meta babies being born to normals remained, especially since so many of Islay's inhabitants had Celtic genes. (This meant that an exceptionally large percentage of the population were promising latents with unlimited reproductive licenses who might be expected to engender operant offspring.) But here again Milieu law inadvertently kept the island free of operant residents who might detect the creature. Since there was no metapsychic preceptorial facility on Islay, normal parents with meta newborns were obliged either to move to the mainland in order to live near such a school or else give up their children to operant foster care. This particular aspect of the hated Reproductive Statutes remained on the books even after the Human Polity achieved full Milieu citizenship, and it served Fury's purposes well. While thousands of meta tourists visited picturesque Islay each year, none stayed long enough to detect the anomalous aura of the Hydra.

Details of the creature's covert years on the island, and of the crimes perpetrated by the Hydra while it lived there, were revealed piecemeal during the intensive investigation into the deaths of Viola Strachan, Robert Strachan, and Rowan Grant. The Magistratum was able to determine from residual DNA traces and circumstantial evidence that the four Hydra fugitives had resided at Sanaigmore Farm ever since they fled New Hampshire. The young quartet officially took up residence on Islay in mid-2054, although it was probable that they had occupied the supposedly vacant farmhouse for some months before that. Sanaigmore was purchased in June of that year on behalf of the Eumenides Corporation of Elysium by one Frederick Urquhart Ramsay Young, a man of unmemorable appearance who represented himself to the local authorities as an interstellar export-import entrepreneur. That the acronymous Citizen Young was filthy rich became evident after he contracted for the extensive renovation of the isolated old farmstead, turning it into a handsome country residence with all mod cons and then some, including an independent power supply and a satellite uplink.

The youngsters, who had assumed the names Celia and Magdala MacKendal and John and Arthur Quentin, were alleged to be two sets of nonoperant orphaned siblings with mild mental and physical disabilities. They were the wards of the above-mentioned F. U. R. Young, their maternal Uncle Fred. Their caregivers included a governess-therapist named Philippa Ogilvie (also of eminently forgettable appearance) and a pair of close-mouthed locals, Rod and Judith Campbell, who functioned as live-in cook-housekeeper and man-of-all-work until their "accidental death" in a fiery groundcar wreck five years later.

No merchant, contractor, day laborer, repair person, regional official, or other Islay citizen ever saw Uncle Fred or Ms. Ogilvie together, nor were any photos, digital likenesses, fingerprints, mindprint IDs, or genetic material of theirs ever tracked down. All known details of their background, including their names, were later found to be fictitious. Scores of witnesses claimed to have seen them and dealt with them during various business transactions, but no one could give a distinctive description of either one. It was as though they were ghosts, drab and instantly forgettable, who went abroad in daylight, performed certain mundane operations, then reentered the oblivion from which they had sprung.

Magistratum investigators speculated that the Fury persona itself might have played both roles using "sendings," psychocreative simulacra projected from a distant locale, when it seemed desirable to demonstrate that the four orphaned adolescents did indeed have adult protectors. From what I myself learned later about Fury's activities, I can affirm that the monster never physically set foot on Islay; but whether Young and Ogilvie were living dupes later disposed of by Fury or only illusions is anyone's guess.

Frederick Young made only sporadic visits to the children and the farm after the new household settled in, since his business supposedly required him to travel to the human colonies of the Milieu. On his rare sojourns in Islay he sometimes took the four youngsters out for dinner at one of the fine hotel restaurants that catered to tourists, or went walking with them in the wild moors of the uninhabited northern parts of the island. The extended family would exchange polite greetings with any birdwatcher, botanist, or cross-country stroller they chanced to meet. Sometimes the family would walk on . . . and at other times, if circumstances were propitious, it evidently paused to *feed.*

Now and again Uncle Fred would drop into a pub in Bowmore,

sipping a dram of Islay's finest and keeping himself to himself, except for a bit of inconsequential chitchat. No one ever suspected he was not what he appeared to be. No one seems to have thought very much about him at all—not even when suboperant island residents began to disappear and rumors of the Kilnave Fiend resurfaced after a hiatus of nearly two hundred years.

The Ogilvie woman was even more shadowy than Young, coming into Bowmore to shop only every two weeks and declining every overture from friendly local folks eager to recruit her into political, social, or charitable groups. Any busybodies bold enough to come knocking on the door at Sanaigmore were invariably confronted by one of the surly Campbells and told that "Miss Pippa and the young people are at study" and not to be disturbed under any circumstances.

For the first two years of their stay on Islay, the Hydra-children were schooled at home by a series of private tutors, each with impeccable credentials in a wide variety of academic disciplines. One of the farm outbuildings had been converted into an elaborately appointed schoolhouse, complete with laboratory and shop facilities. A fine gymnasium, a game room, a handball court, and a heated swimming pool had been tucked within the shell of the old barn. The educators, all nonoperant, were mostly recruited from mainland Britain and paid exorbitant salaries to compensate for their tour of duty in the lonely Hebrides. They would drive to the farm each schoolday, work with the four youngsters, then drive back to their lodgings in Bridgend or Bowmore or one of the other south-shore villages when classes were over. They rarely saw Ms. Ogilvie and almost never encountered Uncle Fred—except when they were hired or dismissed.

The tutors never suspected that their unusual students were metapsychic operants with exceptionally powerful coercive and creative abilities. The psychologically astute did note the atmosphere of profound sexual tension that seemed to prevail among the young people, and some of the more susceptible teachers found themselves hopelessly smitten by one or another of their charges—but to no avail. The Hydra-children had no casual affairs with their teachers or with any other residents of Islay who lived to tell about it, nor did they socialize with the islanders, except in the most perfunctory way.

When the children attained their majority at age sixteen they were legally free to dispense with home tutoring. They set about to acquire their higher education working independently at four different institutions via satellite, never leaving their island of exile.

While the former tutors' later testimony to the Magistratum proved virtually useless as a source of information about the mysterious governess or the children's skittish guardian, it did provide valuable insight into the developing characters of the four Hydras themselves.

Magdala MacKendal (a.k.a. Madeleine Remillard, the third child of Paul and Teresa and Marc's younger sister) was the most brilliant of the quartet, and the only one with whom I was more than casually acquainted during the pre-Islay years. (The total offspring of the Dynasty numbered forty, and at family gatherings they tended to blend into an amorphous rainbow-auraed mob.) I remember Maddy as a calculating minois—a pretty little thing—who was tactfully compliant to Marc and her bossy older sister Marie, but often inconsiderate and even cruel to her brother Luc, who was a year younger and a rather shy and sickly child at that time. When baby Jack arrived, Maddy took an unusual interest in him and spent a lot of time ingratiating herself. In hindsight, she was probably attempting to bring Jack into Fury's orbit—a futile enterprise that the monster seems to have abandoned once Ti-Jean was diagnosed as having cancer. With her ebony hair, compelling blue eyes, and pale perfect complexion, Madeleine Remillard grew up to be a stunner by any standard, and—according to one wistful jobbing pedagogue, who didn't realize how lucky he'd been to escape with his goolies intact—she was as distant and cold as the aurora borealis, while at the same time reminding him of a barely dormant volcano. She later graduated summa cum laude from Harvard's home-study division and earned an advanced degree in Milieu law.

John Quentin (Quint Remillard, youngest son of Severin by his third wife Maeve O'Neill) was characterized by his teachers as an amoral charmer with blond curls and carnivorous eyes. Although not quite as talented as his first cousin Maddy, Quint easily managed degrees in psychophysics and philosophy from Cambridge's Open University branch.

Celia MacKendal (Celine, Maurice Remillard's fourth child and the firstborn of Cecilia Ashe) struck all of her tutors as mentally disturbed, for all that she was wanly pretty and winsome as a porcelain figurine, with hair the color of clover honey and darting, evasive turquoise eyes. Her manner was superficially prim, almost timid, and the tutors claimed that she suffered wildly fluctuating mood swings, lapses of memory, and other evidences of mental instability. Celine had once been discovered by a scandalized science instructor naked as a jaybird in the high meadow adjacent to the farmhouse, apparently having blatantly satisfying sadomasochistic sexual congress with an invisible being. The instructor was promptly discharged, but he received a consoling bonus and kept his mouth shut until the Magistratum interview. Celine's college work was mediocre except in metapsychology, and she got a satellite-study B.A. sheepskin from Stanford in California.

Arthur Quentin (Parnell, son of Adrien Remillard and co-murderer of his older sister Adrienne) was apparently the low head on the Hydra totem pole. His teachers characterized him frankly as a lout, and he barely scraped a nanotech engineering degree from the Extension Division of Tiranë Polytechnic. In young manhood Parni had the tall, burly physique and dark hair of his cousin Marc; but where Marc's body was massively elegant, Parni's was brutish. When Dorothée showed me his memorecalled image years later, he reminded me of that classic stereotype, the raging, bearlike Canuck brawler who would duke it out with Sergeant Preston of the Mounties at the climax of the antique television show. His role in the Hydra metaconcert was mental muscle, not subtlety, and he was an insatiable gobbler of lifeforce as well as the designated reality-partner in Celine's demented sexual romps.

When the young Hydras were about eighteen, their governess was seen less and less frequently in town and the young people began to do the shopping and deal with all the other household affairs on their own. The two Campbells died during the following year and were not replaced. Ms. Ogilvie was said to have left to take another position shortly thereafter. Uncle Fred also made fewer and fewer appearances on Islay, and in the year 2059 a brief notice appeared in the *Islay Guardian* newsbase: the peripatetic businessman Frederick U. R. Young of Sanaigmore Farm and Erinys House, Elysium, had died tragically in a hotel fire on the "Russian" planet Chernozem, leaving his four wards as his only heirs.

It was expected that the bereaved young people would sell the farmhouse and move away. But to everyone's surprise they carried on as reclusively as ever.

And so did the Kilnave Fiend.

The Magistratum would eventually number the unaccounted-for victims of the Hydra on Islay at approximately twenty-nine, averaging three or four a year from the time that the Remillard children first came to the island. All ages and both sexes were sacrificed to the creature's hunger for human vitality, and the victims shared only one characteristic in common: they were all suboperants, persons born with extremely strong but latent metafaculties. Most of them disappeared without a clue. Only in three of the earliest cases were peculiar areas of scorched earth or rock discovered, together with DNA traces and bits of burnt clothing belonging to the missing persons.

These circumstances had prompted tales of the resurrected Kilnave Fiend. The amused Hydra decided to reinforce the legend, and from time to time island children or other susceptibly imaginative persons caught glimpses of a weird, dwarfish person lurking about in lonely places.

The local police dismissed the Fiend sightings as tosh and taradiddle. But in spite of their best efforts at the time, the disappearances remained unsolved until the deaths of the three Edinburgh researchers brought in the full resources of the Galactic Magistratum and the First Magnate of the Human Polity.

However, the homicide suspects were not then or ever identified publicly as Remillards. Once again the Lylmik Supervisors acted to protect the reputation of Paul and the other distinguished members of Humanity's First Family of Metapsychics. This chronicle of mine is the first to reveal the truth.

Professor Masha MacGregor-Gawrys underwent rigorous conventional mind-probing following the three deaths and she also freely submitted to testing with the Cambridge machine. The principal objective of the examining authorities was to determine whether there had been a significant motive for the latest killings, or whether the victims had been only casually slain by the Hydra, in the manner of the luckless Islay suboperants who had preceded them.

Nothing in Masha's mind indicated that the triple slaying was anything but coincidental. It was troubling to Paul Remillard that she seemed to believe that the dead researchers had been working on a CE operator safety study that was expected to show severely *negative* conclusions—when examination of their encrypted raw data files at Edinburgh University demonstrated that users of highly advanced cerebroenergetic equipment faced only a moderate and acceptable risk, about as much as xenoplanetologists or urban firefighters. But Masha had, after all, recently undergone rejuvenation, and six months in the regen-tank was known to induce a temporary discombobulation even in the brain of a Grand Master. The professor herself decided in time that she was probably honestly mistaken about the research results that had been discussed by the dead trio.

Paul Remillard, however, experienced a lingering uneasiness about the subject of the Edinburgh study, although he said nothing about it to Throma'eloo Lek or the other Magistratum officials.

Little Kenneth Macdonald was questioned with the utmost gentleness by Paul himself, but the boy knew almost almost nothing of value, other than confirming the fact of his sister's proleptic anticipation of mortal danger and her uncanny knowledge that Sanaigmore Farm was the source of it.

Dorothée was in a state of severe shock in the wake of the killings; but unlike her brother, she had not yet wept or manifested any other emotional outburst. The examiners realized that they would have to treat her with extreme caution if she was not to break down. She answered all verbal questions willingly, and even worked with a police computer artist to provide depictions of the two suspicious adults who had spoken to her on the ferry and introduced her to the story of the Kilnave Fiend. (The book-plaque they left behind was devoid of clues.) She also described her vivid dream of the murders and assisted the artist in producing likenesses of the third and fourth units of Hydra.

Both Paul and Throma'eloo Lek were convinced that Dorothée had not dreamed about the killings at all, but rather had experienced a rare type of symbolic excorporeal excursion—an out-of-body experience—instigated by some metacoercive impulse of her mother or the other victims. The authorities were very eager to perform an exhaustive examination of the girl's memories, not only to retrieve more details of the auras of Madeleine and Quentin, which would aid in the manhunt, but also to glean other possible clues to the murders that Dorothée might have forgotten or repressed.

Paul explained very carefully to her how important it was that they probe her mind. He told her that they would give her a hypnogogic drug that would put her into a peaceful, drowsy state. She would not remember the least bit of discomfort when the procedure was over.

"Would it be like the medicine that the latency therapists use to get inside patients' minds?" the little girl asked Paul. When he conceded that the drug was similar, Dorothée reacted with unexpected vigor, refusing absolutely to permit the probe. No appeal from the First Magnate, the Krondak Evaluator, or her grandmother Masha could shake her decision.

"The doctors used that medicine on me when they tried to push their way into my mind," she said. "It hurt and it made me terribly sick."

"But this is a different medicine." Paul tried to soothe her. "I promise that it won't be painful."

"No!" The small face was adamant. "I told you everything I know." Then, displaying an amazing dignity for one so young, she asserted that her mind was her own and she would allow no outsider to enter . . . "except the angel."

This amazing qualification to her refusal precipitated a considerable fuss. Evaluator Throma'eloo, unfamiliar with childish human religious fantasies, feared that the putative heavenly guardian might be some kind of indwelling aspect of Fury itself. But Paul quickly reminded his monstrous colleague that no mature operant persona could take over a latent child's mind, not even the unconscious, without altering her bioenergetic aura. A very simple test showed that Dorothée's vital field, while extraordinarily complex for a nonoperant and deformed by unarticulated grief, was well within normal parameters. She was *not* a creature of Fury. (Whether or not an actual angel resided within the girl's mind was deemed irrelevant to the investigation, but Throma'eloo remained intrigued by the possibility.)

Paul, on the other hand, was quietly furious. A stubborn five-year-old could not be allowed to impede the investigations of the Galactic

Magistratum—especially in a matter touching so closely upon the Family Remillard itself. Nevertheless, little Dorothée had the First Magnate cold when she pointed out:

"You can't probe my mind unless I say you can. That's the law."

It was indeed—and the only way to circumvent it was to obtain the permission of the girl's legal guardian. Professor Masha MacGregor-Gawrys would have readily agreed, but she was not Dorothée's next of kin under Milieu law.

Ian Macdonald was.

Paul had a subspace communicator flown to the little Bowmore police station from the Scottish mainland, for the island boasted no such amenity. The following day, with Throma'eloo Lek, the professor, and Dorothée herself present, he put in a call to the planet Caledonia. As the visage of Ian Macdonald flashed onto the screen, the little girl gave a soft cry. It was the same man who appeared in the cherished old photo her brother had found, looking older and more careworn but still handsome and very strong. Her Daddy . . .

When Paul Remillard broke the news of Viola Strachan's murder Ian turned away briefly, cursing, his eyes filled with sudden tears. Then he cried out: "Who did it? What bastard killed Vi? . . . And what the bloody hell is the First Magnate of the Human Polity doing telling me about it?"

"I can't discuss that with you at this time, Citizen." Paul's voice was steely. "But you may be able to help us track down the assailants. Your daughter Dorothea had an EE experience at the time of the murder and her unconscious may have retained important clues. I'm officially requesting from you, her legal guardian, permission to interrogate her with coercive-redactive techniques."

"Daddy, don't let them!" the little girl shrieked. She pushed past Paul before her grandmother could stop her and appealed to the image on the monitor. "Don't let them dig into my mind! It'll hurt! I'm afraid! I already told them everything I know!"

Ian Macdonald looked stunned, then blackly furious. "What the fuck are you trying to pull, Remillard? You want to *mind-ream* my little Dorrie? God damn it, she's not even operant! You've got a fine friggin' nerve asking my permission to torture her."

"Not at all. With the latest medications—"

"Daddy—no!" the girl wailed, and broke into wild sobs. Masha took hold of her granddaughter and pulled her out of range of the communicator's scanner, but the child continued her terrified weeping.

"We've got to have Dorothea's evidence." Paul was urgent. "Her memories may contain data vital to the investigation. The people responsible for your ex-wife's murder are serial killers who have taken the lives of scores of other persons. They may threaten the security of the Galactic Milieu itself. You've got to give us permission to probe the girl."

"I've got to give you bugger-all, Remillard. I know my rights and I know the kid's. I *forbid* you to ream Dorrie! Is that clear, you mealy-mouthed mindfucker?"

"Quite clear," said Paul dryly.

Abruptly, the little girl broke free and dashed back within range of the communicator scanner. Relief transfigured her tear-drenched face. "Oh, Daddy, thank you! . . . Can Kenny and I come live with you now that Mummie's dead? We want to so very much."

Ian Macdonald was struck speechless. Rage melted into astonishment and he hesitated for a long moment. Then he glared out of the screen at Paul, his lips drawn back from his teeth in a smile of fierce triumph.

"Come to Caledonia, Dorrie," he said. "As soon as you can. I'll order your ticket and Ken's right now."

And with that his image vanished.

Forensic anthropologists comparing Dorothée's depictions of the four Hydra units with early Tri-Ds of Madeleine, Quentin, Celine, and Parnell Remillard confirmed that the girl had described the assailants accurately, but there seemed little likelihood that the fugitives would be foolish enough to go about undisguised while they were on the lam. All four might be expected to alter their features drastically—at least during the early hue and cry. Plastic surgery or regen-tank alteration of their appearance were distinct possibilities; but the easiest method of disguise was metacreative masking—the technique used by Throma'e-loo and others of his race when they assumed a human aspect. This involves the spinning of an illusion, pure and simple, and any reasonably competent operant child with a modicum of creativity can pull it off . . . for a short time. Long-term illusion-projection, however, is an energy-draining exercise that no meta can be expected to continue indefinitely. Mug shots, DNA samples, and copies of the original mental signatures of the four Hydra-units circulated Milieu-wide against the day that the Hydra might shed its camouflage or make some criminal mistake that allowed official scrutiny; but no one had high hopes for an early apprehension.

Police teams continued to comb Islay for weeks, searching for the bodies of the missing suboperants with the aid of the most advanced equipment. Later, archaeologists would sing the *Hallelujah Chorus* over the thousands of bones and other human remains—Neolithic to Modern—that the searchers turned up and meticulously left in situ after determining that they were immaterial to the case at hand.

But no other Hydra victims were positively identified. The investigators were morally certain that Fury's creature had killed the missing suboperants of Islay, leaving only charred husks that could easily be disposed of in the sea or in some deep and secret cave impervious to any technique of geophysical detection or farscanning.

However, there was never any proof of that hypothesis until years later, when the adult Dorothée had her encounter with Madeleine, Parnell, and Celine Remillard after coming for the second time to the island of her forebears.

[7]

CONCORD, HUMAN POLITY CAPITAL, EARTH, 4 JUNE 2062

The evening was exceptionally warm for early June in New Hampshire, and Paul Remillard suggested that his brothers and sisters bring their drinks outdoors while they awaited the arrival of their father, Denis. The flowers in the large informal rose garden behind the new residence of the First Magnate were already in full bloom, perfuming the still air, and there was also a smell of freshly cut grass.

"I hate designer-gene turf that never grows higher than three centimeters," Paul said, when his oldest brother Philip commented on the unusual lawn. "Oh, the modern grass is easier to maintain and the landscapers just love it. But to me it looks like green bath-toweling and it feels so stiff and crunchy when you walk on it. I had this good old stuff seeded in while I was away at the last Concilium session and it's looking quite decent by now. It's even guaranteed to have a dandelion or two."

"But how do you keep it clipped?" Catherine asked. "Surely it's too short for the laser-reapers that farmers use."

"Fitch's nephew cuts it with a modified antique tractor mower—when I don't beat him to it. It's a very soothing thing, cutting grass. Just driving up and down while rotating blades do the work, breathing in the scent of new-mown hay."

Philip shook his head in mock disbelief. "This man can't be the hard-charging workaholic First Magnate we all know and love."

"I've turned house-proud in my middle age," Paul said. "Now that Human Polity administration is finally out of the learner-permit stage, I intend to take life a lot easier. I've even learned to cook."

"Good God," said Philip.

"I don't believe a word of it," said Catherine.

The other members of the Remillard Dynasty laughed warily. None of them had seen Paul for months, and they knew he had not summoned them tonight so that they could admire his grass and flowers and indulge in polite chitchat. Something was wrong, and beneath his bantering façade the First Magnate frankly exposed a stratum of grave concern.

Paul was forty-eight and the climacteric of his individual self-rejuvenating gene complex had come when he was in his mid-thirties. Except for the quirky silvering of his black hair and neatly trimmed beard, he had apparently aged no further. He wore dark slacks and a white, open-necked pirate shirt with balloon sleeves.

For a time they strolled along in silence. Only two of the guests, Severin and Adrien, had the remotest idea what this family council might be about. Unlike the First Magnate, they were keeping their mental aspects closely shrouded.

The sky was deep purple with the first stars beginning to come out. At the garden's perimeter was a woodland of mutant elms, butternuts, and sugar maples that did not quite conceal the softly lighted, soaring stratotowers of the administration buildings situated a couple of kloms to the north. The capital city of the Human Polity of the Galactic Milieu spread over the Merrimack River valley adjacent to Old Concord, the venerable capital of the state of New Hampshire. In the nearly half-century since the Great Intervention, the seat of human government had expanded as the population on Earth and in the colonial planets approached nine billion. Concord had long since overflowed its original site; but the necessary growth had been handled gracefully, with most of the new offices hidden in an enormous underground complex, called the Ants' Nest by the irreverent, carved out of the native rock. Lower-echelon government officials and workers lived in the quaint old villages of New Hampshire, Vermont, and even Maine, commuting via a maze of high-speed subways. Only bureaucrats at the very highest level had homes in the parklands of Concord proper. These lately included the First Magnate.

In 2054, when the Human Polity was freed at last from the hated Simbiari Proctorship and finally admitted to full citizenship in the Galactic Milieu, Paul Remillard abandoned the pretense that his official

Earth domicile was the old family home on South Street in Hanover, New Hampshire, the college town where he and his children had grown up . . . and where his troubled wife Teresa Kendall had taken her own life. In the peculiar egalitarian oligarchy of the Concilium, there was at that time no such thing as an official mansion for the Human First Magnate, and so a simple apartment in Concord served as Paul's literal pied-à-terre during the brief periods he was on Earth. A similarly modest place in the Golden Gate enclave sufficed as his residence in Concilium Orb.

Unlike the historical chief executives of Earth nations, the First Magnate of the Human Polity was unburdened with time-wasting ceremonial duties. His statutory obligations were considered formidable enough. The first five years of human enfranchisement had been wildly hectic for Paul. He arranged for his four children to be supervised by operant housekeepers and governesses when they were not away at school and saw them only rarely. Paul's parents, Denis Remillard and Lucille Cartier, both semiretired from the faculty of Dartmouth College, became increasingly concerned about the motherless brood of their brilliant youngest son. Eventually the two of them rented out their elegant farmhouse and moved back into the old place on South Street that had been their original home in order to act as surrogate parents to their grandchildren.

Paul did meet frequently with his six siblings during the thirty-three-day plenary sessions of the Galactic Concilium that took place about once each Earth year. All of his brothers and sisters were magnates who had come to occupy high positions in the Milieu's primary governing body. But Paul's attendance at purely social family gatherings had for a long time been infrequent. What snatches of leisure he did enjoy were almost invariably spent in the company of his lover, Laura Tremblay, the wife of a complaisant Hibernian magnate named Rory Muldowney.

In 2059 Laura died suddenly, under curious circumstances. Along about the same time Human Polity administration finally attained a fairly satisfactory condition of homeostasis, chugging along without the need for urgent executive action or reaction at every other turn. The First Magnate discovered that his crushing burden of work was easing. It was no longer necessary for him to spend interminable months in Orb overseeing the extraparliamentary affairs of the Human Concilium and its fledgling Directorates. Less and less was he required to rush from one colonial world to another staving off brushfire crises, or forced to undertake visits of appeasement to exotic planets in order to smooth over some atrocious solecism committed by members of his race.

As the Golden Anniversary of the Great Intervention approached, it seemed that human magnates—except for the contentious Rebel faction—had finally learned to conduct their legislative business with reasonable facility and diplomatic aplomb. In the colonies, the system of Milieu-appointed Dirigents, combined with multilevel elected representational government, had shaken down to the point where special Concilium action—and Paul's personal attention—was only rarely required.

The Human Polity's relationship with the exotic races was largely cordial. The Simbiari now cooperated with humans in a wide variety of scientific works and at the same time resigned themselves to being forever unappreciated by their ungrateful ex-wards. The bonhomous little Poltroyans had become humanity's most enthusiastic trading partners and closest allies. The Gi love affair with human arts and entertainment persisted, while Earthlings had learned to tolerate that strange race's flamboyant and outrageous behavior. The Krondaku were as ever ponderously benevolent, and as ever skeptical of long-term human potential. As for the wise and evanescent Lylmik, they remained enigmatic and were hardly ever at home to callers.

Two sessions ago, the plenary Concilium had adjudged that the Human Polity was in such good shape that it was time to think about redefining the office of Human First Magnate, pruning it of autocratic and troubleshooting accretions that had been necessary during the formative years and making it more of a true presidency. Paul Remillard enthusiastically supported the decision and was reelected by a huge majority. He then decided it was time for him to settle permanently again on Earth. He was tired of apartments and felt he had worked hard enough to deserve a real home and some sort of normal social life.

But where would he live?

The old family place on South Street in Hanover was out of the question. Two of Paul's adult children, Marie and Luc, still lived there together with Denis and Lucille. So had young Jack, until he entered Dartmouth College as a ten-year-old prodigy and took up residence in the freshman dorm. Marc, Paul's oldest child, having earned a string of advanced degrees and immersed himself in CE research financed by the family foundation, had dipped into his all-but-untouched investment fund and bought a tiny, isolated house in the hills east of Hanover. Paul's brothers and sisters also had permanent residences in and about the lovely old town and they now urged him to build his new home in the vicinity and rejoin the close-knit family circle.

Unspoken was the Dynasty's hope that the First Magnate would marry again and have done with the series of well-publicized sexual liaisons he had pursued since the death of Laura Tremblay. But Paul was not about to let the family cramp his style. He chose to live in Concord, a safe 90 kilometers away.

When Paul was not presiding over his metapsychic peers at Concilium sessions or otherwise engaged in Polity affairs, he was supposedly a private citizen just as the other magnates were, free to enjoy any lifestyle and engage in whatever personal or professional business he chose. Practically speaking, however, it would have been unseemly for the First Magnate to resume his career in the North American Intendancy as just another IA. Even under the new order, there were still semiofficial calls on Paul's time when he was away from Orb, notwithstanding the fact that the turmoil of the shakedown years had subsided.

Paul suggested that he set up an unofficial headquarters for the First Magnate, separate from the bureaucracy of the Concilium and having no ties to the Office of the Dirigent for Earth. He would hold himself available for extraordinary consultation and use his free time to study Milieu law and human-exotic relations. His proposal was accepted, and the Human Polity voted to provide him, gratis, whatever kind of dwelling he fancied.

The First Magnate might have chosen to live in splendor. A replica of the Château de Versailles or even Mad King Ludwig's sumptuous Neuschwanstein Castle could have been his for the asking. His family and colleagues assumed he would at the very least erect some stately home appropriate to his exalted position.

But instead Paul Remillard indulged his notorious whimsy.

When Lucille Cartier, renowned in the Dartmouth academic community as an arbiter of good taste, first clapped unbelieving eyes on her son's new home in Concord, she pronounced it to be a bastard cross between a Swiss chalet and a wedding cake.

"It's nothing of the kind." Paul had been polite but firm in the face of his mother's disapproval. "It's an authentic reproduction of a carpenter-gothic New England cottage, in the style of the mid-nineteenth-century American architect Andrew Jackson Downing. The original version of this little beauty is still standing downstate in Peterborough."

His mother said, "It's preposterous!"

"But it suits me," the First Magnate had gently replied, "and I paid for it myself just so that I can take it with me when the Concilium lets me retire."

The white-painted wooden "cottage" had ten rooms—not including the west wing with its little ballroom, informal executive offices, and domestic apartments. Beneath the 20 hectares of landscaped grounds was a sophisticated subterranean complex that included everything from garages and a private subway terminal to a subspace communicator station. The quaint main house sported pointed-arch windows with pointed black shutters, handsome square columns on the porches and rear veranda, and scrollwork bargeboards dripping from the edges of the roof like ornate wooden lace. The overall exterior effect was conceded even by hostile architectural critics to be warmly human.

The dayrooms featured polished oak floors, stone fireplaces, sprigged wallpaper, and a cosy, eclectic mix of colonial and Victorian furniture. Paul's private bedroom was in the simple Shaker style; but the four spacious guest chambers were decorated in frontier rustic, baroque Federalist, nineteenth-century Chicago cathouse, and 1930s Hollywood Art Deco. Robots in the woodwork and a small staff of nonoperant employees did the housework.

Paul's cook was a laconic Yankee named Asahel Fitch, whose culinary specialties were New England boiled dinners, lobster salad, coq au vin, and pot roast. Fitch's wife Elsie did desserts and flower-arranging and also supervised the wine cellar, the only area of the cottage where the vast Remillard family fortune proclaimed itself. It was a repository of the Galaxy's rarest and most costly vintages and ardent spirits—plus a case or two of good old Wild Turkey for the times that Uncle Rogi came to visit. When the First Magnate entertained semiofficially, he hired the best caterers in Old Concord, or flew them in from other Earth cities as far away as Kuala Lumpur. If a more intimate supper for two was appropriate—as it often was—the Fitches got the night off and Paul whipped up crêpes or a fancy omelet himself.

About 100 meters from the First Magnate's cottage, at the margin of the surrounding woodland, stood a frivolous wooden summerhouse furnished with white-painted wicker chairs and settees and a number of discreet high-tech appurtenances. Paul indicated this structure to his brothers and sisters as they walked across the darkening lawn.

"We'll wait for Papa there. The place has a dumbwaiter to keep us supplied with drinks, and a state-of-the-art sigma-field installation we can activate for complete privacy during the family council. We might see some luna moths while we wait if we're lucky." He led the way among the irregularly shaped rose beds.

"A sigma?" Adrien was taken aback. "You really think someone might eavesdrop? What the hell is this confab about, anyhow?"

Paul glanced back over his shoulder, smiling without mirth. "There are a number of matters we need to discuss. One particularly involves you and Sevvy."

"Is that so?" Adrien spoke lightly, but there was a hint of defiance in his mien. He resembled a less polished version of Paul with a small mustache and no beard; but his immortality genes had climaxed at a much earlier age, giving him a boyish air almost as incongruous as that of his father, Denis.

"So we're going to get political," groaned Severin. "I was half afraid of something like that when you summoned all six of us to Concord like a gang of wayward prep-schoolers."

"Paul did nothing of the sort." Catherine's defense was prompt and wholehearted. "What in the world's got into you two?"

Maurice said, "Perhaps the loyal opposition to Unity is feeling just a trifle bumptious after its boost in the last constituent poll."

"A disgrace," Anne said. "You lot never would have got that high a vote percentage if you hadn't stooped to disinformation."

"Disinformation—?" Severin exploded. "Look who's talking. What well-known petticoat-Jebbie legal scholar tried to twist the Pope's arm so he'd issue an encyclical saying that Unity doesn't pose a threat to human free will?"

"It doesn't," said Anne.

"Que tu dis," sneered Adrien. "We've got tame theologians on our side who'll match your guys jot for tittle swearing it does. Psychologists, too! Anytime you Jesuits and swamis want a *real* debate on the Interstellar Tri-D Forum instead of an eye-glaze contest on the Philosophical Channel, we'll bring on Rabbi Morgenstern and Cardinal Fujinaga and Doctor Aziza Khoury to clean your clocks."

Briefly, Anne's composure slipped. "Unity is a serious subject for debate. You and your Rebels won't be allowed to trivialize it by treating it like some game show!"

"No," Severin said. "But the matter's not going to be decided behind closed doors by your clique of operant mystics, either."

Paul had thus far ignored the bickering, but now he broke in to thank his siblings for coming to this emergency family conference.

Anne's tone was cynical. "There was a choice? I had to egg in from a meeting of theologians in Constantinople. My paper will have to be delivered by Athanasius Wang, and he'll drone on and put everyone to sleep."

"Surely not," Catherine said. "What's the subject?"

" 'The Unanimisation Concept of St. Teilhard de Chardin as a Prefiguring of Unity.' "

"Ye gods and little fishes," croaked Adrien.

Anne shrugged. "Unity's going to happen, no matter how much you latter-day Sons of Earth piss and moan. Full participation in the Milieu by humanity demands that we embrace a consonant mental relationship with the Galactic Mind."

Severin's chuckle was ominous. "Think again, little sister. There are alternatives to the lockstep mentality of Unity, and you can be damned sure they're going to be discussed openly and exhaustively. Humanity has a right to *choose* whether or not to risk its racial individuality in a permanent mind-meld with exotics."

"Of course it does," Anne retorted. "But if your faction continues to spew distortions and half-truths instead of helping to clarify the issue, how in the world will people be able to make an informed choice? The tirade that Annushka Gawrys spouted before the Concilium last session was full of calculated misstatements—"

"You mean," Adrian broke in, "she raised points that hit too close to the mark for comfort! You ought to come down from your ivory tower once in a while and listen to what the normals and the metas opposed to Unity are saying. It's not operancy that worries the ordinary folks, it's the notion of being controlled by inhuman *humans*!"

"Please." The First Magnate held up an admonitory hand. "There are good reasons why we should wait until we're behind the sigma before discussing this any further." As Paul spoke aloud, his formidable coercion gently touched their minds. They were all Grand Masters, all Magnates of the Concilium, all among the most powerful human minds in the Galaxy. But at that moment, their youngest brother's will was irresistible.

For a time they continued walking in silence.

Finally, Philip ventured to say: "You made some changes in the rose garden, didn't you, Paul?"

"I had the gardeners rip out all the trendy new varieties the landscapers stuck in. The sky-blue ones, and the blacks and purples and lime greens, and the ones with fringed petals and polka dots and stripes."

"Once again . . . you surprise me. I never realized you were such a traditionalist at heart." The firstborn of the Dynasty had a pleasant homely face with a receding hairline, and he tended slightly to portliness. Philip Remillard was sixty-five years old but seemed to be in his late forties. The only one of the family who was not physically impressive, he had long ago decided that none of his bodily flaws was serious enough to warrant wasting time having them corrected in a regen-tank.

"Traditionalist?" Paul seemed surprised at the accusation. "Hardly! But a rose is a rose is a rose, dammit. It should look like one and smell like one. Now the only varieties growing here are pre-Intervention."

"Good for you," said Catherine. "The plant engineers for the big nurseries seem to think that the more outlandish the flowers are, the better. There were roses in the catalog last fall that were the size of dinner plates, with more colors in each flower than a stained-glass window. They call them Chartres hybrids. Ridiculous."

"Just part of the general trend toward the baroque and outré," Maurice remarked. "Flowers, clothing, vehicles, music . . . all kinds of things getting more and more intricate and fussy. Some popular-culture theorists think it's a reaction against the austerity of the Simbiari Proctorship years."

Catherine nodded. She was tall and blonde like Maurice, Severin, and Anne, but without the studied judiciousness of the first, the panache of the second, or the cool intellectuality of the third. She often seemed to be the most vulnerable of the Dynasty, passionate in her opinions and imperious in manner, but paradoxically chilled by melancholy, never able to forget that her late son Gordon McAllister had been exposed as one unit of the Hydra who had killed her beloved husband, the boy's own father. When the Human Magnates of the Concilium were finally able to assume a lighter administrative work load, Catherine Remillard had once again taken up her original profession of clinical metapsychology, the work she had once shared with Brett McAllister. She was now acknowledged to be one of the principal latency research scholars in the Polity.

"I rather like the new Regency look in men's clothing," she said. "Those buckskin breeches and hussar boots are very dashing on you, Sevvy."

"Oh, well," muttered Severin, a trifle sheepishly. But he kicked at an imaginary pebble in the grass to make the boot-tassels swing.

"Better watch out, Paul." Adrien's sardonic smile was almost phosphorescent in the deepening dusk. "You'll find yourself displaced as First Fashion Plate of the Polity if Sevvy gets any more gorgeous."

"Quel dommage," Paul drawled.

Severin sketched a mock bow in Paul's direction. "No, you'll always have the edge with the ladies. Won't you, little bro? Nothing's quite as sexy as unlimited political power."

"Did you say there were luna moths hereabouts?" Philip interposed quickly. They had finally reached the summerhouse.

"I'd love to see one." Anne relaxed on one of the chintz-cushioned settees and picked up the dumbwaiter zapper. Her lemonade glass was empty. Anne's aging had halted in her early forties and her features were as austere and precisely chiseled as those of a Greek statue. Except on the most formal occasions, she eschewed the clerical collar and black rabat of more conventional priests. Tonight she wore a fashionable royal-blue linen trouser suit with a silk blouse the color of caramel, making Catherine in her simple beige cotton shirtwaist dress look almost mousy.

"Perhaps the First Magnate will order a command performance of his little creatures of the night," Adrien suggested archly.

Not in the least put out, Paul dropped into a wicker chair, set his beaker of iced tea on the low table, and assumed an intent expression.

Severin nudged Adrien. The pair of them sat side by side on a second settee. "The regal coercive summons! Or is he cooking bug pheromones, do you suppose? And if he is, *where is he getting the raw apocrine components from?*"

"You're the ex-doctor," Adrien said. "Elucidate the disgusting possibilities—starting at his armpits and moving south."

Paul grinned. "Sorry to disappoint you two filthy minds, but coercion's a lot easier than creativity when you're dealing with sex-crazed males . . . and here they come."

"Oh!" Catherine's face brightened with delight. She instinctively held out both her hands.

Full night had now descended and the only illumination came from the windows of the distant residence and from the starry sky; but all of the grandmasterclass operants of the Dynasty could see as well in darkness as they could in broad daylight if they chose to exert their visual ultrasense. What they now perceived was a fluttering squadron of large pale-green moths emerging from the canopy of trees nearby. The insects were about the size of a human hand and delicate as moonbeams. Their wings had long tails, narrow purplish margins, and four transparent eyespots. Prominent feathery antennae confirmed that the moths were indeed males. They flew into the summerhouse and orbited Catherine with exquisite precision. Then, released from Paul's mental control, they flapped about uncertainly and began to scatter.

"How marvelous!" she said. "Thank you, Paul."

"It was actually young Jack who decided that my new place needed some special pets. He salted the forest with cocoons last fall." The

First Magnate chuckled. "I'm glad his tastes run to Lepidoptera rather than fruit bats."

"How's your little boy doing?" Maurice inquired. "Settling in at Dartmouth? I don't think Cecilia and I have seen him since Marc's birthday party in February. Amazing, the way the two of them seem to relate almost like colleagues rather than big brother and kid brother."

"One of the matters we're going to discuss involves Jack's collaboration with Marc," Paul said.

"Oh-oh. That'll be the new CE rig," Philip guessed shrewdly. "Marc told me he'd had flak from the Concilium Science Directorate already, and the news of the proposed design modification isn't a week old."

Paul cocked his head, listening to something inaudible, then let out a sigh. "Papa's finally here. Elsie Fitch is aiming him in our direction. Now we can get on with this bloody damned conference."

Maurice said, "Are things really as serious as all that, Paul? I realize that Marc's mind-booster research is ethically problematical, and Sevvy and Adrien's anti-Unity faction has embarrassed you before the media. But surely—"

"There's more," the First Magnate broke in. "And it's as serious as it gets . . . Anne, if you're sending in drink orders, make mine a Scotch rocks. Double. Somehow I don't think plain iced tea is going to do me much good this evening."

DENIS: Hello, children.

PHILIP+MAURICE+SEVERIN+ANNE+CATHERINE+ADRIEN: [Murmurs of greeting.]

PAUL: Good evening, Papa. I'm glad you could join us. Can I offer you a drink? A Hawkeye? Certainly. Excuse me for a moment while I turn on this sigma . . . There. Now we're ready to begin our family conference.

DENIS: You're shielding us, Paul? For heaven's sake, what's wrong?

PAUL: What we're going to discuss concerns the family and the innermost circle of the Concilium. It's vital that no one else hears about it—most particularly not the Planetary Dirigent of Earth.

DENIS: Davy MacGregor? But—

PAUL: Please, Papa. I'll explain. I've just returned from Scotland. Three unusual murders were committed there a week ago. I have positive proof that the killer was Hydra.

VARIOUS: [Expletives and gasps.]

ANNE: The four missing Remillard children? . . .

PAUL: My own investigators, a forensic evaluation team from the Galactic Magistratum under Throma'eloo Lek, and the local police have gathered a fair amount of information about the perpetrators—although Lek and his Krondak associates in Orb are the only ones aside from the Lylmik Supervisors who know their true identity. Quentin, Parnell, Celine, and my own daughter Madeleine have been living on Islay in the Inner Hebrides ever since they disappeared eight years ago on the night Uncle Rogi and Jack were attacked.

SEVERIN: Son of a bitch.

PAUL: The Hydra-children fabricated new identities with the help of some unknown adult who has access to nearly unlimited, untraceable funds. Since the planet-scan done at the time of their disappearance failed to pinpoint them, we have also assumed . . . that they were able to change their mental signatures.

CATHERINE: Impossible!

PAUL: According to current Milieu technology, yes. But it was done. We're virtually certain that the children themselves lacked the expertise to manage the alteration. It must have been done by Fury, Hydra's adult controller. It was probably also Fury in an illusionary aspect who posed as the guardian of the four children during their stay on Islay. And no one but Fury could have helped them escape again after these latest killings without leaving a single clue to their whereabouts.

MAURICE: And the Galactic Magistratum has the whole story?

PAUL: Evaluator Throma'eloo Lek was practically a material witness.

SEVERIN: Oh, shit.

PAUL: The Evaluator was vacationing on the island when it happened. He recognized Hydra's modus operandi from his investigations of the earlier deaths and immediately called me. Here's a précis of the findings.

[Data.]

As you can see, Lek's bureau of the Magistratum knows almost everything except Fury's identity and a plausible motive for the murders—

CATHERINE: And where the fugitive Hydra-children have gone.

PAUL: [Nods.]

MAURICE: This opens the old can of worms all over again. Any one of us could be Fury—or none of us! What does the Galactic Magistratum intend to do about the Dynasty?

PAUL: In this matter, as in the earlier crimes, Lek and his people ceded authority to the Lylmik Supervisors. I offered them our joint resignation from the Concilium and suggested that we all accept voluntary preventive incarceration.

[Stunned silence.]

My proposal was turned down. The Lylmik were adamant that we retain our official positions, and they intend to keep the continuing investigation as confidential as possible so that we won't be tainted by scandal. But their protection will cease if the truth somehow leaks out. If Davy MacGregor or some other hostile magnate finds out about this matter and formally demands our impeachment, we'll have to put it to a special vote of the plenary Concilium.

SEVERIN: And end up fucked to a fare-thee-well.

MAURICE: *Is* there a chance of keeping it under wraps?

PAUL: The Hydra-children were living in Scotland under assumed names. They'll keep those names as far as lower-level law-enforcement bodies are concerned. The manhunt will go on—but not for young Remillards. Their DNA assays have been transferred to the fictitious identities along with all of the other forensic material.

ANNE: [troubled] It's the same kind of cover-up that we had eight years ago. At the time I thought the deception was despicable. I don't like it any better now!

PHILIP: Disclose the fact that the Hydra has killed again and Davy MacGregor will surely make the entire affair public—including the fact of Fury's existence and its probable relation to us. At the very least, we'll all be forced to resign from the Concilium. And to what end?

ANNE: Truth. Honesty. The prevention of further killings! . . . Oh, God, Phil, I don't know. Why are the Lylmik so determined to protect our family—to the point of letting five homicidal maniacs remain at large?

PAUL: Annie, it's useless to agonize about this unless you're prepared to defy the authority of the Supervisors and condemn the lot of us to disgrace and probably to imprisonment as well. All for the sake of a moral abstraction! No matter what we may suspect, there's no more evidence now that one of us is Fury than there was eight years ago. Of course, we'll all be interrogated again by Lek—but it's largely pro forma. The Galactic Magistratum doesn't expect to learn anything new.

PHILIP: What about Marc?

PAUL: He'll also be put to the question, since he's also a Grand Master who was a suspect in the earlier crimes. We'll have to swear him to secrecy as well.

MAURICE: Has the Magistratum had any luck tracing the movements of the Hydra-children after the crime?

PAUL: No. The four fugitives could have escaped from Earth by assuming the identities of genuine human passengers after having disposed of the originals, but we think it's more likely that Fury created completely new identities and inserted them into the Human Vital Statistics Database.

ADRIEN: No way! Do you know how many layers of encryption would have to be penetrated in order to accomplish that? How many backups would have to be modified? And to make the sneetch foolproof, Fury would have to cook *every single human vital-stat database in the Galactic Milieu.* We're talking more than seven thousand planets, exotic as well as human, to say nothing of the Lylmiks' central database at Concilium Orb!

PAUL: There was a brief anomaly noted at Earth VitalStat in Geneva just before noon on the day after the Scottish murders. The same kind of momentary glitch affected the database at Orb pip-two-six Galactic hours later. We've since learned that every other vital-statistic system in the Milieu experienced an anomalous data modification in a cascade of impulses propagated via subspace from the Orb central system. The modification was complete within twelve nanoseconds. All of the databases are currently in complete accord. It took a Lylmik to uncover the cascade and deduce what must have happened. There's no way of identifying the fudged data.

PHILIP: Good God. The hack couldn't have been electronic. It had to be mental . . .

PAUL: Hitting the computer at Geneva must have been child's play for Fury. But to reach the base at Orb, he'd need a shaped PK-creative impulse in the gigawatt range.

SEVERIN: *I'm* impressed.

ADRIEN: Paul, not to put too fine a point on it, but who among us, with the possible exception of you and Marc and Jack, has the potential to perform a humongous mind-ploy like that? God knows I couldn't zorch a computer system four thousand lightyears away with a shaped thought to save my soul. Maybe Fury's outsmarted himself by showing off! A simple review of our metapsychic armamentaria should show who in the family is a go and who's a no-go in the PK and creativity necessary to pull off the stunt.

SEVERIN: Don't forget Marc's new brain-bucket. What's it supposed to do? Augment creativity thirty times?

CATHERINE: But he only has a design as yet—nothing operable.

ADRIEN: Marc gongs out of sight in creativity with only his naked gray. So does Jack.

PAUL: [irritably] Dammit, Jack's not a suspect! He wasn't even born when Brett and Margaret Strayhorn were killed, and he wasn't *conceived* until twelve years after Vic died. There's no way that boy could be Fury.

SEVERIN: Marc was there at Victor's deathbed, though. He was a baby, but he was near enough for Victor to have . . . infected him. His mind surpasses all others in our family in every metafaculty. If we concede that Fury must be a Remillard, then Marc is the most logical suspect.

PAUL: I—I had reluctantly come to that conclusion myself.

ANNE: No. It won't wash.

PAUL: Why not?

ANNE: You've all forgotten the reason why we weren't exonerated by Davy MacGregor after twice passing the truth tests on the Cambridge machine.

CATHERINE: The possibility of multiple-personality disorder. Of course!

DENIS: That does constitute a very plausible hypothesis for Fury. I've devoted a whole chapter to the dysfunction in my new book, *Criminal Insanity in the Operant Mind.*

[Data.]

If one of us has this affliction, a second persona—normally submerged and imperceptible to the core personality—could be the malignant entity called Fury. This second persona might possess an entirely different metapsychic complexus. It could be much more powerful than the core as well as driven by a different moral imperative: Victor's . . .

CATHERINE: Papa, there is no psychiatric evidence whatsoever for the transfer of a persona from a dying mind to a living one. In the recognized forms of multiple-personality disorder, the additional personas are generated in reaction to some profound trauma suffered by the core, and they split off from the core.

DENIS: That's true. But—

SEVERIN: A last-ditch assault by Vic was enough of a trauma to stitch five fetal minds into a homicidal monster and turn poor old Louis and Leon and Yvonne into cold meat. Who can tell what else Vic might have done, striking out at the rest of us?

PAUL: And finding the one who was unconsciously vulnerable.

DENIS: If only I had not brought us all together that last Good Friday! If I had not led that presumptuous prayer! If I'd simply withheld water and nourishment when it was obvious that Victor would never emerge from his coma—

ANNE: Papa, don't castigate yourself all over again. You did what you thought was best at the time. You aren't to blame.

ADRIEN: If anyone is, it's Vic. How the flaming hell could such a depraved thing be born of man and woman?

ANNE: The engendering of a moral monster is one of life's great mysteries. But there's one thing that psychologists and theologians agree on: In almost every case, monsters are *made,* not conceived.

SEVERIN: Then who or what made Vic?

DENIS: I've thought a lot about that. And I've talked the subject into the ground with Uncle Rogi, sifting through some of his memories of Victor's childhood and of our parents, Don and Sunny. You all know that my poor father had a neurotic dread of his own metabilities and also a profound self-hatred. It turned him into an alcoholic and ultimately led to his death. I was Don's firstborn and my very obvious powers terrified him. Victor, the second child, was more subtle in his operancy from the very beginning and Don adored him. Made him his pet. My mother was an old-fashioned Catholic who thought birth control was sinful. She had ten children, one after another, and each time she was pregnant Don's alcoholism intensified—perhaps from his sense of inadequacy because he was unable to earn a decent living, perhaps from sexual frustration if Sunny denied him or if he found her repugnant when she was with child. Don might have turned elsewhere for gratification, especially when he was crazed by alcohol. It's taken me a long time to admit this to myself, but I now suspect that Don might have had good reason for self-hatred during his sober moments.

CATHERINE: Oh, sweet Jesus. Not that.

DENIS: Uncle Rogi says there was never any hint of it. I remember nothing of the sort. But by the time Vic was a toddler, he was already a mental thug. He coerced every one of my siblings into latency when they were infants, and played sadistic games with them. Whatever unspeakable trauma turned my brother into a monster first happened when he was very young. He would have repressed the memory of it, of course.

CATHERINE: [abstractedly] It affects different victims in different ways. Many of them survive to live almost normal lives. Some are left emotional cripples until therapy helps them drain away the old poison. A few are so wounded that their only release is in wounding others. The wickedness isn't completely involuntary, however. We psychologists took quite some time to concede that. Always, somewhere along the line, the nascent monster chooses to do what he or she knows is evil. Genuine insanity and lack of culpability may follow, but in the beginning there is always that fatal *yes.*

[A long silence.]

PHILIP: [doggedly] Victor Remillard is dead. His sins—his guilt or innocence—are beside the point. The thing called Fury, whoever and whatever it is, is alive but apparently inaccessible. As I understand it, we have no idea how to uncover and eliminate Fury, but its creature Hydra is another kettle of fish. What are we going to do about those four wretched young people? Simply hope that the Magistratum will eventually track them down?

ANNE: *I* think we have a moral obligation to hunt them ourselves.

PAUL: I think so, too . . . but maybe not for the same reasons Anne does. I've been considering possible long-range motivations that the Fury-Hydra combine may have. Certainly it's slaughtered people casually, apparently for no reason other than to slake its beastly appetite. But the killing of Brett seemed consequential, and so did Margaret's murder. And if Rogi and Marc and Jack had died, Fury would have been rid of one inconvenient old man who knew too much, and two highly independent, extremely righteous Remillards who are arguably the most powerful non-Lylmik minds in the galaxy. Now we have the latest atrocity: the killing of three Scottish researchers. Was it simply feeding time at the zoo? Perhaps not. The Scots had nearly completed a detailed study on CE operator safety. Not starship control-hats or other conventional cerebroenergetic applications but the most sophisticated kind of mind-boosting.

PHILIP: Like Marc's.

PAUL: Exactly. Do you realize what would happen to Marc's E15 research project at Dartmouth if a highly reputable study condemned his work as unacceptably hazardous to the human mind?

SEVERIN: At the least, there'd be a departmental review and Marc's enemies on the faculty would have a field day sniping at him. At the worst, the whole E15 project might be axed . . . and Marc would very likely resign his professorship.

PAUL: I checked out the work of the murdered researchers. It seemed to conclude that there was *no* serious risk in using upper-end CE. But when I talked to a close relative of one of the victims, who is a respected scientist herself and a grandmasterclass operant, she recalled conversations implying that the research had pointed to the opposite conclusion.

ANNE: The hyperhacker strikes again, altering the data?

PAUL: I can't prove it. But suppose Fury sees Marc and his work as potentially useful?

ADRIEN: Hydra's creativity brain-boosted! Christ . . . that's the way the thing kills, isn't it?

DENIS: There is a redactive component to Hydra's lifeforce-draining procedure as well as a perversion of creativity, but the creative metafaculty has the greatest potential for misuse. It might be directed into any number of destructive activities, including mental lasers and fire-raising—the kind of thing your mother did inadvertently when she was a disturbed young woman. The faculty is present on the Remillard side of the family as well. I don't know if Uncle Rogi ever told you children, but he managed a bit of energy-projection himself many years ago. He melted a hole in a windowpane. The mental wattage wasn't large, however, and Rogi only accomplished it under conditions of extraordinary stress. I've never had any indication that you children or I have this aspect of creativity, but it's certainly possible.

PHILIP: [quietly] It's part of the family heritage, even if we've never been crazy enough to sharpen the faculty up and use it.

SEVERIN: Yet! The possibilities are verrrry intriguing.

CATHERINE: Don't joke about it, Sevvy. Don't you *dare* joke about it. I saw what that damnable power could do—did!—to my husband. I'll see it for the rest of my life . . . And if we've judged correctly, the monster's only motive for murdering Brett was to force me to become a Magnate of the Concilium. But why is Fury dedicated to this—this twisted notion of Remillard family aggrandizement?

MAURICE: If Fury is one of us, as we suspect, he or she might have some mad scheme to manipulate the rest of the family. Not by bald-faced coercion but by other, more subtle means.

CATHERINE: But *why*?

PAUL: To dominate the Milieu.

SEVERIN: [laughs] Seems to me that we're doing fair to middling along those lines already: six well-polarized magnates; one Lord High Panjandrum of the entire human race; our revered sire the Grand Old Man of Metapsychology—who keeps getting nominated to the Concilium and keeps turning it down; and young Jack the Amazing Superbrain. Remillards über Alles! And if Marc isn't nominated to the Concilium and affirmed a Paramount Grand Master next session, then I'm a monkey's uncle instead of his.

[Uneasy chuckles.]

DENIS: [testily] Paul, you must convince the Concilium to stop nominating me to be a magnate. I'm not interested in politics. I don't think that Marc is, either.

ADRIEN: I hope Marc does get nominated and I hope he accepts. We Rebels could use a big gun on our side—

ANNE: What makes you think Marc would go along with your undermining of the Milieu?

SEVERIN: Ask him yourself, Reverend Sister.

ANNE: I certainly shall!

PAUL: [forcefully] The fact that Sevvy and Adrien are prominent in the anti-Unity party poses a very serious problem when taken in conjunction with the reappearance of Fury and Hydra. Objective observers—such as the Lylmik—might now see the Rebel movement as the beginning of an attempt to dissociate humanity from the Milieu altogether. A scheme like that, using Remillards as catalysts, would seem to play right into the hands of Fury . . . if the monster really does aim to dominate the galaxy.

ADRIEN: [hotly] Wouldn't you and your gang of exotic ass-lickers like to think so! Is *that* what you've got up your sleeve? Using the Fury thing to discredit the loyal opposition? Well, lotsa luck, Number One! The Rebel party is no more dependent upon Sevvy and me than the pro-Unity gang is dependent upon you and Annie!

SEVERIN: Your idea won't fly, Paul. Before the Human Polity got the franchise, opposing Unity was high treason. Now it's a perfectly legitimate political option. The exotics don't like it, but they've conceded our right to hold the position.

ADRIEN: And that position is getting more viable by the minute! The whole damned galaxy knows that our group isn't a gang of crazed anarchists coerced by some shadowy Satan. We're honest magnates and respected citizens. We simply believe that Earthlings shouldn't trade personal freedom and individuality for an exotic security blanket guaranteeing peace and happiness forever in the Great Unified Beehive.

ANNE: Unity isn't like that!

SEVERIN: Blow it out your asymptote, Annie.

ADRIEN: Amen with knobs on.

PAUL: For God's sake, you two! You *know* that the Great Intervention took place only because the Milieu anticipated eventual Unification with humanity. If you think we can split off from the confederation and go our merry, unreconstructed way you're as crackbrained as Fury!

SEVERIN: Don't bet on it. The way our human colonists are increasing and multiplying, we'll outnumber all races except the Poltroyans in less than a hundred years. And the little purple people just might fancy joining our side. They're damn near human themselves—not like the other exotics.

PHILIP: The majority of human operants don't share your views, Sevvy.

ADRIEN: But the deadheads are more and more gung ho for Rebellion! Can't blame them, can you? They know that someday they'll have operant descendants—and they prefer their grandchildren human, not brainwashed into some alien mind-set.

ANNE: Humanity has only just gained acceptance into the Milieu—and already your Rebel faction is scheming to destroy it!

SEVERIN: We don't advocate violence. We believe in friendly persuasion over the long haul and a peaceable separation at the appropriate time. You Milieu daisy-chainers can go your way and the rest of us Earthlings will go ours.

ADRIEN: And devil take the hindmost.

[A simmering pause.]

DENIS: Children. Please listen to me for a moment. Paul's opinion of the Rebel movement deserves to be taken seriously. Sevvy and Adrien are undoubtedly sincere in their beliefs and not overtly influenced by any machinations of Fury. But it remains plausible that the politics of Unity might be part of a larger, more sinister picture orchestrated in some subtle manner by the monster. Uncle Rogi claims he was present when Fury was born. You may recall that he was exconcert at Victor's deathbed. Rogi says he asked Fury then what it wanted, and it said *all of us.* Is it possible that Rogi's thinking was too limited in scale when he concluded that Fury only coveted the souls of the Remillard family?

PHILIP: It wants the entire Human Polity? That's preposterous!

MAURICE: Not to a megalomaniac.

ANNE: Fury could be afraid of Unity . . .

DENIS: Perhaps this being prefers its own style of mental conjugation. We've seen a sample, and its name is Hydra! A many-headed monster, only fourfold now—but who can tell what it might become?

CATHERINE: And if it includes Remillard minds, it could be immortal.

PAUL: I can't help but feel there's a terrible kind of synchronicity at work here. This is why I called the family conference, and why I sequestered us beneath the sigma-field so that no one else would know what we discussed.

ANNE: We seven have our differences. But we *must* attack this Fury-Hydra problem together.

SEVERIN: [sighs] Yes.

PAUL: Can we agree on this—that Fury and Hydra pose an unacceptable danger to the family, the human race, and the Galactic Milieu—and therefore they must be destroyed?

PHILIP+MAURICE+SEVERIN+ANNE+CATHERINE+ADRIEN: Yes.

DENIS: The Hydras are your own children. Fury may be one of you. Do you still agree with Paul's assertion that they must die?

[Mutual affirmation.]

PAUL: Do you also agree that we, personally, must take upon ourselves the responsibility for hunting these entities down and killing them?

[Reluctant mutual affirmation.]

DENIS: And what if Marc is Fury? He fits the psychoprofile for multiple-personality disorder more closely than any of you.

CATHERINE: Marc has Paramount Grand Master potential. If Fury resides within such a mind, it may be that only another paramount of equal or greater mental potential would be a match for him.

ADRIEN: A Lylmik?

CATHERINE: Nobody knows how their wispy minds check out. But the other exotics have no paramounts—and in all the human race, Jack's the only other person that we know of so far whose mental assay approaches the paramount level. But he's years away from maturity and psychologically fragile as well. We can't draw him into this. You know how he adores Marc.

PAUL: Marc is my son and I love him, too. But we must keep in mind that the latest Hydra murders may have been committed solely to protect him and his CE research. If high creativity enhancement is ever perfected and put to use by Fury and his creatures, the entire Milieu might find itself enslaved by a metapsychic tyrant . . . I'm seriously considering shutting down Marc's project by executive fiat. I have the authority.

PHILIP: If you do it, Marc will be devastated—and you'll also deprive the Milieu of a technology that could be extraordinarily beneficial. I won't bore you with the details, but the Commerce Directorate that I chair has estimated that the gains in geophysical modification alone would be stupendous. We could double the number of habitable worlds for all races except the Lylmik through the utilization of CE creativity in crustal-plate adjustment alone.

MAURICE: Marc is destined to be more than a scientist, Paul. He's going to be a leader. Perhaps even more formidable than you! If you quash his research high-handedly you'll alienate one of the greatest minds in the galaxy—

PAUL: I'll do what has to be done to protect the Milieu! And I'll make certain that Marc understands my motivation.

CATHERINE: You'd do Marc a terrible injustice and he'd *never* understand. Surely you can see that, Paul! Marc lives for his work and he's convinced it will benefit the Milieu. I know him better than all the rest of you do, and I'd stake my life that he's not Fury. For the love of God, Fury tried twice to kill him!

PAUL: [stubbornly] There's also the matter of Marc's Rebel tendencies—

CATHERINE: He's no Rebel, either . . . Sevvy, tell us the plain truth without bullshitting: Do you have any good reason to believe that Marc is sympathetic to the Rebel faction?

SEVERIN: Maybe Paul should take time out from his power-politicking and just ask him.

PAUL: [wearily] I'm asking *you.*

SEVERIN: All right, I'll give it to you straight: We've approached Marc several times. He listens, he seems to agree that human mental autonomy is necessary—but thus far he's declined to join our group. He's a damned cold fish, if you ask me. No passionate commitment to anything or anybody except himself.

MAURICE: Marc deserves to be treated justly, whatever his political views or emotional shortcomings. We may have our suspicions about him, but they're only that. *We have no proof that Marc is Fury.* Any action we vote upon here tonight must be predicated on that.

DENIS: [sighs] You're absolutely right, Maurie.

PHILIP: No, Papa. He errs in one important matter. We can't simply take a family vote on this matter. Paul alone will have to decide. He's the First Magnate, and he reports to the Lylmik Supervisors.

[Mutual affirmation.]

PAUL: [after a long pause] Very well . . . *One*: Marc will be allowed to continue his research without hindrance. The full Concilium will debate the applications of CE creativity when and if the E15 equipment is perfected. *Two*: Subject to Lylmik approval, I summarily condemn Fury and the four Hydra-units to death. *Three*: Each one of us, insofar as he or she is able, will devote significant time to some aspect of the hunt for these creatures. I'll draw up a schedule of your individual roles, based upon personal expertise. You'll coordinate all significant action with me, reporting progress or lack of it at times and places that are prudent. I'll see that you all receive unedited data from the Galactic Magistratum pertaining to the case.

PHILIP: And if one of us should locate Hydra?

PAUL: We'll all have to deal with the creature, working in metaconcert with Marc if it's at all possible. Under no circumstances should any of us attempt to act alone.

CATHERINE: What if we turn up a significant clue to Fury's identity?

PAUL: Report it only in a meeting where all except the suspect are present. *Remember that the core personality of Fury is probably innocent.* The Lylmik Supervisors will have to advise us on how to deal with this entity if we ferret it out. God knows, I haven't the faintest idea. It may be possible to excise the malignant Fury persona without harming the core personality.

DENIS: And what if that's impossible? Will we ask the Enforcement Arm of the Galactic Magistratum to put the innocent persona to death along with the guilty one?

PAUL: I don't know. I simply don't know.

[An interval of silence.]

Thank you for coming tonight, Papa, sisters and brothers. Evaluator Throma'eloo and his people will be interrogating us—and Marc also—tomorrow afternoon in the Magistratum offices of Concilium House at thirteen hundred hours. I'll leave you now. Excuse me if I don't see you out. I want to prepare our Fury-Hydra search plan and have it ready for discussion tomorrow evening—if our reamed-out brains are still compos mentis after the interrogation. Good night.

DENIS+PHILIP+MAURICE+SEVERIN+ANNE+CATHERINE+ADRIEN:

Good night.
[Paul turns off the sigma-field and exits into the darkness. A single male luna moth blunders into the summerhouse and flaps about the heads of the silent occupants until Catherine gently sends it on its way.]

[8]

CSS DRUMADOON BAY [Hu 12-201]

GALACTIC YEAR: LA PRIME 1-382-401/422 [6–20 JUNE 2062]

Dee was very nervous about the starship voyage . . . but not for the reason her grandmother supposed.

As the children settled down in their stateroom before lift-off, the professor did her best to reassure them.

"Most of our journey to Caledonia will be no more uncomfortable than a trip on a rhocraft bus. We fly out beyond the Moon under subluminal power, just as though the starship were a gigantic egg, and then jump into the gray limbo for the first time. But you needn't worry about feeling pain when we go through the superficies. There's a new minidose for nonoperant children that completely eliminates the discomfort of passing from the real world into hyperspace. Isn't that nice?"

"Great!" Ken was all enthusiasm, but Dee said nothing.

Gran Masha showed them a package of little green dosers, explaining that the medication would put them into a deep sleep during the few moments the ship took to cross over, then leave them pleasantly drowsy for a half hour or so afterward.

"Can I do it to myself?" Ken asked. "Please, Gran?"

The professor thought about it for a moment. "Very well, I'll let you try administering the dose yourself the first time. If it works out you can continue . . . Now I must speak to the purser about something. I'll only be gone a short time. You two stay here and watch our preparations for takeoff on the cabin monitor." She went out of the stateroom and closed the door behind her.

Ken sat on the edge of his recliner-bunk, zapping from channel to channel on the monitor. The big screen on the stateroom bulkhead provided views of the command bridge, the cargo loading bay, the passenger boarding area, and several other regions of the starship's interior, as well as a long exterior view of the ship patched in from a remote groundside transmitter. In a few minutes, those aboard the Drumadoon Bay would be able to watch themselves take off. Now the remote showed the huge vessel held fast in its complicated cradle-dock, looking something like a shackled skyscraper lying on its side. Tiny tenders and inspection vehicles buzzed around it.

"I'll bet Gran's going to try another subspace shout to Dad," Ken said. "He never did get back to her when she sent him the message saying she was going to bring us to Caledonia herself."

"Kenny," Dee ventured uneasily, "I've got something to tell you."

But her brother swept on. "You know what? Gran's worried. I think she's afraid Dad's place might not be—you know—safe for little kids to live in. His farm's in a part of Caledonia that was opened up to settlers only ten years ago. It's still a hairy wilderness." He grinned. "Erupting volcanoes! Maybe man-eating exotic critters, too!"

"Kenny, I'm scared."

"Aaah, I'm only bullshitting you, midgelet. Dad won't let anything happen to us. He never would've told us to come to Caledonia if it was really dangerous."

"That's not what I'm scared about."

"Well, what then? Gran told you that it won't hurt when we pass into the limberlost—"

"The minidoser medicine. I don't want to be knocked out! It—it turns off my mind-screen."

"So what?"

"Gran will look inside my head. I know she will. She thinks I might have some clues about—about Mummie and Uncle Robbie and Aunt Rowan hidden in my mind. So did the First Magnate and the Krondak policeman. That's why they wanted to probe me. If Gran pokes around, she's sure to find out my secret mindpowers."

"Don't be a thickie. Self-redacting is just a dumb little power. It doesn't mean you're *operant.* Masses of normals have the healing thing."

Dee was beginning to cry. "No—not that! I've got another new mindpower. I didn't tell you. It came all of a sudden, when I didn't even want it."

"What, for chrissake?"

"I—I can farsense now. Hear people's thoughts. It happened right after Mummie died."

"Oh, shit," whispered Ken. His breezy condescension gave way to real concern. "You're sure?"

Dee nodded miserably. "And I think Gran suspects something. Maybe my aura's different. A couple of times, she tried to ream me while I was asleep. Drilling really hard. She couldn't get in, because a long time ago I learned to wake up whenever anyone poked at my screen while I was sleeping and not able to keep it strong. But if this minidoser medicine knocks me out, I won't be *able* to wake up."

Ken scowled, thinking hard. "Probably not . . . Damn! You know, if you really can farsense, even a little, then the law says you're a head."

"I know," Dee wailed. "What am I going to do?"

Ken pondered the matter for a few moments more, and then a wily grin brightened his pale features. "You could try this," he said, and told her his idea.

She was dubious. "What if Gran finds out that I tricked her?"

"Then you've given away one secret. But you said yourself that the other one was the most important."

Dee sighed. "All right. I'll try it. It *might* work . . . "

The new power had come upon Dee quite unexpectedly ten days earlier. Ever since then she had tried with all her strength to force it back into its mind-box—but she had failed.

Occasional flashes of this perilous metability had happened before, especially with Ken, but it had never lasted long. The permanent change had occurred on Islay, as she lay in bed in the hotel on the night after Mummie and the others were killed. By then, the awful events of the afternoon seemed more and more unreal, like a Tri-D horror show that was over and done with. She had cried a little when she said her prayers and was tucked in, since Gran had seemed to expect it. But lying there in the dark by herself, Dee didn't feel terrified or ill anymore—only very tired and plagued with worrying thoughts.

Dead. Mummie was dead. She would never come back.

Dee had never known anyone to die before—not even a pet, since Mummie would never allow her to have one. Gran Masha had told the children that their mother's mind had not simply vanished like a blown-out flame when her body died. Mummie's mind was still alive. She had gone to join the great Mind of the Universe, Gran said, together with all the creatures who had ever lived, in the special and very mysterious way that God had planned. Gran assured Dee that Mummie was very happy now.

The girl found that hard to understand, but she did not express her doubts to Gran Masha. Why was Mummie happy to have gone away from her and Kenny? Was it because they were not the sort of children she had really wanted? Had Mummie really not loved them at all, even though she said she did?

If Dee had not been so proud and stubborn, if she had done what the latency therapists had wanted—what her mother had wanted—would everything have happened differently?

"Would it, Mummie?" she whispered. Real tears scalded her eyes as she felt for the first time a pang of piercing loss. Was it somehow her own fault that the Kilnave Fiend had killed her mother and her uncle and aunt?

Dee listened with all her might, hoping for a reassuring answer.

And heard something.

The world inside her head was no longer silent.

At first there were only weird hisses and howling noises, seeming to become louder and louder, that did not sound human at all. Dee was terrified, thinking that it might be the Fiend itself. What if it had followed her and was lurking somewhere in the darkened hotel room? She lay frozen in her bed, too scared even to cry out. Then little by little the mental jumble softened and clarified into muttered words. Only words. Like many people talking all at once over a communicator.

Could it be Mummie after all, trying to speak to her from inside the crowded Mind of the Universe?

As the mental sounds became more distinct, Dee realized that someone was talking *about* Mummie . . . and about her . . . and about Ken . . . and about the police looking for the killer . . . and about being responsible for two motherless children while still doing her work at the University unless she let Dee and Ken live with Ian . . . and about Ian (who was Daddy) being hopelessly unsuitable . . .

Gran!

Dee was overhearing Gran's thoughts as she lay sleepless in the next room.

It was farspeech—telepathy—and Dee hadn't even opened any box!

She concentrated harder. The other peculiar noises became bits of thinking from other people in the hotel who were still awake. Some thoughts were faint but exquisitely precise and clear, while others were blurry or twisted or rambling or an incomprehensible hodgepodge. Some of the hotel guests whose thoughts Dee could understand were worrying about things, like Gran was. Others were giving off wild and chaotic mental sounds and seemed to be very happy. A few were praying. One person was planning to sneak away without paying his bill.

When Dee got tired of listening she shut off the strands of farspeech one by one until her mind was quiet again. Then, awed and fascinated (but not yet frightened) by this new ultrasense, she brought the thoughts all back in a great snarl and practiced focusing on them individually. It was fun, and she quickly became adept.

Did operant people hear things like this all the time? And why had the new power come upon her so suddenly, without her wanting it?

Unfortunately, the angel remained silent as ever, although she did have the feeling that he was smiling triumphantly at her as she finally fell asleep.

The next day, before she and Gran and Ken went to the Bowmore police station to be formally questioned, Dee crept into the little hotel snuggery and called up a reference on farsensory latency from the data unit. The plaque she obtained from the dispenser turned out to be an article written for grownups, but she understood enough of it to realize that the shock and fear she had suffered had probably caused the telepathy box in her mind to open all by itself. Neither the therapists nor Gran Masha had ever hinted to her that this sort of thing might happen.

From the article she also learned that there were different kinds of mental speech with differing degrees of "loudness" or perceptibility. Blatant subvocal speech, farspoken shouts on the imperative mode, and casual declamatory mode conversation were so intense that even nonoperants might sometimes perceive them. The hardest to pick up were private narrow-beam thoughts precisely directed along another operant person's intimate mental pathway. She had obviously been hearing the loudest kind of telepathy.

Then she had read the words that made her heart sink: *Farsensing is the major indicator of metapsychic operancy.*

She knew what that meant. She was no longer a deadhead, no longer a normal, even though most of her powers were still safely imprisoned in their boxes. If Gran or any other operant adult ever found out that she was telepathic, she would surely be sent back to the therapists. And even worse—

Ken might be allowed to go live with Daddy on Caledonia; but unless she kept this new power of hers a secret, *she* would be forced to stay on Earth.

By acting dazed with grief (which wasn't really very hard to do), Dee managed to fool everyone at the police station. She hid behind her blue mind-screen almost all of the time and only came "out" to answer direct questions. Not even the handsome, grandly dressed First Magnate or the Krondak Magistratum official realized that she could read their minds when they made casual declamatory telepathic comments to each other about the case.

Dee found out that the terrible black dream-monster she'd called the Kilnave Fiend was really a thing named Hydra, somehow made of the put-together minds of four wicked adults—including John Quentin and Magdala MacKendal. The Hydra had lived in the spooky big farmhouse at Sanaigmore, just as she had suspected. Dee learned the names of the other two people who made up the Hydra, and she discovered that it had killed many other people, not just Mummie and Aunt Rowan and Uncle Robbie.

All the while that she eavesdropped on the others' thoughts, she kept perfect control of her features and her actions so no one would realize that she was listening. It had been hardest of all for her to keep a straight face when the Krondaku told the First Magnate that the Hydra had escaped and was no longer on Earth.

Now she didn't have to worry about it getting her!

When the questioning was finally over, Dee and Ken and Gran had been allowed to go back home to Edinburgh. Two days later, they all dressed up and went to church, even though it wasn't Sunday. The place was full of people from the University, and up front, on a stand in the sanctuary, were three small boxes that Gran said held the ashes of Mummie, Uncle Robbie, and Aunt Rowan.

After the Requiem Mass they got into groundcars and went to the cemetery, where the boxes were put into little holes in the ground, surrounded by bouquets of flowers. The priest said in his last prayer that the chemical elements that Mummie and Uncle Robbie and Aunt Rowan had borrowed for a while to use in their bodies now had to be returned to the Earth to be used again by other living things. He reminded everybody that those same elements had been made billions of years ago, long before there was even a solar system, when an ancient star exploded in a supernova and scattered its ashes into space. All living things, the priest said, had bodies made from the recycled dust of dead stars; but the minds that bloomed spontaneously into the vital-mental lattices when elements from the matter-energy lattices combined in space-time to make a living thing were completely unique and immortal.

Dee found the notion of being made from stardust very interesting. While the people standing around the graves were saying goodbye to each other, she whispered to Ken that she thought it was too bad that Mummie's elements would only become soil for cemetery flowers and trees to grow in.

"When *I* die," she confided, "I want my elements to help make a new star!"

"You're daft," Ken hissed angrily. His face was stained with tears. "Stark staring crackers." He stooped, picked up something from among the tree roots, and thrust it into her hand. "This is what you'll make when you die. Squirrel food!"

"Hush," said Gran Masha. "Behave yourselves for just a little longer."

Dee had looked at the acorn for a long time. Then she had put it carefully into her coat pocket.

. . .

The children were allowed to bring only a few things along with them on the starship journey to Caledonia. Dee had been content to let Gran pick out her clothes. The things she chose for herself included her goosedown bed pillow, a little plass boîte of flecks that held her favorite books, a china cat called Moggie that was her mascot, the acorn from the cemetery, which she intended to plant on Daddy's farm, and her most prized possession—a lapel pin with a bent clasp that she had found glittering on an Edinburgh sidewalk one rainy day last fall. It had the shape of a domino mask and was entirely encrusted with rhinestones. Even though Ken had scoffed, Dee remained convinced that it was a piece of valuable lost treasure, and she was sure that the stones were real diamonds.

She also begged Ken to let her carry Daddy's picture. Looking at it, she told him earnestly, would help her not to be scared on the trip. He made fun of that idea, too, but finally gave in when she promised to let him look at the old photo whenever he wanted to.

When everything was finally ready, Gran had taken Dee and Ken to Unst Starport in the Shetland Islands, where the three of them boarded the ship that would take them to Caledonia. It was going to take fourteen Earth days to travel the 533 lightyears in daily leaps of about 40 df.

Every single day they would go in and out of hyperspace. And Gran would make Dee take the medicine that would leave her mind and her secrets exposed . . . unless Ken's idea worked.

When the captain's image appeared on the Tri-D monitor in their stateroom about an hour after subluminal lift-off, warning that the first hop into hyperspace was imminent, Gran Masha got out the packet of minidosers. She let Ken hold one of the tiny green pillow-shaped things to his temple and press it with his thumb. A hair-thin needle sprang out of the doser's underside, pricked him painlessly, and injected the drug. Ken fell at once into a deep sleep.

"Let me do it to myself, too," Dee pleaded. "I'm not afraid."

"Very well," said Gran. "Be sure to put the side with the white circle next to your skin, and then press hard."

But Dee only pretended to inject herself, letting the little green doser fall into the crevice between her recliner-couch's seat and armrest just as she had planned, so Gran would not see that it was still full. She flopped back dramatically and closed her eyes with a slight sigh as Ken had, then she withdrew into her comforting rosy redactive pool and awaited the passage into the gray limbo. She heard faint noises as Gran sat down at the stateroom desk and rustled some durofilm printouts. The ship's low displacement factor would hardly bother Gran at all. She had said she would try to get a little work done while the children had their nap.

There was a peculiar snapping sensation, a *zang* and then a *zung.* And then the ship's captain announced that they were through the upsilon-field gateway and safe on their catenary, taking a shortcut through space-time faster than the speed of light.

Dee had felt no pain. None at all, although Gran had said that even the most powerful adult operants usually experienced a little twinge as they entered hyperspace—

"Oh, Dorothea. Why didn't you tell me?"

Dee lifted her eyelids the least crack. Gran Masha was standing over her. "Don't bother pretending. I know you're not asleep. Why have you hidden this from me?"

Dee opened her eyes the rest of the way. "Hidden what?"

"Your self-redacting ability. That's what it is, isn't it?" Gran knelt beside the couch. "You silly, silly child! If you'd taken the medication, your aura would have changed—and it didn't. And since you obviously felt no pain at the translation . . . How long have you been operant in the self-redacting metafaculty? Tell me the truth!"

"Since—since the ferryboat trip to Islay," Dee admitted.

"How did it happen?"

Dee avoided her grandmother's trenchant gaze. "I—well—I just wanted not to be seasick anymore. And I wasn't." She could feel Gran trying with all her strength to get inside her head, trying to find out the truth. Gran's coercion was much more powerful than that of Mummie or the therapists, but the blue shield held fast. Because of the new power, Dee could also "hear" Masha's blaring telepathic questions:

Can you perceive my mindspeech Dorothea can you hear me? Can you use the redactivepower on others as well as yourself? Do you have other new metafunctions? Are you breaking through into fulloperancy? Answerme Dorothea answerme!

The five-year-old girl's face was a picture of childish sincerity. Her desperate fear was masked by the impregnable mind-screen. "The redact power isn't really special, Gran. I just found out I could wish away bad feelings. Like when something hurts or makes me feel yucky."

Dorothea can you hear me?

Dee sat up and carefully put the minidoser she had concealed onto the table beside her couch. "Can I go to the observation lounge? The captain said we could look at the gray limbo there. Will Kenny wake up soon? I know he'd like to see the limberlost, too."

ANSWER ME CHILD CAN YOU HEAR MY MINDSPEECH?

Yes, she could. And she was so terror-stricken that she could hardly speak—but she was careful to give no outward sign of it.

"Please, can I go to the observation lounge?" she repeated in a tremulous whisper, edging toward the stateroom door. "I—I really want to see the gray limbo."

Gran caught her by the hand, her green-crystal eyes bright with a compulsive power that Dee had never before experienced. Telepathic questions amplified by coercion thundered in Dee's mind, smashing against her blue barrier like storm waves battering a cliff.

ANSWERANSWERANSWER! "Dorothea, listen to me!" *YOU MUSTANSWER!* "If there is a chance that you are becoming spontaneously operant to a significant degree, then it's important that we continue your therapy. On Earth. We won't go to the doctors in Edinburgh anymore, the ones you don't like. We'll go to Catherine Remillard in America. She's a kind, wonderful woman. You'll like her. Please, dear! You must let me know if you can perceive farspeech. You must." *TELLME TELLME TELLME!*

No! I won't! Angel, make me stronger! Help me . . .

TELL ME THE TRUTH! Gran's full coercive strength demanded. *ANSWER ANSWER ANSWER!*

Dee's mind-screen held in spite of her mortal terror. The angel helped her prop it up.

Dee managed to smile at her grandmother. Her face was open and innocent. "I really want to live with Daddy, not on Earth. I'm mostly normal, Gran. Just like him . . . Can I go to the lounge now?"

Gran let go of Dee's hand. "Yes," she said in a dull, defeated tone.

The formidable coercer had retreated. "You may go. But there's nothing much to see. Limbo is really a very frustrating state. Neither being nor nonbeing."

She turned away to take care of Ken, who was tossing and mumbling as he began to regain consciousness.

Giddy with relief, Dee hurried off along the narrow, silent corridors, stopping from time to time to look at illuminated diagrams with blinking YOU ARE HERE dots. She only met one other person, a member of the crew who grinned and gave her a playful salute before entering one of the cargo holds. Before the door closed behind him, Dee caught a glimpse of yellow rhocraft with checkered belts standing in rows like gigantic Easter eggs: new flying taxis bound for Caledonia. Gran Masha had told the children that the ship carried vital necessities such as road-building equipment, embryonic livestock, medicines, and also things that simply made life more pleasant on a frontier world—Monopoly games, Italian shoes, Swiss wrist-coms, and special foods like oranges and pineapple and chocolate that would not grow on the Scottish planet. Perhaps the strangest cargo was a shipment of empty sherry barrels from Spain. They were needed for one of Caledonia's most important industries—whisky-making!

The CSS Drumadoon Bay was gigantic, like most commercial starships, over 400 meters long. It was also very old, being one of the first colonial merchantmen built by humanity after the advanced science of the Galactic Milieu revolutionized Earth astronautics overnight. A freighter with limited and spartan passenger accommodations, it had offered the cheapest fare to Caledonia. Masha had been quietly furious when she discovered that Daddy had sent a pair of economy-class tickets for Dee and Ken, relegating them to the open cabin. Fortunately, the professor was able to upgrade and get the three of them a small stateroom. The first-class accommodations had mostly been snapped up by miners, xenobiologists, civil engineers, salvage archaeologists, medical specialists, and other professionals who had contracted for limited tours of duty on the rugged ethnic planet. There were also sixty new settlers among the passengers, but most of them traveled in economy class, sleeping in cubbyholes hardly larger than teleview booths when they were not amusing themselves in the recreation rooms or eating in the common mess.

Dee thought the starship was marvelous and never noticed the threadbare tartan carpeting, the scuffed and dented plass bulkheads, or the unpleasant chemical smell pervading their cramped en suite bath.

The observation lounge, when she found it, was much smaller than the one on the ferryboat to Islay and more modestly furnished. Two dozen scruffy easy chairs, all empty, faced a viewport of transparent cerametal five meters in diameter.

Outside the window was . . . nothing.

Dee stood transfixed at the sight of the hyperspatial matrix. It was not really gray, nor was it black or white or any other color she could name. It shone at the same time that it seemed to soak up the artificial light from the lamps in the lounge, making the place seem dim and cavelike but eerily lacking in shadows. If one stared keenly at the gray limbo it was featureless; but a sidelong glance seemed to detect minute trembling motions and larger ghostly waveforms racing in all directions. At irregular intervals the cryptic nothingness seemed racked by an enormous *throb* that overwhelmed the lesser pulsations. Hyperspace seemed to Dee to be alive, and she could not take her bedazzled eyes off it even when they began to hurt and she felt increasingly dizzy. It never occurred to her to call upon her self-redaction. She dared not look away from that bewitching window! Any moment now, something stupendous would surely happen—

"Now then, lassie. I think that's enough."

Someone took hold of her shoulders gently and spun her about, away from the maddening, irresistible gray.

Dee blinked and the spell was broken. She shivered, wiped her eyes, and saw that her rescuer was a tall man wearing a black velvet jacket with silver buttons. He had on a fancy white shirt, a black bow tie, and a kilt of scarlet with a lattice of black stripes and thin lines of gold. His sporran was white leather with silver tassels, his shoes had silver buckles, and there was a small knife with a jewel in the hilt tucked into the top of his right stocking. He guided Dee to a chair near the snack bar, sat her down facing away from the viewport, and ordered the bar to produce a cup of sweet milky coffee.

"The gray limbo's a fascinating thing," the man said, "but it can drive a body clean daft if you keep staring at it."

The steaming drink arrived in a thickish plass mug with no saucer or spoon. The man presented it to her with a theatrical flourish and a charming smile that lifted one side of his mouth higher than the other. His chin had an attractive cleft and he was very good-looking, with hair that was completely white and glittering eyes so deeply sunken she could not tell their color.

"My name is Ewen Cameron and I'm going to Caledonia to see some friends," he said. "Drink this and the dizziness will go away. Experienced star-travelers know that if you want to look at the limbo, you must always make an effort to turn away every few minutes. Coerce yourself if need be."

Dee took brief sips of the drink to be polite. She really didn't much care for coffee and wished that the man had ordered hot chocolate. "Thank you, Citizen Cameron. I'll remember what you said."

"What's your name, lass?"

She told him. The drink made her feel better almost at once. How funny, she thought. It was delicious, and now it really did taste very much like chocolate! Perhaps it was a special kind of Caledonian coffee. She drank it all and set the cup aside. Her fellow passenger had ordered coffee for himself as well, but she caught a whiff of something else in the steam wafting from his cup. He'd put brandy in it, just like Uncle Robbie did—had done—sometimes.

"Does that stuff make the coffee taste better?" she asked.

"Yes—if you're an old man with creaky bones, brandy makes it much better." Are you feeling all right now?

"Yes, thank you."

Good. Now tell me: Why didn't you take the dose of pain-killer that's provided for nonoperant children?

She giggled, still feeling slightly light-headed. "I thought I'd see if I could dodge the pain instead. And I did. It was easy."

So you redacted yourself, did you?

"Only a little bit," she said quickly. "A very little bit. I'm not really an operant at all."

You mean you would like not to be one. But you'll have to do much better than this if you want to continue hiding your powers from your grandmother. She *will* bring you back to Earth if she finds out, you know. The Milieu law regarding metapsychically talented children takes precedence over the rights of a nonoperant parent. Any adult operant who discovers that you are capable of farspeech has a legal obligation to report the fact to the authorities. So you'll have to be very careful. Especially around strong coercers like your Gran who might try to diddle you into demonstrating your ultrasensitivity. Do you understand what I'm saying?

"Yes. I'm a child prodigy and very mature for my age. But you're wrong about me being ultrasensitive. I—" She broke off, her eyes widening in sudden dismay, realizing what she had been doing. "No!" she moaned.

Yes. You answered me when I spoke telepathically.

She sprang to her feet. "It's not fair! You tricked me!" She would have run away, but her feet seemed glued to the tatty carpet.

"Quite right," he admitted, speaking aloud. "I tricked you to show you that you're very young and very vulnerable, and without help you'll never be able to deceive Gran Masha and stay with your father on Caledonia. You do want to stay, don't you?"

"Yes." YesyesYES!

He stretched out his hand, laid it gently on top of her head, and smiled in sudden bemusement. "An angel! How apropos. Let's delegate the job to him, shall we?"

Completely mystified, Dee was taken by surprise when a new thing bloomed within her mind. No . . . it was not really a thing at all: it was a *way.* A linked series of steps leading to a goal she desperately desired. Following that way, she need never fear that she would inadvertently disclose her last great secret to Gran or anyone else. The angel would help keep her mind's mask in place and he would also stop her from making stupid mistakes—as she had just done by responding to the tall man's farspeech.

"Did you put those things into my head?" she asked him timidly.

He placed both their empty cups into the bar's disposal and then headed for the door leading to the corridor. "You would have learnt to be cautious about farspeech and found the proper counteraction to coercion yourself after a while. I simply helped you along so that nothing would prevent you from staying with your father. It's important that you live with him now."

She stared up at the man in the kilt, overcome with wonder. "Are *you* my angel?"

He laughed. "Only this once. But you'll have others when you need them." He left the lounge, closing the door behind him.

Dee's wrist-com peeped. She pressed RECEIVE and Gran's voice said: "Your brother is awake now and the captain has invited all the first-class passengers for a visit to the command bridge, to show us how the ship is run. Would you like to come, too?"

"Oh, yes! I'd love to! Wait for me, Gran. I'll be there in just a second."

She pulled the door open and dashed out into the corridor, all memory of the man named Ewen Cameron erased from her mind.

The ship's final exit from the hyperspatial matrix into the star system of Caledonia was a moment of magic for Dee. Poor Ken lay drugged in the stateroom and so he missed experiencing the event live, as did the other zonked-out normals aboard. But Dee and Gran and twenty or so operant passengers sat watching in the observation lounge when the ship burst out of featureless subspace for the last time.

The mesmerizing gray outside the window shattered into a blaze of turbulent color. And then a planet appeared, very large and three-quarters-lit against a backdrop of diamond-flecked black. Sparkling artificial satellites hovered about Caledonia like fireflies, and seeming to look over its shoulder was the world's natural moon, Ré Nuadh, appearing to be shiny and flat as an oval silver medal.

"Crikey!" exclaimed one of the indentured doctors, impressed in spite of himself. "She's a beaut."

"As long as you don't get tired of raindrops falling on your head," said a female engineer. "Will you look at that cloud cover?"

"Mostly cirrus," somebody else said in an authoritative tone. "Ice crystals, and also a fair amount of high-altitude volcanic dust. I've heard the surface gets hazy sunlight about half the time."

And the other half you drown.

Most of the operants laughed. Dee was very careful not to.

She had seen pictures and Tri-Ds of Caledonia's island-strewn surface, but none of them prepared her for the view from space. Unlike the familiar white-splashed blue marble that was Earth, the Scottish world seemed to be a gigantic misty opal mounted on its nightside crescent of black velvet. In contrast to the harsh blaze of its quartered moon, the planet was softly luminous, shadowed with pale lilac and milky aquamarine. Scattered small openings in the nearly universal cloud mantle decorated it with slashes, spirals, and ragged holes that glowed vivid azure—or, rarely, a dark brownish-green splotched with ochre.

"This is your captain speaking. We have emerged into an orbit above Caledonia and shut down our superluminal drive. In a moment we will switch to ordinary inertialess rho-field propulsion and begin the planetary approach."

A dim web of purplish fire enveloped the window for a split second before fading to invisibility. The planet seemed to swell like a rapidly inflating balloon until it filled the entire opening with mother-of-pearl luster. Then the scene outside darkened as the ship curved around to the world's nightside. The window showed only blackness, broken by what seemed to be hundreds of scattered small bursts of flickering fuzzy light that rapidly grew in size and intensified in brightness. The captain informed the passengers that most of these silent explosions were huge thunderstorms. Certain deep crimson pulsations, rarer than the lighter-colored ones, signified the presence of active volcanoes.

When the starship broke through the high cloud deck Dee saw the Caledonian ocean shimmering faintly in the blaze of incessant lightning from towering ranks of cumulonimbus cells. The captain told them that the storms reached nearly 21,000 meters into the sky and were so powerful that they could tear an ordinary small passenger-egg to bits. As the starship flew much more slowly above the night sea they saw their destination on the horizon, the continent of Clyde, a black jagged landmass rimmed and spangled with the lights of human habitation. Then came the oddest sight of all, when a myriad of miniature yellow and blue flashes battered the observation port like a sudden snowstorm of fireworks.

"The sparks that you see," said the captain's voice, "are due to a natural phenomenon unique to Caledonia. They are caused when the ship's unshielded rho-field makes contact with aerial plant life called looyunuch anower that float in a zone around six thousand meters above the planetary surface. We do our utmost to avoid passing through drifts of these lifeforms, since they are a special part of Caledonia's ecology, but sometimes it's impossible to avoid them."

"And the space line's too cheap to shield its old scows with sigmas that'd push the wee airplants aside," growled a man in a tam-o'-shanter hat who sat in the seat next to Dee's. His name was Lowrie, and he was an immigrant of the most desirable type—an operant geochemist come to work in the fast-growing fullerene processing cooperatives.

"Airplants!" Dee exclaimed. "My Daddy grows those on his farm!"

Lowrie glanced at her briefly. "Your Daddy doesn't grow the luib-heannach an adhair, lass, he only harvests them. Skyweeds grow wild—and most of them are verra, verra wild indeed!" There was laughter from the other adults.

The ship now decelerated with startling suddenness, as though it had come up against a glass wall in mid-air, but the passengers felt no discomfort because the rho-field abolished external gravity-inertia. They floated toward a region of patterned lights, where the vessel would land softly in the sea and be towed into a dock. Caledonia's only starport was not prosperous enough to have the huge sigma generators needed for shielded starship cradles.

"We are entering our final approach and splashdown," the captain said. "We'll dock at Wester Killiecrankie Starport at approximatcly twenty-five-thirty hours Planet Mean Time. Thank you for traveling the MacPherson Line. Safety and economy are our prime directives."

With an emphasis on the latter!

[Laughter.]

You tell 'em Tam! No live cabaret on the bloodyboat the swimmingpool down for repairs and the hough-magandy cubicles with a fleck selection 4years old.

The kitchen recycled that fewkin' tureen of Scotch broth so many times it could qualify for historical landmark status! Next time I'll fly United.

And pay your own bloodyfare? That'll be the day Charlie.

Try flying Astro Gi you lads. At least the food's edible and hey there's worse things than a 2week orgy with the googlyeyed SexTurkeys.

Like what? Circumcision with a grapefruit-knife?

[Laughter.]

Cool it ye hairyarsedgowks! None of your clarty mindtalk in front of the wee lassie.

She's no TrueHead can't farsense atall her gorgeous Gramma here told Aylmar so. Ain't that right Green Eyes darlin'?

[*SILENCE.*]

Ohright be like that YourRoyalEffingHighness and next time take the QE3 if you don't fancy the company of honest workingblokes.

"Come along, Dorothea," said the professor frostily. "There's nothing more to see and we must all get ready for decon."

"Yes, Gran." Dee took her grandmother's hand and the two of them hurriedly left the lounge.

It had been very interesting, listening to the other passengers' telepathic conversation throughout the voyage. The miners' talk, especially, was completely unlike any that Dee had ever heard before. Ken had sometimes been rendered speechless at the things she reported overhearing.

"The decon procedure is very simple," Gran was saying briskly. "We put on paper clothes, and then step under lights that zap any stray Earth organisms on our skin or hair that might not be compatible with the Caledonian ecology. Our regular clothes and other things will be decontaminated separately before we get them back."

The carpeted deck beneath Dee's feet shuddered briefly. Suddenly, she felt slightly heavier.

"They've turned off the artificial gravity," Gran said. "We've splashed down."

"Do you think Daddy will be waiting for us?" Dee asked eagerly.

Gran only said, "We'll see."

[9]

SECTOR 12: STAR 12-337-010 [GRIAN]
PLANET 4 [CALEDONIA]
6 MIOS GAILBHEACH [21 JUNE] 2062

A moving walkway carried the professor and the two children and the other passengers from the Drumadoon Bay toward the terminal and their first true experience of the planet Caledonia. It was past midnight local time and a violent storm had just broken out, filling the atmosphere with jangling ions and making it impossible for Dee to get a proper feel of the new world's aura. Through the concourse windows she could see a rain lashed tarmac and tossing trees down by the seashore where their starship and three others had just docked. Egg transports, hop-lorries, groundcars, and scuttling people in raingear gleamed wetly under the starport's halide lights. Every few moments the exterior scene was lit up and bleached colorless by blasts of lightning. Thunder made the concourse walls tremble, but its noise seemed almost insignificant compared to the telepathic tempest that began to assault Dee's mind once she got within "shouting" range of the crowd swarming within the terminal.

Tuning out the mind-chatter of the crew and the other passengers on the Drumadoon Bay had become second nature to Dee by the time the voyage ended, but this fresh attack on her immature ultrasense left her shocked to numbness until she finally managed to regain control. The mental voices had never seemed so loud before, not even back on Earth. Were there more operants on Caledonia? Surely not. More people lived in Edinburgh Metro than on the entire Scottish planet. Were the minds here more powerful then?

No. You are simply becoming more sensitive to farspeech.

She gave a great start. (Fortunately, it coincided with a deafening thunderclap and Gran never noticed.) The telepathic voice seemed to be that of the man named Ewen Cameron, but when Dee cautiously looked about there was no sign of him among the other disembarking passengers on the walkways. How odd! Up until this moment she had completely forgotten the mysterious stranger who had inexplicably promised to help her. Holding tight to the walk's rail, she closed her eyes and tried to summon up a mental picture of him; but all she perceived was a shadowy figure who appeared to be wrapped in a huge pair of folded wings, standing before a rampart of glowing, multicolored boxes.

. . . Angel? Was it YOU talking to me?

Yes. When you really need the answers to questions about your metapsychic abilities, you may ask me.

Are you really Citizen Cameron?

No. I am a preprogrammed response with psychoanalytic discretionary options. Now open your eyes. You are at the end of the moving walkway and you don't want to trip and fall down and look silly.

Dee hadn't the least idea what a "preprogrammed response" with all the rest of it was. But she did as she was told and saw that they had reached the terminal's luggage-claim area. Gran herded the children ahead of her once they stepped off the walkway. The air inside the building was chilly and humid and had an unfamiliar perfumey smell that Dee decided she liked. Even the canned music playing on the public address system was pleasant, a woman's voice singing a haunting tune:

Let me tell you that I love you,
That I think about you all the time.
Caledonia, you're calling me,
Now I'm going home.
But if I shall become a stranger—
No, it would make me more than sad.
Caledonia's been everything I've ever had.

The aura of the place was invigorating, hopeful, friendly. Here and there among the tourist-services booths, rent-a-rho kiosks, roboporter stands, and banks of televiews were glazed crocks with odd little trees growing in them. They reminded Dee of the colorful coleus plants that grew in shady nooks of Gran's garden during the summer. The big leaves had crisped edges and were blotched and spotted and striped with every conceivable shade of green, and also with purple, pink, white, orange, yellow, and rose red.

Ken poked her in the ribs. "Those trees. They're like the ones in Dad's picture. Aren't they weird?"

"I think they're pretty. Most of the plants here on Caledonia have colored leaves. I read about them in the ship's library. They make food from sunlight with chlorophyll just like green plants on Earth do."

Ken pulled a face. "Ooo! Aren't you the clever clogs!" But an instant later he forgot about teasing her and began anxiously searching the crowd that awaited the arriving passengers, trying to find their father. The welcomers were all human and all of caucasoid appearance. Dee recalled that exotics and humans of non-Scottish heritage were allowed to visit Caledonia freely and even work on the planet for a limited time, but they were forbidden to settle permanently. Hardly anyone among the natives wore kilts (perhaps because of the weather), but a kaleidoscope of tartan patterns graced everything from raincoats to baby bonnets.

Some Caledonians held up small signs with names on them or messages written in English or Gaelic. Others rushed forward calling greetings when they managed to locate friends or relatives. A tremendous gabble of farspeech filled the aether, some of it emanating from operants using the declamatory mode and even more being broadcast inadvertently by nonoperants. Of course Daddy was latent, so Dee knew there was very little chance that she would be able to pick up his subvocal speech even if he did chance to farspeak her name. But no one called her, and finally she shut out the crowd-thoughts altogether.

The professor led the way to the nearest roboporter kiosk, where she and the children joined a queue to retrieve their checked luggage. Gran Masha's face was serene and her thoughts remained in the intimate mode, screened almost as perfectly as Dee's own and quite unreadable; but the little girl did perceive that her grandmother was becoming increasingly apprehensive and irritated because Ian Macdonald had failed to appear.

A number of people in the queue were talking Scots Gaelic, and Dee was both shocked and delighted to discover that she understood the spoken language quite well, even though she had learned only a few words and phrases from teacher-flecks at her day school in Edinburgh. However, the written Gaelic on the bilingual signs in the terminal remained as difficult to decipher as ever.

Dee asked the angel why this should be, and he replied promptly:

Farsensors who are very talented, as you are, perceive the meaning of spoken foreign languages easily. All words are symbols for meaningful thoughts. When people speak to each other, they think the meaning of the words at the same time their lips pronounce them, and this meaning is evident to you. But written words are only accompanied by thoughts when they are first put down by the writer. You will also find that your ultrasenses will not enable you to speak Gaelic without studying. You will still have to learn the vocabulary, grammar, and pronunciation, or else use a Sony Translator.

I see. Am . . . am I really very talented?

But this time the angel did not reply, and before she could formulate another question her brother spoke and brought her back to the reality of the starport terminal.

"Do you think something might have happened to Dad?" Ken was asking Gran.

The professor had finally been able to take her turn at the roboporter. She handed Ken the release token the machine had spit out after it scanned her ticket. "Stand over there and accept the luggage when it comes up. I'm going to make a phone call and see why we weren't met."

She went into one of the nearby teleview cubicles. The children could not see the screen, but they saw Gran's face tighten as she carried on a conversation for some minutes. Unfortunately, Gran's thoughts were shielded and Dee was still unable to eavesdrop with any other ultrasenses.

"Maybe Dad was delayed by the storm," Dee said. "It's the beginning of autumn here. The sixth of Mios Gailbheach. That means 'blustery month.' "

"Quit being such a show-off," Ken muttered grouchily. He was feeling badly let down. "I hope Dad still talks Standard English. What a stone dragola it'd be to have to learn Gaelic right away."

"I could help you," Dee said eagerly. She would have told him about her new translation talent, but one of the floor-doors of the roboporter suddenly opened and up popped a carrier with their bags and the big trunk on it. The carrier's mechanical voice said: "The citizen claiming this baggage must deposit the claim-token in the slot below the red light." When Ken did, the light turned green and the thing said: "Thank you. Shall I follow you to your ground transport? Or do you wish the baggage transferred to the egg platform via tube? For other options, please consult my command menu."

"Wait," Ken snapped. The roboporter blinked its green light at him and rolled a short distance away from the lift so that the next batch of bags could be delivered. The two children followed it. Then Gran came striding back, pale and tight-lipped and obviously trying to hold her temper.

"We will spend the night at the terminal hotel," she said, "and go on to Glen Tuath Farm tomorrow. It seems there was an extraordinary bloom of airplants. According to your father's housekeeper, the phenomenon represents an opportunity for him to earn a great deal of money. He and every other qualified person on the farm have done nothing but harvest and process the plants for the past two weeks. He has been working night and day with very little sleep and could not spare the time to come for us since the harvesting season will end tomorrow. Someone else will meet us in the morning and fly us to Glen Tuath."

"Who?" Ken asked.

But the professor had turned to address the roboporter, instructing it where to take the luggage. Then she was off to Tourist Services to book rooms, with Dee and Ken trailing slowly behind.

"I know who's coming for us," Dee said in a low voice. "Gran's thoughts about him were really loud."

"Who cares," Ken retorted, "if it's not Dad."

"It's Grandad. He's coming from the University of New Glasgow and flying us to Daddy's farm himself."

The next morning there came a great pounding on the door of their hotel suite. Dee and Ken ran together to open it and there he stood, seeming to fill the entire doorframe.

"Fàilte," bellowed Kyle Macdonald, dropping to one knee. "Bhur beatha an dùthaich! D'you know what that means? Welcome to my country—to my world!" He flung out his arms and swept the pair of astonished children into a bear hug before they had time to think. "And do you remember your old grandfather at all?"

"Yes! Yes!" Ken shrieked happily. Dee knew her brother was lying, wanting to please Grandad and succeeding. She herself was overcome with shyness, and she could only stare wide-eyed at the burly newcomer after he had put her down, hiding her confusion behind a tentative little smile and her adamant mind-screen.

The famous fantasy writer had on a hairy tweed jacket and rumpled cord trousers stuffed into muddy half-Wellingtons. A waistcoat made of the ancient hunting tartan of Macdonald of the Isles strained to confine his paunch without bursting its staghorn buttons. He wore a flat cap, and a thatch of bushy gray hair straggled out from under it, covering his ears. His face, imperfectly shaven below the jowls, had once been strikingly handsome but now the brow and cheeks were ravaged and furrowed. Great pouches of flesh hung below his rheumy eyes, and capillary webs reddened his thickened, arched nose.

Dee heard her grandfather's clumsy, subvocal musings distinctly:

The lass seems sonsie enough for all she's pokerfaced and no oil painting but Christonacrutch the lad is a poor shilpit thing pale as milk and no more meat on him than a bloodybroomstick I wonder if he's got a decent brain behind those whippedpuppydog eyes? . . .

"Who's ready to fly to Glen Tuath Farm?" Kyle Macdonald cried heartily. "The trunk and your big bags are all stowed in my egg, the room tab's paid, and we've sixteen thousand kloms to travel so let's be off! Where's your grandmother hiding? Masha! Maire nic-cridhe! Where are you, old wumman?"

The professor's voice, cool and penetrating, replied "Coming." A moment later she emerged from the inner bedroom, carrying the children's anoraks. She had put away the sensible cotalene skirt and blazer she had worn most of the time on the starship and was now dressed in a dramatic formfitting bodysuit of metallic hunter-green nebulin with an ornate golden belt. Over this she wore a long hooded cape of amber cashmere, lined in green silk. She had changed her hairstyle, loosening the familiar severe braided coronet so that two thick, wavy auburn tresses fell over the cape's golden clasp onto the high swell of her breasts. Her face, slightly shadowed by the hood, glowed with skillfully applied cosmetics.

Dee and Ken gawked at her, never having seen Gran Masha in this amazing aspect before. Grandad's incoherent subvocalizations revealed his own shocked incredulity. He staggered back a step and for a moment was lost to words.

"Great God in heaven," he whispered at last. "Can it be *you*, Maire a ghràidh? Young again and so beautiful you tear the heart out of a man?"

She swept past him, ignoring his outstretched arms, and began bundling the children into their jackets. "Rejuvenation therapy is a common thing in the more civilized parts of the Milieu. It's safe, reasonably priced, and requires only a few months' sabbatical"—she looked him up and down critically—"provided that one has maintained a reasonably healthy lifestyle. You might present more of a challenge to the genetic engineers, Kyle, but they're accomplishing the most remarkable things with difficult cases. Even regenerating pickled livers."

Wagging his head sadly, the writer appealed to the little boy and girl. "Do you hear how unkindly your dear Grannie speaks to me? But it's all a sham, you know. All these years we've been apart, she's never lost her love for me nor I my heartfelt devotion to her. That's why she's come with you to Caledonia."

Masha uttered a brittle laugh. "I'm only escorting the children, Kyle. And I'll only stay long enough to make certain that Ian is in a position to give them proper care. I have no intention of burying myself in a provincial backwater with a gaggle of kiltie barbarians. Now, if you're quite sure that you're feeling up to it, let's be on our way. I'll meet you and the children at the egg park on the roof after I find the hotel's subspace transmitter and send off some work I managed to finish on the voyage."

Waving aside Kyle's offer to take her overnight case, she sailed into the hallway and headed for the lifts.

Dee said, "I don't mind if you carry *my* bag, Grandad." She held it out and smiled shyly when he took it from her. "Kenny and I are very glad to be here. We think Caledonia is . . . an interesting place."

Ken shot an anxious look at his grandfather. "It'll be all right, won't it? I mean, Dad really does want us, doesn't he?"

"Of course he wants you," Kyle declared aloud. But his mind said: Ha! He's cursed himself for a sentimental berk ever since the black day he shot his mouth off but he's too pigheaded to go back on his word.

Ken giggled with relief. Dee's smile never wavered even though she felt her heart turn to ice.

Kyle Macdonald lowered his voice and bent down to speak more confidentially. "Now you listen up, bairns. Your Dad's a hardworking man who's doing his best to earn a living in one of the most rugged places on the whole planet. He won't have time to cosset you or waste time playing kiddie games. He'll expect you to help with the farm work as best you can and take care of your satellite-school studies without being nagged over it. He's a fair man, but he can't abide crybabies or layabouts, and he'll be disappointed and impatient if you get squeamish or frightened about the new things you're going to encounter out in Beinn Bhiorach. Do you hear what I'm saying?" . . . You'd better hear or you'll find yourselves well&truly up it!

Ken nodded gravely but his thoughts were a panicky howl: I'm going to be eversobrave for Dad yes even if I have to eat creepyfood but whatabout Dee she could make Dad angry doing her scaredybabyshit and whatabout her damnstupidmindpowers if she gets sent back to Earth then Dad might make ME go too it's not fair why did I have to have a weirdheadsister like her I think I *hate* her—

"Glen Tuath's in a very lonely part of the world, but the big house is comfortable and there's lots to explore and do in your spare time. A pair of paleontologists are staying at the place and digging up fossils. You can go boating on Loch Tuath, and visit the diamond and buckyball mines, and watch Ben Fizgig volcano blow its stack. There'll be other children for you to play with—the workers' kids and the three nonborn fosterlings that Ian's taken in. They're older than you, but you'll manage. Every few weeks your Dad'll take you to Grampian Town or Muckle Skerry for a wee bit of excitement while he gets supplies, and I'll egg in now and then and steal you both for a holiday in New Glasgow or in some other amusing place. As soon as you're a bit older you can learn to fly and tend the skyweeds."

Ken said, "Wow! I'd love that!" But I bet Dee would be tooscared to learn and toodumb besides.

"You must promise me not to fash your Dad by moping or getting homesick for big-city Earthside ways," the writer warned them. "He won't take kindly to that sort of hassle." He's got troubles enough keeping the farm from going under and fending off Thrawn Janet . . .

"I understand," Ken said.

"Me, too," Dee added quietly. "I'm very mature for five."

"We're in luck," Kyle told them, as they all boarded the egg. It was a sporty white Porsche, nearly new, with stubby heat-dissipation fins. Dee overheard Gran Masha thinking: How in the world can he afford it? Or has he found a way to make Rebellion pay?

When the writer took off his cap, he revealed a polished dome of bare freckled scalp protruding from an encircling tangle of gray. Dee stared at the unusual disfigurement, fascinated. She had seen pictures of bald men, of course; Shakespeare was bald! But a simple genetic engineering procedure developed over forty years earlier had all but abolished male pattern baldness on Earth. Why hadn't Grandad grown new hair?

"We'll have decent weather for sightseeing as we fly across Clyde and also at northern BB around the farm," Kyle said. "In between's rather a filthy mess with one storm after another, but we'll fly high above them until we put down for lunch on Strathbogie. I'll do a little travelogue in the clear spots and you bairns can decide for yourselves whether or not Caledonia's a barbarian backwater as your lovely Grannie says. Of course she's never been here so she might possibly be wrong."

"H'mph," snorted the professor. She had the rear banquette of the egg to herself while the children sat on either side of their grandfather in front.

Hazy sunshine had turned the Caledonian sky the color of skim milk. Except for the colorful foliage, the environs of Wester Killiecrankie did not seem particularly exotic when seen from the air. The clusters of warehouses, offices, and industrial buildings near the spaceport did not look much different from those in the commercial parts of Edinburgh, while the houses and apartments resembled those of the Scottish metro hinterlands. Many dwellings were built of handsome white-painted stone and the majority stood in the midst of spacious gardens or fronted onto landscaped commons. As the egg followed an urban Vee-route northward along the coast the children saw a golf course, a big glass-roofed shopping mall, and business parks adorned with plantings and tiny lakes.

"Are all the cities on Caledonia as pretty as this?" Ken asked.

"Hardly," said the writer with a wry grin. "The Wester Killiecrankie Starport's quite new, only twenty years old or so, and it was carefully planned to be a showplace for arriving visitors, with quakeproof buildings and all . . . We do get the occasional temblor now and then! The older settlements like my own hometown of New Glasgow have some run-down parts that need spiffying up—and some of the mining towns are ugly as sin. But by and large, we Callies have kept the planet tidy."

"Is that what the citizens call themselves—Callies?" Ken asked.

"That's right. And in the Gaelic 'caladh' means 'a safe haven,' so we often call the planet Callie, too."

"The steep hills with the patches of different colored trees look like they're wrapped in great big tartans," Dee said softly.

"Right you are, lass." Kyle gave her an approving nod. "Back in the beginning, after the Great Intervention, the Simbiari Proctors were setting up the first batch of ethnic worlds, and the Scots being an especially dynamic group had their pick of three or four that were all surveyed and had reasonably high human compatibility. This planet won hands down, even though it's a wee bit rugged and shy of dry land, because of the plaidie look of its forests and the fine crags and waterfalls and louring mountains."

"Sheer romanticism," huffed Gran Masha. But Grandad only laughed.

Once they were out of the controlled airspace around the city, the writer began to show off his piloting ability, free-flying the powerful Porsche along the Clyde coast at barely subsonic speed so that they could admire the dramatic fringe of steep, tusklike islands north of the starport. With nonchalant skill he zigzagged among the towering skerries at a perilously low altitude with the sigma off. Their wind-of-passage made an eerie howl, Ken shrieked with excitement, and Dee used her redaction to keep from becoming ill. Gran Masha ignored the aerobatics while she read an academic journal.

Then Kyle turned inland and ascended into a mid-altitude transcontinental Vee-route, relinquishing control of the rhocraft to the computerized traffic system. There were only moderate numbers of other vehicles moving with them in the arterial airway—nothing approaching the congestion of central Scotland, where the skies always seemed circus-bright with endless streams of colored flying eggs on hundreds of intermeshing programmed vectors.

Traveling now at nearly 2000 kph they traversed Clyde's interior Lothian Range, a wilderness of jagged black-and-red peaks that comprised the remnants of extinct volcanoes. The highest of them had glaciers on their northern slopes even though the continent was near the planetary equator. Fast-flowing rivers, gleaming like twisted platinum threads, carved out precipitous valleys heavily forested with bronze-colored, bluish-green, and scarlet trees. Nestled amongst the high ridges were chains of lakes, often bordered with vivid golden patches of vegetation that the writer called "fearsome bottomless peat bogs." Very few roads traversed the highlands, and the settlements there were small and widely separated. Kyle kept up a running commentary, telling the children the names of the geographical features below and making them laugh by describing adventures of the first intrepid settlers, who had had to contend with "fierce skelly-eyed native beasties," tsunamis, volcanoes, and now and then certain peculiar eruptions called diatremes.

"But things are fairly calm nowadays except for the occasional ground-rumble," he reassured them. "Sixth-degree ecological modification lets us grow quite a few Earth crops, and we also have wholesome local veggies thanks to genetic engineering. The most enthusiastic of the hostile critters have been herded off to preserves in uninhabited regions, and the seismic shivers we can't nip in the bud are mostly predictable well in advance so that they don't endanger people."

East of the Lothians the terrain was rolling and more congenial to civilization, obviously longer-settled with larger towns, extensive agricultural areas, and spectacular stretches of rainbow-hued deciduous woodland. The planetary capital of New Glasgow was situated on a great arm of the sea, predictably named the Firth of Clyde; but a small patch of storm clouds unfortunately hid most of the city from view as they passed to the south of the estuary. The writer did point out the verdigris-copper dome of the Caledonian Assembly, Dirigent House, where intrepid old Graeme Hamilton worked to keep his planet of hardheaded Scots toeing the Milieu line, and the University of New Glasgow, a cluster of white stratotowers in the midst of a multicolored campus.

The fertile lowlands along the firth shores were parceled into neatly delineated farms. Some crops were conventionally green, while others were an exotic purple, pale pink, and even orange.

"Full of beta-carotene, the bloinigean-gàraidh," Kyle remarked about the latter. "Very good for a body. We eat the plant like spinach—in salads or cooked with baconfish."

"Ick!" Ken grimaced. "I hope there's Earth food here, too. We had some really foul swill for brekkers. Poached eggs with brown yolks, kippers with the heads still on so you could see the fishies' ugly little teeth and dead white eyes—and the milk was yellow!"

"That's because of harmless pigments in the local silage our cows eat," Kyle said, chuckling. "You'll get used to it, laddie." *Or else.*

"The food tasted very good," Dee said quickly. "I just wish I could have had porridge."

"They'll have that at the farm, lass. Oats are one Earthside crop that does very well on Caledonia. And barley, too, God-be-thankit." Or there'd be no lovely malt and I'd die from having to quench my thirst with naught but beer.

To the children's astonishment, Gran spoke up sharply from the backseat in fluent Gaelic. " 'S an t-ol a chuir an dùnach ort!"

Grandad shot back a reply in the same language. "Mo nuar! 'S e do bhoidhchead a leòn mi."

Then the two of them started a fine argle-bargle back and forth that left Ken utterly mystified; but Dee made the translation with ease, eavesdropping on the exchange while pretending to study the masses of islands that clogged the mouth of the firth. Gran Masha had scolded Grandad for drinking, and he had said she was so beautiful it made him sick.

"Save your honeyed flattery," Masha told her husband in Gaelic. "Both of us know you're only interested in embalming your brain in alcohol and cooking up feckless conspiracies with your drunken friends. Your thoughts betray you as always."

"I'm happy you remember the mother tongue I taught you," Kyle retorted. "But I'll thank you to stop reading my poor leaking mind and putting your own cruel interpretation on what's in there. I do what I have to do and do it quite well, thank you."

"But you don't! All you write now are political diatribes against the Milieu. You haven't done a decent piece of fiction for years, and what a pitiful waste of talent it is. You were never a great literary light, but at least you were competent and amusing. Fit for better things than trying to teach creative writing to adolescents and fomenting sedition in your spare time to keep from being bored to death."

"Abah, you gorgeous hag! I've had a bellyful of your bitching. How much more must you shame me before the children?"

"The little girl knows only a few words of the Gaelic, the boy next to nothing. And the shame is your own if you're still a slave to the drink and still talking treason."

"If I do tip off a mutchkin from time to time it's you who've driven me to it, Mary my jewel. As for the treason, remember what the Poet said: 'Freedom and whisky gang thegither!' You were once sympathetic enough toward the Rebel cause yourself—a worthy daughter to your learned and valiant mother. You're the one gone astray, lovely creature, not I."

"Don't talk nonsense."

"Is it nonsense that you still care for me?"

"Nar leigeadh Dia!"

"Oh, aye! Then tell me why you're here with your hair down and gold rings in your ears and perfume on, dressed to the teeth in that scandalous suit? As if you didn't know what the sight of you, bonny as the buds of May, would do to me! Ah, Mary, Mary, all that's needed for my salvation is you, best-beloved, warming my bed and charging my loins and lashing me to creative frenzy again with your luscious forked tongue. And you're young! *Young!*"

"And you're a pathetic, sodden, baldpated wreck of a bramaire and I loathe you."

"Do you! One part of me's still as youthful as ever, and eager and ready to take you to the seventh heaven and beyond. You can't have forgotten! As for the rest of my battered carcass . . . it could be cobbled back together, given proper incentive. I'd swan-dive into the vat of rebirth in a trice if I knew you'd be waiting for me when I crawled out.

Waiting and ready to help me fight for humanity's freedom from the exotic seducers."

"It's too late, Kyle. Not only for you and me, but for your callow seditious schemes as well. The vast majority of metas and nonoperants on Earth believe that—"

"Earth!" He let loose a bark of rough laughter. "An old, tired world blinded and led astray by the mighty Galactic Milieu! The generous Milieu! The tyrannical Milieu! But you're not *on* Earth anymore, woman. Out here among the far stars is a new kind of humanity—swelled-heads and deadheads working together to build worlds that we'll do with as we please."

"Kyle—"

"Tosd! We've havered enough in the Gaelic. The children are getting restless."

"Oh, no! You don't go fobbing me off quite yet. Is Ian involved in this damned conspiracy with you?"

"He's my true and firstborn son. Not like the three bread-and-milk operant brats you turned against me, sgoinneil! And if you think you can change his mind—"

"I may try just that."

"Aha! So you *are* thinking of staying here. I might have known you were up to miching mallecho! But I'll remind you, my lovely darling, that Rebellion is quite legal these days."

"For now," Masha said sweetly. "Just wait until the next session of the Concilium."

"And what's that supposed to mean, Madam Magnate?"

"Burraidh!" she snapped. "Na lean orm na's faide!"

And Dee knew that the fascinating and baffling conversation in Gaelic had come to an end, for Gran Masha had called Grandad a bumbling fool and told him not to bother her anymore.

They left Clyde behind and ascended to 20 kilometers altitude so that they could fly at top speed above the violent weather of the northeastern sea. Ken engaged his grandfather in conversation about the history of the colony, but Dee pretended to sleep while she consulted the angel.

Is it true, she asked apprehensively, that Daddy wishes we hadn't come?

She saw an unmoving silhouette deep within her mind. Behind it the imprisoned lights inside the neatly stacked imaginary boxes seemed to flare in mockery at the foolish question to which she already knew the answer.

Her mind cried out to him: I didn't want to eavesdrop on Grandad's thoughts. Why don't you help me so I don't have to listen to bad things that make me sad and afraid? Now I know that Daddy doesn't want me. And Grannie is worried about us living here, and still thinks I might be a head. Even Kenny is thinking awful thoughts about me. I hate being able to read minds. I don't want this power. It's awful! Please take it back. Please!

The angel was silent. The boxes glowed, three of them open, including the big new violet one, and all the rest shut.

Angel, I want Daddy to love me! Tell me how to do that if you can't do anything else.

For a long time there was no response. The angel was entirely wrapped in his wings, hidden as completely as a cob of maize within its shuck. Finally his mind-voice bespoke her reluctantly.

You will have to be the kind of child Ian Macdonald finds lovable: quiet, obedient, uncomplaining, useful. And you must give no hint of your operant metafunctions nor even of the latent ones, for they will frighten your father.

Frighten? . . . But Daddy is a grownup man! The powers scare me, but—

Grownups can also be frightened by them. And it is impossible to love what you fear.

At least help me keep the closed boxes shut up tight forever!

Someday you will need what is inside them, and so will many other people. Not for a long time yet, but someday. And when all the powers within the other boxes are freed you will have to become a grownup yourself and leave Caledonia and learn how to do your life's work.

No! I'll stay here forever! I will I will and I HATE my rotten powers and I'll always keep them hidden so that—

Enough. Be still, little Illusio. Rest behind your blue rampart. Sleep in the peace of your rosy pool.

I don't want to! I won't! You're not my good old angel at all. You're HIM and I don't like you anymore!

Sleep. Forget . . .

She felt herself sinking, sinking into warm calmness walled round with impenetrable safety. She forgot the angel, forgot the man called Ewen Cameron who seemed to speak through her mind's guardian, forgot all the things that had vexed and worried her.

Dee did not awake until hours later, when Grandad landed the egg for lunch on the continent of Strathbogie.

They came down in the crowded public egg park of a compact town situated on a bay between two curved promontories. A number of large container ships were moored in the deeper water and many smaller craft—commercial fishing vessels, motor sailors, and a few private yachts and runabouts—were tied up at the docks or moving slowly about the harbor.

It was raining lightly. Torn swatches of cloud straggled down the slopes of immensely tall mountains that seemed to shoot up almost vertically a kilometer or two inland. The close-packed houses and shops were painted in bright colors, as if to liven the somberness of the landscape. Many of them had fences of whitened stone, and coleus trees and cheerful flowers had been planted in the dooryards and on the median strip dividing the busy high street.

"This is Portknockie," Kyle said. "We're still nine thousand kloms southwest of Beinn Bhiorach continent, and there's naught but a few strings of volcanoes between Strathbogie and there." He took Gran Masha's arm in spite of her disapproving look and led the way into the bustling town center. The heads of both men and women turned to stare at the striking female visitor in her haute couture.

"Hee hee hee!" The writer strutted along the sidewalk, smirking with pride. "The ladies will be dashing for their sewing modules and the men cranking the shank over the glamorous sight of you, Maire."

She shook off his arm and drew the cape closer about her without saying a word. Kyle was unfazed.

"There's a seafood house on the quay that I fancy. Let's have a leg-stretch and a good lunch, since it'll be six hours or more before we put down at the farm. The damned express Vee-route between here and BB is out of service, and it's unsafe to fly free in stormy weather. You have to expect that kind of thing, the farther away from Clyde and Argyll you travel. The other ten inhabited Callie lands fall pretty much into the wild frontier category."

The groundcars on the streets of Portknockie were mostly pickup trucks, Ford Broncos, Toyota Land Cruisers, and other sturdy vehicles suited to primitive roads. In spite of the drizzle, large numbers of people were going about their business on foot, not bothering with umbrellas or minisig shelters. Their dress was more extravagant than that of the Clyde folk. Both men and women were as likely to wear kilts or gaudy trews as ordinary street clothes, and some had tartan plaids wrapped around their shoulders, fixed in place with huge Celtic brooches studded with amethysts, cairngorms, and striking colored pearls that Dee exclaimed over.

"You probably know that pearls are one of Caledonia's principal exports," the writer said to the children. "Portknockie is one of the pearling centers of this continent, and there are gold and silver mines in the outback as well. Jewelry-making is a big cottage industry here. Would you like to stop at one of the shops and look over the whigmaleeries? I'd been meaning to get you some welcome-to-Caledonia prezzies, and a body gets better value for the money here at the source than at the big stores in New Glasgow or the pokey little places at the Muckle Skerry Mall on Beinn Bhiorach." He turned to the professor. "What d'ye say, Maire a gaolach? There's a fine shop right here."

They had paused at a window display that seemed to Dee like the open mouth of a pirate's treasure cave. Strings of richly glowing pearls in every color imaginable hung from perches and gleamed in overflowing baskets. There were pearl bracelets, pearl earrings, armlets, pins, hair ornaments, and rings designed for humankind, while fantastic collars of woven seed pearls, wedding diadems with gems the size of cherries, and enormous pearl pendants larger than hen's eggs were intended to lure Poltroyan tourists.

"How kind," said the professor, not bothering to hide her lack of enthusiasm. "But I think not. Perhaps you can find something less extravagant for the children later. These things are much too ornate and expensive."

Kyle shrugged and they continued on to the restaurant. It was an unimpressive-looking place that stood on rickety pilings in the tidewaters, but the food turned out to be delicious and very Earthlike. Gran Masha had a bowl of hog-clam chowder and hot soda bread, while Grandad had a platter of local oysterish creatures that he called eisire and gobbled raw, winking at Gran all the while and sending very odd thoughts at her. Ken and Dee had something called portan au gratin on toasted muffins, which tasted just like the best Dungeness crab with melted Cheddar cheese. The milk served to the children was still primrose yellow, but the pot of tea that the writer insisted Masha share with him was authentic Twinings Darjeeling with slices of real Brazilian lemon.

The professor shook her head disapprovingly at the extravagance. "Twenty dollars for a pot of real tea! The menu has Caledonian mint for a tenth of the price."

"Or two wee drams of the local deoch làidir for half." Kyle's eyes were twinkling and Dee knew he was talking about whisky. "But I remembered how you love tea, and you won't get it at Ian's. He's dead set against letting Thrawn Janet serve expensive food and drink—not that Miss Vinegar-Moosh would have any notion how to cook gourmet goodies if you gave 'em to her. Or other food, for that matter. Only Scots cook I've ever known who always ruins the scones." He sighed. "But she's a stone whiz with computers and keeps the hired hands and the nonborns toeing the mark." If only she'd face up to the fact that Ian'll never fancy her for sweet houghmagandie!

The image that accompanied Grandad's appended thought was so extraordinary that Dee nearly gasped aloud. Her grandmother caught the involuntary remnant of farspeech, too, and another sharp argument in Gaelic commenced. But Dee had had enough of grownup squabbling and overhearing nasty secrets. She shut both the spoken words and the thoughts of the adults out so she could enjoy her food in peace.

Dee had come to the conclusion that Gran Masha was not nearly so hostile toward Grandad as she pretended to be. Why then did she continue arguing and pretending to be stuck up? It was baffling.

Toward the end of the meal the writer excused himself, saying he had an errand to do and would meet them back at the egg. He was gone before the professor could object. Gran seemed to have some idea of what he was up to, however, because her face tightened into a frown, and on the way back to the parking lot she let slip into the aether a surprising string of powerful subvocal profanity that Dee could not help perceiving. The words were new and interesting.

The reason for Gran's ill temper became evident when Kyle reappeared at the egg carrying a string bag with three parcels in it. Grinning like a wolf, he thrust one package into Dee's hands, one into Ken's, and tossed the third carelessly into the backseat with the professor. Then he lit up the egg and sent them rocketing into the sky.

The children exchanged glances and opened the presents. Dee's was a delicate gold chain with four iridescent peach-colored pearls spaced on it. Ken received a little silver model of a Strathbogie decapod sea monster. Its claw-studded tentacles writhed realistically and its six eyes were black pearls.

"Thank you, Grandad!" the children chorused happily.

Gran Masha said nothing and her gift was left unopened. But she used her deepsight to inspect it, and Dee suddenly heard a farspoken exclamation: *Kyle you fool you obstinatebloody fool!* And for the briefest instant the girl beheld what her grandmother's ultrasense perceived—a curiously wrought necklet shaped like the letter C. It was formed from thick twisted strands of gold and at the ends were two dragon heads facing each other. The eyes of the beasts were glowing crimson pearls and their teeth held two diamonds.

During most of the remainder of the journey, their egg flew at an altitude of ten kilometers in a lonely zone of sky having an undulating floor of unbroken rain clouds and a ceiling of very thin cirrus. From time to time they saw strange atmospheric phenomena that Kyle said were common on Caledonia: vast elliptical rainbows suspended above the cloud deck, brightly colored haloes and arcs drawn in the ice-haze that veiled the sun, and patches of luminescence near the solar disk called parhelia or sun dogs, which sometimes appeared to jump magically about the sky.

Toward the end of the afternoon, when both Ken and Gran Masha were napping in the backseat and Dee was thoroughly tired of watching game shows, cartoons, and news broadcasts on the egg's Tri-D, the sea of cloud below began to break apart, revealing tantalizing glimpses of a deep-green sea and occasional strings of islands clothed in sparse vegetation. Then a formation of towering clouds reaching all the way to the cirrus ceiling appeared ahead of them and to the left. In the midst of the cloud-mass was a billowing shape that appeared darker and somehow more solid than an ordinary thunderhead. As the course of the egg brought them even with the heaped clouds the sinking sun, which up until then had resembled a whitish paper cutout or a dazzling ball made fuzzy by ice crystals, was completely blotted out. When the sun reappeared it had turned an amazing azure blue color.

"Oh, Grandad! Look!" Dee exclaimed.

"It's the dust from that erupting volcano floating in the stratosphere that does it," he said. "The mountain's name is Stormking. We're flying around sixty kloms east of the Reekie Isles, an active chain south of Beinn Bhiorach. A major volcanic zone extends northward all along the western rim of the continent. There's even a small belcher called Ben Fizgig a hundred kloms or so from your Dad's farm, in the Goblin Archipelago."

"Is it dangerous?"

"Nay, it puffs off harmlessly now and then and the prevailing winds carry the ash out over the sea. The only habitation anywhere near it is the Daoimean Dubh Mines, and they're safe enough tucked in a gorge of the Tuath Peninsula. But there are other volcanoes in southern BB that bear careful watching. Not only for lava flows and ashfall, but because their eruptions can melt snow and glacier ice and cause lahars—terrible fast-moving mudflows. The reason Beinn Bhiorach was the last continent to be settled is because it has the most active volcanoes. But they do good as well as ill. Their gases and drifting bits of mineral dust help make good soil in some places and also nourish the airplants. It's when the fiery mountains are quiet that the luibheannach an adhair grow scarce and the airfarmers have hard times."

"Has—has it been hard like that for Daddy?"

Kyle nodded. "He's been struggling in poortith for over five years, not even able to afford a full slate of workers. It's been a long dormant period for the local firepots. They're cooking nicely now, though, and things will be fine at the farm once this bonanza harvest is safely in. But listen to me, lass. You mustn't shame your Dad asking questions about the bad years." It was one of the reasons your mother left him.

"Oh, no! I'd never do that."

Dee was silent then, thinking about what Grandad had told her and sometimes watching the view of Beinn Bhiorach below. Frequent openings in the clouds revealed an elongated landmass with high mountains and glaciers calving icebergs into the sea. More volcanoes, smoking gently, appeared now and again along the continent's western coast or among the islands offshore. Masha and Ken awoke and admired the blue sun, which gradually became greenish, then golden, then brilliant vermilion. As it finally sank beneath the thickening cloud deck great fan-shaped rays of purple and red appeared, expanding until nearly half the sky was dyed the color of burgundy and the backlit dark clouds nearest the western horizon looked like a bed of glowing embers.

The navigation unit of the Porsche chimed and said: "ETA Glen Tuath Farm airspace five minutes. Cirrostratus veil eleven-pip-three kloms, broken stratocumulus layer two-pip-three with base at zero-pip-niner. Visibility below clouds twenty-one, precipitation none, sea-level wind north one-zero, sea-level air temp plus zero-eight. Attention! Abundant aerial vegetation vicinity Goblin Archipelago, Daoimean Mountains, Loch Tuath, Rudha Glas, and Tuath Peninsula between eight-pip-three and six-pip-seven kloms altitude may constitute a hazard to unshielded rhocraft, reaction-engine flyers, and powered aerostats. Please select auto or free flight landing option now. Failure to exercise navigation decision within five minutes will result in your vehicle being inserted into a holding pattern."

Kyle keyed the RF communicator. "Eesht, Glen Tuath! It's Kyle Macdonald here ready to drop down your chimney with some rare cargo! Ian! Are you there, laddie? Can I fly in free as usual?"

"Janet Finlay comin' back," a grating female voice responded. The accent was strange—definitely not Scottish or British. "Ian's still out but he and the rest of the crew have full cargo cells and we expect 'em any minute. Use the auto landing option and be damn sure your sigma is activated this time."

Kyle rolled his eyes, but his voice was cordial. "Why certainly, Janet, luvvie. I wouldn't dream of frying the darlin' wee floaters! Tell me you've set aside a plass baggie of the finest for the two of us to share tonight."

"Save your lame humor for your sleazy books," the voice snapped. "Glen Tuath out."

Kyle burst out laughing and Gran Masha said to him in Gaelic,

"You should be ashamed of yourself, teasing the poor woman like that."

Kyle replied in kind. "Och, Thrawn Janet will survive, whether or not she ever succumbs to the lure of the flirting-weed."

"You will *not* discuss the pharmacology of airplants or make vulgar jokes about them in front of the children! Is that understood, you great blabbermouth?"

The egg navigation unit said: "ETA Glen Tuath airspace one minute. Please select auto or free flight landing option now. Failure to—"

"Aye, you bloody thing," Kyle growled, using Standard English. "Auto landing. Go!"

What in the world had Gran Masha and Grandad been talking about in Gaelic? Dee hadn't a clue, but it didn't matter. The egg was plummeting down and soon she would meet her Daddy.

"Watch now!" Kyle exclaimed. "You see those patches of greeny-pink fog? There, we're into it. It's the airplants!"

Dee and Ken plastered their faces against the transparent part of the egg's dome. But they were descending so rapidly that the drift of strange organisms seemed to flash past in an instant. This time there were no destructive flashes; the slick sigma force-field Kyle had turned on deflected the plants without igniting their flammable gases or otherwise harming them.

"I see something bigger out there!" Dee exclaimed. "A bird!"

"Likely a faol na h-iarmailt, a sky-wolf. But he's not after the weeds. Those things prey on the daoine sìth—the tiny grazing creatures that feed on the airplants. Their Gaelic name means 'fairy folk' and they're fascinating and a wee bit dangerous as well. Sky-wolves are usually harmless to people unless they catch a pilot climbing around on the superstructure of the flitter. Then they can be vicious devils, dive-bombing you with their stony excrement and trying to bite with their toothed beaks."

"Slow the egg down, Grandad," Ken pleaded. "We want to see the fairies and the airplants close up."

"Sorry, laddie. We're in the grip of the farm's NAVCON and Thrawn Janet would wax my tail if I did an override. You'll see processed specimens of the airplants soon enough, and when your Dad has a free moment he'll likely enough take you up in the big flitter to see the whole aerial ecosystem live."

Hesitantly, Ken asked, "Who's this Janet, Grandad? And what does that word 'thrawn' mean?"

Kyle began to hem and haw and looked embarrassed. Gran Masha said reprovingly, "It's a derogatory term in Scots dialect that your grandfather mistakenly thinks is funny. You children are never to use it in connection with Citizen Janet Finlay, who is your father's house and office manager. She—she seems a rather a stern person, from what little I know after talking to her on the teleview, but you are to be polite and respectful to her. Is that clear?"

"Yes, Gran Masha," they said meekly. But Dee had readily discovered the meaning of the odd word from overtones of the professor's thoughts: thrawn meant "unpleasant" or "misshapen." Grandad had intended both terms to apply to Daddy's house manager, and Dee felt a slight shiver of apprehension. In her concern about her father, Dee had never considered what the other people living on the farm might be like. Not only Janet, whom Grandad made fun of because he was a little afraid of her, but also the other farm workers and the three nonborn children Daddy had taken as fosterlings when Mummie left him and took her and Kenny away. Gran had willingly explained the Caledonian custom of fosterage on the starship. But she had changed the subject when Dee wanted to know what a nonborn was, and the professor's associated thought-image was so complex that Dee had been unable to understand it. Kenny hadn't the foggiest, either, but he pretended he did and declared that a nonborn was some kind of orphan. Dee knew there was more to it than that, but there was no such entry in the Drumadoon Bay's library and so her curiosity had remained unsatisfied.

The egg reached the cloud deck, decelerated, and began a long, slow, 180-degree turn through thick clouds. Eventually they emerged into a clear zone of gray twilight and saw the northern end of Beinn Bhiorach spread out below. The Porsche continued to descend at greatly reduced speed, flying now on a southerly course down a huge fjord with steep walls of dark rock interrupted here and there by scree slopes or canyons. Dee knew from her studies of the egg's map-displays that it was Loch Tuath. Snow-tipped peaks and sawtooth ridges rose on either side and the calm black water was dotted with picturesque wooded islets and rocks. Kyle pointed out the massive extinct volcano called An Teallach that loomed 50 kloms to the east, its summit hidden in the clouds.

At the head of the sea-loch the land opened out and became somewhat less precipitous and barren. A medium-sized riverbed, clogged with boulders and having very little water in it at this time of year, ran through the valley. To the left of its mouth was a small cove with a dock where two cabin runabouts were tied up. A dirt road led up the left bank. Further to the east was a snug portable cabin set up next to an excavation among the rocks. Lamplight shone from the plass dwelling's windows. A Range Rover, a hop-lorry, and several large pieces of equipment covered with tarpaulins stood beside it.

"Those are the fossil-diggers," Kyle said to Masha. "Salvage archaeologists named Logan and Majewski from the Old World. They've been working there nearly half a year. Ian plans to level that area eventually for a new warehouse, and by law the fossickers have to pick it over first so that nothing of scientific interest is lost or destroyed. We must invite ourselves to a nosh-up at their place while you're here, Maire a ghràidh, for they've got the only supply of decent plonk on this end of Beinn Bhiorach—and the Logan woman makes barbecued ribs to die for."

The course of the river up the glen into the misty southern highlands was marked by bordering stands of the multicolored coleus trees, already beginning to shed their leaves at this far northern latitude. The farm fields, completely enclosed in repellor-fencing, began about three kloms upstream from the sea-loch where a small bridge crossed the river. On both banks were pastures of proper green grass that gave way to rock or moorland as the terrain rose. A double-rut track zigzagged away westward into the Daoimean Mountains, leading to the mines. Little red West Highland cattle as shaggy as yaks grazed in one meadow and a herd of black miniature horses dotted another. Sheep wandered the stonier uplands. A flight of white birdlike creatures soared below the slowly drifting egg, heading north toward the open sea.

Ian Macdonald's establishment consisted of more than a dozen sturdy buildings, all with steep, silver-striped black roofs that would heat up to melt winter snow or ice. The elegant gabled farmhouse that Viola Strachan had designed stood on a rise surrounded by rock gardens and genuine gnarled Scots pines. The house was painted light Wedgwood blue picked out with white and was discreetly crowned with two satellite dishes, a navigation dome, and a podded device that looked for all the world like a small laser cannon. At the foot of the knoll lay an unusually large egg-pad with two rhocraft parked in front of an open hangar. Across the landing area from the house was an important-looking barnlike structure. Steam vented in a thin plume from machinery at the rear of it.

"That's the primary processing factory for the airplants," the writer said. "Mostly automated. Over there's the main stock barn, a warehouse, and a combination pub and general store that Janet operates for the sake of the workers and the occasional drop-in patron. Nearer the river are three cottages for the farmhands and their families, who usually move into apartments in Muckle Skerry when fast winter sets in up here. The other buildings are the implement shed, the repair shop, and the utility-powerhouse."

"Kyle, some sort of very odd aircraft are coming." Gran Masha was gazing intently up the valley, obviously exerting her farsight. "A large yellow one and four smaller ones of different colors. They're flying very slowly. I've never seen anything quite like them."

"Flitters," he said, tapping away at the pads of the console viewer, "more formally known as aerostatic harvesters."

A close-up of the parade of flying machines appeared on the viewscreen and the children leaned forward eagerly to look. The craft were shaped like fat wedges of cheese with blunt, bullet-shaped fuselages suspended beneath.

"The top part of the flitter is a rigid hydrogen balloon with inflatable external storage compartments for the airplant harvest," Kyle went on. "The operator rides in an enclosed cockpit below, but he sometimes has to climb outside in mid-air to fix things that go wrong with the pumps up in the balloon that slurp the floating plants. The fairy-critters clog the intake all the time, even though the farmer zaps as many of them as he can with thread-beam lasers, and once in a while the harvester sucks up a certain kind of really bad plant that can drill holes in the thin walls of the storage cells and let the other plants escape. Och, airfarming isn't a job for the fainthearted."

"Now I can see the flitters coming!" Ken said. "Does Daddy fly the big yellow one?"

"Not usually," his grandfather said. "It's slow and clumsy and usually acts as a storage dump for the others at the same time it chugs along harvesting. Your Dad usually drives the silver jobbie. It's so maneuverable that the wee things have a hard time escaping it. The three other flitters belong to the hired hands."

"Are flitters rhocraft?"

"No, lad. There's some technical reason why even sigma-shielded rhocraft can't be used to harvest airplants. The flitters maneuver by means of high-compression air jets, but the machines are held up by hydrogen in the balloon section. Your Dad knows more about how they work than I do."

The Porsche egg flew slower and slower, until it hovered motionless 200 meters above the farm. Kyle explained that the loaded flitters had priority to land first, then NAVCON would let their egg come down. The aerostats arrived in a stately train: yellow, red, blue, and Ancient Gordon tartan, with the silver flitter bringing up the rear. They landed neatly in a row with their noses at a white line drawn on the tarmac in front of the factory. Two people emerged from the building to meet the harvesters. Through the egg's panel viewer Dee watched a man and a woman in coveralls pull corrugated tubes from small hatches in the pavement and begin attaching them to the superstructures of the aircraft.

"Unloading the skyweeds," Kyle explained. "Have to sip 'em out very, very gently or they—hah! Now it's finally our turn."

Their egg descended sedately under control of the farm navigation system. It landed more than a hundred meters away from the five flitters on the opposite side of the pad, not far from a flight of wide, shallow steps that led up to the house on the knoll.

Dee climbed out stiffly with the others. It was cool and very quiet, with a light breeze blowing from the direction of the southern mountains. An unfamiliar, faintly musky scent mingled with the smell of pines and the heated patches of asphalt beneath the egg's unshielded landing-gear soles.

So this was her Daddy's farm! From the ground, many of the outbuildings were partially screened by trees and colorful bushes. The rock garden forming the house knoll was planted with what Dee recognized as familiar fall flowers from Earth—purple asters, gold and white and ruby chrysanthemums, dahlias in every hue imaginable.

Suddenly an unobtrusive metal door set into the hillside whisked open. Out stepped a young woman with a hard-favored face and ginger hair cut in a short bob. She wore a blue denim skirt and jacket, a tartan shirt, a beautiful silver necklace studded with turquoises, and cowboy boots. A cream-colored Skye terrier at her side broke into a bouncy run, yapping with shrill ferocity as it charged the visitors. The woman put two fingers to her mouth and emitted a piercing whistle. The long-haired little dog skidded to a halt. "Sit!" the woman commanded. "Stay, you goldarn mutt."

"Citizen Janet Finlay was originally from Arizona," Kyle whispered to the children. He sidestepped the growling terrier, hauled off his cap, and flourished it in a sweeping bow. "As radiant and charming as ever, Janet m'annsachd! And how about a big wet smùrach for the auld pòitear?"

The domestic manager strode on past him without a word and extended her hand to Gran Masha. "How do, Professor MacGregor-Gawrys. I'm Janet Finlay. Welcome to Caledonia and Glen Tuath Farm." As the two women shook hands, Janet's narrowing gaze swept over Masha's fashionable outfit. Her subvocal disapproval was perceptible to both Dee and the professor.

"We're happy to be here at long last," Masha said in a neutral tone. "Let me introduce Kenneth and Dorothea."

Thrawn Janet smiled thinly. "Hi there, Kenny. Hi, Doro." She gestured to the dog. "That there's Tucson. He's got a fancy-schmancy Scotch pedigree name I forgot soon's I got him. Better not pet him till he gets to know you, less'n you don't value your fingerbones."

The children nodded mutely.

"You kids must be tuckered out and starving," she went on. "There's a mole-car just inside that door that'll take us through the burrows to the main house's elevator. The burrows are what we call the tunnel system we use for transporting supplies and for getting around the farm in really bad weather." She gave a grim little chuckle. "You'll find that winter here's a whole lot tougher than it was back on Earth in dear ole Edin-berg."

Dee and Ken gave gasps of dismay. With a sweet smile, Gran Masha corrected the manager's mispronunciation.

"Why, thanks all t'hell, perfessor! I 'preciate that." Janet was almost gleeful. "It'll be a real treat having somebody fresh from Scotland clearing up my ethnic boo-boos. They like t'drive ole Ian off his nut. A lot of Callies are like me—enough Scotch genes to qualify for emigration here, but five, six generations removed from life among the bagpipe tootlers. Too bad you're not staying longer. You could prob'ly teach me a whole lot."

"I may," said Gran Masha casually, "stay a bit longer than I had originally intended. Just to make absolutely certain that the environment is congenial to the children."

"Swell! We'll find a way to put you to work." Janet's daunting gaze flicked to Dee and Ken, who had continued to stare at her in frozen fascination. "And you li'l ankle-biters'll earn your keep, too, after we fatten you up a tad. Count on it! Now let's get up to the big house. Ellen and Hugh'll bring along your bags and traps later."

Dee said in a small, clear voice, "I'd really rather go meet my Daddy first."

"He's busy. He'll be along when he figgers up the day's take. You can see him at supper." Janet turned away abruptly and headed for the door in the hillside. A snap of her fingers brought Tucson the terrier to heel. Dee heard the manager's subvocal grumble: Homely as a mud fence and sassy too! That little brat better learn to do what she's told.

Wordlessly, Dee lifted her eyes in appeal to her grandfather, who had been standing with his hands thrust into his pockets, glowering. The writer perked up. There was a sly grin on his face as he seized both children by the hand.

"Còir càir e!" he said. "To think Ian would be too busy to see his own bairns! Havers! It'll be a grand surprise." Leaving Janet and Gran Masha standing there, he hauled Dee and Ken off across the tarmac at a brisk canter. But after they had gone only a few dozen meters, Kyle pulled up, winded. "Don't wait for me!" he wheezed. "Run on ahead!"

Dee shrieked with delight and went dashing away, outdistancing her less sturdy brother easily. Ken soon gave up the race and dropped back to join his grandfather, but Dee rushed on, heading straight for the five parked aerostats. They were much bigger than they had seemed from the far side of the landing field. Even the small ones were more than twice the height of an egg, and in the gathering dusk they looked more like otherworldly animals come to their night roost than flying machines.

The two coveralled ground crewmen were talking to four other people who wore half-unzipped flight suits and carried bulky helmets under their arms. They all grinned when little Dee came running up. Suddenly seized by shyness, the girl found herself unable to speak. But the workers knew who she was, all right.

A woman pilot pointed to the silver aircraft. "Your Dad's still inside his flitter, sweetheart. Just go knock on his boarding ladder and he'll come down in a jif."

"Zonked out after a killer day," another pilot said, laughing. "Or maybe he's just floating on cloud nine because he finally figured out how rich he's gonna be when we get this humongous crop of screw-weed tallied and shipped."

Dee managed to thank them and scurried away. The aircraft were still tethered to the exsufflation hoses that gently sucked out their fragile cargo. A soft humming sound came from invisible machinery and the musky odor was stronger. The silver flitter was the last in line. A dim greenish radiance illuminated its cockpit, which was still covered by a transparent canopy. Like the others, her father's aerostat rested on retractable jointed legs similar to those of an egg. A plass ladder had been extended down to the tarmac from the left side of the fuselage.

Dee could see a figure sitting inside, but it looked scarcely human, for its face was hidden behind a shiny lowered helmet visor and a strange mask. Was it really Daddy? Carefully, she reached out to touch the pilot's mind.

Tired . . . tired enough to die.

For the briefest instant she perceived his outermost layers of thought—the harvest of airplants; a vast burden of physical exhaustion shot through with flashes of pain like a dark cloud stabbed by lightning; and below that the hint of an enormous, all-consuming sorrow that she could not understand and flinched away from examining any closer.

Poor Daddy! He had been working so very hard, thinking of nothing but gathering up the precious, unexpected masses of plants, working night and day almost without a break. His subliminal thoughts revealed to Dee that the arduous job was finally done. Harvest season was over, and tonight shifting winds would scatter the airborne treasure; but Glen Tuath Farm, after tottering for years on the brink of ruin, had been saved. As for Ian Macdonald, he was home with his crew and he could shed his responsibilities at last. What he wanted most of all was to go to sleep.

Escaping it all—including the greater pain that had nothing to do with his weary body.

Dee felt a pulse of dread lance through her. If the farm had been saved, then why was Daddy still so unhappy? Was it because she had come? She knew that her father's deeper, secret thoughts probably held the answer, but she shrank from looking any further into his mind. She could not bear to learn the truth about his feelings for her before even seeing his face.

Hesitantly, she rapped on the plass ladder. The masked figure did not move.

"Daddy?" she called. "It's me. Dorothea."

For a little while nothing happened. Then, just as she lifted her hand to knock again, the cockpit canopy slid back. The green light inside was extinguished and the masked man climbed out very slowly and began to descend.

She backed away apprehensively as he reached the ground and turned to look at her there in the twilight, slowly removing his gloves.

"Daddy?" she whispered.

His flight suit was silvery like the ship, fitting his body tightly, having elaborate ridged and corded patterns like an insect's armor. He had lifted the reflective visor of his complicated helmet, but the lower part of his face remained concealed behind a silver oxygen mask. His eyes were hazel like Dee's own, bleared by fatigue and deeply creased at the corners. When his hands were finally free of the gloves he clipped them to his belt, then unfastened one side of the mask and slipped off the helmet and its self-contained breathing apparatus, setting it on one of the ladder steps. His hair was damp and plastered to his head. A thin bruise ran across his upper cheeks and nose where the mask had pressed into his flesh during long hours working high in the air. He had a dark stubble of beard and dry, cracked lips.

Was he really the father she could not remember, the handsome young man in the old photo, the furious, heroic protector whom she had seen so briefly on the subspace communicator in the Islay police station back on Earth?

He stared at her, unsmiling. As the silence lengthened between them Dee's throat tightened. She tried to speak again but apprehension had rendered her mute. Sudden tears transformed the motionless tall figure to a dim blur.

Daddy? Are you—

Oh, no! She must never use farspeech, just as she must not try to read his private thoughts! She must be careful to give no hint of what she was, must try to be the kind of daughter he would find lovable—a child who was quiet, useful, obedient, and uncomplaining. She blinked away the tears and tried to smile, seeing his careworn face clearly again in the dusk.

He was hurting so much inside. Poor Daddy.

The urge to share her healing redaction with him, to really know him, suddenly became irresistible to Dee. She had to find out whether this man could love her, no matter what price she paid.

Instinctively continuing to shield herself, she looked directly into her father's eyes, into the deepest wellsprings of his emotions, hoping she would be able to understand what she found.

Oh, yes. There it was.

A knot of misery greater than his physical suffering, greater than any of his persistent anxieties about the farm. The root of the pain was twofold: part of it was despair over twice-lost Mummie, the rest an even greater and older grief for himself, the one latent child among three operants, rejected both by his mother and by the woman he had loved most. The capacity for happiness still resided within Ian Macdonald, but it was horribly damaged, almost buried beneath a black mountain of loss, rejection, and heartache. How could he possibly be expected to free himself from its burden and embrace a plain-looking little girl?

Poor Daddy. It wasn't his fault that he couldn't love. Dee was very sorry that he had been so badly hurt. There had to be some way she could help—

She possessed more than one kind of redactive power. The personal healing force was operant, but the external redaction that could affect other minds and bodies still lay imprisoned within its imaginary box. A very large box. The surging huge crimson thing inside could change others and it was also capable of changing her in some unknown, fearsome fashion if she released it and put it to use.

Ian Macdonald continued to stare at her blankly. Did he even realize who she was?

Daddy, I'm Dorothea. Your daughter. Please feel better!

She opened the new box. The angel appeared immediately, showing her in a split second what she must do.

As the invisible crimson flood surged out and engulfed him, Ian Macdonald gave a sharp gasp. For a moment his silvery figure went rigid. Then his shoulders slumped and he swayed, taking hold of the aerostat's boarding ladder to steady himself. The spasm passed and he uttered a profound sigh and wiped his forehead with the back of one hand. He looked down at the little girl in puzzled surprise.

When she was sure that her redaction had done its work, Dee withdrew it and hid once again behind her blue mental armor, lowering her head and squeezing her eyes shut so Daddy would not see the triumph shining there. She had done it! He was not completely healed, but she had helped him.

The new mindpower was out of its box and she would never get it back in again. It was one more thing she would have to hide from Gran Masha's prying. But Daddy no longer hurt so badly. She was certain that he would never know she had touched him with her red comfort. And he would never hear if she bespoke him now:

It's all right if you can't love me, Daddy. I understand. But may I stay here with you anyway?

Hands beneath her thin little arms.

Powerful hands lifting her high, high.

Holding her against a broad, hard chest and shoulder that were not cold and metallic at all but warm. Sounds of hoarse breathing, slight leathery creaks from the environmental suit, smell of plass, smell of grownup sweat, a whiff of the exotic musky odor that she had decided must belong to the mysterious airplants.

A hand pulled back the hood of her anorak and moved slowly over her hair. She was afraid to open her eyes, afraid even to breathe.

Rough lips brushed her forehead.

She opened her eyes and saw him, battered and grubby and human inside his awesome garb. His silver arms tightened about her and she clung to him fiercely, not making a sound even though tears were once again streaming down her cheeks.

Somewhere far away she heard the voices of Ken and Grandad calling. The floodlights on the factory building flicked on and the noise from the pumps suddenly stopped.

"Little Dorrie," Ian Macdonald said. "Time to go home, my lass."

And finally smiled.

[10]

FROM THE MEMOIRS OF ROGATIEN REMILLARD

Like most other ordinary people during those immediate post-Proctorship years of the mid-twenty-first century, I had become extremely curious about the Lylmiks' wonderful artificial world called Concilium Orb and the activities going on inside it. From Orb came the laws and major public policy decisions that shaped the long-term course of human racial destiny . . . but people like me had no say whatsoever in the process. We did not elect the Human Magnates of the Concilium, much less the exotic magnates who greatly outnumbered them. The whole crowd was appointed by the Lylmik, and ordinary citizens—operant and non—knew very little about Conciliar operations.

No official policy of secrecy prevailed. There were plaque-books and Tri-D documentaries galore that seemed to describe in detail the way that the central galactic government functioned. Everyone knew that magnates were individually skimmed from the crème de la crème of human operants by the Lylmik Supervisory Quincunx itself, those five demigodly paragons of wisdom and virtue. Magnates conducted their Conciliar business mentally, with open minds. It was therefore supposedly impossible for them to lie, dissemble, or otherwise betray the public trust.

Human and exotic magnates went to Orb about once every 334 Earth days to participate in plenary Concilium sessions. Magnates also attended single-Polity sessions and committee and Directorate meetings whenever these were deemed necessary.

No law held that the deliberations of the magnates were secret. Nevertheless, human news-gathering organizations were barred from having offices in Orb or otherwise attempting to cover the Concilium proceedings in any systematic way. Sympathetic human magnates (especially those belonging to the Rebel faction) leaked the occasional piece of hot poop, and privileged visitors, nonoperant human service employees who worked in the Orb enclaves, and even friendly exotics spilled what beans they could. But most news from Orb consisted of canned material disseminated from the Information Directorate of the Human Polity.

Humanity was unique in fretting over a star-chamber Concilium. The other five Milieu races, secure in a tranquil Unified state that seemed to preclude outright contention or even serious dispute (making it automatically suspect to free-spirited Earthlings), would never have dreamed of questioning the activities of their magnates. The perseverant bumptiousness of humans struck them as strange, immature, and disquieting.

More than once the very admission of humanity into the Milieu was called into question by the other races; but the almighty Lylmik had insisted that our acceptance was necessary. They had gone to ingenious lengths to bring us into the confederation in the first place, and as time passed and the Metapsychic Rebellion seemed more and more inevitable, they used means both fair and foul to prevent us from getting chucked out. Only in hindsight can we understand why.

Since the entity reading these memoirs (like all too many busy people) may not have been a keen student of Milieu governmental structure, I will do a fast overview in the hope of rendering this account of mine a trifle less opaque. Those who are already familiar with it may want to skip ahead directly to the raunchy bits and the violence.

The thousands of individual planets of the Galactic Milieu are not governed on a day-to-day basis by the Concilium, but by republican Intendant Assemblies made up of elected representatives of the populace. On human worlds, the Intendant Associates include both metapsychic operants and nonoperants, and the legislation they debate and decide upon encompasses most of the nuts and bolts of local planetary law and has minimal impact upon the vaster tapestry of interstellar civilization. Intendant Assemblies may discuss high matters of public policy, but only in order to pass recommendations on to the Planetary Dirigent, the highest authority and ultimate local arbiter on each world, who in turn may forward the matter to the Concilium.

The Dirigent, who is always an extremely powerful operant and an influential magnate, is appointed by the Lylmik. She—or more rarely he, for human females have shown a special talent for this arduous job—serves as the principal channel for Milieu policy on each planet and guardian of the Milieu's rights. She may summarily and even secretly overrule any action of the local Assembly deemed contrary to the best interests of the confederation.

Oddly, the Dirigent is also required to act as a World Ombudsman. The most humble nonoperant citizen may petition Dirigent House and have a point of law adjudicated on the spot if simple justice seems to demand it. Most often, petitioners are directed by the Dirigent's staff to the appropriate government officer having the authority to deal with their problem. But on rare occasions (as I myself can testify), the Dirigent may personally intervene, with the result that all hell breaks loose and heads—even those of the most exalted and Magnified kind—may threaten to roll.

Some Dirigents are revered and even loved by their constituents. Greater numbers are feared, despised, or endured as a necessary evil.

The Concilium is the principal executive, legislative, and judicial body of what is officially termed the Coadunate Galactic Milieu, a federation consisting at the present time of six racial Polities having significant numbers of metapsychic operants among their population. Magnates of the Concilium are presumably selected from among the most exceptional minds of their Polity—although some of the human contingent strike one as odd choices indeed. They are all operants and may come from any walk of life, including their planet's Intendant Assembly. While some magnates are full-time bureaucrats, the majority devote only part of their time to the Concilium and work at other occupations as well. Magnates serve terms of indefinite length, according to the whim of the Lylmik. Unlike the Planetary Dirigent appointees, who are required to accept the office whether they want it or not, magnates-designate may decline the honor if they feel they do not wish to serve in the Concilium.

When the Human Polity was first enfranchised, the membership of the Concilium was as follows:

Lylmik	21	[with veto power]
Krondaku	3460	
Gi	430	
Poltroyans	2741	
Simbiari	503	
Humans	100	
TOTAL	7255	

Human representation grew steadily as we pulled our act together, until there were nearly 400 humans serving on the Concilium around the time of the Metapsychic Rebellion in 2083.

One doesn't simply drop in at the legislative center of the galaxy as part of a grand tour. Concilium Orb is strictly off limits to casual travelers, with only the magnates of the six Polities and their immediate families and administrative staff permitted unlimited access. (Humanity's unique cultural requirement for living, not robotic, service workers has been accommodated by hiring nonoperant personnel for limited terms of employment and restricting them to the human enclaves most of the time.) Other citizens of the Milieu may come to Orb only when invited by a magnate, and even then only on very special occasions.

I would have been eligible, along with Denis and Lucille and the Remillard Dynasty spouses and children, to attend the inaugural session in 2052, when the founding magnates of the Human Polity first took their Concilium seats. Unfortunately, I was unavailable at the time, being on the lam in the British Columbia wilderness abetting the felonious pregnancy of the Human First Magnate's late wife.

The next opportunity for me to visit Orb did not take place until the unforgettable session of 2063, when my great-grandnephew Marc Remillard became a magnate and a galactic celebrity to be reckoned with in one fell swoop, and when the world-class randan between Paul Remillard and Rory Muldowney marred (or enhanced, depending upon one's point of view) the festivities at the Poltroyans' party.

On that occasion I happened to travel to Orb on the CSS Skykomish River, the same starship that carried Marc's four young operant friends Alexis Manion, Guy Laroche, Peter Dalembert, and Shigeru

Morita. Like me, they had been invited to be Marc's honored guests at his accession to the Concilium.

I was already fairly well acquainted with these worthies, who frequented my bookshop in Hanover, New Hampshire, and called me Uncle Rogi, as most of my customers did. They were all around Marc's age, all outstanding minds, and all destined to become magnates themselves someday. Manion, Dalembert, and Laroche were Hanover natives who had attended Brebeuf Academy along with Marc, and they had known one another since early boyhood. Shig Morita had joined the gang when they all roomed together at the Mu Psi Omega operant fraternity at Dartmouth College.

Alexis Manion was Marc's best friend in his younger years, and I had once enjoyed a brief affair with his widowed mother, Perdita, when she worked in my bookshop. During the Metapsychic Rebellion, Alex was Marc's closest advisor and confidant; and if Cloud and Hagen are to be believed, he also became Marc's most implacable enemy long after the Rebellion ended . . . or aeons before it began, if you want to be nitpicky.

Like Marc, Manion was a towering genius with an IQ classed as "unmeasurable." His field of expertise was dynamic-field research, and he became an authority on the relationship of the mental lattices to the Larger Reality. Manion did his postdoc work at Princeton in New Jersey but spent most of his mature years on the faculty of the IDFS at Cambridge, England, where he was a colleague of the famous Annushka Gawrys. In 2080 he was on the short list for the Nobel Prize in physics when his denunciation of Unity and public conversion to the Rebellion put him beyond the pale.

Alex possessed grandmasterclass creativity, masterly coercion and PK, and adequate farsensing. He was a rather awkward individual physically, of medium height, with a jaw like a concrete block. An air of preoccupation gave his rugged features an incongruously dreamy look. Alex had a fine light baritone voice and was especially fond of Gilbert and Sullivan. He was much more contemplative than Marc, resisting nomination to the Concilium for ten years until irresistible pressure was put on him by his peers at IDFS.

Guy "Boom-Boom" Laroche had much the same blue-collar Franco-American heritage as the ancestral Remillards and seemed less of an egghead than Marc's other close friends. He was a powerfully built young man, an enthusiastic skier, fisherman, and skirt-chaser, who favored T-shirts even in winter so that he could show off his gorgeous pecs and 55-cent biceps. The face topping that magnificent body was so ugly it was splendid—joli-laid, as we Froggies express it. In later life he had himself resculpted into more conventional handsomeness, but I'll always remember him as he was in his youth. When Boom-Boom grinned with his pearly whites, flummoxed with his long eyelashes, and let loose a blast of winning metacoercivity, strong men would trust him with their lives and strong women would go gooey as chocolate éclairs. Piss Boom-Boom off, on the other hand, and you either got out of town at escape velocity or ended up knitting your bones in a regen-tank.

Laroche's only grandmasterly functions were creativity and coercion. He studied Milieu jurisprudence and law enforcement, and in 2063, fresh out of college, he was an inspector-intern for the New England Zone Police. In time he joined the Human Division of the Galactic Magistratum, where he quickly made his mark and was appointed to the Concilium. He was in line for the top cop position and would undoubtedly have become Human Evaluator General had not circumstances led him in a completely different direction.

Peter Paul Dalembert, Jr., was the great-grandson of the late Glenn Dalembert and Colette Roy, both of whom had been part of Denis Remillard's original "coterie" at Dartmouth long before the Great Intervention. His father, Peter Paul, Sr., became the Chief Executive Officer of Remco Industries when Philip Remillard retired from the family business to become a Magnate of the Concilium and head of the Human Commerce Directorate. Young Pete's Aunt Aurelie married Philip, and his late Aunt Jeanne was Maurice Remillard's first wife.

Pete was one of those hyper little guys who had his life organized down to the last byte. When he and Marc and Alex and Boom-Boom were kids, it was always Pete who took care of the logistic details for their fishing and camping trips, or rustled up the makings for the outrageous gadgets they built, or knew how to manipulate the system and do a fix whenever one of them got into trouble. Another creator-coercer, Pete was probably the most skillful bullshit artist I have ever known. Women thought he was sensitive and adorable. He studied computer science at Dartmouth and took an MBA at the Amos Tuck School of Business Administration. Pete Dalembert might have become a hotshot executive just like his father if Marc had not convinced him early on to apply his talents elsewhere.

Shigeru Morita was born in Japan and educated at Dartmouth, Johns Hopkins, and Cambridge. His metapsychic talents included grandmasterclass redaction and creativity. He was a quiet, scholarly youth who grew up to be an outstanding biophysicist, and his hobbies included piano jazz and fly-tying. In person, Shig was slyly witty, modest, and seemingly unaware that he was very good-looking. His area of professional interest was the microanatomy and electrochemical functioning of the human brain, and he shared Marc's and Alex's interest in cerebroenergetic enhancement.

It was Shig Morita who eventually demonstrated how the infamous Mental Man project might progress from theory to practical application. Without his assistance, Marc would never have become the leader of the Rebellion, never brought about the deaths of four billion people, and never metamorphosed into my Family Ghost.

The CSS Skykomish River had a df of 180, which was a whole lot brisker than I liked, but by scarfing anodyne pills and lubricating myself with frequent coups de gnole in between hops I kept discomfort at bay. My well-basted condition had an additional advantage. When Marc's four buddies judged that I was safely hors de combat from overindulgence, they did not bother to screen me out when I happened to be in a position to overhear their telepathic bull sessions. The ship's swimming pool, solarium, gym, and garden-bar provided me with many a diverting hour's worth of entertainment as I pretended to nap with a Wild Turkey highball close at hand, all the while secretly eavesdropping on what the metapsychic Jeunesse Dorée—including Marc himself—was getting up to. A lot of their conversations involved sex, with Boom-Boom and Pete regaling their comrades with the number of notches added to the handles of their six-shooters, while Shig and Alex stressed quality over quantity.

And then there was the sex life of their glorious leader . . .

At this period in his life, Marc was still fairly close to me, sharing accounts of his running battles with the Dartmouth trustees and his squabbles with Paul, who kept trying unsuccessfully to steer his oldest son into more politically acceptable areas of research and away from left-wing Dynasty members such as his Uncle Severin and Uncle Adrien.

But even though Marc kept me informed about his work, he was reticent about his private affairs. Far from being a loner, he attended parties, dances, and other social events regularly, often squiring lively females of high metapsychic quotient. As far as I knew, he had never had any deep romantic involvement with any of them, but I had naturally assumed that the invincible Franco hormones had done their stuff.

I assumed wrong.

My eavesdropping during that voyage revealed that Marc was still a technical virgin at the age of twenty-five and intended to remain so indefinitely. He had told his incredulous friends that he considered sexual activity a monumental waste of time and energy that dulled the mind's keen edge.

I suppose I should not have been so surprised. I was a rather late bloomer myself, and Denis had told me years ago that he probably would have remained celibate if his eyes had not been opened to his "procreational duty" by an old mentor. Sex being the ultimate in addictive behavior, Denis had gone on to fulfill his obligations with zest, siring the seven stalwarts of the Dynasty and writing, together with his wife Lucille, a brief but cogent monograph on the sexology of operants. (I was a bit disappointed not to be credited as the pioneer of doing it in mid-air.)

Denis's most brilliant offspring, Paul, had also been sexually inhibited until the grand-opera superstar Teresa Kendall ignited his passion. When their love died, Paul seemed to compensate by fucking every presentable operant woman in sight until he settled into a stable liaison with Laura Tremblay. The fact that she was already married to an Irish magnate named Rory Muldowney, later the Planetary Dirigent of Hibernia, seemed not to bother either of them. Poor old Rory apparently bore his cuckoldry with old-fashioned complaisance. After Laura's strange death, Paul played the field again, ultimately siring thirty-eight natural children in addition to Marc, Marie, Madeleine, Luc, and Jack.

When Marc was very young he told me about his impatience with what he called "the inherent limitations of the human body." Puberty was a considerable shock, but he claimed that he had found ways to conquer the worst of the distractions inherent in being an inefficiently engineered male human.

I had tried to talk some sense into him, had told him that it was dangerous to mess with hormones and other precious bodily fluids, had even warned him that human nature was likely to nail him in the end no matter how successfully he thought he had repressed it. But he only gave me that maddening one-sided smile of his and suggested that I mind my own business and get my own ashes hauled whenever necessary. I knew all too well what his abhorrence of his father's promiscuity must have done to his unconscious mind, but I could not believe that he was genuinely asexual.

When the right woman came around, I reassured myself, Marc would happily discover that he was human after all.

As it happened, the wrongest woman possible would shortly prove me mistaken, and Marc would have to wait seventeen more years for the redemptive love of the right one to cancel out the effects of the disaster.

Marc had described Orb to me and so had his sister Marie and his brother Luc. All three of them had served as pages and junior administrative assistants either for their father or for their Aunt Anne during their adolescence, earning poli-sci college credits as they performed what was basically prestigious dog-work during the weeks the Concilium was in session. The best kind of Orbicular fun was to be had after office hours, they told me, exploring or participating in the recreational opportunities of the hundreds of residential enclaves of the planetoid where the six racial groups were housed in clever simulations of their home environments. There were thirty-two different human enclaves alone; and this session, for the first time, a Lylmik enclave would be open to visitors. We would also be able to attend some of the Concilium sessions—including the all-important seating of the new magnates and the appointment of the new Dirigents—watching the proceedings from the visitors' gallery.

. . .

Most of the operant passengers on the CSS Skykomish River, myself included, crowded into the eight big observation lounges in order to catch a first eyeball glimpse of Orb and its unusual star, Telonis. Stupidly, I had decided to forgo the pills and the booze during this final passage from hyperspace into the vicinity of the artificial world so as not to miss anything. The abrupt *zang-zung* of the translation through the superficies felt like someone had hammered a couple of ninepenny nails through the top of my skull. Manfully, I refrained from howling out loud. Since my mind-screen is the only reliably powerful metafaculty I possess, I thought I could shriek all I pleased inside my head without making a spectacle of myself, but I must have shown some physical indication of distress perceptible to a keen redactor, because Shig Morita put a solicitous hand on my shoulder.

"Are you all right, Uncle Rogi?"

The other three young men came over and hovered about me in the dimly lit observation chamber, looking anxious.

"Course I'm all right," I grumped. "Just a little twinge caught me by surprise there."

"At your age, you really should use anodyne pills," Alex Manion reproved me. "Or better yet, a knockout minidose for big hops like these."

The damn kid had never forgiven me for boffing his mom. "I'm only a hundred and seventeen, and I've got the same immortality genes as the rest of the Remillards, and I'm doing just fine. Quit treating me like a basket case." Boom-Boom's bulk was blocking my view of the Telonis system so I shouldered past him, not wanting to miss what was said to be one of the scenic wonders of our galaxy.

But where was Orb and its star?

The sickmaking void of the gray limbo had given way to the usual jewel-strewn black velvet of deep space, but there was no sun to be seen and no planetoid, either. I wasn't much of an interstellar traveler in those days but I'd already gone to the cosmop worlds of Avalon and Okanagon, the planet Assawompsett (originally ethnic "American" but now grown so populous and important that it had been recently reclassified cosmopolitan), the lovely "Japanese" world Ezo, and the inadvertently euonymous "French" planet of Blois. Like almost all of the worlds explored by Milieu scientists ages ago and designated suitable for human habitation, they were warmed by G-type yellow suns. I had known that Orb's sun Telonis was a peculiar dwarf, but nothing prepared me for the stellar object that Alex Manion now pointed out.

It seemed at first to be just another bright pinpoint star, presumably many lightyears distant. But as my eyes accommodated to the darkness and the window's polarization I saw that Telonis was golden, not pure white, and certainly close by, for I could perceive that its tiny disk was fringed by orange and red prominences that rippled with languid slowness, like the pseudopods of some fiery microorganism. A luminous double corona surrounded the dwarf sun. The inner halo was diminutive and pearl-colored, consisting of spiky rays at either pole that curved and eventually blended into a filmy donut-shaped gas cloud about the equatorial plane. More striking was an immense, very faint, almost perfectly spherical nebula that nearly filled the area of sky visible through the huge viewport. The glowing gas was mostly green, but there were dim filaments and diaphanous patches of crimson, violet, and blue as well. I can compare the vision only to a huge broken bubble of frozen, iridescent smoke with the ornately coiffured miniature sun at its center. The longer I stared at the stellar anomaly, the brighter and more beautiful it seemed.

"My God," Shig Morita whispered. "What is it? Surely the Lylmik wouldn't have built their artificial world in a T Tauri system—"

"It's not a T Tauri," said Alex Manion. "It's been fairly stable for at least six million years. It's a conventional white dwarf star that the Lylmik meddled with. An artifact."

The others uttered awed obscenities. I, not having the least notion what Shig and Alex had been talking about, asked the obvious question. "But why did the Lylmik do it? And how?"

"Apparently," Alex said, "they tinkered with this sun just to make it pretty. No one is sure how they managed it, not even the Krondaku, but Marc and I have been working on a theory that I won't bore you with now. Telonis itself is smaller than Earth. The radius of the outer sphere of nebulosity is roughly five hundred million kloms. Orb is the only planetary body in the system, another A.U. or so further out . . . and we're almost on top of it."

I strained my eyes—and sure enough, occulting the marvelous star-spangled colored veil near the bottom of the window was a fast-swelling circle of dead black. As we drew nearer it was transformed into the familiar dark sphere depicted in every schoolchild's first book-plaque about the Galactic Milieu. Concilium Orb is about 500 kilometers in diameter, sparsely dotted with points of light. We swooped in smoothly toward one of them, which turned out to be the colossal entry portal of the Human Terminal. Our ship entered at a good rate of knots and we docked with a minumum of fuss and disembarked at the most important place in the Milky Way Galaxy.

Marc was waiting for us, wearing his old green Rangeley parka, jeans, and Bean boots, looking as sardonic and debonair as the Devil himself. Standing at his side was one of the most gorgeous women I have ever seen in my life. She was nearly as tall as Marc, with a marvelous long neck emphasized by her upswept hairstyle and scarlet polo jersey. Raven curls sprang like a dark fountain from an ornamental clasp at the crown of her head and fell nearly to her shoulders. The skin of her face was utterly flawless, the color of milk, making a startling contrast to jet-black brows and lashes and wide-set eyes of electrifying blue. A faint, charming dimple graced her chin, and her full lips were tinted a glossy coral pink. Her body in its simple black-and-white ski suit was that of a mannequin, willowy rather than voluptuous.

This exquisite creature projected no sexually provocative vibes at all and her mind was hedged about by a grandmasterclass shield. Nevertheless I felt the hairs at the back of my neck prickle and my blood pound as I goggled at her shamelessly, my three-piece set roused from torpor to a most embarrassing bandaison. Tonnerre de dieu, but she was magnificent!

. . . But why was my understandable surge of lustful admiration somehow tainted with aversion?

The goddess was having an effect upon my four young companions as well. You could almost smell the surging testosterone and hear the frantic slamming of mental barriers. Marc did not seem to notice as he presented us formally to her, and then introduced her to us.

"Citizen Lynelle Rogers is from Okanagon. She's a special assistant to that planet's Dirigent-Designate, and she has very kindly found time to help me out of a very tough spot. Be grateful to her."

The marvelous Lynelle lowered her dusky eyelids. "It's nothing at all, Marc. It would have been such a shame to disappoint your friends and your Uncle Rogi."

The five of us grinned like apes.

"Let's all get on the tube," Marc said, "and I'll explain as we ride. Your bags are being sent on ahead."

"This way," Citizen Rogers said sweetly. She and Marc led us onto the correct terminal walkway, and the conversation continued in colloquial farspeech.

Marc said: I ordered my accommodation here on Orb months ago, when I first received my nomination, and I specified the Alpenland enclave so we could all enjoy some winter sports when you came as my guests. Unfortunately, I got totally wrapped up in my CE work at Dartmouth because I wanted to have a working model of the E15 ready to bring with me to Orb. I left the finalization of the accommodation details to a departmental secretary—and he goofed. When I arrived here in Orb with Marie and Luc and Jack last week, I discovered that I'd been assigned a chintzy little A-frame chalet that slept only one. And the billeting flunkies claimed there was no larger place available anywhere in Alpenland.

Lynelle Rogers said: This Concilium session marks the Fiftieth Anniversary of the Great Intervention on Earth. Over a hundred new human magnates have just been been appointed. Most of them have brought along numbers of invited guests as well as operant staff members. The result is that facilities in the human enclaves are strained to the bursting point.

Marc's mind-tone was wry: We can blame Lylmik absentmindedness for not anticipating a crush. They've promised to triple the amount of human-enclave accommodation by next session—but that's no help now. I cast around among the other family members and got my three sibs beds in Papa's big apartment, but only Uncle Phil and Aunt Aurelie had any extra room for you. Somehow, I didn't think you'd appreciate bunking with their teenage kids over in Paliuli.

Lynelle flashed a radiant smile over her shoulder as we got off the moving walkway and went into the tube station. She said: Paliuli enclave is ever so twee if you like sunny tropical beaches jammed with boogie-boarding children. And slack-key guitar music coming out of the hibiscus bushes. And hordes of middle-aged Russian magnates sitting under coconut trees sipping Mai-Tais and banana daiquiris.

There was nervous laughter from the lot of us and once again I experienced that peculiar frisson. What was it about her that made her seem simultaneously desirable and menacing? Her beauty was unusual, but she had nothing of the classic femme fatale about her; her manner was friendly, intelligent, almost modest for all that she was obviously an operant of the highest rank.

I dismissed my uneasiness as we entered an inertialess tube capsule. We were the only ones aboard and I had failed to note its posted destination. There was no sensation of speed as the windowless thing whizzed through Orb's guts. We relaxed in the comfortable seats and were able to indulge in verbal conversation again.

"I promised you some fun in the snow," Marc said, "and Paliuli didn't fill the bill. Of course I could have booked you into one of the big hotels in the central core, but they're so bland and cosmop that you might as well be in Boston. I'd just about resigned myself to building a large igloo in the front yard of my A-frame when I happened to meet Lynelle at a bash Davy MacGregor threw. She made a suggestion that solved our problem in the best way possible—as you'll see in just a minute or two."

And the pair of them exchanged glances.

I said to myself: Qu'est-ce que c'est que ce bordel?! Which may be roughly translated: What the *fuck*?

Not a single thought had escaped from behind either of their invincible mind-screens. I'm sure no one else noticed a thing. Shig Morita was asking Marc some damn fool technical question about Orb's weird sun, and Marc was answering with breezy aplomb.

Had I imagined that nanosec flash of mutual affinity between my cerebral great-grandnephew and the enigmatic smasher?

Before I could ruminate further on the topic a bell tone sounded, the door of the inertialess capsule opened, and Lynelle Rogers said, "Here we are, everybody!"

We emerged into another tube-station waiting room and were nearly blinded by the sudden razzle-dazzle. A silver-gilt sign on the wall gave the name of the place in ideographs and in more familiar Roman script: BIRITON ENCLAVE—AMALGAM OF POLTROY.

Boom-Boom Laroche looked around and said, "Holy flaming shit!"

Shig Morita giggled.

Pete Dalembert murmured, "Welcome to the Arabian Nights!"

Alex Manion said, "Compared to Poltroyan homes, this is drab." He'd studied on the Poltroyan planet of Fomiron-su-Piton.

Even if one has had some experience with this charming race's mode of accommodation through Tri-D presentations or books, the first view of actual Poltroyal glitz is apt to bring on terminal flabbergast—to say nothing of scorched retinas.

Imagine a quaint little old nineteenth-century railway depot . . . with a décor that blends Black-Forest-Disneyland kitsch with the dizzying jewelry-box extravagance of a Balinese temple. Imagine intricately carved woodwork picked out with gold and silver leaf, rafters tarted up with finicky curlicues and gem-encrusted gargoyles, gilt-leaded stained-glass windows, an unbelievably lovely ceramic stove glowing like a great plique-à-jour lantern, golden filigree benches with red leather cushions set cosily near the source of heat, and an honest-to-God Chinese cloisonné floor. The Purple Folk love human fripperies. Everything from doorknobs to teleview cubicles in the tube station had been floridly embellished with lashings of colored enamel doodads, precious sequins, inset tiny mirrors, and faceted glass rondelles. Glitter, shimmer, sparkle, blaze, flash—time out to reset the fuses. That's Poltroy, citizens! After a while you even get to like it.

The place was toasty-warm, but there was thick frost on the lower part of the windows and a clot of melting slush on a fish-fur mat near the outside door.

Lynelle Rogers beckoned and headed toward the exit. "It's a bit nippy outside, but you can all turn up your body thermostats for a few moments, can't you? There's a sleigh waiting."

Laughing and chaffing, we all stumbled out into the wintry night. A simulated starry sky with a brilliant, Y-branched Milky Way shone overhead. The Poltroyan station seemed to be situated in the midst of a snowdrifted forest clearing. Polished brass lamps cast a glow on icicles fringing the stationhouse roof and struck diamond glints from a light dusting of hoarfrost clinging to the platform and steps. A closed vehicle waited in the station forecourt, a kind of gussied-up Cinderella coach mounted on sprung sled runners that had ample space for seven people. Hitched to the sleigh was a foursome of high-rumped exotic quadrupeds in bejeweled harness. They had branched horns, long laid-back ears, and puffy tails.

"Good God," drawled Pete Dalembert. "They look just like giant jackalopes! You know, those mythical critters of the American West—jackrabbits with antlers."

"The Poltroyans call the animals yingi," Marc said. "These are robotic, of course. On their own worlds, Poltroyans have mechanized snow vehicles and flying rhocraft for everyday transport. But the yingi are as traditional with them as horses are with us. Now they keep the creatures as pets."

"All aboard!" caroled Lynelle Rogers. "I'll drive."

We piled in, glad that the interior was heated since the outside temperature was well below freezing. Lynelle took the reins, which entered the coach through a befurred slot, shook them, and gave a command in the Poltroyan language through a speaking tube. The mechanical jackalopes galumphed off in comical unison and we all rolled about laughing. The beasts even had sleighbells, another feature that the Poltroyans had borrowed from humanity.

The trip was a short one, but the illusion of an expansive snowy countryside was nearly perfect. The road went up hill and down dale, and on either hand were clusters of gigantic trees, gnarled and leafless branches lifted toward the stars, and lights scattered among the monstrous buttresses of their roots and dotting their trunks.

Our sleigh turned onto a neatly plowed lane and entered one of the groves, pulling up before a particularly impressive tree. Nestled within the shelter of its roots was the entrance to a typical Poltroyan abode, an antechamber built of mortared stone. The margins of its sloping roof were hung with festoons of fairy lights—another adopted human novelty. The rest of the home was carved out of the living tree, and small lighted windows were visible higher on the massive bole.

Lynelle pulled up and we all got out. The patient robots appeared to snuffle and twitch their furry ears as they settled down to wait indefinitely. Realistic breath-clouds came from their nostrils.

Either Marc or Lynelle must have sent out a farspoken announcement of our arrival, for the front door of the tree-house was abruptly flung open and a diminutive lilac-skinned male Poltroyan dressed in jeweled robes bounded out to meet us.

"You're here! You're here! A thousand welcomes to my hearth, honored guests!"

The exotic ran up to me, seized both my hands, and forced me into an impromptu ring-around-the-rosy there in the snow. "Rogi, Rogi, mon vieux! Surely you remember me? Fritiso-Prontinalin!"

"Batège!" I cried. "It's old Fred!"

Of course I knew him. The ever-perplexing Lylmik had forced the poor guy to rescue me and Teresa Kendall and newborn Jack the Bodiless from the snowbound fastness of British Columbia. Fred was a longtime academic colleague of Denis, a former Visiting Fellow in Psychogeomorphology at Dartmouth. He and his wife Minnie had become dear friends of our family during their tenure at the college, but I had not seen them since they returned to their own planet four years earlier, at the time that they were both named magnates.

Marc introduced Alex, Pete, Boom-Boom, and Shig, and the genial Poltroyan urged all of them to call him by his Earthling nickname. Then he led us inside, apologizing for Minnie's absence; one of her Concilium committees was sitting. We crowded into the little stone foyer, stamping the snow off our feet, then followed Fred up a very long, steep, and narrow (for bulky humans) stairway into the main part of his tree-home.

Once again there were exclamations of awe and amazement. Alex Manion was right: the fantastic tube station didn't have a patch on Fred's parlor when it came to eye-popping Byzantine splendor, but for all that the place was comfortably untidy, strewn with book-plaques, discarded mukluks, outdated news printouts, and other homey clutter.

We all made admiring comments, but our little host hurried us up another stairway to our individual guest rooms on the upper level, each one small but tricked out fit to titillate Louis Quatorze. Our luggage had already arrived. Fred invited us to freshen up and come down to the parlor in an hour or so for drinks and a simple fondue supper.

Then he turned to Marc. "Are you sure I can't tempt you to move in, too? Minnie and I have oodles of room and we both adore house parties. The enclave's Wintergarden is just across the grove from our place and it has facilities for every kind of cold-weather sport imaginable."

"Do it!" I enthused. "You've been overworking yourself for months."

But Marc shook his head. "It's kind of you, Fred. But I've got to finish preparing a critical piece of CE equipment for demonstration before the Science Directorate. And there are still details connected with my new magnateship that I need to sort out. I certainly will drop by for skiing and mind-mashing with this gang of loafers as often as I can. Thanks again for taking them in."

"The warmth of my abode is always yours to share," Fred replied rather formally. Marc had never been quite as matey with him as Denis and Lucille and the other children and I.

"I'll have to be leaving now," Marc said. "But I want everyone to join me for dinner at twenty hours tomorrow at Les Trois Marches in Versailles Enclave. Lynelle will be there and I hope Minnie will be able to come, too."

Fred went to see him and the Rogers woman off and I retired to my room, where there was a compact teleview with a data terminal. I did a bit of fast research and found out that Citizen Lynelle Rogers was a very high-ranking staffer of Dirigent-Designate Patricia Castellane of Okanagon. She was only twenty-three years old, and had lived on the cosmop world all her life. Her educational background was outstanding (political science, economics) and all of her metafaculties were grandmasterclass. She had never been married.

Well well well!

But I still felt vaguely uneasy.

Later, space-lagged and ready to relax, we sat in the parlor eating, drinking, and schmoozing while Fred attended to some domestic matters. The buffet our host had laid on was simple but delicious, and outside a preprogrammed snowfall was adding four cents of crispy new powder to the winter wonderland.

Boom-Boom and Shig lounged like Roman emperors on gilt-wood divans upholstered with blue sea silk, snacking desultorily from a low table with golden legs and a top of priceless lapis lazuli that was now splattered with melted cheese and strewn with dirty dishes. The lads were still munching ambrosial Gi candies and slices of some exotic melon that tasted like perfumed custard. The big fondue pot was almost empty, as were the baskets of mauve Poltroyan bread and the big dish of Earth-style crudités.

Alex Manion had finished eating. Perched on a carved stool, he was doing a rather good job of hammering "The Flowers That Bloom in the Spring" on an exotic dulcimer inset with what might have been emeralds. Pete Dalembert, elected bartender, was making a round of killer shooters from the collection of outlandish liqueurs and flavored brandies on Fred's sideboard. Poltroyans are crazy about syrupy booze.

I lay on the fish-fur rug at the far side of the room, replete, sipping a B&B and studying a big wall-hung Sony Tri-D masquerading as a reproduction of Fra Angelico's *Madonna and Child with Saints.* The faces of the holy folk and angels had been modified to give them lilac complexions and ruby eyes, and their uncovered heads were bald and painted with delicate designs in the best Poltroyan fashion. It was sensitively done and the Fra would have approved.

After a while Fred came in, poured himself a stein of eau de vie de Danzig, and joined me on the floor. "Minnie won't be back tonight." He sighed and gazed moodily at the flakes of gold leaf floating in the clear, oily liqueur. "All of the Ethics and Philosophy Directorates are stuck in extraordinary session. Debating the morality of creativity enhancement."

I h'mphed. "Marc's E15 project?"

"Exactly."

"Ti-Jean wanted to help plead his brother's cause but Marc wouldn't hear of it. How are things looking?"

Fred shrugged. "Poltroy is for it, the Simbiari are violently opposed, and the Gi and Krondaku lean toward conditional approval. Your Human Polity is split down the middle. A lot of humans seem to be more dubious about Marc himself than about his project. There are rumors that Paul Remillard prevailed upon the Lylmik not to nominate Marc to the Concilium two years ago when they were inclined to do so."

"Afraid he might join the Rebel faction, I suppose." Or was it just envy? I told Fred: "Marc's mental assay is cosmic. He's about the best we've got. But Paul's wrong if he thinks Marc would side with the Rebels. He's above politics. All he's interested in is that CE project of his."

Fred took a hefty gulp of goldwasser and I tried not to cringe. "Minnie says that if Marc's demonstration is a success and his brain shows no damage from the device, his research will probably be granted restricted approval. Great benefits could accrue."

"So they say." For a time we were silent. Alex Manion was softly singing "Poor Wand'ring One" from *The Pirates of Penzance*, accompanying himself on the Poltroyan instrument. The others were drinking Pete's appalling shooters and cooking up exploration plans for the morrow.

"What are your feelings about Marc?" Fred inquired softly. "He was a remarkable person even when I knew him as an adolescent. Imagine! Defying the Galactic Magistratum in order to save his mother and unborn brother . . ."

Behind my own mental barricade, I reflected that Fred didn't know the half of it! I confessed: "There were times, when Marc was very young, when I wondered whether he was really human. He was more withdrawn then—colder—and it was obvious that he was awesomely intelligent in addition to having those stupendous metapsychic powers. Neither his mother nor his father took the time to understand him. Teresa was sweet but neurotic, the lark who'd hatched an eagle egg, if you catch my analogy. And you know what Paul is like—passionate, driven, putting humanity's success in the Milieu above every other consideration. The sexual games Paul plays have led Marc to despise him. He underestimates the tremendous things Paul has accomplished and his importance to the Human Polity."

"Perhaps now that Marc is to become a magnate himself, seeing his father at work, he'll be more forbearing."

"If only the young hardass wasn't so judgmental and self-righteous! But he thinks he's got all the answers—and to hell with people who make mistakes or don't meet his standards of perfection. I tried to do what I could with him. When he was a kid I let him hang around my bookshop, encouraged him to talk about himself, tried to be his friend. But he doesn't confide in me the way he used to. I think his closest confidant now is his little brother Jack! And that's weird."

Fred pursed his plum-colored lips, thinking. "Perhaps not. Both Minnie and I got to know the little boy very well. In spite of his great mindpowers and his ghastly mutation, Jack is a warm, loving, very *human* person. Perhaps his older brother unconsciously seeks to emulate him. To discover Jack's successful adaptation to—to superhumanity and apply it to himself."

"Maybe," I conceded. Then I brought up the thing that had been eating away at me ever since I arrived in Orb. "Fred—is there anything going on between Marc and Lynelle Rogers?"

His ruby eyes widened. "What an interesting notion! But I see that the idea troubles you—"

I explained Marc's aversion to sexuality, and the warm-blooded little Poltroyan was all sympathy. "I see. You think a love affair would help Marc's psychomaturation."

"You bet your precious purple ballocks I do! But something about Rogers gives me the willies. How did you get to know her? What do you know about her background?"

"Minnie and I went to your cosmopolitan world, Okanagon, where I was to check out a stalled research project conducted by some of my students. It was—let me see—about five of your Earth months ago. The old Planetary Dirigent had died and the newly nominated Dirigent-Designate was to be fêted at a grand garden party. We were invited, and there we met Citizen Rogers, who was the new Dirigent's special assistant. Lynelle was particularly kind to us when an inebriated human guest made—uh—xenophobic remarks to Minnie. Coerced the boor right out the gate and smoothed things over nicely. We made arrangements to meet her again when we all came to Orb for the Concilium session. Evidently Lynelle made Marc's acquaintance here and learned of his embarrassment of hospitality, and when we had her to dinner she asked for our help. Our friendship with the Remillard family is rather well known in operant circles. Of course we were delighted to oblige. Marc should have thought of asking us himself."

"Not him," I muttered. "But you don't know anything else about this woman? Or her relation to Marc?"

"I'm sorry, no. I really think," he added with a twinkle, "that it would be best if you asked Marc himself about that."

I did, the very next day at the dinner party. But he only smiled his charming asymmetrical smile and told me again to mind my own damn business.

[11]

SECTOR 15: STAR 15-000-001 [TELONIS] PLANET 1 [CONCILIUM ORB]

GALACTIC YEAR: LA PRIME 1-382-692 [17 MARCH 2063]

The Poltroyans had terraformed nearly 150 hectares of their enclave to accommodate the Saint Patrick's Day party, creating a surreal but charming Irish never-never land. Gnarled oaks, lush rolling meadows, standing stones, Celtic crosses, and strategically placed artificial crags evoked a fantasy landscape of Eire. An evening sky with an improbable luminous rainbow overarched a small ruined castle on a "distant" knoll. Flowers clambered over stone walls and bloomed in the dooryards of thatched white cottages that stood beside a dirt track heading toward the "Irish village" where the festivities would take place.

Luc and Jon Remillard and their grandparents, disembarking at the tube station with scores of other human and exotic guests, were greeted by a giggling mob of Titian-wigged Poltroyan females garbed in their quaint conception of eighteenth-century Irish peasant dress: dark brocade skirts fluffed out with lots of petticoats, blouses of emerald silk georgette, gold-tissue aprons, and glistening shawls of fine wool embroidered with Celtic motifs in precious metal thread. The pretty little lilac-skinned colleens pressed shamrock boutonnières, blackthorn walking sticks with green ribbons, and buttons that said KISS ME, I'M IRISH upon the arrivals before guiding them to a fleet of gilded jaunting cars, open vehicles with twin benches facing toward either side, bedizened with green pompons and bunches of daffodils. The drivers were diminutive Poltroyan males in green lamé leprechaun costumes who grinned and shouted welcoming phrases in what was arguably the Irish language.

Jack and Luc took the left seat in a car and Denis and Lucille took the right, whereupon their genial gnomish reinsman cracked his whip and a clockwork Connemara pony set off at a smart trot. Music swelled on the breeze, mingling with the scent of peat smoke, wild roses, and very inviting food.

"Faith and begorrah, but we've got a fine night of merrymaking ready for yez!" the Poltroyal driver caroled. "And are any here true sons or daughters of the Auld Sod?"

Lucille Cartier flinched minutely at the excruciating brogue, but neither her composure nor her mind-screen wavered. "None of us has Irish blood, but I'm sure we'll enjoy your party all the same. It will be a very pleasant way to wind up our visit to this Concilium session. We're most grateful to the Amalgam of Poltroy for its thoughtfulness."

"Saints be praised! And ye know how we Purple Pipsqueaks love a good frolic! Ye'll have a grand time, I'm sure, if music and dancing and eating and drinking appeal to yez. We've got pipers and drummers and harpists and tin-whistle tootlers, and a feast of corned beef and cabbage and seventeen different kinds of praties and bedad if I know how much more yummy Irish food, and enough green beer and other tipple to jollify every soul in Orb . . . saving the wee gossoons, o' course. They get a special bun-fight with sweet cider and green milk shakes and a chance to hunt for a genu-wine pot o' gold."

"Great!" said Jack.

"And the Dirigent of Hibernia, the glorious Irish ethnic planet, is our guest of honor and grand marshal of the parade," the driver continued. "I suppose you know the lovely gentleman: Rory Muldowney is his name."

"Oh-oh," murmured Luc.

Denis was calm. "We're acquainted with him."

Just then three larger carts full of Gi went clattering by at a full gallop, the feathered passengers waving stone jugs in the air while they warbled "Cruiscìn Làn" in several different keys. It was obvious that they had brought their own supply of poteen. Under cover of the hullabaloo, Jack queried his older brother on the intimate telepathic mode.

What*what* about the IrishDirigent? Why you leak anxietyvibes Luco?

Didn't you know? Muldowney was LauraTremblay's husband

and SHE was Papa's paramour for years&years while pooroldRory grinned&bore it.

Oh . . .

She finally got tired of asking Papa to marry her and used her own creativity to commit suicide afewyearsago in a totallybizarrissimo way. [Image.]

Batège! That must have hurt. Is DirigentMuldowney angry with FamilyRemillard because of—of what happened?

He never said WordOne. It seems he kept on loving Laura allthetime she was unfaithful and they had 4kids and even when she died that way after having the last baby Rory never blamed Papa it was passed off as postpartumdepression . . . but that's enoughofthat morbidstuff. Just look what we're getting into!

"Whoa, ye spalpeen!" cried the Poltroyan leprechaun, hauling back on the reins. The robot pony reared and stamped and rolled its eyes as it halted in the midst of a crush of dozens of other golden cars and laughing guests. "Lady and gents, we're here! A hundred thousand welcomes to the Poltroyan Saint Patrick's Day gala, and please to step down lively now so I can fetch the next batch of revelers."

They had arrived at what appeared to be a village green at eventide, surrounded by clusters of brightly lit dwellings and inviting taverns with their doors wide open. Tricolor green, white, and orange flags and emerald banners bearing the harp of Tara flapped from garland-wound standards. Pseudoflame torches and lanterns illuminated the crowded streets and party grounds. A floodlit statue of the patron saint of Ireland looked down benevolently from a central plinth on the green, where strolling groups of mauve-complected little musicians in outlandish parodies of traditional Irish clothing fiddled and piped and harped and sang airs in clear falsetto voices. Back among the trees, which were festooned with green and white lights, were three big open areas of turf dedicated to archaic, nineteenth-century, and contemporary dancing, each with a Poltroyan band in appropriate garb. More Poltroyans dressed as servers raced to and from the cottages, bearing platters and bowls of food to a huge dining pavilion. Just beyond the village was a lighted hurling ground with a boisterous football game in progress, and a picturesque little racecourse where spectators cheered the efforts of bionic steeds.

"What a lively scene," Lucille said politely to the driver. "You must have worked very hard to achieve an air of authenticity."

The Poltroyan winked and tipped his green stovepipe hat. "Not too authentic. We made it Ireland as we'd *prefer* it to be." He cracked his whip and drove off.

"This might be fun," said Jack. "Can I go watch the races?"

Luc checked out the course with his farsight. "They've got bookies!" he exclaimed. "Come on!" The lanky twenty-two-year-old and his little brother hurried off into the crowd.

Denis and Lucille watched them go. "It's good that Luc is finally coming out of his shell," she remarked. "When Paul first brought him to Orb the boy hardly left the enclave except to do his junior staff work. Of course his health was still precarious then."

"Having Jack to look out for this time has been good for Luc," Denis said. He and his wife extricated themselves from the mass of jaunting cars and skirted the throng streaming toward the green. "It's got him out from under Marie's overprotective big-sisterly thumb and given him a real responsibility for a change."

"Jack has been a handful." Lucille smiled, remembering the boy's escapades during the month spent in Orb. "He's explored every square meter of the planetoid except for the Lylmik Sequestrations, and he's pestered the life out of the family magnates and God knows how many others finding out how the Concilium operates. Keeping Jack under control hasn't allowed Luc much time to brood or mope. What a pity the two of them weren't close earlier in life."

"Jack's always been Marc's pet. But now Marc has . . . other matters to distract him." Unspoken but prominent in Denis's vestibular thoughts was a note of deepening concern. The newly confirmed young magnate had declined to come to the party, saying that he had business to take care of before the family's scheduled return to Earth tomorrow. Denis had an uncomfortable premonition what Marc's "business" might be, but thus far he had said nothing about it to Lucille or the others.

They walked up a little hill and found a quiet place beside a spring trickling from some rocks where they could survey the party scene. Water tinkled pleasantly into a rough basin below a carving of St. Brigit, and there was a mossy bench to sit on.

Denis loosened the black-tie formal wear that Lucille had insisted he wear, plumped himself down, and trailed his fingers in the cool water. "I think Luc will get on much better now that his physical rehabilitation is complete. He never said anything to anyone but me, but he was always worried that his own genetic abnormalities would eventually cause him to metamorphose into—something like Jack."

"Oh, the poor boy! But surely you showed him that his genetic heritage is completely different."

"Of course. And I redacted the irrational fears as well as I could. But Luc has too many memories of his childhood as an invalid. He never felt truly self-confident until his body and brain functions stabilized. I'm delighted that he's been accepted as an intern at Catherine's latency clinic."

"Luc is a very caring person. His intellect is superior and his metafaculties are nearly up to full grandmasterly level now. He should make an excellent therapist. Overcoming his own disabilities should help him to empathize with others who need help in achieving their mental potential."

Denis nodded. "I agree."

"It was good of Anne to help him with his sexual identity crisis. I'm afraid Luc thought he was letting the family down by not being a breeder."

"That's nonsense, of course—but we Remillards *have* been rather a philoprogenetive lot."

Lucille laughed softly. "Including some of you who needed a bit of a jump-start."

She was wearing a flowing gown of black with a dramatic wide collar and cuffs decorated with pastel Caledonian seed pearls. Her dark hair was cut in a French bob, and her strongly drawn features had the bloom of youth—thanks to a third regeneration a year earlier.

Denis said, "I had sense enough to get what I needed, at any rate. Unlike a certain son and grandson who shall remain nameless! Without you, I'd have been an inhuman, heartless freak, living only for my work. With you, I became a man." He bent across the fountain bowl and gently kissed her lips.

"Oh, yes," she said, serious now, "and what a man!" She lifted her hand to push a strand of his blond hair back into place. "It's been a mad and fascinating sixty-eight years, being married to you, mon brave. I don't even want to think about what the future may hold."

Denis put his arm around his wife and drew her close. He was ninety-six years old, but he seemed to be only a shy, appealingly gauche young man in his mid-twenties . . . so long as he kept his terrible blue eyes veiled. Research into the Remillard "immortality" gene complex was incomplete, but the consensus was that his body—and those of his descendants—would probably self-rejuvenate indefinitely. The prospect was one that Denis and his progeny almost never thought about, much less discussed, for reasons that were political as well as personal. From time to time some genetic researcher would take another stab at unraveling the bewildering interaction of thousands of genes that produced the immortality effect in hopes of making it available to the rest of humanity; but thus far all their efforts had failed. To the family's great relief, most people had forgotten about this peculiar aspect of the Remillard heritage now that rejuvenation was becoming nearly universal among humans.

"Well, I suppose we'd better socialize," Denis said with reluctance. "Let's try to steer clear of Rory Muldowney, shall we?"

"Heavens, yes." The two of them rose and dusted off their clothes.

There was an inscription carved on the rock above the spring. Lucille studied it, then held out a cupped hand, caught some of the falling water, and sipped from it. "There. According to this sign, now I can make a wish at the holy fountain. I wish . . . I wish we could all have a few quiet years for a change—without any crises rocking the galaxy or the family." She stepped back to give Denis room. "Now it's your turn."

Obediently, he drank from the spring. "I wish I could do more for the Milieu. Find it in me to be the kind of statesman the Lylmik keep urging me to be." But then he shook his head, pulled out a linen handkerchief, and briskly dried his hands. "No. Abort that wish. It would never work. I can't bear the idea of opening my mind to a telepathic colloquium as the Magnates of the Concilium do. Masses of mentalities, exotic and human, all debating and consulting and trying to coerce others to their point of view, everyone knowing the motivation and reasoning of everyone else! No dishonesty—but no room for face-saving diplomacy or decent reticence, either."

Lucille regarded him with concern. "Is that so repellent?"

"It is to me. The Concilium working relationship is wildly chaotic. It's not at all like the order and elegance that characterize metaconcert." He tucked away the handkerchief and adjusted his cuffs. "I realize that I should try to overcome my feelings—but I can't. Perhaps if Unity prevailed amongst the Simbiari and the Human Polity things would be different. As things stand, if I agreed to become a magnate I'd go bats before a single Concilium session wound up."

"Never mind. The work you've accomplished isn't too shabby." Lucille's smile was teasing. "And you can be especially proud of our children."

Denis turned a little away from her, gazing at the nearest dance-ground where partygoers of three races were jigging hilariously to the strains of "Father O'Flynn." Only the poor gloomy green-skinned Simbiari were ill at ease, standing on the sidelines with glassy smiles and sipping from beakers of fizzy water.

"Our children," Denis murmured. "They're right over there, most of them. Philip and Maurie and Adrien and their wives, and Sevvy dancing with Catherine. I'd certainly like to wish peace and happiness for them. But there's this damnable Hydra thing! We haven't the least notion where those renegade creatures are hiding, and the identity of Fury is still a complete mystery. I've had no luck with my own investigations and none of Paul's schemes to uncover the monsters has panned out, either. It seems that all we can do is wait for a new crime having the Hydra modus operandi—and pray that Davy MacGregor or Owen Blanchard or some other hostile magnate doesn't find out about it first."

"Paul and Throma'eloo Lek will see to it," Lucille said soothingly. "And the Lylmik Supervisors are on our side. They know how important the Remillard contributions to the Milieu are."

"They may not protect the family much longer." Denis's tone was grim. "Not with two of our sons becoming more and more vocal in opposing Unity. And now Marc has managed to rock the Human Polity to the core by defying Paul in that damned maiden speech of his before the Concilium. And he doesn't even sympathize with the Rebel separatists!"

"Paul should not have taken Marc for granted," Lucille said tartly.

"He can't get it through his head that Marc is a grown man now with a vital agenda of his own—and the only Paramount Grand Master metapsychic in the Human Polity."

"Whatever that means," muttered Denis.

"It means he's a force to be reckoned with, my darling. Marc's no Rebel. He believes that humanity must remain part of the Milieu in order to survive, but he also believes in intellectual freedom. That's why he spoke up in opposition to Paul's motion to outlaw the anti-Unity faction. People paid attention because of Marc's rank and the brilliance of his argument. And Paul lost."

"Fury must be delighted! . . . Damn Marc."

"Nonsense. He was only standing up for his principles. I have a certain sympathy for the Rebel faction myself. We didn't *ask* for the Intervention. The Milieu had to drag us into their marvelous interstellar confederation. And when we agreed to join them back in the beginning, there was never any explicit condition made that we would have to embrace Unity."

"It was implicit. And given the relatively high power of human metafaculties, it's a practical necessity. Luce, I've devoted my life to metapsychology and I'm positive that we must eventually be Unified. If—if I were part of a network of benevolent, coadunate minds, I wouldn't feel so uneasy about the future. And neither would Sevvy or Adrien or the rest of the Rebel group."

"But the exotics don't seem to be able to give us a clear picture of how Unity would affect us." Lucille's voice was troubled.

"Unity is one of the principal goals of human evolution, as Teilhard de Chardin and so many other philosophers have maintained. It just can't be the soul-destroying hive-mentality that its opponents claim. I know too many wise, kind, *individualistic* Unified exotics to believe that. Who would ever accuse good old Fred and Minnie of being zombies? Or Dota'efoo Alk'ai and that uxorious husband of hers? Sweet Jesus—the entire Gi race is an argument against Unity as a lockstep mind-meld!"

Lucille giggled. "Do you know Uncle Rogi was propositioned by a Gi last week—and almost succumbed?"

"No!"

Lucille took her husband's arm. "I'll tell you the whole story. But first I want you to take me into that cute little shebeen down there and get us both a nice drop of Black Bush."

"Whatever you do," Luc warned his little brother, "don't let yourself exert mindpower on the robot horses. They're bugged, and any PK or creative meddling by the spectators will disqualify the entry."

"I understand," said Jack. He clutched the receipt the Poltroyan bookie in the orange-checked suit and green bowler hat had given him. "One places bets according to the fictional handicap information provided in the form-plaque, analyzing past performance of the horse, so-called breeding, and the other factors. It was rather complex, determining the best entrant, but I solved the equation. The winner will be Tipperary Tensor even though he's rated 30 to 1."

"We'll see, wiseass," Luc growled. He had bet on Shillelagh Sprig, the favorite.

The small mechanical equines with their Poltroyan jockeys were at the post, pawing and snorting. A bell chimed and they were off to the screams and plaudits of the crowd, kicking up clouds of dust and moving as realistically as living animals.

At first Shillelagh led by two lengths. Tipperary Tensor was third going into the turn and fell to fourth in the back stretch. The second runner, Knockmealdown, began to overtake Shillelagh Sprig, whereupon Tipperary Tensor's jockey guided him outside the bunched front-runners and plied his whip. The spectators gave a collective shout of surprise as the long shot suddenly pressed forward, passed number three, Wild Oscar, and continued to accelerate in the last turn. Thundering into the home stretch, their tiny legs twinkling, Tipperary Tensor, Knockmealdown, and Shillelagh Sprig were neck and neck. But at the finish Tipperary pulled away and was the clear upset winner by half a length.

"I told you so," said Jack smugly.

Luc grunted in disappointment and tore his ticket into pieces. "Self-congratulation at the expense of another person is odious."

Instantly contrite, Jack offered to show his brother how he had calculated the winner.

"It doesn't really matter," Luc said. "What does matter is that you learn how to behave in a polite and kindly manner. It makes no difference how smart and talented you are: if you behave like an asshole you're either thoughtless and immature or acting with deliberate or unconscious aggression. In either case, people won't want to socialize with you."

"But Marc is rude to me rather often—and to others as well—and no one ostracizes *him.* People may get angry with Marc, but they still admire him. I can tell. I do it myself."

"Marc is different." Luc spoke bitterly. "Marc's magic. He doesn't have to play by the rules like the rest of us poor chumps."

"What do you mean by that?" Jack demanded. "Is magic some kind of super-coercion?" Open your mind Luco and let me analyze the thought!

NO! . . . Oh well maybe later. I'm jealous of him you know and I have other mixedup feelings about him that you're not ready to understand.

They were trudging side by side to the bookie's stand for Jack's payoff and the racecourse was becoming more crowded by the moment. All at once Jack halted and stood staring at a group gathered around Tipperary Tensor and its jockey, who were being adorned with green carnations and orange roses.

"Look. There are Marco's four friends. Can I tell them that I won?"

Luc tightened his lips fastidiously. "Well, if you must. But I don't really care for their company very much. That Boom-Boom Laroche is a vulgar barbarian, and Pete Dalembert acts so snotty and superior."

"Marc's going to make Pete the Chief Executive Officer of his new private CE laboratory," Jack said casually. "And Shig Morita will be in charge of development and manufacture."

"What?" Luc was thunderstruck. He grabbed his little brother by the arm and swung him into an alcove behind the saddling enclosure. "Marc is leaving Dartmouth College?"

Jack nodded. "I heard him bespeaking his friends. They had a thought-screen up, but it was easy for me to get around it. Marc is tired of having the college threaten to limit his CE research. He asked Alex Manion and Boom-Boom to work with him, too, but they said they have to do some other things now. They said they'd think about joining Marc later."

"But what the hell is Marc going to do? Where will he work?"

"He has lots of money in his trust. He's going to move the E15 project into a place near Seattle as soon as we get back to Earth. I hope he'll still let me help with the design modification. I've got a *really* neat idea for improving the SIECOMEX."

"This is going to cause big trouble," Luc said, "in the family and outside it. You'd better not say anything about Marc's plans to anyone else. Let him make the announcement when he's ready to." And let him take the flak!

Jack's eager face fell. "Why should there be trouble?"

"Just remember what I said. Come on, we'll get your winnings and see if we can place a bet on another likely long shot with a different bookie. They'll be on to you pretty soon, but we can probably manage another winner or two before they warn you off."

Atoning Unifex had exhorted Its fellow Supervisors not to miss the St. Patrick's Day party, promising that it would have an unusual and important climax. The Lylmik might have overseen the affair from their own enclave, of course; but their leader had strongly urged a material manifestation and they had eventually agreed to attend wearing Poltroyan bodies and the bogus Irish costuming sported by true members of that race. As they had done on previous occasions, Noetic Concordance and Asymptotic Essence assumed female form while Homologous Trend and Eupathic Impulse became males. The sexuality of Poltroyans was so similar to that of the Earthling bodies they had worn before that the four entities felt reasonably comfortable.

"Have fun," said Atoning Unifex, "and keep a sharp eye out for impostors." With that It withdrew to Omega knew where, leaving Its four colleagues bemused but resigned.

"What was *that* supposed to mean?" Impulse inquired grumpily.

Noetic Concordance adjusted her wig's orange curls, which had become entangled in one golden earring. "I suspect we'll find out. You don't suppose that the Hydra creatures have been presumptuous enough to invade Orb?"

"By the Prime Entelechy! Surely one jests!" The bluish-violet cheeks of pretty little Asymptotic Essence faded to a grayish lavender.

"If the monsters are here," Homologous Trend said, "we'd better get along and find out what they're up to. If we can find them, that is. They're getting devilishly clever at screening."

"What good will it do to spy them out," sighed Eupathic Impulse, "when Unifex has forbidden one to interfere? It's maddening, enough to discourage one from contemplating the situation at all until bifurcation is imminent."

"There are hints of a stupendous skew in the noögenetic curvature," Essence noted balefully. "One hesitates to predict calamity, but . . . see for yourselves." She projected a complex probability graphic.

Homologous Trend was more equanimous as he modified the equations to produce a more happy result. "The Hydras and Fury have taken on the aspect of strange attractors and may prove to be even more maleficent than we originally supposed. Or again—thus!—they may not. There is always a chance that the dynamic they introduced will paradoxically advance the Protocol of Unification rather than cause its disintegration."

"One can only continue to have confidence in the judgment of Unifex," Concordance declared. "It is so much older and wiser."

"And capricious," grumbled Impulse. "Oh, very well. Let's get along to the shindig."

No sooner had they arrived at the party than they were dragooned into joining an overly energetic group dance. Twirling and prancing with humans, Gi, and legitimate Poltroyans through one merry tune after another, they found themselves unaccountably exhilarated. When the set ended and the pipers and fiddlers bowed and skipped off to refresh themselves, the four Lylmik applauded as enthusiastically as the rest of the dancers before staggering to a table outside one of the taverns and ordering a round of green crème de menthe.

"How strange," said Noetic Concordance, "that rhythmic, repetitious physical activity should be pleasurable to so many different races."

"Well, one may *resonate* for the fun of it in Lylmik form," Eupathic Impulse noted, "even though some may deem it childish."

"It's not quite the same," Asymptotic Essence said. "The rhythmic irregularities and changing tempi of dancing have an appeal all their own." Her ruby eyes twinkled at her partner. "You dance very well, you know."

"A paragon of agility compared to this one," Homologous Trend added, with a ponderous laugh.

Noetic Concordance sipped her sugar-laden liqueur appreciatively. In a Poltroyan body, one had Poltroyan tastes. "There is also an indefinable delectation in dancing with a partner of the opposite sex, even though that person exhibits more enthusiasm than expertise."

Homologous Trend toasted her ironically.

"Have any of you perceived lurking Hydras?" Eupathic Impulse inquired of his colleagues. The responses were negative. "Or the entity called Fury?" Again, the disguised Lylmik shook their heads. Thus far, the oscillations in the mental lattices were entirely benevolent.

"There's the boy Jack," Essence said, giving an imperceptible nod. "Haring about with his Uncle Rogi now that Luc's gone off to celebrate with some older chaps. The child seems psychologically sound in spite of his horrendous mutation. I'm glad we had the family bring him to Orb so the Quincunx could look him over."

"One had the oddest feeling examining him," Noetic Concordance admitted. "That powerful young mind—unaware of our scrutiny and yet having such . . . appealing affinity."

"One knows what you mean," said Homologous Trend softly.

Concordance called up a memoreplay of the experience, which they all studied once again. "Is this entity the only one who experienced a warm reiteration of Fa-Time when contemplating the immature human?"

"I felt it," Trend said.

Essence only frowned, picked up a green pretzel in her enameled talons, and nibbled it thoughtfully.

"Curious," said Impulse. "Very curious indeed. If my fading recollection is accurate, there is no physical similarity whatsoever between newly generated Lylmik and the anomalous Jack."

"No," Concordance agreed. "And yet, of all members of the human race—of all other races—this boy alone reminds one of *us* in the fundamental structure of his mentality. The girl Dorothea Macdonald, for instance, has suboperant metafaculties equal in potential to Jack's but her mental patterns are fully human. Jack's emotions and actions are human, but he thinks differently."

Asymptotic Essence uttered a disbelieving gasp. "Does one suggest that the Lylmik physical aspect might once have been similar to Jack's disembodied brain? Or does one dare to carry the conjecture even further?"

"Not at all," said Concordance. "No member of our ancient race recalls our origins. To speculate is idle. Nevertheless one might ask what relationship young Jack, this prochronistic mutant with the most extraordinary mind his race has ever produced, has to us . . . and to the rest of humanity."

"One cannot respond to that yet," Trend said, after finishing off his minty bumper. "But one is certainly entitled to one's suspicions."

They sat without communicating for some time, scanning the scene and gently probing those minds that were unguarded, while the party grew more and more uproarious. The aether was a cacophonous babble. Even the Simbiari had begun to loosen up and numbers of them, dazed from overindulgence in carbonated water, were heedlessly dripping emerald mucus into the shamrock patches. A kilted marching band of humans, led by a heavily perspiring Rory Muldowney, tramped twice round the square playing "Amran na bFiann," "Garryowen," and "Mick McGilligan's Ball."

The shining green satin cutaway tailcoat and knee britches worn by the Dirigent of Hibernia were getting a bit rumpled toward the finish and his top hat slid askew; but he was a fine figure of a man for all that, big and broad-shouldered, only a little gone to pot, with a goodly turn of leg in his white silk stockings.

When the parade ended, music struck up again on the dancing grounds. Humans and Poltroyans began howling with laughter as a chorus line of Gi tricked out in green-dyed filoplumage and funny hats performed a travesty of Irish step-dancing to the tune of "Finnegan's Wake." The tall hermaphrodites tipped and tapped neatly with their oversized avian feet, batted their huge eyes saucily, and wound up their act to riotous applause with a dazzling flourish of external genitalia.

Over on the village green the original pair of Rebel conspirators, Annushka Gawrys and Owen Blanchard, were surrounded by a triumphant group of like-minded magnates celebrating the defeat of the gag bill. Unexpectedly, Annushka had come to the party accompanied by her aged and unrejuvenated mother, the metapsychic pioneer Tamara Sakhvadze. All evening long the distinguished old lady had enjoyed the adulation of a host of admirers. Among those attending her at that moment were Davy MacGregor, his sister Katharine, the Poltroyan magnates Fritiso-Prontinalin and Minatipa-Pinakrodin, the new Dirigent of Okanagon, Patricia Castellane, and the slightly winded guest of honor himself, now drinking steadily from a large Waterford tumbler of neat Tullamore Dew.

For some reason Paul Remillard had come to this final party of the session unaccompanied by a female friend. The four Lylmik Supervisors watched with increasing interest as he mingled with the throng, flashing his inimitable smile and looking splendid in an iridescent magenta dinner jacket. He was slowly making his way toward Tamara.

A Poltroyan dressed as a serving lad came up to the Lylmik table. "Will ye have another round of likker?" he inquired. "The tavern's got usquebaugh, heather ale, porter, stout, mead, and green beer. And if ye feel peckish I can offer the specialities of the house! (It all comes from Orb's central provisioning depot, you understand, but we've gone to great pains to program authentic Irish fare!) There's grand corned beef sandwiches loaded with tasty nitrites, mulligatawny soup or Dublin coddle with hot griddle bread, Irish stew, colcannon, champ, and pickled salmon. If ye fancy a sweet there's flummery, spotted dog, tipsy trifle, gooseberry fool, or carraghìn mousse."

"Spotted dog?" Essence murmured qualmishly.

The purple-faced leprechaun laughed. "Faith, and 'tis only a cake with raisins in it."

Trend said, "I don't believe I'm up to the consequences of serious alimentation."

"We'll just have heather ale and some dulse to munch on," Noetic Concordance told the server. He bobbed his head and presently returned with the drinks and a snack bowl of seaweed.

Two pipers and a concertina player launched into an infectious version of "The Irish Washerwoman" right there in front of the tavern, and numbers of the patrons left their tables to dance in the street.

Eupathic Impulse said, "One could sit here comfortably for the rest of the evening waiting for the climactic event promised by Unifex."

"Not on one's life!" said Essence, rising and seizing her partner's arm. "Let's dance!"

. . .

"I really don't want to leave the party, Uncle Rogi," Jack protested. "Something interesting is about to happen. I'm sure of it."

"It's late, Ti-Jean," Rogi said. "You've had enough, and so have I." The old man pinched the bridge of his nose and squeezed his eyes shut, fending off a headache. "I shouldn't have drunk all that poteen after the hurley game. Filthy stuff—it sneaks up on you. First the glow, then the mule kicks you in the skull."

Jack remained prudently silent. He knew better than to offer a redactive cure. Uncle Rogi never let other people into his head. The two of them passed a tavern where people were jigging in the street, then found a jaunting car and climbed in. As the driver cracked his whip and they set off for the tube station, Jack looked back with keen interest.

"Guess what, Uncle Rogi! There are four Lylmik dancing back there—disguised as Poltroyans."

"I'll be damned," said the old man. He exerted his nearly useless farsight but saw nothing unusual. "You sure?"

"Oh, yes. What's more, I recognize their mental signatures. They were part of the group that probed me just after I arrived."

"Merde! They did? Why didn't you tell us?"

"It didn't hurt. They were just checking me out. They installed a memory block, but I was able to override it. It was really interesting, hearing them discuss my mental assay. Do you know that there's another kid who has mindpowers almost as enormous as mine? A girl on the planet Caledonia. Her name's Dorothea Macdonald. She's still not completely operant, but the Lylmik said she would be someday. I wish I could go to Caledonia and meet her."

"Maybe if you learn how to behave yourself and stay out of trouble, Grandmère and Grandpère will take you."

"I was good at the party," Jack protested. "I didn't even go for the pot of gold, even though I knew where it was hidden almost as soon as the game started. To hog the single prize because of my superior metafaculties would have been vainglorious and contemptible. It was different with the horse races where others had a chance to win, too."

Rogi gave a snort of laughter, then patted Jack's shoulder. "Well done, Ti-Jean. You're learning."

Not many guests were inclined to leave the party early. Among the sparse group of passengers waiting in the tube station were Marc's four friends Alex, Pete, Shig, and Boom-Boom.

"Don't tell me you guys are packing it in already!" the bookseller said.

"I get to stay at Fred and Minnie's tonight with you and Uncle Rogi," Jack piped up.

Alex Manion said, "We're not exactly heading back to the tree-house just yet." His mind-screen, like those of his companions, was fully arrayed. "There's another party we want to drop in on. A smaller one."

"Adults only. We'll see you later," said Boom-Boom, winking. "We got heavy dates. You know?" The quartet boarded a capsule destined for the human enclaves.

When they were gone, Jack said quietly, "They're going to Marc's. But I promised Luc not to tell anybody why."

"A conspiracy, eh? I suppose the gang of 'em are plotting to turn Rebel."

"Oh, no," said the child. "That's not it at all. Please don't do any more guessing, Uncle Rogi. I really can't tell you and it would be a sin for me to lie."

"Perish the thought that I'd lead you into temptation," Rogi said huffily. "Toi, t'es un vrai p'tit Saint Jean le Désincarné!"

The capsule that would carry them to Fred and Minnie's house pulled into the station and they got in and sped away.

Paul Remillard bowed formally over the withered hand of Tamara Sakhvadze. She was 105 years old and wore a chic suit of dark worsted with a high-necked white blouse and a fine cameo. Thick-lensed old-fashioned spectacles perched on the end of her button nose and her snowy hair was cut short. Throughout the evening she had held court beneath the statue of St. Patrick, seated in a motorized chair, attended by her grandchildren Gael and Alan Sakhvadze and lionized by Rebels and Milieu loyalists alike.

Operant etiquette made it unnecessary for Paul to introduce himself after the old lady extended her hand and invited him telepathically to approach. He simply opened his mind, revealing his identity in the unlikely event that she had not recognized him, and said: "It's a great honor to meet you in person at last, Madame Sakhvadze. I hope you have enjoyed your visit to Concilium Orb."

"Please, First Magnate," she protested in heavily accented Standard English. "You must call me Tamara and I will call you Paul. It is my first—and probably my last!—visit to this astonishing place. I have been both impressed and bewildered by your marvelous interspecific legislature."

Paul laughed. "It's not nearly as disorderly as it seems."

Tamara shook her head slowly in disbelief. "That humanity and five exotic races can actually cooperate in a galactic government still amazes me. I remember, you see, the spectacular failure of my own late Soviet Union, which attempted to unite a multitude of different human ethnic groups through imposing an idealistic philosophy. It never worked. The weaknesses of human nature prevailed and not even the emergence of higher mindpowers was able to save us from civil war. From what I have heard during my visit, I fear that something similar may lurk in the future of your Galactic Milieu."

"Nonsense, Mamenka," said Davy MacGregor. "The two situations are quite different." The lanky, dark-haired Dirigent of Earth wore the spectacular Highland dress of his clan. His sister Katharine, in a long Regency ballgown with a shoulder sash of the MacGregor tartan, had married Tamara's son Ilya. Their progeny included not only Gael and Alan but also Masha MacGregor-Gawrys. Both Davy and Katharine, tragically deprived of their own mother years before the Intervention, had accorded maternal honors to Tamara for years.

Davy MacGregor spoke now with a voice full of hearty optimism. "The misunderstandings about Unity are bound to be resolved before humanity reaches its Coadunate Number and a final vote must be taken by the population. We've got at least twenty years to study the matter and put any feelings of misgiving to rest."

The little old lady cocked her head and peered up at Paul with an earnest expression. "And what do you think? Will it be so easy?"

It was a long moment before the First Magnate replied. "I hope Davy is right. The great majority of human magnates and others of our race having metapsychic powers believe that Unity would be wholly beneficial to our mental evolution. A fair number of nonoperants fear that it would compromise the mental integrity of the individual and make operants less human in their thinking. The so-called Rebel faction of metas is also opposed to Unity, and their numbers have been slowly growing. I personally think we Milieu loyalists have our work cut out for us disproving the Rebel thesis, but I'm confident we'll prevail in the end. The notion of divorcing the Human Polity from the rest of the Milieu is unthinkable."

Tamara turned to the little Poltroyan pair in their droll Irish fancy dress. The smiles had left the kindly faces of Fred and Minnie and their ruby eyes had clouded. "Both of you are exemplars of Unity," Tamara said. "If the situation came to this—this Bill of Divorcement, would the Milieu let humanity go its way alone?"

Minnie temporized. "The Concilium has never actually debated the contingency."

"There was considerable opposition to admitting humankind to the Milieu in the first place," Fred said somberly. "Your race has a long way to go before reaching the level of psychological and social maturity already achieved by the coadunate peoples. It's true that the Simbiari are also imperfectly Unified, but their race has never been exceptionally aggressive—merely insensitive—and their minds continue to coadunate smoothly into the Whole. With humanity, there has always been the danger of fundamental incompatibility."

"We Poltroyans faced rather a similar situation when we were initiated," Minnie said. "Like you humans, we have a predatory past which we overcame only with great mental effort. This is doubtless why we feel such sympathy for you."

Patricia Castellane, the recently appointed Dirigent of Okanagon, spoke up sharply. "But your friendship doesn't extend to the point of being able to show us exactly what Unity entails!"

Fred and Minnie's distress was obvious. The Poltroyan female said, "Unity cannot be demonstrated, Patricia. It can only be experienced. It can be compared somewhat to the way sexual beings fall in love. No description can adequately portray its reality. Persons may yearn for it, be indifferent to it, or even fear it. But when it happens, its effects are inexplicably transfiguring."

"That," said Alan Sakhvadze, an admitted member of the Rebel faction, "is what we're afraid of: being transfigured to the point of losing our identity."

"One's ego remains intact," Fred said, "but egocentricity becomes impossible within Unity, as does the potential for hostile action toward one's fellow beings. One is not coerced into abandoning these attitudes, you understand. They simply become inconceivable."

"And what," Tamara inquired, "might a Unified operant human do if confronted by a life-threatening *unUnified* human?"

"Resolve the situation peacefully," said Paul Remillard.

"Or die?"

The First Magnate inclined his head. "The ethic is not unfamiliar to the human race."

The old lady's hands, clasped in her lap, were trembling slightly, but her shuttered mind and immobile face betrayed nothing of her emotions. "Long years ago, when human operants were forced to conceal their mindpowers for fear of hostile normals, my dear late husband Yuri and I were lectured on that very point by a Tibetan lama. He told us that aggression—especially the aggressive use of metapsychic faculties—is never morally acceptable. To the day that he died, Yuri refused to accept this teaching. He had seen too much evil that could not be conquered except by extirpation. I *did* believe in the philosophy of nonviolence for a while—until we operants of the Soviet Union were given the choice of fighting for our lives or bowing to martyrdom." She shrugged. "We fought. We lived. Was it wrong?"

Paul searched her fathomless dark eyes. There was no coercion in Tamara Sakhvadze, no defiance, only stone-hard endurance.

"Tamara, our world has changed. The horrors you faced have vanished forever. The Galactic Milieu is far from perfect, but most forms of injustice, oppression, and want are extinct. Human beings—operant and non—are free to fulfill their potential, to live happy and productive lives—"

"So long as their choice falls within the parameters of Milieu Statutes!" said Alan Sakhvadze, interrupting without apology. "But human reproduction is still licensed, certain religions and certain traditional lifestyles are banned, and migration to the colonial planets is hedged with onerous restrictions. Operant human beings have their liberty even more severely restricted. We're required to develop our mindpowers to the fullest extent whether we want to or not. We can also be compelled to pursue an occupation or profession that's deemed most beneficial to the Milieu—even if we have strong personal inclinations in other directions."

"Humans have always been willing to accept limitations on freedom for good and sufficient reason," Paul said. "The more complex the society, the more often the individual human ego must bow to the requirements of the common welfare. Ethics and morality must evolve along with society."

"And you know all about ethics and morality, don't you, boyo."

For the first time since Paul had joined the group, Rory Muldowney spoke. The voice of the "Irish" planet's Dirigent was mild and lilting for all that his features were deeply flushed and his eyes ablaze with some well-muffled passion. He lifted his glass high.

"Then here's to you, First Magnate! Paul Remillard—leader of the polity . . . guardian of humanity's best interests . . . font of swift justice . . . troubleshooter extraordinaire. Slainté to you, Number One! You'll see the lot of us safely wrapped in Unity whether we want it or not, won't you, you darlin' noble man! All the human planets and good old Earth to boot." He emptied the half-full glass in a single heroic belt, set it carefully at the feet of St. Patrick, and stood there swaying in his green formal wear with his head lowered between his shoulders like a befuddled bull. His bloodshot gaze never left the First Magnate.

Paul chuckled uneasily. "Rory, you're pissed as a newt. Let me give you a shot of redaction so you can carry on with your guest-of-honor duties in proper style."

Wagging his head in firm refusal, Muldowney surveyed the group with an expression of lugubrious rue. "Yes, by God, I am by drink taken! How else can I find the balls to speak the *truth* about humanity's distinguished First Magnate?" He raised his voice to a ringing shout. "Listen, everyone! Let me tell you about Paul Remillard's great devotion to our race . . . especially to the sweet females of the species."

Patricia Castellane took a step toward him, her face gone pale with alarm. She seemed to collide with an invisible barrier surrounding the Irishman and staggered back in pained dismay. Davy MacGregor steadied her but made no attempt to intervene. A tiny sardonic smile quirked the corners of the Scotsman's mouth. Tamara Sakhvadze uttered a feeble sound of protest. A few of the others also halfheartedly voiced disapproval at the same time that they strengthened their mind-screens to the maximum so their own thoughts would remain imperceptible.

Rory Muldowney ignored them, flinging his arms wide in a grandiose tragic gesture. He continued his oration at the top of his lungs and with all the might of his declamatory farspeech. Around him, the noisy throngs of revelers were falling into dismayed silence.

"Let me tell you," Rory said, "about the way our First Magnate enticed a good woman away from her man and her children with his fine coercive ways! Bewitching her and then breaking her heart so all she could do was long to die. She was a Grand Master Creator, was my poor wife Laura Tremblay. So when Paul Remillard cast her away she went to a high green hill on our Hibernian world and bade every drop of blood within her to turn to solid ice."

He projected a hideous image into the minds of his audience. The luckless Laura had not caused her body to freeze instantaneously; her body fluids had congealed more slowly once she had irrevocably commanded the fatal process to begin, expanding as they solidified. There were cries of horror and revulsion and many of the hypersensitive Gi uttered faint wails and fell unconscious.

"And thus I found her," Rory said, canceling the ghastly vision, "deformed and lifeless, all beauty fled along with her tormented soul. Our First Magnate said he was so very sorry. He sent lovely flowers."

Slow tears trickled down the Dirigent's florid face. "No one was to blame at all. That's what they said. The storms of love come and go among us human beings, and nary a one can command them—not me, not my Laura, and certainly not the grand First Magnate of the Human Polity. Still, I want you all to know what happened. Remember it when Paul Remillard speaks of ethics and morals and the greater good. I will, and so will the children Laura gave me. And now I've said what I had to say. Beannachtaì na Fèile Pàdraig daoibh! A happy Saint Patrick's Day to you all."

After a beat of utter stillness the party guests began to murmur. Some were frankly weeping. Paul, his face gone livid, took a step toward the Irishman.

"Rory, for the sweet love of God—"

Paul never finished. The Dirigent of Hibernia cocked his right arm and delivered a short uppercut to the jaw with blinding swiftness, knocking the First Magnate of the Human Polity of the Galactic Milieu cold.

. . .

"I presume that was it," said Asymptotic Essence.

"Indubitably," said Homologous Trend.

"One will have to spend some time appreciating the nuances of the event," sighed Eupathic Impulse. "A nodality exists, as Atoning Unifex implied; but one is justifiably suspicious of jumping to the most obvious conclusion."

[12]

SECTOR 15: STAR 15-000-001 [TELONIS] PLANET 1 [CONCILIUM ORB]

GALACTIC YEAR: LA PRIME 1-382-693 [18 MARCH 2063]

He was there alone, just as the Hydra had planned it, sitting by the fire with a cup of hot buttered rum and a magazine-plaque programmed with back issues of some flyfishing publication. His four friends were long gone. The units of the multiplex monster watched him from a darkened snowmobile parked in a lane of Alpenland Enclave a hundred meters or so from the little A-frame hut. The snowdrifts were silvered by a small, chill, illusory moon. Most of the nearby dwellings were dark.

I'm ready. Whatdoyouthink Quint?

He's relaxed and as susceptible as he ever will be. The equipment has already been packed for the trip back to Earth tomorrow but he can easily set it up again if you're persuasive enough.

Just watch me! I know I can do it he won't suspect a thing to him I'm just one more casualfemaleacquaintance the selfcenteredarrogantshit—

Ooo! He's really *your* kindaguy allright Maddy!

[Petulance.] I could handle him better. I'm sexier. I don't see why Madeleine has to have all the fun.

You? Cope with a paramount? Not bloodylikely Celine he'd squash you like a roach if you went exconcert Sweetcakes.

WILLYOU2SHUTUP?

—is wellsoftened after our DREAMTHERAPY what a

marvelousidea of Fury's it never occurred to me/US that he ofallpeople would be vulnerable through that particular limbicpath.

He likes you Maddy. The consanguineal affinity is extremely powerful. There was already a softening of resolve even before I/WE worked on him . . . and males are so much more vulnerable than females in this respect. Even a unique male like Marc can't completely control his hormones like the GreatEnemy can. If this ploy fulfills Fury's expectations the effect on Marc's psychological stability should be devastating. It's going to take a lot to soften up the bastard but this will be a useful start. The rest of us will join you in metaconcert afterward to delete every trace of the invasion.

Until the day I\WE refresh his memory.

And finish him once&forall!

If I'm not successful if he recognizes me or even realizes what I'm trying to do he may kill me. He could probably fry me to a cinder with his unaugmented creativity alone.

Yes. It would probably be inadvertent but the remote possibility is there if he feels himself integrally threatened he must *not* perceive any danger until it's too late. Use the utmost caution.

[Apprehension.] Maddy Quint's right be careful if I\WE lost you the most powerful Hydraunit then Fury's great scheme would suffer a terrible setback.

Don't worry Parni I know what I'm doing just keep a good hold on Celine when the going gets hot I can't have her crashing in halfcocked—

I'd *never* do that damnYOU!

No? You nearly fucked our snuffjob of the old Okanagon-Dirigent losing control from sheerlifeforcegluttony and we had to blow the ship to kingdomcome instead of doing the switch&feeding.

That was an accident . . .

WE WON'T HAVE ANY MORE ACCIDENTS LIKE THAT.

No . . .

No!

NO!

Understand: In the physical sphere Fury depends upon Hydra. I/WE depend on Fury for our life and fulfillment. Hydra must never forget that! Now open the cabdoor Quint. It's time for me to go.

She felt his seekersense flick over her as soon as she stepped onto the walk leading to his hut, but the convenances governing polite behavior between nonintimate operants forbade that he take any notice of her arrival until she actually tapped on the door of the A-frame.

There was an Escheresque snowman in Marc's front yard, a fantastic Strange Loop creation of dizzying entwined spiral limbs and multiple faces. No hands could have carved it: it had been fashioned by an operant mind. Marc's?

The area around the sculpture's base had been trampled by small feet. The Great Enemy had been here, visiting his elder brother. She repressed a shudder.

Making certain that her mental shield was strengthened to the utmost, she forced a smile and reached for the brass knocker.

Marc opened the door. His expression was cordial and his aura benign. "Hello, Lynelle. Not celebrating St. Patrick's Day with our little purple friends?"

"The party's over. And not with a whimper, but with a considerable bang! I think I'd better let your family tell you about the paddywhacking, though . . . The real reason I came by was to wish you bon voyage. Meeting you was one of the more memorable events of my first trip to Orb."

Marc's asymmetrical smile broadened. "Come in—if you're sure you're not afraid of being compromised by associating with a scandalous character."

Her laughter bubbled richly. "That's ridiculous. No one was scandalized by your speech except a few dreary archconservatives. And they're just envious because the Lylmik named a brand-new magnate to be the one and only Paramount Grand Master of the Human Polity."

He lifted a dismissive shoulder. "The honor and two bux will buy me a tall latte at an Alpenland deli. It isn't as though a paramount had any real political status."

As he helped her off with her black velvet evening cape, she looked at him mischievously over her shoulder. "Oh, but he does, you know. When the most powerful metapsychic mind in the human race expresses an opinion strongly, people listen. When you spoke against the outlawing of the Rebel faction, it tipped the balance in the Concilium and helped defeat the First Magnate's bill of attainder. Dirigent Castellane told us staffers that the gag bill might have squeaked through if it hadn't been for you."

Marc only shrugged.

She unbuttoned the wrist slits of her long black kidskin gloves and slipped her hands out, then fluffed up the extravagant corkscrew curls of her gorgone hairstyle. "I'm not a Rebel myself, but there are a good many people on my planet who are. They should be able to speak their minds freely. Calling an honest difference of opinion treasonous—trying to outlaw open debate—is an outrage. We might as well be back under the Simbiari Proctorship. The First Magnate made a serious mistake cosponsoring that bill."

She was dressed in an Empire gown of white silk gauze, high-waisted, with short puffed sleeves and floating panels embroidered in silver and red. A black ribbon centered with a tiny silvery Medusa encircled her pale throat.

Together they went to the fire. Before Marc could pull up another chair Lynelle Rogers sank down gracefully onto the hearthrug, pulled off her red dancing slippers, and arranged them so that the snow-dampened soles would dry. "You should keep your walk shoveled," she chided him, "or turn on the melting grid. Does summer ever come in Alpenland Enclave?"

"Sorry. For that, you have to go to Edelweiss on the other side of our fake Swiss mountains. Would you like something hot to warm the cockles?"

"I'd love it. Alcoholic, please. It's cold out there." She drew off the gloves and set them aside.

He got two clean mugs and added sweet butter, cinnamon sticks, and Jamaica rum, then swung the crane away from the flames and tipped the spout of a steaming cast-iron teakettle with his bare fingers.

She gave a cry of warning. "Look out! You'll burn yourself!"

"No, I won't." He added boiling water, stirred with his PK, and handed the cup to her.

"Oh . . ." Her laughter was apologetic. "How silly of me. Of course a little thing like a red-hot iron teakettle wouldn't faze a Paramount Grand Master Creator. I suppose you could pick up the flaming logs in the fireplace if you felt like it."

"You must forgive my momentary breach of decorum. The potholder was accidentally burnt up when my little brother was messing around here last week and I forgot to order another. I try to conform to civilized operant behavior most of the time."

"What a shame," she murmured slyly. He was wearing a flannel shirt, jeans, and a pair of beaded moccasins over bare feet. When he had finished making his own drink she patted the rug beside her. "Sit down here with me and tell me what you'll be doing now that the Concilium session is over. Someone said you were thinking of leaving academia and taking your E15 project into the private sector."

He settled himself so he could look into the fire and sipped the aromatic drink. "I may as well tell you. It won't be a secret for long. I'm resigning my professorship at Dartmouth College. The trustees and faculty have always regarded me as a maverick who doesn't play by the rules—and that's almost a hanging offense at an Ivy League Earth college. They've been scared to death by the political implications of high creativity enhancement. The fact that creativity is the most fundamental of the metapsychic powers, able to influence all of the others and embracing an enormous spectrum of faculties, shivers their livers. They're afraid my E15 might be misused by some galaxy-class nutcase bent on causing a new Ice Age or a modification of continental drift or some such thing."

Her eyes widened. "Does the equipment have that potential?"

"Hardly. Not even an augmented paramount mind could do those things—if it was mad enough to want to. It's true that the E15 might be abused, but so might any number of other sophisticated devices or processes."

"You'd find a very different attitude toward your project on my world," Lynelle Rogers said softly. "Dirigent Patricia Castellane was fascinated when she learned about it. Okanagon is one of those planets with anomalous crustal plates—like Caledonia and Eskval-Herria and Satsuma. As I understand it, high-creative CE might eventually provide a way of stabilizing the planetary lithosphere and preventing seismic disasters—if enough grandmaster operators learn to use the equipment properly and focus shaped energies in metaconcert."

Marc eyed her with surprise. "You're right—but I don't recall anything published in the literature that mentions *metaconcerted* CE. My own paper on the subject is still going the rounds of the journal editors and being viewed with jaundiced eyes."

"We aren't hicks on Okanagon. We have an outstanding science establishment and we keep a close watch on research topics that are likely to be of critical interest to our survival. Including yours."

"I had no idea your spies were on to me," he teased.

But Lynelle was deadly serious. "Metaconcerted creativity is obviously the next step once the limits of individual enhancement of the faculty are reached. One presumes that you don't intend to limit the E15 to Paramount Grand Masters."

"Certainly not. A grandmasterclass creator would be able to use it safely even now. The only serious hazard would be to an operator who lacked focusing ability or badly misjudged his creative talent. But it will be years before metaconcert programs can be designed for CE equipment. Even bare-brain operants are still fumbling around, trying to get the hang of choral thinking. In theory, a genuinely efficient combination of minds would produce a synergistic effect: a whole greater than the sum of the individual parts."

Lynelle was staring at the leaping flames. "Yes. I understand that."

"But even without multiple operators, CE creativity shows great promise for minor geophysical applications. Seismic forces are delicate and subtle. No conventional energy-beam or explosive that we have is fine enough or immediately variable enough to exert the tuned and shaped pressures needed to avert dangerous earthquakes or change the devastating nature of volcanic or diatrematic eruptions. But an enhanced mind, working like an intelligent, large-scale laser scalpel, just might do the job. Of course that's only one possible application of creative CE. Uses for the equipment are virtually unlimited."

"I wonder why the exotic races never developed cerebroenergetic enhancement."

"God knows. Lack of imagination, perhaps. I'll tell you another of my disreputable opinions: I think the Milieu is rather stodgy, and the Lylmik who run it are a senile race of mystics on a downhill slide. Maybe their motive for dragging humanity into their confederation was to give it a well-needed shot of élan vital."

She nodded slowly. "It's plausible. They've said often enough that they need us. But I wonder if we really need them? So much of the Galactic Milieu smacks of well-intentioned tyranny. The Rebel faction believes that humanity is actually being retarded in its psychosocial evolution by exotic restrictions. It's true that the exotics probably saved us from self-destruction fifty years ago and gave us a great scientific leg up. But by now our science and technology have passed theirs in almost every area, our social problems are nearly solved, and our larger colonial planets are completely self-sufficient. Is the Milieu still good for us *now*? I don't know the answer."

Marc did not offer an opinion. They were both silent for several minutes, savoring the fragrant rum. Finally she said: "Here's just one example of Milieu bungling: Our world Okanagon is really a great place—provided that you don't look too deep underground. It never should have been granted cosmop status and made a main focus of colonization because it has an unstable crust. The Krondaku team that checked it out four thousand years ago were incompetents. A whole group of other worlds in the same stellar region—Satsuma, Yakutia, Eskval-Herria, Caledonia—were also improperly surveyed and suffer the same kind of instability. Of course we humans never doubted the Milieu evaluation when they told us to colonize those planets. Serious anomalies on Okanagon weren't discovered until 2058, when a comprehensive geological survey was done with new equipment developed on Earth. By then our population had mushroomed to over a billion. Okanagon is a Sector Base and the home of the Twelfth Fleet and one of the most highly developed human colonies. It would be economically disastrous to abandon the planet and start all over. Nobody seriously suggests that we should . . . yet. Most exotic Milieu geophysicists think that the likelihood of a truly catastrophic incident is small. Our late Dirigent, Rebecca Perlmutter, accepted that judgment and was inclined to minimize the danger. But a significant minority of planetologists—all human, of course—believe there's room for real concern. Dirigent Castellane takes their opinion extremely seriously.

I'm certain that your research would receive unlimited funding if you'd relocate to our planet."

"Castellane told you to sound me out." It was a statement, not a question.

"Yes. Even though we knew nothing of your problems with Dartmouth College." Lynelle set her cup down. She examined one of her drying shoes, then moved both of them further from the heat. "You'll be receiving an official invitation once we return home. As a senior member of the Dirigent's staff and an acquaintance of yours, I was asked to introduce the idea to you before you left Orb."

"I'm sorry, but I can't accept. I've made other plans."

"Please reconsider! We'd appreciate your genius on Okanagon, Marc. There'd be no irksome academic or political restrictions. You'd have an unlimited budget, carte blanche in facilities and personnel—"

"You probably know that I come from an affluent family. I have abundant funds of my own in trust that are available, and the Remillard Foundation is one of the wealthiest on Earth. I intend to ask the Foundation to help fund the new independent research institute that I'll head." He hesitated, then added, "When the time comes to test the E15 equipment on geophysical applications, I promise to give Okanagon top priority."

"Oh, thank you! Thank you so very, very much . . ." She flung her arms around him and kissed his lips. He was momentarily taken aback, but then laughed and gently extricated himself from the embrace. But she insisted on nestling close beside him and somehow he could not find it in himself to object. For a time they discussed technicalities of the crust-modification process, but then they sat quietly together staring into the flames. Her head with the mass of gleaming ebony curls rested against his shoulder. The firelight had turned her filmy gown and pale skin to gold.

"Dearest Marc," she said finally. "I knew you'd be willing to help us. The people of my planet will express their gratitude later. But I—I wish you'd let me show my own appreciation now."

Her hand began to move along his thigh. It was caught by his psychokinesis and held immobile. She gave a soft moan of frustration.

"Marc, I want you so very much! More than any man I've ever

known. I've felt an attraction from the first moment we met. We'd be so good together! You know we would."

"You're a lovely woman, Lynelle, and very appealing. But I think not."

She sighed, withdrawing her hand reluctantly as his mind released it. "Are you gay, then, like your brother Luc?"

"No. But I'm different from the other men you've known. With very different needs. Perhaps someday I'll welcome the physical pleasures of sex, but not now. It would be a distraction, a diversion of vital energies needed elsewhere."

She rounded on him sharply. "Paramount Grand Masters can't be bothered with vulgar fucking! Is that the way it is? Or are you like Merlin—the greatest wizard of them all unless you succumb to a woman?"

Marc only tossed off the last of his rum and climbed to his feet. He did not offer to help her up. "Thanks for coming to say goodbye. And I appreciate your telling me about Okanagon's support of my work. No hard feelings?"

Her voice was tremulous now as she looked up at him, forcing a smile. "No hard feelings. I'm sorry I barked at you. I hope we can say au revoir rather than goodbye. I—I'd like to show you Okanagon someday. As a friend." Still seated on the rug, she began to put on her shoes. Suddenly she halted, as if struck by a thought, and gazed up at him in eager hopefulness. "Marc, there is one other thing you could do, if you would. A consolation prize."

One winged eyebrow lifted quizzically.

"Show me your new E15 helmet," she pleaded. "All Orb was buzzing about it after you did your demonstration before the magnates of the Science Directorate. Would you—could you—show me just a little of how it works?" Say you will do it!

Say you will do it!

SAY YOU WILL DO IT.

Marc's deep-set gray eyes seemed to glaze for an instant. When he spoke, the words came haltingly. "It . . . might be . . . possible . . . if you're really interested."

She was standing now, charged with excitement. "It would be thrilling to see you demonstrate it. I could give my own confidential report to the Dirigent."

"That might be . . . useful."

He turned away and went to the other side of the little hut's main-floor living area, rooting among a stack of luggage awaiting transfer to the Human Terminal. A moment later he returned carrying an impressive-looking transport pod with a prominent label:

CAUTION—INTERNAL SIGMA SHIELD
DO NOT ATTEMPT TO OPEN THIS POD WITHOUT CODE
OR CONTENTS WILL BE DESTROYED

He gently bit his lower lip to dislodge a few cells, then licked his finger and poked it into the code aperture. There was a ping and the container cracked open like a clamshell. A small puff of smoke confirmed that the decoder had sterilized itself and awaited the next DNA sample.

Lynelle said, "You protect your valuables well. But what if someone simply ran off with the entire pod? There are surely ways of breaking the code or deactivating a sigma that small, given time and resources."

"Not in this setup. I designed it myself. It responds to my DNA, my fingerprint, and my mental signature. The sigma itself has fifteen backup levels—and five are programmed to micronuke at the least hint of tampering. Illegal to ship a pod like this on a civilian transport. It'll go home to Earth on a diplomatic courier."

"Oh, my," she whispered.

Marc opened the pod fully. Inside the padded interior was the prototype CE helmet, a grotesque golden thing with portions of its operating systems mounted nakedly on the exterior for ease in experimentation. The container also held a small fusion power generator with cables, and a device resembling a handheld computer. Marc carried the equipment to his chair by the fire, plugged the helmet into its energy source, and fiddled with the handset. When he was satisfied he sat down and donned the helmet. It engulfed all of his head except the facial area below the eyes and was nearly as bulky as an old-fashioned hard-hat diving helmet.

"Damn prototype still weighs a ton. When it's perfected it'll be more comfortable."

"What does the handset do?" She crept over and knelt beside him.

A fine dew of perspiration had dampened the fine tendrils of raven hair in front of her ears and at her brow. Her lips, painted blood red, were tongue-dampened and the pupils of her eyes had become enormous.

"It's a systems monitor that analyzes this and that and backs up the brainboard controls. It also has a deadman switch. If I drop it or if my hand pressure exceeds a preset level, the CE rig shuts down and a medic-alert squeal goes out."

She reached out tentatively to touch the handset but he moved it out of reach. In spite of having his eyes covered, he was not at all blind inside the awesome golden casque. "Don't be concerned about my safety. The thing works beautifully. Ready for a demo?"

"Oh, yes!"

"Here we go. Remember that what you see is no illusion, such as I might project with my ordinary gray cells, but an actual modification of matter and energy. I'll need to concentrate. You sit still and just watch."

She sank back onto her heels, her hands folded tightly over her breasts. The nipples were prominent and aching. She felt herself swelling and becoming moist as the anticipatory tension grew. Could he detect it? Probably not. His mind was completely rapt in his marvelous machine—

Oh my God.

Something was climbing out of the fire.

It was doll-sized, less than half a meter high, human in shape, but apparently composed entirely of flames. She could see its tiny features, its fingers, even its miniature male sex. It glided over the fender, not touching the floor, and bowed with comical gravity toward the two human beings. Then it turned about and lifted both fiery arms like a dancer posing. A charred chunk of wood some ten centimeters square popped out of the grate and floated above the manikin's hands. Rapidly, the charcoal shrank, glowing strangely blue as it hissed and smoked. When it resembled a black pea the fiery homunculus plucked it from mid-air and held it in both diminutive hands.

"Now for the difficult part," Marc said.

The flame-being appeared to be compressing the ball of carbon, squeezing it and kneading it until it shrank further and was lost to sight within the little hands. Then the manikin bent down, placed something very small on the floor in front of the hearth, bowed again, and whisked back into the fireplace where it disappeared.

The log fire burned as usual. Marc took off the CE helmet, exhaled a deep breath, and ran his fingers through sweat-dampened curls. A line of bloody pinpricks was stitched across his forehead. On the floor, something crystalline sparkled.

"It's quite cool now," he said. "You can pick it up."

In spite of herself, Lynell Rogers cried out, "It can't be! You couldn't possibly have done it." She knelt and retrieved the glittering thing, a sharp-edged octahedron less than two millimeters long that flashed rainbow colors in the firelight. "Good Lord—it is!"

Marc shrugged, grinning. "It's a diamond, all right. Very strange internal structure because I wanted it large enough for you to pick up easily. Take it and have it analyzed. Show it to your Dirigent. You might leave out the fiery sorcerer's apprentice, though. I got a bit carried away."

He set the helmet on the floor upside down, crouched beside her, and pointed out the crown-of-thorns electrodes inside the apparatus that had penetrated his brain. The wounds on his head were fast fading, healed by his redaction. At his suggestion, Lynelle opened her mind to his concise mental diagrams of the cerebroenergetic enhancer. Although Marc withheld critical technical details, the images were explicit in showing the CE rig's mode of operation.

"It's absolutely incredible," she breathed. "What do you estimate is the maximum energy output you might generate at a macro level?"

"That kind of testing will have to wait until the prototype is completed. This hat is only a crudely built demonstration model. It wasn't even operating at full capacity."

Lynelle Rogers shook her head in wonderment, studying the little diamond in the palm of her hand. "Incredible," she repeated in a whisper.

The Hydra struck with its coercion again: *Marc the fire is burning low. Put more wood on it. Now!*

He arose, pulled an armful of logs from the caddy, tossed them into the grate, and bent down with the poker to restore a brisk blaze. When he was satisfied that the fresh fuel had caught fire, he turned back to Lynelle.

And found her wearing the helmet.

"Christ!" he exclaimed. "What the hell do you think you're doing?"

Her graceful, elegantly attired figure was incongruously crowned and blinded by the heavy metal headpiece. She held the controller in one hand and the diamond in the other. Her lips were slightly parted and her mind said:

Marc darling come to me this way.

MyGod *NO* you crazyfool you can't—

Her natural creativity must have been enormous. Enhanced, it took possession of every extracerebral neuron in his body, paralyzing him, rendering him speechless. Momentarily, at least, he was unable to utter a farspoken cry or touch her with his psychokinesis. He might have broken the spell if he had called on the brute force of his coercion. Even creatively enhanced, her mind was no real match for his. But he held back. She offered no threat. What she wanted was glaringly clear, depicted in a dizzying series of erotic images that flooded his senses and ignited his imagination. What he had repressed, what he had denied now came alive with overpowering intensity. There was no anger or fear in his response, only tremendous excitement and need.

You see? she said, laughing. You are human after all. This will be very instructive very humbling and even though you are to forget the details of the catalysis the resultant will remain with you always!

Now come to me Marc.

Even at that point he might have withdrawn, sealing his mind behind a safe, impermeable barrier until he was able to regroup his faculties and regain self-control; something deep inside him was shouting a warning and urging him to do just that. But still he hesitated.

She lifted the tiny crystal.

The diamond, held before his eyes by two slender fingers tipped with gleaming scarlet lacquer. The diamond . . . seeming to expand until it filled the world with hot scintillation, the prismatic rays bathing him with exquisite pleasure.

He felt a delicious pain swell in the root of his being. Vital energies began surging up his spine in slow, ever-amplifying waves. His brain seemed to catch fire within a fierce, thundering rainbow. The crystalline lattice of the diamond was alive, piercing him, trapping him, becoming him. Crucified in light, his entire nervous system burned and screamed and sang, ultrasensitized to the point of torture. She was re-creating him and it hurt and it was marvelous and he wanted it more than anything in the world.

She was with him inside the diamond's kaleidoscopic colors. They were twinned crystals, conjoined and vibrating to inhuman harmonies. The anguish and joy were consuming him, bringing him willingly to the edge of death.

Why are you doing this? he groaned. How do you know me so well to use me to torment me to make me *want* this?

I love you, she said. I hate you. And some day my dearest I'll kill you in just this way.

Yes! he said. Oh, yes. Please.

Fool, she said from amidst the dreadful light, separating herself from him and abandoning him at the very brink. Someday, but not now. This is only to teach you who you are.

Alone, he fell willingly into the abyss.

The living diamond that was himself shattered. He came and all energy was spent and it was over.

Marc awoke. He was lying prone on the hearthrug in front of a grate full of dead ashes. The helmet and its accoutrements were on the floor next to him and the cabin was frigid and silent. He remembered nothing.

Pulling himself up, he muttered an obscenity. Every joint and muscle throbbed with pain. What the hell had happened? And what was the CE rig doing here, out of its pod?

He couldn't possibly have used it to . . .

God.

But he must have. The signs were unmistakable.

Cursing himself and consumed with self-loathing, he limped off to the bathroom. Puzzling out this piece of idiocy could wait. All he wanted now was a long, hot shower.

[13]

FROM THE MEMOIRS OF ROGATIEN REMILLARD

The wish Lucille Cartier made at St. Brigit's spring on St. Patrick's Day, 2063, came true. For five years the affairs of the Human Polity of the Galactic Milieu seemed to run peacefully, even though the Rebel faction continued to flourish and gained some distinguished new adherents. Human colonies grew apace, exotic-human relations continued to be cordial, and human philosophers and ethicists noodled away at the concept of Unity, making it more and more acceptable to the majority of operant Earthlings.

Rory Muldowney's attack on Paul was a nine days' wonder that was never publicized outside of Orb. A good many people took secret satisfaction in the dapper First Magnate's comeuppance, and I admit to sniggering over it myself. It's only human, after all, to enjoy the discombobulation of the high and mighty! But the Dirigent of Hibernia apologized handsomely once he sobered up, and no one believed Paul was actually responsible for Laura Tremblay's death—even though nasty comparisons to the demise of Teresa Kendall were inevitable. Once the brief hullabaloo died down, Paul carried on his official duties effectively and efficiently.

However, he may have subsequently vetted the mental health of his mistresses with more care. No more ladies died for love of him.

The rest of the Remillards also dwelt in relative tranquillity during that half-decade, thanks largely to the fact that Marc had left New Hampshire and immured himself in his spiffy new CE laboratory in the Pacific Northwest, barring every family member except young Jack from the premises. Throughout this time Marc was very closemouthed about his research progress. He did some kind of seismic tinkering on the planet Okanagon that allegedly staved off a large earthquake, but the event was publicized only in a paper he wrote for *Nature.*

He socialized with the family only on special occasions and carried out his Concilium duties punctiliously but without distinction. Having turned Orb on its ear during his freshman outing, he now seemed content to rest on his oars. He apparently had nothing whatsoever to do with the Rebel faction.

The Dynasty was grateful but had no illusion that Marc's quiescent phase would last for long. They had reluctantly agreed to let the Remillard Family Foundation finance the lion's share of Marc's mind-boosting research since the alternative—he had threatened to move the project lock, stock, and barrel to Okanagon—would have given them no control over him whatsoever. As it was, from time to time Marc's associate Pete Dalembert, Jr., would unveil a formidable new piece of cerebroenergetic equipment to the admiring metapsychic establishment and license its manufacture by Remco Industries or some other commercial outfit.

The Concilium passed stiff laws regulating the use of creative CE. Certain viewers-with-alarm still voiced their opposition to the entire concept of artificial augmentation of creative mindpowers. But the equipment proved exceptionally useful in many different fields, and fatalities among its operators were within reasonable limits, so Marc was able to carry on his work virtually without interference. He fulfilled his promise to Dirigent Patricia Castellane by training numbers of Okanagon's Grand Master Creators in CE techniques. Their crudely metaconcerted modification of an unstable chunk of crust on that planet in 2066 was hailed as a geophysical triumph of the first order.

Jack the Bodiless absorbed every single academic discipline that Dartmouth College had to offer within three years of matriculation, and then turned his voracious, polymathic young mind loose upon other top institutions of learning. He simultaneously did clinical work with his Aunt Catherine, wrote a book on colonial economics with his Uncle Maurice, and coauthored a monograph on novel aspects of metaconcert design in collaboration with Denis. Although Ti-Jean rarely spoke of it, he also worked closely with Marc for many years, until his older brother's increasing obsession with the Mental Man concept caused a tragic rift between the two of them.

All throughout his life, Jack would continue to absorb knowledge as though it were an essential nutrient—and perhaps, to him, it was.

Ti-Jean was scrupulous in maintaining his simulacrum of physical normality in the presence of outsiders and grew up to be an attractive teenager, of medium height and build and pleasant but unexceptional appearance. His hair was usually black and his eyes vivid blue, and he ate and drank and peed and shat and breathed and perspired and slept and behaved just like a natural boy . . . some of the time.

We in the family did have to put up with episodes of adolescent experimentation, in which he concocted and wore every sort of body imaginable in order to "attain empathy with fellow beings," going about incognito behind his totally impregnable mind-screen. Sometimes he became female; sometimes he disguised himself as an adult. He took on the decrepitude of extreme old age and also inhabited forms that were diseased or imperfect so that he could experience the limitations of the human condition. He tried out exotic bodies, too, and even experimented with animal shapes—confessing to me once that he greatly enjoyed being feline, prowling the back fences of Hanover with my Maine Coon cat, Marcel LaPlume.

His one great frustration was his failure to make mental contact with the girl Dorothea Macdonald. Jack's stupendous farsight had been able to view her ever since he first learned of her existence by eavesdropping on his Lylmik examiners in 2063; but if she was aware of his persistent telepathic calls she never gave any sign.

"I'm positive she can hear me, Uncle Rogi," the boy complained to me, one day in 2067. He was at that time fifteen years of age and Dorothée was ten. "But she refuses to respond. I've got to find out if her mind really approaches mine in its potential, as the Lylmik hinted. They've refused to confirm or deny it, and they also say that they won't intervene to help establish communication between us. It's very frustrating. I've decided that the only way to resolve the situation is to go to Caledonia and confront her."

We were mooching around my bookshop on a rainy autumn afternoon in the company of Marcel. Jack was helping me to shelve a new shipment of carefully preserved, shrink-wrapped antique volumes that had just arrived—real rarities like *The Green Man* by Harold M. Sherman, a beautiful first edition of Lovecraft's *Beyond the Wall of Sleep*, a signed copy of Stephen King's *Night Shift*, and—rarest of all—a VG

1964 paperback copy of the mildly pornographic *Sin Service*, written under a pseudonym during his hungrier years by a science-fiction immortal. (If you wish to know who, the revelation is included in the price. Write for a brochure.)

"Have you considered," said I, when Jack began to detail his callow scheme to visit the Scottish planet, "that this little girl may not want to farspeak with you—or even meet you in person?"

"Why not?" Obviously, the thought had never entered Ti-Jean's titanic mind, any more than he had thought to simply write Dorothée a letter or call her on the subspace communicator.

I shrugged. "You told me she's not fully operant. She may think you're some kind of delusion: a nightmare . . . or even a ghost. You may be scaring the poor little girl to death farshouting her across the lightyears."

Jack was crestfallen. "But I've tried to make it plain that I'm a friend. That I only want to talk to her, to get to know her, because we might have a great deal in common—both being so out of the ordinary. The Lylmik have told me that I'll be nominated to the Concilium next year when I turn adult—the youngest magnate in human history! I'll be designated a Paramount Grand Master just like Marc. This little girl has the potential to become a paramount, too."

"Lucky her," said I.

But Jack wasn't having any of my cynicism. "Do you know how Dorothea lives? It's a crying shame. She's on this farm way out in the middle of nowhere on Caledonia, getting an ordinary education from satellite school and spending the rest of her time doing silly prosaic things like feeding chickens and cattle, weeding gardens, and patching holes in the farm's landing pad. She isn't being given the opportunity to develop her metafaculties at all!"

"Maybe she doesn't want to, Ti-Jean." I set the last book in place, closed the armor-glass door of the display safe, and set the combination. You can't be too careful in a college town.

Jack stared at me, aghast and disbelieving. "Doesn't *want* to? But why on earth not, Uncle Rogi?"

He trailed after me as I headed for my little office in the shop's back room. Mr. Coffee had just brewed a fresh batch, which I served out to us. We sat at my desk in two comfy broken-down chairs with the cat in his favorite spot, overflowing my OUT basket with his gray shaggy bulk.

"Not all humans are at ease with higher mindpowers," I said, careful to keep my deepest thoughts veiled. "I'm not—even after all these years. The powers complicate life. They're scary. Normal people will always be uneasy with operants. Even afraid of them . . . at the same time that they expect us heads to be more noble and altruistic than they are. The Milieu is more explicit on the bounden duties of operants: Noblesse damn well better oblige—or else! During most of my early life I tried to conceal and deny my powers. When I got wild one day in 1991 and demonstrated them for the first time in public, I had a nervous breakdown. I realized I'd never be able to pretend I was normal again. And it was horrible."

"But—that was before operants were accepted. Before the Great Intervention. Now things are different. You have no valid reason to feel uncomfortable with your operancy anymore. No one persecutes you. I daresay most of the customers who come into The Eloquent Page don't care what kind of mind you have—unless they're planning to shoplift one of the rare books. I've tried to tell Dorothea that she has nothing to be afraid of. Why won't she believe me?"

I drank some coffee before I answered him. Marcel was broadcasting requests for food, as usual, but I ignored them. "The little girl may be timid. In very young people, the emotions outweigh reason. It could frighten her to think she has weird powers that could go out of control. I know it used to scare the shit out of me! I don't worry about it now because I realize I'm only a low-class head. I'm not even adept—much less masterclass—so who gives a damn?"

Jack's voice had an odd timbre as he said, "Your creativity is much more powerful than you may realize. I could help you develop it—"

"God damn it, no!" I slammed my clenched fist on the desk in panicky fury, nearly upsetting my cup and terrorizing Marcel so that he levitated out of his perch and streaked to the top of a storage shelf.

"That's exactly the kind of thing that bugs the hell out of me!" I shouted. "*You* want to help me develop my powers. *Marc* wants me to develop my powers. Even the fucking Family Ghost wants me to get real and attain my full MP potential. Denis wants to redactify my love of the bottle and make me sober. Lucille wants to coerce bourgeois restraints into my skull so I won't mortify our famous family acting like a sloppy old loufoque. But I won't stand for it—you hear me?"

"Who is the Family Ghost?" Jack blurted out, mystified.

"None of your damn business!" I roared.

Jack said: I'm truly sorry to have reopened this old psychic wound UncleRogi please forgive me [comfort + love] I won't meddle with your private mind again.

"Bon, bon," I muttered, squeezing my eyes shut so I wouldn't break down and bawl. "It's not your fault. You are what you are and I can't expect you to understand how lesser mortals feel."

"I've been trying," he whispered. A strong young hand squeezed my bony shoulder. "I really have been."

I opened my eyes and let my gaze lock onto his. "Try harder. Let this poor little girl alone, Jack. For God's sake, forget about traveling to the Scottish planet and harassing her. She's only ten! Give her the chance to grow up before you force her to confront her operant obligations."

Jack retrieved the spooked cat and sat down again with Marcel on his lap, scratching the base of the cat's ears. "Leaving Dorothea alone . . . might be dangerous."

"Don't be ridiculous. Who'd think of harming an innocent suboperant child?" Another thought occurred to me. "Or is the Mind of the Galactic Milieu in such dire need of her talents that it might fall apart without her?"

"The Milieu needs every powerful loyalist mind it can get." Jack spoke with grave insistence. Marcel had closed his gray-green lynx eyes in ecstasy as the boy continued scratching his head. "Caledonia is one of those ethnic planets where the Rebel faction is especially well entrenched, and Dorothea's father and grandparents are firmly committed to separatism. She loves them very deeply. The longer she remains within their circle, the more likely she is to grow up prejudiced against Unity and the Milieu."

"Hogwash. If the kid's as brainy as you say, she'll make her own decisions no matter what influence her relatives try to exert. Nobody's managed to coerce *you*, buster."

"There could be another danger," Jack said. "If her mind is destined to be in the paramount class, she might be perceived as a threat by Fury and Hydra."

I felt my guts plummet. "Merde alors, I almost forgot about those salopards."

Neither the Dynasty nor Denis and Lucille had apprised me of the terrible events that had taken place on Islay; but I'd found out the bare fact of the monsters' renewed activities from Marc, who had warned me to be on my guard. He had also warned his little brother. Since no member of the Dynasty could keep data in their conscious minds secret from Jack's peerless redactive power, he had gently probed them from time to time to keep tabs on the Hydra hunt.

It had gotten exactly nowhere. If the Hydras were killing and feeding in their customary vampiric fashion, they were doing it so artfully that they left no clues.

Jack said, "Dorothea's mother, Viola Strachan, and her uncle and aunt were killed by the Hydra. Since Dorothea herself was left unharmed, we might logically conclude that Fury and its creatures didn't think she was a danger to them at the time. Perhaps her paramount potential hadn't yet manifested itself. But it might occur to Fury to look her over again now that she's older—perhaps to see whether any memories that might incriminate Hydra have resurfaced in her mind."

"That doesn't seem likely. Why bother? We know the Hydra-children have altered mental signatures. They could change their appearance even more easily. What have they got to fear from a little girl on a backwater ethnic world? They're probably hiding out on some planet in the Perseus Spur, fifteen thousand lightyears away."

"I doubt it," Jack said quietly.

"If you're really concerned about Dorothea Macdonald's welfare, you can always tell the Lylmik. They'll protect her."

Jack sighed. "You're right, Uncle Rogi. About everything. I promise to leave the little girl alone until it's possible for us to meet in a nonthreatening, casual manner. And I'll confer with the Lylmik on the other matters and let them decide what to do."

"Good," said I with bluff approval. "You want to go over to the Peter Christian Tavern for supper? They've got cheese soup and baked turkey drumsticks tonight."

Marcel meowed plaintively.

"I promise to bring back most of my share for you, Fur-Face," said Jack the Bodiless, and the big Maine Coon cat nestled against the boy's warm, inhuman chest and purred.

. . .

At the same time that Jack and I were tramping companionably through the rain in downtown Hanover, sheltered beneath the umbrella of his creative bubble, the nemesis of our family was watching us. How do I know? It told me, of course, during our confrontation when I—

No.

That revelation must await its appropriate place in these memoirs. For now, the reader will have to take my word for it that Fury was mulling over what Jack and I had just discussed in the bookshop and thinking these thoughts:

< A Second Great Enemy? How could I have missed detecting her with my sweeps? The Lylmik knew about her damn them and their mindscreen penetration is no more efficient than mine . . . OF COURSE you imbecile *It* would have known would have told Its colleagues would perhaps even have warned the child herself years ago. Is It guarding her overtly now? . . . No. I thought not. That lies even beyond the power of the Lylmik unless they were to meddle with the child's free will . . . AH! but I perceive Its crafty strategy the Second Great Enemy is hedged about with mundane protectors and complicating circumstances most of her faculties are still latent but she is invulnerable to coercive or metacreative attack by Hydra and yet a physical assault upon her now might pose an unacceptable hazard to my dearest little one . . . Let me think . . . Let me think . . . As she grows older a suitable opportunity to eliminate her will undoubtedly present itself. But on the other hand . . . Why did I not think of *that* possibility before? Not a Second Great Enemy at all but a potential new creature! As I once hoped Marc or Jack would be . . . Yes. She is a proud little thing full of vainglorious dreams. A suitable candidate for temptation once she is forced into operancy. But the Lylmik not I will accomplish that! All I need do is bide my time. >

[14]

SECTOR 12: STAR 12-337-010 [GRIAN] PLANET 4 [CALEDONIA]

22 MIOS AN FHOGHAIR [14 APRIL] 2068

The acorn Dee had picked up in the Edinburgh graveyard sprouted and flourished in the exotic soil of Glen Tuath Farm. She had planted it in a special place down near the river where the irrigation system didn't reach, a sunny meadow where the shy wild coinean burrowed and transplanted butterflies and bees sought nectar from unearthly flowers. It was a part of the farm where the nonborns and the hired farm workers rarely went, west of the airplant processing building and screened from the other structures by a grove of spindly, maroon-leaved fearna trees. The oak would dwarf them when it was full-grown and make a welcome patch of shade.

She had watered the young tree all through this unusually dry summer, even though the three fosterlings and Thrawn Janet told her she was wasting her time—that an oak would never thrive in this far-northern latitude. The tree had come close to dying after last year's severe winter, but Dee had redacted it secretly (just as she redacted her father when his depression became too painful) and it had pulled through.

Now the Harvest Month had come and she knew she could safely leave the oak to drop its leaves and go dormant; but since today was going to be very special she came out early and dipped a bucket from the River Tuath and gave the tree a last drink for luck. She was also wearing her lucky pin, the domino mask encrusted with rhinestones that she had brought from Earth.

Grian, the sun, was just rising over the Daoimean Mountains. A few streamers of mist sagged down the slopes and pooled in the little swales across the river. The sky had a pearly overcast, and faint patches of greenish pink drifted high in the air. The luibheannach an adhair were blooming in vast quantities. It was going to be a beautiful day on Callie, and Dee was eleven years old at last and ready to help with the airplant harvest.

She heard the *whoop-whoop* of the ready siren and ran all the way back to the pilots' locker room. Her father was out on the pad, already dressed in his flight suit, inspecting the waiting line of flitters. She waved to him and dashed inside. The place was crowded because Glen Tuath Farm was prospering and this season Ian Macdonald had hired four extra free-lance harvesters in addition to the three regulars. Her brother Ken, looking sad and dreamy as usual, was suiting up. So was the oldest nonborn, Gavin Boyd, who called out in a jeering voice:

"It's about time you showed up, Dodo! We were all set to take off without you. Since you were so late, Dad says I'm going to fly The Big Cheese after all."

"Ian said nothing of the sort," said Sorcha MacAlpin, one of the resident workers. She was a massive, kindly woman who strained the seams of her forest-green environmental outfit to the maximum. "You stop teasing your little sister."

"Aww. Would it make Daddy's Little Princess cry?"

"No," Dee said quietly, and that made Gavin's face turn red with anger. Ever since she had finished her flying lessons and Ian Macdonald announced that she would pilot the yellow flitter this year instead of Gavin, the big fosterling had been unbearably rude, putting Dee down every chance he got. He opened his mouth to make another cruel remark, but Dee's big brother Ken briefly touched Gavin's shoulder.

"Let her alone. You know the reason why Dad gave The Cheese to her. She's a better pilot than either of us, and she'll bring in more weed."

Gavin looked suddenly startled, as though Ken's light tap had hurt him. But he recovered in an instant and offered Dee a mocking salute. "Just try not to screw up too much on your first day out, Baby Dodo." He swaggered out, helmet tucked under his arm.

"Your brother doesn't mean anything," Sorcha said. "He's a wee bit jealous, is all."

Dee tried not to show her anger. In spite of the Caledonian fosterage custom, she could never think of sullen Gavin Boyd as a real brother. He was fifteen, two years older than Ken, and he had been hostile to her from the beginning. The two younger nonborns, Hugh Murdoch and Ellen Gunn, were more friendly, but they were Thrawn Janet's favorites rather than rivals for Ian's affection as Gavin and Dee were.

All five of the children worked hard at domestic and landside agricultural duties when they weren't attending the farm's tiny school, where lessons were piped in via satellite from the Education Center at New Glasgow. There wasn't much time left to play, and the fosterlings usually made it plain that they preferred their own company to that of Dee and Ken.

She'd tried to be understanding. It was hard being a nonborn—gestated in a laboratory from the ovum and sperm of anonymous donors, knowing that the only reason you'd been made was to help build the planet's population quickly. Ken had explained it all to Dee when she was eight and he felt she was old enough to understand: The two of them had been made during an act of sexual love between Dad and Mum, but the poor nonborns had only been *cooked*. Grownups tried to pretend that it didn't make any difference, but kids knew better.

"Let me help you with your lovely new flight suit," Sorcha MacAlpin offered. "It'll be harder to get into than that old baggy thing you used during practice. You know how the plumbing works, don't you? You'll be staying up all day long now, not just an hour or so at a time."

Dee blushed. "I understand." She had thrown off her jacket and Wellingtons and sat on a bench in long underwear just like the other pilots wore, putting on extra socks to pad out the boots of her flying kit, which were not as stretchy as the rest of the outfit. Mercifully, Ken and the men finished and left the room before Dee had to wriggle into the unfamiliar skintight silvery garment and adjust it with Sorcha's help. Ian Macdonald had bought his daughter a flight suit of the highest quality, the same type as his own. Gavin and Ken, being so much taller, had been economically furnished with adult castoffs. The nonborn boy had made no bones about his envy.

Dee looked herself over in the cracked and dusty old mirror above the washbasin and felt a thrill of satisfaction. Except for her size, she looked just like an adult, ready to do an adult's job. Children were ordinarily permitted to work only three hours a day outside the schoolroom, but during the harvest season an exception was made for those who lived on farms and enjoyed good health. Ken, who was still far from strong and prey to every mutant strain of cold and flu germ that came along, would have to return to home base around noon, when his aerial storage-craft was full. But Dee, who was as sturdy as a Sheltie, would labor a full nine hours just like Gavin and the grownups.

"There now, nic-cridhe! You look just fine. Very professional."

Sorcha clipped Dee's gloves to her belt and handed her the silver hard hat and mask. Following the female pilot outside, Dee felt a twinge of anxiety. Briefly, she turned inward to her mental guardian.

Please, angel! she begged. Let me do everything right today. Don't let me be nervous or do anything silly or stupid. I want Daddy to be proud of me.

The angel, as usual, did not reply. He had been silent for over a year now, and it probably had something to do with that awful Jack.

Jack was some kind of horribly powerful operant who had tried many times to farspeak Dee all the way from Earth. He claimed he was just a boy, but she doubted it. No child could farspeak such a long way. Dee had decided that Jack must be a person in league with Gran Masha and the latency therapists, trying to trick her into demonstrating her operancy. When she did, they would force her to go back to Earth. But Dee had been too clever for Jack. She never answered him, never gave a single sign that she even heard him—not even when the angel appeared in her mind and said it would be all right.

Jack finally stopped calling her, and the angel went into a sulk and wouldn't talk to her, either. Dee didn't want to believe that the angel was part of the plot; but he *had* told her, back in the beginning, that she would have to become operant someday . . .

She wouldn't! She was going to be as normal as she could, and keep on hiding the overt powers that had already escaped from their boxes. She used her healing only when it was absolutely necessary (to help Daddy and Ken, and when nice old Domhnall Menzies burned himself so badly in the processing factory during the last earthquake), and she farspoke her brother only when she had some really important secret to tell him.

Once, Dee had believed that farspoken thoughts were private. She knew now, from studying about telepathy after Jack began bothering her, that it took special skill to shield thought-messages from clever operant eavesdroppers.

Dee didn't know whether she had that skill or not, so she was careful not to take chances. No one was going to trick her into betraying herself, as she once had done with the man who called himself Ewen Cameron.

Never again.

The others were already climbing into their flitters, and Dee hurried down the tarmac to her own ship, the last in line. There were eleven brightly colored aerostats: eight harvesters manned by the adults, two larger bin-flitters piloted by Ken and Gavin, and the beat-up yellow machine combining both functions that Dee was going to fly. It was the oldest aerostat on the farm, the first one Ian Macdonald had ever owned and the one he always used for flight training. Because of its color and the wedge shape of its semirigid superstructure, it was nicknamed The Big Cheese.

All summer long Ian Macdonald and Sorcha MacAlpin had patiently taught Dee how to fly the venerable aircraft. Her lessons had taken place at low altitudes for the most part, and she had practiced catching buoyant drifts of degradable confetti rather than actual airplants, which were protected by law during the off-season. It was going to be much more tricky pursuing weeds that actively tried to get away! She would also have to learn how to cope with the pesky fairy-critters and watch out for sky-wolves and the dangerous torachan. Her father had promised to stay close by until she felt confident doing the work, and he alone would be dumping his accumulating harvest into her storage cells.

Sorcha gave a farewell wave as Dee ascended the boarding ladder of The Big Cheese. The compressor that operated the propulsion system and slurper of the aircraft was already humming, having been switched on earlier by the ground crew during the servicing period. Dee settled into the cockpit, closed the canopy, and looked up at the bulgy, much-patched yellow envelope, held within a rigid superstructure frame that was attached to the fuselage by a stout pylon. She fastened her safety harness. A seat cushion helped her see outside and pedal extensions enabled her to operate the floor controls. She put on the visored hard hat with its self-contained oxygen concentrator and fastened the mask. The breathing equipment was necessary because the luibheannach an adhair—the "weeds of the air"—lived mostly at altitudes between six and nine kilometers where the atmosphere was thin. The plants were also poisonous if one inhaled their concentrated essence.

But when the wee things were processed and their essence greatly diluted, they were the safest and most effective human aphrodisiac known.

Dee had learned all about human sexuality in satellite school; but it still mystified her that mature adults—apparently even including operants—were willing to pay extraordinarily high prices for weird chemicals like *that.*

"Glen Tuath Leader requests harvest team systems check and verbal affirm," said Ian Macdonald over the RF com.

Dee went through The Cheese's flight checklist swiftly, then verified her life support. One by one the pilots called out their affirmation and number. Last of all, Dee said in a loud little voice: "GT-11 checked and ready."

"GT Leader says lift-off in sequence via NAVCON. Today all work areas are preassigned and any deviation or hot pursuit of the weeds must repeat must be cleared with Leader. Torachan have been reported in the vicinity of Ben Fizgig, so keep alert." After everybody affirmed, Ian said, "Team enter NAVCON."

Dee put on her gloves and then hit the console pad that would transfer control of her machine to the farm's navigation system. Now she could sit back and relax while The Big Cheese mounted into the sky and flew automatically to the airspace it had been assigned to harvest.

As their ground-locks deactivated one by one, the flitters rose, buoyed by the hydrogen in their envelopes. A series of caged air jets with internal rudders, mounted on both the superstructure and the fuselage of each aerostat, controlled ascent, descent, and maneuvering. All working parts of the fusion-powered fans and compressors, as well as the pump that sucked the crop into expandable storage-cells in the skin of the envelope, were carefully shielded so that the highly flammable gases generated by the fragile, drifting organisms would not be accidentally set on fire—a disaster that might also ignite the hydrogen in the flitter trying to harvest them. This kind of accident was fortunately very rare. Aerostat envelopes were fireproof and had an internal quenching system. If the skin ruptured by accident or as a result of torachan attacks, the pilot could explode bolts in the pylon, separating the fuselage from the gas-bag. A huge parafoil would then pop out and lower the fuselage safely to the ground. Dee had practiced this maneuver on virtual video, feeling reassured by the knowledge that Glen Tuath Farm had a perfect aerial safety record. Its own machines were meticulously maintained, even those that were old, and Ian Macdonald only hired free-lance flitter operators whose standards were as high as his own.

Shortly after arriving at the farm, Dee had asked her father why airplants could not be harvested by ordinary flying eggs. At the time Ian was in no mood to be bothered, so instead of explaining, he told Dee to find out for herself. To Ian's surprise, the little girl found the answer by evening on the same day.

"Eggs have rho-fields all over their outsides," Dee told her father at the supper table. "That's how they counter gravity. A rho-field looks like a net of purple fire you can barely see. It can burn organic matter like airplants to a crisp if they touch it."

"And you, too, Dodo!" Gavin Boyd had said, with a wicked smirk.

But Ian Macdonald had silenced the nonborn boy with a stern gesture and asked Dee if she knew why sigma-shielded rhocraft could not be used for harvesting.

"Because the rho-field has to cover the whole egg, or it won't fly," she said triumphantly, "and the sigma-field has to cover all the rho-field to make the egg safe to touch. But then the person inside the egg can't harvest airplants because you can't usually make holes in a full sigma."

"Very good, Dorrie," Ian had said, without smiling. But Dee knew he was pleased with her.

"Everybody knows that," Gavin muttered. Ken, sitting next to him, gave him a sharp elbow in the ribs.

"Not every five-year-old," Ian said. He asked his daughter: "Did you call a satellite teacher for the answer?"

Dee shook her head. "I looked up the way inertialess aircraft work in the schoolhouse database. Then I figured it out."

"Well, don't that beat all!" said Thrawn Janet archly. "Looks like our little Doro's a real cackleberryhead. I s'pose you know all about how flitters work, too."

Dee flinched at the animosity radiating from the minds of the woman and the oldest nonborn. But instead of holding her tongue, she took a deep breath and said to her father, "I'm going to study about flitters. I'd like to learn to fly more than anything else in the whole world. Will you teach me, Daddy?"

"Yes," Ian Macdonald said curtly. "And the rest of you children, too. Just as soon as you're old enough."

"But *I'm* going to be your harvest foreman when I grow up," Gavin protested. "You promised, Dad!"

Ian surveyed the table with a thunderous scowl. "That was before Dorrie and Ken came to Glen Tuath. Whoever of you becomes the best pilot will be foreman—eventually. But that's years away. Now eat your supper. I don't want to hear another bloody word!"

Ian Macdonald kept his promise. First Gavin learned to fly and then Ken—though he didn't enjoy it. The other two children, Hugh and Ellen, disliked flying even more than Ken and quickly washed out. But Dee was a natural and had proved much more adept than either of the older boys. That was why she flew the dual-purpose Cheese this year while Gavin, in spite of bitter protests, was demoted to driving an unexciting aerial cargo-bin.

Dee fingered the controls gently while the autopilot did the actual flying en route to the harvest site. Her aerostat, the last in the procession, lofted higher and higher as the team headed northward, finally leveling off at an altitude 500 meters below the level of the lowest drift of airplants. The view through her polarized helmet visor was magnificent. On her left, she could even see the clearing in the tartan-forested mountains where the diamond mine was. She had only visited it once, and had been very disappointed to discover that the freshly mined stones looked dull and glassy, not even as bright as the rhinestones on her pin.

Flying as fast as the lumbering bins could go, the harvest team left the fjord, passed above the sharp-nosed cape called Rudha Glas, and moved out over the wave-pounded islets and reefs of the Goblin Archipelago. (Their official name was Eileanan Bòcan, which no one ever bothered to use. Dee had quickly found out that even though Gaelic was a required subject in school, Caledonians spoke Standard English most of the time, and their pronunciation of the ancient tongue was often strange and their usage ungrammatical. No one minded except a few ultraethnic fanatics.)

The farm's computerized tracking system had calculated that today the volume of airplants would be most dense in the area just north of the Goblins, where a thin stratum of smoglike volcanic ash from Ben Fizgig had spread out, providing a perfect concentration of nutrients that the weeds craved. One by one, the individual flitters were guided to their hunting grounds. Dee watched their images on her console monitor as they scattered over an area of 800 square kilometers. Finally, her own machine reached its assigned block of airspace and a mechanical voice said: "Glen Tuath NAVCON to GT-11. You have entered Block 4 of preassigned harvest area. Resume manual control of aircraft within two minutes or your aircraft will be inserted into a holding pattern."

"GT-11 on manual," she said, and felt a little shiver of joy as the control stick came alive. Block 4, which she would share with her father, was at the northeasternmost corner of the rectangular search area.

"You keep to the bottom of the box, Dorrie," Ian said inside her helmet. "Go easy at first. There's a nice cloud seven-pip-niner kloms high that should be showing bright and clear on your target display. See it?"

"Affirm, Leader."

"Go for it, lass. Sonas is àdh ort!"

"Good luck to you, too, Daddy," she said, and soared off in pursuit of the precious weeds.

. . .

By lunchtime, Ian Macdonald pronounced his daughter to be "more or less competent," but she knew he was really saying that she was very good indeed.

"I'm going to Block 3 now to help Aonghas," he said. "You eat your lunch and then carry on here. Remember to ascend to an altitude safely above the weeds before hovering, and be alert for wandering torachan. And don't forget to put your oxygen mask back on between bites of food. We don't want you blacking out."

"Affirm, Leader."

Her father's new black aerostat moved off to the west and was soon lost to sight among the small cumulus clouds that had begun to form. Dee neutralized the thrusters of her flitter and let it seek its altitude of equilibrium, rising among the swirls and drifts of aerial organisms, gently sucking them in as it ascended.

Individual plant species of Caledonian balloon-flora ranged in size from minute specks like red pepper to rarer things as big as apples that resembled masses of greenish soap bubbles. The commonest kinds of airplants had balloons the size of cherries or large peas, mottled bubblegum-pink and iridescent green. Photosynthetic organs provided most of the energy for their life-processes, and they also took up water vapor and gained essential minerals from airborne dust and debris. All airplants stayed aloft by means of thin-walled pneumatophores, float-chambers containing lighter-than-air gases. The "body" of the plant might hang from its balloon, or be embedded within the float, or spread over the pneumatophore's exterior like a weird growth on the surface of an odd-shaped little plass bag.

The luibheannach were highly sensitive to abrupt pressure changes in the atmosphere around them that might signal the presence of predators. When airplants perceived danger, special organs generated additional gases that enabled them to zip about under jet propulsion. The largest and most commercially valuable plants were also the speediest and most apt to drift around in a solitary fashion at lower altitudes. Dee had managed to capture respectable numbers of them this morning in spite of The Cheese's clumsiness.

Now that her flitter had reached the upper section of the harvesting space, blue and brick-red fairy-critters began sailing into view, feeding on the abundant smaller plants. The aerial grazing animals looked something like elongated little jellyfish with complex bodies and dangling branched tentacles, with which they gathered their food. Dee knew she was supposed to blast every fairy she encountered with her thread-laser, not only because they fed on the valuable airplants, but also because their tough trailing arms could clog the pump mechanism of a harvester, making it necessary for the pilot to clear the intake orifice by hand. This meant climbing out of the cockpit, up the pylon, and out onto the exterior framework of the superstructure, secured by a lifeline. Dee had practiced the maneuver often. It was not especially dangerous, only a tedious waste of time.

No fairies had turned up during her first hours of work. Dee had been glad, because the creatures were strangely beautiful and she felt squeamish about killing them. Now, instead of firing the laser, she urged the little animals to get out of her way.

"Shoo! Truis! Mach as m'fhianuis! Get lost!" *GO SOMEPLACE ELSE!*

As she formulated the final coercive thought, every one of the fragile grazers whisked away, leaving behind tiny puffs of vaporous "exhaust."

Well done! said her angel.

Dee gave a cry of dismay. What had she done? "No," she whispered into her mask. "I didn't!" But she did not dare to look inside her head to see if she had opened another of the dreadful boxes.

You did! the invisible angel crowed. *And about time, too! Your coercive metafaculty was ready to break out spontaneously, and that might have been embarrassing, or even dangerous.*

"I won't use the power again," she declared obstinately. "You can't make me. I'll hide it like I did the others and go on being normal forever!"

Don't be silly. You'd better tell your brother about this. His own coercion became operant over four years ago. It's not as strong as yours—but he's been using it very effectively to keep Gavin Boyd from hassling him.

"Oh!" Dee felt oddly betrayed. Why hadn't Kenny stopped the nonborn boy from being mean to *her*?

The angel said: *He did this morning, so that Gavin wouldn't spoil your first day of harvesting. Don't you remember? Before that Ken was afraid to. Don't be hard on him. Not everybody can be brave . . . Now go ahead and farspeak him. He's going to need your help in a few minutes.*

"Oh, all right! Now go away and let me alone! You're not fooling me at all. I know what you're *really* up to. You and that Jack."

The angel said nothing.

The ascending Big Cheese finally emerged from the last billow of airplants into a clear region nearly ten kilometers above the Caledonian surface. The cirrus veil was very thin and the sky overhead was nearly blue. Below, little cumulus clouds seemed to float like miniature marshmallows in a crazy mix of vapor that looked like melted pistachio and strawberry ice cream. There was no sign of any of the other aerostats.

Feeling rather glum, she unwrapped her peanut-butter sandwich, unhooked her mask, and took a bite. Oh, yuck! Janet had put bacon in it again, even though Daddy had said it was all right for Dee not to eat meat. Well, perhaps Janet just forgot . . .

Dee nibbled around the edges and discarded the rest in the cockpit's little fairy-incinerator. Then she summoned the position of Ken's aircraft on the console monitor. The labeled blip showed that GT-10 had already departed the harvest area and was heading back southeast over the Goblins at an altitude of 5.5 kloms.

Kenny?

Uh? Oh it's you is it.

Yes. Did you get a good load?

Jammed to busting . . . Don't you think it would be smarter if we switched to RF com?

No. Listen Kenny . . . my coercing faculty came online.

Troch ort!

I know you've got it too.

[Hastily squelched obscenity.] Well for chrissake keep a lid on it dumbunny or both our asses will be Earthbound&down . . . not that the idea seems so tumturning to me anymore. This place is the pits. More weird viruses than I can ever learn to redact away. If I lived somewhere with decent medics maybe I wouldn't be such a rotten sickie bréochaid. And it's stone boring here in wintertime. I miss AuldReekie something chronic never a dull mo in Edinburgh. Didja ever think that it might be *fun* bringing our powers up to snuff and having other operant kids for friends?

No! Don't even think about it!

[Envy.] Why not? *I'm* not ★★★ {**Daddy's Little Princess**} ★★★ like you.

Kenny please don't be horrid. I can't help it if—

AAAACK! OshitOJesusOmyGod . . . Dee!

[Fear.] Whatwhatwhat? Kennyanswerme! *Answer me!*

Thingstherearethings pokingholesBIGHOLES God THINGS inside my storagecells insideALLthe cells tearingthewalls letting the plants out—

Dee used all her coercion: *Kenny call Daddy now.*

Yesyesallright. "Mayday mayday GT Leader GT-10 has torachan!"

"Torachan!" said Sorcha MacAlpin's voice. "Mother of God!"

An anonymous voice cursed and abruptly cut out.

"Kenny," said Ian Macdonald, "be calm. How many storage-cells have ruptured?"

"The—the readout says twenty-seven. That's all except three!"

"I'm on my way, laddie. Go into hover mode. D'you hear me? Hover!"

"Dad, something's really wrong. The flitter is spinning around all crazy and—and I'm losing H-2 pressure besides venting cargo!"

"Roger, I'm coming," said Ian. "Sit tight."

Dee sat frozen in reaction to her brother's disaster. The torachan were uncommon and insidious floating organisms, resembling medium-sized airplants except for their distinctive grayish color. They had developed a unique defense against the predatory fairy-critters. If they were seized they extruded long augerlike spines that impaled their aerial attackers. Torachan that were accidentally sucked into a harvester might remain dormant; but if the storage compartment was tightly packed with weeds, sooner or later the torachan would be irritated enough to explode into frenzied activity, puncturing and slashing the tough plasticized fabric like little high-speed drill bits going through gauze.

Having even a single tora trapped in a storage-cell meant losing all of its cargo. Large numbers of them were sometimes able to cut through the reinforced inner wall of the gas envelope itself, releasing the hydrogen that provided lift to the aircraft.

Ken's bin-flitter had evidently taken on a cargo contaminated with hundreds of the things. One of the pilots had been criminally careless.

Dee said: Kenny I'm coming to help too Daddy's ship is faster but I'm a lot closer to you than he is!

She put The Big Cheese into a power descent. Once she was below the airplant stratum she went full-bore toward her foundering brother, continuing her telepathic reassurance.

Ken's voice rang out piteously over the intercom. The torachan were cutting all of his cargo-cells to pieces. He was blinded, engulfed in a billowing cloud of escaping airplants. Jets of hydrogen gas venting from holes in one side of the envelope caused his flitter to spin and wallow as it sank.

"What's your altitude and rate of descent, Ken?" Ian's voice was grim. "All that mess around you is futzing your ponder."

"Four kay high," the boy wailed. "ROD nearly two hundred meters a minute. Daddy—I'll crash into the sea!"

"Blow the pylon bolts. Do you understand? Cut the fuselage free."

"Yes . . . all right . . . Dad! It doesn't work. I pulled off the cap thing and punched the button, but nothing happened. And I'm going down faster! Three kay—"

"Sweet Christ," said Ian. "Use the backup. Far right side, under the console. You'll have to pry loose two safety clips to get the switch open."

Dee's mind's eye could see the sinking bin-flitter, its gas-bag nearly collapsed. There was a sudden bright flash, followed a moment later by a stuttering detonation. He'd done it! The fuselage separated and tumbled end over end, falling free of the cloud of weeds while what was left of the envelope drifted off. Ken screamed over the intercom. He was less than 500 meters above the surface of the sea.

Ian Macdonald's black aerostat came into Dee's view, flying in from the west. She herself was now less than half a kilometer away from Ken. She could hear her father's shouts of encouragement. The parafoil would deploy and bring the falling fuselage down safely—

Something colored red and white burst out from behind Ken's canopy. Instead of opening into a supporting mattress shape it streamed flat and fouled, its cords hopelessly twisted. The fuselage continued its fatal fall.

Help him, said the angel to Dee. *You can. Reach out and take hold of the fuselage with your psychokinesis. Steady it and slow it. Use your enormous creativity to thicken the air.*

Time stopped.

Dee saw a shrouded figure and two huge, glowing boxes. One was the golden color of a halide lamp and the other shone like an incandescent emerald. She seemed to be standing in a dark room in her silver flight suit with her hands at her sides, breathing the cool oxygen. There was silence. Nothing moved. Nothing in the world would move until she made her choice: her brother or herself.

It wasn't a real choice at all.

Kenny.

Two masses of colored light erupted in a dazzling flare and faded, giving way to an eerie seascape. The fuselage with Ken inside was close by Dee's flitter, utterly motionless. Scattered drifts of airplants halted in the gelid air and the waves of the sea less than a hundred meters below seemed frozen. Only Dee's mind was able to move.

With her PK she untangled the parafoil's lines, and then spread its fabric so the giant kite could fill properly. Time resumed and the world came to life once more. The waves leapt, the airplants swirled, and rushing atmospheric molecules filled the huge candy-striped parafoil. Dee held it and its suspended fuselage quite still until she was certain that the discarded superstructure frame with its rags of fabric had crashed into the sea. Then she made the wind blow. The parafoil carried Ken toward a flat little islet covered with grass.

The fuselage landed softly, rolling at an awkward angle because its landing struts were still folded inside their compartments. Dee reached out with her mind, collapsed the kite, and unlatched the canopy. The figure strapped inside lifted its visored head and stared up at The Big Cheese, which was slowly descending. Ian Macdonald's aerostat was a few hundred meters offshore, hovering just above the waves. He had seen everything.

Ken's unsteady voice in her helmet said, "Sis?"

You're fine. Just relax. It's all right.

"You did it, didn't you! You used your powers . . ."

She didn't reply. Moments later her own aircraft landed. She extended the boarding ladder. Two white sea mews that had flown off in alarm circled above, calling. Waves crashed on the rocks surrounding the little island. There were yellow flowers growing in the grass.

Dee pulled off her gloves and unfastened her mask. She climbed out of her aircraft and went slowly down the ladder, her muscles aching with stress. Ken was scrambling out of his fuselage, waving, as the black flitter approached the island and landed on the grass. Other aerostats were converging from the north.

There would be no way to hide what had happened. The flight recorder in Ken's cockpit would have logged every word, every maneuver performed by the disabled flitter.

Even its uncanny halt in the middle of the air.

For the first time she thought to ask herself how the miracle had happened. How in the world had she actually *done* that?

Her mental feats had been virtually instinctive, performed in a desperate response to her brother's peril. Could she do it again if she simply willed it?

She turned to The Big Cheese, stared at it intently, and ordered it with all her might to rise a short distance into the air.

Rise! she told the flitter. *RISE!*

It remained where it had landed, not budging a millimeter.

She tried again, this time focusing her volition on a rock near her feet. It was slightly larger than a potato. As she continued to stare at it and strain, it stirred slightly in its bed of soil, then fell back inert.

Dee sighed. She obviously had a lot to learn about metapsychic operancy. But she'd catch on eventually.

She sat down on the bottom rung of the aircraft ladder and waited for her father.

[15]

SECTOR 12: STAR 12-337-010 [GRIAN]
PLANET 4 [CALEDONIA]

35 MIOS MEADHONACH A' GHEAMHRAIDH
[28 AUGUST] 2068

New Glasgow, the rowdydowdy capital of Caledonia, had no robot taxis, and all of the manned groundcabs lined up in front of the modest hotel where Professor Masha MacGregor-Gawrys was staying looked deplorably clapped out and dingy. She considered calling for a chauffeured egg; but that would be costly, and on a cold, rainy night like this it would probably take forever to arrive, and she was already half an hour late for her meeting. It had been stupid of her not to insist on being picked up at the hotel.

Clutching the hood of her raincoat, she entered the first taxi in the rank. Two scarlet furry dice and a miniature sporran hung from the rearview mirror, and the windscreen ionizer was barely functional in the downpour. The cab was suffocatingly hot. Both safety harnesses in the passenger compartment were broken, nameless grunge littered the floor, and a pervasive odor combining fried fish with the driver's bodily effluvia assaulted her nostrils. Quad speakers that were unfortunately in excellent working order poured out a flood of raucous music.

The professor sighed. "Take me to the Granny Kempock Tavern. It's somewhere in the university district."

The scruffy old driver set aside the packet that held his fish and chips supper, chewed up and swallowed a handful of potatoes, and wiped his greasy mouth on his sleeve. "Ye're sure ye wanna go to Granny's, luvvie? It's a wee bit raunchy for a fine lady like yerself."

"Carry on," said Masha crisply, and let him have a brief sting of coercion. She had no difficulty compelling him to shut off the blaring stereo, but nothing could be done about the heater. Its control was broken. And that smell! Her nanocreativity was inadequate to obliterate stink-molecules, and she knew she would never be able to manage self-redaction of her olfactory glomeruli, a hopelessly delicate piece of work, because she was still space-lagged from her trip. And if she opened a window to air the cab out, she'd be drenched. Oh, well. She rummaged in her bag, thinking that it might help a little to suck a menthol lozenge.

Then she remembered she had left them in her room.

Miserably, she settled back on the taxi's rumpsprung seat to brood. She was not looking forward to this meeting. The principles of human liberty were one thing, revolutionary conspiracy quite another. I am a mild-mannered academic, Masha told herself, not an apprentice gunrunner!

If only she hadn't let herself be talked into this side excursion . . . But Tamara Sakhvadze had looked upon her granddaughter's trip to Caledonia on family business as a God-given opportunity to pass along the latest intelligence from Rebel headquarters on Earth to the stalwarts in the hinterworlds. Masha could not turn down the request of the desperately ill old woman, so she had agreed.

Worst of all, she was being forced to meet Kyle along with the others.

Heaven only knew what sort of a dive this tavern was. Probably one of Kyle's haunts, where he and his drunken normal buddies did their half-baked scheming and he cooked up plots for his scandalous anti-Milieu novels. New Glasgow teemed with low-echelon Rebels, notorious characters who proclaimed their beliefs stridently; but the more exalted members of the cabal, the operants holding high positions in the government, kept a lower profile for reasons of political expediency. They were wary of being seen together in places frequented by other operants and by loyalist normals. When Masha passed on Tamara's request to Kyle, asking him to arrange a special meeting with the Rebel honchos of Caledonia, Okanagon, and Satsuma, he'd said it was Granny Kempock's or nothing.

The taxi rumbled and bounced and splashed over potholed pavement, eventually entering a run-down quarter between the University and the waterfront along the Firth of Clyde, where the narrow and twisting streets had a quaint, Dickensian squalor. Masha felt herself relaxing in spite of her discomfort, her mind turning to thoughts of her rakish estranged husband.

Kyle Macdonald had been stunned when she called him on the subspace communicator and told him she was coming to Caledonia in four Earth months for the children. Evidently Ian had said nothing to his father about having discovered that both Dorothea and Kenneth were operant. As was required by law, Ian had reluctantly reported the fact to the authorities and then to his mother, the professor.

But that news was nothing compared to the second surprise Masha had sprung on Kyle. When she announced that her mother Annushka and grandmother Tamara had finally converted her to the Rebel point of view, Kyle was astonished to the point of incoherence. If only she could have seen the old reprobate's face as he gawped and spluttered! It would almost have been worth the hefty extra charge for SS com video.

The rain was starting to turn to sleet when the taxi finally pulled up in front of the Granny Kempock Tavern. Masha peered out of the taxi window, her heart sinking. "This is *it*?"

"As ever it's been, for goin' on forty year," the driver replied. "Ane o' the auldest groggeries in town. Mind the bustit kerb."

"Who was Granny—some kind of dockside madam?"

"Nay. 'Tis not a wumman atall but an ancient magical rock near the original Glasgie, on Earth. I saw it when I was a wee sprat. That'll be twenny-six bux."

Grimly, Masha gave him her credit card, then made a dash for the door of the dingy pub across a cracked and icy sidewalk. The windows of the place were so filthy that she could barely tell there were lights on inside. One of the door panes had been replaced by a piece of ill-fitted particleboard covered in Gaelic graffiti. A hand-lettered sign proclaimed:

TONITE!

SLIMEMOLD!!!

ALSO MUNGO THE TRON-DOODLER

She went inside and paused for a moment in the vestibule to dry her hair and banish the wet from her raincoat. She was not adept enough to fend off driving rain with her metacreativity, but this particular trick was easy enough, and harmless so long as no nonoperant was watching. If a normal had been present, Masha would have stayed wet rather than risk provoking envy by a gratuitous display of mindpower.

She poked her head into the fug and clamor of the barroom. A hulking youth, undoubtedly the second-billed Mungo, was playing "The King of Pain" with minimal talent on squealing electronic bagpipes. The tavern was jammed with young people drinking and talking and laughing. They were all nonoperant. Casting about, Masha failed to detect Kyle's aura anywhere in the mob. The tavern vestibule also boasted a rickety stairway with a sign saying FOOD and an arrow pointing upward. A chalkboard listed the day's specials: hogget stew, baked adag in cream sauce, and grilled rhamphorhynchus with garlic butter.

Yes . . . he was up there, sitting at a big round table in the far corner of the busy dining room with his Rebel companions, four men and a middle-aged woman. Kyle was bent over a steaming plate, feeding his face. The others seemed to have finished eating—or maybe they had not been brave enough to begin.

Keeping a firm hold on her shoulder bag, Masha climbed the stairs and made her way through the closely packed tables. Insolent students leered appreciatively at her and called out mildly salacious compliments in Gaelic. She sat down without a word in the single empty place across from the rumpled, tweedy figure of her husband and shrugged off her coat.

For a beat, the fantasy writer kept his head bowed over his plate of stew. Masha noted that he was eating with his old cap on, the lout. The other people at the table, all stalwart metas indeed, if one could judge from the clever suppression of their auras, watched the professor with an odd sense of amused anticipation.

Then Kyle looked up at her, grimacing in triumphant glee, with food all over his fine white teeth.

Masha gasped. "My God! Look at you!"

He was rejuvenated.

The operant Rebels began to laugh. Downstairs, the piper had done a segue into "Mull of Kintyre." Kyle took a gulp from his glass of stout, used his napkin, and swept off his cap, revealing a full head of wavy brown hair.

"D'ye like it, Maire m'annsachd? I'm fresh out of the tin womb and still wet behind the ears, and a few little items nobody can see aren't exactly up to snuff since the engineers had too short a time to finish the job. But it's a great improvement over my old bod, don't y' think? And I did it all for your sweet love's sake."

Masha was speechless. The regenerative treatment had nearly restored Kyle Macdonald to the brawny, handsome roisterer she had fallen in love with thirty-nine years ago. His skin was unwrinkled and his eyes were clear and unencumbered by droopy bags. The nose that had gone red and bulbous from overindulgence was once again a keen Highland blade. He appeared to have shed over four stone of flab.

The others at the table were still chuckling at Masha's reaction when a young waiter came up and unceremoniously flung a ragged menu in front of her. "What'll ye have, then?"

"Get this poor stricken woman a double dram of Dalwhinnie," Kyle ordered. "And the rinkie special with buntàta and a salad with oil and vinegar." He said to her, "You'll like rhamphorhynchus, lass. A Mesozoic-type birdie with a long tail. Fills the sea-gull niche here on Callie and tastes like chicken."

Masha gave a minimal nod, still unable to take her eyes off him.

"And for my other friends," Kyle instructed the waiter, "a round of Drambuie cheesecake! No beggin' off now, you villains. This is my favorite eatin' spot and you're steppin' on my corns just drinkin' and nae takin' a single mouthful. And how about some tea or coffee?"

Kyle's companions opted for various beverages and the waiter went away.

Kyle lowered his voice. "We'd best get the business over with, since three of our fellow conspirators, here, will have to be moving along soon to catch the midnight shuttle to the starport. You were a wee bit late arriving, Maire a gaolach."

Masha didn't apologize. She pulled herself together with an effort. "Is it going to be safe talking aloud in this place?"

"It is," said Kyle. "Only deadhead students and other low types like me come here. And even if it wasn't safe, we'd tongue-talk anyhow. I'm no operant and I'm damned if you longheads are going to shut me out of the confab. I'm here representin' the normals."

"Whether they know it or not," said one of the Rebels with suave good humor. "Let me introduce myself, professor. I am Hiroshi

Kodama, the Dirigent of Satsuma and a member-at-large of the Human Directorate of the Concilium."

"I recognized you, of course, Dirigent Director," Masha said. "I also could hardly believe my eyes. Your sympathy to the Rebel cause is hardly public knowledge."

Hiroshi's smile broadened. "Perhaps the Lylmik would not have appointed me to oversee the newest 'Japanese' planet if it had been."

"Now let me present Clinton Alvarez," Kyle said, "Special Assistant to the Dirigent of Okanagon. Pat Castellane couldn't come and I'm glad. Clint's a more congenial drinkin' buddy."

The blond and striking Alvarez nodded coolly. He had a smooth manner that was almost feline, and was dressed, like all of the others except Masha, in clothes much the worse for wear.

The other three quickly introduced themselves. The woman whose tatty rainsuit could not disguise her commanding aspect was Catriona Chisholm, First Deputy to the Dirigent of Caledonia. She was widely believed to be the designated successor to sickly old Graeme Hamilton, who stubbornly refused to step down.

Masha had also recognized the thin, bearded man sitting next to the First Deputy, even though he was wearing an incongruous tam-o'-shanter and wrapped in a voluminous old plaid. He was Jacob Wasserman, the Intendant General of Okanagon, a distinguished metapsychiatrist as well as the leader of his planet's legislature. The fifth conspirator was his opposite number, Calum Sorley, the fiery young IG of Caledonia, who had yet to be tapped for magnateship. His attempt to disguise himself as an impoverished student was somewhat negated by his designer haircut and a blue diamond pinkie-ring.

Kyle made a bravura gesture with his fork. "As you see, dear Maire, we have quite a collection of treasonous movers and shakers assembled expressly to hear the important communiqué you bear from dear old Tamara. And now, you may ask, why don't I stop haverin' and let you deliver it? So I shall!"

The waiter brought Masha's tumbler of Scotch and went off again. She tasted it and let her gaze rove from face to face, seeking clues to the minds hidden behind them. Only Kyle was readable, leaking semi-intoxicated sedition and renascent lust like a colander. The mental barriers of the others were tightly locked. Only the lingering hints of their suppressed auras betrayed them as stalwart operants—and the most formidable of all seemed to be Castellane's young henchman. Strange that he was not a magnate. As a professional metapsychologist, Masha kept tabs on the more powerful young minds in the Human Polity and had acted as an advisor when the Lylmik put together the last list of Concilium nominees. How had this remarkable young man escaped her notice? She decided she would have to find out more about Clinton Alvarez when she returned to Earth.

"First I must tell you some very sad news," Masha began. "Tamara Sakhvadze is dying."

There were exclamations of distress and sorrow. Kyle dropped his fork and sat stricken while Hiroshi Kodama lowered his head and took out his handkerchief. Only Alvarez seemed unaffected.

"My dear grandmother is a weary woman who fears for the future, and she has declined rejuvenation in spite of all the family's urging. She is more convinced than ever that we Rebels will eventually have to fight for our freedom, and she says she has had enough of war. She wishes us well and asks me to offer her apologies for being unable to take up the burden of a new lifetime."

"You must reassure her on our behalf," Catriona Chisholm said. "No one has been a finer exemplar of mental liberty than she. Tamara has earned the right to rest, although we'll miss her greatly."

Masha paused while the waiter set a plate of broiled white meat in front of her. It smelled tempting, but she found she had lost her appetite. The others were served their dessert and hot beverages and seemed similarly unenthusiastic—again excepting Alvarez, who tucked into the cheesecake with gusto.

"The second piece of news comes from my mother, Annushka Gawrys. As you know, she is the head of the Institute for Dynamic-Field Studies at Cambridge. Her people at IDFS have confirmed experimentally that Marc Remillard's enhanced-creativity equipment may indeed be modified to produce the so-called 'mental laser' effect."

"Losh!" exclaimed Calum Sorley. "Does the Concilium Science Directorate know about this yet?"

"Certainly not," said Masha curtly. "Not even Marc knows. Annushka had Severin Remillard filch the design specs from Marc's new lab. Severin was once a rather decent neurosurgeon and Marc has been consulting him occasionally on technicalities of brain implantation. A reproduction of Marc's latest model CE rig was built by Gerrit Van Wyk and Jordan Kramer under conditions of greatest secrecy. Both of them have wide experience with cerebroenergetic enhancement—as well as with unorthodox versions of the Cambridge lie detector. Producing a destructive beam of mental energy required only a slight modification of Marc's design."

"Excellent!" Alvarez exclaimed. "There'll be no stopping us now!"

Masha frowned at him and continued. "Annushka believes that creative CE is a perfect weapon for our self-defensive purposes—compact, mobile, and versatile. However, she asked me to remind you that the equipment will not be truly effective until numbers of grandmaster creators are able to use it in metaconcert."

"We'll get them," said Jacob Wasserman, showing small teeth in a foxy smile. "Okanagon alone has thirty stalwart creators in the Rebel camp. We'll get twice that number from the Japanese worlds, won't we, Hiroshi?"

Kodama nodded. "Most of the powerful creators on Satsuma sympathetic to our cause are still young. But they will mature. Atarashii-Sekai and Ezo have twenty-two stalwarts who may be suitable."

"Every year more concerned operants join the Rebel party," Kyle said, his eyes glittering. "When the time comes for the break—"

"It will have to be before the Human Polity attains its Coadunate Number," Clinton Alvarez said. He had an actor's voice, well modulated and deep. "That's a population of roughly ten billion, which we should reach in the early eighties. At that point, a vast metapsychic complexification will take place—if Milieu Unity theory is correct in assessing the evolution of the Human Mind. Other Milieu races have already experienced this so-called coadunation. It's not Unity per se. But in some ineffable way, a coadunate race is pressured *internally* to Unify—to make a quantum-style leap to a higher level of socialization. We must attain our independence before this complexification begins."

"That's an interesting idea, Clint," Calum Sorley said, letting his skepticism show. "I've studied the pros and cons of Unity rather extensively myself—but I don't remember running across the notion of an inevitable change in the human mental paradigm. What's your source?"

Alvarez smiled. "At the moment, it prefers to remain anonymous.

I've been analyzing the criticality of coadunation in some depth myself. I'll have a report ready in about fifty Galactic days. If you'd care for a copy, I'll send one on."

Jacob Wasserman blinked sardonically from beneath his tam. "I hadn't realized that Pat Castellane's new staff included psychophilosophers."

"The Dirigent is interested in everything that may affect the welfare of our home planet, Intendant General. She'd welcome closer liaison with you and the Assembly on this and . . . other matters."

"It's about time," Jacob grumbled. "The woman's spent so much time reorganizing, she's been practically incommunicado."

"That's about to change," said Alvarez easily. "The transition following the sudden death of the Dirigent's predecessor presented serious problems, but things are well in hand now."

"Wonderful," Jacob growled. "Then what do you say we talk some practicalities? We're going to have to build these new brain-blasters secretly, train people in their use, and spread them about where they'll be most valuable. That'll be expensive and very difficult to keep secret—at least on Okanagon. Even with Castellane and me in the Rebel camp, you have to remember that our cosmop world is a Sector Base for the Magistratum and the home of the Twelfth Fleet. In time, that last may work to our advantage. Owen Blanchard is packing the Fleet with Rebel sympathizers. But at the present Okanagon is simply not a place where clandestine factories or training facilities could operate for very long without being detected."

Hiroshi said, "I doubt that we could do much now on Satsuma, either, Clint. We are still a newly founded colony with an unsettled economy and serious geophysical problems. Less than a year ago we suffered a devastating earthquake in one of our principal cities, which was inadvertently constructed in a zone of instability. The city is going to have to be moved, at great expense. In addition, seismic analysis suggests that other areas may also be in danger. Satsuma will be swarming with scientists, inquisitive strangers, and exotic Milieu loyalists for a number of years."

"Plenty of isolated corners on Callie," said Kyle Macdonald happily. "Plenty of sympathetic folks, too! Now, you take the continent of Beinn Bhiorach, where my son Ian farms. Nearly half a million square kilometers with a total population of less than twenty thousand souls."

"We don't dare risk it," Catriona said, "so long as Graeme Hamilton remains Dirigent. His office oversees high-tech imports and exports. Graeme has vowed to make Callie self-sufficient, and he personally goes over balance-of-trade figures with a toothcomb. Sooner or later he'd twig to the fact that unauthorized manufacture of a sophisticated kind was going on. Building CE rigs isn't exactly a cottage industry."

"Hamilton should be persuaded to retire," said Clint Alvarez. "Then *you* would become Dirigent, and there'd be no problem."

"We don't know for certain that the Lylmik would appoint me," said the First Deputy.

"No," Calum Sorley agreed. "It's quite probable that Catriona would get the job—but the Lylmik are notorious for their unpredictability. You would have thought they'd replace Hamilton—but the old man's sticking like a tick. He can't take time out for rejuve, though, so he's bound to kick the bucket sooner or later when one of his dicky vitals craps out."

"Let's hope," Clint murmured, "that it happens sooner. We were more fortunate on Okanagon."

There was a silence. Operant insiders knew about the rumors that the late Dirigent of the cosmop planet had been murdered, even though the Magistratum had been unable to prove it.

Yes, Masha thought. I *must* find out more about that young man!

"Graeme is a kind and brilliant person," Catriona said, "and he's done a splendid job for most of his years in office. But there's no doubt he's slowed down. The Intendant Assembly has petitioned the First Magnate as well as asking the Lylmik to replace him. He could be gone tomorrow—or he may remain Dirigent for years. We can only wait."

Masha said, "There is one other piece of intelligence I have for you. Paul Remillard's sixteen-year-old son Jon is to be made a magnate at the next Concilium session. He'll be designated Paramount Grand Master, just as his older brother Marc was. But where Marc has only three metafaculties at the highest level, young Jack is paramount in all five."

"Och, if we could only recruit either of those superbrains!" Calum groaned. "Especially Marc. If we had that one on our side, we'd win any fight, walking away!"

"Marc may be suffering from multiple-personality disorder," Hiroshi Kodama said very softly. "And the abnormal persona within him may be a sociopathic fiend—a serial killer of the most atrocious kind."

"What?" Calum was incredulous. "Are ye joking, Dirigent Director?"

Catriona gave a shrewd nod. "You're talking about the Fury-Hydra affair, aren't you, Hiroshi? The Remillard family's 'worst-kept secret.' "

"Except among the Rebel operants," Jacob Wasserman commented. "But I thought the killers and their mysterious puppeteer had been dormant for over fourteen years."

"Hydra is back," the Satsuma Dirigent said. "It's killed again and then dropped out of sight, just as it did before."

"What the hell is a Hydra?" Calum was increasingly impatient.

Hiroshi continued as though the Caledonian IG had not spoken. "Adrien Remillard told me some time ago about the latest murders. I regret I cannot give you any particulars at this time." He glanced uneasily at Masha, wondering whether she knew the truth about her daughter-in-law's death. "Adrien's revelation came as a result of certain . . . imprudent attempts to recruit Marc Remillard into our Rebel faction. Adrien strongly advised that we avoid doing so, since Fury, the controller of Hydra, must certainly be a prominent member of the Remillard family and Marc is a very strong suspect. If Marc is Fury he could destroy our movement. We would never know whether the sane or insane persona was in control of his mind. Both Adrien and Severin have recommended that we make whatever use we can of Marc's brilliant CE research, but avoid taking the man himself into our inner circle."

"What the fuck are you lot talking about?" Calum exploded. "What's all this Fury-Hydra cack about?"

"Bi ad thosd," said Catriona, hushing him. "I'll explain it to you later." She turned to Masha. "The lad Jack: Has he indicated where his sympathies lie on the Unity question?"

"No," the professor replied. "Annushka says he's very cagey. Keeps his thoughts to himself and plays the prodigious innocent, skipping all over the map picking up advanced degrees as though he were gathering nuts in May, and spending a lot of time meditating. My mother has heard rumors that there may be some serious physical abnormality in the boy that he masks with his high creativity. She says Severin and

Adrien will neither confirm nor deny the matter. Given Jack's so-called 'miraculous' recovery from the genetic horrors of his infancy, some sort of teratism in the remissive state is all too likely."

"It will be interesting to see how Jack behaves at the next Concilium session," Catriona said, "when several thousand top-caliber operant minds are focused on him."

Jacob asked, "Is there any possibility that this totipotent little pisher could be part of the Fury-Hydra combine?"

"Adrien was emphatic on that point," Hiroshi said. "No member of his family believes Jack is involved in the killings."

"Then perhaps," Wasserman murmured, "one of our Rebel mavens who is adept at psychological subtleties might carefully sound the little momzer out."

Calum's grin was wolfish. "Go get 'im, Jake."

Kyle Macdonald had no interest whatsoever in Jack Remillard. He had finished both entrée and dessert and now ogled Masha in a manner that required no mind reader to interpret.

"Has this Jack indicated what profession he plans to follow?" Clint Alvarez asked the question offhandedly.

"Evidently not," Hiroshi replied. He stirred his tea, tasted it, and returned the mug to the table with a disappointed sigh before addressing Masha. "Kyle has told us that you are here on an exciting family mission, professor. You must be proud and happy that your two grandchildren have spontaneously emerged from latency into the operant state."

"My happiness is mixed, Dirigent Director. Because Caledonia's Metapsychic Institute lacks the facilities to train young metas of very high assay, I must take the children to Earth. We're leaving in two days. This will be especially painful for my granddaughter Dorothea, who is eleven. She's deeply devoted to her father, who is a widower, and now she'll have to leave him."

"Do the youngsters have masterclass potential, then?" Catriona inquired.

Masha hesitated, then finally said, "According to the preliminary test results done here on Caledonia, Kenneth appears to have Grand Master farsensing and coercing abilities. Dorothea . . . may have all five faculties at levels surpassing that."

"¡Puñeta!" Clint Alvarez whispered. "Do you mean she might possibly mature to be another paramount?"

Masha looked away. "Both she and her brother are to receive therapy and training at Catherine Remillard's preceptor establishment in New Hampshire, on Earth. It remains to be seen whether Dorothea reaches her full potential. Because both children will be lonely and confused, I've taken sabbatical leave from Edinburgh University in order to be with them. I may even assist in their therapy."

"Another paramount!" Calum was elated. "And this one a good Scots lassie instead of a fewkin' Yank-Froggie Remillard!"

"Oh, for heaven's sake," said Catriona, rolling her eyes.

"New Hampshire . . . " Clint Alvarez seemed to be thinking deeply. "The home ground of the Remillard Dynasty. You might turn up some information important to our cause during your stay, professor."

Masha appeared to be studying the grubby tablecloth. "I'll continue to do whatever I can."

"Get as close to Catherine as you're able to." Jacob spoke urgently. "She's the most private member of the family. Not even Adrien and Severin know how she stands with respect to Unity."

Masha nodded, and then they sat without speaking for several minutes, the mental façades of the operants adamant and that of Kyle Macdonald leaking maudlin sorrow, for he now realized that Masha would be leaving the Scottish planet almost as soon as she had arrived. Catriona sipped her mint tea pensively. Alvarez finished his cheesecake and then ate Wasserman's. Jacob huddled inside his plaid with the tam tipped down nearly to his nose, looking like a trapdoor spider in ambush. The waiter came, slapped down a single bill, and ambled off.

From the floor below, a monstrous bass chord thundered out of amps cranked up to the max and settled into the teeth-jarring 16-beat rhythm of neutronium rock. The foundations of the tavern trembled and the inmates of the barroom applauded, whistled, and screamed. Slime Mold was beginning its set.

Hiroshi lifted his voice above the din and asked Masha, "Are there any other things you would like to tell us, professor?"

She shook her head. "Remember that I'm still fairly new at this game. Annushka let me attend Rebel meetings on Earth for less than half a year, even though I passed my 'entrance exam' last winter." She shuddered. "That Cambridge mechanical mind-prober is a devilish thing. I was a total wreck for weeks afterward."

"But ever so blithe and bonnie now," her estranged husband said in a broken voice. "Maire, Maire, mo chuid d'en t-saoghal. Ach tha uaibh falbh!"

To her intense annoyance, Masha found she was blushing—and that wasn't all—at the Gaelic endearment and his sorrow at her leaving him.

Damn Kyle for looking at her with those woebegone calf's-eyes! The last thing she needed was to have the old passion force its way back into her carefully ordered life.

Ah, but see what a precious pair the two of them made! Rejuvenated, Kyle Macdonald was magnificent, even in his worn-out jacket, frayed shirt, and the limp tartan tie with fresh stains of hogget stew. There she sat with her perfect makeup and her auburn hair neatly arranged, the quietly expensive suit she wore a complete contrast to her young husband's dashing seediness. The two of them were so unalike they were two poles of a magnet, inevitably attractive to each other as they'd been so many years before . . .

Masha damned her betraying body that knew what it wanted. She brought herself under control but she knew that Kyle had already caught her out, discovering her vulnerability through that concupiscent ultrasense even nonoperant men possessed. In an instant his melancholy vanished, giving way to perfervid hope. The sexual tension building between them was becoming as palpable as the grinding music assaulting their eardrums.

Hiroshi Kodama rose from his seat and inspected the check. "Please allow me this favor," he shouted. "I have brought plenty of cash. Shall we say our adieux outside? Otherwise we may have to resort to farspeech after all."

He put down a neat stack of durofilm money while the others quickly got up and donned their outerwear. Kyle insisted upon helping Masha into her raincoat, behaving with the utmost decorum. They trooped downstairs and out into the appalling weather. When the heavy old door closed, Slime Mold's musical efforts were still audible—but the decibels no longer approached the near-fatal range.

Sleet had turned the sidewalk and street into a grubby skating rink of black ice. Since nobody except themselves was there to see, Jacob Wasserman erected a psychocreative umbrella above them all and adjusted the ice's coefficient of friction. He folded up the huge plaid he had wrapped himself in and gave it back to Kyle.

"It's been a great pleasure meeting you, Professor MacGregor-Gawrys," he said, taking hold of Masha's soft hand in his sinewy one. He was wearing a shabby scarlet sweat suit that matched the tam. "Keep your courage up and take good care of those grandchildren of yours and Kyle's. Be sure they get the proper kind of mental nurture."

"At the appropriate time, I'll certainly try to convert Kenneth and Dorothea to our Rebel cause. And anyone else I can influence."

Hiroshi bowed to her. "We're fortunate to have such a distinguished new comrade. I look forward to meeting you again at the Concilium session, Masha. I would like you to meet my own dear wife and children."

Kyle looked at his antique windup wristwatch and cursed. "You offworlders are going to miss the Killiekrankie shuttle if we don't egg out of here right now. My aircraft's in the alley around back. It'll carry four."

Then Kyle realized what he had just said. Wasserman, Kodama, Alvarez, and him! There was no room in his damned old Porsche egg for anyone else. "I—I'm afraid the rest of you will have to call taxis." He looked at Masha despairingly. "See you again sometime, luv."

A totally unexpected pang of disappointment stabbed her, and she was certain that the dismay must have shown on her face. She was scheduled to take the children to Earth in two days. There was enough time for the flight to and from Beinn Bhiorach, but none to spare.

"So very kind of you to volunteer to fly us, Kyle," Hiroshi said. He gestured skyward with a gloved hand. A glint of humor shone in his eye. "But we would not dream of imposing on you. Fortuitously, I managed to coerce two egg-limousines into providing us with transport. And here they come. Perhaps you would like to take Masha back to her hotel."

A miracle! The writer and the professor stood side by side in the freezing rain (the creative umbrella having been abolished for prudence's sake) as two luxurious rhocraft materialized out of the torrent like ghostly illuminated Easter eggs and landed without a sound on the icy street. Hiroshi, Clint, and Jacob climbed into one and Catriona and Calum got into the other. An instant later the aircraft were gone, leaving Kyle and Masha alone together.

"Come on!" he cried, and grabbed her hand. They skidded and slid through a dark gangway, past disposal units, dustbins, and heaps of rubbish covered with a gleaming, glassy shell. His Porsche egg was waiting in the mews, encrusted with ice nearly a centimeter thick.

"Allow me," said Masha. Her creativity was feeling distinctly better. She pointed a finger at the frozen lockpad and a faint beam of metapsychic energy shone forth, melting the icy covering. Kyle poked through the resulting hole and quickly tapped out the DEFROST and OPEN codes. Within moments the door gaped with a tinkle like breaking crystal.

He tossed the bundled plaid inside and they fell in after it, laughing. He slammed the door behind them, lit up the rho-field, and the rest of the ice crust vanished in a great cloud of steam.

"My place," he said, "or yours?"

"I'm out of my mind," she wailed. "Oh, you great gowk! I can't believe this—"

He opened the console storage compartment. "And what, to my wondering eyes, should appear?" He extracted a vial of clear plass and held it before her face. There were greenish-pink spherules inside. "But some poppers of screw-weed for you and me, dear!"

"Hah! You never *used* to need such things."

"You're right!" He tossed the vial aside, seized her, and kissed her until the two of them half suffocated.

"For God's sake—not here!" she moaned. He was tearing open her raincoat and fumbling at her blouse.

With difficulty, he controlled himself. "High in the stormy sky, then! Into the backseat with ye while I get 'er up!"

"I think," she said primly, "that you already have." They both howled with laughter and collapsed into another embrace.

A sobering thought struck her and she pushed him away. "The children! Dorothea and Kenneth—I hired an egg to fly me to Ian's farm tomorrow. It'll be at the hotel at five in the morning and we'll have to—"

"No we won't," he bellowed, turning away from her to the rhocraft console. "I'll cancel the bugger and take ye myself!" He plucked the command microphone out of its clip, called up a map reference, then barked out a flight plan. The Porsche lofted into the sky with inertia-less ease: one moment they were in the sleet-clogged alley and the next they were arrowing toward the black stratosphere.

"But, my things—" she protested.

He pressed some buttons and the front seat metamorphosed, merging with the rear banquette to form a single flat padded surface. He began to hum "Roamin' in the Gloamin'."

"Kyle, this is madness!"

"What's the name of the transport service you hired?" She told him and he transmitted the canceling message. "We'll get other clothes and all the rest on the way to Beinn Bhiorach." He shook out the big length of tartan wool, singing:

> *"What a wondrous time we had on that old MacGregor plaid,*
> *Oh, it's lovely roamin' in the gloamin'!"*

"Nach bu tu an t-urraisg," she whispered. "What a fool you are!" And came to him.

[16]

SECTOR 12: STAR 12-337-010 [GRIAN] PLANET 4 [CALEDONIA]

36 MIOS MEADHONACH A' GHEAMHRAIDH [29 AUGUST] 2068

<Dody! Dody, lass, it's me.>

Mum? *Mummie?* But . . . you're dead.

<Death is only another kind of life. You know that. I'm alive in heaven—in the All in all and outside it as well. I exist beyond the matrix fields and also within them. I'm real and I want very much to talk to you now that you've become operant.>

This is a dream, isn't it.

<Some dreams come entirely from your own imagination. This one is different. I'm really, truly talking to you. My image comes from your memories because I have no physical body anymore, but my *self* is real.>

Then you're not like my angel.

<Your [apprehension] what?>

My angel. [Image.] He's a preprogrammed mental response who acts as a kind of psychic counselor and guide to my metafaculties. Not a real person. But he was installed by somebody real.

<Who, Dody?>

I don't know.

<*It's very important that I know who!*>

Mum, please don't do that! You can't coerce me like you did when I was a baby.

<No, of course I can't. [Remorse + affection.] I'm so sorry, Dody. You're a big girl now, an outstanding operant . . . or you will be when your training is complete. It was all such a surprise to me. I knew you had strong latencies, but I never dreamt you had paramount potential.>

What's that?

<The preceptors on Earth will explain it all to you. It means that your mind is going to be very, very powerful. I'm so happy and so very proud of you.>

. . . That's why you came?

<I'd like to be close to you again. To help you and advise you and be your friend. I love you so very much. Much more than your Dad does. He can't understand how it feels to have metapsychic powers. When I was alive, he was afraid of me because of them. Now he'll be afraid of you, too, and stop loving you.>

No he won't! I've . . . redacted some of his fear away. He doesn't know how to show love very well because that's the kind of person he is. But he loves me as well as he can, and I love him.

<Yes, of course. But *normals* can never fully understand the way we True People think and act. We can do so many things that are impossible for them. There are marvelous experiences ahead of you, Dody. You can't imagine how exciting your life is going to be—>

I wish I could stay here! I wish I could have kept the powers hidden.

<Dody, you're being silly. Spend your whole life on this lonely farm, working with coarse-minded itinerant harvest hands and cloddish nonborns? Gavin Boyd hates you, you know. He was your father's favorite before you came. Janet Finlay doesn't like you, either. She wants your father to marry her, and she thinks you disparage her to him behind her back.>

I don't! I never did such a thing!

<Well, *we* know that. But if you stayed, she'd be more and more unkind to you the older you got, and Gavin would be even worse . . . No, it's a good thing you're leaving. Just bide a wee bit and you'll see I'm right. Your brother's glad to leave the farm, isn't he? Ken's always been a sensible lad>

Dad wishes . . . that Kenny had been like Gavin. Strong and outspoken. But he never treats Kenny badly, and he does love him.

<Ken will be happier on Earth, using his metapsychic powers for the good of the whole human race. And so will you. Farming is only an occupation—something any normal can do. But metas have vocations! Do you know the difference?>

Yes. A vocation is when a person is called to do something important.

<Exactly! Oh, Dody, I'm so very glad that you have a vocation. I'll come and talk to you about it often and help you when you face hard decisions.>

Mummie, that would be nice. But I wish you wouldn't for a while. I'm all mixed up inside—

<I know. My poor baby. That's why I want to help.>

I have to work it out for myself. [Obstinacy.] Otherwise it won't be . . . done right.

<But I love you! I want to be with you now! Be your special friend.>

Now that I'm operant.

<Yes, dear.>

Will you be Kenny's friend, and come into his dreams, too?

<Well, I'd certainly like to. It would depend on whether Ken really wanted me. Whether our minds were consonant—whether we really fit together. I'm positive about you and me, Dody, and we'll see about Ken. For now, it would be best if you kept our dream-talks a secret. This is a very special privilege I've been given, coming to you. Because our talks are so unusual, some people might misunderstand them. Even Ken.>

Mum, I want to ask you something. I hope you won't be angry.

<Of course not, darling.>

Did Jack send you?

<*Jack?*>

He's a person who's tried to bespeak me. Not lately, but a while ago. His mind is so powerful that it frightened me, and I refused to answer him. He says he's a boy, living on Earth. Do you know him? Is he the one who told you I was operant and sent you to me?

<I know Jack. He doesn't know me and he didn't send me. He's . . . a dangerous person, sweetheart. I'm very relieved that you ignored his calls. Pay no attention to him at all.>

I'm glad I did the right thing.

<Listen carefully, Dody. Jack wants to get control of powerful operant minds and make them his slaves. He pretends to be friendly and kind, but he's actually a liar and a very wicked person. Never let him into your mind under any circumstances! Oh, dear lass, thank God I was able to warn you [solicitude + fear].>

Don't worry, Mum.

<I must go now. It's nearly time for you to wake up and there are so many things you must do before you leave Glen Tuath. Goodbye, my dearest little daughter. I'll come and talk to you again soon. There are wonderful secrets I have to share with you. Marvelous things! Goodbye, Dody dear.>

Goodbye . . . Mummie.

A dream?

Dee opened her eyes. Her room was still winter-dark, but the clock on her nightstand said 6:00 A.M. Time to get up for breakfast. Then she would have to do her last chore, bringing feed to the cattle and horses in the lower pastures. How she'd miss Pigean and Cutach! . . .

What kind of a dream?

. . . She'd make a brief stop at the schoolhouse for the fleck with her transcript, then come back to the house and finish the last of the packing so she'd be ready when Gran Masha arrived . . .

A worrying dream. About what?

. . . It was going to be strange, living on Earth where a day was twenty-four hours rather than twenty-six. And the months would be all different, too, because Earth's moon went through its phases faster than Ré Nuadh. Not even the year would be the same length. She could hardly remember what life on the Old World was like . . .

Never mind that! What was in the dream?

. . . All the trees would have green leaves, and the grass would be green, and the sky would be blue rather often, there'd almost never be earthquakes, and—

Stop that, mind.

The unwanted thoughts that had been flooding her head shut off as she finally exerted self-coercion. She was finally able to concentrate.

The dream had been very odd.

What had it been about? Why couldn't she remember? It was important, she was sure of it.

Slowly, Dee crawled out from the warm bedclothes, lowering her feet to the carpeted floor. She waited before telling the room lights to turn on, went to the window, parted the drapes, and looked out.

It had snowed during the night, the first snowfall of the winter. The rocky knoll on which the farmhouse stood was covered with spotless white, like a plumped-up pillow, with a twisting line of small lights marking the buried pathway and steps. No one had turned on the melting grids yet. The landing pad was a smooth white tablecloth and the two eggs parked outside the hangar had fat white berets. Exterior lights mounted on the stock barn, the factory, and the utility buildings made yellow-orange pools on the unbroken snow around them. More lights twinkling through the skeletal trees indicated that Domhnall Menzies and his wife Ciara Brown were up. Theirs was the only inhabited cottage at this time of the year, when most of the airfarm employees returned to Grampian Town or Muckle Skerry until the next harvest season . . .

The *dream*!

Why was she having so much trouble concentrating? It was as if her mind rebelled at furnishing her with the memory she demanded.

Softly, she said aloud, "Angel, help me."

And then she remembered.

Staring down at the whiteness, she recalled the figure she had seen so clearly in the dark of her mind. Her mother, Viola Strachan, wearing the same outdoor clothes she had worn on the day of her death, smiling at her and speaking. Speaking urgently about . . . what? An icy chill seemed to strike at Dee through the triple-glazed window. She hugged herself, shivering, and addressed her old mentor with growing fear.

"Angel, was that really Mum in my dream?"

No.

"I didn't think so. The aura was wrong. What she said was wrong. Who was she, and what did she really want?"

The person who bespoke you is named Fury. It is neither a woman nor a man—only a mind. A mind overflowing with rage against the entire universe and its Creator. In some ways, Fury is exceptionally powerful. Besides insinuating itself into your dreams, it can farspeak across interstellar distances—

"Like that awful Jack!" Dee wailed.

Fury is not Jack. It hates Jack and is afraid of him, as it is beginning to be afraid of you. Fury is the one who controls the Hydra.

"The monster who killed my mother?"

Fury is the one who really caused the death of your mother and uncle and aunt.

It told Hydra to kill them. Without Hydra, Fury is nearly helpless. This is its great weakness. Almost always, it must act through Hydra except when it interfaces mind to mind.

"This Hydra . . . there are four of them! I know it. I saw them when Mummie and Aunt Rowan and Uncle Robbie died."

Yes. Fury's great physical power results from the four Hydra minds working in metaconcert, as Fury has taught them. Fury's ultimate goal is the destruction of the Galactic Milieu, and for this it will require other stalwart helpers besides the Hydra-units.

"But why does it want to destroy the Milieu?"

It schemes to establish a new galactic confederation, which it will rule. It hopes to trick you into doing its work, just as it once tricked Hydra.

"How can I make it let me alone?" Dee cried.

Now that you are aware of its mental signature and pattern of metapsychic emanation, you will be able to shut it out of your dreams if you wish. But since you are a brave and resourceful girl, you might wish to consider something else.

"What?" she asked suspiciously. She left the window, called on the lights, touched the bed-making button, and began to get dressed. The angel seemed to be thinking things over. Finally he said:

You might let Fury continue to come to you.

"Let that awful thing that pretended to be my mother into my mind? Angel, have you gone crazy?"

This alternative course of action would be somewhat dangerous. But you are in a unique position to help save the Milieu from this monster. At the present time Fury does not want to harm you. It would rather convert you. You see, Fury cannot easily coerce people into doing its bidding. The Hydra can exert very strong coercion for short periods of time, but that would be no help in getting you to become a follower of Fury.

"I see . . . It would like me to become its disciple of my own free will."

That is correct. But if you resisted it tactfully—while at the same time gaining its confidence and encouraging it to reveal the details of its scheme to you—you could help destroy it.

Destroy her mother's killer! Could she really do such a thing?

"How?" She had put on cord pants and a heavy shirt, work clothes she would not be taking with her to Earth, and now she went to her dresser for a fresh pair of wool boot socks. "If Fury is only a mind, it must be as indestructible as—as an angel!"

Not quite. Fury's mind shares a human body with a second mind that is unaware of its evil companion. I do not know whose brain Fury hides in and neither does anyone else. Not even the Lylmik know. If they did, then the monster could be destroyed.

"By the Lylmik?"

No. By the Remillard family. Acting in metaconcert, they would have the power to kill Fury. And the obligation to do so. Because this much is known about the monster: it is the product of a Remillard mind.

Dee paused in the act of putting on her thermal boots. "I've heard of them. The First Magnate belongs to the Remillard Dynasty. And Dad says Gran Masha will be taking Ken and me to an operant training institute run by one of the Dynasty women named Catherine . . . So if I discover any important clue about Fury, I'm to tell the Remillards?"

No! Under no circumstances. You will tell me, and I will see that the family is notified.

Frowning, Dee combed her hair and began to braid it into a single plait. "I—I suppose if Fury pushes me too hard, I can always shut it out of my mind."

You could shut it out right now without too much danger to yourself. Later, closing your mind to Fury would probably rouse its suspicions. It might decide you were a threat to its plans and attempt to kill you. You must understand this clearly before you agree to my suggestion. I am confident that you will succeed—but there is danger.

Danger, she thought, but not much satisfaction. Fury could harass her for years without her being able to learn anything useful! On the other hand . . .

Guiltily, Dee looked over her shoulder in the mirror, half expecting to see either the tall figure of Ewen Cameron or the shrouded apparition that spoke with his voice, expressing stern disapproval of the startling possibility that had just sprung into her mind. But there was nothing reflected there except her own self and the familiar furniture of her room.

The angel was no more able to read her secret thoughts than Fury was. He would not be able to stop her from—

The small, heart-shaped face with the intent hazel eyes turned to a mask of stone.

"I'll do as you suggest, angel. I'll be very careful."

Good. Call on me if you require advice.

She nodded, and the angel was gone.

Dee opened the jewelry drawer of her dressing table. The pieces she had made herself with real gold and silver and semiprecious stones were packed in her trunk, ready for the trip to Earth. Only Grandad's pearls, which she was going to wear on the starship, and the old rhinestone pin remained, glittering in the shadows. She fastened the diamond mask to her shirt and smiled.

Breakfast at Glen Tuath Farm was unusually quiet. Gavin Boyd was unable to hide his triumph; with Dee gone, he would once again be cock of the walk. Hugh Murdoch and Ellen Gunn, the other non-borns, ate their porridge, smoked goose breast, and hot fruit compote with resentful expressions, knowing that they would now have to do Dee and Ken's chores as well as their own. Ian was more dour than ever, ignoring Thrawn Janet's attempts at conversation. The domestic manager was in a sunny mood, clearly overjoyed to be rid of the two young flies who had infested her ointment for the past six years.

When the children finished their meal and Ian left the table to go to his office in the factory, Janet gave out the work assignments as usual.

"Gavin, Domhnall will need your help overhauling the broken animal waste conveyor. You go meet him in the stock barn. Ken, you finish putting in the new section of melting grid on the school walk. Hugh, do the regular monthly maintenance on the fairy-gun and be danged sure you wear your safety harness when you're up on that roof. Ellen, sort the clean laundry and route it to the proper rooms. The clothes-tag reader's on the fritz again. Then give the mole-cars a good mop-out. We don't want Citizen Kyle and Doctor Mary getting all mucked up coming through the burrows from the landing pad to the house. Doro, you truck feed down to the livestock in the winter pastures as usual. And for corn's sake don't dawdle around! I want you and Ken back here, washed up squeaky clean and packed to go, by lunchtime. Okay? Ever'body got their beeper?"

"Yes'm," chorused the children. All of them except Ellen trooped to the cloakroom to put on their outer garments.

"Hughie!" Gavin said. "Trade jobs. Nice warm barn instead of freezin' your butt off on the roof."

Hugh gave a scornful laugh. "Nice warm cow-shit to scrape off the busted conveyor, you mean! Keep it, sucker."

"I'll trade if you like," Ken said. "I think I'm getting a sore throat. It might be better if I worked inside."

"Aw riiight!" Gavin said. "You're on, Lavender Lips. The grid tools still in the school shed?"

Ken nodded. "You'll have to apply the top layer of sealant as well as hook up the power. The mini-dragline, the mixer, and the bags of stuff are with the tools." He turned to his sister. "Will you pick up my transcript fleck at school when you get yours? You'll probably finish sooner."

"Sure, Kenny." She fiddled with the control of her environmental suit, then pulled on her mittens. "I'm going to walk instead of taking a mole-car. See you guys."

"Aww." Gavin pulled a lugubrious face. "Does little Dodo want one last slog through the Callie snow so she can store the memory in her giant brain?"

She smiled sweetly at him. "Yes. But I'll be coming back to Caledonia, Gavin. You remember *that*." She went out the door and closed it carefully after her.

The snow was 20 cents deep and fluffy, not too difficult to walk in. The veranda lights gave the snowbound farmhouse a cosy look, and when she had tramped halfway down the knoll she stopped and looked at the place for a long time. Her mother had designed the house and supervised its construction. She and Ken had been born in it. It was not only a beautiful building but also sturdy enough to resist the hurricane winds of Beinn Bhiorach winters and the frequent earthquakes that shook the land. She loved the house and the farm. She would come back.

There was no wind now and the buried stone steps were firm beneath Dee's boots. She continued down, singing quietly.

> *"But if I shall become a stranger—*
> *No, it would make me more than sad.*
> *Caledonia's been everything I've ever had."*

Down on the freshly snow-covered pad, she delighted in being the first one to make a dotted line of prints across it to the stock barn.

Then she continued on to the big storage shed next door to pick up the tractor. She could use the sledge this morning instead of the wagon. Ken met her at the side door of the barn when she drove up and quickly loaded bales of hay and sacks of feed with a forklift. She would have had to do that work herself if surly Gavin had been working there.

Thanking her brother, she drove off to the main farm road, headlamps illuminating the snow. It quickly became warm inside the tractor cab and she took off her gloves and unzipped her suit. Dawn was breaking over An Teallach, the huge extinct volcano that most people knew by its Standard English name, the Forge. At 7350 meters, it was the highest point on the continent, with a short but formidable glacier on its eastern slope that fed icebergs into the sea all year round.

The River Tuath on her left was still unfrozen, steaming amidst the snow-capped boulders in its bed. A flock of white rinkies bobbed and paddled in the Big Pool, semireptilian native "birds" that usually remained out among the fjord islets in good weather. There was probably going to be more snow soon, and it would get colder.

Dee backed into the lane, bordered by repellor-fencing posts, that lay between the horse and cattle pastures. The sledge fetched up at the heated trough that provided water for both groups of animals. Snowy humps in the cattle field stirred and turned into shaggy little red beasts with long horns that came ambling toward the load of fodder. They were incredibly hardy and almost never took shelter in their stone bàthach.

The small herd of coal-black miniature horses had been huddled in a three-sided open shed on the western side of their field. They let out shrill whinnies and milled about for a moment after emerging. Was it really breakfast arriving, or were the stupid cattle merely reacting to a fence rider or some other false alarm? Suddenly a tiny filly broke away from the group and came hurtling toward Dee at a full gallop, throwing up a great cloud of fine snow. Electrified, the other horses followed.

Cutach! Dee farspoke the horse, and then called *Pigean!* to the West Highland bull who trailed protectively after his harem of cows. The girl fastened her suit, hauled on her gloves, and jumped down from the tractor cab. Cutach came to the fence's invisible barrier and hung her head over it so that Dee could embrace her. Like her herd-mates, she was a perfectly proportioned true miniature, not a pony, with a withers only slightly higher than Dee's waist. Tiny horses were raised as companion-animals on many human planets and sometimes used for chariot races, trotting contests, or pulling wagons on festive occasions. Ian Macdonald kept the horses only for the pleasure of their company, for they would follow humans through the rough terrain like dogs, carrying packs of supplies for the two-legged walker as well as for themselves.

Cutach had a bobtail (hence her name) and a thick, furry coat. As a newborn foal two years earlier, she had not been expected to live. Only Dee's nursing and clandestine redaction had saved her, and she had become the girl's special pet.

"I'm going to miss you," she told the little horse, kissing its nose. "But I'll be back and we'll climb An Teallach together."

She checked the drinking trough to be sure the defroster was working, then put out the oats and hay and horse-chow. By the time she had finished with the horses the bull named Pigean had shouldered his way through the eager cows, snorting and tossing his horns. His coat reached nearly to his hoofs. The small Highland cattle were also raised mostly as pets, but in spring the cows gave rich but meager milk that was a marvelous accompaniment to fresh strawberries or the equally sweet golden native berries called oidhreag. None of the other children had been able to approach fierce Pigean, but he had gone instantly tame when first confronted by Dee.

She patted his muzzle. "I'll miss you, too, old potbelly. Don't you dare chase Gavin while I'm gone. Hear me?" She smiled. "Well, maybe you can chase him a little."

She gave the cattle their food and stood for a few minutes amidst the cloud of sweet animal breath, checking each horse and cow over carefully, as she always did when it was her turn to feed them. One mare, flighty Aigeannach, had a small cut on her left rear shank. Dee healed it easily. Then, before tears at the thought of leaving them could come, she got into the tractor and drove back to the road.

It was full light now and there was still plenty of time, so instead of returning to the farmstead Dee continued northward to the shore of Loch Tuath, passing between ranks of leafless coleus trees. There were coinean tracks everywhere, but no creatures visible. The furry, long-eared reptilians had fled at the sound of the approaching tractor.

At the sea-loch's edge Dee stopped and climbed out again. It was low tide, and the seaweed on the exposed rocks smelled like iodine and Earth oranges. There were more animal tracks, the large four-toed footprints of a fish-eating dòbhran and the smaller marks made by sgarbha, larger birds resembling red cormorants. Then, on the other side of the dock, she made an exciting discovery. In the wet sand were drag-marks, wide as a wagon, where a female teuthis had scrambled out of the sea to plant one of her amazing homeothermous egg-cases on the upper strand. Dee wished she could have seen the huge, tentacled decapod emerge at high tide. She had never seen a living teuthis, although bits and pieces of the sea monsters, killed by zeugloids, often washed up on Beinn Bhiorach shores. Ken still treasured the model of the creature that Grandad had given him when they first came to Caledonia.

Dee's deepsight found the barrel-sized packet of embryos buried beneath a big pile of shingle and debris that now blocked the doors of Daddy's new boatshed cum warehouse. But it didn't matter. By springtime, when the building was in use again, the fierce babies would have hatched and crawled back into the sea.

The waters of Loch Tuath were black, lapping as turgidly as oil against the beach and the snow-bonneted rocks. Soon the north wind would blow small icebergs into the fjord and it would freeze into slush for nearly half its length.

A single rhamphorhynchus flew overhead, trailing its long bony tail with the feathered tip and uttering melancholy shrieks.

"I will not cry," Dee said firmly.

She got back into the tractor and headed south at top speed. After returning the equipment to its place, she trudged around the stock barn and across the white-blanketed truck garden to the schoolhouse. Gavin was flat on his stomach in the snow at the edge of the road, connecting the new section of melting grid to the subterranean power main. A small dragline, a composite mixer, bags of sealing compound, and an open kit of tools were scattered around him.

"For chrissake stay off my sidewalk," he growled at her. "It's taking forever to set in this cold."

She decided not to remind him that the freshly poured sealant mix would harden instantly once the melting grid was turned on. Entering the school, she took off her suit and boots and padded to her study carrel in stocking feet. Today was Di-sathuirne, when satellite school was not ordinarily in session; but the Education Ministry in New Glasgow was expecting Dee to log on and obtain her transcript data. It was much more economical for Gran Masha to carry the data-fleck to the new school on Earth than for the Caledonian school system to transmit it via subspace.

Dee took up the command microphone and summoned the office of her form. To her surprise, the round, smiling face that appeared on her monitor was that of Tutor Una MacDuffie, her favorite teacher.

"There you are at last, Dorothea! I arranged to come in so I could say a very special goodbye. You must never say a word about this to the other children in your school . . . but I've always thought of you as a very special pupil. So creative and bright! I'm not at all surprised that you've gone operant."

Dee could not help showing her surprise and uneasiness. "Nobody was supposed to know."

The tutor laughed merrily. "Not know? Oh, lass, it's been the talk of Tutorial House ever since your metapsychic assay was done last month. Even Dirigent Hamilton got word of it and called us. Didn't your father tell you that your quotient is the highest that's ever been recorded on Caledonia?"

"No, ma'am," Dee whispered, stricken with dread.

"Well, don't go getting a swelled head over it. Just do your best at the Preceptor's on Earth and make us Caledonians proud of you."

"I'll try, ma'am."

"Bless you, dear. Be sure you keep on with your clothes-designing and jewelry-making, too. It's good to work with the hands when one has to spend overmuch time cudgeling the brain."

Dee nodded. "I think you're right, Tutor MacDuffie. And I will."

"Now I'd better transmit your fleck data. You've more important things to do this last day on Callie than chunnering with me."

Dee asked the tutor to send Ken's data as well. When the two flecks—transparent squares no wider than thumbnails with a microscopic data-carrier sandwiched in the center—popped out of her computer, she put them into a boîte, said a final goodbye to the tutor, and shut her computer down.

She left her carrel and wandered around the schoolroom for the last time. The half-finished projects of the other children—the printouts, the science experiments, the artwork, and the other hands-on assignments that were part of satellite school—were still strewn about the worktables. None of her things or Kenny's remained. No one would ever know they had studied here.

Outside, the sky had darkened again and a few snowflakes were falling. Gavin was still working on the power connection. Looking out the window, Dee let her ultrasense flick over him and learned a few new obscenities. Why should she walk past him again and endure more insults? She decided to use the burrows.

Retrieving her suit and putting on her boots, she descended in the lift to the tunnel system that connected all of the farmstead buildings. The burrows were brightly lit and warm, with smooth gray cerametal walls. A mole-car came trundling along a few minutes after she tapped the call-pad.

Her father was already seated in it.

"Get in, Dorrie. Your grandparents just arrived. I was on my way to meet them. Livestock all in good fettle?"

"Yes, Dad. They're fine. I went down to the loch shore after I finished with them. A teuthis buried its egg-case right in front of the warehouse door! I'm sure of it. The track was just like ones I've seen on the Tri-D."

Ian Macdonald laughed. "Well, the nerve of the brute! That hasn't happened around here for years. Not since before you came."

Dee found that she couldn't reply. She turned her head toward the tunnel wall and once again willed that tears not spill from her eyes. A moment later the car slowed and stopped at the farmhouse.

Ian climbed out and extended his hand to her. After she had disembarked he stood there, silent, looking down at her. As always now, she permitted herself to know only the outermost thoughts in his mind. They were puzzling. She had expected the fear mixed with love, the deep disappointment, even the suppressed anger. But why was his mental image of her superimposed upon the image of her mother?

"Dorrie, I'm going to ask a strange thing of you." He hesitated.

It's all right Dad. I'll do anything! Anything! Ask! . . .

"Your mother. Find out why it happened. I can't believe she and the others died only by chance, as they say, just picked at random by those anonymous murderers. There was some reason. Find it! You mustn't say anything to the other operant adults, though. Don't let anyone know that you're prying around. You could get into serious trouble . . ."

He broke off, as if suddenly aware of the burden he was placing on an eleven-year-old child. "Och, God, no! What am I saying?" He was shaking his head, his face twisted with emotion, moving away from her toward the lift. "I've no right to ask this of a wee lass! Forget what I said, Dorrie. I'm a glaiket loon."

Daddy. Wait.

He halted and turned back to face her, startled and then suddenly terrified at the realization that he had been coerced. He spoke in a hoarse whisper. "But you're not just a child, are you? You're not even like *her*. You're more than she ever was. God only knows what you are."

"I'm your daughter," she said. "I love you and I'll do as you asked. Find out about Mum and the others. I was going to do it anyway."

He stared at her.

"Please, Daddy," she whispered. "It's all right. I'm the same as I always was." The same.

"Yes." There was despair in his eyes. "I know that . . . now. Go ahead then and see what you can find out. It's driven me half-daft, you see, thinking it was a stupid casual killing. That God let Viola be snuffed out for no reason, like some ant getting stepped on . . ."

"I don't think it was like that. I can't tell you why, but that's what I think. I'll find out, Dad, and I'll tell you." And if it's possible, I'll do even more.

He nodded, seeming to understand.

The lift car was waiting. The two of them got into it without speaking further. She handed him the little plass box with the school transcript flecks and he simply nodded. At the first floor, Ian Macdonald got off. Dee continued up to the third floor, to her own room.

Quickly, she washed and put on the pleated Macdonald tartan skirt she had made herself, a white silk blouse, and a hunter-green blazer with silver buttons. They were her best clothes. Grandad's pearls went around her neck and she put the rhinestone mask pin in her skirt pocket. It took only a few more minutes to pack a seat-bag with pajamas and personal things, and to tuck a clean handkerchief into the new leather purse that had been a farewell gift from Janet.

Her other things were already in the small, tightly packed trunk standing near the bedroom door. Had she forgotten anything? She looked in the bath, checked the dresser drawers, opened the tall wardrobe.

Her handsome silver flight suit hung there, with the helmet and boots on the wardrobe floor. She had intended to leave it behind, but now . . .

"Kenny!" She grabbed the outfit, dashed out of her room, and went into her brother's, across the hall. "You've got to help me! I don't have any more room in my trunk."

He looked up with a startled expression, his arms filled with folded shirts and jerseys. "You want to take that? What the hell good will it do you on Earth?"

"Please," she begged. "I just *have* to take it."

Muttering good-naturedly, he made room in his trunk. "Good thing for you I'm not a clotheshorse."

They went downstairs together after sending the baggage to the pad on the goods conveyor. Masha, looking more gorgeous than ever, and Kyle, seeming to be younger than his own son, were having tea in the front parlor with Ian. Janet came in from the direction of the kitchen, carrying a basket.

"Well, better late than never," drawled the domestic manager. "You kids got all your stuff together?"

"Yes'm," said Ken. "Down at pad level ready to be put in the egg."

"Good. Your Grampaw and Gramma don't fancy sitting down to eat. They want to get started for Clyde right away. Seems the both of 'em are going back to Earth with you, and Gramps has to rush through some business if he's to make it. I packed a picnic lunch for you to eat aloft. Ken, you can carry it." She shook hands with the boy, then handed him the covered basket. "Hasta luego, muchacho. And good luck. I think you're gonna need it."

Janet turned to Dee and pumped her hand. "So long, Doro. Sorry we didn't get along better. My fault, I think. Come back when you're older and maybe we'll give it another shot." She grinned at Masha and Kyle. "Lots of things to get done around here. Be seeing you." And she was gone.

"What an amazing woman," murmured the professor, setting down her teacup.

Kyle snorted. "You could almost suspect there was a heart under that barbed-wire brassiere."

"There is," said Ian shortly. "Ken, Dorrie, get your coats and things."

They obeyed. Then they all made their way down to the pad exit. Kyle and Ian loaded the baggage into the egg. It was snowing harder. The pad was wet but clear, with the melting grid now programmed for automatic winter mode.

After Ian said goodbye to his parents, he turned to the children. Ken, who was thirteen, was relieved to be offered a handshake. But Ian kissed his daughter on the forehead. His eyes were wet as he said, "I'll take care of the oak tree while you're gone." Then he put both children into the egg and slammed the door.

The Porsche took off in free flight.

With her farsight, Dee saw her father go back into the hillside door. He took a mole-car to the house lift and ascended to the second level, where his bedroom was. Janet was waiting for him there with some of the little greenish-pink popspheres that held airplant essence, and so Dee stopped watching.

[17]

FROM THE MEMOIRS OF ROGATIEN REMILLARD

I first met her in the March of 2069, when she was twelve. It was late afternoon on a dark, blustery day in New Hampshire that had the Dartmouth College students and Hanover townsfolk scuttling anxiously about, bundled to the eyeballs in anticipation of one of our notorious spring blizzards. The little bell mounted on the door of my bookshop jingled and in came a solemn-faced waif wearing a scarlet enviro parka and a knitted white cloche. The place was understandably empty. I had been sitting with my feet up before the working antique woodstove I had recently installed in the readers' nook, perusing a classic issue of *Unknown Worlds*. My cat, Marcel LaPlume VI, was asleep on the rag rug under the footstool.

"Good afternoon," the child said, looking around at the shelves of paged books somewhat apprehensively. From her small stature, I had judged her to be nine or ten, but the mature inflection of her voice suggested she might be three or four years older. I was half asleep and didn't immediately notice that she was an operant. "I'm looking for something special. For a gift."

I was not going to disturb my carefully arranged old bones for a mere slip of a girl who might have mistaken my specialty bookshop for the local plaque dispensary. "I sell mostly rare science fiction and fantasy books dating from the twentieth century. Collector's items."

"I know. I'd like to find a birthday present for my brother. He's turning into a rather keen bibliophile. You may remember his coming into your shop a few times. Kenneth Macdonald."

I woke up at that, and so did my cat. Marcel lifted his gray-maned head, stared at the girl with interest, and decided she was ripe for his scam. He began broadcasting strong telepathic requests for food.

She was a meta, and a powerful one from what little I could discern of her "social" aspect. Her reference to her brother and her slight Scottish accent let me place her: Dorothea Macdonald, the prodigy from the planet Caledonia who'd entered Catherine Remillard's Preceptorial Institute last fall.

There had been a brief flutter in the operant community about her at the time, but the little girl had stayed out of the limelight since then. Naturally the Remillard Dynasty was extremely interested in the newcomer, and all of them found excuses to visit Cat's place from time to time to check out the wiz-kid and keep abreast of her progress. Only Denis, Lucille, and Jack had exercised decent restraint and respected the poor child's privacy. Marc, hard at work on the other side of the continent when he wasn't off among the stars, ignored her completely. I had gleaned from family scuttlebutt that the girl was a potential paramount, if she could only manage to overcome some serious inhibitions that still kept portions of her creativity, redactive power, and coercivity latent.

"Any book in particular you're interested in?" I asked.

The enfant formidable had an unassuming and winsome manner and she obviously liked cats. She pulled off her gloves and took a packet of potato chips out of her pocket. "These crisps are barbecue-flavored. Do you think Marcel would like some?"

Yes! said my furbearing gourmand, cantering over to her with slavering chops. *I love you!*

She hunkered down and opened the snack-pack. Marcel's first eager chomp nearly took her fingers and she wisely decided to scatter the chips on the floor for him.

I lurched upright, cracked a few joints that had developed mild rheumatiz, and restored the valuable old magazine to its protective envelope. The long-haired lunchbucket gobbled away, uttering telepathic sighs of appreciation. The only thing he loved better than potato chips was canned sweet corn.

"You've made a friend for life there, young lady," I said, "and you'll probably regret it. That beast is the worst food cadger in northern New England."

She looked up at me. Her hazel eyes were a bit too closely set but fringed with attractive dark lashes. No one would have called her pretty, and yet she had a gamine charm that had nothing to do with the coercive power she almost, but not quite, managed to conceal behind her mind-screen.

"The only pets I ever had were larger, outdoor animals—a horse and a bull." She stroked the cat's head and emptied out the last of the chips. Marcel was scarfing them down like a starving thing in spite of the fact that he'd eaten most of the nuked macaroni and cheese that had been my midday meal. "Cats are wonderful creatures, aren't they? So telepathically responsive."

I reallyreallyreally love you, Marcel said to her. *More food in pocket?*

Gently, she removed his huge furry paws from her lap and got to her feet. "Sorry, boy. You've eaten it all."

"He hogs the blankets in cold weather and sheds like a molting bison when it's warm," said I. "But I keep him around to control the mice and spider population." Thrusting forth my hand, I introduced myself. "Everyone in town calls me Uncle Rogi, so you might as well, too."

"My name is Dorothea Macdonald." She gave a tiny shrug. "People have given me all kinds of nicknames, but I don't much care for any of them."

"H'mm." I cogitated for a moment. "May I call you Dorothée? It's the Franco equivalent of your name. Comes off the tongue more trippingly, n'est-ce pas?"

She brightened. "Yes. I like it."

"Well. Now that's settled, let's talk about books. How much do you want to spend? Not all antiquarian books are priced sky-high, but some are. I hope your brother's not a collector of early Stephen King firsts."

"Oh, no. He likes older fantasy and horror. The fifties and before. I can't spend more than about twenty-five dollars."

I went striding into the M section, plucked a shrink-wrapped volume from the shelf, and handed it to her. "How about this? *The Rival Monster* by Sir Compton MacKenzie, in the Clarke Irwin Canadian edition. It's a humorous piece about the Loch Ness monster being hit by a flying saucer."

She burst out laughing. "Kenny should love it."

"Only fifteen bux. A steal for a Very Good copy. I'll throw in a plass bibilope your brother can keep it in. Prevents the old high-sulfur-content paper from deteriorating any further. Tell him to turn the pages carefully."

We went to the desk to complete the transaction, followed by Marcel, who still hadn't abandoned hope. Her credit card had been issued by the Bank of Caledonia.

"You're a long way from home," I remarked. "How do you like the Old World?"

"I lived here from the time I was a baby until I was five," she said, after a brief pause to sweep my mental vestibulum for traces of senile overfamiliarity. As usual when I was tending the shop, I hadn't even bothered to put my screen up and I was readily classified as a harmless old coot with no motive other than commercial bonhomie for questioning her.

"But I hardly remember anything about my early life on Earth," she went on. "Our home was in Edinburgh, Scotland. It's very different in North America. Especially . . . here."

"And a far cry from Caledonia, I betcha."

She eyed me in silence for a moment. Then: "You know who I am, don't you." It was a flat statement.

I nodded, handing back her card, and indicated a boxlike gadget I had recently acquired for the business. "Would you like some free instant gift wrap? This machine here can do anything from eco-sensitive to high camp."

For the first time, the corners of her lips turned up in a hint of mischief. "Can you make it really weird?"

I put the book inside the dojigger, selected the BAD TASTE—MILD option, and hit the pad. A few moments later the finished present plopped out: screaming orange paper imprinted with motifs from *Bambi Meets Godzilla*, all tied up with a glittering cerise ribbon. Dorothée was delighted.

Outside, the sky had started to spit snow pellets, those horrible little white bits like micro-popcorn that sting the face so badly when the wind is strong. I asked the girl if she would like to wait in the shop for a while and have a cup of cocoa by the fire until the nasty stuff either stopped or turned into honest snow.

Again I felt the brief touch of her prudent mental scrutiny, affirming that I was only a Kindly Geezer rather than a Dirty Old Man. She accepted my invitation—and at that point our long friendship began.

Marcel, purring like an outboard motor, sat happily on her lap as we chatted, and by the time she left, nearly an hour later, I had learned a fair amount about her background and she had cleverly extracted from me information about the Remillard family that I was not accustomed to share with casual acquaintances.

In the three years that followed, Dorothée came to The Eloquent Page every other week or so. At first she feigned an interest in my wares, but finally she admitted that she just liked to talk to me. She needed an adult operant with no axe to grind as a confidant, and none of the personnel at the Preceptorial Institute filled the bill. Neither did her grandmother Masha, who had taken a Visiting Professorship at Dartmouth's Department of Metapsychology in order to remain close to the girl and her brother. The professor and her husband, the subversive comic novelist Kyle Macdonald—my ancient drinking buddy, as you may recall—had made a nice home for the children in a rented house on the south side of Hanover. But neither Masha nor Kyle were types who invited childish trust. I apparently am, as any attentive reader of these memoirs may have deduced, and it has got me into a peck of trouble for my pains.

But what the hell.

At that time in my life things were tranquil enough. The bookshop was almost profitable, I was having a protracted no-strings affair with a delicious sloe-eyed librarian named Surya Gupta who worked at the Public Database around the corner, and the Remillard family members were engrossed in their own arcane machinations and not in need of a cantankerous but sympathetic father figure. Little Dorothée was.

So I got to hear blow-by-blow accounts of her painful progress from suboperant to adept metapsychic, and from masterclass operant to Grand Master Farsensor, Creator, Coercer, Redactor, and Psychokinetic. The ultimate accolade of paramount status waited in the wings, dependent upon her rootling out the last of the inhibiting dross in her unconscious and activating the full potential of her mind. Besides lending a sympathetic ear to stories of her travails at the Institute, I made sure she learned the civilized behavior patterns and important bits of "metiquette" that kids raised in operant homes take for granted.

Dorothée was Cat Remillard's star pupil, and at the same time she acquired an education in our local ivy-clad halls of academe, majoring in higher mathematics and theoretical physics. Her hobbies were bird-watching (of which more anon), skiing, and hiking. She also enjoyed sewing her own clothes and creating jewelry, grinding the gemstones and doing the metalwork, too. Her favorite piece was a reproduction, in white gold and the relatively inexpensive diamonds of Caledonia, sent to her by her father, of a piece of costume jewelry she had cherished as a young child. She wore the small diamond-studded domino mask on a thin chain around her neck as a good-luck charm.

Dorothée sometimes came to the bookshop with her brother, a pleasantly nerdish youth two years her senior, who was also in training at the Preceptorial Institute. I let Ken Macdonald use my database to hunt inexpensive collectible fantasy books in return for his doing chores such as packing mail orders and cleaning up the cat latrine. (I was never able to train this particular Marcel to use modern kitty sanitary facilities. He demanded, and got, a sandbox.) Ken had chosen to major in metapsychology. It bothered him not a whit that his mindpowers weren't as phenomenal as those of his baby sister.

My peaceful interlude as mentor to a saint in the making came to a crashing end in October of 2072.

Dorothée was fifteen years old by then and just finishing her post-graduate work. She had matured physically into a young woman of small stature, and was still too shy and preoccupied with her studies to be much interested in boys. Her manner was restrained—even enigmatic—but she had already developed the personal attribute that normals call "presence." No one would ever have mistaken her for an ordinary operant girl.

Like other powerful metas, Dorothée routinely suppressed her aura; but there was still a palpable air of specialness about her that she was unable to disguise—even though she tried. It was by no means the "odor of sanctity" that her legend imputes to her. Neither did she have Marc's daunting charisma nor Jack's fey and quasi-mystical aspect. The closest I can come to describing the quality she projected is . . .

steadfastness. Behind that little face, nearly expressionless for much of the time, was a person bound and determined to pursue her own Grail in spite of any obstacles the world or her own mind or body put in the way.

Now that her metafaculties were confirmed to be grandmasterclass or above, it was expected that she would be nominated to the Concilium when she reached adulthood at sixteen, just as Jack had been. She was not looking forward to magnateship and the public revelation of her mental talents. Her near-paramount status had been kept quiet, and most of the operant students and faculty at Dartmouth knew nothing about it; but the fact of having all five of the higher mindpowers in the top category would be enough to make her a galactic celebrity. "High Five" metapsychics were rather common amongst the Krondaku (and the Lylmik, of course), but the other races boasted only a handful of them. Humanity, at that time, only had eleven (not including the two paramounts) that had been verified by MPC testing. The only adults in the group were Paul and Anne Remillard, Davy MacGregor, Cordelia Warshaw (née Warszawska), who was the Intendant General of Earth, and Edward Hua-Kuo Chung, the Commander-in-Chief of the Fourteenth Fleet.

I had been aware for some time that Dorothée had a mysterious antipathy toward Jack, which he admitted was "his own fault" but declined to elaborate on further. She had continually refused to meet him face to face and he had not forced himself upon her. I never suspected that Dorothée's soul-struggles actually involved any person other than herself and the imaginary demons each one of us must confront, nor had the thought ever crossed my mind that she had been less than honest with me.

Then I made a very unpleasant discovery.

I had gone down to Concord, the Polity capital, to visit Severin Remillard in his spiffy new townhouse. I'd known Sevvie from the time he was a scrappy infant rebelling against the pacifistic philosophy espoused by his parents and most of the other pre-Intervention operants. I'd stood by him through the breakup of three marriages (one his own fault, the other two not), and surreptitiously encouraged him to follow his conscience and his younger brother Adrien and join the Rebel faction of magnates. Like me, Sevvie had a happy-go-lucky streak that went against the High Seriousness considered appropriate in the most exalted operant circles. He hip-hopped from one Concilium Directorate to another without ever seeming to find a committee with work he genuinely cared about, which drove his brother Paul and his straitlaced sister Anne to distraction. A tall, fair-haired, rather cynical individual, he was actually happiest plotting with his anti-Unity cohorts. It was inevitable that he would stand at the forefront of the Metapsychic Rebellion in 2083.

Since Sevvie was the least priggish of the family stalwarts and a sometime professional redactor and neurosurgeon, I had gone on this occasion to seek his help in a delicate problem peculiar to the masculine gender. My adorable young librarian, Surya, had tried to be patient and understanding with me, but I had disappointed her far too often of late, and I feared that if I didn't find some way to stiffen my resolve, she would seek a more talented bed companion.

To his credit, Sevvie didn't laugh when I told him my predicament. We sat together on his balcony overlooking the autumn colors of the Merrimack Valley, he considering treatment options and I observing morosely that it was a long, long while from May to December, and my days weren't the only thing growing short as I reached September.

"Well, you *are* a hundred and twenty-seven years old, Uncle Rogi," Severin observed.

"And you're sixty-nine and I'm as immortal as you are, dammit! I feel just fine otherwise and I haven't even been overindulging all that much. But my libido's sagging like a tired soufflé."

"You could try some poppers. Caledonian Sunrise would tumefy an Egyptian mummy."

"I don't like those things," I grumped. "Might as well be goosed by a moose. Can't you redact whatever's wrong? It's gotta be all in my mind. Maybe I'm just tired of the lady and don't want to admit it."

Severin sighed and rose from his wicker chair. "Come inside then, and let me rummage around inside your brain-pan. Maybe you're suffering from a mild depression."

I shuffled in after him and arranged myself on a white leather sofa strewn with black petit-point pillows. He pulled up a matching leather pouf, ordered me to close my eyes, and put his hand on my forehead. My lights went out.

When I came to, my grandnephew was pacing the floor with a fierce scowl on his face. My groin ached dully. I elbowed myself up and bleated, "What's wrong? Is it prostate cancer?"

"Don't be an idiot," he snapped. "You're healthy as a horse." He helped me to my feet. "And hung like one, too. I fixed what was wrong. You'll stop hurting in a minute. Your block and tackle went into action mode in anticipation after the redact job. I had to put the brakes on a bit crudely."

Oh, joy! I was a man again! I limped after Severin to the well-appointed wet bar behind his gilded grand piano. "What was the matter with me?"

He poured a double shot of Wild Turkey and handed it over. "Uncle Rogi, somebody has systematically subjected you to a very subtle type of powerful coercive-redactive probing. Apparently, it's been going on over a period of two years or more. The reaming was probably imperceptible to you while it was being done, but it had adverse and cumulative side effects on the hypothalamus and limbic septum, which I've repaired. Your love life is now back on the rails . . . but I suggest that you review the Grand Master Coercer-Redactors of your acquaintance and find out which one is the likeliest to have tossed your cerebrum."

I choked on my booze. "No!" I cried. "She couldn't have!"

Severin shrugged. Fortunately, I had not attached my words to a legible mental image. "Get another girlfriend," he advised. "One who's too weak in coercion to slip into your mind when your bells are chiming. God knows your mind-screen's strong enough to repel all boarders when you're not shtonkered or orgasmic."

"Merde," I groaned. "Merde et contremerde!" And then I had sense enough to keep my mouth zipped and my mind shut tight. Sex and drinking had nothing to do with my violation. There was only one person aside from my great-grandnephew Ti-Jean who could have perpetrated a ream-job without a trace, and only one who would have had the opportunity, the talent, and the blatant chutzpah to do it in a public place, in the course of a casual conversation:

Little Dorothea Macdonald.

I was going to have to confront her with what she had done, even though it might mean the end of our friendship.

. . .

I have mentioned that Dorothée, like myself, was an enthusiastic birdwatcher. Both of us belonged to the local branch of the Audubon Society, met frequently at its meetings and outings, and tipped each other off when a rara avis blew into town. On a certain lovely Sunday in mid-October we made a date to go down to the evergreen woodland bordering the Connecticut River after 11:30 Mass. I told her about an uncommon pileated woodpecker that had been reported lurking among the towering white pines, and we planned to photograph it.

We sat on rocks beside the river, eating the Jarlsberg sandwiches and molasses cookies she had brought and drinking my contribution, winesap apple cider. Serious peckerwood hunting was supposed to commence after lunch.

I got down to the real business at hand right off the bat.

"Dorothée, I've learned something that disturbs me very much. Some person, a very powerful coercer-redactor, has been probing my mind without my consent. I think that person is you."

"Me?" she exclaimed, all indignant. "Me, prying into your mind? What in the world gave you that idea?"

"Don't try that reverse-question gimmick on me, kiddo," I retorted, looking sad and betrayed. "And spare me the hurt feelings act, too. It's taken me long enough to discover what you were doing—but then I never was accused of being the sharpest thorn on the family rosebush. You've been grubbing around my brain almost from the first day we met, haven't you."

She looked away toward the river. "Yes. It was necessary that I obtain the life-history and detailed psychosocial profile of you and every one of the older Remillard family members, plus Marc and his siblings. The information I got was incomplete, but it sufficed for my purposes. I probed you the most extensively because you've lived so long and made so many objective judgments about members of the family. But I also probed all of the others except Marc and Jack, who stayed out of reach."

Whatever excuse I had expected for the reaming, this wasn't it. "For God's sake, why?"

"The Remillards are the most prominent human family in the

Milieu, but very little about their private lives or mental attributes has ever been published. You know that complete metapsychic assays of operant newborns have only been mandatory for the past fourteen years. For individuals born before 2068, the complete assay is only optional. Since the procedure is likely to be painful for an adult, few older operants have submitted to it—and that includes all of the Remillards except Paul and Anne. I needed the information for a very important research project."

"You reamed the lot of us for *research*? C'est drôlement couillon!" I scoffed.

She had no trouble at all deciphering my meaning, which roughly equates to "bovine fecal matter," and her little face flushed with chagrin.

"I'm telling the truth," she insisted. "My—my research project is private, but it's consequential. You may verify my statement coercively if you wish."

"I'm no good at reaming, and you know it." But I *was* capable of erecting and maintaining a cosmic-class mental barricade if my life depended upon it, and I had an uncanny feeling that it just might. Now that I was forewarned, Dorothée would never again probe me with impunity.

"You've been using me, young lady," I continued, "and that's tacky behavior from someone I thought was my friend. Your excavating had side effects, too—knocked some of my mental machinery out of whack. I had to be redacted, for God's sake, and that's how I discovered what you'd been doing."

"I'm sorry you were hurt, Uncle Rogi. Truly I am! I had no idea the probing would do you any harm." Her distress and contrition were genuine, all right. But then she had to spoil the effect by adding, "I did it for a very good reason, though."

"I'll be the judge of that," I said sternly. "I want you to explain yourself right here and now . . . or I'll have to tell Catherine Remillard that her school harbors an embryonic Grand Inquisitor."

"No!" she cried, now regarding me with real fear on her face. "Please, don't! If you tell her, then Jack will surely hear about it. Or even Marc himself."

I goggled at her. "What the bloody hell do they have to do with this? Are you going to tell me what you've been up to, or not?"

She squeezed her eyes shut in some monumental act of emotional self-discipline. When she looked at me again her face was not that of a misbehaving child but of an adult on a mission of capital importance.

"You're different from the other members of your family, Uncle Rogi. You have no . . . dynastic or personal ambition. No need to prove your superiority, no great cause to promulgate. You know your operant talents are insignificant and it doesn't bother you. You accept people as they are, without trying to change them. You have a kind heart in spite of your grumpiness and you were very good to me when I came wailing and whinging to you about my painful therapy. And so I'm going to trust you with the most important secret of my life."

Still seated on the rock, I sketched an ironic bow at the insolent chit and said, "Plût au ciel qu'il en fût ainsi!" Which is more or less the equivalent of "Thanks all to hell for the dubious honor."

She took a deep breath. "Let me tell you how my mother died."

My sarcastic attitude popped like a lighted bulb touched by a wet finger. I said quietly, "All right, Dorothée. If you'd like to."

Sitting there at my side in the pleasant forest park, taking occasional sips of apple juice when her throat dried, the girl told me her own ghastly and fascinating tale of Fury and Hydra—everything she knew, including official data from the Magistratum investigation. (God only knows how she pried out that information.) She not only described Hydra's atrocities in the Hebrides, she showed me explicit mental images that turned my stomach. She also told me how Fury had invaded her dreams back on Caledonia, pretending to be her dead mother.

. . . And she told me how the monster had been appearing to her in her sleep ever since then, at intervals ranging from a few days to months apart, believing that it was slowly converting her to its cause.

When she finished I was in an icy sweat, frightened to death for Dorothée, for myself, and for all the rest of my family. I couldn't speak for several minutes and simply cowered behind my mental shield, willing that it not be true. But clearly, it was. I had nearly forgotten the monster and its multiheaded minion, having assumed that their threat had passed after the Islay incident. But now Dorothée told me that Fury was apparently more determined than ever to destroy the Galactic Milieu and dominate the planets of the Milky Way—not only with the original Hydra-units, but apparently also with a gang of new recruits!

I paused to glug down more cider, wishing fervently that it was a more bracing kind of drink. "What did you mean when you said you were afraid Marc or Jack would find out what you're up to? Don't tell me you suspect one of *them* is Fury."

"They're the only Remillards whom I haven't been able to probe. Whose metafaculties are powerful enough to insert dreams—or any other kind of psychocreative icons—into minds located lightyears away." Her face was set in stubborn lines. "When I had that first dream about my mother back on Caledonia, Jack Remillard was in Orb and Marc was on Earth."

"Dorothée, you're way off the beam on this. I probably know Fury better than most members of my family. I saw the damn thing born, for God's sake! It can't possibly be Jack because he didn't *exist* when Fury first appeared. He was born twelve years later."

I told her about the awful Good Friday epiphany of 2040, which she had obviously failed to retrieve from anyone's memory bank. (Small wonder it had been repressed. It traumatized the hell out of the whole Remillard clan!) I described my own adventures as potential Hydra prey, and told her how the monster had tried to murder teenaged Marc and baby Jack. I also told her the family's conclusion that Fury had to be a manifestation of multiple-personality disorder, probably unknown to the core persona whose body it shared, and having a completely different armamentarium of powers.

"It could be any of the people you've already probed," I pointed out. "Did you come across hints of a second persona in any of the Remillard skulls you poked around in?"

"No," she said, clearly dismayed by this new idea. "I didn't. I never considered the idea of multiple personalities at all! Inside the host mind, a second persona would—would be disguised. It might not even exist except when it was in control of the body! . . . Oh, shit, Uncle Rogi. This could change everything!"

"Exactement," said I.

"Perhaps Jack isn't a viable suspect after all," she conceded grudgingly.

"Damn tootin' he ain't."

Her indignation boiled over. "But he did try to coerce me into revealing my operancy, which was hateful of him! At the time, I was doing everything I could to conceal my powers so that I wouldn't be forced to leave my father's farm, and here was this *fool* trying to start an interstellar mind-pal exchange! He obviously knew about me—perhaps from my . . . from the Lylmik. They know everything, damn them, even if they don't always admit it. And then along came Fury, who was also very eager for me to develop my metafaculties and become part of the Milieu operant community. I was no good to it half-latent, working on a colonial farm. Can't you see why I thought Jack might be Fury? The thing began bespeaking me out of the blue just as he'd done."

"I'm sure Jack didn't mean you any harm. It's only natural that he'd be curious about another person with a mind approaching the caliber of his own. He'd like to be your friend—"

"He had no right to meddle with me on Caledonia and he has even less right to bother me now! I've made that very clear. But I know for a fact that he continues to snoop into my progress at the Institute. I've overheard Luc Remillard discussing it with Doctor Cat."

"I'll just bet you have," I said. "But you're wrong in thinking Jack's your enemy. My Lord, girl—I've known Jack since before he was born! He's a good boy. Not a malicious bone in his—uh—body."

She glowered at me, unpersuaded. In the middle distance I heard an authoritative *tunk-a-tunk-tunk-tak-tak* that could only be the work of the rare feathered pile driver that backwoodsmen call the Good God Woodpecker, an amazing bird nearly half a meter in length with black and yellowish-white plumage and a jaunty red crest.

I couldn't help perking up and opened my pack in search of my camera. But Dorothée was not about to be distracted from the main chance.

"Never mind the bloody bird," she said. "There's other game afoot. What about Marc?"

There she had me. What about him? He had always been the top Fury suspect, even though his cousin Gordo, a proven Hydra, had run him down with a spike-wheeled motorcycle, killing himself in an attempt to murder Marc when both of them were teenagers.

In maturity, Marc Remillard was prodigiously intelligent, blessed with devastating good looks, and the acknowledged leader of a growing clique of exceptional young grandmasterclass operants. His research in metacreative CE had spawned a whole adjunct industry—geophysical engineering through mindpower. Lately he had turned his talents to the design of complex metaconcert programs based on the work of his grandfather Denis and his brother Jack. At that very moment, Marc and Jack were on the planet Satsuma attempting to fend off potentially devastating crustal movements using the latest-model CE equipment in dual metaconcert. It was a much trickier piece of work than the Okanagon operation.

"Marc's a genius," I asserted stoutly. "He has his flaws, but I'd stake my life that he's not Fury. If he intended to conquer the galaxy, he'd just *do* it—not whomp up some psychopathic alter ego to go about the job underhandedly."

With withering expertise, Dorothée pointed out, "One doesn't choose to develop multiple-personality disorder, so that argument won't wash." I waved one hand in disgust, but she continued. "I've used the material I got from your mind and from the others to calculate the probability that each member of the Remillard Dynasty is Fury. Even if a multiple personality is involved, I think my research may still be valid. Are you interested?"

"Oh, why not? I suppose you've got the odds calculated for me, too."

"Of course. I won't bore you with the details of my equations, but they include objective as well as subjective criteria. Marc checks in at a probability of 74 percent, the most likely suspect."

"Poppycock!"

She went on relentlessly. "For the others, Philip's probability is 23 percent, Maurice 26, Severin 51, Anne 68, Catherine 22, Adrien 49, and Paul 64."

"Paul?" I croaked. "Anne? The First Magnate and the Jesuit priest? Those are your other top suspects? Child, you're two bubbles shy of plumb—and I don't care if you're an apprentice paramount or not! Sevvie and Adrien I could understand. Both of them have had their doubts about the Galactic Milieu from Day One. But Paul and Anne have been its greatest champions in the family and in the Concilium."

"True," Dorothée said. "Both are nearly fanatical in their support of the Milieu and their advocacy of eventual Unity for the Human

Polity. But, don't you see, Uncle Rogi? This is the very reason why they're the likeliest to have a shadow persona insanely opposed to the Milieu! That's basic psychiatry."

"Basic bollocks," I growled.

She ignored me. "Paul and Anne also have metapsychic complexi that assay much higher than those of their siblings, which also weights their plausibility as Fury candidates. What's more, both of them—if your deep thoughts concerning them and the professional opinions of Catherine Remillard are valid—have significant emotional warpage. Anne, especially. Not nearly as serious as Marc's, but definitely sufficient to generate an abnormal persona."

"You must have really done a job on poor Cat to root out that kind of sensitive data."

"And Luc Remillard as well," she admitted. "He furnished most of my psychological profile on Marc, although he had nothing much of value on Jack. Both Catherine and Luc acted as preceptor-therapists to my brother and me, opening their own minds as they sought to open and integrate ours. With Kenny, as with the other partially latent clients at the Institute, there was no danger of coercive-redactive backlash."

"But not with you . . . "

I regarded the girl with a well-churned mix of awe and stark fear. It was not an unfamiliar sensation. I'd felt the same way at certain periods in the lives of Marc and Ti-Jean.

"I have no animus against Catherine," Dorothée said warmly. "She's a kind, sweet-natured woman and a brilliant psychiatrist. If I do achieve paramount status, it will be largely because of her. But I would have been a fool not to make use of her insights into the minds of her brothers and sister. Essentially, she has come to the same conclusions as I have regarding the Fury probabilities."

"Has she told other members of the Dynasty?"

"No. Only her mother and father, Denis and Lucille. They advised her that nothing is to be gained at the present time by revealing the information. They're right, of course."

"Oh, of course." I began collecting the remnants of our lunch and stuffing them into my daypack. "How likely am I to have a secret Evil Twin?"

"Your probability of harboring Fury is 52 percent. Denis Remillard and Lucille Cartier have a probability roughly the same. As you know, they've never intruded upon me at the Institute. I'll need more data from their minds before completing their analyses. You'll be glad to know that the probability of Luc Remillard or his older sister Marie being Fury is vanishingly small. Their talents are intellectual, not metapsychic."

I sighed. "What now? Do you plan to blow the Dynasty out of the water by revealing your statistics in your maiden address at the Concilium next session? Or will you just send on your bit of homework to Davy MacGregor or Chief Evaluator Throma'eloo Lek and watch Remillards tumble like bowling pins?"

"Probabilities aren't proof. I have no intention of making trouble for your family at the present time. That would be counterproductive to my own plan to track down the persons who killed my mother."

I felt a sudden infusion of ice water in my veins. "Your plan to *what*?"

"I intend to keep all this data secret for the time being. Meanwhile, with your help, I hope to collect additional information that will refine my focus. Not on Fury, but on Hydra."

"Hydra?" I reiterated hollowly. "My *help*? Don't tell me reaming my brains out wasn't sufficient—"

"I've told you more of my secrets than I've told any other human being. Not even Ken knows what you know. I was afraid . . . that Fury might also have approached my brother in an effort to get at me."

"It's possible."

"Now that you know the truth, you've got to help me! There's important information about Hydra that I've been forced to keep on hold because I couldn't act on it. A solid clue to the new identity of one of the fugitive units—and its whereabouts. If you help me, I can finally follow through on my investigation. Please, Uncle Rogi!"

The intent hazel eyes brimmed with appeal and she took hold of my hand in a pleading gesture. But I wasn't fooled. Maybe she didn't want to coerce me, but she would if I balked. Tonnerre de chien! I was cornered again.

"What's this clue?" I asked gruffly.

"My grandmother, Professor Mary MacGregor-Gawrys, came upon some very curious information that she's kept to herself because she doesn't realize its implications. I've been probing her just as I've probed the Remillards, but I only found this clue in her memories last week."

I opened my mouth to make another snide comment, but she silenced me with a brief coercive jab.

"Just listen to me! . . . Are you familiar with the political situation on Okanagon?"

I shrugged. "Supposed to have lots of Rebel sympathizers in high places, isn't it?"

"Yes. Do you remember how the former Dirigent of that world, Rebecca Perlmutter, died under suspicious circumstances? She was on her way to tour one of the orbiting Twelfth Fleet installations when a miniature fusion generator in the new courier ship carrying her inexplicably malfunctioned. The ship and everyone in it were vaporized."

"I remember. There was talk of sabotage. Leaders of the Rebel faction on Okanagon were interrogated with the Cambridge machine."

"There was no proof Dirigent Perlmutter was murdered, but she had been one of the most implacable foes of the anti-Unity movement. Along with Anne Remillard and Paul and a few others, she was a cosponsor of the Concilium bill to silence the Rebels."

"Stupid move," I observed. "Humans were fed up with thought control after the Simbiari Proctorship. As I recall, Okanagon's new Dirigent makes no secret of her own Rebel sympathies."

"That's correct. And Patricia Castellane has surrounded herself with like-minded officials, although the fact isn't trumpeted about. Now here's where Gran Masha comes in: At a meeting on Caledonia back in 2068, she met a man from Okanagon, one of Castellane's top aides. My grandmother is a highly skilled clinical metapsychologist and she can pick up clues from a person's aura that most operants would never notice. She noticed that this man was an extraordinarily powerful meta. Perhaps even a High Five! And yet he wasn't a magnate, only an administrative assistant. She was curious about him and did some quiet investigation of his background. She discovered that some of the data were inconsistent. His metapsychic assay, for instance, was pegged much lower than it should have been. That made her worry that he might be a Magistratum spy, infiltrating the Rebel movement on one of its strongest planets."

I had been listening doggedly to her recitation, but now I did an incredulous double take. "Are you saying that Masha is a closet *Rebel*?"

"Of course," Dorothée snapped. "She told the Rebel leaders here on Earth her suspicions about this chap, and they checked him out. They have their own spies in the Human Magistratum, you know. But apparently Castellane's aide vetted clean. A fair number of operants have been inaccurately calibrated; and while the possibly bungled mental assay of a High Five is outrageous, it poses no threat at all to the Rebel movement. Castellane had her aide get his marbles recounted, and it supposedly turned out that he wasn't a High Five at all, only a masterclass fiver with a quirky aura. That was the end of it as far as the Rebel investigation went. The matter rested for over three years—until I probed Gran Masha's mind and found the story and learned that she still has doubts about the man. She met him again a year or so after his second calibration, and *his aura was entirely different from what Gran had perceived at their first meeting.* Now Gran's afraid he might be a Lylmik spy!"

"Et alors?" This spy stuff didn't seem very relevant, and I wished Dorothée would get to the point.

"Suppose," she said softly, "that this overly modest High Five who can tune his aura at will is an infiltrator, all right—but not for the Lylmik. Suppose he's one of Fury's Hydra-units, manipulating the Okanagon Dirigent and the Rebels on her planet for Fury's purposes. Up to a point, the Rebels *are* Fury's allies, you know. Both want humanity out of the Milieu."

I had to agree. "But how the devil could you prove your spy is a Hydra?"

"By going to Okanagon and checking out this character's mind myself," she replied, cool as you please.

"A Hydra on Okanagon—and you want to *check him out*? Ne dis pas de conneries!"

"Don't worry, it won't be dangerous. This person will never know I've touched his mind. No more than you or the other Remillards did. I can even do an MP assay without a trace. I'm a top-gun redactor, Uncle Rogi."

I lifted my eyes to heaven at this piece of offhanded conceit, but the cherubim with the fiery swords were out to lunch.

"There are a few little problems connected with the Okanagon trip," the little idiot admitted. "I can easily get away for a couple of weeks without my grandparents or the Institute preceptors knowing it, but I'm still a minor and I have no legitimate excuse to leave Earth. I need an adult traveling companion to stave off suspicion during the starship voyage and the port formalities at takeoff and landing—to say nothing of help getting into Dirigent House once we're on the planet. My father, the only other person I trust absolutely, can't go with me. It's harvesttime on Caledonia, and after that's over he'll have to attend Assembly sessions. He's an IA now."

I gave a horrified squawk, finally seeing where all of this was leading. "Absolutely not! I refuse categorically—"

She sailed on. "Dad will be happy to pay for the starship tickets, though. He's as determined as I am to apprehend my mother's murderers. You and I can travel to Okanagon on a Poltroyan ship with a very high df and be there and back inside of six days. I can redact any pain you might suffer during the tight-leash hops."

"Why don't you just go to the goddam planet invisible? Or fuzz your identity psychocreatively!"

"Neither would work. Sensors on the ship would detect my mass. And I wouldn't be able to conduct the probe and mentally conceal myself at the same time. I'll have to get reasonably close to the guy wearing an ordinary wig-and-makeup disguise. You could stay at a safe distance, of course."

"When were you intending to make this trip?" I cleverly conveyed seesaw vibes, hinting that I might be starting to cave in.

"Just as soon as I finish my dissertation on hierarchical lattices in tau-field coupling. Say, two weeks from now. The first week in November."

I uttered a sigh of spurious near-capitulation. "Did it slip your mind that there are three more Hydras hiding somewhere in the woodpile? They're probably *all* High Fives! In metaconcert, the quartet would certainly be able to zap you to scrapple—even if you are a bush-league paramount. And Hydra would cook my poor old goose for damn sure if you roused its suspicions—no matter how I tried to hide."

My cowardice provoked a pitying smile. "If I can probe members of the Remillard Dynasty without their knowing it, I can do the same to a Hydra."

"You've got to promise," I muttered, "that you won't try anything with this suspect unless we can get close to him in some public place."

Quick as lightning, she flung her arms around me and planted a kiss on my cheek. "I promise! You won't be sorry you helped me, Uncle Rogi."

"I hope to hell not . . ." The woodpecker was at work again, and I got out my image recorder and started fiddling with it, careful to keep my mental screen at max.

"There's no assurance this man is a Hydra-unit, of course," Dorothée said in an odd tone of voice. "He could be perfectly innocent or even an agent of the Lylmik like Gran thought. But if he does turn out to be one of Fury's henchmen, I'll be well on the way to nabbing the rest of them as well."

"How? The others could be on any human world in the Milieu."

"I have something Fury wants very much. *Me!* And if it can't have me, if I break off the games I've been playing with it and tell it to go to hell . . ." She turned away, but not before I had seen a new look on her face, as grim as that of a mountaineer who must conquer a lengthy, mortally dangerous pitch if the climb is not to end in failure.

Suddenly I knew what Dorothée's long-range scheme was. My appalled expression gave away what my screened mind concealed.

"That's right, Uncle Rogi. If I deliberately reject Fury, it will send Hydra to kill me. But if I know the true mental signature of even one of the units, I'll be ready for them."

"Jésus! You're hardly more than a child, Dorothée! The Hydras are—"

"I know what they are," she said bleakly. "I met two of them face to face and I . . . perceived . . . all four of them just after they'd committed the murders in Scotland. Fury can change the superficial mental signatures of the Hydras, which is why they've been able to remain at large. But it can't change their true metapsychic complexus—the total assay of higher faculties in each mind. The MPC is unique in every mature operant. Even more individual than a DNA scan. Ordinarily, only an expert in coercive-redactive probing can fully analyze an adult mind, and Milieu law requires the consent of the probee before the procedure can be carried out. But of course, *I* don't face those limitations."

"Ça n'a pas de nom!" I wagged my head at the gall of her.

She flashed me a sudden smile, supremely self-confident. But an instant later her mask was back in place and when she spoke, her voice was low and intense. "I'll never forget what my ultrasenses showed me that day in the Islay death-cave. At the time, I couldn't understand what was happening. I was like a baby hearing some horrible off-key chord of music played by a symphony orchestra. I had no idea what kind of instruments were making the sound, much less the harmonic pattern of the metaconcert—which is analogous to the intricate vibrations of the air molecules that actually produce musical sounds."

"But you did remember the whole? The—the song of the Hydra?"

"I remember."

"Could you transfer the data to another operant mind?"

She shook her head. "I won't."

"I see." But something still puzzled me. "Why do you need to go to Okanagon, then? Why risk probing this guy when you could flush the Hydra out at any time simply by telling Fury to take a flying fibrillation?"

"It would be a safety precaution. If I probe this individual and discover that he's a Hydra-unit, my knowing his true mental signature will enable me to track him with my farsight. In time, I'd learn the identity of the other units through him—"

I brightened. "Then you could blow the whistle on them without baiting a trap with yourself!"

She shook her head. "I'd still have to let Hydra come after me. My evidence would have been obtained illegally. My private convictions are insufficient grounds for making a citizen's arrest—or even reporting the suspects to the Magistratum as possible perps of the Islay murders."

The pileated woodpecker hammered again, drilling after some hapless grub that thought itself safe deep within a mass of solid wood.

"For the final confrontation," I said, with forlorn hope, "I presume you'd find some way to bring in the authorities."

Dorothée brushed lunch debris from her jeans. She opened her daypack, took out her own camera, and peered through it, adjusting the settings using me as the subject. Her face was concealed behind the device as she said, "I haven't decided yet. I won't let Hydra escape, if that's what's worrying you."

That was hardly my principal concern, but I had no intention of letting her know that. Secure within my mental ramparts, I tried frantically to think of the best way to stop the child from committing this piece of suicidal folly. And of course there was my own precious ass to consider, too. All very well for her to say I could keep out of the way while she did her mental assault; but Hydra *knew* me. If Mister High Five caught Dorothée in the act, it would be child's play for him to discover who'd brought her to Okanagon. Then good night, nurse!

Two weeks.

I had a little over two weeks to come up with some way to forestall the trip to Okanagon. I couldn't stop her all by myself. I needed help—and from a magnum cranium that couldn't possibly be Fury.

Only one person filled the bill. If I called him today, he'd either come to the rescue in his private express starship or think of some other way to checkrein Dorothée. Meanwhile, I'd have to hide out so the crazy kid couldn't catch me with my screen down and uncover my ploy.

I'd go to Kauai! To Malama Johnson, pretending it was just an innocent visit to an old friend. Dorothée might be able to track me there with her ultrasenses, but the powerful Hawaiian kahuna woman would keep me safe from kidnapping or premature bean-spilling.

Until Ti-Jean came to the rescue . . .

"Would you rather go home now, Uncle Rogi?" Dorothée had the grace to look slightly ashamed of herself for having bullied me.

"Not on your life!" I said cheerfully. "Let's go snap that damned woodpecker. You get a farsight fix and I'll work out the best way to sneak up on it without scaring it away. I'm pretty good at that sort of thing."

Ti-Jean figured out a way to save both of us, but it was a close squeak.

He was on Satsuma with Marc, winding up an important CE geophysical project. When I called him via subspace from Kauai, got him to focus his ultrasense on me, and farspoke him the lunatic scheme of Dorothée, it took him a full half-minute to figure out how to salvage the situation.

His mind said to me: Our work here on the Japanese world has been a great success. We managed to avert a seismic catastrophe and we're heroes. I don't think there's a piece of fireworks left unburnt on the entire planet. Now here's my plan: Marc wants to celebrate the triumph with his research associates and friends as soon as we get back to Earth. He's going to throw a big Halloween party at his place on Orcas Island. See that you and the girl come, and I'll take care of the rest.

When I televiewed Dorothée and invited her to the party, she very nearly refused to attend. But I wheedled her insidiously, pointing out that she'd asked for my help—and here I was, offering her an unprecedented chance to catch the entire Remillard Dynasty off guard and further refine her Fury probability researches.

"Nothing lowers inhibitions like a masquerade," I asserted with a telling wink, "even when the participants are hotshot operants. They'll all be drinking and dancing and carrying on and trying to fool their friends with mental disguises. You can slither around in the thick of the wingding, slipping in the mental shiv. I'll introduce you as my girlfriend Surya. All you have to do is fake the aura of a barely operant person when you're first introduced and then keep your own walls up."

Dorothée finally agreed to go . . . if only because it presented her with a perfect opportunity to examine the otherwise inaccessible psyches of Marc and Jack. She also told me that on the day following the party—which was Halloween proper—she and I would be off like a couple of bats out of hell, en route to Okanagon.

"I'll meet you at the masquerade on Orcas Island," she said, crackling with authority. "Wear a decent costume. I guarantee I'll have one that'll knock your socks off."

[18]

ORCAS ISLAND, WASHINGTON, EARTH
30 OCTOBER 2072

<Go to Marc's party my dear little ones. There is no need to bother about invitations. Many of those invited plan to use psychocreative disguises and you will not be conspicuous if you do too.>

May I/WE ask why we should go dearestFury?

<I am concerned about the Girl. I sense a lack of sincerity in her continual temporizing. She is too strong for me to penetrate to her CoreofTruth and I have no proof she has rejected me but I worry. I wish you to observe her carefully at this party and see if she has contact with the Great Enemy. Thus far she has avoided him but . . . *I worry.*>

[Jealousy.] She's not to be trusted. She should have been killed as soon as her paramount potential was identified. I/WE have told you this again and again. Why must you even consider recruiting another unit? We've become invincible! Any two of us can control the most powerful Grand Master in the Human Polity. Celine and Quint are progressing splendidly on Okanagon and Parni and I have the EuroRebel contingent eating out of our hands. It was laughably easy to eliminate the Sánchez woman before she reported the Cambridge mental laser experiment to the university authorities.

<You did well my darlings.>

Thank you. It would be more . . . gratifying if I/WE had more of your personal attention.

<This is not always possible. You know the reifying limitations I face until I am able to take charge of the body. I had hoped that the superlatively powerful mind of the Girl might have helped to alleviate that problem . . . but now [sorrow] I fear she is slipping away from me. I may have no recourse other than to endure what must be endured until the day when I am free and One.>

I/WE can give you all the help you need! You never should have approached *her.* She's dangerous and her full metapotential is still unclassified. She may even exceed the Great Enemy in certain faculties. If you let her live long enough for the Lylmik to initiate her and affirm her paramount status she may discover exactly what you've been doing. She may discover YOU.

<There is still a small glimmer of hope. Provided she remains steadfast in her antipathy toward Jack.>

Let me/US kill her! I/WE are afraid of her! She's as dangerous as the Great Enemy. More dangerous!

<You two will do as I say: Attend the party tonight and *observe.* Now farewell.>

"Just one minute more," Masako Kawai said to her husband. She stood before a dressing table scattered with cosmetics, studying herself in the mirror. "This awful rice powder isn't covering properly. My face should be whiter for an authentic Samurai-lady look." She took up the powder puff again.

"You're a dream of beauty, Masa," Hiroshi Kodama reassured her. "That peach-colored kimono is quite the loveliest one I have ever seen. How fortuitous it is that the Seattle area has so many citizens of Japanese ancestry. These costumes Shigeru Morita borrowed for us are marvels of authenticity." The voice of the Satsuma Dirigent was muffled by his mempo, a demonic iron mask that was part of the magnificent reproduction bushi armor he wore. The fierce Samurai walked his gloved fingers up the exquisite lady's silken back and tickled her neck beneath the elaborate black wig.

"Stop it, Hiro! It took me half an hour to anchor that thing properly." She applied more powder to her nose.

The warrior chuckled wickedly, abandoning the Standard English of the Human Polity to speak in Japanese. "You forget, Masako-chan, that I am now your lord and master! Your very life belongs to me to dispose of as I wish." The hands crept beneath her arms, onto her breasts.

"If you attempt an assault on my ivory citadel wearing that armor," she said, speaking the ancient language with considerably more precision, "you will destroy my borrowed costume and possibly do your own precious jade stem an irreparable injury." Wriggling out of his grasp, she tucked a small dagger called a kaiken into her obi along with her fan, turned to him, and reverted to English. "I'm ready. Let's have a look at you."

Docile now, the Dirigent of Satsuma let his wife retie the cords of his kabuto helmet in a more symmetrical bow, after which she kissed his iron nose. "You'll be roasting inside that mask before long," she said, "but I must say that you look madly sexy. Let's buy some costumes like these and take them back to Satsuma with us for our private amusement. We've endured frontier hardships long enough. Now that the quake danger is defused, I'd like some attention paid to my own seismic stresses."

He bowed formally to her. "As you command, Lady."

Hiroshi Kodama and Masako Kawai had come to Earth for business reasons, together with several other Satsuma officials, on the same starship as Marc and Jack Remillard. Later in the week there would be meetings in Seattle at CEREM, the new corporate affiliate of Marc's research establishment that was headed by Pete Dalembert and Shigeru Morita. The Japanese planet was prepared to open negotiations for an important sale of cerebroenergetic equipment. Meanwhile, Hiroshi and Masako were houseguests in Marc's huge, many-leveled home.

They left the bedroom and made their way down the long, windowed upper hall. The house was constructed in Pacific Northwestern style from cedar, stone, and glass and seemed to grow out of the western flank of Orcas Island's Turtleback Mountain. Almost every room commanded a view of the moonlit President Channel, other islands of the San Juan group, and even Vancouver Island far to the west. Flurries of moving lights in the air and among the tall Douglas firs down along the seashore signaled the arrival of guests by rhocraft or by groundcar from the submarine tunnel interchange at West Beach a few kilometers away.

Nearly two hundred metas had been invited to help celebrate the triumph of the Remillard brothers on Satsuma. Marc had arranged for the chef of the famous old Rosario resort on Orcas to cater a sumptuous buffet, and an amateur combo of operant musicians, all friends or associates of his, was tuning up on the awninged terrace. Hiroshi and

Masako went down two flights of stairs to the ground floor and found themselves swept up in a colorful mob.

"To be a correct ancient Samurai woman," Hiroshi whispered to his wife, "you should trail behind me by several respectful steps."

"Jodan desho!" she retorted, snapping open her fan and taking his arm. "There *are* limits."

Some masqueraders made no attempt to conceal their identities, while others had gone to extremes of mystification. Impromptu guessing games, accompanied by a good deal of raucous laughter and shouting, were de rigueur. With no nonoperants present who might be scandalized, the metapsychic partygoers were clearly ready for unrestrained tomfoolery. Historic ethnic dress seemed particularly popular, but there were plenty of traditional North American Halloween costumes as well—witches, wizards, Frankenstein monsters, ballerinas, cartoon animals, comic-book superheroes, pirates, nuns, and clowns. A rotund Falstaff escorted a bangled belly dancer, a top-hatted Marlene Dietrich clone fluttered false eyelashes seductively at a matador, Marie Antoinette simpered through a mask-on-a-stick at a vizarded Sherlock Holmes, a Lakota chief in war paint offered a drink to a demure Wonder Woman, the Mad Hatter cackled at a joke told by a Chinese dragon with a two-meter tail supported by psychokinesis, Achilles and Patroclus strolled together arm in arm, clad in golden Greek armor, and the band—with beaming Shig Morita conducting from the piano—launched into "Stray Cat Strut."

It was a fine autumn evening, not too chilly. As Masako and Hiroshi came out of the house onto the terrace they encountered Lucille Cartier and Denis Remillard. Both wore doctoral academic gowns trimmed with the spruce-green and gold velvet of the School of Metapsychology.

"Komban wa!" said Denis, bowing cheerfully. He had recognized the pair from Satsuma at once. "You two look smashing. Lucille and I opted for just grabbing something out of the closet."

"Shame on you for looking so comfortable," said Hiroshi.

Masako, looking over Lucille's shoulder, suddenly gave an unbelieving gasp. "Good heavens! Can that be Marc in the E16 helmet?" She indicated a bizarre tall figure in white-tie evening dress dancing with a Valkyrie. His head was almost entirely enclosed in a grotesque black CE headpiece with jack-o'-lantern features pasted on.

Lucille shrugged. "Who else? He says he's a high-tech Brom Bones from *The Legend of Sleepy Hollow*. I suspect he'll do tricks with the equipment at the shank of the evening."

"And is young Jack also among the masquers?" Hiroshi inquired.

"We haven't found him yet," Denis admitted, "although he's certainly here. That was a fantastic piece of work those two did on your world. As I understand it, Kagoshima Metro is now safe from major tremors for at least fifty Earth years."

"So the Milieu scientists say. We're all very relieved that the largest settlement on our world is finally out of danger." Hiroshi shook his armored head. "I still find it incredible that two human minds could have modified the crust of a planet. Even twenty years ago, such a feat would have been called impossible. Naturally, we cannot expect the two Paramount Grand Masters to come to our rescue regularly, so we're establishing a CE training facility that will emphasize the geophysical applications of metaconcerted creativity. The governments of other worlds suffering crustal instability are helping in its financing and staffing. Okanagon will contribute teaching personnel. Your metaconcert programs, Denis, will be a valued part of the curriculum."

"Utilizing many minds in large-scale CE metaconcert projects will require tweaking the designs about considerably. Jack will be working closely with me for several months in order to make some very necessary modifications." Denis's youthful brow creased in a slight frown. "It's hard to argue with success—but I'm still not altogether certain that artificial augmentation of human brainpower is a good idea, especially in metaconcert. Marc narrowly escaped serious injury in the untested new configuration he and Jack used on your world."

Hiroshi drew in his breath sharply. "I had not realized! That's appalling! Why was nothing said to me?"

"He didn't want to rain on your parade," sighed Lucille.

"Jack was leading the metaconcert and Marc was the focusing agent," Denis said. "The focuser is almost always the one at greatest risk in such a situation because his role is essentially passive. Jack called for a certain change in configuration and Marc responded with an unexpected surge of power that temporarily overwhelmed the metaconcert design. The potentiality for dysergism is high enough in barebrain metaconcert programs using two such extraordinary minds. When such brains are hyperenergized, the hazard becomes acute unless the program is given very fine tuning. Ordinary grandmasterclass minds would not be nearly so much at risk because they can be strictly calibrated and fitted into the design structure. But paramounts are still full of surprises, unfortunately."

"I'm not familiar with the dysergism phenomenon," Hiroshi admitted. "Would it be the opposite of synergism, where the action of the whole is greater than that of the sum of the parts?"

"There's more to it than that," Denis said. "I'd be happy to explain it to you . . ."

"By all means!"

Lucille and Masako exchanged resigned glances.

A robot waitron came by with a tray of full champagne flutes and each of them took one. But while the others drank, the iron-masked Samurai regarded his inaccessible beverage with consternation. "I believe that ancient warriors accoutered in armor drank through broken arrow-shafts, which were hollow reeds. I refuse to make a fool of myself drinking champagne through a straw. Wife, kindly help me to remove this confounded mempo at once!"

Masako, Lucille, and Denis burst out laughing. After Hiroshi was freed, he and Denis went off into the garden for a professional discussion while the two women remained on the perimeter of the dance floor.

"I certainly didn't take hours getting dressed in order to spend the evening talking shop," Masako murmured crossly.

Lucille made a sympathetic noise as she finished her champagne and immediately snagged a refill from another robot. "Not when there are so many presentable young men to dance with! . . . But let's play the guessing game for a little while first."

They quickly found the First Magnate heaping a plate of hors d'oeuvres at the buffet table, costumed as Zorro and surrounded by a bevy of operant beauties. Adrien Remillard and his wife Cheri Losier-Drake danced by, dressed as Robin Hood and Maid Marian. Anne Remillard, tall and awesome in the scarlet robes of a medieval Catholic cardinal, boogied expertly with Alex Manion, who was got up as the captain of H.M.S. Pinafore. Boom-Boom Laroche, a hulking executioner with a black hood and a hangman's noose tucked into his belt, partnered Vampira—alias Marie Remillard. And then Lucille recognized Uncle Rogi.

"He makes a rather decent Abraham Lincoln," she decided. "But who in the world is he dancing with?"

"Her costume is . . . very unusual," Masako said.

That was a gross understatement. Rogi's petite companion was clad in an impressive silvery outfit that might have been a genuine high-altitude flight suit—except that it was extravagantly decorated with glittering rhinestones. Even the visored helmet and the mask that covered the lower part of the woman's face shone with faux diamonds.

The "Stray Cat Strut" ended and the dancers applauded.

"There's something rather odd about her aura," Lucille said thoughtfully. "Let's go make nuisances of ourselves and inspect her at close range."

But before the two of them could make a move the music started up again, this time with "Jalousie," and Honest Abe and his scintillating lady tangoed off at a smart pace.

"Drat," muttered Lucille. Then she saw a red-nosed clown cut in on Rogi and take his partner away. The bookseller watched the pair for a few minutes and then retreated in the direction of the bar. At the same moment a strapping Cossack and King Henry VIII asked Masako and Lucille to dance, and they forgot all about Rogi's mysterious companion.

Rogi spotted Kyle Macdonald, inevitably wearing Highland dress, glumly nursing a tumbler of amber liquid on a cedar bench off in the midst of some potted azaleas.

"Well, well! Who let the deadhead in?" Honest Abe chortled. "Don't you know this bash is for Homo superior only, my good man?" He took a seat beside the fantasy writer, doffed his stovepipe hat, and sampled his own drink.

Kyle grimaced. "Argh. Don't remind me, ye decrepit Canuck rumdum! Ever since we moved back to Earth, Masha's worked me over with the newest tortures of latency therapy. Me! The great champion of normalcy! Would ye believe I'm now classed as a minimally operant farsensor? It was either that or get chucked out by Her Nibs all over again . . . The woman's damn near irresistible in dominatrix mode."

"Serves you right falling for a coercer," Rogi said. "I warned you."

"Just look at the shameless bint!" Kyle pointed out the voluptuous figure of Professor MacGregor-Gawrys, bent over backwards nearly to the floor in a tango dip by a masked Lawrence of Arabia. She wore a black-and-white Erté ball gown of the 1920s, dripping with strings of crystal and jet. Her auburn hair had been frizzed and bound about with a magpie-silk bandeau.

"Devastating beyond belief," Rogi agreed. "Who's the Sheik of Araby?"

"Goddam fewkin' Severin Remillard. Who pinched *your* popsy?"

"You got me. One of the clowns. Identity-fuzzed."

"Weird outfit your bird had on," Kyle commented. "Reminded me of something, but I couldn't put my half-spifflicated finger on it. Who the hell is she?"

"You don't want to know." Rogi downed a swig of bourbon.

"Och, there she goes now: Lucy in the Sky with Rhinestones. Queen of the glitz-bikers." Kyle screwed up his craggy face as he attempted to bolster his exiguous, liquor-befuddled farsight. "God damn, I *thought* that outfit looked familiar! It's a tarted-up Caledonian air-farmer's flying kit, and that means the girl must be my own—"

Using what coercion he could conjure, Rogi socked it to his friend. "Shut up, Kyle!"

The Scotsman nearly fell off the bench. His drink went flying into an adjacent azalea tub. "Hey! Wot th' flamin' hell d'ye think—"

Rogi whipped his hand over Kyle's mouth, stifling him. "I'll tell you what's going on if you swear to keep your big haggis-trap shut forever."

"I shwear," Kyle said through Rogi's fingers.

The band played "If the Devil Danced in Empty Pockets, He'd Have a Ball in Mine." Numbers of the partygoers joined Marc Remillard's lead and formed into bouncy, finger-snapping country lines.

"This kind of choreography isn't quite my style," said the clown. "Shall we sit this one out, Diamond Mask?"

"I don't mind."

They made their way off the terrace into the big living room. It was dimly lit with scores of carved pumpkins with candles inside. In one alcove, a noisy variant of spin-the-bottle was being played with an empty champagne magnum. People were conversing in standing groups, sitting on the overstuffed furniture, and lounging on the floor. Pieces of discarded costume were beginning to litter the nooks and corners.

"Would you care for a drink or some munchies?" the clown asked as they passed an open bar.

"No thank you. But do have one yourself."

He took a glass of designer water and ice. "It's pretty noisy in here. Let's go across the hall to the library. It's got a balcony overlooking the sea."

"Perfect."

No one else was in the book-lined sanctum. The balcony doors were open and there were cushioned Woodard chairs waiting outside in the shadows. A cool breeze rustled the giant fir trees that framed the spectacular view.

The clown plopped into one of the metal chairs and his sparkling companion took a seat more gracefully. The dark visor of her ornate helmet was up, but her face was entirely concealed except for the hazel eyes. The clown wore traditional whiteface with a broadly drawn smile and a red rubber ball for a nose. His suit was white with big colored polka dots and he had a pleated ruff around his neck. His multicolored fright wig was topped with a floppy pointed hat.

"You're a great dancer," he said. "Hope I didn't step on your toes too often. I don't go to very many parties. A bit of a workaholic, I'm afraid." He had his mind-screen up, but it was only casually constructed and she had no difficulty sliding through it.

"You're very light on your feet," she said. "What kind of work do you do?" She took special care in fashioning the probe, holding it ready until the appropriate moment.

"A little of this, a little of that. I'm sort of an apprentice in the family sweatshop. Boring stuff. Money, power, interstellar commercial intrigue . . ."

She laughed. "I don't suppose you want to dispense with the games and tell me your name?"

"Why, sure! Just as soon as you show me your face, Diamond Mask."

"Not yet. I'm surprised you can't see it already with your deepsight."

Hunching over his knees, he leaned closer to her, squinting. "Oof! Gimme a break. You're hiding behind the Great Wall of China!" Shaking his head, he fell back into his seat and pretended to fan his brow. "That's what I call a real face-blanking headscreen! What are you—an axe-murderer on the lam? Or some famous Planetary Dirigent come slumming?"

She slid the probe home and began to weave the bypass structure.

"I'm only a college student," she said. "Math and physics. Boring . . . like your old family business, Mister Bozo the Clown."

There! Now she could begin the ream while they nattered on, making idiotic boy-meets-girl small talk. She would be able to ask him questions as well as extract data from his memories, just as she had done with the members of the Dynasty, and he would never suspect.

"I'll bet you're lovely behind that mask, little Diamond." He grinned hopefully. "Come on. Give us a peek."

"Oh, no. Not yet. Tell me more about yourself first. Do you know Marc Remillard well? This house of his is really a showplace, isn't it?"

"Kind of ostentatious, if you ask me." The clown waved a hand in lofty dismissal. "I've found that people who need to surround themselves with excessive amounts of material goods are—"

Show me your metapsychic complexus.

[Profoundly esoteric image.]

What is your name?

Jon Paul Kendall Remillard.

How old are you?

Twenty.

Where do you live?

My domicile of record is 4480 Lawai Beach Road, Poipu, Kauai, Hawaii. I am not often in residence there.

What is your current occupation?

I am a Magnate of the Concilium, a member of the Panpolity Unification Directorate, an occasional participant in academic research concerning the design of metaconcert programs, and a codeveloper of cerebroenergetic equipment with my older brother Marc.

Are you participating actively in the search for the criminals known as Fury and Hydra?

Not at the present time.

In your opinion, which members of the Remillard Dynasty are most likely to harbor the entity called Fury within themselves? List them in order of probability and include Marc and Uncle Rogi in your calculations as well.

1. Marc
2. Anne
3. Paul
4. Severin
5. Adrien
6. Maurice
7. Philip
8. Catherine
9. Rogi

Give me the complete background information that leads you to your conclusions.

[Data.]

Do you know a person called Clinton Wolfe Alvarez, a resident of the planet Okanagon, who serves as an executive assistant on the staff of Dirigent Patricia Castellane?

No.

Have you ever personally encountered this particular metaconcert configuration? [Data.]

No.

Why did you attempt to farspeak the child Dorothea Mary Macdonald at her home on Caledonia?

I was curious about her. I had been told of her existence by [untranslatable Lylmik name], who indicated that she was potentially a mind of the paramount grandmasterclass, like me. I was lonely. I hoped we might become friends. I still do.

Why do members of your family call you by the nickname Jack the Bodiless?

Because my normal physical form is that of a disembodied brain. This body and certain others I wear are metacreative constructs.

!!! Who . . . knows about this outside of your family?

The Lylmik Supervisors, a handful of exotic and human friends.

You will recall nothing of this probing.

Yes—

"—but when you're a nine-hundred-kilo canary like Marc, you get to sing anywhere you damn please, right?"

She laughed appreciatively at the conclusion of the joke. "Oh, abso-bloody-lutely!" She got to her feet. "This has been ever so much of a giggle, Mister Bozo, but now I'd like to go dancing again."

The clown's face fell. "Aw, you promised, Diamond Mask. First let me see you for real." He reached for her jewel-encrusted breathing equipment, but she skipped out of range, laughing again, and dashed away toward the terrace. The band was playing a fair imitation of the famous George Benson cut of "This Masquerade."

The clown closed and locked the library door, then went into the adjacent room that served as Marc's home office. A credenza yielded up a powerful subspace communicator at the touch of a button. The clown called Chief Evaluator Throma'eloo Lek at the Office of the Galactic Magistratum in Orb.

"Lek? Get ready for an intimode mind-squirt. I'm gone."

Shutting off the communicator, the clown relaxed in Marc's big leather chair, closed his eyes, and extended his mind 4000 lightyears to bespeak the waiting Krondak official on his intimate telepathic mode:

Lek, this is vitally important. I want you to arrange the immediate arrest of one Clinton Wolfe Alvarez, an administrative assistant to the Dirigent of Okanagon. He is an unusually powerful Grand Master with all five faculties up to snuff, so you'd better send a Krondak team. Hoke up some civil charge like suspicion of vehicular homicide. Groundcar hit-and-run. You'll have to arrange a major computer hack-job, but I know you're capable of it. See that Alvarez is held without bail and with as much publicity as possible until you and I can get to Okanagon to interrogate him. I especially want the Earth media to find out that this guy is in the slammer just as soon as it happens. And make it happen soon! Within hours, not days. Can you do it?

Certainly, if you say so. What is the actual reason for detaining this individual?

I'm virtually certain he's part of Hydra. Catch you later . . .

The clown opened his eyes and sat there for a few minutes, thinking. Then he left the office and went out to find Rogi.

The bookseller was at the bar, filling a glass of ice cubes with straight Wild Turkey. "She do her number on you okay, kid?"

The clown nodded. "And she was very good, Uncle Rogi. Too damned good. Once I deliberately let her in, I was almost dead meat. I was actually forced to tell her the truth. Thank heaven she didn't ask the wrong questions. Or maybe I mean the right ones."

"Well, well. So she really is paramount-class."

"Beyond a doubt . . . She fingered a Hydra-unit that her grandmother had inadvertently stumbled over and showed me the monster's metaconcert config."

Rogi brushed all that aside. "But am *I* off the hook? Did you fix it so she won't drag me off to Okanagon and get us both killed?"

"All you have to do is make certain she checks out the interstellar news tomorrow. A certain Citizen Clinton Alvarez is about to be framed on a capital charge and locked up howling his head off in the Chelan Metro chokey on the planet Okanagon. Dorothea will call off the trip like a shot when she finds out."

Rogi let out a sigh of relief. "What next?"

The clown gazed out at the dancers. Brom Bones and Diamond Mask were waltzing to Wes Mongomery's "West Coast Blues." Near them was a couple in strikingly beautiful Shakespearean costume—a burly Moor of Venice and a delicate, pale-skinned Desdemona with scarlet lips. For an instant, Rogi thought he recognized the woman. But then he realized he was mistaken. Both she and her companion wore impenetrable mental disguises.

"I'm taking my own starship to Okanagon," the clown said. "You make sure our mutual female friend goes to Kauai after she gets the news. Drag her there if you have to, and see that the two of you stay on the island under Malama's protection until I find out what Clinton Alvarez has to say for himself."

Dee nabbed Marc during the Ladies' Choice waltz. At first he had attempted to demur because of the difference in their heights: he was over 40 centimeters taller than she, and the black jack-o'-lantern of the CE helmet made him even taller.

But she said, "You can't back out of Ladies' Choice, Big Boy!" She took both his hands in hers and gave him a coercive nudge that made his eyes widen. Then he laughed at her audacity, and they swung out onto the floor together. She was so light on her feet that they seemed to complement each other perfectly, a pair of graceful grotesques, and many of the other couples stopped to watch.

But she found it impossible to get into his mind.

No fair! she said. You've got the *hat* energized haven't you.

He said: The E16's internal power source won't move mountains, but it's quite adequate to Diamondproof me. You'll simply have to take my word that I'm neither Fury nor part of Hydra.

"A likely story," she said aloud. She tried to pull away from him but he held her gloved hands tightly. "Let go."

"Don't make a scene. You wanted to dance. Do it."

"You big bully!" The diamond mask hid her fury at being momentarily outmaneuvered, but after a moment's hesitation she submitted.

Marc only laughed. He had not bothered to extend his augmented power to an external disguise, and she could easily see through the bulky CE helmet with its zany stuck-on features to the ironically smiling face beneath. It was safe to assume that he could see her face, too.

"I'm delighted to meet you, Dorothea Macdonald. Since you've had a go at probing the other Remillards, I believe it's only fair to give me a turn with you."

Her dancing feet never missed a beat but the eyes above the glittering mask hardened. "Try it."

He did, gently at first and then with building intensity, calling at last upon the maximum enhancement potential available with the limited power source of the helmet. His mental probe would have cracked a Krondaku Grand Master; it did not faze the fifteen-year-old girl.

"Bonté divine! You are a prodigy, aren't you, Diamond Mask! Your mind-screen's as strong as Jack's."

"Good."

"You're hostile . . . what a shame. And we've just met."

"Let's not pussyfoot," she retorted. "You were expecting me to do just what I did. Your CE equipment is set for the augmentation of coercion—not creativity."

The black jack-o'-lantern nodded. "The helmet is capable of enhancing only one metafaculty at a time. Switching it over requires the insertion of a different brainboard. It's not difficult. The original interface will be plugged back in before I perform my bag of tricks later in the evening."

"What are you going to do to me now?" she asked calmly. "Prosecute me for felonious mental trespass against members of your family?"

"I'm going to waltz with you," Marc said.

"No warning me off the Remillard preserves with threats of legal retaliation?"

"Your enemy is ours. Believe me! We should join forces, not work at odds. My brother Jack would like to—"

"No!" For the first time, her silver-clad body faltered. "I don't want anything to do with that—with him."

"He's human," Marc said softly. "He was very impressed by your probing this evening. He says he couldn't have done anything approaching it without cerebroenergizing. You're an appalling young woman, Diamond Mask. I hope the Lylmik waste no time magnatizing you. You'll join our elite little club then, whether you want to or not."

"If they make me a paramount, I'll carry out whatever duties the position entails." Her tone was stilted.

"Paramount Grand Masters have no special obligations aside from the usual duties of a magnate, but sometimes suggestions are made. It was suggested that Jack and I take a bash at the Satsuma seismic problem. We did and we got lucky. But I nearly died."

"How?"

Marc showed her. "In this configuration, I was the prime focus, the one actually directing the flow of energies. Unfortunately, we had failed to calibrate our atypical mental potential precisely enough, and because of this the metaconcert suffered a dysergistic failure. What we call an all-systems zorch—a funny name for a not-so-funny phenomenon. The pressurized atmosphere inside the deep-drilling machine we rode in suddenly ionized into white-hot plasma because of misdirected creativity. Jack might have had a pico-sec's warning through the proleptic metafaculty—the one that allegedly sees the future—or perhaps his mind just outraced the expanding ions. At any rate he cut out of the concert and spun a psychocreative shield around me that saved my bacon. The ionization was gone as fast as it came but the cab of the driller and part of its instrumentation were fried. The surface crew descended and rescued us within two hours. Then Jack and I modified the config of the concert, climbed into a new deep-driller, and tried again. The second time was the charm. We were able to diminish the friction within the fault zone—to 'lubricate' it with a creative injection of carbon—and minimize the danger of a serious quake in that area for a useful number of years."

"Why wasn't your brother burnt to a crisp in the plasma blowout?"

"He was in his natural mutant form. It seems to be invulnerable. At least, nothing's ever been able to harm him yet."

The music ended and Marc and Dee applauded.

"Thank you for the dance," she said. Will I be expected to undertake mortally dangerous work like this if I'm named a paramount?

Marc said, "It was my pleasure, Citizen Macdonald." Only if you feel you must. You're free to make your own choice.

The band began to play a techno variation of "Pompton Turnpike" and Lucille Cartier and Denis Remillard materialized out of the crowd.

"Your mother insists on having a whirl with you, Marc," Denis said. "I think she wants to make certain you're all in one piece." He bowed to Dorothea Macdonald. "If you'll accept a default partner, my dear?"

"I'd be honored, Professor Remillard," she said.

As they danced away she slipped carefully through Denis's mind-screen, slid the probe home, and began to weave the bypass structure.

<My poor little one.>

Fury. I expected you earlier. It's a goddam catastrophe.

<Yes.>

Is it ruined then? Your great scheme for the Second Milieu?

<No my darling boy not if you are willing to save it.>

The other units can . . . carry on successfully without me until you recruit more?

<They can. Some of them are not so mature and unselfish as you. They have resisted my need to regenerate. But now the need will be more than self-evident. I shall carry on. And bless and remember you always as you rejoice with Gordo in the abode of reward I have prepared for you. If you wish, you can wait until tomorrow—>

I'm ready to do it right now. Farewell Fury. Farewell *SELVES* . . .

. . .

The man known as Clinton Wolfe Alvarez died in his sleep of a massive myocardial infarction approximately three hours after he was arrested and placed in a holding cell in the Metropolitan Jail of Okanagon's capital city. The body was not discovered until the next morning, by which time there was no possibility of resuscitating him in a regeneration-tank.

DNA analysis eventually identified the deceased as Quentin Frederic O'Neill Remillard, the fugitive son of Severin Remillard. This information was kept confidential by the Galactic Magistratum. The vehicular homicide case fabricated against the erstwhile Citizen Alvarez was classified as "solved" by the death of the suspect.

[19]

KAUAI, HAWAII, EARTH
2 NOVEMBER 2072

The dream came to her for the last time while she waited on the island with Uncle Rogi for Jack to complete his investigation on Okanagon. After two nearly sleepless nights as a result of Malama Johnson's huna therapy, she found herself finally relaxing on the breezy lanai of the little house in Kukuiula. Her eyes closed and she slept.

<Dody . . . >

Mummie? You're crying. What's wrong?

<I'm so disappointed. In you, my dear. We had so many fruitful conversations. You seemed to be so excited about the plan for the Second Milieu and your role as the leader of it. But now I find that you've been consorting with the Great Enemy. You promised you'd never listen to his lies, never have anything to do with that godless inhuman tool of the Lylmik slavemasters. You broke your promise, Dody. Betrayed my trust. I'm so unhappy.>

There's no need, Mummie. The Halloween party was a perfect chance to probe Jack's mind. To know just what kind of threat the Great Enemy poses. You can't contend against a foe you have no data on. Surely you realize that.

<The Cosmic All designated *me* to be your guide and mentor, Dody. I am the only conduit of God's truth, the only one who can show you how to fulfill your destiny and bring about the new Golden Age for humanity. Trusting in your own judgment is arrogant and foolhardy, a sign of childish pride.>

I didn't think of it that way.

<The time is growing so short! You seemed nearly ready to make the Choice. But now I suspect . . . that you have doubts.>

Nothing has changed in our relationship. I'm as committed to you and the Second Milieu as I ever was.

<Then why have you gone to Kauai, to consort with the Great Enemy's two lackeys?>

Uncle Rogi is no one's lackey, Mum. And Malama Johnson is simply a friend of his that we're visiting—

<The Hawaiian woman is a kahuna! Don't you know what that means, you foolish child?>

She's a traditional Hawaiian healer. A practitioner of natural redaction. She's been helping me with the inhibitions that prevent me from using the full spectrum of my metafaculties—

<She's an ignorant witch doctor! A primitive thinker with no conception of the Cosmic All, who toys with malignant psychic phenomena that she doesn't understand. Do you realize that the Lylmik have used more sophisticated variants of this "huna magic" from time immemorial in order to control the minds of their Unified slaves?>

Oh, Mum. Malama Johnson is a Catholic, just like I am. She's a dear, harmless old soul who teaches me how to make flower leis when she's not helping me sweep out the last of my mental garbage. She's a kahuna lapaau, not one of the black-magic anaana kind. Her use of the higher mindpowers is restricted to her work as a healer amongst her people here in the islands.

<Dody, Dody, what a simpleminded lass you still are, for all your education and operancy. This woman Malama practices a dark, soul-destroying art that lets her control those around her. Heaven only knows what damage she'll do if you allow her inside your mind! She's been instructing the Great Enemy how to use an amplified version of her huna power, so that he'll eventually be able to obliterate the human opponents of Unity. The Lylmik have concealed the existence of this ultimate mental evil from all except a handful of their most trusted servants. Jack is one of them and so is his brother Marc. There are others as well, subverting the human freedom movement on every world our people have colonized.>

I—I find that hard to believe.

<Do you? Do you really? My dearest daughter, have you finally turned your back on the holy vision I was privileged to bring you?>

No. I only want to study it scientifically from all aspects, to make certain—

<You persist in clinging to false notions of reductionist objectivity when you should be embracing the tapestry of the Whole, which is mystery! You're a mathematician, Dody. Have you forgotten what Gödel's Theorem tells you? Axioms cannot describe a world that is both provably complete and consistent. There *is* a truth that lies beyond! One that can be grasped only through faith.>

I know. I still must ask whether the Second Milieu exemplifies this truth. And whether I'm the one to promulgate it.

<I weep for you . . . Your lack of vision is on the verge of condemning Earth's children to a future of mental bondage. Unless you make the Choice, humanity will never prevail against the horror that is Unity. Our race will be engulfed by the oppressive exotic Mind, and it will be your fault! For doubting. For lacking courage. For toying with uncertainty and paradox rather than making the leap of faith—the Choice.>

You know I'm not . . . a person of unswerving self-confidence. When you tell me I must lead the human race into the Second Milieu all by myself I feel overwhelmed—

<But you needn't! Because *you won't really be alone.* That's the most consoling, the most beautiful thing about the Choice. Up until now, I haven't spoken of this aspect of the glorious mystery, but now I must. Because this is your last chance, Dody.>

I—what do you mean?

<I am empowered to offer you the Choice *now*, for the first and only time. If you accept, you will know instantly how the Second Milieu is to be accomplished. Your doubts and fears will evaporate—together with that malignant preprogrammed response you call your guardian angel, that poisonous thing the Lylmik planted within you when you were an unsuspecting child, hoping to make you their slave.>

How . . . do I make this Choice?

<All that's necessary is for you to say, "Mother, let it be done," and mean it with all your heart and mind.>

You mean I must open myself?

<Yes.>

Without reservation?

<Yes.>

What will happen then?

<My dearest, most fortunate child! The Cosmic Afflatus will fill you—the very Life-Breath of the All. You will find yourself sharing your body with the Mind of the Universe itself.>

That's incredible. It's like . . . the Annunciation.

<No. It's greater. The Entity dwelling within you will make you the instrument of human freedom and happiness without your having to sacrifice anything of your self. You will never be called upon to suffer. You will only know ineffable joy.>

With the Cosmic Mind residing inside my body.

<Yes.>

Whose body does the Mind inhabit now?

< . . . What?>

The Mind. Where is it now?

<*WILL YOU MAKE THE CHOICE?*>

Will you answer my question?

. . .

Mummie?

<So . . . All these years, it has been a game. You hoped to trick me, you perfidious damned child! You know who I really am. You've always known. And *you* are the one responsible for the death of my poor Quentin!>

That's not true, and you know it.

<Shitfacedliar! Stinkingputridcunt! Mindfuckingwhore! It was your fault—>

I'd like to help you, Fury. Neutralize the anger and relieve the unending pain. There must be a way to reintegrate the broken parts of you. To heal you.

. . .

Tell me whose body you live in.

<You'll find out, Dorothea Macdonald. As you die. Be assured that I am going to kill you, in precisely the same way that your dear mother was killed: slowly, in the most intense mental and physical agony that human beings can experience. Wait for it! It will happen when you least expect it. Au revoir.>

Rogi came out of the house carrying a tray with two frosty glasses of pineapple juice and a durofilm printout of the island newspaper. "So you're awake after all. I was hoping you'd finally get a few hours of rest."

Dee managed a wan smile. "I did doze a little."

He gave her the drink and sat down in one of the other chairs with the paper. "You ought to reconsider letting Malama help you with the insomnia."

"There's no need. I don't think I'll be troubled with sleeplessness again. Malama has enough to do, teaching me the huna discipline. It's fascinating the way she's been able to release some of the most intractable of my residual mind-blocks in just the two days I've been here. Things Catherine and her people couldn't touch."

"Well, Jack told you she was special. He says she worked with him even before he was born. I don't know whether to take him seriously or not. It sounds pretty peculiar."

Dee's expression darkened. "*Jack* is peculiar. I still can't believe I agreed to come here and do this. You're a very persuasive man, Uncle Rogi. If it had been only Jack urging me to come to Malama, I'd have turned him down flat."

"You don't have to be afraid of Ti-Jean, Dorothée. He has your best interests at heart."

She sighed. "So people keep telling me." She set her untouched drink aside, got up from the chaise, and stretched. Her hair was in two braids and she wore a pair of tattered shorts and one of Rogi's gaudy old Hawaiian shirts knotted beneath her small breasts. "I think I'll take a walk down along the shore. The surf ought to be spectacular this morning after the storm."

"I'll go with you," Rogi said with a smile, throwing his newspaper aside and climbing hurriedly to his feet.

"No, thanks. I have to sort some things out in my mind. I'd really rather go alone. I know you and Malama mean well, but you two have hardly let me out of your sight since I arrived. And that's silly. She verifies the MP ID of everyone on the island each night when her mana's strongest. There are no Hydras here. And even if there were, I'd know them the instant they combined in metaconcert to attack me. And I'd get them."

Rogi sat down again, glowering. "You're too damned sure of yourself. How can you be so positive you're stronger than they are?"

"For starters, there are only three of them now. One of the Hydras is dead. Jack will find out that the DNA of Clinton Alvarez matches that of Quentin Remillard."

"How do you know that for certain? You been watching Jack on Okanagon with your farsight?"

"No . . . but I'm sure of it, all the same. And there's another reason why I'm confident I'm a match for the remaining Hydras. They consider Jack to be Fury's Great Enemy. If they could have drained the lifeforce from him with mindpower, they would have done it years ago. They haven't—ergo, they *can't.* My own mental defenses are at least the equal of Jack's, but the Hydras don't know it."

"Smart-ass female!" The old bookseller retrieved the newpaper and took a hefty slug of his own drink—which she noted was by no means unadulterated fruit juice, as her own had been. "Go ahead and take your walk, then! But just remember there are lots more ways to eliminate people than by burning 'em up and sucking their minds with highfalutin kundalini metawhatsit! A Hydra could just drop a coconut on your head with PK, for chrissake. You'd be just as dead!"

She couldn't help laughing. "I'll keep my farsenses alert. Where's Malama?"

"Gone to the supermarket in Poipu. She figured you'd nap for a while longer. I was supposed to keep an eye on you."

"That's very sweet, and I appreciate it. But I'm going to go over to Spouting Horn Park and sit on the rocks and do some heavy thinking. I don't want to be followed. Agreed?"

Rogi rustled the newspaper reproachfully, but he said, "Agreed."

She left Malama's house and walked along the shore road until she came to the parking lot and viewing area above the formation called the Spouting Horn. It was a gray, chilly morning and the surf was monstrous. There were a few tourists leaning on the railing, taking pictures of the famous natural wonder. Below the lookout were dark, flattened masses of lava periodically inundated by the surging sea. From time to time an especially high wave forced its way beneath a submarine shelf with a large lava tube in it, compressing air within the narrow tunnel and ramming a mass of water through it. With a roar, a spectacular fountain would erupt from a blowhole amongst the flat rocks, spraying saltwater over 15 meters high and causing the drenched tourists to shriek. The Spouting Horn was one of Kauai's best-known scenic attractions.

Smiling, she moved further down the shore and found a niche among the rocks and flowering shrubs where she could watch the sea in privacy. It was still windy and cold, but she fixed that by slightly increasing the temperature of the air flowing over her bare skin. Thermal modifications were among the more easy metacreative actions.

Three brave sailboarders in shorty wet suits had come from the small boat harbor at Kukuiula Bay and were zipping up and down a few hundred meters offshore. Now and then one of the colorful craft would capsize, only to be righted again and resume its perilous dance on the waves.

I've got to be like that, too, Dee thought. I mustn't brood about what's finally happened with Fury and get all in a state. I've got to pick myself up, make sure all the bits and pieces are working properly, and then refine my plan to trap Hydra.

It was going to be a great deliverance, finally being able to shut Fury out of her dreams, even if the trade-off was unending vigilance against Hydra attacks. Fury would certainly send its remaining minions after her soon, now that she had defied it. With Alvarez dead and no clue to the identities or location of the others, she would never recognize her assailants until the last moment, when they combined in metaconcert, singing their deadly mindsong as they prepared to drain the life out of her.

Was she really a match for them, as she had so glibly assured Uncle Rogi? The probabilities were favorable—providing she was awake, alert, and not diminished by bodily injury or any other disability. Malama had promised to teach her a more sensitive version of her own "instant wake-up" program that would sound a mental alarm if an intruder touched her mind or body while she slept. That would ensure her safety during her most vulnerable time. She could even hide inside a small sigma-shield if she became ill or weakened—but of course it was quite impractical to use such a device when she was awake and going about her daily life. Nor would she want to. Luring Hydra out of hiding—not barricading herself against it—was her principal priority.

The most worrisome aspect of the hunt was what she now decided to call the Coconut Factor, after Uncle Rogi's shrewd insight. Unlike Fury, the three human minions were not limited to subtle mental assault. They could come at her individually, without using their telltale metaconcert, and attack her in some purely physical way—with a laser gun, a bomb, poisoned food, even the dreaded falling coconut. Jack, that creepy Superthing, might be able to clothe his brain in invulnerable psychocreative armor, but she was not yet capable of such mental virtuosity.

Jack Remillard had gone to Okanagon in his personal starship, not only to identify the body of "Clinton Alvarez" but also in hopes of finding clues to the identity of the other three killers. Dee doubted that he would learn anything of value. Even if the other Hydras had lived on the cosmop planet, they would surely have fled as soon as Alvarez was arrested. Fortunately, it was unlikely that any fugitive Hydra-units could have already reached Earth from Okanagon. Only the ultra-express starships operated by the Krondaku—and Jack the Bodiless—would have been able to make the trip in less than four days. Humans booked passage on such vessels only rarely. It was unlikely the killers would have risked their new identities by doing so and calling attention to themselves.

There was another reason why Dee thought she would probably remain safe from the Hydras for some time yet. Up until this morning, Fury had at least harbored a forlorn hope that she would accept its blasphemous Choice.

She shuddered. To be condemned to share her body with that monster! What an abominable fate! But how in God's name would Fury have been able to move from its Remillard host to her? It had no life except as an abnormal adjunct persona hiding within a human brain.

Didn't it?

She shivered again. The wind had increased slightly and she was obliged to thicken her warm, creative shelter. One of the windsurfers seemed to have given up after being dunked continually, but two valiant sails still hurtled at high speed out among the swells.

What I must do, she told herself, is set myself up as soon as possible in a perilous situation impossible for Fury and the Hydras to resist . . . It will have to be before my sixteenth birthday on January

20. The Lylmik are bound to call me to Orb then for my initiation, and after that there'll be the Concilium session. And heaven knows what work assignment if they do designate me a magnate and a paramount. I'll have to do my best to set my trap during Christmas break.

Where? . . . No doubt an opportunity will present itself.

Should I take Jack into my confidence?

No, she decided. Remillards were responsible for producing Fury and Hydra. One of them *was* Fury. Besides, if she asked for Jack's help, he'd want her to yield up the Hydra metaconcert score—less one voice—so that he would have an equal opportunity to identify the killers. She would not make it possible for him to cheat her of doing her solemn duty. It was her obligation to bring her mother's killers to justice, not Jack's.

Should she notify the Magistratum?

Again, she decided the answer was no. Local police could bring the Milieu Enforcement Arm in fast enough once she'd done her work. Let the Magistratum use the Cambridge machine on the villains once she'd captured them and forced them to identify Fury at last. She was willing to leave *that* monster to the Remillards. Its paradoxical existence was utterly beyond her experience. Let Jack deal with it. He was as inhuman as Fury was, and he was the only one of his family above suspicion.

Or was he?

What had Fury said in the last dream, castigating so-called evil servants of the Lylmik? *Jack is one of them and so is his brother Marc.*

Then Marc Remillard was not Fury, either.

But she couldn't possibly ask that sardonic older man for assistance or even confide in him. He'd outwitted her very nicely out on the dance floor at the party, and he'd certainly betray her plans to Jack. There was also the distinct possibility that Fury had lied about Marc being its enemy. No. There was only one way for her to undertake her crusade, and that was alone.

She canceled the warm air, got up from her rocky seat, and followed the path back to Spouting Horn Park. There were a few curio peddlers among the trees beyond the public lua, their stands shielded from the wind by flapping plass tarps. Only a single tourist vehicle remained in the parking lot. The periodic hissing roar of the blowhole punctuated the sound of the booming surf.

Then she heard shouts over by the lookout.

"Oh, God—Mikey!" a man cried out. "Help! Somebody get help! Mikey! Get up! Run! Quick!" He moved clumsily toward the end of the railing as he continued to shout, a tall and strong-looking man but one who was rather overweight and encumbered with flopping zori sandals.

Dee dashed across the grass verge and looked down toward the Spouting Horn. A boy six or seven years old wearing a red-and-white striped shirt was lying facedown on the rocks less than two meters away from the big blowhole. Foamy water was draining away over the slippery black surfaces into the heaving sea and into the sinister crevice in the lava.

"Get help!" the man shouted, catching sight of Dee. He started down the rocky embankment. "My little boy—he must have slipped away and gone down there while I was in the john! Maybe one of the spouts knocked him over and—oww!" He tripped and fell, uttering curses. The boy still hadn't moved.

"Do something!" shrieked the father. "If that thing goes off again, it might wash him right into the blowhole!"

Without stopping to think, Dee vaulted over the rail and began to slide down. The man, halfway down the slope among the tumbled chunks of lava and dried sea grass, was still trying to struggle to his feet.

Dee lashed out at the child with her coercion, but he was unconscious and did not respond. Before she could muster the creative-psychokinetic energy to lift him she, too, lost her footing on the slippery rocks and fell headlong toward the half-submerged lava bench.

As she tried to arrest her fall she was aware of an eerie, anticipatory moaning sound. Then the Spouting Horn erupted and she was enveloped in spray. Something struck her a sharp blow on the head and she saw a burst of brilliant light. Roaring water smashed her against the rocks, pushing her, pulling her, tumbling her helpless body over and over until she was sucked down into a whirling maelstrom.

Somewhere underwater she regained consciousness, lifted her head into air, and coughed and spat until she breathed again. She seemed to be down in a well more than three meters deep. The sides were weed-encrusted black rock studded with barnacles and other razor-sharp shellfish that sliced her hands as she instinctively clutched at them. The water around her surged up and down, reflecting the pattern of the lesser waves that always preceded and followed the biggest, but it was clearly becoming more shallow as the blowhole drained. Occasionally her feet, still encased in trainers, touched the rocky floor.

Suddenly she saw that the lava tube was L-shaped. Its horizontal section became visible, filled nearly to the top with water as each swell marched shoreward. The outlet terminated many meters away in the direction of the open sea. Something red-and-white bobbed on the dim, foamy surface halfway down the tunnel.

Oh, sweet Jesus. It was the little boy.

She was still disoriented, dizzy, nauseated from the seawater she had swallowed. Her head was a throbbing drum of pain and her higher mindpowers seemed inaccessible, as though she had forgotten everything she had ever learned about their use. All the lifeforce she possessed persisted in functioning at the most primitive level of being: that of bodily survival. She had to escape from the blowhole, taking the child with her, before the next great wave pounded and smashed both of them to death against the walls of the lava tube.

But how?

Psychokinesis. The mind's power over matter. Focus the PK impulse internally, not externally. In her injured condition, the metapsychic force she could muster was pitifully feeble; but it might be sufficient to bolster her flagging muscles.

She took a deep breath, surface-dived, and headed toward the small drifting body. The tunnel pinched to less than a meter in diameter in some parts. Its walls harbored other forms of marine life—anemones, starfish, mussels, anchored seaweed. Many small rocks and white chunks of broken coral rolled about the tube's bottom in murky water full of sand and other suspended matter. Perhaps one of those rocks, flung out by the last eruption, had struck her on the head.

Her right arm was going numb, not functioning properly. She kicked with all her diminishing strength against the increasing buildup of water pressure. Another huge storm-swell was beginning its leisurely progress toward shore.

She touched human flesh under water. Saw a wavering shape.

The boy seemed to have drowned. His eyes and mouth were wide open and his hair streamed like pitiful strands of algae. The red-and-white shirt had turned to black-and-gray in the underwater twilight. She grasped one of his limp arms in her good left hand and attempted to swim toward the spot of bright water marking the seaward mouth of the tunnel.

The pressure of the inflowing water was growing harder and harder to resist. She was making no progress. Then she was actually moving backwards! Her PK, once rated beyond grandmasterclass, had dwindled almost to nothing.

Angel . . . help me!

You must help yourself this time. Pray. But not to me.

Help us! For the love of God, we'll die—

To coerce God is to coerce reality and answer your own prayers.

The weight of the sea was forcing her inexorably backwards. In despair, she yielded to the pressure and was flung head over heels against one of the tunnel walls, almost losing her grip upon the child. The water around her had become a chaos of swirling bubbles, nearly opaque. Once, when her head was above water, she saw another opening in the solid rock of the tunnel roof—the dead-end chamber where the air would be compressed by the largest waves, eventually causing both the sounds and the fountain of spray.

A mighty surge slammed her into the roof, sending new flashes of pain through her skull. She refused to relinquish her grip on the boy, even though her increasing weakness made it seem that he was actively pulling her toward the blowhole.

An uncanny basso moaning sound, like some huge sea beast in agony, began. In another moment the Spouting Horn would erupt again.

Show me how! Please . . .

Not psychokinesis. Creativity. Heat. Cold.

Of course! It was self-evident. Her joy and triumph at finding the solution lent her the strength to accomplish the miracle inside of a few seconds. To freeze a volume of water in the direction of the blowhole, plugging the lava tube for a critical instant. To encase her body and that of the child in thick salty ice at the same time.

Then to superheat the air and the rising water within the compression chamber above the tunnel roof.

The resulting great blast of steam sent them rocketing through the lava tube and out into the open sea nearly 80 meters from shore. Their icy shrouds melted before they drifted to a halt. Behind them, the Spouting Horn roared skyward like a geyser as the plug of frozen water burst.

Dee managed a single farspoken call for help before letting go of the other body and slipping into black unconsciousness.

Malama Johnson, driving back from her shopping trip to Poipu on Lawai Road, exclaimed, "Auwe! Oh, my goodness!" She tromped on the accelerator and sped toward the park.

The two windsurfers still plying the offshore waters near the Spouting Horn were mildly operant Hawaiian boys. Coerced by Malama, they came speeding over the waves to the rescue at more than 50 kph.

Dee woke hours later in her own bed in the tiny number-two guest bedroom of the kahuna's house. Her head still ached horribly, but the rest of her body was pain-free. A brown face peered around the doorframe and smiled.

"You saved my life, Malama," Dee whispered. "Mahalo nui, Tutu."

"You bet," said the kahuna brusquely. She came in and touched Dee's forehead and it stopped hurting. Then she said, a trifle crossly, "Fine t'ing, Makana Lani, Jack come back find you pau! He going show Tutu Malama stink-face, even if it you own fault you mek A."

Rogi stood in the door, beaming with relief. "You didn't even break any bones. Just a little sprain in the right arm. Malama will finish fixing it and your bruises and scrapes tomorrow."

"Now try sleep, Makana Lani," the kahuna commanded, using the Hawaiian name she had bestowed upon Dee. Like Dorothea, it meant "gift of God."

"The little boy," Dee murmured, letting her eyelids close as the woman's healing redaction soothed her. "Is he all right?"

"What little boy?" Rogi asked.

"His name was Mikey. I pulled him out of the Spouting Horn with me. Don't tell me he wasn't found!" Dee was wide awake again, half risen from the bed in agitation. "That's the reason why I was caught in the blowhole—trying to save him."

Malama and Rogi looked at each other.

"No keiki in da breaks wit' you," the Hawaiian woman said. "Nobody in da park at all when da two kanaka pull you out and bring you to me."

"But his father . . . " Dee fell silent. "Yes. I see. There was a third sailboarder when I first arrived at the park. Later he—or she—disappeared."

"Sleep," said Malama Johnson. "Tomorrow we going do some extra-special huna, then I teach you how spahk Jack wit'out subspace radio. You tell *him* all about da kine at Spouting Horn, yeah!"

"And the Coconut Effect," Dee said.

<Love. Regret. Yes I see. My precious little ones! You failed but the plan was well conceived. It might have worked. There will be another time.>

Two units were enough to plant the idea in the Girl's head and nudge her to act on it but we were unable to follow through. If only Celine had been here with me\US! Parni is a dolt he bungled the stone. If he had impelled it to hit her squarely on the temple or even at the point of the jaw she might never have regained consciousness.

You weren't too swift yourself Maddy Jeez I nearly plotzed when the Girl did that steamheat thing and dragged you with her damngoodthing she went blotto at the end of the line sweetsurprise to find out she'd rescued Maddyinawetsuit instead of poorlittleMikey.

<You avoided the temptation to strike out at her mentally Madeleine. That was admirable. The Girl would have known you . . . and perhaps obtained your true mental signature.>

Yes. Well she&kahuna certainly know what happened by now.

[Laughter.] Fat lot of good it does 'em we were out of there slickerthanhogshit before the HawaiianWitch arrived.

I tried to deflect the two boys on the sailboards from rescuing her but the kahuna's compulsion was too strong. If we are to dispose of the Girl by nonfeeding means we'll have to use more conservative tactics and pick the next time&place of attack with the utmost care.

No kahunas ready to ride to the rescue! And have *all* Hydraunits on board and cooking.

<Yes Parni you are quite right. Celine will be with you soon.>

It's safe for her to travel? I mean won't the cops be watching traffic from Okanagon to Earth?

<She will take a roundabout way to Earth and arrive undetected. I will deal with the matter. No grand gestures this time however. Only quiet alterations of computer data.>

Fury . . . do we still have the watts to snuff the Girl even with Celine's input? [Doubt.]

<I will be honest: You do *not* unless she is first diminished in some manner. But this can be accomplished by physical injury by mental trauma by excruciating fatigue even by distraction. As you saw today. She is not a mature Paramount-GrandMaster with wellhoned survival experience. She is still a child.>

She won't be much longer. Not after the Lylmik get hold of her.

<That is why you must make your ultimate assault before the Girl goes to Orb. Celine will be on Earth in thirty-three days. Plan well. I cannot tell you the most efficient course of action but I have full confidence in you. I love you but now I must leave you. Farewell.> . . .

Maddy?

Yes.

I really got the willies about this new act. ExQuint. KnowwhatImean?

It's understandable Parni. We're all shaken by his death. Celine nearly went to pieces. You know she had fixated on him sexually in the last year or so [bitterness] the thieving little bitch.

Hey sweetheart you started it giving her the boot don't come crying to me . . . But delete that and listen: There are some things that have really pissed me off lately. You know Fury would have installed that Scotchtwat over us if she hadn't put her foot in it.

Yes.

And poor old Quint! Had to fall on his sword just because Fury told him to. Maximum bummer.

He was happy to sacrifice himself in the cause.

Oh right. And we're left threeheaded! What happens if Fury digs up another BabyParamount and starts the same shit all over? You remember how Fury went after Marc.

Yes . . .

It tried for Jack in utero too. Might have got him if the HawaiianWitch hadn't stepped in and taught him to shut Fury out. And then there was that Remillard woman! *Four times* Fury's made it perfectly clear that WE'RE NOT GOOD ENOUGH TO LEAD THE SECOND MILIEU. How thickheaded do we have to be to figure?

Fury . . . knows best.

Maddybaby Fury can't do zilch without us. What is Fury anyhow? A goddam syndrome! A sicko persona hiding fuckknowswhere. You ever stop to think what we could do working on our own?

IMBECILESHITFORBRAINS! Parni don't you understand? *Without Fury we're nothing.* Without Fury *WE DIE.*

Panic. No—I don't believe it that's total bullshit! . . . Fury created us Fury can destroy us! And we'd go happily. Just like Quint.

Denial. Terror. WrongwrongnoIdon'tbuyit!

Exasperated resignation. Never mind sweetheart. It's all going to work out. No ParamountBabies anywhere else in the HumanPolity. Not yet. All Fury has to work with is US. Love you BigLug! What say we go have a mondomojo twoheaded feed&fuck?

Kaleidoscopic.

[20]

SECTOR 15: STAR 15-000-001 [TELONIS]
PLANET 1 [CONCILIUM ORB]

GALACTIC YEAR: LA PRIME 1-385-969
[15 DECEMBER 2072]

Paul Remillard didn't much like the new Lylmik enclave. When the Supervisors required vis-à-vis encounters with human magnates in the earlier days of the enfranchisement, they would simply summon them to a quiet section of the Administrative Sphere, more or less materialize in a severe golden room, speak what was on their wispy minds, and then disappear. It was a direct, no-nonsense approach that the First Magnate had appreciated.

That had changed, perhaps because the Galactic Overlords had become concerned about the negative psychosocial effect their otherness might be having on skittish humans. They decided to mend their image, creating a Lylmik enclave in Orb where visiting was encouraged—even though the inhabitants were rarely perceptible to ordinary senses or to ultrafaculties. The artificial environment called Syrel supposedly reproduced conditions on the prehistoric Lylmik home world. (The actual planet, a barren rock orbiting the strange star Nodyt more than 27,000 lightyears from Earth, was deemed too aesthetically forbidding—and lethal to air-breathers—to be re-created.)

Paul exited the Syrel tube station into a world of crystalline pastels and elusive herbal scents. A thin opaline mist filled the superoxygenated air, and only in his immediate vicinity was the landscape clearly visible. It was as though he were the principal light source, illuminating the enclave as he walked along, while a violet scrim obscured details more than a few meters away. Most of the ground was covered by a yielding turf of what seemed to be cellophane grass, in which transparent, feathery organisms continually sprouted and grew rapidly to heights of a dozen centimeters or so. After producing pale, glassy fruits that exploded soundlessly and released glittering spores, the things crumpled and seemed to vanish, only to begin their brief life cycle again a few minutes later.

Paul went along a pathway made of rose-quartz flagstones that passed through a patch of larger, faintly glowing, sessile lifeforms. Some were like living plass umbrellas flecked with dew; others resembled plump terrestrial jellyfish with sparkling fringes. Tall, stalked ribbon-bearers reminiscent of white or pale-pink kelp undulated languorously, now and then reaching out a gentle tendril as if to inspect the exotic passerby.

Stepping-stones led across a brook that flowed over tinted pebbles. Moon-colored little water-creatures with shining eyes zipped evasively among rock-crystal boulders at the stream's margin. Further up the banks grew lucent fungoid shapes with diamond spikes, vitreous "reeds" topped with gauzy plumes, and organisms that mimicked exquisitely carved white-jade flowers.

The residence of the Supervisory Body stood in a twilit grove of many-branched "willow trees" that seemed to be formed of twisted, milky glass. Their lanceolate, hanging foliage was also glassy, clashing and tinkling faintly in the vapor-laden breeze. The house might have been an enormous gold nugget with a brushed finish. Its shape was irregular and no door or windows were immediately evident.

The First Magnate had visited the place many times now, doing his best to respond cordially to the awkward Lylmik attempts at sociability. These often took the form of annoying inquiries into his intimate affairs. Lylmik notions of privacy did not equate with Paul's own, and he also disliked being reminded that the entities possessed the godlike ability to oversee anything and anyone in the galaxy if they felt like it. Fortunately (and occasionally unfortunately), they were usually disinclined to do so.

Paul followed the path to its termination before a featureless golden wall and announced:

I am here.

Immediately an iris doorway opened in the nugget's side. He stepped over the threshold into a single softly lit room where all surfaces were subtly curved and formed from some transparent substance. The walls were slick but the floor was ribbed for comfortable walking. Within and behind them flowed currents of deep green and indigo liquid shot through with whorls of bubbles. In the center of the room stood a golden armchair of human design. Before it, formed from extensions of the floor-ribbing, was a low dais. The metaconcerted voice of the Lylmik Supervisors spoke:

Welcome and high thoughts to you, First Magnate. Please be seated.

As Paul sat down five faintly visible whirlwinds formed in the air above the dais, making the familiar Quincunx pattern—one at each corner and one in the center of a squared diamond shape. The aerial phenomena quickly materialized into five near-humanoid heads of amiable aspect that trailed ectoplasmic filaments from the occipital region.

The central entity, the Lylmik leader called Atoning Unifex, had eyes of luminous gray and seemed to be much older than the others, even though Its illusory appearance was almost identical to theirs. It rarely spoke, apparently preferring to leave intercourse with vulgar humanity to Its associates. The eyes of the other four Supervisors were the color of backlit aquamarines.

Although they manifested a similar appearance, Paul had discovered early on that the Lylmik personalities were quite distinctive. The one called Homologous Trend was a slightly ponderous, avuncular logician, while Noetic Concordance had a serene character and was prone to mystical digressions. Asymptotic Essence was an incisive critic who did not bother to hide a biased view of humanity. Eupathic Impulse played the gadfly, had a rather slangy manner, and was not above twitting the other four—even the awesome leader—for perceived flaws in judgment, absentmindedness, or conversational vagaries. Paul rather liked Eupathic Impulse.

Ominously, it was the gray-eyed Unifex who addressed the First Magnate in a soft voice:

"We must confer with you on matters of the utmost gravity, Paul, and so you must forgive us if we forgo the usual pleasantries and get right down to brass tacks."

"Right," said the First Magnate aloud. And to himself: Oh, shit.

"My colleagues and I," Atoning Unifex continued, "have been discussing the advisability of condemning the so-called Rebel movement and requiring an oath of loyalty to the Milieu from all Human

Magnates of the Concilium. Please tell us your reaction to this proposal."

"I think it would be a tragic mistake," Paul said immediately. "Even though I myself once cosponsored a bill that would have forbidden debates about Unity in the Concilium, I now believe that such gag-rule legislation would be futile—possibly ruinous to Human Polity discipline. It would be even more disastrous to label anti-Unity sentiment treasonous."

"You believe that your race values free discussion so highly?" Noetic Concordance asked.

"Yes," Paul replied. And then: "What penalty do you propose for refusing to take the oath?"

"One would have a choice," said Homologous Trend. "Redaction of the magnate to the latent state and expulsion from the Concilium . . . or euthanasia."

"You would very likely lose nearly a quarter of the two hundred human magnates," Paul said, "including some of the most brilliant and influential. A significant percentage of the others would be so scandalized by the draconian action that their own loyalty to the Milieu might waver. I know my own would. I've undergone a change of heart about this business—"

"By the Prime Entelechy!" Eupathic Impulse exclaimed. "Does one mean to say that one has converted to the Rebel point of view?"

"Certainly not," said Paul sharply. "I'm more committed to Unity than ever. But I firmly believe that it is impossible to *force* the Human Mind to accept the Unity of the Coadunate Milieu. Humans must be persuaded—shown that Unity does not pose a danger to their free will or mental integrity. This is the purpose behind the recent establishment of the Panpolity Directorate for Unity, in which my son Jon and my sister Anne are prominent."

"But the Rebel movement is spreading apace—especially amongst nonoperants in the human colonies," said Asymptotic Essence. "Never before in the history of the Galactic Milieu has a precoadunate race presumed to question the value of Unity."

"Humans are unique," said Atoning Unifex. "I warned you about that at the time of the Great Intervention."

"One remembers." The voice of Noetic Concordance was soothing.

"These were your words concerning Earth: *This small planet occupies a critical place in the probability lattices. From it may emerge a Mind that will exceed all others in metapsychic potential. It is known to us that this Mind will be capable of destroying our beloved Galactic Milieu. It is further known to us that this Mind will also be capable of magnifying the Milieu immensely, accelerating the Unification of all the inhabited star systems. For this reason we have directed this extraordinary attempt at Intervention . . .*"

Unifex inclined Its head. "I said further that the step involved great risk. But all evolutionary leaps are hazardous, and without risk-taking there can only be stagnation, the triumph of entropy, and eventual death."

Asymptotic Essence said, "Nevertheless, there remains the dire new resultant of the latest probability analysis, which prompted one to offer the drastic remedy: If the Rebel movement continues to grow at its present rate amongst operant and nonoperant humans, the Unification of that race may never take place. Instead of merging with our Coadunate Galactic Milieu, humanity will be constrained to declare war upon it."

"Nonsense!" Paul exclaimed. "Not even the most xenophobic of the anti-Unity faction advocates that course. At the worst, they'd simply drop out of the confederation to go their own way—"

"Even if we would allow it, this is not likely," said Homologous Trend. "Why does one think the Great Intervention eradicated the last vestiges of the old nationalism on Earth before enfranchising its populace? Why does one think the Simbiari Proctorship suppressed—sometimes ruthlessly—those Earth sects and political movements that had bigoted mind-sets or advocated so-called holy or preventive wars to eliminate opposing points of view? Why has the Milieu been obliged to forbid certain types of commercial activity by human entrepreneurs even now? Why does it severely limit governmental autonomy of human colonial planets, and control their operant/nonoperant population mix?"

Calmly, Paul said, "In order to prevent the kinds of bloody conflict that traditionally prevailed among human beings in pre-Intervention years. If humanity wasn't restrained, the probability is that we'd fight for what we perceived to be our self-interest. Asymptotic Essence's calculations are correct." He fixed his gaze on the gray-eyed Lylmik

Overlord. "But there's a paradox here. Don't tell me *you* don't see it, Unifex."

"Certainly I do: In order to protect itself from humanity while the race is still immature and dangerous, the Milieu has behaved in a despotic fashion. By limiting human freedom, it has provoked the very kind of behavior it sought to prevent. The Milieu took a great risk in admitting humanity. It may have overreached itself."

"I don't think so." Paul's mental aspect shone with stubborn hope. "Aside from the Unity issue, there are only minor pockets of human discontent. If Unity can be proved to be the right and proper goal of human mental evolution, the Rebel movement will most likely evaporate. The new Directorate will bring together the best minds from all six racial Polities to discuss every aspect of Unity and deal with legitimate Rebel objections to it. Forget the notion of outlawing the Rebels—at least until you've given the more conservative course a chance."

Unifex said, "This is my recommendation also, colleagues. My reasoning is perhaps not the same as Paul's—but I say again that without risk there can be no evolution, only torpidity and finally extinction. Our own Lylmik race is a melancholy exemplar of that truth. We believe we have reached the pinnacle of our evolution, and there we stand, most of our number now content to think their own grand and unutterable thoughts, alone and self-sufficient. The excitement engendered by my original Protocol of Unification has long since dwindled to ennui in all except a handful of Lylmik minds. We do not reproduce. Except for this small Quincunx, we do not create. The Twenty-One Worlds each send a single delegate to the Concilium but there is little genuine interest in Milieu affairs remaining amongst us. Shall I tell you the true reason why the Galactic Milieu needs the Human Mind? . . . It is because the Lylmik Mind is dying, as I am dying Myself. When I go, our race will retreat into aloof senescence and will perish inside of a single millenary. But by then I foresee that the Human Mind, fully coadunate and Unified, will have taken our place. The magnification of the inhabited star systems in the Milky Way will continue under Human Polity direction until all thinking beings within it are loving siblings, as they are in the Duat Galaxy from which I originally came. And then, if it pleases the Cosmic All, another Unifex may move on to a younger whirlpool of stars and begin again."

Paul listened, stunned into speechlessness. Nothing of this had ever been hinted at during his long years as a Milieu official. Each Polity had its own legends and speculations of Lylmik origins and destiny. Each had debated why the nonconformist humans were declared to be necessary to Milieu survival. None had suspected this rationale.

"You can't tell a soul, Paul." Atoning Unifex was smiling, almost playfully apologetic. "Not until I give you permission. But you, of all people, have a right to know."

The other four Supervisors exuded resignation.

"One must trust Unifex," said Noetic Concordance. "The decision is made: there will be no further attempts to outlaw or restrict the Rebel faction of the Human Polity."

"Even when the probability of a successful human Unification seems to grow more and more remote," said Homologous Trend, sighing.

"This does not mean, however, that the First Magnate should diminish his efforts to bring the Rebels into conformity." Asymptotic Essence spoke sternly.

Eupathic Impulse delivered the kicker. "Most particularly, the First Magnate and his family must restrain the malevolent persona called Fury and its execrable servant, Hydra, from using the anti-Unity faction for their own evil ends. The obliteration of one Hydra-unit is a cause for rejoicing. But the other three—and Fury itself—are more dangerous to the Milieu than ever."

"But who the hell *is* Fury?" Paul cried. "I can't believe you Lylmik don't know!"

The Quincunx only stared at him sadly.

"Is it Marc? Is it *me*? Isn't there anything you can do to help us find this—this family devil?" Paul had sprung up from his chair and stood with his fists clenched at his sides. Sweat dampened his hair and he thrust a graying lock impatiently out of his eyes as he glared at the silent exotic heads.

Unifex said, "Go talk to your sister Anne. An ancient sin lies at the heart of Fury's generation and a terrible moral dilemma attends the monster's destruction. Perhaps a priest can help you with the problems."

"Very well." Paul spoke wearily. "Is there anything else you require of me now?"

The heads were beginning to fade away. The eyes, as always, remained visible longest. The Quincunx spoke in metaconcert:

No. May the All sustain you, First Magnate, and bring you success.

Unifex made a sudden capricious decision to go to Earth and performed hyperspatial translation without even bidding Its colleagues goodbye. There were still matters to discuss, and so the four remaining members of the Supervisory Body convened out by the brook, wafting in and out of the dew-dripping "willow" leaves to gather the occasional molecule for sustenance.

Asymptotic Essence ventured a mild complaint. "Unifex might have stayed with us to consider the matter of young Illusio."

"It's probably gone to keep an eye on her," Trend observed. "That girl is surely cooking up another mad scheme to entice Hydra. She has a right to do so, but if she dies in the process some very important nodalities will have to be scrapped."

"If Hydra kills her," Essence noted astringently, "we certainly can't appoint her Deputy Dirigent of Caledonia."

"She's almost as much of a wild-card factor as Jack," said Impulse. "A pity she seems to loathe him so. He might have been a useful ally in her quest against Hydra."

"One suspects Jack might not scruple at acting without her knowledge or permission," Concordance remarked. "His starship has left Orb, you know."

"No!" said the other three entities.

They all thought about the anomalous young human magnate for a time, speculating upon what he might do to help Dorothea Macdonald. Thanks to Dorothea's probing at the Halloween party, Jack now knew the Hydra metaconcert configuration; but he did not know the identities and whereabouts of the Hydra-units, as the Supervisors did. It was most likely that his only option was following the girl, either mentally or physically, in hopes of coming to her assistance if he was needed.

"One wishes one could intervene personally in this matter," Noetic Concordance said, with regret. "Jack could dispose of the Hydra-units in a trice if we pointed them out to him."

"Unifex's prohibition must take into account factors that one is unaware of," said Trend.

"One has been mulling it over," Eupathic Impulse said. "There may be more to this situation than the simple survival of the girl and the apprehension of Hydra. One should also consider Jack's relation to Illusio, and vice versa."

"She can't stand him," Asymptotic Essence said. "She finds his mutation repulsive and his manner cheeky and superior. He thinks that she is rash and immature. One may recall that Jack, while an estimable person in many ways, does have certain unfortunate mannerisms. His great success on Satsuma, saving the life of his brother Marc when their metaconcert faltered, bolstered his self-esteem higher than ever. Now he is determined to become Unity's greatest champion. One fears Jack is in some danger of becoming a wise guy."

Reluctantly, Noetic Concordance agreed.

"One suspects Illusio would bitterly resent any well-intentioned interference on Jack's part," Trend said. "Perhaps it is necessary to her spiritual maturation that she face the Hydra monster alone, and either vanquish it or die in the attempt."

"One has it in a nutshell," Essence said. "We shall so instruct Jack."

"One can certainly pray for the girl, however," Concordance put in. "Poor thing, with so few friends! If she becomes Dirigent at a young age, she risks becoming even more lonely. But great things are required of those possessing great talents."

"An apt sentiment," Impulse remarked. "Original?"

"Luke 12:48," the poet admitted.

"One is inclined to vote that Illusio become Deputy Dirigent of Caledonia," Aymptotic Essence decided. "How say you, colleagues?"

"Affirm," said Noetic Concordance. "She flirts with Rebellion, but her deepest inclinations are toward Unity."

"One also affirms," Homologous Trend added, "while hoping devoutly that she survives until her inauguration to the Concilium. However, once Illusio is installed in office on Caledonia, the probabilities are strong that she would be secure from Hydra's menaces for many years to come."

"One is pleased to contribute the final affirmation," said Eupathic Impulse. "In spite of Jack's low opinion of her maturity, one finds her most suitable to be the eventual successor of Graeme Hamilton. She will have a lot to learn, but she can scarcely do worse than that worthy dotard. The Scottish planet is an attractive world and Illusio loves it. She should be happy there for a little while, until the next nodality."

"Provided that the major planetary cratons behave themselves," Essence said.

"A pity the besotted and neglectful Krondak surveyors never got what was coming to them for botching those crustal evaluations four millenaries ago," Impulse remarked, showing a trace of righteous indignation.

"The lithosphere may remain stable for hundreds of Caledonian orbits," Trend said. "One should attempt to look on the bright side . . . not only of that probability, but also of the Great Bifurcation involving Jack, Illusio, Marc, Fury, and all the rest of them."

"Anent that concern," said Concordance, "one proposes that we turn our thoughts to prayer. It may take a bit of coercion to jolt the Prime Entelechy into resolving this fine mess."

"Years, maybe," Asymptotic Essence sighed.

"All the more reason to get on with it," said Eupathic Impulse.

"Amen," said Homologous Trend.

Anne was not in her apartment in Rive Gauche, and it took Paul several minutes to track her down with his seekersense. He found her alone in the little Eglise St.-Julien-le-Pauvre, and rather than disturb her with farspeech he strolled through the quaint streets and byways of the Parisian enclave mulling over what the Lylmik had said.

The trouble with them was that they were too damned subtle. More often than not, it was necessary to find the meaning-behind-the-meaning in their rambling discourses. Unifex was apt to be blunter than the rest, but Paul suspected that Its lofty talk about "sin" and "moral dilemma" was a camouflage for something else.

There was some compelling reason for him to question his oldest sister about Fury, but it probably had little to do with gaining her priestly insight and a great deal to do with Anne herself.

It was past "midnight" in the enclave and most of the nonoperant humans who ran the place for the benefit of the operant tenants—the restaurateurs, shopkeepers, concierges, and other service personnel—were asleep. When the Concilium was in recess the enclaves hosted only magnate bureaucrats and meta staffers working on special projects in the Human Polity offices. A month from now Rive Gauche would be bustling; now it was nearly a ghost town.

The church of St. Julian the Poor was a replica of the smallest and oldest church in Paris, dating back to the twelfth century. The Rive Gauche version was reasonably authentic in its exterior but more modern inside to accommodate the needs of worshipers in the Galactic Age. The door opened without a sound and Paul went into the vestibule, dipped his index finger in the holy water stoup, and crossed himself. The Greek Uniate ornamentation and other accretions in the original Parisian edifice had not been reproduced, leaving a vaulted chamber with elegant stonework, a statue of the original St. Julian and another of St. Julian of Norwich, ranks of cushioned oak chairs and kneelers, and a tiny baptistry. In the sanctuary a simple contemporary wooden table-altar stood before the old-style stone one with its gilt candlesticks. The tabernacle was also modern, but above it hung an ornate silver lamp of medieval design. Its flickering ruby light, and the dim luminosity from the stained-glass windows, revealed a figure prostrate on the stone paving in front of the sanctuary.

Paul's mental vision identified her at once. It was Anne. The sound of her weeping was almost inaudible.

The First Magnate moved quietly up the center aisle, inclined his head toward the tabernacle, and sat down in one of the chairs. His sister was clad in a long black gown of some roughly woven fabric, grayed with dust. A hood covered her hair, and she wore sandals on her bare feet.

For at least ten minutes she continued the vigil with her mind tightly shut, although she certainly knew Paul was there. He waited patiently. A soft tapping of rain on the leaden roof marked the start of the nightly shower that refreshed the air of the urban enclave. There were bouquets of old-fashioned roses on the stone altar together with the unlit candles. Their fragrance reminded Paul of his own garden in Concord, 4000 lightyears away. He wished to hell he were there, even though it was winter in New Hampshire and perpetual spring in Rive Gauche.

The woman on the floor finally stirred and drew in her arms, which had been outflung in the ancient cruciform posture of penitential entreaty. She got to her knees, remained there a moment with her hooded head bowed, and then came over to Paul, unceremoniously wiping her tear-stained face on her sleeve.

"Hi," she said. "Let's go to my place. I'll give you coffee or whatever."

She momentarily lost her footing and Paul steadied her and took one arm. For the first time he noticed that Anne had become excessively thin. Her face was normally gaunt and austere, but he was shocked at the boniness of her arm. When they were outside the church, walking down the wet cobbles beneath a psychocreative umbrella, Paul said:

"The Supervisory Body called me on the carpet tonight. I might have helped to talk them out of condemning the Rebel movement. On the other hand, the Lylmik kingfish seemed ready to veto the others and none of them were especially keen on a pogrom. So they may have had other reasons for the meeting. Sometimes I can't help thinking that the Supervisors secretly approve of the Rebels . . ."

"What form was the condemnation to take?"

"Loyalty oaths for all magnates. Those who came up treasonous would have had to choose between a snuff-job and having their operant lights put out."

"Flaming idiocy!"

"I more or less told the Lylmik the same thing and gave them a quick refresher course in the psychology of our perverse race. Anyhow, they've agreed to bag the inquisition. The Panpolity Directorate for Unity will be instructed to get the lead out and begin propagandizing pronto."

"We'll be rolling by the time the Concilium convenes. Got a lot of good stuff from the Poltroyans, bless their purple pellicules."

The rain shower stopped. Crickets chirped in the flower beds fronting the little Musée de la Terre, a popular spot for nostalgic colonials. There were lights on in the boulangerie where the breadmaking was about to begin. Small robot cleaners on noiseless treads sniffed around the gutters and scavenged fallen leaves.

"The Lylmik also told me that the family had better make damned sure that Fury doesn't infiltrate the Rebel movement. I asked them to help in tracking the thing down, but I got the usual stonewall treatment."

Anne snorted. "They don't *know* who Fury is."

"I have a sneaking suspicion they know the new identities of the Hydras, though. Damn their eyes! Why won't they tell us?"

"We persist in thinking of the Lylmik as omnipotent and all-seeing. They're not. They're a pack of lazy effetes—except for that busybody Unifex. They have one valuable idée fixe that has saved humanity's neck time and again: that we're vitally important to the future of the Milieu, and the rest of the Polities jolly well better put up with our imperfections. Other than that—"

"They've also saved our family from disgrace," Paul pointed out. "But I get the idea that they may withdraw their protection if we don't do something about Fury soon."

They had reached the quaint building where Anne lived on the top floor. Paul had not been there for years. They climbed three long flights of creaky, carpeted stairs and she opened her door and turned on the lights. The place was mostly as Paul remembered it, a sizable replica of an artist's studio with a few finished canvases lying about or propped against walls. A tabouret with brushes and a mess of oil paints stood next to an easel bearing an unfinished double portait of Denis and Lucille. In a corner was a large and messy table loaded with tins of turps and oil, stretchers, rolls of canvas, and other art supplies. One entire wall of the loft was devoted to research equipment: library and newspaper units, plaque-dispensers, a huge Tri-D screen, a subspace communicator and data retriever. There was even a shelf of paged reference books that Paul's deepsight identified as theological tomes borrowed from the Vatican Library. In front of the huge "north" window was a tiny altar. A red LED glimmered on top of a little silver-gilt pyx that held a consecrated host. The domestic furniture of the place was almost monastic and the kitchen fitments rudimentary.

Anne took off her hooded robe and hung it on a wooden clothes tree. She wore a short denim skirt and an old red blouse beneath. Her limbs were almost skeletal, the knees raw and reddened.

"My God, Annie!" her brother exclaimed. "What have you been doing to yourself?"

"Something archaic." She went to the little kitchen and began to make coffee. "Fasting, praying, physical discipline. Don't look at me like that. I'm doing no serious damage to myself and I'm not in need of a psychiatrist. I wish it were that easy. Go light a fire for us."

He did as he was told. There were two raddled easy chairs and a small table in front of the iron hearth. A scuttle held kindling and split billets of artificial wood. Glancing uneasily over his shoulder at Anne, he asked, "Is this business at the church part of it?"

"Yes. I go there whenever I can, usually late at night. Old Père François has been very good about mopping up the puddles of tears." She brought the Melior cafetière, two plain mugs, and the sugar she knew Paul preferred. When the coffee was brewed she pushed down the piston, poured for both of them, then finally relaxed in her chair. "I suppose you want the story."

Paul shrugged. "The Lylmik must know you're up to something. Unifex Itself told me to come here when I begged for help in finding Fury."

"The Lylmik do know, because I've told them. I asked for their help, too, and when they didn't vouchsafe it I turned to another Authority."

It began late in 2054 [Anne said], at the time the Human Polity finally finished its probation and was admitted to full citizenship in the Milieu. I began to have a series of very interesting dreams. I seemed to be in an attractive place that I recognized as one of the academies of ancient Greece—all white marble columns and splashing fountains and trees with zephyrs blowing through them. I was young, perhaps in my early twenties, and I wore one of those classic chiton and peplum outfits of white linen.

I was obviously a student of philosophy—never mind that women were forbidden to attend the Greek academies—and my teacher was none other than Pallas Athene herself.

You remember that little statue of the goddess that I used to keep on my desk in the Human Polity offices. Athene was the embodiment of wisdom and learning, the invincible protector of warriors, the defender of states and cities. She was the virginal daughter of Zeus, sprung from his forehead. She sat next to him on Olympus and she was the only one besides him who could fling lightning bolts and use his terrible shield. Athene was also a spiritual mother to human beings and the patron of conception. Without her blessing, there would be no human offspring.

Above all she was a goddess of mentality, of right reason and sanity. I was never much of a Catholic when I was young, and Athene was a more appealing patron saint for me than any of the submissive women the Church once held out as models of sanctity.

I was delighted with my dreams of the goddess. (They were appropriately Jungian, as well!) When I woke up, I could never quite recall her lessons, but I did retain a feeling of self-confidence and righteousness as a result of them. I knew I was a very special and important person—a Remillard, a Doctor of Jurisprudence and a scholar of Milieu law, a Grand Master in all of my metafaculties, a Magnate of the Concilium, and finally a member of the Human Polity Judicial Directorate. My personal life was both Spartan and Athenian. I lived for the Golden Mean and was a model of objectivity. I was never distracted from my work by banal family matters, nor had I ever engendered a child who turned into a Hydra, a potential Fury, or a problematical mutant.

I was obviously the cream of the Dynasty! I was neither bourgeois and virtuously plodding like my two older brothers Philip and Maurice, nor plagued with self-doubt like Severin and Adrien. I was coolly reasonable, not prone to fly off on emotional tangents like Catherine. I was chaste, not flawed by a promiscuous sex drive as you are, my dear little brother . . .

I would not have recognized hubris if it bit me in the gluteus maximus.

Deep in my heart I envied you, Paul, and I was convinced that the Lylmik had named the wrong Remillard to be First Magnate. Failing that, they'd at least chosen the wrong Dirigent for Earth! I had always been bitterly disappointed that Davy MacGregor was picked for the job instead of me.

The dreams of Pallas Athene went on for several years until finally, in 2058, their character changed. I began to remember them when I woke up, and their content filled me with incredible excitement. I knew the goddess wasn't real; but the vision she had introduced me to might very well come to pass.

It was a vision of a Second Milieu. And if I chose, I might play a crucial part in its foundation.

What exactly did the Athene figure mean by a Second Milieu? At first, I wasn't quite sure, but I knew it was wonderful and I knew it was *right*—as the galactic confederation we now live in is not.

Gradually the goddess revealed its details: The Human Polity would have to free itself from the present governmental structure, which was dominated by exotics. Above all, we would have to avoid the diabolical snare of Unity. The goddess assured me that Unity would destroy not only human individualism but even our very human nature.

Under a new leader—c'est moi, naturellement!—the Human Polity would sever its connection with the First Milieu and go its own way, peaceful, prosperous, and free.

I liked the concept very much. I had chafed bitterly during the Proctorship at the indignities and hardships our race suffered under those humorless green Simbiari nannies. It was all for our own good, they said to us, and only temporary. Stalin told his oppressed people the same thing.

Then Pallas Athene revealed the ultimate mystery, the means by which I was to lead humanity into the Second Milieu. As she described it, I would become a new Blessed Virgin—except that Divinity would be implanted within my brain rather than my womb. In my dream, I was overjoyed. The goddess smiled at me and withdrew.

I awoke from that dream screaming.

And aware of who Athene really was.

What had I done? How could I have been such a blind, arrogant fool? Athene was Fury, and for over three years I had permitted it to range freely in my unconscious mind, instilling its poison! I had let my pride lead me to the verge of becoming another Hydra—or perhaps a new host for the Fury parasite itself. If I had submitted to it, I would have given the monster a foothold within the highest levels of galactic government. I really *had* been willing to destroy the Milieu! I would have broken and cast aside the confederation of benevolent minds that has done so much for Earth and replaced it with . . . God knew what.

I was in my home in Hanover at the time that I finally came to my senses. But you can hardly call it that! All day long I alternated between fits of hysterical weeping and demented rage. I almost destroyed the inside of the house and I nearly committed suicide in my despair and self-hatred. Fury had chosen well when it picked me out of the Dynasty to become its new acolyte. I would have been ideal.

I still don't know why I didn't succumb.

After two days without sleep, unable to kill myself as I knew I should and loathing myself even more for my cowardice, I called our parents.

Denis and Lucille came at once. They seemed to know immediately that my demon was real, not a product of insanity. They took me to the old house on South Street where they were living and put me to bed in my old room, the one I had slept in as a child. They sat beside me, redacting me and comforting me, for four days. Denis assured me that I would be able to banish the Fury-goddess from my mind now by a conscious effort of will. Unless I wanted her to return, she would vanish forever. Finally I was able to believe him and I slept, exorcised.

It took me another two weeks to pull myself back together emotionally and physically. Fortunately, it was high summer and your children, who usually lived in the house, were all at the shore. Denis and Lucille never told any other members of the family about my breakdown.

When I was fully recovered I knew what I would have to do. Our parents, poor darlings, thought I was still deranged and tried to talk me out of it—but I finally convinced them I was sincere. My work as a magnate and Milieu legal scholar could continue at the same time that I began my new career.

I went down to Concord and spoke to the Jesuits who run Brebeuf Academy. They sent me to their seminary in New York and in due season I presented myself to the world as Anne Remillard, S.J.

"I still don't understand the penance and fasting you're putting yourself through now." Paul said. "What's it in aid of? Surely you—uh—worked off your sin of pride and suchlike long ago. Nothing did happen, after all. You have no reason to continue feeling guilty."

"The penance and prayer aren't for myself," she said. "I'm storming heaven on behalf of someone else."

His eyes narrowed as he understood, and then his coercive-redactive probe came at her like a bolt from a crossbow. But she was ready. The First Magnate could not penetrate his sister's mental shield. She was as good a coercer as he was.

"Annie, tell me what you know!" he cried, seizing her by the shoulders. "Tell me who Fury is!"

"There have been quite a few clues, to say nothing of the insights obtainable from psychological deduction." Her voice was level. "But I'm not absolutely certain and so I can't tell you. I *won't* tell you. As Papa said, the core persona is innocent. If I share my suspicions, you would feel obligated to act on them in some way or another. I believe this would eventually cause more objective evil than if we permit Fury to remain at large. It may even be true that Fury's evil is destined to bring about an even greater good."

"You have no right to make that judgment," he told her coldly. "As First Magnate, I overrule you and demand your evidence."

She gave a little humorless chuckle. "I know Milieu law better than you, Paul. You do *not* have the right to force me to reveal unconfirmed raw data. When . . . the prevailing conditions change and my conscience tells me it's time to talk, I will. To the entire family, including the suspect."

"Fury's after a little girl," Paul said, turning away from her. "Dorothea Macdonald, the fifteen-year-old metapsychic prodigy. Jack told me that a pair of Hydras almost got her in Hawaii. Are you willing to leave the child at risk?"

"Yes. At fifteen, she's a moral adult, not a little girl. If what Jack has told me is true, she's deliberately called Hydra down on herself in hopes of trapping it. She's a near-paramount and ready to take the chance. I have no obligation to interfere."

Paul's lips twitched in spite of himself and he turned back to her. "Sometimes, Annie, you're positively . . . Jesuitical. Give us a kiss goodnight."

They embraced, and then Paul Remillard left his sister and clumped down the three flights of stairs, brooding.

A greater good. *What* greater good?

He himself continuing in office as First Magnate?

Marc's machinations with metaconcerted CE?

Safeguarding the Milieu's laissez-faire policy for the Rebels?

Keeping the Unity Directorate unsmirched by scandal? . . .

"Jesus," Paul said to himself, suddenly stricken. He stopped for a moment beneath a lamppost and looked up at the building's top floor. Even from the street he could see the tiny red LED in her window, a pinprick of light that symbolized the Divine Presence in Anne Remillard's apartment.

Had she really said no to Pallas Athene?

[21]

ISLAY, INNER HEBRIDES, SCOTLAND, EARTH, 17 DECEMBER 2072

Dorothea Macdonald stood above the deep rocky cleft called Geodh Ghille Mhóire and sampled the aetheric vibrations.

Are you here Fury? Are you here Hydra? . . .

The late-rising winter sun shone from a cloudless sky. Islay's land-aura was placid and the gray-green ocean waters were unaccountably calm. Even with the sea breeze blowing, Dee was almost too warm in the cotton crew-neck sweater and Eddie Bauer mountain parka she had brought with her from New Hampshire. She had expected the Hebrides to be cold at this time of year—after all, they were at the latitude of Labrador —but the egg-bus driver who had brought her from the Scottish mainland told her that Islay rarely had snow or even frost because of the moderating effect of the Gulf Stream. The bright sunny weather was a wee bit unusual, he admitted, but not freakish. It was expected to hold for several days until the next gale blew in.

Dee hoped the fine weather was a lucky portent.

She had finished her doctoral dissertation and now only her orals remained to be dealt with after the New Year. When time came for her to embark for Orb, where she was to be inaugurated into the Concilium in February, she would have completed her formal education at Dartmouth College. What remained for her to learn she would have to learn by herself.

Hence the journey to Islay.

Malama Johnson had done all she could, but a stubborn residue of latency still remained in Dee's mind. It would prevent her from utilizing her full spectrum of metafaculties, prevent her from becoming a paramount, unless it was neutralized.

"But you hafta take care da kine pilikia you self, Makana Lani," the Hawaiian woman had told Dee earnestly. "No kahuna, no mainland shrink going do dat, eh? Ass' *your* kuleana."

"But how am I going to heal myself, Tutu? Through self-redaction? I've tried to get at the really deep inhibitions many times, but I just can't reach them."

"Nevvamine redact, li' dat. Mo bettah you go moku hikina!"

Dee shook her head, refusing to understand.

Malama rolled her eyes in exasperation and abandoned the Pidgin dialect that even the most educated Hawaiians loved to use among their closest friends. "You know perfectly well what I'm talking about, Dorothea. You must return to Islay in the Hebrides, to the place where your mother was murdered, and resolve the traumatic event in your mind. Live it again and purge the horror, the useless guilt, the rage that continues to fester in the deepest core of your being."

"I healed myself of all that years ago. The latentizing factor must be something else."

"Mebbe so, mebbe no! Go anyhow and do the healing journey. But this time begin at the end and go back to the beginning . . ."

Masha and Kyle had been very dubious when Dee told them about her plan to visit Islay. First they tried to dissuade her. Then, after she explained the reason for the trip and its potential therapeutic nature, her grandparents wanted to go along and lend her their emotional support. They had no idea of the danger she might face, nor were they worried that she was too young to make the journey by herself. Their only motive was to be available if she should need comfort.

"That's kind of you and very sweet," she had said. "But if Malama Johnson is right, then I have to do this alone."

And also face the Hydra alone.

She checked into a hotel in Bowmore village on the island and dealt with some preliminaries she felt were important. Taking advantage of her new status as a magnate-designate, she visited not only the police station where she had been interrogated, but also the farmhouse at Sanaigmore. The local police inspector, Bhaltair Chaimbeul, furnished her with interesting data she had never heard before, including the fact that the remains of only a few of Hydra's earlier victims had ever been found.

Her visit with the inspector to the farm where the Hydras had lived was disappointing. Because of its evil reputation no one had wanted to live in the place and it had been partially destroyed by a fire seven years earlier. The thrifty islanders had voted to raze it if funds could be pried from the Zone Council, but money had not been forthcoming and so the ruins remained.

On her second day on Islay Dee began the journey of healing. After sending her rented groundcar off to meet her at the end of the trail, she hiked up a rolling expanse of moor to Geodh Ghille Mhóire, the deep cut in the northwestern sea-cliffs where the remains of her mother, her uncle, and her aunt had been found.

She stood now just above the scene of the murders, a well-equipped daypack on her shoulders and a metal-tipped walking stick in her hand. At Gran Masha's insistence she wore a wrist-communicator. The rough region around Gilmour's Chasm was deserted except for a hen harrier scouting a late breakfast.

Nothing had responded to her farspoken call to Fury and Hydra. The aetheric ambiance was tranquil.

Gripping her stick and keeping her mind resolutely blank of memories for the time being, she began the tricky descent into the cleft. Tumbled rocks along one side served almost as giant steps. Her PK helped waft her down the steepest parts, an acceptable fiddle provided that no normals were there to witness it. It was low tide, and with the sea almost dead calm the flat rocks where the victims had fallen and the Kilnave Fiend had come scuttling after them were completely above water. The way into the narrow cave was unimpeded.

At the bottom she negotiated areas of slimy wrack and stood finally at the cavern entrance, probing the darkness with her farsight. What had seemed eerie and otherworldly in her dream had a more prosaic aspect in fact. The chamber was typical of Hebridean sea-caves, a simple excavation in Precambrian gritstone accomplished by wave action, having no stalactites or other picturesque features. Its damp walls were streaked with the white excrement of birds that had nested in the crevices. On the level floor were a few pools of water, areas of rippled sand between smooth, flattened slabs, piles of seaweed, and a few bits of driftwood and other flotsam. The smell of marine growth was strong.

Still keeping her imagination reined in, she went deeper into the cave, finally reaching the place where she had "seen" the three smoking mounds and the hideous creature standing over them. No trace of the atrocity remained. The rocks where her mother and her uncle and aunt had died were long since washed clean by the tides. Half a dozen meters beyond them the cave walls met in a dead end.

Dee closed her eyes then, and let the memories flood back into her mind. This time they would be complete, without any merciful hiatus or deletion. She would relive exactly what had happened in her terrible experience of ten years ago.

She saw the white gyrfalcon that symbolized her own spirit in excorporeal excursion come flying down the chasm to defy the Hydra. The bird pursued the monster into the cave's green shadows, then confronted it as it prepared for its appalling feast.

Who are you? WHAT are you?

I am Hydra the servant of Fury.

What are you doing?

Watch.

She saw the great black body with its grasping limbs, the four heads with eyes like evil stars, the red mouths opening, ready to feed on the lifeforce of the first helpless victim.

The discordant shriek of Hydra's metaconcert reverberated in Dee's mind, that obscene mental symphony that enabled four human beings to metamorphose into a single devouring entity with more power than the sum of its participants.

Held fast in multiple arms, Robert Strachan looked at Hydra.

Not Uncle Robbie! No . . .

Yes. Watch and learn.

From the four gaping mouths came shining golden tongues that braided together into a single probe that affixed itself to the crown of Robert Strachan's head. His body was suddenly enveloped in purple radiance. He underwent a galvanic spasm and uttered a hopeless cry as the beast began to drink from the first vital source. Deprived of all willpower but still hideously aware, he could only convulse and suffer as Hydra moved to the second source at the rear of his skull, to the third at the back of his neck, and on down his spine. As the feeding progressed the writhing body's aura changed in color and the skin darkened, as though the flesh and bone within were burning in astral fire. Each emptied chakra point was imprinted with a different, intricately detailed pattern having radial symmetry.

Dorothea Macdonald watched, helpless to interfere; but this time she inhabited the vision with full sentience, experiencing the pain of her dying uncle through redactive empathy.

Finally, when the lifeforce was drained from the seventh chakra at the base of his spine, Robert Strachan died. So did the agony Dee had shared with him. Hydra dropped the seared husk, which lay steaming on the damp floor of the cave.

That was well done, Girl! Now for the next one. Watch! Learn!

It turned to Uncle Robbie's wife Rowan Grant and consumed her vitality in the same way. Again, Dee shared the pain, not knowing why.

It was easier that time, wasn't it?

Last of all, Hydra took Dee's mother.

Not my Mummie no no please . . .

Her most especially. Ready? Begin.

For the third time Dee knew that incredible pain, inflicted deliberately by the Hydra to enhance its own pleasure and for another reason as well.

Why did you kill them that way WHY you filthy misbegotten thing?

But the monster only said: *Find your own food!*

Find your own anger. Find your own pain.

Oh Mum no. I did love you. I'm sorry I was so angry. You thought the therapy would do me good. You thought the pain would be worthwhile if it made me operant. I didn't understand then. I really would have saved you if I could. But I was too young too weak too selfish too unaware—

Pain unending. Not for the three victims but for her.

It wasn't my fault that you suffered! It was Hydra's fault and Fury's. I couldn't stop them!

Liar.

Pain.

Hydra laughed at her and her tardy pilgrimage, and as it laughed its monstrous form changed and divided and it became four human beings. One woman was a dark-haired, scarlet-lipped beauty, the other a frail-looking blonde with the glint of madness in her eyes. The taller of the two men smiled like a satisfied cat that had consumed its prey. His brawny companion was the young "father" who had besought Dee's help at the Spouting Horn.

I know who you are! Dee cried. *I know you're here on this island hoping for a chance to destroy me. BUT I'M NOT A HELPLESS CHILD ANYMORE. Go ahead! Try to feed. See what will happen!*

She showed them. And in the dream-vision, pain turned against the paingivers.

The Hydra faces screamed soundlessly, together with Dorothea Macdonald. She saw them squirming, dying, and was filled with joy.

Abruptly the four Hydra-units became motionless, like holoforms in a frozen Tri-D display. "John Quentin" lost his solidity, turned to a wraith, and faded to nothingness. Yes, of course. He was already dead. Safe from her, damn him! But not the others . . .

COME AFTER ME HYDRA COME SO I CAN KILL YOU EVEN MORE PAINFULLY THAN YOU KILLED MY MOTHER!

The Hydra survivors in her dream returned to life. Linking hands, they howled at her in a metaconcert of pure hate. *Too late! You should have done it the first time. Coward! Hypocrite!*

They vanished.

Joy vanished as well, and with it the beginnings of an awful understanding.

Dee came to her senses, alone in the dank reality of the cave, standing in water up to her ankles. The tide had turned and the sea was streaming slowly into the Geodh Ghille Mhóire. The memorecall of the old traumatic experience was dim, confused, troubling. There had been no catharsis. She inspected the innermost portions of her mind with redactive scrutiny and discovered that the deep mental inhibitions were still in place. Reliving the old nightmare had apparently accomplished nothing.

A few gulls wheeled overhead, their melancholy cries echoing from the walls of the chasm. She wanted to shout her disappointment and anger to the soaring birds. Somehow she had managed to bungle the initial part of her healing journey. Understanding had slipped away from her at the last moment—or else she had let it escape.

Very well. She'd try again.

But not immediately. There was no real danger in the rising tide, but she would have to leave the cave at once. The high-water mark on the wall was above her head. She went splashing out, using her stick, and climbed onto dry rocks above the inundated bench. The sea was still nearly calm, heaving gently up and down as she began the ascent of the blocky "steps" leading to the moorland above the cliffs.

Now the cave would be inaccessible for nearly twelve hours, and to start over at the beginning she would have to wait until long after nightfall for the next low tide. She could see in the dark, of course, but that required continuing mental effort that would seriously detract from the experience.

"Damn!" she said as she reached the chasm's top. "What am I going to do?"

A wry female voice seemed to say: First you try dry out da boots an' socks, eh?

Dee had to laugh, and bent her creativity to the task. Then she made the only possible decision. She would ignore her apparent failure and proceed along the north-shore path as she had originally planned, retracing the route she and her family had taken on the fatal hike. Whatever happened would happen.

First, though, a bit of prudent reconnoitering.

She traveled a few hundred meters northeast, circling the steep slope above the geodh, and climbed to the top of Cnoc Uamh nam Fear, a small hillock that was the highest point on this part of the island. From its vantage point she let her ultrasenses range out. Westward was only open sea that stretched all the way to Canada. North across the water lay little Colonsay and Oronsay, and Mull, where the invading MacLeans had launched their invasion force centuries earlier. A few scattered bright emanations indicated the presence of harmless nonoperant human life. She turned, scanning Islay itself, and found the northern parts of the island almost deserted. At this time of year, only a handful of hardy visitors came, and the locals stayed mostly in snug villages on the southern and eastern shores. She found no operant minds nearby, no threat to her safety.

. . . But what was *that*?

As she faced in the direction she must travel she felt for the merest fraction of a second the weird aetheric disturbance that had frightened her when she visited Islay as a child. It was neither an aura nor the metapsychic resonance of minds working together. It was certainly not farspoken communication. It touched only the emotions, not the intellect, wordlessly urging her to fear for her life . . . run away . . . give up the journey before it was too late.

As swiftly as it came, the ultrasensation disappeared.

She cried out: *I'm not afraid of you! I won't run from you, Hydra!*

But was it Hydra? She replayed the elusive fragment, analyzing it with all the skill of a Grand Master Creator. Its source was not Hydra, not even Fury, but something else.

Something. Many things? Not threatening, only warning.

A frisson of unease touched her as she found herself remembering certain stories Malama had told her, frightening accounts of genuine "ghosts" whose unquiet spirits the Hawaiian woman had laid. One of them had been the unfortunate mother of Jack and Marc Remillard. With a dismissive shrug, the kahuna had admitted that the more sophisticated metapsychic practitioners of the Human Polity did not acknowledge the existence of "malignant personality aspects" that were able to survive death and bedevil the living. But kahunas knew better.

Standing on top of the hill, Dee let her mind range out again, seekersense honed to the keenest. This time there was no evocation of deadly danger, no warning.

She thought of farspeaking Malama, even briefly considered asking her angel for advice and reassurance. But then a hot rush of resentment welled up in her, sweeping away any temptation that smacked of continuing childish dependence.

No one could help her except herself.

Malama had done all she could. The angel, that preprogrammed Lylmik artifact, had also told her she was on her own. Her mother, her uncle and aunt, even the other murder victims were quite dead and beyond communicating with her. *She* was alive and strong and ready to begin her life as an adult. If irrational fears or even genuine enemies stood in her way, she would have to remove them.

She set off for the Tòn Mhór headland a couple of kilometers to the northwest. As she strode along in the sunshine, she realized with a sudden burst of hopefulness that the Tòn, not the death-cave, marked the proper starting place for her journey. Perhaps she had not failed after all. Perhaps she had been a fool to think that she could accomplish her goal before completing the full pilgrimage.

When she reached the headland she sat for a time, resting against the same rock that had sheltered her and Ken and Gran Masha. She relived the original gyrfalcon dream in memorecall once again, this time without empathy, as though it were some fantasy drama and she an objective critic. She suffered no pain or fear, made no attempt to analyze the experience.

Next she retraced her panicky flight down the steep path where she had met Throma'eloo Lek. Before returning to the clifftop, she scanned the blackened ruins of Sanaigmore Farm and the lands around it. There was nothing unusual to be found. The nearest human beings were at Loch Gorm, six kilometers due south, and her farsight showed that they were only biologists taking a census of the swan population.

Staying as close to the precipitate shore as she could, she hiked down to sandy Sanaigmore Bay, passing roofless, abandoned crofts with stone walls that seemed to be slowly sinking into the ground. There was still hardly any wind, but the air seemed colder and more damp. Haze was slowly bleaching the blue sky to milky gray. Far offshore the horizon was beginning to blur. As she continued her resolute tramp through sand dunes, small bogs, and areas of dead bracken, she marked the absence of seabirds that had been so abundant on her childhood trek. Even the ubiquitous "peeps"—the shore-runners that should have been rather common in winter—seemed to have disappeared.

After walking for over two hours she stopped to scan the sullen sea. It had turned leaden as the high overcast moved in. When she extended her farsight she encountered a bank of fog about a dozen kilometers offshore.

"Uh-oh," she muttered, and switched her wrist-com to the weather channel. As she had feared, the fog was expected to move inland within a few hours. Still, if she stepped along briskly she might still reach the beach picnic shelter at Tràigh Nòstaig, completing the journey before visibility was too badly impaired.

She had not yet stopped for lunch. The other sea-cave, where she had seen the white gyrfalcon, was not far off.

When she came to the area above it she sat at the rim of a small gully and unwrapped her peanut-butter sandwich and orange. While she ate, her childhood musings over the splendid Greenland falcon drifted back into her mind. The bird had killed in order to live, and that had troubled her young conscience very much. When Dee grew older, she chose to minimize her consumption of flesh in order to spare the lives of higher animals. Janet and the nonborns had mocked her resolution, and most of her fellow students at Dartmouth had thought her a squeamish sentimentalist.

But she had felt that the abstinence was necessary.

At this time in the Galactic Age, the majority of philosophers and ethicists had rejected as illogical the idea that humans should not kill and eat living things. Milieu physics had demonstrated that *all* life, not merely that of higher animals, was enmeshed within the vital lattices. Even so-called inanimate objects were known to have a minimal share of vitality, and so if one avoided the consumption of life, one would consume nothing. Logic dictated that the proper food for the human species was that which had nurtured it throughout its evolution. Dee's moral preceptors taught her that "Thou shalt not kill" really meant "Thou shalt not kill thine own kind—those who think." The stewardship of other lifeforms and prevention of their needless suffering was properly regulated by prudence and logic; only the lives of sapient beings, whether human or not, fell under a solemn commandment.

Now, for the first time, Dee thought to ask herself why she was so anxious to spare animal life, when at the same time she would have gladly killed the humans who comprised Hydra.

Hydra is a murderer! A torturer who deserves to die.

. . . Is that why you're trying to trap it?

I want to bring it to justice. Stop it from killing again.

. . . And if it tries to kill you?

I wouldn't hesitate for a moment to strike back with all of my mental strength! Kill it in self-defense. It's perfectly justifiable.

. . . And if you captured it and it didn't try to harm you?

It would try. Of course it would. I'd have to kill it. *KILL IT EVEN MORE PAINFULLY THAN IT KILLED THEM!*

. . . There. Now you understand!

The section of orange she had just taken seemed to turn to dust in her mouth, half choking her and setting her to coughing. She had to drink quickly from her canteen to restore herself. Still breathing raggedly, her heart thudding in her breast, she stared at the stony ground.

Understanding.

Knowing the truth not only about her culpable witness to Hydra's crime in the sea-cave, but also the truth about the promise she had given her father. There were mitigating circumstances for the first sin: overwhelming fear, and the egocentrism of a very young child. But the second action, back on Caledonia, had been quite different. Hearing her father's agonized plea, she had decided just what she would do when she found her mother's murderers. She would not simply capture them and bring them before the Milieu authorities, but—

"Oh, God," Dee whispered, and covered her face with her hands.

Later, when the last fragment of the thing that had shattered inside her was gone, she was amazed to discover that it was late afternoon. Fog was stealing over the water, into the bays and coves, and making its first tentative foray onto the land. Dee packed up her things and climbed to her feet, aching all over, realizing that she must have been sitting there without moving for over two hours.

"Right," she said aloud. "Definitely time to leave."

It was a little over three kilometers to her journey's end, where her car would be waiting. Once beyond Falcon Cave (and the ravine where she once thought she had seen the Kilnave Fiend) the walking would be fairly easy. She would have to stay close to the cliff edge in order to avoid bogs, but her farsight would keep her safe in the thickening fog.

When she had passed this way as a child, she and the others had remained on the height above the beach and obtained only a partial view of the bird-cave. This time there was no surf, and she decided to take the low route to get a look at the cavern's interior. A strong air current streaming from the large opening in the rocks blew the encroaching mist away. It was still very quiet except for the sound of her boots squeaking on the sand. Inside, the grotto was spacious and deep, much more impressive than Gilmour's. The doves had unaccountably abandoned the place but their guano whitened many of the rocks protruding from the sandy floor.

The wind from within the cave was steady and it bore a peculiar musty scent quite unlike bird droppings. Dee progressed to a point where the fading daylight did not penetrate. Her farsight seemed to show that the cave ended another thirty meters or so further in, but when she reached the back of the chamber she noticed that the airflow had become stronger and had changed direction. It was now blowing from somewhere above her head. When she "looked" up she saw a ledge about six meters high interrupting the sloping, rough-surfaced wall. Above it was a crevice that seemed wide enough to admit a human body. A nonoperant person exploring the cave with artificial light when the cave-wind was not blowing would likely have missed the crack entirely because of the way it was shadowed.

There was a way up. Using her stick and her PK, she negotiated the climb, then pushed her way through the tight crevice. Its sides were unpleasantly wet from dripping groundwater. After she had penetrated ten meters or so the passage opened into another large chamber. Dee straightened and stepped inside, scanning upward with her farsight to see how high the ceiling was.

And stepped on something brittle that crunched beneath her boot.

She did not scream when her mind's eye discovered the bones. The only sound she made was a low moan of sorrow.

So many bones! Skulls and rib cages, the long bones of legs and arms, perforated pelvic basins, disarticulated small bones that had been the framework of hands, feet, and vertebral columns. The skeletal remains were white and clean, and all of them were human. Dee counted the skulls. There were thirty-three, some adult and some belonging to children.

Inspector Chaimbeul had told her that the presumed victims of the "Kilnave Fiend" still unaccounted for numbered twenty-nine. Dee wondered who the other four had been. Lonely day-trippers from the mainland with no one to report them missing on Islay? Boaters who had come unsuspecting to shore for a picnic and instead found death lurking on the pretty beach of Falcon Cave?

The underground wind still blew, this time from another opening at ground level that was less than a meter in diameter; but Dee was too distraught now to do anything but retreat. She turned and re-entered the cramped slot leading to the main cavern.

A light was shining at the other end.

With a sharp intake of breath Dee stopped to focus her farsight in the darkness.

Not one light, but six! Small brilliant pinpricks like three pairs of stars . . . or glowing eyes.

Two women and a man were standing shoulder to shoulder on the ledge just beyond the tunnel's end. The Hydras—Madeleine, Celine, and Parnell Remillard—dressed in ordinary outdoor clothing, were waiting for her to come out.

"Oh, dear Jesus!" she whispered, nearly paralyzed with dread.

Whatever confidence she possessed had evaporated at the sight of those pathetic bones. She was no longer a brilliant, highly educated young woman, a grandmasterclass metapsychic nominated to the Galactic Concilium, but only a panic-stricken fifteen-year-old girl who had grossly overestimated her own bravery. Pressing back the way she had come, she staggered into the bone-room heedless of the relics crackling underfoot. The old sense of dire warning thundered in her brain, urging her to flee for her life.

They came after her then. One at a time and slowly, because they were larger than she and the passage very narrow.

The wind still blew.

Dee ran to the entrance of the next tunnel, threw off her backpack, dropped her stick, and crawled into the opening on her hands and knees. Where did the passage lead? Desperately, she probed ahead with her ultrasenses, not expecting to learn much. Seeing through expanses of solid rock was formidably difficult even for a Grand Master Farseer—and yet she accomplished the task now with an ease that astounded her. The tunnel she was in slanted steeply upward and entered another underground chamber having two other exits. The larger passageway, which was the source of the wind, angled off, twisting and turning, for nearly half a kilometer until it abruptly plunged into unknown depths. The smaller tunnel, up near the ceiling, was only three or four meters in length. It terminated at the surface.

Dee wriggled madly up the incline, dislodging loose chunks of rock that rolled and rattled behind her. Why weren't the Hydras combining in metaconcert, trying to stop her with their mind-devouring ploy? Working together, they might be able to kill her with psychokinesis or some bizarre manifestation of creativity. Instead, they seemed determined to apprehend her physically.

One of the Hydra-women, Celine, was more slender and agile than the others. She came eeling up the passage after Dee with incredible rapidity, uttering monotonous telepathic obscenities.

Dee reached the third cave-chamber and began to scramble up the steep wall. She struggled onto a rocky shelf eight meters above the floor and tried to gather her shaken wits to decide what to do next. The exit shaft was another four meters up and there were no more footholds.

Celine Remillard appeared, screaming vulgar insults out loud. For a moment she paused, irresolute, staring up at Dee. The Hydra was fair-haired and sweetly pretty and the mind that looked out through her turquoise eyes was mad. Giving a final maniacal cry, she changed into a soot-black monstrosity with glowing eyes, a serpentine neck, and multiple arms—a smaller version of the metaconcerted Hydra. A split second later the thing conjured up a hissing ball of energy and flung it at Dee.

Without thinking, the girl spun a psychocreative shield. The lightning-ball hit the barrier and disintegrated into a shower of embers that rained onto the cavern floor. Roaring, the Hydra lifted a broken piece of rock the size of a small desk and hurled it without effort. Dee's shield held and the deflected missile fell with a great crash, cracking apart into sharp-edged fragments. The Hydra shrieked in frustration. An inhuman leap carried it across the rubble-strewn floor to the base of the wall. It began to climb like a huge spider, slowly and carefully.

At that moment the head of Parnell Remillard appeared in the opening of the lower tunnel. Crawling awkwardly into the chamber, he shouted, "Get her quick, Cele! That's the way out!"

By now the creature was nearly halfway to Dee's precarious perch. It seemed unable to climb as fast as a human. As Dee cowered behind her mental shield her farsight perceived the third Hydra-unit, the woman she had first known as Magdala MacKendal, enter the chamber and speak urgently to her male companion.

Abruptly, Dee's protective barrier evaporated. The three units had not combined in true metaconcert, but Dee knew instinctively that the other two had lent the black monster sufficient creativity to neutralize her mental shield. The thing slowly raised one limb and pointed it at her in a purposeful manner.

Dee tensed, shifting all her mindpower into the psychokinetic mode. Levitation was all that could save her now—a maneuver that operant preceptors considered ostentatious and déclassé, one that was never taught to PK-adept students. Most powerfully operant children learned it anyway. But before Dee could carry out the levitation sequence the Hydra pitched another lightning-ball at her with blinding speed. This time the mass of raw energy struck Dee's right thigh, burning through the denim of her jeans and searing the leg almost to the bone.

She screamed in agony and nearly fell, but peripheral PK steadied her feet and the redactive metafaculty that automatically responded to injury cut off input to her sensory nerves. What her redaction could not do immediately was restore the ruined sartorius and rectus femoris muscles of her upper leg. And with the greater portion of her mental potential diverted willy-nilly to self-redaction, Dee found she was unable to levitate.

Huddled on the ledge with tears of pain streaming from her eyes, she watched the Hydra continue to creep upward toward her. Viewed by farsight, it was shadowless.

Kill me if you can! the insane creature said, almost gaily.

No. I won't deliberately try to kill you Celine. Not now.

Then you are a fool, said the Hydra.

Confident that it would now be able to penetrate whatever mental protection Dee could erect, the monster had not bothered to put up a psychocreative screen of its own. It seemed to think its quarry had surrendered. With a wild giggle, it produced another globe of deadly energy and held it up for the girl to see.

Instead of cringing, Dee picked up a fist-sized stone and propelled it with all her remaining physical strength, striking the Hydra squarely between its blazing, demented eyes. The lightning-ball winked out in the onslaught of unexpected hurt and the monster faltered, black limbs scratching frantically for purchase. But before it could recover Dee threw another stone, again striking the misshapen head. Wailing, the Hydra lost its grip and fell, landing heavily on the jagged rocks below.

"Cele!" the other two cried. Unaccountably, they did not rush to the aid of their fallen companion. Instead they remained standing side by side, motionless.

The Hydra stirred. Its body flickered and for an instant Dee farsaw the human form of Celine Remillard staggering upright, her face twisted with pain. Then the woman straightened and gave a triumphant cry, apparently reinvigorated by some unconcerted mental ploy of Parnell and Madeleine. She underwent her terrible metamorphosis, and Hydra reappeared. It immediately began to climb the wall again, and this time it wore a mental shield of its own.

The terror and confusion that had afflicted Dee earlier had passed away, leaving her in control of what faculties she could still muster. Even if she managed to divert mental energy from the redaction, there would still be only enough vitality remaining to fully activate a single higher mindpower.

Very well. Then let it be creativity, the strongest of all.

The agony from her ghastly burn returned as her redaction withdrew, and so did the traumatic shock. She was seized with a sudden attack of dizziness and a profound weakness. At first her body refused to obey when she ordered it to move, but a roar from the advancing monster, intended to intimidate her, had the opposite effect. Still crouching on the ledge, Dee stretched out her right arm and thrust her fingers into the nearly featureless rock face.

Her creativity softened the stone like putty. She gouged out a foothold at knee height, then a second somewhat higher, then a third and a fourth. Once her hand withdrew, the rock rehardened instantly, leaving a useful hole. Dee began to swarm up the wall, letting her injured leg hang free and supporting most of her weight with her arms.

The Hydra reached the rock shelf, extinguished its shield, and extended its upper limbs, ready to seize her. Dee clawed out a final hold and heaved herself up into the tiny passageway, gasping from pain and exertion. The tunnel was barely wide enough for her shoulders. The cave-wind hissed past her, seeming to push her gently toward freedom, and she began to worm her way upward. Ahead lay a dim gray area of light that had to be the evening sky.

Then something took hold of her right ankle and pulled at her hideously burned leg.

In hindsight, she knew she should have switched to the coercive mode and forced the Hydra to release her. But the abrupt blaze of new pain canceled all rationality. Her creativity was available and so she used it, accelerating the exhalation of the cave-wind to hurricane force. Her small body was propelled through the passageway like a human cannonball. The Hydra's grip tore loose from her ankle. She flew out of the tunnel mouth on a roaring blast into the foggy night, tumbling head over heels through the air like a discarded doll.

There was a stunning splash. She had landed in a shallow bog. Before the pain could render her unconscious, she called on her redaction. Crawling on her elbows and one knee through the yielding muck, she was able to reach the bog's edge and haul herself onto dry ground.

She had emerged in a region of nearly level moorland all swathed in mist. Her farsight, used gingerly, revealed that less than 30 meters away the land abruptly terminated in a precipice above the sea. The north shore trail skirted the cliff's edge. Behind her was the bog, to the left a dale with a tiny burn that flowed down into Falcon Cave cove, and to the right lay a jumble of rocks surrounding the subterranean shaft. Gnarled old heather bushes grew in rank profusion over much of the area. If she had fallen in them she would very likely have broken every bone in her body.

The roaring wind had stopped. Dee heard her own pounding heart, the trickling of the stream, and the distant sigh of the sea. Another noise, a very faint splashing, seemed to come from the other end of the bog. After a few moments it stopped.

Dee's wrist-communicator was smashed and inoperative, but she would not have chosen to use it even if it worked, nor did she intend to send out a farspoken cry for help. She stripped off her muddy parka, her sweater, which was hardly wet at all, and her cotton flannel shirt. Dipping part of the shirt in the stream's clear water, she bound it carefully about her wounded leg and tied it in place. She put the sweater back on and hung the parka over her shoulders. In its capacious pockets were a bandanna handkerchief, a damp Hershey's chocolate bar, her wallet, her hotel room key, and the encoded plass strip that would unlock and activate her rented groundcar.

She tied the bandanna on her head and ate the chocolate. A swift, circumscribing beam of seekersense assured her that there were no

Hydra-units in the vicinity. It was no use searching for them underground. Deep beneath the rocks of Islay, their auras would be imperceptible to her. It didn't matter. If they were hiding in the tunnel network they were no danger to her.

Dee's injured leg was as useless as a length of wood, but her mental strength was returning and she knew she would be able to hobble to the car park where her rented vehicle waited. The village of Bowmore was only 20 kilometers away. She would first make a report to Inspector Chaimbeul, then drive to the little hospital and check in.

The authorities could deal with the Hydra. Dee didn't give a damn about it anymore. Strangely, the inhibitory barriers deep in her mind seemed to have crumbled, perhaps as a result of the moral insight she had experienced earlier. She felt no special increase in her powers, but in her present traumatized state that was to be expected. She'd let Catherine Remillard investigate her expanded metapsychic complexus when she had recovered.

Only one thing still puzzled her. Why had the Hydra-units failed to combine in metaconcert when they attacked her, rather than trying to subdue her physically? Even two of them working together would have been a match for her after her injury.

The solution to that mystery would have to wait.

Marshaling both her redaction and her farsight in the most efficient way possible, she set off on the trail to the car park.

Jack watched her go, then said a prayer of thanksgiving. Noiseless and invisible, he glided over the surface of the bog until he reached a dark shape half submerged in the water. It was the body of a young woman, naked except for a pair of stout hiking boots and so fearfully abraded that it seemed to be one vast open wound. Nearly all of Celine Remillard's skin was torn away, and both arms had been ripped off at the shoulder as she was sucked and battered through the constricted rocky shaft by Dorothea Macdonald's metacreative blast. She had no face.

Jack probed the brain of the Hydra carefully to make certain that life was extinct, then sent his powerful seekersense underground. His sister Madeleine and cousin Parnell had disappeared completely. It was to be expected that the Hydra had other secret exits from its death-cave.

Jack moved up into the sky, tracking Dorothea as she trudged doggedly along. She might deduce in time that the Hydras had avoided using metaconcert for a very good reason. They had suspected that Jack might guard Dorothea surreptitiously, and they knew that the emanations of their life-devouring mental combination would have drawn him to them like a beacon.

What they had not known was that Jack had been forbidden by the Lylmik Supervisors to interfere, even if Dorothea had died. It was only when she had escaped by her own efforts that he allowed himself to divert her falling body toward a safe landing place. Once she had admitted herself to the hospital in Bowmore, he would go to her and show her how to heal her injuries quickly.

Fury would withdraw into siege mode now, guarding its two last precious links to physical reality. The mental signatures of the units would be changed again, and Madeleine and Parnell Remillard would eventually surface again with new identities and a fresh focus for meddling.

No matter how ingenious their disguise, however, Jack was confident that he would eventually find them and confine them. Then Fury would be all alone, forced to reveal itself. It would have no recourse but to take over the body it secretly shared with an innocent mind.

Father of Light, Jack prayed, help me learn how to kill it before then.

[22]

FROM THE MEMOIRS OF ROGATIEN REMILLARD

Of all the higher mindpowers, creativity is the strangest.

Its expression differs greatly among the races of the Galactic Milieu—as anyone familiar with the slaphappy Gi and the anal-retentive Simbiari will attest. I've been told I have a goodly dollop of creativity, although I never allowed anyone to measure it—or any other contents of my skull, for that matter. I can recall only a few occasions that the power has been really useful to me. On the other hand, creativity may have influenced me more than I realize if my Family Ghost turns out to be a figment of my imagination and I, myself, am actually responsible for everything you have read.

Qu'à dieu ne plaise!

In human operants, metacreativity is the power most likely to be made latent and unusable by deleterious factors. Even when you've got it beaucoup and up the wazoo, you can lose it or have it seriously diminished by fatigue, illness, physical or mental trauma, or even getting up on the wrong side of the bed. Conversely, some emotions—fear, anger, lust!—can hype it all to hell. Not always, worse luck. But sometimes when you'd least expect it, a creative brainstorm can save your neck or win you a bundle.

Creativity is the faculty most likely to be very strong in normal humans, where it's called talent or genius. In the days before metapsychology, hardly any educated Earthlings thought of creativity as a higher mindpower at all. But the primitives knew, and wisely identified it as the touch of the gods.

Every creature with true willpower possesses a modicum of it. Creativity is the integrator and modulator of the entire mind, forming the linkage between thought and matter. It's literally the inspiration —the "breathing in"—of the divine into what would otherwise be mere mud molecules. Le bon dieu had to tell us himself that humans are most godlike when they love one another. Left to ourselves, we equate godliness with creativity because human beings appreciate *results*.

Psychologists and good schoolteachers know that creative potential is elusive and inborn. It doesn't necessarily equate with high intelligence. It can be nurtured but it can't be implanted when the inherited faculty itself is puny. There's no way a person can acquire it by studying; but if you've got it and you work at it, overcoming obstacles in its pursuit, it grows muscles. Ignore it or suppress it and it withers and may even die. You can lose it due to aging or bodily infirmity, and grief is the greatest creativity slayer of all.

Creative insights can strike in an abrupt coup de foudre or be wrung painfully from the psyche over long periods of time. Creativity can sneak into the mind in a dream, sleeping or waking, but it doesn't often fly in the window when you're drunk or stoned . . . it only *seems* to, and then comes the cold gray dawn.

In normals, when left-brain creativity flags, it can often be spectacularly revived if one pursues a right-brain activity—and vice versa. Play music or drive a vehicle and the literary muse will be resuscitated. Read a book or balance the accounts and the artistic inspiration may return. It's as though the creative stew must sometimes be left to cook on its own, undisturbed by mere ratiocination or willpower's whip.

When creativity is frustrated or warped, the effect upon the possessor and the environment can be appalling, because creativity's flip side is destruction.

It's not necessarily true that great creativity in humans is closely allied to madness. This is discredited folklore. There have been human geniuses who suffered severe mental illness, particularly the manic-depressive kind; but by and large they seem to have been creative in spite of their disorder rather than because of it. Schizophrenia, a disease affecting the imagination, is most spectacular when the person's imagination is extraordinary.

The loonies depicted in these memoirs of mine have often possessed high creative talent; but try to remember that the consummate creative villain of them all was eminently sane.

Metacreativity is the queen of metafaculties, more awesome in its potential than any of the others. The creativity of normals yields ideas that may indirectly influence matter and energy. That of operants brings forth an idea that may *be* matter and energy.

The simplest aspect of creativity is the special aura that all living things have. Elementary metacreative tricks include such things as producing flames or lights through the chemical decomposition of organic or atmospheric molecules. Heating and cooling matter is also pretty easy for the average longhead, as is drying off things that are wet, which depends partly on creativity and partly on PK. Making a creative umbrella or other external shield is trickier because it depends upon the mental generation of a sigma-field, but most human masterclass metas learn how to do it eventually. Shape-shifting (which isn't fully understood, involving as it does both "sender" and "receiver"), the generation of conventional illusions, and going invisible are middling creative. Actually putting together a physical body—even the shell of one—the way Jack did is gonzo-class creativity, on a par with the external assembly of organic matter, directing metaconcerts, and producing mindbolts of psychic energy.

I did that a few times by accident, but it's easier with a CE hat. So are lots of other kinds of creative mischief-making, which is one of the main reasons why the Galactic Milieu outlawed cerebroenergetic enhancement after the Rebellion.

But now I'm getting ahead of myself . . .

Dorothée's healing, assisted by Jack, stupefied the medical staff at the little Islay hospital. With no operants on the island, the medics were unfamiliar with the spectacular way in which powerful redactors can cure serious injuries. The operant community kept this information, and a whole lot more besides, more or less confidential in order to avoid "invidious comparisons."

A normal Islay citizen of modest means suffering a deep muscle-destroying burn like Dorothée's might have had to spend a month in a regen-tank—when one became available in a larger hospital on the mainland. (Healing through genetic engineering was not as routine in the seventies as it would be twenty years later.) Such expensive facilities were always available to operants who needed them, however; it was one of the side benefits the Milieu quietly vouchsafed to those it deemed the most important members of the human race.

With Jack's redaction added to her own, Dorothée was discharged within three days—not fully restored, but able to function normally and without pain. She would have plenty of time to deal with the cosmetic aspects of her wound herself during the starship flight to Concilium Orb.

In his statement to the police, Jack said only that he had come to Islay in search of background information on the original crimes, as had Dorothée herself. It was tacitly inferred by the locals that the famous young Remillard magnate and the hugely talented young woman were great and good friends, and he had been helping her investigate the old crime committed against members of her family.

The two of them did nothing to contradict this notion, but Dorothée was actually furious with Jack for shadowing her. It was only after a nasty telepathic wrangle that she consented to let him help with her healing—and then only because she didn't want to stay in hospital any longer than necessary.

To the great exasperation of Inspector Chaimbeul, agents of the Galactic Magistratum converged upon the island to take charge of the latest investigation. The First Magnate himself put in an appearance, and he was mightily pissed off with the two young people for setting a Hydra trap without notifying him. But there was really nothing Paul could do about it; Dorothée had been completely unaware of the Dynasty's secret search and Jack was a law unto himself.

All proceedings of the new Islay inquiry were sealed, with the exception of a terse announcement saying that Celia MacKendal, believed to be the perpetrator of the numerous killings that had taken place on the island in earlier years, had been found dead in a cave, together with the bones of her victims, by a girl hiker. The presence of the killer on Islay was not explained, but *The Scotsman* speculated that she might have been overcome with remorse and committed suicide at the scene of her grisly crimes.

The DNA of the woman who had attacked Dorothée yielded a positive identification of Celine Mireille Ashe Remillard, daughter of Maurice Remillard and Cecilia Ashe. The information was not made public, nor was it shared with the local police. The body was released to the custody of the First Magnate himself. After a private Catholic memorial service attended by certain anonymous operants, the ashes of the murderer were scattered over the Atlantic Ocean.

On 20 January 2073 Earth computation, her sixteenth birthday, Dorothea Mary Strachan Macdonald became a Magnate of the Concilium and was named a Paramount Grand Master in all five metafaculties. Her maiden speech, delivered a couple of weeks later, was brief but moving: a plea that all operant members of the Human Polity renounce forever the use of higher mindpowers as weapons, even in a cause that might be deemed "just," such as self-defense.

There was enthusiastic applause for the young woman's naive idealism, plus a certain amount of trepidation among the Rebel contingent, who feared that Dorothée might become a new and vocal member of Anne Remillard's pestiferous Unity Directorate. But instead the new paramount was quickly named First Deputy Dirigent of Caledonia, which effectively removed her from the forefront of Concilium politics.

Dorothée was both astounded and troubled by her unexpected appointment. She tried to decline the honor, insisting that she was too young and inexperienced for such responsibility, but the Lylmik Supervisors were adamant. The only concession she wrung from them was an agreement to review and evaluate her work critically in two years' time, and remove her from office if she proved incompetent.

When she returned to the planet of her birth, she had a warm reunion with her father Ian, who had recently married Janet Finlay. Her nonborn adoptive siblings Ellen Gunn and Hugh Murdoch were overawed at her new position of authority, while the onetime bully Gavin Boyd was scared shitless of her until she assured him she held no grudge.

Dorothée lived in a simple apartment in Dirigent House in the Caledonian capital, New Glasgow, and spent the first year of her term learning her duties while acting as all-around dogsbody to the aging planetary executive, Graeme Hamilton.

His former First Deputy, Catriona Chisholm, was transferred to the populous cosmop planet Avalon, where she became Deputy to Usha Singh. Although this was technically a promotion for Chisholm, she was furious at being replaced by a raw teenager, even one with paramount faculties. Chisholm had expected to succeed Graeme Hamilton, but there was small chance of that happening now. Calum Sorley, the Scottish planet's Intendant General, was livid at the thought of a youthful idealist "usurping" a position that the radical anti-Unity faction had counted heavily upon. Their scheme for manufacturing illegal CE equipment on Caledonia once Hamilton was out of the way had to be abandoned, with the result that the active phase of the Metapsychic Rebellion was put on hold for nearly a decade, until Satsuma was finally able to produce the mental weaponry.

Hamilton had been Dirigent since 2054, when the Simbiari Proctorship finally ended in the colonies. Before that he had served in the planet's Intendant Assembly for over thirty years, he and his late wife having been among the first settlers. Graeme was a rugged old haggis-walloper who scorned rejuvenation, claiming that he had no time to waste floating in a vat of artificial amniotic fluid when there was work to be done. He knew every nook and cranny of Caledonia, was personally acquainted with almost every first-generation settler, and had tinkered and goosed the Scottish world's economy to an unexpected state of prosperity, considering its paucity of natural resources.

His health had remained excellent until his wife's accidental death in 2064. Then, like a lot of brilliant but careless old farts, he let himself go to pot physically once there was no dedicated spouse in the house to keep an eye on him. He ate wrong and drank wrong and kept the doctors and the genetic engineers at bay declaring he'd redact any little aches and pains that bothered him.

Hamilton was a hell of a coercer but a bush-league redactor. By the time Dorothée came to Callie in 2073 he was seventy-nine years old. He had been fitted with a bionic heart, liver, and kidneys, and also suffered from a maverick strain of chronic lymphocytic leukemia that defied treatment. He had been dying for at least two years and was fated to hang on for another four.

There was nothing whatsoever wrong with his wits.

He recognized at once that Dorothée was the successor he had been waiting for—a young woman endowed with a full bag of extraordinary mental talents who was loyal to the Milieu and fiercely devoted to Caledonia itself. Unlike Catriona Chisholm, she was ready to put the welfare of her planet and its inhabitants above galactic politics. Her extreme youth made her malleable and eager for Hamilton's counsel; her energy and intelligence provided him with fresh insight and made him feel confident that when he cashed in his chips, he'd be leaving Callie in the best possible hands.

No wonder the two of them got on together like a house afire.

Ideally, the office of Dirigent involves ombudsmanship, fiscal oversight, the expediting of communication between the citizens and their government, and liaison between the Intendant Assembly of the planet and the Milieu. The Dirigent has a large staff of assistants, but most of them report directly to the top, so that the chief executive and First Deputy are able to keep their fingers on the planetary pulse at all times. Although the Dirigent and the deputy are both empowered to use coercion, deep-probing, and the other metapsychic powers in the course of official investigations, good old horse sense is apt to prove a more effective tool in the long run.

The Dirigent's deputy is expected to act as the boss's sampler of public opinion, troubleshooter, and inspector general. Sophisticated Catriona Chisholm had spent most of her time in the capital city; but Dorothée was almost compulsively on the move, interviewing citizens in the frontier regions of the planet as well as the centers of commerce and culture.

Nobody knew where she and her souped-up Lotus egg would turn up next. One week she'd be prowling the farmsteads of Argyll, the next she might be visiting pearlfishers in Strathbogie, buckyball mines in darkest Caithness, or checking out tourism in the sportfishing resorts of Cairngorm.

Her paramount status made her an object of pride to the operant Callie citizenry; but the normals didn't really give a hoot about her awesome mindpowers. It was her unassuming manner, intelligence, and genuine interest in their lives that won the hearts of those crusty kiltie hinterlanders. They called her the "Dirigent Lassie" and accorded her a fondness that the aloof Chisholm had never enjoyed.

Not everyone thought Dorothée was a superstar, however. Certain

Caledonian Assembly bureaucrats with private agendas, professional sharpsters, sleazy corner-cutters, and thimblerigging entrepreneurs came to view her as a holy terror. She'd come poking around some trouble spot, winsome and innocent-seeming, and when the lowlives were confident they'd pulled the wool over her young eyes—whammo! Wyatt Earp rides into Dodge City disguised as a girl in a tartan culotte. She could read the minds of flimflam artists like they had windows in their skulls, and she was merciless with the exploiters and environmental spoilers who always seem to infest the planetary frontiers.

During her four years as Graeme Hamilton's deputy, she played an important part in helping her world to achieve its long-sought goal of a positive balance of payments. The time finally came when the old Dirigent saw his beloved Scottish planet no longer dependent upon Milieu subsidies. Thanks to him and his tireless young deputy, Caledonia proudly took its place among the dozen or so ethnic worlds in the Human Polity that were prosperous and financially secure.

Dorothée remained dubious about her own performance, however, suspecting—perhaps correctly—that the citizenry viewed her more as a beloved mascot than as a competent executive. She continued to beg the Lylmik to demote or remove her, feeling that she had failed to measure up to her high office. Some of her insecurity was due to Calum Sorley and his Rebel allies, who waged a subtle and persistent campaign designed to belittle and discredit her. But even aside from this subversion, the nagging feeling persisted in her heart that she was only a jumped-up prodigy who had been thrust into high office through an exotic whim. No reassurances by Graeme Hamilton or any other close associates in Dirigent House could convince her otherwise.

Much later, Dorothée confessed to me that each morning during those early years, when she looked at herself in the mirror and combed her hair, she felt a pang of anxiety and disbelief. The person looking back at her from the glass was a freak and a fraud. This plain-faced, very small, very young woman did not deserve to be Deputy Dirigent and could not possibly command the true respect of the planetary populace. She was only a celebrity, not a genuine leader. The Lylmik had made a terrible mistake, and one day she would surely be exposed as the incompetent she felt herself to be. Each morning and night she prayed for deliverance from a situation she felt was hopeless.

But during her working days, she continued to do the very best she could.

I did not see Dorothée again until 2076, three years into her term as deputy, when she returned to Earth for the marriage of her brother. News about her doings came to me mostly from my old drinking buddy Kyle Macdonald, who shared many an ethanol-tinted evening with me in my favorite Hanover oasis, the Sap Bucket Tavern, just about the only bar in town that actively discouraged college students.

It was there that Kyle converted me to the Rebel cause. Not that I wasn't already tilting toward sedition on my own, what with Sevvy and Adrien's shining example to poison my willing mind. Not even Jack's devotion to the Milieu and keen advocacy of Unity was able to overcome my own long-standing sense of unease at the prospect of humanity getting into some sort of permanent mind-meld with the exotic races. The Poltroyans were fine and dandy, regular folks if you could forget their purple skin, ruby eyes, and painted little bald heads. But who would seriously want to share mental intimacy with a gang of green-dripping, technocratic crepehangers like the Simbiari? Or be mind-buddies with the nightmarish Krondaku? The Gi were a hoot at parties, but they were alarmingly oversexed and so sensitive they were known to drop dead just to make an aesthetic statement. The Lylmik were probably the scariest of all, and I had my own Family Ghost to prove it.

Fortunately, le Fantôme Familier had left me in peace during most of the years since Jack's birth. But I knew It was still out there, ready to bedevil me again when I least expected it.

So I felt right at home when Kyle Macdonald gradually introduced me into the local Rebel sewing circle. The activities of the Hanover Disunity Club at that time weren't especially exciting, concentrating as they did upon refuting the propaganda of the Panpolity Directorate and subverting operant Dartmouth students. Kyle's wickedly anti-Milieu fantasy satires enjoyed a wide readership throughout the Human Polity and he was once again rolling in money. Even his passage into low-grade operancy didn't harm his popularity among the xenophobic normals, who would eventually become cannon fodder in the Metapsychic Rebellion.

One prime objective continued to elude the Rebel leadership: they still hadn't managed to net Marc! Believe it or not, I was given the assignment of brainwashing my paramount great-grandnephew and converting him to the cause. Laughable in excelsis, you'll agree, but at that time no one else among the insurgents had ready access to him. I at least visited Marc now and then in his Pacific Northwest home, and even joined him on fishing excursions to Belize, Christmas Island, the Yakima River, and even the Irish planet. I did my insidious best to put across the Rebel party line when we were together; but Marc, while sympathetic to anti-Unity philosophy, seemed quite uninterested in doing anything about it.

He mocked my fellow conspirators (especially the magnates) as a bunch of cocktail-party mutineers with no viable alternative to the Milieu they were so anxious to escape. Anyone possessing higher mindpowers, said he, needed to be part of a highly structured, altruistic civilization; Homo superior was too dangerous to be let loose in the kind of old-fashioned laissez-faire society the Rebels advocated.

Yes, I recognize the irony here! But Marc would remain a staunch supporter of the Milieu for years—until his own precious ox got gored, whereupon he revised the Rebel manifesto and assumed leadership of the movement himself.

Kenneth Macdonald and Luc Remillard were married in the same fieldstone church where Denis and Lucille had wed eighty-one years earlier. Anne officiated, Dorothée was maid of honor, and Catherine, the boss and professional colleague of both young metapsychologists, served as best woman. There was a reception at the Hanover Inn following the ceremony, and it was there that Dorothée and I managed to renew our friendship after its long hiatus.

"It's too bad Ian couldn't make it," I said, having danced her onto the hotel terrace away from the noisier celebrators. We found an empty wrought iron table with four chairs in a corner under an ornamental tree and took possession. It was June and the weather was perfect. A waitron came along with sloe gin fizzes and made it even better.

"Dad still believes the farm can't function without him," she said.

"And he's an active Intendant Associate for Beinn Bhiorach as well."

Although she hadn't grown a cent since I'd seen her last, she was most definitely a woman now at nineteen, poised and mature and still very private behind that grave little face that never betrayed what she was thinking. She wore a trouser suit of cherry-colored linen and a white blouse with a froth of lace at the wrists. Around her neck on a gold chain hung the little diamond-mask talisman.

"Do you get to spend much time with Ian yourself?" I asked.

"Not as much as I'd like." She pushed back a lock of straight brown hair that the breeze had disarranged. "I did break the news to him about Ken and Luc. Dad was slightly . . . disconcerted. His attitudes on marriage are still rather old-fashioned, like a lot of people who live on outlying ethnic worlds. But he came around in time and even sent wedding rings of Callie gold inset with black diamonds from the local mine."

"The stones didn't look black to me," I remarked in surprise.

"No, they're really brilliant gray. Lovely things. I suppose the Callie diamond merchants think black sounds sexier. Our mines produce diamonds in all kinds of odd colors, but black is the rarest. Our pearls are tinted, too. Even the trees on the planet come in outlandish tartan colors. Caledonia's a wonderful place. I want you to come and visit soon, Uncle Rogi. The Deputy Dirigent gets a quota of free transport tickets as an official perk and I'll send you one."

"I'd like that. How's the fishing?"

"Fantastic!" She actually smiled. "Angling is one of our prime tourist attractions. We have genuine Scottish salmon, of course, but the real prizes are some naturalized blue Siberian trout as long as your leg planted years ago on Clyde by a chap named Vladimir Ilyich MacNaughton."

"Send three tickets," I chortled, "and I'll bring Marc and Jack."

"If you like." She looked away and the smile disappeared.

"Batège!" I exploded. "Are you still on the outs with Jack after all these years?"

"Certainly not." She took a prim little sip of fizz and gazed out at the college green across the street. Young women her own age, college students dressed in Levi's and T-shirts and bright cotton shifts, were lounging about on the grass as carefree as meadowlarks. I wondered if Dorothée ever took time off to birdwatch anymore—or even to relax.

"Director Jon Remillard and I conferred at the last Concilium session about some of Callie's geophysical problems," she went on matter-of-factly.

"Anything really serious?"

"We hope not. The studies have only just begun, and they'll take over a year. Human scientists are conducting them this time rather than the Krondaku, who did the original survey thousands of years ago."

"Another one of their fuck-ups like Satsuma and Okanagon?"

"Evidently," she said. "Dirigent Hamilton has been after the Milieu to do a complete new lithospheric evaluation for ages. Work finally began in earnest about five Earth months ago."

"After you put the arm on Jack," I remarked.

She nodded uncomfortably.

"Speak of the devil," I muttered.

Two men, one towering and dark, the other medium in height and so unexceptional that he almost faded into the woodwork, had come out onto the inn terrace. They were looking about in that offhanded operant way that invariably means you are the target of subliminal attention and had better acknowledge the overture unless you have a damned good reason not to.

I waved and grinned, Dorothée produced a dutiful social smile, and the two Remillard brothers ambled over carrying drinks and little plates of dessert.

"May we join you?" Marc inquired, looking dapper as the devil in a Brummelesque outfit with a dark green tailcoat, fawn breeches, shiny boots, and a white stock. Jack wore the only *brown* nebulin suit I've ever seen in my life. The glittery fabric actually looked drab on him.

"Certainly." Dorothée was gracious. "Please sit down."

Jack took the place next to her and made small talk about the lovely wedding and the happy couple. Dorothée produced similar pleasantries and then remarked that his goodie looked delicious.

"It's Almond Mademoiselle wedding cake," he said eagerly. "Please share it with me."

The fork, the plate, and the cake all fissioned like mutant amoebae, yielding half-sized replicas of the originals. Marc and I rolled our eyes and heroically refrained from snide utterances, but Dorothée might have been young Queen Victoria confronted with a flower-bearing guttersnipe.

"How very kind of you," she murmured. She began to eat, the very paragon of politesse.

"Dorothée was just telling me about the great sportfishing on Caledonia," said I.

"Cosmic class, so I've heard," said Marc. "I've always meant to give it a whirl, but the new E18 project at CEREM seems to be taking all my time."

"A new cerebroenergetic application?" Dorothée inquired.

Marc nodded. "We'll crank the enhancement of innate creativity up to nearly three hundred percent if I can get the bugs out of this model."

"Why, that's amazing!" She hesitated momentarily before continuing. "I wonder if your brother has mentioned the spot of seismic bother we've been experiencing on Caledonia? If your organization should ever need to field-test your new equipment in a geophysical application, we'd give you a grand Scottish welcome . . . and take you fishing besides."

"The offer sounds irresistible," Marc agreed, smiling his charming asymmetrical smile.

"Mind if I tag along?" Jack asked diffidently.

"You'd both be welcome, of course," she said. "Shall I keep you posted on the progress of the new survey?"

"Oh, CEREM's been keeping an eye on you ever since the crustal studies began," Jack said, with bland innocence.

"Then you must know," she said a bit more stiffly, "that we may have reason for grave concern. Within the last three years, deep-seated seismic activity has increased throughout the entire northern hemisphere, especially in the vicinity of the Clyde continent. We've even had a kimberlite diatreme for the first time in thirty thousand orbits. Fortunately, the pipe was less than a meter wide and the eruption took place in an uninhabited region."

"What's a diatreme?" I asked.

"A cold eruption of gas," Jack said, "usually carbon dioxide or water vapor. The phenomenon undoubtedly accounts for the abundant diamonds of Caledonia. The crystals form at great depths beneath ancient cratonic landmasses and are blasted to the surface when diatrematic activity forms a kimberlite pipe. It's fascinating—"

"Unless it takes place in the midst of a densely populated area," Dorothée broke in gently. "But we're not so much concerned with the diamonds as we are with a possible threat to cratonic stability. A craton is a very ancient chunk of crust that forms the nucleus of a continent. On Earth, each continent is made up of a number of cratons. Caledonia has nineteen small continents with a single craton for each. We've left the seven most seismically active landmasses uncolonized. The twelve populated ones were supposed to have cratons that stabilized aeons ago, but as you may know, doubts have been cast on the validity of the original Krondak survey."

"A charitable way to put it," Marc murmured.

"We're not sure yet," Dorothée continued, "but there may be a sizable reservoir of magma with an extremely high volatile content just below the lithospheric mantle of Clyde's craton. If signs of imminent instability turn up in the new study, then CE modification of the reservoir contents could be critically important."

"Sounds challenging," Jack said. "Do you have many trained CE ops with grandmasterclass creativity who could work on geozap planning with Marc's CEREM people?"

"We have three," she said.

Jack was taken aback. "That sounds like a *considerable* challenge!"

"Forty-two Caledonian grandmaster geophysicists are undergoing training on Satsuma," Dorothée said, "but it will be some years before they're all fully certified for cerebroenergetic enhancement. Dirigent Hamilton is adamant about safety considerations."

"So am I," Marc said tersely.

"My brother and I have developed some interesting new metaconcert programs for multiple grandmaster heads," Jack said, "but we don't usually participate personally in CEREM geophysical projects these days."

"Oh." Dorothée was plainly disappointed. "You see, it would be very difficult to get additional experienced grandmasterclass creators to come in to Caledonia from other worlds. Those planets that have CE operators trained in geophysical creativity paid a fortune and waited a long time to get them certified. They're understandably anxious to keep the workers at home, where there tend to be more projects than they can handle. That's why I thought—that is, I hoped—that you two might consider working with our Caledonian operators in order to test your new equipment."

Jack shook his head with real regret. "Frankly, tacking just three grandmasters onto my own metaconcerted input and Marc's would hardly produce an appropriate configuration."

I let loose a derisive guffaw. "Be like hitching a trio of mice alongside a pair of Clydesdales!" But I shut my fool mouth and mentally kicked myself when I saw the look of dismay on the poor girl's face. It vanished immediately, however, and she appeared as composed as ever.

"I see," she said. "I apologize for the misunderstanding." She pushed back her chair and prepared to leave. We all politely climbed to our feet. "Whether or not you choose to test your new equipment on Caledonia," she said to Marc, "it would make me very happy to welcome you and Jack and Uncle Rogi for the fishing. Now you must excuse me. I promised dances to Ken and Luc before I left."

She nodded pleasantly at each of us and went back to the ballroom.

"Nice going," Marc said to me, with heavy irony.

"Aw shit," I muttered wretchedly. "I didn't mean to make fun of her dinky little CE corps."

Jack said, "Three GMs on their own wouldn't have a prayer of defusing a deep-seated high-pressure magma reservoir—even using CEREM's new E18 brain-booster." He lifted his inhuman eyes to his older brother. "Would they?"

"No," said Marc. "I thought the problem on Caledonia was typical subduction-zone volcanism, ten to fifty kloms deep. If Caledonia's mantle and crust are nearly terrestrial, then a subcratonic reservoir of the type she spoke of would likely lie one-thirty to two hundred kilometers below the surface. Deep-drillers can descend that far, but getting the metacreative impulse focused and shaped under those conditions of heat and pressure would be a real bitch. It may not be feasible under *any* circumstances, and it would certainly be bloody dangerous."

"But you and I might be able to pull it off using the new hats." Jack's tone was almost pleading.

"Creative CE is finally gaining acceptance with the Milieu conservatives," Marc said severely. "A fiasco now would put us back to square one . . . or worse."

"But if a big subcratonic reservoir blows, it could be a major disaster for the affected planet."

"Dammit, Jack, I'm not touching this thing with a barge pole! I almost barbecued myself once before doing experimental geozap CE with you. Pardon me if I can't get all worked up at the notion of a fresh try! If the boil on Caledonia pops, they'll just have to evacuate the region and pick up the pieces."

"Poor Dorothée," I said.

"Poor CEREM," Marc retorted, "if I get myself killed or tangled in a no-win mess because Bodiless Bozo, here, thinks he's in love."

I gaped at Jack. The paramount naked brain and little Diamond Mask? The absurd contingency had never entered my mind.

"You know, Marc," Jack said in a friendly fashion, "sometimes you're really a primo prick."

"At least I've got one to call my own," Marc snapped, and he went stomping off, coattails and hackles both flying high.

Jack's mind said: [Freakish obscene image] + [utter dejection].

I tried to force some hearty optimism. "Cheer up, Ti-Jean. Maybe there won't be any rumble on Caledonia. Maybe those half-assed Krondak surveyors got it right after all."

"And maybe bears will build latrines in the woods."

I couldn't resist asking, "Are you really in love with her?"

The inhuman blue eyes had a sardonic glitter. "What a ludicrous idea. Me, in love? Why, that's positively sickening. Right?"

"Oh, Ti-Jean . . ." I whispered, and my vision began to blur.

"I really can't stand people who cry at weddings," Jack said. "See you later, Uncle Rogi."

I stayed there alone for a good long time, then snuck away to the Sap Bucket Tavern and got paralytic.

A little over a year after Dorothée returned to her home world, Graeme Hamilton died peacefully. She was immediately appointed Planetary Dirigent of Caledonia by the Lylmik Supervisors.

Late in 2077, the team of human geophysical surveyors confirmed the presence of an enormous high-pressure magmatic reservoir beneath the continent of Clyde. In their report to the Dirigent, the scientists estimated that the thing would blow off catastrophically within two to three years unless something drastic was done to modify its development.

Dorothée thanked the surveyors and promised to take the matter under advisement. Then she called me.

And I called Jack.

[23]

SECTOR 12: STAR 12-337-010 [GRIAN] PLANET 4 [CALEDONIA]

13–14 AN GIBLEAN [24–25 NOVEMBER] 2077

By the time Rogi revived from the state of enforced hibernation he'd endured throughout the tight-leash trip from Earth, Scurra II was dropping through the aurora-streaked ionosphere toward the cloudy Scottish planet.

Scratching himself and yawning, the old man made his way to the flight deck. His great-grandnephew was no longer in the brainboarded fishbowl that was his resting place of choice while disembodied, but sat instead in a command chair like a decent human being, dressed in a blue jumpsuit and a pair of Sauvage Hikers. The blinking light on the terrain display before him indicated that their landing site was nowhere near either of Clyde's metro areas.

"What's happening?" Rogi inquired. "You're not putting down at the Wester Killiecrankie Starport?"

"We've got emergency clearance to land at the geophysical operations site," Jack said. "Callie Traffic Control decided Scurra II is small enough to be designated an honorary egg-bus. We won't have to transship the equipment to a rhocraft for atmospheric flight."

"Some bus!" the bookseller snorted. "Damn thing'd leave a Krondak clipper in the dust. I can't believe we hopped over five hundred lights in two days."

"Actually, I held back a little to be sure you'd survive. You're the first passenger I've taken in the new ship."

The old man flexed his arms again and groaned a little. "I'm glad you didn't tell me that before we started out. I might have thought twice about wanting to come along."

The bus driver showed immediate concern. "Are you in pain, Uncle Rogi?"

"Just creaky from being zonked out for two days. You redacted me just fine. Didn't feel a thing. All I need is a square meal. You get any word from Dorothée while I was out for the count?"

Jack turned back to the display. They were swiftly approaching their destination, a plateau situated between two sizable rivers that was labeled WINDLESTROW MUIR. It lay about 700 kilometers south of Caledonia's capital, New Glasgow, below Clyde's Lothian Range. There were dozens of small cities and villages in the valleys near the sea, but the moorland itself seemed almost devoid of settlement.

"I farspoke the Dirigent when we emerged from the first subspace vector," the young man finally said. "I wanted to find out if she'd had any luck recruiting additional CE operators from other worlds. She only got three from Satsuma and one from Yakutia . . . and now she wants to call off the operation."

"Merde." Rogi heaved a disappointed sigh. "But what else can she do? You told her before we ever left Earth that fifteen trained geozappers would be the minimum to fit the E18 metaconcert for a big operation like this."

"I want to check out the situation myself. Confer with the chief surveyor of the planet. Maybe I can think of something—design a new config for the seven operators or find some different way to tackle the problem."

The ship said: "Entering planetary tropopause. Opening viewport shutters. ETA Windlestrow Auxiliary Landing Area five minutes. Do you wish a summary of surface conditions?"

Jack gave a sad little laugh. "Why not?"

"Scattered cumulonimbus cells with heavy precipitation and limited visibility at surface. Wind three-six gusting to five-five. Air temp plus-oh-four. Local time 1732 hours. Windlestrow NAVCOM clears us for immediate landing. Shall I proceed?"

"Go," said Jack. And to Rogi, "Break out a couple of rain jackets, would you, please? And one E18 unit for show-and-tell."

They touched down in a thundering deluge and near-total darkness. The portable buildings of the geophysical operations camp stood on high ground above a hollow containing a lake about a kilometer in width. Down at the water's edge, high-intensity floodlights on tall standards illuminated four huge machines and a similar smaller model, sigma-shielded deep-drillers capable of penetrating far beneath the planetary crust.

Scurra II shuddered slightly as it came into gravity's grip, touched down, tilted, then modified the landing-struts' extension to compensate for the soggy, unstable ground. The pad was nothing but roughly graded earth, scored with shallow erosion channels full of running water. A single big-wheel Bronco, headlights dim in the rain, came lurching and bouncing toward them from the cluster of buildings.

The starship said, "This area is experiencing microseismic activity as well as soil instability due to water saturation. I advise you to leave my systems activated at level two rather than commanding full shutdown. In the event of an emergency, I will assume a holding pattern in the planetary ionosphere and await your mental summons."

"Go," Jack agreed. He stared through the ship's forward port for a moment, checking out the approaching truck with his farsight. The Dirigent was driving and Intendant General Calum Sorley sat in the backseat. Her face was without expression but her eyes had dark smudges beneath them, betraying anxiety and lack of sleep. She looked years older. Poor little Diamond Mask! She had pleaded with the Supervisors not to appoint her to the dirigentship, but they had been adamant. And now her beloved home world was on the brink of ruin, and she would have to preside over its demise.

Jack joined Rogi and donned a jacket. When the big Ford four-wheeler pulled up he opened the starship's air lock. The waiting vehicle had cleated tires nearly a meter in diameter and stood in mud up to the hubs. Jack propelled Rogi and the carrier with the CE equipment into the front seat with unceremonious PK, levitated himself into the backseat, and slammed the truck doors after them.

"Welcome to bonnie Caledonia," said Dorothea Macdonald, lifting her hand in the open-palmed operant greeting. "Sorry about the wee sprinkle. It'll pass by in half an hour or so." She introduced IG Sorley, a well-built man in his late thirties. Both of them wore Day-Glo orange environmental suits without headpieces. Their hair was soaked and their faces beaded with raindrops.

The Bronco began to wallow toward the lighted buildings. "Thank you for coming, Jack," the Dirigent said, rather coolly. "Uncle Rogi should never have pressured you to involve yourself, but—"

"He didn't. I'm glad to be here and I'll do anything in my power to help. I can't understand why you didn't ask me yourself."

She was staring straight ahead, clutching the steering wheel in a white-knuckled grip. "I wouldn't have presumed. You have so many other demands on your valuable time. I asked Rogi to approach your brother Marc about lending us the new CE equipment from CEREM, but I never dreamed he'd ask you to come here."

"Oh, for God's sake," Jack muttered. "Would you really put Caledonia at risk just because you can't stand me?"

"I have the greatest respect for you. I simply didn't feel it was proper to involve you in a hopeless situation."

"How do you know it's hopeless?" he challenged her.

"You can see for yourself in just a few minutes. Our chief surveyor is ready to give you an overview. I told you in our subspace conversation yesterday that you were only wasting your time—"

"Dammit, let me be the judge of that!"

"I'm responsible for this world, not you, Jack!" she snapped. "And the final judgment on this project will be mine!"

"Then be sure that judgment is based on reason and not on your stubborn pride!"

"Will you two cut it out?" Rogi pleaded.

"One piece of good news," Calum Sorley put in hastily. "Another geozap recruit signed on. From Okanagon. She'll be here by suppertime."

"That's eight qualified CE operators all told, then," Jack muttered. "Better, but still not enough for the fifteen-head metaconcert the job probably needs."

"The Yakutia operator made a suggestion this morning," Sorley went on. "She said that we might abandon the metaconcert approach and attack the subcratonic reservoir with multiple individual creative impulses instead. It seems they've had some success with the technique on their world, coping with smaller magma chambers. The beastie under Clyde is much larger and deeper, of course, but with the added power of your E18s . . ."

"I'll need a better picture of the reservoir," Jack said.

"We'll give you a full Tri-D model with all the bells and whistles right now—unless you'd rather freshen up first."

"Not at all. Let's go for it."

Sorley nodded. "Narendra has it all set up."

They were approaching a large portable building crowned with antenna arrays. The Dirigent skidded to a stop in front of it, flinging a sheet of muddy spray. The four of them climbed out and raced through the rain to the entrance, where they were met by a dark-complected man with a dazzling smile. The Dirigent introduced Caledonia's chief surveyor, Narendra Shah MacNabb. He greeted Jack and Rogi with effusive enthusiasm and led the way to a holographic display chamber.

"Are you familiar with the latest geophysical graphic models?" the scientist inquired. "No? Well, you should find this interesting. I'll just start the simulation." He glanced at a little monitor just outside the chamber, took a portable keypad from its holder, and tapped away for a few moments. Then he opened the door.

To a three-dimensional vision of hell.

"Christ de tabernacle!" Rogi gasped, backpedaling in dismay.

But the surveyor only laughed, beckoned for them to follow him inside, and shut the door. The holographic representation of the tectonic environment beneath Caledonia's crust filled the entire room, so that an observer seemed at first to be immersed in flaming chaos. Only gradually did the scene take on a sense of order and even stark beauty, with semitransparent streams of fiery scarlet, vermilion, and yellow forming dynamic three-dimensional patterns that one could examine at close range, from any angle.

At the other end of the room a platform with shallow steps running along its entire length was barely visible through the simulation. Narendra Shah MacNabb led his guests through the midst of the conflagration and up onto the platform, where it seemed as though their heads broke through the illusion's surface and into open air. They became giants, looking at the southern shore of Clyde landmass and the adjacent sea. Then, as they moved down one shallow step at a time, they effectively descended beneath the lithospheric crust and into the depths of the planet. Clyde grew a massive root, solid in the top 30 kilometers or so and stiffly molten to a depth of about 160 kilometers. The entire continental lithosphere was embedded in the much thinner oceanic lithosphere that formed the floor of the sea.

"The fiery, moving portion of the model below the lithosphere," MacNabb said, "represents an upper part of the planetary mantle called the asthenosphere. It behaves more like a liquid than the more rigid lithospheric mantle that generally stays coupled to the continent. The swirling areas in our model asthenosphere are convection currents—greatly accelerated in the simulation, of course. Note that they're very complex. The individual convection cells change shape and also exhibit changing velocity in response to heating and cooling and alterations in the density of the circulating material. Now let's move down the rest of the steps and inspect the asthenosphere immediately underneath Clyde. Very soon now, the simulation is going to demonstrate the catastrophe scenario."

They took up a position just "south" of the continent, where they were able to look up through the semitransparent root.

"The umber-colored area with the deep crimson lower portion represents the Clyde craton and its associated lithospheric mantle. We're right on top of it here at Windlestrow Muir. The craton is the southerly, most ancient part of the continent, which was presumably formed when Caledonia first solidified some three billion years ago. The lighter-colored continental regions around the edges and to the north are younger rocks that accreted to the craton throughout the aeons as the landmass slowly grew."

"Largish craton," Jack observed.

"Callie's continents have grown much more slowly than those of more Earthlike worlds," said MacNabb. "But never mind the reasons for that. Look lower now, into the asthenosphere right in front of us. Notice how that very large convection cell beneath Clyde is losing stability—actually fissioning while we watch! (Of course the event actually took place over a period of several million orbits.) Now look down here. Ascending amidst the turbulent area is an elongated thermal anomaly that looks a bit like an inverted fiery raindrop. It's less dense and much hotter than the surrounding area of mantle."

"A plume!" Rogi exclaimed.

"No, a diapir," Dorothea Macdonald said. "A rising blob, not a persistent upwelling stream."

"Exactly," the surveyor agreed. "We've speculated that the diapir resulted from the remobilization of very ancient, so-called 'fertile' mantle material that never previously surfaced and outgassed. Whatever its origin, it contains a high percentage of volatile material—mainly carbon dioxide and water. Now watch what happens when it reaches the lower boundary of the lithospheric mantle at the hundred-sixty-klom depth."

The rising portion of magma, colored a brilliant golden-yellow in the simulation, reached the stiff mantle of the cratonic root and halted, spreading out and partially penetrating the crimson. After a moment the ascending diapir pinched off from below and its matter formed a reservoir at the deepest part of Clyde's lithospheric mantle.

"At this point," Narendra Shah MacNabb said, tapping his portable keypad, "I'll speed up the simulation. In actuality, the high-pressure reservoir of volatile magma remained lurking in place for an unknown length of time."

"Just peacefully cooking up diamonds," the Dirigent said, "as carbon-laden diapirs are accustomed to do."

The surveyor nodded. "It stayed relatively dormant until natural changes in the ordinarily stiff and resistant lithospheric mantle allowed it to resume its ascent."

In the simulation, a tiny thread of magma began to travel upward from the reservoir's top.

"That ascending queue seems to have begun to move only about ten years ago. What we are about to see now is an extrapolation that will be valid if no CE modification is accomplished . . . That is, if human intervention proves impossible."

The crimson part of the cratonic root swirled in minute turbulence. Instantly the thin filament of golden magma enlarged and pushed upward at an accelerating velocity. It smote the underside of the umber cratonic crust, broke it, and burst forth at the surface. In moments, the reservoir contents were drained. The observers stood silent for a moment, and then the Tri-D simulation winked out, leaving them standing in a featureless empty room.

Rogi spoke hesitantly. "What happens on top when the thing blows? Aside from a shower of diamonds, that is."

"Imagine," MacNabb said gently, "the eruption of fifty Krakatau volcanoes—but because of the adiabatic decompression of volatiles in the magma, the eruption would be cold, not hot. What we call a diatreme."

"There would be stupendous earth tremors," Dorothea Macdonald said. "Clyde itself would be devastated, of course, but that's not the worst of it. Airborne ash, carbon dioxide, and vapor would pollute Caledonia's atmosphere and render it nearly opaque to sunlight for an indefinite period. A Great Die-Off would very likely ensue. The planet would have to be abandoned."

The surveyor opened the holographic chamber door and held it politely. "I hope the brief simulation has been of use to you, Director Remillard," he said to Jack. "Detailed information on the volatile-magma reservoir is available in the survey data bank, and of course I myself will be entirely at your disposal if you should decide to attempt a modification."

Jack hesitated, reluctant to ask the obvious question. He had no doubt that Dorothea Macdonald already knew the answer. "I wonder if I might I ask you for a snap opinion, Dr. MacNabb—quick and dirty."

The chief surveyor gave a small shrug.

Jack took the E18 carrier from Rogi and hefted it casually. "I know you're familiar with the conventional type of CE geozap modification. We now have eight grandmaster operators available, and I've brought experimental CE equipment that will boost their metapsychic output by a factor of three hundred—as opposed to the older-style helmets that augmented a hundred times. You know the volume of the reservoir and its constituents. In your opinion, will we have enough creative energy available from unconcerted joint output to bleed off the volatiles and sink the magmatic residue back into the asthenosphere?"

Narendra Shah MacNabb knit his brow in a courteous imitation of earnest thought. Finally he looked Jack straight in the eye and said, "Not a prayer."

The Dirigent of Caledonia, looking very small in a bulky white sweater and a pair of tartan trews, was a little late for supper. She and the newly arrived CE operator from Okanagon, a slender black woman named Tisha Abaka, came to the table in the scientists' mess where two chairs had been saved for them. They plumped down after minimal vocal greetings to Jack, Rogi, and the CE operators and fell like wolves upon the roast lamb with rosemary-anchovy sauce, bashed neeps, and butter-drenched baked potatoes. Everyone else seemed equally hungry and the conversation was entirely telepathic.

DOROTHEA MACDONALD: If Director Remillard can check out the crew on the new E18s tomorrow, we may be able to initiate Neelya Demidova's attack scheme the next day.

JON REMILLARD: This is the plan predicated upon the deployment of individual operators exconcert?

DOROTHEA MACDONALD: Yes. Neelya, would you please show us the finalized version?

NEELYA DEMIDOVA: [Image] This would be the first phase—a final recon of the southern side of the reservoir, done by Jim MacKelvie in the small driller. As chief CE geophysicist of Caledonia, he's best qualified to determine the optimal point for lateral drainage of the magma into the Sgeirean Dubha subduction region south of Clyde. The ancient island system associated with the sinking oceanic plate there has the potential to form a back-arc basin if diverted magma interferes with the old arc structure and ruptures it. Once the small driller has established the optimum attack pattern—this might take a day or more—the rest of us in the four larger machines will join Jim for the diversion. The result will be a new slow-growing island arc. There would still be devastating volcanism over a period of decades, but it could be coped with, whereas the present situation is cataclysmic and quite hopeless.

TISHA ABAKA: I've never heard of such a thing. We've never tried anything like it on Okanagon, that's for damn sure.

NEELYA DEMIDOVA: [cheerfully] Perhaps that's because Okanagon is an older and more stable world with relatively few island-arc situations. Our poor little Yakutia is filthy with them! Of course, we've never had such a large, deep magmatic reservoir to cope with. The ones we've diverted were continental—at a depth of seventy kloms at the most—and only a tenth as large.

JAMES MACKELVIE: I'm not sayin' I doubt ye, Neelya, and I agree your scheme seems to be our only chance . . . but look again at the horizontal component of the diversion! It's nearly three hundred kloms under the sea from the south edge of the Clyde craton to the Sgeirean Dubha island arc. Ailsa and Tormod and I spent the day goin' over the convection patterns in the intervening asthenosphere. We're worried that we won't be able to keep the diverted magma in a coherent blob, pushin' it that far. Part of it's bound to get away from us—especially if we're not in metaconcert where we can react instantly to anomalies in the thin A/LM boundary zone beneath the oceanic plate.

TORU YORITA: My three colleagues and I did a similar analysis, also taking into consideration potential fracture zones in the intervening small piece of thin oceanic crust. Zannen desu! But in our opinion, the diverted magma is all too likely to ascend and break through the sea-floor before we can trap it beneath the more rigid island-arc structure.

MIDORI SAKAI: We're not prepared to predict the effect of a huge submarine diatrematic eruption, but it would certainly be very nearly as disastrous as a continental one, with the added effect of a massive tsunami engulfing every continental shore.

AILSA GORDON: [looking up from hand-computer] It might even be worse if the erupting shit is ultrapotassic with a large water-soluble component. Then you might poison the sea as well as blotting out the sun with ash and vapor clouds.

NEELYA DEMIDOVA: [slightly huffy] Well, I offered the plan as a potentially workable hypothesis, that's all.

INTENDANT GENERAL CALUM SORLEY: And we deeply appreciate your desire to help us, Neelya Alexandrovna. All of you . . . [looking around the table] . . . willing to risk your reputations and even your lives to aid Caledonia in a situation that the Milieu Science Directorate has officially categorized as hopeless.

YOSHIFUMI MATSUI: We have had to cope with official skepticism on Satsuma as well, Intendant General. Our entire corps of geophysical CE operators would have volunteered to assist Caledonia if it had been possible. Since it was not, we drew lots—and Midori, Toru, and I were the winners. We are honored to be here.

DIRIGENT MACDONALD: Even if Caledonia must be abandoned and a new Scottish planet established elsewhere, we'll remember our friends.

NEELYA DEMIDOVA: We don't want a memorial or a footnote in a history text. We want to *do* something!

TORMOD MATHESON: The greatest difficulty, lass, is our low level of creative strength. Even with Director Remillard's E18 super hats—

JON REMILLARD: Call me Jack, for God's sake.

TORMOD MATHESON: [nods] Even with Jack's 300x CE helmets, our energy output exconcert is going to be too low to move the beastie with safety over that great distance. Now, if we could only tie all eight minds together in a new metaconcert config, Neelya's scheme just might work. It'd still be iffy, mind ye, but at least there'd be a fightin' chance.

TORU YORITA: How about it, Jack? Could you whip up a new program?

DIRIGENT MACDONALD: Toru, I don't think you appreciate the difficulties of metaconcert design. I never anticipated asking CEREM for more than the loan of the new equipment. Jack volunteered to bring the hats when his brother reluctantly agreed to assist our experiment. But there was never any question of his doing a—

JON REMILLARD: Yes.

DIRIGENT MACDONALD: [incredulously] Yes? . . .

ROGATIEN REMILLARD: Hot damn! You really think you can do it, Ti-Jean?

JON REMILLARD: [apologetically] Not following Neelya's plan, I'm afraid. There really is too great a probability that the volume of magma would escape if we tried to divert it metacreatively.

AILSA GORDON: What the devil *else* could you do but divert it?

JON REMILLARD: Alter its composition.

AILSA GORDON: Jack, pardon me if I seem rude. But you're not a geophysicist. The magmatic components of the reservoir can't be altered in any useful way. Not unless you can design us a metaconcert for the transmutation of elements—

JON REMILLARD: If the extremely volatile materials—the CO_2 and water—are segregated at the top of the reservoir, what's left will be denser than the asthenosphere immediately below the cratonic root.

JAMES MACKELVIE: [awed] The laddie's right. Degassed, it'd sink right back into the mantle!

AILSA GORDON: How the devil do you plan to effect the separation? We're talking sixty kilobars of pressure, for Christ's sake! And given that you *do* figure out how to perform the miracle—do you realize what would happen as soon as the volatiles began to bubble out?

MIDORI SAKAI: [mildly] The cork would fly out of the champagne bottle.

TORMOD MATHESON: [to Jack] Both Ailsa and Midori are right, you know.

JON REMILLARD: We would need not one metaconcert, but two. One to effect the separation, and another to delay the eruption until the process is complete. Then we allow the volatiles to outgas through a diatreme vent. There would be a rather powerful temblor, but the volatile ejecta would almost surely be essentially harmless to the atmosphere and the land.

DIRIGENT MACDONALD: Two metaconcerts. Of course! The eight grandmasters working together to effect the separation—

JON REMILLARD: And two paramounts in tandem to hold down the lid until the volatiles are allowed to blow. You and I, Diamond.

DIRIGENT MACDONALD: [inscrutably] I'd do it willingly. But I know nothing about CE operation and very little of metaconcert.

JON REMILLARD: I could teach you enough . . . and act as the executive [image] in the concert. You would handle the focus.

ROGATIEN REMILLARD: But—that's the way Marc nearly got himself killed! Doing focus!

JON REMILLARD: Yes. But his mind hadn't been accurately calibrated to fit the dual configuration. I checked with Orb last night: Diamond's mind was calibrated by the Lylmik before they named her paramount.

DIRIGENT MACDONALD: Yes. [She smiles ruefully.] It was quite an experience.

INTENDANT GENERAL SORLEY: [beside himself with excitement] But, that means . . . if *you* two joined in . . . then Caledonia—

DIRIGENT MACDONALD: Might be spared after all.

TISHA ABAKA: Jack, how long will it take you to get everything ready?

JON REMILLARD: Two days should do it. I'll need an in situ analysis of the magma to complete the calculations. I'm afraid I can't use the old figures. I need to know what the composition is right now.

JAMES MACKELVIE: Tormod and Ailsa and I will take the small driller down at once. We'll have the beastie vetted inside of fourteen hours.

JON REMILLARD: Training the lot of you—and the Dirigent—will take most of two days. [Rises from the table.] I'd like you to excuse me now. It would be a good thing if I got just a bit of sleep and studied up on igneous petrogenesis at the same time. I'll get started on the preliminary metaconcert designs in the morning. If you all agree, we can start training when Jim and the others come back with the magma specs.

DIRIGENT MACDONALD: [also rising] Let me show you and Uncle Rogi to your rooms.

[Verbal adieux and expressions of enthusiasm as Macdonald and the two Remillards exit.]

NEELYA DEMIDOVA: [worriedly] I know Jack is the greatest mind in the Human Polity . . . but I hope he knows what the hell he's doing. Genius or not, one can't learn everything there is to know about magma dynamics overnight.

TORU YORITA: [sighing] Nor can a group of Grand Master Creators, and one brilliant young female Paramount, learn to perform perfectly in a novel metaconcert without long months of practice. But I think we are all going to have to try.

The rain was over, watery morning sun shone through the high cirrus veil, and quasi-Mesozoic birds with pink plumage squawked in the exotic heather as they gathered bits of vegetation to pad their subterranean nests. It was spring on Windlestrow Muir and the Dirigent asked Rogi to go for a walk with her to calm her nerves before the return of the small deep-driller.

The old man was suitably impressed with the multicolored foliage of the rolling moorland—mostly baby-blue and peach, softened by generous amounts of dark green. Large flowers resembling buttercups bloomed among the rocks and were visited by insectile fliers with transparent wings. The ground beneath the gnarled bushes was coarse, yellowish in color, and nearly dried out in spite of last night's downpour. In the gullies and other eroded areas were drifts of wine-colored sand and heaps of light green and garnet stones. Sixty kilometers to the northwest, the Lothian Range loomed on the skyline as a saw-toothed shadow.

Keeping a friendly silence, they followed a game trail along the broken perimeter of the cup-shaped depression that held Windlestrow Loch. After they had walked a couple of kilometers the Dirigent gave a little triumphant cry and stooped to pick up something from the side of the path.

"Look, Uncle Rogi—a diamond."

"You're kidding."

She dropped the crystal into his open palm. It was a pea-sized dodecahedron with rounded edges, oddly greasy-looking and faintly blue in the diffused sunlight.

"If this operation is succesfully concluded, I'll have it cut and polished for you as a keepsake. We'll call it the Star of Windlestrow." She peered closely at it for a moment. "My deepsight shows it's a VVS blue-white—with only tiny flaws. Diamonds are very common on Callie." She indicated the surrounding area. "That little lake is right on top of a very ancient kimberlite pipe. You know—the material diamonds are found in. The old pipe goes clear through the Clyde craton right down to the magma. Millions of years ago, there was another, much smaller diatreme on this site."

"Batège! It's been a long time since anyone gave me a diamond." Rogi fished in the pocket of his chino pants and came up with the key-ring fob known to three generations of Remillard youngsters as the Great Carbuncle. "When I first got hold of this, it was worth millions. I suppose you could buy another for only a few thousand dollars nowadays. It's been my lucky charm for God knows how many years."

She examined it with interest. "But it's gorgeous! That unusual clear red color—and polished into a perfect sphere. Where in the world did you ever get it?"

"From a Lylmik," the old man said playfully. And when she eyed him askance, he said, "Oh, all right. I found it in a gutter in Hanover. Very mysterious. But I swear it's saved my life a couple of times." His face lit with sudden inspiration. He detached the fob from the key ring and pressed the glowing little silver-caged gem into her hand. "Let's trade, Dorothée. You keep the Great Carbuncle for luck during this operation, and I'll hang on to the Star of Windlestrow."

She froze, and for a moment it seemed as though she had stopped looking out of her eyes and had turned instead to some somber inner vision. Then her face lost its haunted aspect and she smiled.

"I'd love to carry the Carbuncle, Uncle Rogi." She pulled a gold chain out the neck of her sweater. A glittering little mask-charm hung on it. "There. Your good-luck piece can hang next to my own talisman."

She tucked the chain back into its hiding place. Then her gaze met that of the tall old man and she threw her arms around him and buried her face in his chest, not making a sound.

Rogi felt his heart plummet. She was twenty years old and she might very well die within the next few days, consumed in a split second by the fires inside her world. Last night, after they had left the others, Jack had confessed to him and Dorothée that even using the double metaconcert, there was only a fifty-fifty chance of the new plan succeeding. The Dirigent had nodded calmly. She had not asked Jack why he was willing to sacrifice himself for the sake of a rather ordinary colonial planet.

Do you know why, Dorothée? Rogi asked her. Would you like me to tell you?

But she pulled away from him, not answering, and stood staring down at the little lake.

"Look," she said.

The waters were suddenly roiled and bubbling. At the same moment Rogi felt a faint tremor underfoot. In the survey camp on the other side of the depression, people were running out of the buildings and down the steep embankment to the shore, where they waited expectantly. A few minutes later a vast eructation of steam broke the water's surface. A bullet-shaped black machine the size of a bus thrust up vertically in the middle of it like a broaching leviathan, then fell back with a resounding splash that echoed over the heath. A pair of frightened pink birds burst out of the shrubs and took wing, squawking. The humans down on the lakeshore jumped up and down and their faint cheers reached Rogi and Dorothée on the ridge.

Still steaming gently, the driller floated sedately toward land, deployed its treads, and crawled ashore. It halted next to the four larger machines parked there, and in a few minutes its ventral hatch opened and three people emerged.

The Dirigent watched them with narrowed eyes. "They have the analysis. It's time for me to go back and learn how to boost my brain. Pray for me, Uncle Rogi!" She turned and ran off along the path.

"I'll damn well do more than that," the old man growled to himself. He waited until the Dirigent was far away, then looked around furtively and addressed the open sky. "Ghost! You hear me? . . . Do something! You can't let those two young people die. Help them!"

He stood with his head cocked, listening. The pearly sky glowed, the spring wind blew softly over the moor, and the archaic pink birds uttered relieved clucks and returned to their nursery hole.

"Don't play coy! I know you're watching, mon fantôme."

The breeze seemed to sigh in resignation.

The old man smiled then and set off for the survey camp, fingering the slippery little diamond in his jacket pocket and muttering to himself in French.

[24]

SECTOR 12: STAR 12-337-010 [GRIAN] PLANET 4 [CALEDONIA]

17–18 AN GIBLEAN [28–29 NOVEMBER] 2077

The ten of them assembled at dawn, dressed in silvery Nomex suits as a partial precaution against creative flashback and carrying the matte black CE helmets under their arms. The drill-rigs had been equipped with every piece of safety equipment the CE operators could think of.

It was raining again, and rather than waste mindpower erecting an umbrella they stood together beneath the belly of one of the huge machines listening to Jack's final instructions.

"If everything goes according to plan, the job should be completed in approximately fifty hours, including the fourteen needed for ascent and descent. This is well within the safety margin for our four full-sized drill-rigs. Keep in mind, however, that the only possible way we can abort is for the Dirigent and I to hold the lid in place until the volatile components return to solution in the magma. I must warn you that the reabsorption process might take over twice as much time as the separation did, and she and I might find ourselves unable to contain the pressure. So we'd damn well better *not* abort."

"We understand, Jack," said Jim MacKelvie. "We do the job right the first time or risk complete disaster."

The others murmured in acknowledgment. Unspoken was the fact that every settlement on Clyde was now on full seismic-alert status, ready to deal as best they could with the catastrophic results of failure.

"Let's get on with it, then," Jack said. As they all went off to the different vehicles, his mind reached out to his great-granduncle, who had withdrawn with the other survey personnel to a safety bunker 20 kilometers away.

Goodbye Uncle Rogi.

Bonne chance Ti-Jean et Dorothée et dieu vous bénisse.

"After you, Madame Dirigent," Jack said, gesturing to the ladder of the drill-rig he would share with Dorothea Macdonald. Tight-lipped, she climbed into the machine without a word and went immediately to the control room, where she halted in sudden consternation.

Before the command-console was a single chair. Beside it stood a pedestal bearing what looked like an open-topped spherical fishbowl.

"Sorry," said Jack, coming up behind her. "I forgot to warn you that I'll have to do this job bodiless to conserve my mental energy. I don't usually say too much about this aspect of my life to people I work with. It distracts them."

"I . . . see." She sank into the chair and watched, blank-faced, as he set his CE helmet aside, slipped off his boots, and began to remove the rest of his clothing. The deep-driller, which like the other three was temporarily under the command of Jim MacKelvie for the descent below the planetary crust, suddenly came to life.

"Attention," it said in a Scots-accented voice. "This vehicle, designated D-4, is now being activated via remote control from D-1. Checklisting of operating and environmental systems will proceed silently unless a verbal override is given."

Jack said nothing as he unzipped the fireproof coverall, stepped out of it, and tossed it aside. His PK folded the suit in mid-air before it hit the deck, and stowed it tidily in an open locker. He stripped off his boots, socks, and air-conditioned underwear and disposed of them in the same way. The Dirigent waited in some apprehension for him to remove the last white formfitting garment.

Reading her thoughts, Jack shrugged. And she knew then with sickening certainty that he was already naked.

Except for his normal-looking hands, head, and neck, his body was smooth, hairless, and completely without wrinkle, crease, or blemish. He had no genitals, umbilical scar, or toes. His appearance was that of a man-sized doll made of plass, with human parts inexplicably grafted on. Involuntarily, she gave a low cry of pity.

"It's all right," he said with casual reassurance. "I don't usually bother with body-construction details if it's not absolutely necessary. But all the usual humanoid equipment is optionally available. And then some!"

She gasped. For the merest instant his body had grown an astonishing coat of light brown fur, curled ivory horns, and membranous wings that stretched between his wrists and ankles. The fantastic embellishments disappeared almost as soon as they were created, and Jack's pale pseudoflesh began to dissolve, flowing to the deck like heavy smoke and gathering in a grayish-pink puddle. The fluid contracted into a gelatinous lump the size of a large melon, then bounced into the locker where the clothes were. The door slammed behind it.

Hovering in mid-air was a glistening silvery brain.

The driller said: "Checklist completed. Prepare for inertialess descent."

As the Dirigent continued to watch, stunned and disbelieving, the thing that was Jack floated to the crystal fishbowl and fitted itself neatly inside. Outside the forward viewport, the rainy landscape seemed to be in motion as the driller entered Windlestrow Loch.

"But . . . your physical form isn't disgusting at all!" she blurted at last.

There was a disembodied laugh. "I hope not. But aesthetic standards vary quite a lot, don't they? When I was very young and just getting the hang of living with the mutation, I made my share of social errors cooking up weird bodies to nauseate my elders. Marc and Uncle Rogi made me—er—shape up rather quickly."

She could not take her fascinated eyes off the brain. "Does—does it hurt when you come all apart?"

"Certainly not. Physical sensors are lacking in the bodies I create unless I have some special need to install them, which I rarely do. Ultrasenses deliver a full spectrum of external stimuli to my brain, and my metacreativity and PK modulate the output."

"And the sound of your voice is only—"

"My PK vibrating the atmosphere molecules. I do usually create vocal cords, lungs, and all the rest of it when I incarnate. It gives a more natural vocal timbre. And I do a partial gastrointestinal tract to accommodate social eating, and a set of male plumbing when I'm put into a situation that requires social peeing. You know how men are. The camaraderie of the porcelain."

She had to laugh in spite of herself, and then looked away. Turgid gray water now covered the viewport, and light from the surface was rapidly fading. The rig was descending into the lake at an angle of nearly sixty degrees, but there was no sensation of tilting or falling in a vehicle with intertialess propulsion.

"Activating penetration beam and level-one sigma-field in preparation for entry into lithospheric overburden of the maar," the driller announced importantly.

"Just shut up and drive," Jack told it. "You can let us know when we arrive at our destination, but don't bother us with details en route unless there's an emergency. Understand?"

"Affirmative." The mechanical voice had a slight overlay of wounded pride.

The Dirigent regarded the brain with a little smile of approval. "That's telling it."

"Life's too short to waste time chitchatting with machines for no good reason," Jack said.

"I agree . . . but I thought all members of the Remillard family were essentially immortal."

"All except me. My mutation made a mess of the self-rejuvenating gene complex. The brain will age. Its hardware will deteriorate more or less in the normal human fashion as redactive processes fail, and I'll die after reaching the biblical three score and ten years. Or thereabouts."

Her face was unreadable and her voice calm. "The regeneration-tank can't help you?"

"It operates at normal human parameters, and I'm not normal. Don't feel sorry for me, Diamond. I plan to accomplish a thing or two before I go to glory. Provided that we survive this little adventure, of course."

She nodded, and pretended to study the console's instrument readouts. After a few minutes, there was nothing but darkness outside the viewport. The drill-rig was capable of illuminating the ancient kimberlite pipe as they descended, but the formation was uninteresting except to a specialist, and neither Jack nor Dorothea cared to be reminded that they were plunging deeper and deeper into solid rock.

"I suppose we should practice our metaconcert," she said without enthusiasm.

"It'll be hours before we reach the magma reservoir. Later, we ought to put the hats on and review the program. But I'd rather talk about other things now. That is, if you don't mind."

"I . . . No, of course not. Would you think I was prying if I asked you about your life? I know from talking to Uncle Rogi that you weren't born . . . that way, but he didn't tell me much else. He saw that the very idea of your mutation frightened and repelled me."

"And you were angry," the brain said softly, "because of my stupid attempts to farspeak you. I'm sorry about that."

"I thought you were trying to trick me into demonstrating my operancy. That would have meant my leaving Caledonia. I pretended to be latent as long as I could."

"I was a tactless idiot. Adolescents are apt to be insensitive and I was probably worse than most. It went with the territory. It was Rogi who finally got me to back off."

"He *said* you farspoke me because you were lonely."

The brain produced a dry little laugh. "And then there are those who remain insensitive even though they're centenarians! I love Uncle Rogi, but sometimes he's a damned blabbermouth."

"Loneliness is nothing to be ashamed of. Or defensive about. It's a human thing."

"Reassuring, you mean? Proving I'm not a monster?"

"I'm glad you can be straightforward about your condition. And laugh." She lifted her chin in a small defiant gesture, to show she didn't much care. "That's probably a sign of mental health."

"Maybe. I've never let shrinks mess with me. How about you?"

"I simply locked the snoopy bastards out. The one who really troubled me was my mother . . ." And she began to tell him about her.

Later, she wondered if he had managed to coerce her when she was distracted by the emotion-laden thought of Viola Strachan. Or was there another reason why she suddenly felt compelled to tell him all about her difficult early years? The words came tumbling out almost without volition, her terrible time with the latency therapists, her fears that her powers would destroy her if she failed to keep them locked away, her struggle between wanting to please her mother and wanting to be true to herself.

She described the ambiguous trauma of Viola's death, the appearance of the mysterious guardian angel, the escape of one metafaculty after another from the bonds she had imposed on them. And then she told him about her encounters with Fury and the Hydras.

When she finally ran out of breath she felt both relieved and furious with herself. "I—I don't know why I told you all that. It's none of your business."

"Yes it is," Jack said. "I want to know everything about you. Not only your life story, but what you like and dislike, what your ambitions are, even your fears—"

She fixed her intent gaze on the brain. "I'll tell you one thing I'm afraid of: an inhuman mutant who can force me to reveal my secret thoughts!"

"I swear I didn't! And to prove it, I'll tell you my own cerebral tale."

"H'mph."

She got up from her seat and went to make some coffee in the drill-rig's tiny galley. Jack oozed out of the bowl and floated companionably after, and began to spin the improbable story of his birth and childhood. He was a bewitching raconteur, embroidering his amazing autobiography not only with slapstick humor but also with a poignancy that brought tears to her eyes. By the time they returned to the control console, the drill-rigs had passed the Moho and entered the lithospheric mantle.

They continued talking for hours, he about himself and she about herself. She was now quite sure that he was not coercing her. A real compassion for the disembodied brain began to stir within her, and reluctant sympathy as well. He was so full of quixotic ideals, so determined to use his awesome power and influence for the good of the human race . . . to which he only marginally belonged.

So eager for her approval.

Why? What did he want from her? Did it have something to do with his family's attempts to track down Fury and Hydra?

More hours passed. They practiced their metaconcert, she had a meal and a nap, and then they talked again, this time more easily. By the time the drill-rig reached its destination in the red-hot magma far beneath the surface of Caledonia, she had nearly managed to forget what her companion was.

He was simply Jack, and if they managed to survive, they might become friends after all.

"Attention. D-4 has now reached a depth of one hundred sixty-eight pip two kilometers below mean sea level and has reached its preselected station. Remote-control operation is now suspended. Manual control may be assumed ad lib. Please give the appropriate command if you desire to activate an alternative navigation program."

"Continue hold," said Jack. "Open intervehicular communication channel . . . Hello, everybody. I presume we've arrived."

An armored shutter had closed off the viewport at the 50-kilometer level. The console monitor now showed three blips indicating the other drill-rigs positioned around the equator of the magma reservoir, while their own machine lay slightly above the molten mass.

Jim MacKelvie's voice, sounding faint and hollow, came out of the com speaker. "All units are now deployed at operating station: Drills One, Two, and Three stand at klom-depth one-seven-five-pip-five, azimuth ninety, one-eighty, and two-sixty, range one-pip-five. D-4 stands klom-depth one-six-eight-pip-two, azimuth three hundred, range zero-pip-niner. The asthenospheric temperature outside our sigma-field here in D-1 is a brisk eleven-hundred-ought-six degrees Centigrade and the pressure fifty-eight kilobars—which I might remind our ignorant lay Paramount Creators is equivalent to fifty-eight thousand times that of Earth atmospheric pressure at sea level."

"Eek," whispered the Dirigent.

"I knew that," Jack chimed in, with mock superiority. There were a few scattered laughs from the experienced geozappers. "Any significant change in the mantle roofing the magma reservoir, Jim?"

"No. The extrusion queue has ascended another three meters or so to the one-three-niner-pip-zilch-two. Still on a slow creep. You'll find the complete up-to-the-nanosec data on the rigidity of the superimposed lithospheric mantle in your CE-helmet banks, with pull-up graphics galore to assist continuous mental monitoring. An alarm will sound in your minds at the least shift in mantle-phase or mantle-reservoir boundaries. If the queue starts accelerating you'll also get a shout. The interconcert com-link that provides you with data-feed on the degassing operation—plus jokes, snappy comments, and complaints from all and sundry—is set to activate once we've all slotted in."

"Then," said the brain, "there's no reason why we shouldn't begin. Go for the hats, everybody."

Jack's CE helmet levitated from where he had left it on the instrument console and settled over the bowl, hiding it and its contents from sight. Like a golden snake, a power cable emerged from a deck receptacle and plugged itself into the back of the hat. Small LEDs lit up on the dull black surface, indicating that Jack's brain was energetically enhanced.

The Dirigent put on her own E18 helmet. As always, there was a moment of claustrophobia as the thing covered her eyes, but fortunately this model left the lower part of her face exposed so she could talk and breathe normally. She winced at the brief painful stab of the multiple crown-of-thorns electrodes penetrating her scalp, felt nothing as tiny holes were drilled through her skull and the cobweb-fine wires carried their tiny cargo to the fluid-filled ventricles within her head. The brain-boosting machinery sprouted and activated.

She could see again. Every detail of the drill-rig's control deck was now exquisitely distinct, even though the CE helmet's brainboard was set to enhance only creativity. That metafaculty was so deeply enmeshed in the function of all the other mental processes that they became preternaturally efficient as it intensified.

But there were certain disadvantages. Every nuance of bodily feeling and every ultrasense that she possessed was also sharpened. She heard her heart thud, her lungs inhale and expel air, her guts rumble, even the hissing of blood in her eardrums. The tiny noises filling the control room were magnified into a jarring racket. She felt the helmet's weight, the pressure of the heat-resistant suit intended to protect her in case of mental flashover, even her tongue moving nervously over her teeth in her closed mouth. The distractions would vanish once the metaconcert was established and the work began.

I'm ready, she said to Jack.

The control deck disappeared. She was no longer a human being but a small globe of emerald radiance suspended in darkness. Another green nebula hung nearby. Wispy, crimson mist drifted around them and there seemed to be two lingering musical notes sounding faintly, like a deep chord from some phantom cello. Below, a slowly churning expanse of red represented the magma reservoir. A thin stemlike excrescence, the queue of scarlet molten matter slowly pushing its way toward the surface in an expanding lithospheric fissure, protruded from the top of the reservoir some distance away.

The Dirigent found that if she exerted herself slightly, she could see all the way through the mass of magma below and discern three widely separated groups of little white lights gathered round it that represented the poised minds of the others.

Jack said to her: *Come together.*

Their metaconcert established itself. The two green nebulae began to orbit a common center, describing complex glowing patterns that constantly changed as they moved closer and closer. The sustained notes of mental music became melodies that rose and fell, creating a subtle, coordinated fugue. When it seemed that the two shining globes had nearly metamorphosed into one, a luminous emerald cone flashed into existence, extending from the center of the metaconcert to the upper surface of the reservoir. The beam drew a bright, sparkling circle that rapidly expanded until the entire mass of magma was roofed in scintillating points of prismatic light. The queue extension was a red stalk sheathed in twinkling stars.

Jack was the executive continuously organizing and guiding the creative impulse. Dorothea was the living lens through which it was focused and activated. She felt marvelous. There was none of the frightening tension she had experienced during the practice metaconcert maneuvers. This time the two of them were combined to do real work. They had created something exquisite together and it was very, very good.

The lid is in place, Jack told the other metaconcert. And he asked her, *Are you all right, Diamond? Is the energetic flow consonant?*

Yes, she sang. *Oh, yes!*

The luminous parts of the other metaconcert seemed to come together in the heart of the reservoir, even though the generating minds actually remained outside its boundaries. The eight white lights began their own intricate orbital dance, but their unique harmony was inaudible beneath the adamant vault Dorothea and Jack had made.

Begin degassing operation, said Jim. *We're on our way, people. Mo dia's mo dhuchaich!*

For a long time the effect of the separation effort was imperceptible to the Dirigent; but at last she became aware that a real change was taking place in the magmatic reservoir. It was visible first in the queue, where bubbles seemed to be rising, creating a golden zone free of the scarlet matter as they reached the tip and coalesced.

Slowly, the queue filled with the volatile components of the magmatic mass that were being separated from the molten rock by the other merged minds. The Dirigent watched the process in mesmerized fascination, never interrupting her own metasong, for what seemed to be many hours. When the entire fissure was filled with gold the bubbles began to gather at the ceiling of the reservoir itself. The gaseous brightness expanded like a swarm of fiery organisms, swelling and joining and spreading until the entire top of the magma-chamber turned to a layer of fluid gold.

It's working, Jack said to her. *There are no signs of instability yet in the lithospheric mantle above us. It's staying nicely rigid. But as the volume of separated volatiles grows, there will be a tremendous increase in pressure against our barrier. If the alarm sounds, we'll have only a fraction of a second to alter the structure of the lid—to strengthen it at whatever point the lithosphere has weakened.*

I understand. I won't let myself get lulled by the song. But it's wonderful, isn't it, the way the contrapuntal duet works . . .

Yes. It's a kind of magic. Very satisfying. The pattern is so elegant, so right. It's been a while since I worked in concert. I'd nearly forgotten how exciting it can be. Of course, working with my brother Marc was quite a bit different from this. You and I together are a Bach invention. When you link with Marc it's apt to be either Stravinsky or Wagner at his wildest.

[Laughter.] *Do the E18 helmets make much of a difference?*

Yes. There's an apt analogy, but I don't think I want to go into it just now. [Half-formed image.]

Oh? . . . OH!!

Let's see how the others are getting along: Jim?

MacKelvie said: *Aye. We're keepin' the pot stirred down here. You realize we've been at this for over ten hours? Twenty-six left to go, plus or minus, till we've wrung as much volatile matter out of the beastie as we can. Then you two pull the cork . . . and it's either Party Time or Apocalyse Now.*

Dirigent Macdonald said: *It seems to be working well so far.*

Neelya Demidova said: *Both Tisha and I are amazed, actually. And quite relieved.*

Toru Yorita said: *D-2 crew is gratified that its faith in Jack's ingenuity is being so well repaid.*

Ailsa Gordon said: *Oh, he's a clever wee bugger, for certain. But you just remember that he's got our Dirigent doing the really tough work in the configuration.*

The Dirigent said: *I'm fine. Really. This is turning out to be a very educational experience in more ways than one. Working in concert with Director Remillard is . . . an interesting challenge.*

Tell us! said the women in the degassing metaconcert.

When we're finished, the Dirigent said. *Perhaps.*

The queue began to rupture seven hours later, when less than half the volatiles had been separated from the magma.

Dorothea had tried valiantly not to let herself be distracted, but even the mind of a Paramount Grand Master may be torn by conflicting emotions. She had avoided analyzing her changing attitude toward Jack, telling herself that it was enough to know that her earlier sense of loathing was finally obliterated. His life story had been moving, at times hilariously funny. He had listened to her own tale with sympathy, and his comments had been sensible and unsentimental. He had refrained from commenting on the obvious comparisons between them, while she had had sense enough to stay on firm emotional ground after making the faux pas about loneliness.

There would be time enough for further exploration, she told herself, when the two of them were no longer enmeshed in this perilous situation. Now she must focus entirely upon the job at hand, just as Jack was doing.

But the distracting thoughts continued to come. Could it be possible that he saw their future relationship as more than an alliance against Fury and Hydra? Was he human enough for that? . . .

In the midst of her reverie the mental alarm shrieked. The queue had broken through their metacreative sheath.

Jack's command to alter the configuration of the metaconcert came and she floundered clumsily, trying to regain her concentration. The complex image of the new metaconcert shape that would cap and contain the ruptured queue hovered in her brain, ready for her participation. Jack was saying nothing, only showing her clearly what she must do, but she still tottered off-balance, at first furious with herself and then mortally afraid.

In desperation, she reached deep within her mind, tapping ultimate reserves of metapsychic power that neither she nor the Lylmik examiners had ever suspected were there. A creativity far greater than Jack's responded. A surge of fresh energy more powerful than what he had called for exploded from her mind—and overwhelmed the metaconcert design.

The phenomenon was called dysergism.

Only a fraction of a second had passed. Jack saw the structure they had created begin to collapse—not only the reinforced sheath enclosing the queue but the entire lid of the reservoir as well. The generating beam that had formerly been green flashed an abrupt blue-white. Shock waves rippled the starry roof. A tiny lance of gold spurted up, penetrating it: a newborn second queue.

He realized immediately what must have happened, heard her despairing mental cry. She was completely unaware of the disaster's source, frantic because she was unable to reintegrate her creativity. She did know that something had gone fatally wrong, and there seemed no way she could stop the lid from dissolving.

Jack do something for God's sake DO SOMETHING!

The new metaconcert . . . He decided in an instant that it might possibly be changed to accommodate her higher creative flux. But he would be forced to withdraw his own metacreative output from the faltering lid while he refashioned the framework. In the meantime, the high-pressure volatiles would smash against the unshielded mantle as the reservoir of magma was transformed from a caged brute into one set free and eager to escape.

The lithospheric mantle *might* hold if he was quick enough.

The dance of the twin emerald globes had become stumbling and uncoordinated, the metasong a discordant howl as she tried without success to control the blue-white power surges that were destroying the barrier. A third nascent magmatic queue broke through. Jack heard her mind crying out hopelessly as she tried in vain to steady the flickering green beam—

Flashover.

Energy overflowing from her enhanced brain escaped into the command deck of the drill-rig, ionized the atmosphere, and created a burst of incandescent gas.

Jack cut loose from the original metaconcert, drew the new configuration, flung himself into it, and rechanneled the chaotic metacreative force. The entire magmatic reservoir shuddered and began a diapiric ascent.

Focus now! he cried out to her. *We can make a new lid if you focus now!*

Yes, she said, ignoring the pain, the hideous burning pain. *Now.*

The metaconcerted pas de deux resumed in a blare of triumphant mindsong. A brilliant aquamarine beam thrust down at the rising diapir, expanded into a cone, and created a new starry roof, denser and thicker than the first one.

The slowly moving golden crest of the diapir hit the barrier and expanded laterally. Singing in her agony, she widened the focus, keeping pace with the spreading magma. Finally, when the reservoir was only half its former depth, the pressures stabilized. The new lid held firm. Beneath it, the molten mass contracted slowly into an approximation of its original shape.

Good God almighty! said Jim MacKelvie. *You saved it, Jack! It's holding, stronger than before.*

But Jack wasn't listening. His own invulnerable brain had been unaffected by the flashover, but he knew what had happened to her. He spoke on her intimate telepathic mode.

Diamond—can you hear me?

Yes, she replied. I—I maintain focus now. Myredaction came online as—as flashover dissipated Nomexsuit protected body but—but—Jack! Myface below CEhelmet burntdeep myentirerespiratorysystem damaged flightdeckenvironmental restored depleted atmosphere . . . but I can't breathe Jack somethingwrongnerves can't see either—

I don't dare divert any energy from the metaconcert! Your PK—can you use it?

Perhaps . . . a little. But I'll die soon and then—

Be quiet. Listen. In the locker to the left of your chair, marked

EMERGENCY IPPB, is a positive-pressure breathing apparatus. Get it.

Yes. Ahhh God it hurts! . . . Yes. Oh Jack. Oxygen. Hurts somuch but I can breathe/see again. Jack? . . .

Diamond. My dear, darling Diamond.

She breathed. Intermittent positive pressure from the oxygen mask inflated her ruined lungs, then let them exhale. Fingers shaking, she fastened the mask in place. A hallucination swept over her, and for a moment she was back in the cockpit of the funny old yellow flitter, filled with joy as she flew high above her father's farm as free as a falcon. To fly again! She *would* fly again . . .

Diamond! Come back!

Yes. Sorry Jack. But I didn't drop the concert, didn't stop the dance. I'm still with you.

Of course you are . . .

But Jack knew that she wouldn't continue for long. Her metacreative output was slowly sinking. The oxygen was keeping her alive, but she was too badly injured to maintain her role in the metaconcert for more than another five minutes or so. They would have to abort less than halfway into the operation.

There was time enough for the other eight CE operators to escape, but he and Diamond would certainly be caught by the ascending diapir when the lid failed. They would ride the molten rock to the surface of the planet, accelerating faster and faster as the volatiles expanded. When the eruption broke through the surface, their armored, sigma-shielded deep-driller would be blasted high into the air. Perhaps they would survive.

Caledonia would not. There would still be enough ash in the ejecta to devastate the planetary atmosphere.

Jack? Jack? For God's sake, man, answer me!

Poor Jim MacKelvie was trying to find out what had happened. It was time to tell him.

Jim, the rest of you—listen. The Dirigent has been seriously injured in a flashover event. She won't be able to carry on much longer in our metaconcert. We're going to have to abort the operation.

NO.

I know what a horrible disappointment this is, but we have no choice—

I SAID NO, DAMMIT! DON'T ABORT!

Jim, don't be a bloody fool! Kill your concert! Get out of here while you can!

NONONO! HOLD ON TWO MINUTES MORE!

. . . Jack? Jim here. It's—it's not me talking. There's somebody else! Somebody using CE-enhanced farspeech right down here in the fewkin' asthenosphere!

IT TAKES ONLY TWO MINUTES TO PLUG IN A CREATIVITY BRAINBOARD.

Jack was laughing, nearly hysterical. He knew who it was.

He said he wouldn't have anything to do with this project. God only knows what he's doing here. But I'm going to plug him into this metaconcert of mine and he's going to work with us now whether he wants to or not!

STOP YAMMERING LIKE AN IDIOT AND OPEN UP. I'LL PHASE IN AS SOON AS YOU CUT HER LOOSE. SWITCHING TO CREATIVITY MODE . . .

"Diamond, can you hear me?"

Yes. What—

"It's over. The separation of the volatiles is complete. We're on our way to the surface. We don't know yet whether the operation was successful, but the probability is high."

I'm . . . glad.

"How do you feel?"

It doesn't hurt so much anymore.

"I've been redacting you."

Featherlight kisses on her closed eyelids. She opened them, saw his face bending over her. She was lying on the deck of the control room, her body somehow cushioned and comfortable. She lifted her hand and he kissed the palm. Silken fabric slipped down her arm. She was no longer wearing the Nomex suit but was wrapped instead in some peculiar white material that was soft and warm.

"The suit was scorched and filthy from the flashover," he explained. "I made you a gown and robe. From the food rations. I've had a lot of practice transforming organic matter."

She tried to smile.

She couldn't.

Her fingers touched the mask that still covered her lower face and gently fed oxygen to her damaged lungs. She let her seekersense look beneath the smooth plass and found hideous charred muscle and bone.

Jack's redaction anticipated her shock and horror, neutralizing it so that she only felt a mild sadness.

"I couldn't heal you completely. I'm sorry. Your injuries are too severe and I'm wrung out myself from our ordeal. I didn't want to make any mistakes. I dealt with the pain and certain internal problems and did some superficial tidying. The rest had better wait until we reach the surface and let medic redactors look you over."

All right.

"I just thank God you survived. There was nothing I could do to prevent the flashover from harming you. The E18s are too powerful."

Why . . . did it happen? I know it was my fault.

"No. Blame the Lylmik who did your last MP assay. You had reserves of creativity that were still uncalibrated, and when you fed them into the concert unexpectedly, dysergism resulted. It wasn't your fault. We paramounts are full of surprises, my darling."

Her eyes widened.

He bent closer. There were tears on his face. "My dearest Diamond! I love you so very much. Ever since we first met at Marc's party. I know it's impossible, though, so please don't give it another thought. I promise never to make a pest of myself ever again. But I had to tell you. I hope you'll forgive me."

Her own vision fogged. She tried to bespeak him but her thoughts were too chaotic. He loved her . . . That was why he had come to Caledonia and risked his life. Uncle Rogi had tried to tell her, but she had refused to listen.

Knowing it already. Not wanting to know.

All she could say was: But I look so horrible!

"You're beautiful," he said, and showed her the mental image of her that he treasured.

That's . . . not me.

He laughed softly. "It is, you know! But don't fuss about it. What you need now is rest. It'll be hours before we reach the surface. Go to sleep, little Diamond."

But she continued to stare anxiously at his face instead—that smiling face with the ordinary features and the extraordinary blue eyes. That face that she now realized did not really exist, except in her imagination.

He projected no illusion, wore no creative disguise, and still she saw him, heard him, felt his kisses and his falling tears. How? *Why?*

"Don't worry about it now," said the hovering brain. "We'll sort it out later. When you're feeling better."

[25]

FROM THE MEMOIRS OF ROGATIEN REMILLARD

I was in the Windlestrow safety bunker, where I had spent the previous 48 hours together with a skeleton crew of geophysicists, several government observers, and three media reps, waiting on events below. We played poker and tizz and Monopoly, listened to music, ate nuked pizza, Scotch eggs, sausage rolls, and scones with jam. Some of us, including me, drank to excess.

There was no way we could contact the people in the drill-rigs down in the magma and no way we could tell what progress they were making. Continual microtremors from the subterranean activities made a hash of any attempt at fine monitoring. Only when the diatreme began its ascent would we know for certain whether or not the operation had been a success.

The fifty-fifty odds had first made us optimistic; but as the hours dragged on and the deep seismic disturbances grew more alarmingly intense, our spirits did a one-eighty flip and our once-hopeful vigil turned into a virtual deathwatch. It was futile, we all agreed, to think that ten human minds could forestall the awesome eruption that was going to devastate the Scottish planet.

The Celtic soul has a natural bent toward melancholy fatalism. My kiltie companions and I, by unspoken agreement, began to conduct a wake for Caledonia.

When he arrived I was well on my way to alcoholic oblivion, sitting in a dim corner of the bunker's main seismic monitoring room with Calum Sorley and a couple of sozzled Tri-D reporters. A big wall-mounted screen showed a view of rainswept Loch Windlestrow 20 kloms away, where the eruption was expected to surface.

I was pouring myself another shot of Glenfiddich and wishing somebody would turn off the damned bagpipe music on the intercom when there was a sudden rumpus at the entrance to the bunker—a great metallic clang, confused yelling, and a familiar voice bellowing for people to get out of his way or he'd zap them into piles of dogshit.

A towering figure in black jeans and a buffalo-plaid mackinaw exploded into the room. His gray eyes were blazing and psychic tension made his wet curly hair stand out around his head in a wiry corona. He froze as he caught sight of me lolling there with my tot of Scotch, and the anxiety on his face turned to fury. He came at me and plucked me from my chair like a rag doll. My shot glass went flying.

"What the bloody hell is going on, Uncle Rogi?" Marc said through his teeth.

"The—the CE job, o' course! W-what're *you* doing here?"

He didn't answer immediately. A coercive-redactive probe raced through my drunken carcass like a galvanic shock, causing me to convulse and nearly lose control of my sphincters. I shrieked. My stupefied companions watched with sagging jaws.

Marc dropped me back into my seat and stood glowering with his big fists on his hips. "There's nothing wrong with you except a skinful of booze. No emergency at all! What the fuck do you think you're playing at?"

"I'm getting drunk," I explained with sweet reasonableness.

"You broadcast a telepathic scream for help two days ago that nearly fractured my skull! You begged me to drop everything and come to Caledonia at top df to save your frigging life, then disappeared underground where I couldn't farscan you. I had to commandeer a Krondak research ship to get here from Earth. Explain!"

I was tight as a tick and his mental shakedown had by no means rendered me sober. I shrugged and attempted a winning smile.

"Never farspoke you, mon fils. Nosiree. Can't reach across five hunnerd lights t'save my sin-sodden soul. You know that 's well 's me." I uttered a pixilated titter and laid my finger aside of my nose. "But I betcha I know who *did* make the shout!"

"Who?"

"The Family Ghost . . ."

"Tu foutu biberon, toi!" He came at me again and hauled me to my feet. "I was right in the middle of a crucial experiment and your telepathic call scared the living shit out of me. I ought to punch you senseless!"

"Too late for that," I pointed out. "But 's long 's you're here, why don't you take a li'l ride? Do something truly useful."

I squirmed out of his grip and picked up the hand-control for the big monitoring screen. After a few false pokes at its pads, I got the remote to zoom in on the small drill-rig still sitting forlornly on the shore of the loch.

"Ti-Jean 'n' Dorothée 'n' the rest of 'em are down in the rock soup. You take one of the spare E18s, put a farsense brainboard in, and go keep an eye on 'em." My eyes, overflowing now in spite of myself, locked onto Marc's. "Drive that drill-rig there. You don' have to do a thing if they're noodlin' okay down there. Jus' watch. *Please.*"

Cursing, Marc went.

With him taking the place of Dorothea Macdonald in Jack's metaconcert, the separation of volatile components from the subcratonic reservoir was successfully completed. As had been expected, the outgassed molten rock started to sink back into the deep mantle from whence it had come. The hot carbon dioxide and water vapor, together with a small amount of solid material, began moving toward the surface as soon as the metacreative lid was removed, creating a colossal subterranean commotion.

The flashover that had injured the Dirigent had done no significant damage to the control room of D-4. The drill-rig carrying Jack and Dorothée, together with the four other machines, withdrew to a safe distance from the ascending diatreme and then headed for the top.

For a long time we didn't know whether the folks down there were safe or not, but we knew they'd done what they set out to do. The wild acceleration of the elongated bubble of gas had a seismic spoor much different from that of denser magma. Narendra Shah MacNabb was almost incoherent with happiness and relief when he verified the data and announced the good news about Caledonia's reprieve.

The diatreme was scheduled to erupt within about six hours. I was all for getting out of the stuffy bunker and watching the event live, and so were Calum Sorley and the privileged media people who'd been invited to cover the operation. But MacNabb put his foot down on us fun-seekers with emphatic gusto. Nobody knew yet, he explained, whether the ascending mass was mostly water or mostly carbon dioxide. If it was the latter, any observer downwind of the blowout stood a fair chance of getting suffocated. The chief surveyor also delivered many a discouraging word about the hellaceous earthquake and shock waves that were going to accompany the blast.

My drinking buddies and I decided to stay in the bunker after all and watch the spectacle on the monitor. There was plenty of food and liquor left.

The big belch was going to surface right where MacNabb had predicted it would, right in the hollow containing the little lake. As the volatile mass rose it expanded, and as it expanded it cooled. When it reached the solid part of the lithosphere, the actual Clyde craton, which was about 35 kloms thick, it was still hot enough to melt the rock in its path and turn it into the stuff called kimberlite. Closer to the surface, its heat almost entirely dissipated, the rising diatreme just pulverized whatever got in its way.

It exploded out of the ground in a vent over two kilometers in diameter, the largest eruption of its kind ever to occur on Caledonia. The whole planet vibrated like a gong and the quakes, especially on Clyde, were formidable. Most of the stuff tossed into the air by the eruption was ice, some of it "dry"—solid carbon dioxide—but the bulk was just plain old water ice, like hail, in fairly small bits and pieces. The blast wave scattered it from hell to breakfast all over the area surrounding the vanished lake. We even got 25 cents of icefall at the bunker. When the eruption subsided, ice fragments filled the kimberlite pipe to a depth of nearly 300 meters. It settled and solidified into a plug that didn't melt for years.

The diatreme also spit out some rocks. And pretty near a metric ton of diamonds.

. . .

Calum Sorley farspoke the good news to the government people in New Glasgow, and a fleet of eggs was soon on its way, carrying support personnel, eager geologists, and lots more reporters. Meanwhile, a monstrous, diatreme-induced rainstorm pounded the eruption area and helped to melt the drifts of ice pellets. We all sat tight in the bunker, riding out the aftershocks and praying that the heroic CE ops were all right. Three hours after the blowout, the five deep-drillers broke through the ice-mantled surface of Windlestrow Muir and came trundling to the bunker.

Jack had redacted Dorothée all throughout the long trip to the surface, repairing a good deal of damaged lung tissue and relieving most of her pain. She was fully conscious when he carried her out of the machine in his arms. The two of them came up the slope to the bunker flanked by the eight CE operators, still in their helmets, who now used their creativity only to keep off the rain and provide a nice dry surface to walk on. An oxygen tank floated along behind the triumphal procession, suspended by Jack's PK.

Dorothée was wearing a garment that looked like a long dressing gown of white silk, and a veil of the same material covered the lower part of her face. Her eyes and hair were untouched by the mental fire. The two good-luck charms, my Great Carbuncle and her little diamond mask, lay side by side on her breast, hanging from their golden chain.

Dorothée's serious injuries threatened to put a damper on the wild festivities that were already breaking out, but she would have none of it. Speaking to us with a PK-induced pseudovoice, she related the entire extraordinary story of the operation from beginning to end, telling of her own horrendous role matter-of-factly. When she finished, we all cheered ourselves hoarse. Then Jack and I put Dorothée in Scurra II and flew her to the University of New Glasgow Medical Center.

She declined recuperation in a regen-tank. The quakes had done considerable damage and she had important official duties to attend to. There would be plenty of time later, she said, to restore her face.

Meanwhile, the ingenious medics at the university hospital fitted her with a half-mask that not only facilitated her breathing but also made it possible for her to take liquid nutrients and water. In a fit of whimsy she had the thing decorated with diamonds—then completed the ensemble by donning her much-loved old flying outfit. Over the years, just for fun, she had replaced its erstwhile faux stones with the real thing.

She toured the quake-damaged regions of Clyde in this costume with Jack and me at her side, supervising relief efforts, and the dour Caledonians wept and laughed and adulated their Dirigent Lassie half to death. But there was a subtle new flavor to the popular esteem that secretly excited and gratified Dorothée. Whether it was because of her unprecedented accomplishment and her sacrifice, or simply because of her awesome outfit—she was now accorded not only affection but also the deepest respect.

She was very young and very human, and this change in her relationship with the Callie citizenry touched her profoundly. Before, her great abilities had been obscured, as it were, by the image of a small, plain-featured woman wearing ordinary clothes. But in her diamond mask and sparkling suit she became almost an icon, a telling symbol of strength and authority. While she wore that garb, no one would ever forget what she really was. And neither would she.

That, I think, is why Dorothea Macdonald wore her dramatic costume, and others like it, until the very end of her life.

Marc had managed to disappear almost as soon as he climbed out of his drill-rig. He returned to Earth immediately and declined with thanks the Dirigent's offer to make him an honorary Caledonian. He did agree to return to the Scottish planet during its next autumn, when the fishing would be at its best.

I stayed on Callie with Jack and Dorothée for nearly six weeks, until they bowled me over (along with most of the rest of the Milieu) by announcing that they would marry in the summer of 2078. Then I finally reclaimed the Great Carbuncle, which had done a damn fine job, went back to my home in New Hampshire, and tried to decide what kind of wedding present to give the improbable lovers.

I was feeling wonderful! Le bon dieu was in his heaven and all was right with the Galactic Milieu.

And then Anne Remillard spoiled it all by coming into my bookshop and telling me that Denis was Fury.

THE END

of

Diamond Mask

Book Two of the Galactic Milieu Trilogy

Book Three, entitled *Magnificat*,
tells the story of Jack and Dorothea's life together,
of Marc, his wife Cyndia Muldowney, and Mental Man,
of the Metapsychic Rebellion,
and of the end of Hydra, Fury, and Rogi's Family Ghost.

REMILLARD FAMILY TREE

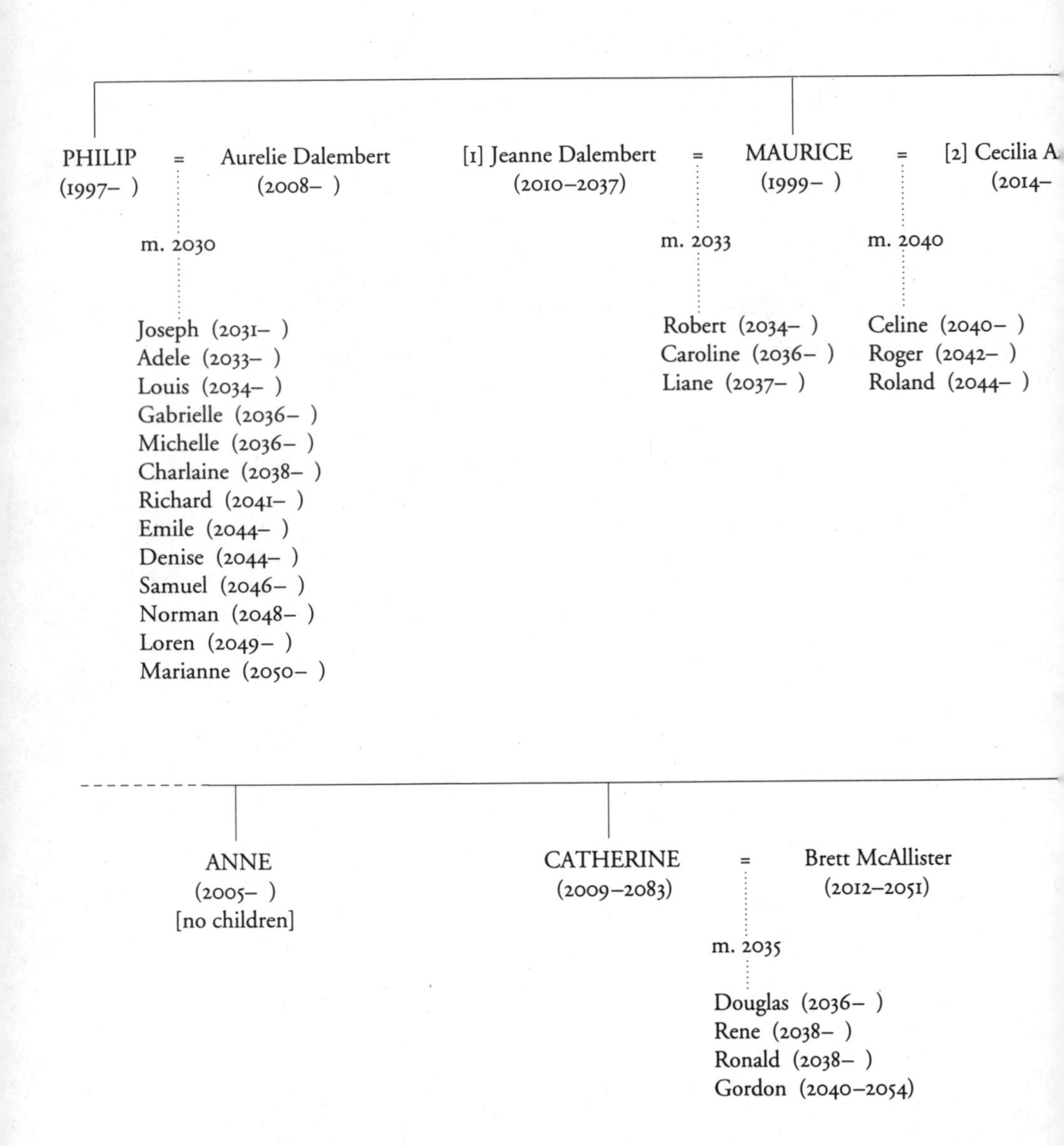

PHILIP
(1997–)
=
Aurelie Dalembert
(2008–)
m. 2030
Joseph (2031–)
Adele (2033–)
Louis (2034–)
Gabrielle (2036–)
Michelle (2036–)
Charlaine (2038–)
Richard (2041–)
Emile (2044–)
Denise (2044–)
Samuel (2046–)
Norman (2048–)
Loren (2049–)
Marianne (2050–)
[1] Jeanne Dalembert
(2010–2037)
=
MAURICE
(1999–)
=
[2] Cecilia A
(2014–
m. 2033
Robert (2034–)
Caroline (2036–)
Liane (2037–)
m. 2040
Celine (2040–)
Roger (2042–)
Roland (2044–)
ANNE
(2005–)
[no children]
CATHERINE
(2009–2083)
=
Brett McAllister
(2012–2051)
m. 2035
Douglas (2036–)
Rene (2038–)
Ronald (2038–)
Gordon (2040–2054)

IIS = Lucille Cartier
082) (1968–)

m. 1995

vieve Boutin = SEVERIN = [2] Galya Miaskovska = [3] Maeve O'Neill
004–2045) (2003–2083) (2006–) (2013–)

m. 2027
div. 2029

Gregory (2028–)

m. 2030
div. 2033

Yvette (2031–)
Natalya (2032–)

m. 2035
div. 2046

Suzanne (2036–)
Quentin (2040–)

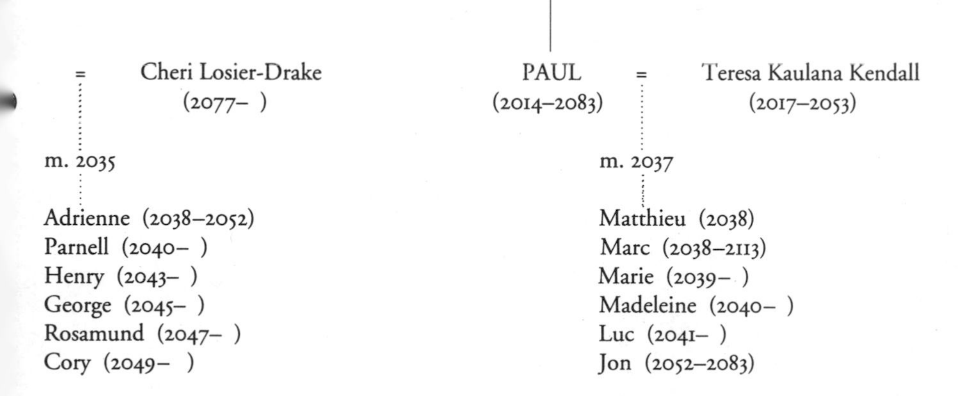

A NOTE ABOUT THE AUTHOR

Julian May was born in Chicago in 1931. She has written numerous books, including *The Many-Colored Land, The Golden Torc, The Nonborn King, The Adversary, Intervention* (Book One: *The Surveillance* and Book Two: *The Metaconcert*). Julian May lives in the state of Washington.

A NOTE ON THE TYPE

This book was set in a digitized version of Garamond. Jean Janson has been identified as the designer of this face, which is based on Garamond's original models but is much lighter and more open. The italic is taken from a font of Granjon, which appeared in the repertory of the Imprimerie Royale and was probably cut in the middle of the sixteenth century.

Composed by Com Com, a division of Haddon Craftsmen,
Allentown, Pennsylvania
Printed and bound by R. R. Donnelley & Sons,
Harrisonburg, Virginia
Designed by Virginia Tan